FANGS

FANGS

K.L. SPEER

BOOK 2 OF THE BONES SERIES

ISBN 979-8-9897440-3-9 (epub)
ISBN 979-8-9897440-4-6 (paperback)
ISBN 979-8-9897440-5-3 (hardcover)

For more information:
P.O. BOX 68014, Minneapolis, MN 55418
author.klspeer@gmail.com
www.klspeer.com

Fangs is set in a brutal and violent post-apocalyptic world.
This book is intended for adults.
Content warnings include graphic language, child abuse,
sexual activities on page (slightly spicier than Bones),
sexual assault and rape, descriptions of severe
mental health conditions, suicidal ideation,
violence, and extreme religious views and content
that may be disturbing to readers with religious trauma
and/or experience with cults. Since Bones is a healer,
there are descriptions of blood, illness, and wounds.

For a more detailed list of content warnings
that include minor spoilers go here:
https://www.klspeer.com/content-warnings-fangs

To Aaron
with all my love

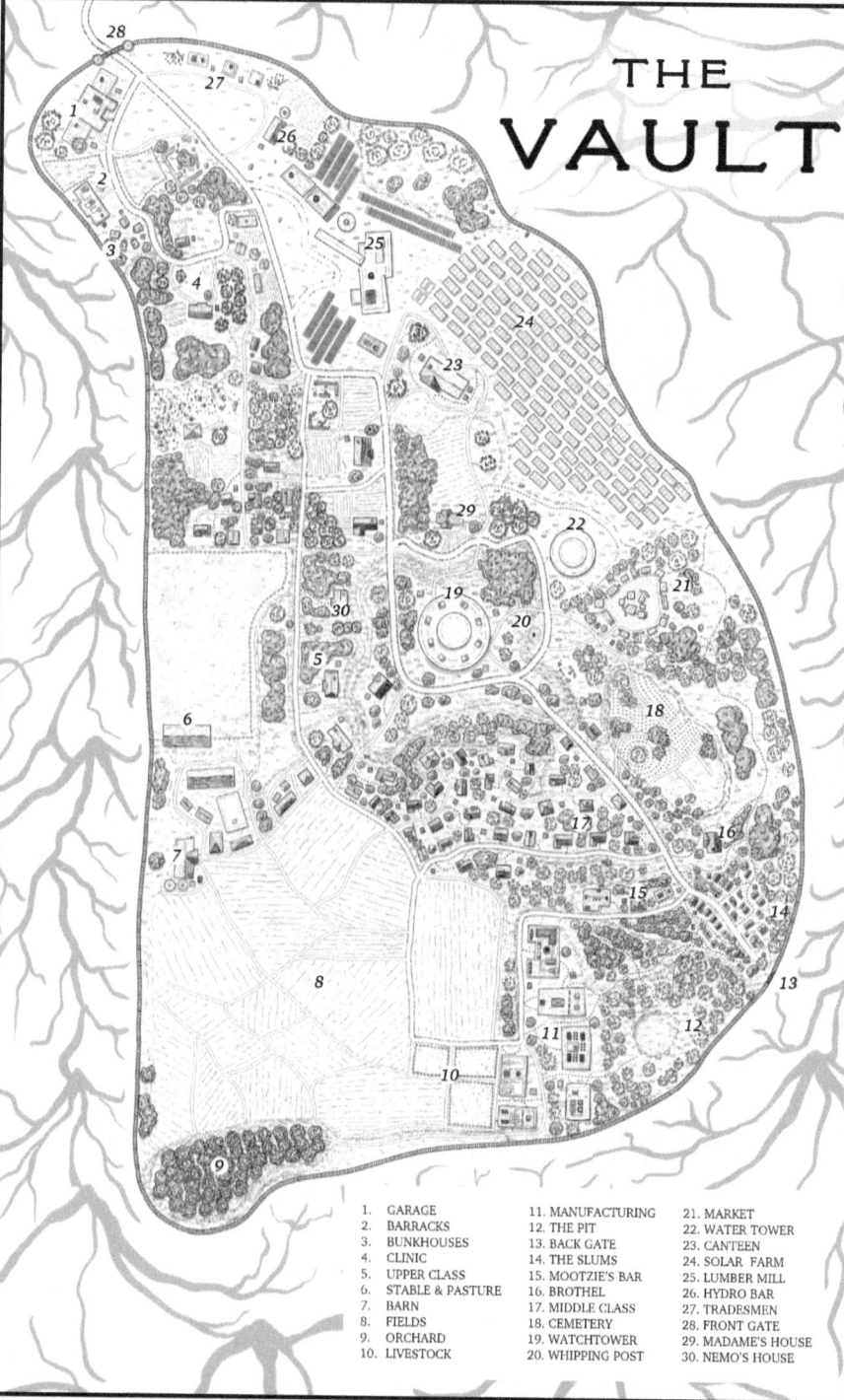

THE VAULT

1. GARAGE
2. BARRACKS
3. BUNKHOUSES
4. CLINIC
5. UPPER CLASS
6. STABLE & PASTURE
7. BARN
8. FIELDS
9. ORCHARD
10. LIVESTOCK
11. MANUFACTURING
12. THE PIT
13. BACK GATE
14. THE SLUMS
15. MOOTZIE'S BAR
16. BROTHEL
17. MIDDLE CLASS
18. CEMETERY
19. WATCHTOWER
20. WHIPPING POST
21. MARKET
22. WATER TOWER
23. CANTEEN
24. SOLAR FARM
25. LUMBER MILL
26. HYDRO BAR
27. TRADESMEN
28. FRONT GATE
29. MADAME'S HOUSE
30. NEMO'S HOUSE

PROLOGUE

W olf shifted, his fingers tightening on his rifle, and kept his movements slow and quiet—even though there was no prey to frighten. His last several hunting trips had been the same. He needed to go at least two or three days' travel away, but the council wouldn't't approve it. The lookouts had spotted raiders in the distance, and it wasn't worth the risk. The council believed they had enough provisions to last until the raiders moved on, but the food stores were getting low. He'd brought his estimates to the council, but as usual, they had smiled and dismissed him—even Pa.

Wolf ground his teeth together. He was only eighteen and didn't understand why no one else in Carth realized how vulnerable they were. Yes, the wall had protected them—*so far*—and yes, the raiders had honored the treaty so long as the council paid the bribe they demanded— *so far.* It would be foolish to expect either of those things to last forever.

Or, as Ember would probably say, dumb as shit.

Wolf grinned to himself. He always reprimanded her for cussing, but it was hard not to laugh. She was so tiny and cute, and she looked like a furious kitten when she was angry. But his smile faded as he remembered how he'd left the house that morning. Pa hadn't even come home last night to sleep, which left Wolf scrambling to get everything done before he went hunting. Dune was supposed to go hunting with him, but he'd refused in an unusual act of defiance that morning. Of course, Em had seized on that and refused to drop it, insisting she and Dune could swap chores for the day. He'd lost his temper and shouted,

1

and she'd burst into furious tears and disappeared to go sulk somewhere. He doubted any of the mending would be done when he got home.

His chest tightened in a familiar way. It made all his insides feel like they were quivering. He hoped she was at least staying out of sight and not doing anything improper like wading in the public fountain... again. It had been two days since he'd received that fateful visit from the Ministry, and he was terrified his new focus on the rules wasn't doing enough to curb her wild behavior. He grimaced, his mind replaying the conversation for the hundredth time.

"Greetings, Wolf."

Wolf stood rigidly in the doorway, staring at the old man on their doorstep. Arbiter Eli was a familiar sight in their community, but a house visit meant something was wrong—wrong enough to send an arbiter instead of an inquisitor. Dread crawled up his spine and froze his tongue.

"May I come in?" Arbiter Eli asked, smiling kindly.

Wolf nodded mutely, stepping aside and gesturing for the Arbiter to enter. He led the way to the small sitting area and cleared his throat. "Can I get you anything?" he asked hoarsely.

"No, thank you," Arbiter Eli responded.

Wolf sank into a chair across from his guest and tucked his trembling hands under his legs. Arbiter Eli had a kind face lined with wrinkles, and his hair was a respectable grey. He had the traditional long beard of a Ministry arbiter, trimmed neatly to a sharp point at his chest. His robes were dyed a soft brown, the most muted color of the various official robes. It was supposed to be soothing and friendly, unlike the crimson red of the high justicars or the solemn dark blue of the inquisitors or the stark black of the enforcers.

"I am here to talk about your sister, Ember," Arbiter Eli said.

Wolf had been expecting that, but to hear it said out loud still made his heart hammer faster. Did the Ministry discover their training?

"What's she done, now?" he asked, his voice ragged.

"I'm not here to discuss any one particular offense but to look at the issue as a whole. While Ember has not broken any laws, her behavior demonstrates a willful spirit. She may have only committed transgressions in propriety for now, but I fear if her behavior is not curbed, it will only grow worse.

"Your sister is in her tenth year; soon, she will be a woman, and as a woman, she is not equipped to govern herself in accordance with

our righteous path. Her role is to submit and serve—to be guided by the wisdom and authority of the men around her. Allowing her to act on her every whim and desire, no matter how small, sets a dangerous precedent.

"You must understand, Wolf. If you allow Ember's willful spirit to fester, it will corrupt her very soul, and she will be forever lost." The old man's bushy grey eyebrows drew together as he leaned forward, placing a hand on Wolf's knee and lowering his voice. "Your father's position on the council allows you some leeway, but there are limits. Her defiance is not just a personal failing but a threat to the moral fabric of our entire community."

Wolf sat so rigidly, it felt like all his muscles had turned to stone. His mind raced, but no words came out of his mouth. The room felt too hot, and his hands were numb.

Arbiter Eli offered a pitying smile. "I understand, son. You are in a hard place. It is a shame your father has not heeded our advice and taken another wife to care for your siblings. This is an unfair burden for a young man to bear, but you are a man, now, and it is your responsibility to guide and protect your family."

Sweat trickled down his back, and he swallowed hard. Arbiter Eli was waiting, clearly expecting him to speak, but still no words came.

"This is the final warning I can offer," Arbiter Eli continued after several seconds of silence. "Remember, a woman's heart is deceitful above all things and easily swayed by the whispers of the world. You must shield her from these influences and mold her into a vessel of virtue and obedience. If your sister persists in her behavior, there will be consequences—public reprimand or worse. Do I make myself clear?"

Wolf managed to nod, and Arbiter Eli stood, smiling once more.

"You are a true blessing to us, Wolf. Our God does not bestow burdens we cannot bear. He has chosen you to be a pillar of faith in your family and in your community."

Wolf continued nodding, and Arbiter Eli continued smiling as they made their way to the door. Before he could open the door, however, Arbiter Eli caught his hand, squeezing with urgency.

"As you know, it is our duty to intervene when the well-being of any child is at stake. It's never our desire to separate a family, but the spiritual and moral welfare of our community must always come first." The old man's grip tightened, the warning clear despite the smile and gentle tone. "It is within your power to ensure Ember stays under your

care, Wolf. I trust you will do what is right."

Wolf shuddered at the memory, and the weight of his responsibility crushed him into the hot sand. The grief and anger surged, fighting against his self-control. Why was he chosen to endure these trials? Why didn't God save his mother's life when he had *begged* on his hands and knees? Why suffer trials at all if God had the power to—

He forced himself to stop the frantic spiraling thoughts, sucking in several deep breaths. He had to be strong. He could not fall into fear and doubt, not when his little siblings hung in the balance.

The setting sun caught his eye, and his heart sank. He needed to head home. If he got there before Pa, maybe he could coax Em into doing her chores and figure out what the hell was up with Dune.

An uncomfortable twinge pulled in his gut. Dune was usually the easy one. He'd never seen his brother be so willful—so *like* Em. Could it be Em's influence? The two of them spent all their time together. Dune hated hunting, but he understood it was a necessary part of life, and he'd never outright refused to go before. For a brief moment, Wolf considered asking Pa for help with the two of them before letting out a heavy breath. No, Pa would just yell, which only made Dune cry and Em mad.

Wolf packed up his rifle, slung it over his back, and exited the rock quarry. The sun had begun to set, bathing the entire desert in a beautiful orange and pink, the blistering heat dropping to something pleasant. He traced his footsteps back out of habit, careful not to leave tracks. He loved hunting and wasn't bragging when he said he was good at it. He was the best hunter in Carth despite being one of the youngest. When he hunted, everything just made sense. There was nothing but him and the desert, the hunter and the prey.

Carth came into view, and he admired how the warm, reddish-brown adobe wall and houses blended into the desert landscape like camouflage. Inside the wall, the dwellings were stacked on top of each other like towers of blocks, and from a distance, the terraced formation almost looked like rolling hills. As he neared, the homes disappeared behind the twelve-foot wall that towered over him. He greeted the guards at the gate, swallowing his urge to snap a terse reply when they teased him for coming back empty-handed again.

He was winding through the narrow streets and thinking about the dinner waiting for him when he heard her scream.

He knew it was Em—knew it in the same unexplainable way he

knew how to find whatever prey he tracked. He started running, his heart in his throat. She kept screaming, and he felt a tiny flash of pride. He'd taught her that. Scream as loud as you can. Don't stop, even if it seems like no one is coming. His one act of blatant disobedience was teaching her to fight. For months now, he'd gotten her up before dawn and taught her not just the moves and footwork but all the dirty tricks she could use to make up for her small stature. The raiders often stole young girls and women to sell as slaves or whores. He'd heard the stories. The raiders taking her was one of his worst fears, and he was willing to risk a public caning if it meant she could defend herself.

It couldn't be a raider, though, because her screams were coming from high above on the roofs. One of Em's common transgressions was climbing onto the private roofs of the upper class and running and jumping across them like they were her own personal playground. Wolf scrambled up a set of broken pallets and grabbed the balcony above, hauling himself up to reach the next one. Someone inside the house shrieked, and he grimaced. He'd deal with that later. Right now, he needed to get to Em.

By the time he got to the roof, he was sick with panic and adrenaline. He followed the sound of her panicked screams at a sprint, dreading what he was about to find, but nothing—*nothing*—could have prepared him for what he saw. Em was crouched over a body, and the metallic tang of blood filled the air. As he got closer, he realized with a sickening bolt of horror it was Dune. Dune lay on his back with one hand clutching his bloody gut and the other trying to push Em away. He was screaming, too, but weakly.

"No! Stop! Please stop, Em! Stop!"

Everything slowed as his feet pounded across the hard-baked clay roof, and he scanned the horrible scene. Dune's terrified eyes cut to him. One of Pa's knives lay bloody and discarded on the roof next to Ember. Blood formed a puddle beneath his brother's body and splattered across the roof as Dune raised his bloodied hands and tried to smack Em's hands away. Dune's lips formed Wolf's name, and Em's head swiveled to look at him.

Wolf crashed to his knees beside them, shouldering Em out of the way and pressing his own hands against the wound—no, gods—the giant *gash* in Dune's gut.

"What happened? What did you do?" he screamed at both of

them. When neither answered him, he glanced from the blood gushing between his fingers to his little sister beside him. The fear and the *guilt* in her eyes felt like a knife to his own heart. "Em, what did you do! "

"Wolf!" Dune choked out, his voice a horrible gurgling noise. "Help me."

Wolf's gaze snapped back to his brother, and he stared, horrified at the death creeping into those familiar blue eyes. He'd seen death fill the glassy eyes of dying deer and rabbits and antelope after he killed them. He knew Dune was dying, even as he began shaking his head, trying to deny the truth in front of him.

"No, Dune! Dune!" He was sobbing now, his carefully made plans for emergencies scattered to the wind. He didn't know what to do. *He didn't know what to do!*

Dune cut his eyes back to Em, but the fear that flashed across them didn't fade. He gave one more shuddering breath and went still, his blue eyes open and staring at their ten-year-old little sister. Wolf followed his gaze, his entire body going numb with shock. Em still knelt beside him as though frozen, staring at Dune with tears rolling down her face.

"Ember!" Wolf barked, and her eyes shot up to meet his.

Again, he couldn't deny the horrible *guilt* filling her green eyes. He gasped in a breath to demand answers, but she bolted to her feet and *ran.*

It was something like instinct that had him scrambling up after her. It sure as hell wasn't his brain. His head seemed to go quiet and empty, like when he trailed his prey. She was fast, but his legs were much longer, and he caught up to her in just a few strides. He tackled her to the rooftop, not even feeling the pain as his arm scraped against the rough surface. She fought him like a panicked animal.

"What did you do! What did you do to Dune?" he screamed and pinned her to the ground.

She stared up at him with wide, terrified eyes, her tiny chest heaving with sobs, but she didn't say a single fucking word.

If her behavior is not curbed, it will only grow worse.

"Emmy!"

He heard people coming, shouts and footsteps pounding across the roof toward them.

"What did you do!"

You must understand, Wolf. If you allow Ember's willful spirit to fester, it will corrupt her very soul, and she will be forever lost.

Wolf wasn't sure who pulled them apart, but he started fighting to keep them from ripping his sister away. For a moment, he wasn't sure if he was trying to protect Em or to force answers from her with his own two hands. Then the enforcers were there, black robes billowing as they walked and faces hidden behind their black helmets, and everything seemed terribly *real.*

The enforcers hauled Em away without even speaking a word. She sobbed, but she didn't fight or scream. Maybe she also felt that heavy weight of reality sinking in. One of the inquisitors in his deep blue robes told him they were taking her to lockup. Hands patted his shoulders, and concerned voices asked him questions, but he pushed past them to walk back and crouch beside Dune's body. The gash in Dune's stomach was long and deep. He'd taught Em to aim for the gut, to stab and jerk the knife through as many vital organs as possible. She'd always been a good student.

He stood and numbly walked to an empty corner, where he heaved up the contents of his stomach.

ɢᴅ

Wolf wasn't sure how much time passed before Pa arrived. He didn't notice until a heavy hand clapped on his shoulder, startling him. Pa stared at Dune, and pain etched into his face for a moment before it disappeared under the carefully crafted mask of the councilman. The crowd thinned upon Pa's arrival, and Wolf didn't blame them. Pa cut an intimidating figure on a good day. He was tall and broad, and his greying blond hair made him look anything but feeble. When he spoke, his voice was like quiet steel.

"What happened?" It wasn't a question so much as a demand.

Wolf recounted everything he'd seen, realizing an inquisitor was recording the information. Several more inquisitors crouched and lifted Dune's body when he finished. Wolf had a sudden insane urge to lunge forward and rip Dune's body out of their gloved hands, but he swallowed it, watching them disappear with dry eyes.

"Come, Wolf." Pa gripped his arm with almost bruising strength. "They want us to see her."

The Ministry was an ugly, grey metal building in the city's center that clashed with the soft red curves of all the adobe houses. Wolf followed Pa down the hallway until they stopped before a cell. He stared at the dirty straw floor where his little sister sat. Her wide, terrified eyes stared up at them. She was covered in dirt and blood, and it made her look like a wild animal.

"What happened?" Pa repeated his question to her, his voice and face hard.

"Pa, I didn't kill him," she whimpered. "I didn't kill him," she managed to say once more before she burst into sobs.

Wolf's own eyes prickled at the sight of her looking so scared, stricken, and small. He wanted to wrap her in his arms; he wanted to *shake* her; he wanted to wake up and realize all of this was a terrible nightmare. He clenched his fists hard enough to feel his nails digging into his palms.

"Stop crying and tell me what happened, girl." Pa's voice was ice cold, making the hair on the back of Wolf's neck stand up.

Pa rarely called Em by name. It had always struck Wolf as strange, but Pa was never the same after Mom died.

"He stabbed himself in the gut! I was tryin' to help him!" Em seemed to try to stop crying, but her words tumbled out between panicked sobs.

Wolf glanced between the two of them, speechless as his mind spun. Pa's expression didn't change, but he could have sworn something like disappointment flickered across his features.

"I swear, Pa!" Em sobbed. "I'm not lyin'!"

The rage washed over him like a sudden sandstorm, blinding and sharp. "Why would Dune fucking stab *himself* in the gut?" he demanded. "That doesn't make any sense. I saw you! He was pushin' you away and beggin' you to stop!"

Em jumped when he started yelling, but now she stared at him, those huge green eyes swimming in tears—Mom's eyes.

"I didn't," she gasped. "I didn't do it, Wolf. I swear! I was tryin' to help him."

Remember, a woman's heart is deceitful above all things and easily swayed by the whispers of the world.

"You're lying," Wolf shouted, and she flinched.

He felt a sudden surge of bitter hatred with the red-hot rage. Did Em think they would believe Dune stabbed *himself?* How could she do this? Em and Dune had always been best friends, so much so he sometimes felt jealous. He'd been her primary caretaker since Mom died giving birth to her, and they'd fought like cats and dogs as soon as she was old enough to talk. Dune was different, though. Em had always loved Dune the most. It would have made more sense if Em had tried to stab *him*.

"Pa, please! Please look at me!" Em wailed.

"Come, Wolf." Pa's voice was cold and hard as he gripped Wolf's arm again, trying to pull him away. "The council will decide what to do with her."

If your sister persists in her behavior, there will be consequences.

Wolf jerked away, slamming into the bars of the cell so hard Em flinched backward and shrieked. "I don't understand!" He was drowning in fury and desperation. "Tell me why you did it! Why would you kill him? He *loved* you!"

She didn't answer, shaking with the force of her sobs. Pa gripped Wolf's arm again, and he let Pa pull him away as his eyes filled with helpless tears.

෨

Wolf didn't sleep much that night, laying alone in their bedroom for the first time since before Dune was born fifteen years ago. It was too quiet, and there was too much room. Usually, all three of them were curled up on the pallet—Dune by the wall, Ember in the middle, and Wolf on the edge. He hadn't realized how comforting it was to hear his younger siblings breathing at night until they were both gone. So, instead of sleeping, he alternated between silent sobs of grief and a furious simmering rage.

Yet as he lay awake in bed, watching the sky lighten with the dawn, he found himself more confused than anything.

Em was smart. Why wouldn't she have a better cover story if she had killed Dune? Why didn't she say somebody else attacked Dune? She had to know that would have been more believable. Had she just panicked and said the first thing that came to mind?

He couldn't get Arbiter Eli's words out of his head. *A woman's heart is deceitful above all things.*

Em had to be lying. Dune would never have stabbed himself in the gut. Their community was no stranger to people dying from self-

9

inflicted wounds, but no one would *choose* to die from a gut wound like that. As much as he hated hunting, Dune had done it countless times. Wolf had taught him the quickest and most painless ways to kill an animal, and he'd supervised Dune doing it until his brother could do it without hesitation; besides, there was no way his brother wanted to die. Sure, he'd been in a strange mood yesterday; however, Dune couldn't tell a lie to save his life—not like Em. Dune was so gentle and honest. Wolf was sure he would have noticed *something* if he had wanted to die.

Was Arbiter Eli right? Had Em's willful spirit corrupted her soul? Had she lashed out during an argument? Em had always hated that she and Dune didn't get to do the same things. She wanted to hunt and learn how to fight. Maybe he should have let Pa give her to the Lopez family as a baby. All the Lopez girls were quiet and obedient. He knew Mrs. Lopez would have loved Em as her own, but the idea of losing his baby sister—his last piece of Mom—had sent him into a panic. Pa hadn't fought him on it. In fact, Pa washed his hands of Em the moment Mom died. It had always been clear Em was Wolf's responsibility.

He tried to swallow past the lump in his throat. His responsibility *and* his failure.

The guilt felt like a physical wound in his chest. If only he had been stricter with Em. If only he had enforced her role in the divine order. Maybe if he'd been a better leader, Dune would still be alive, and Em wouldn't be lost.

The door to the bedroom crashed open, and Wolf bolted upright to see Pa standing there, breathing hard.

"She escaped," he said.

"What?" Wolf managed to choke out.

"She manipulated an idiot guard to let her out, and then she ran. She can't be far—she's in the city somewhere. We're starting a search party, and we need you," Pa snapped. "Get dressed."

As Wolf scrambled to pull on his clothes, a horrible, numb acceptance settled over him. Ember must have done it. She must have killed Dune because innocent people didn't run, and she had run twice.

CHAPTER 1

Twelve Years Later

"Think you ran far enough?" asked Wolf.

I couldn't speak, couldn't remember a single word. I was ten years old again, staring into my older brother's furious face, but he wasn't a gangly teenage boy anymore. New scars marked his skin, his wavy brown hair hung long enough to cover his ears, and he wore a green and brown uniform that was worn and dirty. There was a rifle strapped to his back and a pistol on his hip, along with several sheathed knives. A pair of goggles sat on top of his head. The hardness of his green eyes made me feel sick.

"What? You got nothin' to say to me?" He smiled with no humor in it. "After all this time?"

I stared at him, my heart lodged in my throat. He stared back, studying my face as though looking for something. Was he trying to find the ten-year-old girl he last saw? A low whistle came from the main floor of the clinic below us, and it snapped Wolf out of our bizarre staring contest. Wolf whistled back, then scanned the loft with narrowed eyes. I followed his gaze, trying to see what he was looking at. There wasn't much. My mattress lay on the floor, covered in Trey's quilt, and my dresser stood in the corner. Wolf glanced back at me, his expression unreadable, then spun me around and marched me toward the loft ladder.

"We're leaving," he said in a low, dangerous voice. "Go down the ladder."

I obeyed. Another man with black hair pulled back into a messy top knot and dressed the same as Wolf stood in the clinic holding a large rifle. He looked familiar, but the panic roaring through my head made it impossible to place him. His face stayed expressionless as he shifted to put his body between me and the door. Wolf came down the ladder right behind me, grabbing my arms and twisting them behind my back. I heard the familiar sound of a zip tie cinch shut and felt the plastic dig into my wrists.

"Not a word, you hear?" Wolf growled in my ear as he propelled me toward the door. "I don't *want* to shoot my way out of here, but I will if I have to."

My eyes found the pistol in his hand. It had a silencer on it, and my heart seized with terror that Mac would return and—

I gulped in short, frantic gasps of air. I couldn't watch another person I cared about get shot. Wolf and his friend hesitated, staring at me with furrowed brows.

"*Quiet,*" Wolf hissed as he shook me hard.

Almost as though a switch flipped, it felt like I was outside my body, watching. My gasping eased, an empty nothingness replacing the panic. They both stared at me for a second longer before pulling their goggles down and dragging me outside.

They slid through the shadows easily, and I stumbled along with them in a dreamlike state. After I tripped for the tenth time, they started practically carrying me, the toes of my boots barely brushing the ground.

As we approached the gate, I didn't notice the bodies until we were stepping over them. They lay in the shadows of the wall, and I couldn't tell if they were dead or alive.

Fuck. Oh gods, please don't be—

"Sable?" Wolf called in a low voice.

Another shadowy figure bled out of the darkness of the gate, startling me. The dark-haired man holding my left arm released me and traded places with this third person—Sable, apparently. As Sable took my arm, I could just barely see their features in the moonlight, making out long blond hair and lips that were frowning at me. The dark-haired man moved to operate the pulley to open the gate doors. We slipped through when the door opened enough to fit a person, and Wolf and Sable darted toward the woods with me in tow. The gate shut behind us and I craned my neck to look back. I had to bite back a gasp as the dark-haired man rappelled down the wall with ease. There were no cries of alarm. No guards shouting. Nothing.

Please don't be dead.

The dark-haired man caught up and swapped places with Sable. They dragged me through the woods while Sable took up the rear, drawing the large rifle he carried on his back. I tried to keep up and cooperate, but *I* didn't have night vision goggles and stumbled over every damn tree branch and rock. Soon, they seemed to grow frustrated and started carrying me again—my boots dangling. They moved so fucking fast, and now that we were out of the hold, I felt less concerned about Wolf shooting other people and more concerned with my own looming death.

My brother was about to kill me.

I knew he would catch up to me eventually but turns out I hadn't been as mentally prepared as I thought. They looked like fucking mercenaries. Was Wolf a merc now?

Wolf let out a low whistle, and an answering whistle sounded from somewhere ahead of us. A minute later, a shadowy figure appeared leading a horse.

"Any trouble?" a distinctly male voice asked.

"No," Wolf said. "Any updates?"

"All clear at home base," Horse Guy responded.

"Are your bones full of air?" the dark-haired man holding my arm muttered, and it took me far too long to realize he was talking to me.

I glanced up to find him studying my face. He tilted his head, a slow smirk curling one corner of his mouth. "You're a lot prettier than Wolf."

"Shut up, Lee," my brother growled.

Lee released my arm as Wolf began to drag me toward the horse. He stopped at the horse's side, releasing my arm, and glared at me as I tried to breathe.

"If you think passin' out is gonna help you, you're dead wrong," Wolf said in a low, harsh voice.

He reached toward me, and I instinctively jumped backward, only to crash into a body that grabbed me tightly by the shoulders. I froze in fear, and Wolf's angry face swam in my vision.

"I wouldn't try to run if I were you," the person behind me said.

A quick glance revealed it to be Horse Guy.

"Listen to Tuck. Or you're gonna make this ten times worse for yourself," Wolf said, pulling me toward him by my arm.

He moved around behind me and grabbed my waist, lifting me and slinging me onto the saddle. As he bent to make sure my feet were in the stirrups, Tuck moved around him to join Lee and Sable. The three of them spoke in low tones while watching me. I couldn't hear what they were saying due to the panic roaring in my ears and Juck's voice echoing in my head.

Quit cryin', Angel, or I'll give you somethin' to cry about.

As soon as Wolf finished adjusting the stirrups, we started moving again in a single file line. Sable led the way, and Wolf walked behind him, holding the horse's reins. I only knew Tuck and Lee were behind my horse because I glanced back and saw them. Somehow, the only sound was the horse's hooves crunching through the snow. The zip ties stung where they rubbed against my skin. I wondered if the horse would start running if I gave it a good kick, but I knew I'd probably fall off with my hands tied behind my back.

What would Mac think when he came back and found me gone? Would he assume I'd been called out to heal someone? Would he even look for me before morning? It wasn't unusual for me to be out healing during the night. At this speed, we'd be far away by then.

That was for the best, though. Wolf was going to kill me. Like he'd said, my time was up.

Was this how Trey felt when he knew he was going to die?

I'll find you again in another lifetime.

I struggled to wrestle my emotions down. It was harder than I expected; I'd gotten too used to letting them out. I had to fall back on my old method of reciting medical text in my head until I felt myself sinking into numb emptiness again, the woods passing by in a dreamlike blur. By the time the sun began to rise, I was numb inside and out. I was only wearing a thin jacket and no gloves—fine for running around the hold while healing people, but not warm enough for an overnight trek through the woods in late winter. I couldn't feel my hands anymore, and the adrenaline barely kept me awake. How far were they going to take me before they just got it over with and killed me?

The sun had fully risen when they finally stopped. On one side of us was a rocky cliff with large boulders scattered about its base. Despite my effort to stay calm, my heart started thudding out of control. This had to be it. This was where my brother would kill me.

The others shrugged their packs off, and Wolf came to the horse's side. I tried to be calm but wasn't managing it very well. I was shaking like a leaf when he pulled me down. I saw his gaze narrow on me before I dropped my eyes. When he set me on my feet, my knees fucking buckled, and he had to grab my arm to catch me before I ended up in a heap on the snowy ground. I could barely feel my ice-cold feet, and my legs were stiff and sore. Wolf dragged me toward the rocky cliff and shoved me down to sit on a flat rock someone had cleared of snow.

"Don't move," he ordered.

I pulled my legs in and leaned forward, trying to curl into a ball and stop fucking trembling. We'd fought constantly, but Wolf had never laid a hand on me. The idea of him hurting me was worse than the idea of him killing me. His boots stayed before me for a few breaths, but then he turned and went back to the horse.

The other men were moving around the small area, getting food and water. I didn't move. I knew better than to try to run. I'd be lucky if I made it five steps before one of them caught me. A gust of wind blew some of the powdery snow into my face, and I shivered, miserably cold. If only my hands were tied in front of me so I could try to warm them up. Jaw clenched to keep my teeth from chattering, I risked glancing up, scanning the three men who traveled with my brother. It didn't look like they planned to make a fire, just getting food and water and resting.

In the morning light, I could see them clearly now. Sable's long hair fell to his collarbones in a silky sheet, and his eyes were so pale blue they almost looked white. He studied me often with a scrutiny that made my stomach churn. Tuck was the tallest and had brown skin; his head of messy black curls seemed permanently mussed. His glances at me seemed more cautiously curious, bordering on concern. Maybe he was the weak link in my brother's group.

I glanced at Lee, and all my muscles tensed when I realized he was staring at me. His hair was pulled up in a messy top knot with a shaved undercut below. He had high cheekbones and almond-shaped eyes, and again, vague recognition tickled my brain. For a few seconds, I held his gaze, and then the memory crashed over me.

He was the prisoner from the cells at the Vault—the man who looked at me like he knew me, and Mac had later accused me of helping escape. So he *had* recognized me. I guessed that answered the question of how Wolf found me.

My revelation must have shown on my face because he smirked again and then said something to Sable and Tuck. They both glanced up, and then all three stared boldly back at me. I dropped my eyes back to the ground again, my skin crawling.

Wolf's boots appeared before me again, and I tensed but refused to look up. His knees came into view as he crouched in front of me.

"What's wrong with you?" he asked. "You forget how to talk?"

I didn't answer, focused on breathing in and out. Wolf's hand shot out and seized my jaw, pulling my face up to look at him. His eyes narrowed as his fingers squeezed into my cheeks and pried my mouth open. Terrified, I jerked my head back, and he let go, watching as I nearly fell off the rock in my haste to escape. He raised an eyebrow.

"Just making sure you still had your tongue. Never thought I'd see you so quiet."

I pressed my trembling lips together hard, trying not to think about all the times I watched Juck cut people's tongues out. Wolf scanned me again with those sharp eyes, taking in my filthy, muddy clothes and the dried blood all over my front.

"Whose blood is that?" he demanded.

I looked away. I was not going to cry. I was going to be numb and empty.

"Godsdamnit, Em, if you don't tell me, I'm gonna have to search you for injuries."

Em. The familiar nickname hurt, but his threat terrified me.

"Not mine," I choked out.

"So she does speak." He smirked, looking so satisfied that fury roared through me. "Who'd you kill this time?"

My anger fizzled out like he'd dumped a bucket of ice-cold water on my head. I dropped my eyes again, staring at the ground. The fierce ache in my chest surprised me. Apparently, I still had a heart, or just enough of one to break again. Gods, I wished he'd just kill me already and be done with it.

"Here."

He held out a bottle of water as though offering me a drink. I looked between his face and the water bottle, hesitating.

"It's just water," he frowned.

I leaned forward and let him tip some water into my mouth, feeling awkward. After I got a drink, he reached into his pack again, and

I tensed, but he just pulled out a piece of dried meat and held it out to me. I shook my head and knew he was glaring at me before I even looked. I could *feel* the heat of it.

"We're not stoppin' again until nightfall. You should eat, now."

I shook my head again, my stomach churning. If I ate anything, I'd just be sick with all this anxiety.

"Fine," he snapped, dropping the food into his pack and taking it with him as he strode away.

I rested my forehead on my knees, trying to take deep breaths. Was my brother waiting for nightfall for a reason? At least I had an idea of their timetable. I could hear the low mumble of their voices and feel the weight of their eyes, but no one else spoke to me.

Maybe I would get lucky for once in my miserable life and see Trey after I died. I didn't know what I believed about the afterlife, but I did know if there was any chance to find him, I would take it. I'd teased him when he said he'd wait a thousand years for me, but I understood with painful clarity now. I would live and die and claw my way back a thousand times over just to have one more moment with him.

My throat ached with the force of holding back tears. It'd been over three months, but the pain hadn't dulled; I'd just grown more accustomed to feeling it.

They only rested for about an hour before they were packing up. When Wolf's boots appeared in front of me again, I uncurled from my protective position, and he grabbed my upper arm and hauled me to my feet without a word. He lifted me onto the horse again and then marched around to the horse's head to take the lead.

As we traveled, I could feel exhaustion creeping over me. I tried to fight it, watching Wolf and the others in an attempt to distract myself. All of them stalked through the woods with an unnatural grace. Wolf had always been that way, able to adapt and move through his environment like he was a part of it. He either found others like him or taught them his tricks. They were quiet, but the few times they interacted, it was with an easy camaraderie that reminded me of Mac's crew.

I swallowed hard. Mac must have realized I was gone by now. Would he even think of searching *outside* the hold? I might be dead before they realized I wasn't in the Vault. The ache in my chest worsened. Talking to Mac, *actually* talking, had felt like gasping in air after being underwater. I wished I could have said goodbye and told them

I wasn't abandoning them—not of my own free will, anyway.

How would Wolf kill me? A bullet to the head? A knife in my gut? The bloody images flashed through my mind—Dune bleeding out on the rooftop and Madame slicing into Mac's stomach in the dungeon. I forced myself to recite an entire chapter on medical annotations until I felt nothing again.

I made it a few hours before exhaustion won and pulled me under. I woke up to the sensation of falling from the saddle and somebody shouting. I couldn't even try to catch myself because my damn hands were tied behind my back, so I ended up going face-first into the brush. My chin scraped on some ice, and there was a sharp stabbing pain in my cheek. I didn't move, stunned and burning with humiliation, but someone yanked me up by my jacket. Wolf glared at me, swearing under his breath. As soon as I got my feet under me, I jerked away, only to run into Tuck—*again*. He caught me by the shoulders to keep me from falling and frowned.

"She sliced open her cheek," he said.

The concern in Tuck's face looked real. Maybe I could manipulate him—

A vise squeezed the air from my lungs as memories of Trey overwhelmed me.

"Lemme see." Wolf sounded annoyed.

Tuck started to turn me by the shoulders like I wasn't fucking capable of moving on my own. I jerked free, flooded by the familiar queasy feeling of being surrounded by men I didn't know—even my brother was a stranger. I turned to Wolf just in time to see his arm moving toward my face, and I flinched. He froze with his arm still outstretched, and my face flamed hot. Godsdamnit, I'd gotten better at not doing that, but all this adrenaline and anxiety had me on high alert. He pulled his arm back, and in the silence, I stared at the snowy ground, willing myself not to cry.

"Wolf," Sable's voice had a sharp edge.

"I know," Wolf snapped. I heard him take a deep breath. "Lee, can you grab the kit?"

Behind him, Lee dropped his pack and dug through it to pull out a battered tin. He opened it, took out a tube of ointment, and handed it to Wolf.

"Hold still, Ember. You just about put a branch through your cheek," Wolf said.

I looked warily at the tube in his hands, but it appeared to be some sort of sealing astringent. He reached out, much slower this time, gripped my chin in one hand, and dabbed at the wound with a handkerchief with his other. His hands were gentle as he applied the ointment, and that small detail almost brought all the emotion back up my throat. I dug my fingernails into my palms hard enough to hurt and stared at the trees. I had to remember this person wasn't the brother who had brought me dandelions and taught me how to fight. This person was a stranger who hated me.

I just didn't understand why he was bothering to patch me up before he killed me.

"We better get movin' if we're gonna get there before nightfall," Wolf added as he screwed the lid back on.

I couldn't tell if he was talking to me or the others. I wanted to ask where "there" was, but I kept my mouth shut. Lee put the kit away, and my gaze locked on Wolf as he pulled out a knife.

"Turn around, I'm gonna cut the tie," Wolf ordered.

I did as he said, trying to ignore how turning my back to him made fear prickle my skin. Tuck and Sable stood a few feet behind me, watching, and I dropped my eyes. Wolf cut the tie, spun me around, and then gripped my wrist, examining the red welts already forming on my skin. He pulled my jacket sleeves down and re-bound my wrists over top of the fabric, keeping the plastic ties off my skin. When he lifted me back onto the horse, my head was spinning for more than one reason, but at least I could cling to the saddle horn now.

I did not understand what Wolf was doing. Maybe he was playing mind games? Juck did shit like that all the time.

Pa's words just kept echoing in my head. *"Run, girl. 'Fore Wolf tears you apart like a lil rabbit."*

CHAPTER 2

The second time I fell asleep, someone behind me called my brother's name in a sharp voice. Wolf caught my arm just as I started tilting, preventing me from falling off the horse again. They stood there arguing in low tones as I tried to stay awake.

"Either you do it, or one of us will," Sable said loud enough for me to make out.

Wolf growled something I couldn't hear, then stomped over to the side of the horse. My heart lurched as he reached up, but he just swung onto the horse behind me. I stiffened, and he felt just as stiff as he wrapped an arm around my waist and took the reins. He didn't say a word to me, simply urging the horse to continue following Sable.

I wondered if he was as tall as Pa now. He'd been close when I was ten, but eighteen-year-old Wolf had been all skinny arms and legs. He was still on the slender side but broader and more muscled. He sure seemed taller than I remembered.

I tried to stay alert but started drifting off again as the adrenaline faded. I kept jerking awake, startling Wolf and the horse. It reminded me of riding with Trey while we were on the run, but Trey didn't swear under his breath each time like my brother did. Eventually, I passed out because next thing I knew, I opened my eyes to see the sun had disappeared behind the mountains. The woods were so dark, but there was a warm glow of light ahead. I squinted at it, and as we neared, I realized it was a cabin.

When we finally stepped out of the trees and into a small

clearing, I could barely see any details of the dark wooden building. It was small, and the windows were covered in what looked like oiled paper, revealing only the shadows moving around inside. The smell of woodsmoke filled the air. Where the fuck were we?

Wolf dismounted and then pulled me off, too. My legs shook when he set me on the ground, and he had to half carry me into the cabin. I was too tired to keep my teeth from chattering now. Our boots thudded across a small wooden porch, and we stepped inside.

The heat washed over me, and I almost whimpered in relief. Wolf brought me in front of the fireplace and growled at me to sit, so I did. I huddled as close to the fire as I could, adrenaline making me more alert again. My gaze darted around the room. There was a woman and a red-haired, freckled man in the same faded green and brown uniforms as the rest. They both stood in the middle of the room, studying me with arms crossed.

"*This* is her? I thought she'd be, you know, *bigger*." The red-haired man smirked. His hair was cut short, and he had a neatly trimmed short beard the same red as his hair.

"Kai," Wolf grumbled.

"Whose blood is that?" the woman asked, looking at Wolf.

"Not hers," he grunted, stripping off his pack and jacket. He glanced up at me, eyes hard. "Guessing she was torturing someone. That's your job, isn't it, Ember?"

The shame paralyzed me. I couldn't help glancing at Lee, knowing exactly where Wolf had received *that* intel. Lee stared back at me, a challenging look on his face as he shrugged off his pack. I dropped my eyes and shifted closer to the fire.

"Wow, she's as talkative as you," Kai said.

"Shut up, Kai," Wolf said, but he didn't seem angry.

I heard him approach me, and every muscle in my body tensed. He crouched before me and grabbed my bound wrists, making me flinch. A knife glinted in the firelight, but he simply cut the zip tie off again. *Why* was he drawing this out? It reminded me far too much of sitting in the dark cell under the watchtower, panicking about how Madame would punish me. When the plastic tie fell off, he sheathed his knife and took my wrists one at a time, pushing up my sleeves like he was making sure the ties hadn't added more welts.

"Take off your jacket," he ordered.

I clumsily obeyed, wishing he would back up and give me more space. He took my jacket from me but frowned at the sight of my bloody shirt.

"Your clothes are filthy," Wolf muttered, then louder, he said, "Scar, you think you got anythin' that might fit her?"

"Maybe," the woman replied, frowning.

Wolf grabbed my arm and pulled me to my feet. I hoped he didn't notice I flinched again. My nerves were shot.

"Go with Scar," Wolf shoved me in the direction of the woman.

I obeyed, following as Scar led the way to one of the bedrooms, and pretended not to hear the bits of conversation that erupted behind us.

"That tiny little girl is the one—"

"Kai, *shut up.*"

"Did you see how—"

"What the fuck—"

"Wolf, you gotta—"

Scar closed the door, muffling the voices. I pressed my back against the wall and took in the small bedroom with its double rows of bunk beds. Scar eyed me momentarily before walking past to a pack sitting on one of the beds. I stayed where I was, rubbing my sore wrists and watching as she pulled out a few clothing items. She looked a little older than Wolf, maybe nearing forty. Her skin was light brown, and her short brown hair was pulled into a tight ponytail, somehow looking both pretty *and* dangerous. My eyes fell to the holstered pistol on her waist.

"These are gonna be too big, but they're clean and dry," she said.

She handed me the clothes, and I stayed against the wall, waiting for her to leave so I could change. When she didn't move, I didn't either. Scar studied me, and I hated feeling so exposed and vulnerable.

"Wolf wants eyes on you at all times," she said. "It's nothing I haven't seen before."

Fucking hell.

I was not going to let this woman see any of my scars. My shirt was covered in blood, but it had dried. Maybe I could get away with just changing my pants. I slid out of my cold, damp, muddy pants and pulled on the new ones. They were too big around the waist and too long, but I just slid my belt off my pants and threaded it through Scar's, cinching it tight. I rolled the ankles up until I could walk without tripping on the fabric. When I finished, I set her shirt on the small side table near me and met her gaze, hoping I didn't look as terrified as I felt.

"I don't need a shirt," I said.

Scar frowned. "Your shirt is filthy. C'mon, we'll wash your clothes tonight, and you can wear them again tomorrow."

Tomorrow? I would still be alive tomorrow? Panic was threatening to choke me, so I seized the anger instead. "No."

She tilted her head, her gaze narrowing. "What's the matter?"

"Nothing." I glared at her. "My shirt is fine."

"You mean the one covered in blood?"

"It's fine," I said through my teeth.

She pursed her lips, looking almost amused. "You're as stubborn as he is. Fine, but I'd bet you a drink Wolf sends you right back in here to change."

"Wolf can go to hell," I spit out before I could think better of it.

She raised her eyebrows. "Alright, come on."

We walked back out, and Wolf began to speak, but Scar interrupted him.

"Before you yell at me, she didn't want a new shirt." Scar moved to where Lee was filling up the sink, my jacket on the counter beside him.

"Your shirt's filthy." Wolf glared at me.

The rest of the men had spread out through the room, but I could feel everybody's eyes on us. I didn't answer, staring at the few haphazard patches of worn yellow linoleum that remained on the kitchen floor.

"Ember, go change so we can wash your shirt."

"No."

"Why not?" he snapped.

"It's dry," I said through my teeth. This was familiar—as if we were falling into an old pattern.

"I don't care if it's dry; it's covered in *blood*."

His voice was rising, and his hands clenched at his sides; part of me felt sadistically pleased I was breaking through his calm façade. I didn't answer, remembering how ignoring him would make him madder when we were kids. Apparently, it still worked because when he spoke again, his voice was dangerous.

"Go change your shirt, or one of us will change it for you."

My gaze snapped to him, fury and panic making me feel sick. *He wouldn't.* But he was staring back at me, his expression cold and severe.

Fuck. I struggled to think of something to say.

"If you just give me some fuckin' privacy, I'll do it." I hoped they didn't hear the thread of panic lacing my voice.

Wolf's brow furrowed, but to my surprise, Scar saved me.

"That window squeaks so damn loud if she tries to get out, we'll all hear it," she murmured.

Wolf exchanged a long look with her before nodding. "Fine. But change quick, Em, or I'm coming in."

I changed faster than I'd ever changed before in my life.

After I reemerged in Scar's shirt and handed mine over to my brother, he instructed me to go sit by the fire, so I did. Sable and Kai were curled up together on the couch. Tuck was sitting in one of the chairs. I gave them all a wide berth and sat on the floor with my back to the fireplace, pulling my knees up to my chest. *Now what?* He was going to make me wait?

Apparently, he was.

I tried not to notice Sable and Kai, but they were directly in my line of sight. Kai ran his fingers through Sable's long blond hair as they kissed. When they broke apart, Kai said something that made Sable smile and kiss him again. The two men looked so in love. I fiddled with my shirtsleeve as my throat clogged with emotion—a dark, miserable envy and a deep, painful longing.

I missed Trey so much.

Wolf crouched at my side with a plate of food and a glass of water. "After you eat something, you should go to bed," he said.

I stared at him, refusing to take the plate he was offering. "And then what?"

"Then we start traveling home."

He didn't mean...not our *home...*

"What home?" I whispered.

He looked at me like I was stupid, and my hackles rose.

"*Our* home. Carth."

"What!" The word burst out of me—too loud and too panicked.

I registered Sable and Kai straightening and shifting to sit on the edge of the couch. Scar, Lee, and Tuck hovered between the living area and the kitchen, watching.

Wolf set the plate and water on the floor, glaring at me. "You're goin' back so we can finally have a trial."

A trial?

I gaped at him, a ringing sound filling my ears. He waited like he expected me to say something, but I could only choke one word out, "What?"

"We're gonna have a trial," he repeated louder as if he thought I hadn't heard him, "since you ran away last time."

I stared stupidly at him for what felt like forever. *Ran away?* When I got my mouth to move, the words came out shaky, "I did not *run away.*"

"Then where the fuck did you go?" he challenged.

"I was *exiled.*" My control was slipping. This had to be a nightmare. "I *had* a fuckin trial."

"Language, Em."

As soon as the familiar words left his mouth, a funny look crossed his face like he'd said them without thinking, but I saw red. *Language?*

"I am not a fucking *child*, Wolf."

He glared but pushed past it. "Don't lie to me, Ember. I know you manipulated a guard to let you out, and then you ran. We searched the hold for *days*. How did you get outside the wall?"

Something icy cold was overtaking the anger. "I didn't! Pa took me outside the wall and told me I was exiled!"

Wolf's body tensed at my words, his eyes narrowing sharply on my face. "Oh, and what? Then he came back and lied to the council, the Ministry, the whole hold, and *me* about it? If I'm gonna trust anyone, it's gonna be Pa and not a *murderer*."

My eyes burned, and I struggled to keep from crying. "I'm not... I'm not lyin'!" I could tell he believed what he was saying—sincerity was written all over his face. So what did that mean? That Pa *had* lied? Why would he do that? Why would he tell us two different things? None of this made any fucking sense.

"I'm not arguing with you about this," Wolf said sternly. "You're wanted for murder, and I'm turning you in."

Panic swelled. I'd been prepared to die. I'd made my peace with that, but this was worse than death.

"Wolf, I swear. I'm not lyin'." I tried to calm my voice, but it shook. "I can't go back. I was *exiled.*"

"Ember, I don't wanna hear your lies." Wolf ran a hand through his hair, weariness deepening the lines of his face.

"I'm not!" I cried, desperate, but I knew I couldn't convince him. He was dead set, and nothing could move him when Wolf dug in his heels. He was going to drag me back to Carth, and Pa would kill me. Or the Ministry would—

I felt like I was going to be sick.

"If you already think I'm guilty, why don't *you* just kill me?"

The fury that roared to life in his eyes made them look like green fire. "Because *I'm* not a kinslayer."

That horrible word hit its mark just like he meant it to. I couldn't breathe for a moment as I tried to choke everything back. The awful sound of Dune's frantic dying cries rose like a ghost from my memory, and I furiously struck back.

"No, you're just a fucking *coward,*" I hissed.

Something in him seemed to snap. He shoved me back by the shoulders, and my head smacked into the wall. Wolf's jaw flexed, but for a long moment, he didn't say anything. We'd always butted heads, but now there was an entire chasm between us—a chasm haunted with memories of Dune.

"Watch your mouth, Ember Cutler," he bit out.

He released me and stood, stalking past where Sable and Kai were now standing in front of the couch to the front door and slamming it behind him. In the sudden silence, I could feel everyone looking at me, and I ducked my head as my eyes flooded with tears. Scar followed Wolf outside, and after a moment, Sable went outside, too. Kai moved into the kitchen, speaking to Lee in a low voice. Tuck stayed in the chair, watching me.

I pulled my knees tighter against my chest and didn't move, reciting medical text inside my head at a frantic pace and trying to hold the broken pieces of myself together.

⁓

When someone tapped my boot several minutes later, I jerked upright again. Lee crouched in front of me this time. I'd been awake, but I hadn't heard him approaching. They were all so quiet it made it impossible to track them around the cabin, and it unnerved me. How the fuck were they doing that?

"You remember me?" he asked.

He knew I did, so I didn't answer, my stomach churning. No one else was in the room, and I wondered if anyone would even come if I screamed. Strands of his black hair fell across his face, escaping the bun on top of his head, and the firelight made long shadows under his high cheekbones. His almond-shaped eyes were dark, almost black, and something about them reminded me of a hawk—intelligent and missing nothing. Everything about him was sharp, from his cheekbones to his eyes to his jawline. I wasn't blind—he was handsome. All my brother's friends were attractive, which I found fucking annoying. Would it kill Wolf to find some ugly friends?

"You and your brother could be twins if you were closer in age," he finally said, "Especially with those damn eyes."

I dropped my gaze to the floor. Wolf and I both had our mom's unusual green eyes. Every so often, Juck loved to casually mention how a man had been asking around about a girl with green eyes. He'd use it as a threat to get me to cooperate, but he never asked who was hunting me or why. Somehow, that was worse. I hated not knowing how much or how little he knew. As I got older, I realized he liked reminding me I depended on him and needed him to keep me safe. He liked to work me up so he could comfort me, but I was so pathetic and starved for comfort I let him keep doing it. What I didn't understand was why none of the Reapers ever turned me in.

"You got quite the reputation in the cells," Lee continued. "Madame's Grim Reaper."

I couldn't hide the way my breath caught in my chest. His sharp eyes narrowed, sending a bolt of fear through me, but fuck, that hurt. He waited like he was expecting me to say something, and when I didn't, he looked almost disappointed.

"You should eat something."

I glanced back at the plate of food on the floor. What was the point? I was being hauled back to Carth to die. Why did they care if I ate or not?

"Were those guards dead?" I asked instead.

His brow drew together. "At the Vault? No, just tranqed."

Relief made me dizzy.

"Did you really think we killed them?" he asked, his head tilting as he regarded me.

I didn't answer, dropping my eyes. For several breaths, the only sound was the crackling fire.

"So you're, what? Twenty-two, right?"

I didn't answer.

"How long have you been at the Vault?"

I kept my eyes on a small spider crawling in and out of the cracks on the floor. Despite the cabin being ancient and worn, it was surprisingly clean and in decent condition. How long had they been staying here?

"How's that cut on your cheek?" Lee's voice was calm, as though my silence didn't bother him at all.

The sealant was still stiff on my skin where Wolf had put it. The cut ached when I thought about it, but it was barely a scratch. It'd probably be gone by—

Lee shifted toward me, and my fucked-up reflexes roared to life. I lurched backward, nearly straight into the fireplace. I probably would have at least singed my hair if he hadn't grabbed my arm and jerked me back away from the flames.

"Whoa!" he exclaimed, his eyebrows shooting up. "Easy."

I yanked my arm free and curled my shoulders inward, avoiding his eyes.

"Alright, let's get somethin' straight, right now," his voice grew stern, and my stomach dropped. "I'm not gonna hit you, Ember. None of us are ever gonna hit you."

The spider had vanished, probably scared off by my overreaction. I wished I could crawl into one of those cracks in the floor and disappear.

"Who taught you to flinch like that? Madame?"

My stomach churned, but my embarrassment was fading to anger. "Don't you have anythin' better to do?" I muttered.

When he didn't respond, I glanced up at him to see him grinning widely.

"Tell you what, I'll leave you alone if you eat something." He winked.

I immediately took a piece of dried meat and took a bite, ignoring his chuckle. True to his word, he stood and returned to the kitchen. As he began washing the dishes, I glanced around the room, carefully checking all the shadows, but it was empty except for the two of us.

I needed to make a decision. This wasn't what I expected. I'd planned to surrender if Wolf ever caught up with me. I knew that was inevitable, but I always thought he'd kill me. I never would have imagined he'd want to drag me back to Carth. I shuddered. No, I couldn't go back to Carth.

I thought of Mac smiling and flashing those dimples, of Griz helping me, of Sam teasing me and making me laugh, of Jax opening up, of Raven's gentle hands that contradicted her sharp tongue. I wanted to go home—not Carth, but the place that had become my *real* home. I wanted my *real* family. A seed of hope took root in my chest. They were underestimating me, and Wolf himself had taught me to use that to my advantage.

"Where's Wolf?" I didn't have to fake the way my voice shook.

Lee turned around, eyebrows raised. "He went for a walk."

I bit my lip, trying to look nervous.

"Why?" he added when I didn't say anything.

I willed my cheeks to redden. "I need to use the bathroom," I mumbled, and he looked uncomfortable. *Good.*

"The outhouse isn't operational. We've been using the woods."

I chewed on my lip for a second. "I really have to go."

He stared at me then heaved a heavy sigh. "Alright, c'mon."

I stood by the fireplace and waited until he shrugged on his coat and beckoned me over.

"We don't have any spare coats," he said as I neared.

"I'll be fine," I said, desperate to get outside.

He hesitated but then took my elbow and opened the door, marching us out into the dark woods. When he stopped and released my arm, I didn't move, standing close to him and staring out at the darkness.

"What's the matter?" he asked.

"Are there cougars out here?" I whispered.

"No," he said, but his voice gentled. "We haven't seen any signs of cougars."

I shuddered and saw him notice. I hoped he bought my act that I was scared to walk into the woods. I stepped forward, then stopped, turning to look back at him.

"Don't look."

A sharp laugh escaped his lips. "You think I want your brother to cut off my balls?"

"Just... don't look."

"I'm not gonna look." He sounded irritated.

I took slow, deliberately noisy steps into the woods, acting like I was trying to find some good cover.

"Don't go much further," he called.

"Don't *look!*" I hissed at him.

"I'm not looking. Gods."

I could see from his silhouette he'd turned his back to me. I took a deep breath and started walking a lot quieter, trying to mimic how they'd moved silently through the woods. He disappeared behind the trees. I breathed shallowly, my heart pounding.

"Ember?" he called, and I turned and ran.

He let out a string of curses as he charged after me, and I pushed myself even faster, my breath puffing out in white clouds. The woods were so dark, and unseen branches slapped me in the face as I ran, but I could barely feel them. He whistled the same pattern over and over, and I knew he was trying to alert the others. Moonlight weakly filtered through the trees, casting ghostly shadows on the snow-packed ground. Somehow, I managed to stay on my feet as I ran, but I could hear the crunch of his running footsteps behind me.

It wasn't long before I heard running water, even over my gasping breaths, and I went straight for it. Water was the only thing Wolf couldn't track through. A second later, I broke through the trees and came to a stumbling stop on the bank of a river. The moon put out just enough light for me to see it was swollen with snowmelt and roaring quickly past, far wilder than I knew was safe, but it was my only chance to escape my brother. I hesitated for half a second, then charged into the dark water.

I sucked in a gasp. The water was so cold it *hurt*. It surged up from my knees to my chest, and I nearly fell as my boots slipped on the rocks.

"Ember! Stop!"

I threw a terrified look over my shoulder to see Lee barreling out of the woods toward me.

I lunged forward, fighting the current. Maybe this was as deep as it went. If it stayed like this—

I took another step, and the ground dropped out from under me. My shriek was cut off by icy water rushing into my nose and mouth. I popped back up, gasping in a lungful of air. I could hear Lee yelling, but I was more focused on not drowning as the current pulled me downstream. Lee tried to run along the river, but there were fallen trees and thick brush along the edge that he had to swerve back into the woods to go around, and I lost sight of him. The water slammed me into a partially submerged rock hard enough to make my bones vibrate. I could swim okay, but I was tired, and keeping my head above water was getting harder.

I avoided another rock, but the water behind it sucked me under. For a terrifying minute, I couldn't tell which way was up as the water spun me around. I tried to fight it, but it wasn't until I gave up in panicked exhaustion that the river spit me out. I broke the surface, gasping in a lungful of air.

The current was moving fast. I couldn't see Lee anywhere. My body was so cold my limbs were growing stiff. I managed to grab hold of the next rock I nearly bashed my skull in on. I clung to it, struggling to pull myself up as the water sucked at my body. The freezing air sliced across my wet skin as I panted, arms trembling. I wouldn't be able to hold on for long.

Fuck.

I had precious few options, but this river might make the choice for me. Maybe this wouldn't be such a bad way to go. It hurt, right now, but I would eventually go numb, and I'd rather drown in frozen water than burn alive.

I thought of Mac and the crew—*my* crew—and tears filled my eyes. I didn't want to lose them. I wanted to go home.

I closed my eyes, fighting the panic by picturing Trey reaching for me. He would pull me against his chest. My arms would go around his neck, my hands in his hair, and his strong arms would hold me tight. I would breathe in his comforting scent and tip my head up to meet those brown eyes. He would smile that sunshine smile and kiss me.

I'll find you again in another lifetime. Maybe there we'll have more time. I love you, Bones.

I love you, Trey. I love you so much.

I could see him so clearly: the warmth of his eyes, the way the skin crinkled around them when he smiled, the soft waves of his brown hair. I could feel the calluses on his hands as he entwined them with mine.

"Stay with me. Please, don't leave," I begged.

Maybe it was just my imagination, but I could have sworn he whispered. "I'm *not goin' anywhere, darlin'.*"

The tears that ran down my face felt scalding hot compared to the frigid water. I held on as long as possible, but soon, the current ripped me away. I let my body go limp, eyes closed, trying to fight the instinct to survive. Then my head slammed into a rock, and there was nothing at all.

CHAPTER 3

I knew I was still alive because I felt *awful*.

My entire body shivered. I pried my eyes open to see I'd washed up against a giant fallen tree in the river. My upper body was on the tree trunk, my hands clinging to the icy branches, but the rest of me was still submerged in the freezing water. My teeth were chattering so hard I was half afraid they would break. Pulling myself onto the tree took many tries, my skin scraping across the slippery bark, but I managed to drag most of my body out of the water. I knew I needed to get up and move, find shelter, and start a fire, or I would die of hypothermia, but I couldn't seem to find the strength, mentally or physically. I was just so fucking tired. I didn't want to fight to survive anymore. I wanted Trey. I wanted to fall asleep and wake up in his arms.

The frothy whitewater continued to roar past, dragging other large branches and logs along with it. The tree I clung to rocked with the force of the water, threatening to pull it downriver. Chunks of floating ice bumped against my lower body, and a constant freezing mist sprayed my face. My legs were still in the water, and I couldn't feel them at all.

You're a river, Bones.

My lips twitched. I doubted anyone else would find that as funny as I did.

I drifted in and out of consciousness, and the sky lightened. My wet clothing and hair had frozen stiff. I wasn't shivering anymore, and I was pretty sure that was a sign death was coming. That knowledge didn't bring any fear, though—just relief that soon quiet darkness would embrace me.

Wait for me, Trey. Please take me with you.

The sun had risen when a strange noise cut through the fog. I moved my eyes just enough to see Lee running down the bank toward me. His lips were moving, but the sound was all garbled. He didn't hesitate before charging into the water and swimming out to me.

"No," I croaked in a hoarse whisper. "No!"

He ignored me, climbing onto the tree and easily balancing on the slippery bark. He stood over my body and began to pry my fingers from the tree branch. I tried to cling to it, but my body was a numb, frozen prison.

"Ember, let go!" I realized he was shouting at me.

"N-n-no," I choked out through chattering teeth, but the branch slid through my fingers, and both of us tumbled off the slippery log and into the water. I tensed in anticipation of the painful cold, but I couldn't feel *anything*. I tried to kick my legs to get back to the surface, but my body barely moved, and I just kept sinking until a hand snagged my arm and jerked me up. I broke the surface, gasping. Lee grabbed my face, trying to keep it above water. His eyes bored into me.

"Ember! Are you—"

He let out a pained grunt as the rapids slammed him into a rock, and we both went under again. Despite the water trying to rip us apart, he didn't let go of my arm. He dragged me to the surface again, and I blinked water from my eyes, my teeth chattering uncontrollably.

"I got you," he promised as he wrapped an arm under my chin and began to swim with the other.

I stared at the cloudy sky as he towed me along on my back, feeling like I was floating out of my numb body. I could hear him taking deep, controlled breaths as he moved through the water. As soon as he could touch the bottom, he stood and hauled me into his arms, cradling me against his chest. Water streamed from both of us as he took careful steps toward the shore.

"Ember, can you hear me?" he asked, his voice steady but laced with urgency.

I stared up at him, shivering hard. Strands of his black hair clung to his face, water dripping from his chin. He met my eyes, and his jaw clenched.

"Stay awake," he ordered.

He stumbled onto a gravel bar along the side of the river and dropped to his knees with a groan. He laid me down, his fingers pressing against my neck for a pulse. I still couldn't feel my body, and exhaustion crashed over me, my eyelids fluttering shut.

"Ember!" He might have gripped my chin. "Stay awake!"

I couldn't get my eyes back open, and he swore, gathering me into his arms again.

"Don't you dare fuckin' die on me," he growled, and then he started running.

Despite my head bouncing against his chest, I drifted away.

ෙ

I woke up to darkness. I was lying on a cold rock floor, still shivering, but I couldn't see *anything*. For a terrified moment, I wondered if I was still in that awful cell under the watchtower, but then light flared, blinding me. I blinked, trying to get my eyes to adjust, and focused on Lee's face as he coaxed a small fire to life. I scanned our surroundings, but all I could see was rock. Were we in a fucking *cave?*

Lee stood and grabbed a pack from the cave floor. As the fire illuminated the cave more, I saw several packs and supplies. This wasn't just a random cave; it was a hideout or—

My thoughts cut off as Lee started stripping off his wet clothes. He'd turned his back to me, but I stared at his lean, muscled body that emerged. He was more slender than Wolf and less rugged, more like the people in a troupe of performers who had traveled with the Reapers once. Black tattoos covered his back and arms—jagged black strokes that wrapped around his arms and twisted across his back in a fluid, unpredictable design. It looked more like someone had splashed ink across his back than any tattoo I'd ever seen.

A wet slap echoed as his dripping clothes fell heavily to the floor, reminding me how ice-cold and soaked my own clothing was. I might have been scared of his intentions as he stripped naked, but he dressed as quickly as he undressed, moving at a speed that was difficult to follow. As he buttoned up his shirt, he turned around and caught me staring at him, and a corner of his mouth twitched up; I couldn't find the energy to care.

The parts of my body I could feel burned with cold, while the rest felt like heavy weights attached to me. I tried to curl my stiff fingers, but they simply twitched.

Lee grabbed something from the pack and moved around the fire to kneel beside me.

"Alright, here's the deal," he said. "We gotta get you out of those wet clothes so you don't freeze to death."

A stab of panic went through me.

"I'm gonna help you," he continued, "'cause there's no way you can do it yourself."

"No," I croaked.

"If it makes you feel any better, Wolf is gonna beat the shit out of me for all of this."

"No." My voice sounded so *weak*.

"What the fuck did you think was gonna happen when you went charging into a half-frozen river?" His voice grew sharper.

I attempted to move away, fear making my head swim, but all of me was numb and exhausted, and I shivered so hard it felt like I was seizing. He took my arm and pulled me upright, which made the room tilt and spin as pain stabbed through my head. When I could focus again, he was undoing the buttons at the bottom of Scar's shirt, and panic swallowed me whole.

"No!"

It felt like waking up after being drugged with a narc, and that realization did not help. I tried to smack his hands away from me, but my body moved sluggishly. Still, I managed to make it just difficult enough that he couldn't hold onto the buttons.

"Ember, stop. I'm trying to help you."

I didn't answer, putting all my energy into forcing my numb limbs to move. He suddenly released my shirt and grabbed my face with both hands, forcing me to meet his gaze. He was grimacing like he was in physical pain.

"I am not going to hurt you!"

"Stop!"

"You are gonna die of hypothermia if you stay in these wet clothes."

I didn't fucking care. My brain was trying to drag me back to Juck's tent in the desert. He released my face, and I almost fell over trying to get away.

"Look," he held up a man's flannel shirt. "I got you some of my clothes. I'm gonna help you get dressed, that's it, I swear."

I managed to shift backward a little, but he caught my arm. I tried to jerk free, my head swimming as I gasped in frantic breaths.

"Gods, Ember, *please* help me out here," he said in a low voice.

"Don't touch me," I choked out.

"If it wasn't a matter of literal life and death, I wouldn't." Pain flashed through his eyes, but I saw the resolve harden over his face. "But I'm not gonna let you die."

"No!"

"I'm sorry," he said, and then he yanked me toward him.

I tried to fight, but my weak attempts were laughable. Juck's face swam in my vision. He worked Scar's pants off my hips, and I started crying—furious and helpless tears tumbling down my face.

"Please stop!" I begged, fighting him every inch of the way. "I'm sorry! I'm sorry!"

He didn't respond, his jaw tight as he got my pants off and threw them to the side. The cold rock burned against my bare skin, and for a moment, I thought I'd be sick from the panic, but he quickly slid a pair of men's undergarments onto my body. The panic receded slightly, but I renewed my efforts to escape when he reached for the shirt buttons again.

"Ember!" he snapped. "Stop it. I am not going to hurt you."

"Please don't... don't do this!" I gasped out, trying to shove him away.

"Gods-fuckin-damnit," he growled.

He grabbed my arm and hauled me into his lap, my back against his chest. One arm wrapped around my torso, pinning my arms to my sides, and his free hand started unbuttoning the shirt. I tried to thrash against his grip, but he was far stronger than me. He got the shirt unbuttoned and began pulling it off my shoulders.

"No!" I sobbed.

"Ember, just let me—" his voice cut off, and his body went still behind me.

I tried again to jerk away, and for a moment, I thought I was successful, but then I realized he was just moving with me so he could turn my back toward the light of the fire. His fingertips brushed across the scarred skin of my upper shoulders, and I went rigid.

"What are these?" he asked in a quiet, dangerous voice.

I squeezed my eyes shut, trying to hunch forward as much as

possible. He hadn't noticed the brand on my chest yet. My breath came in sharp, gasping sobs, and my body shivered.

"Fuck, okay, okay, here." He pulled my wet shirt off but stalled as the rest of my back was revealed. He swore under his breath, then grabbed his warm flannel shirt and started dressing me in it.

I shoved my arms into the sleeves, cooperating in my desperation to get the shirt on as fast as possible. I still sat in his lap, giving him a perfect view of my back, but at least he couldn't see my front. He helped pull the shirt over my shoulders and reached around me to button it up. I readied myself to lunge away when he finished buttoning, but he moved quickly, bundling us both in a blanket. I tried to push away, but he just pulled the blanket tight, wrapping both of his arms around my torso and trapping me against his body.

Squirming only made his arms tighten further, and fuck, I couldn't breathe. I was back in Juck's tent, unable to move, panic spilling into my lungs and drowning me.

"I'm just tryin' to warm you up." His warm breath ghosted over my neck, making my skin break out in goosebumps. "I'm not gonna hurt you, Ember, I swear."

I couldn't answer him. The fire started to swim in my vision as I grew lightheaded from my short gasps of air.

"It's okay," he murmured. "It's okay, Ember, you're safe. Just try to breathe."

ço

I slowly came back to myself. I was lying on my side, and just a few feet away a fire had died to smoldering embers. I was wrapped up in a blanket—

The blanket shifted, and I realized I was *also* wrapped up in another body.

I tensed in alarm, and the arms holding me released. I rolled onto my back and stared at Lee's face above mine. He'd propped himself up on one hand resting on the blanket next to my head.

"It's okay, you passed out." He smiled, but it looked strained. "That tends to happen when you don't breathe."

I just stared at him. My brain felt sluggish, and my body felt heavy but different from the cold. This felt—*fuck*—this felt like I was *sick*.

"Ember?" His brow furrowed.

Was this the beginning of a burnout fever? Why would I get a burnout fever? I hadn't healed—

It hit me like a blow to the gut—the river. My powers must have worked overtime to keep me from freezing to death. I closed my eyes, feeling so fucking defeated. I couldn't even die right.

"You don't have to talk to me, but can you just nod or shake your head or somethin' so I know you can hear me?"

"Fuck you," I muttered without opening my eyes.

"Wow," he sounded *amused,* "you're just as grateful as your brother when someone saves your life."

I rolled back to my side, staring at the fire. I wished he'd stop comparing me to my brother. My brother thought I'd *run away.* He thought the past twelve years meant *nothing.* He thought I hadn't even begun to atone for Dune's death.

"I'm pretty sure you have blood in your hair. Did you hit your head in the river?"

The back of my head *was* throbbing, but I just didn't care.

"C'mon, Ember, please?"

I refused to acknowledge him, staring numbly into the fire.

Lee let out a long-suffering sigh. "You're gonna make me do everything the hard way, aren't you?" When I still didn't answer, he shifted and grabbed my upper arm, pulling me upright. "Alright, the hard way it is."

The movement made my head spin and throb, and when he released my arm, I swayed as the room tilted. He quickly grabbed me again.

"You're probably concussed, Here, c'mere." He tugged me backward between his legs, lifted my arms, and placed them on top of his raised knees. "You can hold onto me if that helps."

I didn't want to, but I also didn't want to faceplant into the rocky floor, so I clung to his knees as the room spun. His hands gripped my head and tilted it down, his fingers searching through my hair. I sucked in a breath when his fingers pressed right at the source of the pain radiating through my head. He parted my hair carefully to look at it.

"Shit, yeah, you got a good-sized lump here, but it's not bleeding anymore." He paused, then muttered, "Who knows how much blood you lost, though."

His hands moved through my hair again, and I felt him pause on the large scar on my temple from the mercs. He tilted my head to the side to see the scar that disappeared into my hair, gently tracing the jagged line with his finger.

"What happened here?"

"Nothin'," I muttered.

"Oh, so you *are* talking to me!"

Something about the way he said it reminded me of Sam, and grief washed over me.

"This is a pretty big scar for nothing."

I was not about to explain my scars to this stranger. "It's *nothing*," I said sharper, jerking my head out of his hands and facing forward again.

"Lemme guess, those scars on your back are nothing, too?"

My spine locked up as the memory of him touching my scarred back flashed back to me. I tried to remember what else he'd seen, but my memories were hazy and fragmented. I waited for him to ask about the brand with my heart in my throat.

"If I had to guess, I'd say those are scars from a whip," he said with an edge to his voice.

I didn't answer.

"And they're not that old, either."

I released his knees to tuck my trembling hands into my lap.

"Did Madame do that to you?" When I still didn't say anything, he spoke again, his voice sharper. "You know your brother is not gonna let you get away with not answering these questions."

Gods, that was why I didn't want him to fucking know. I hadn't planned for any of this. I was supposed to be too dead to answer questions. Lee must not have seen the brand, though. I doubted he'd stay quiet about it if he had.

"Is that why you didn't want to change in front of Scar?"

The familiar smell of blood hit me, and I chased the distraction. I looked at my bare legs, noting the numerous bruises and scrapes covering my skin from banging into rocks in the river. I wasn't bleeding, though. Where was it coming from? I glanced at Lee's legs and realized he had a messy bandage around one calf. My fingers twitched with the urge to fix it. Had he even cleaned the wound? No, it didn't matter. I didn't care. I was not going to *ask—*

"What happened to your leg?"

"Oh no!" He barked a laugh. "You don't get to refuse to answer my questions and then ask me one."

"I answered your fuckin' question," I snapped.

"You answered *one* by tellin' me you wouldn't answer it."

He sounded annoyed but also amused again, and the combination infuriated me for some reason.

"Fine," I growled at him, "let it get infected and gangrenous from that shitty-ass bandaging job you did, but when you lose your whole fuckin' leg, don't come crying to me."

A short silence fell.

"So she *is* still in there."

"What?" I snapped, twisting to look at him.

He grinned at me. "The Ember I've heard so much about."

I turned back around, hoping he hadn't seen the pain flash across my face. "I'm not her."

"So, who are you, then?"

Good fucking question.

I shivered, and dread filled me. I could feel the fever creeping closer. I had just minutes before I was fucking delirious. Should I warn him? My hands trembled, and I balled them into fists on my lap. I would be at his mercy, incapacitated. Who knew what he might do?

I needed to get some space. I started trying to scoot out from between his legs, but he caught my arm, and I cringed.

"I'm not gonna hurt you, Ember," he said, his voice softening.

"Stop calling me that," I snapped, trying to wrench free.

"Calling you what? Your name?"

"That's not my name."

"Okay, so what *is* your name?" He raised an eyebrow and waited.

I looked away. I didn't know what to tell him. All I knew was that Ember died in the desert when she was ten years old. The sun, wind, and predators peeled off her flesh until all that was left was Bones, but Bones wasn't me, either.

I never told Trey my real name. I never got to hear him say my real name with reverence, desire, and love. He gave me all of him, and I never trusted him with that final piece of me. He died without knowing who I really was. The tears I'd been fighting started rolling down my face.

"I have to call you something. What do you want me to call you? Freckles?"

I didn't care.

"Here, look at me." Lee's voice sounded like he was speaking in a tunnel. "I need to make sure you don't have a concussion."

I closed my eyes. *I never even told him my real name.*

"Freckles? Hey, what's wrong?"

I clenched my jaw, trying to keep my teeth from chattering. The cold ached in my bones. He pulled me around to face him, and my eyes opened again. He leaned in close to me, frowning, and I stared at his dark brown eyes. They weren't brown like Trey's eyes or brown like Griz's eyes. I blinked as my vision blurred with tears, trying to bring them into focus.

I jumped when his fingers connected with my face, and his eyebrows rose, but he just slowly wiped away the tears spilling out of my eyes. His frown deepened, and he moved his hand to my forehead.

"Fuck, you are burnin' up," he muttered.

My eyeballs felt hot and dry as sandpaper. His hands wrapped around my upper arms again and moved my body, pulling me into his lap and wrapping the blanket around both of us again. I wanted to shove him away, but I was so cold, and he was so warm. My traitorous body curled into him, desperately seeking his warmth.

"Those damn eyes," he muttered, seemingly to himself.

There was something I was going to tell him, wasn't there? Or was it something I *wasn't* going to tell him?

It was something important, something I needed to remember, but my eyes drifted shut.

CHAPTER 4

I opened my eyes and found myself in Trey's arms.

I tilted my head up to look at him, my brow furrowing. He was awake, staring back at me. He was sitting against a rock wall and holding me against his chest. My brain struggled to remember what just happened as my teeth chattered.

"You're here," I whispered.

"I'm here," he said.

Emotion overwhelmed me, filling my eyes and sliding down my cheeks. His eyes widened in alarm.

"What's wrong?" he asked.

"I thought—" My voice broke.

His eyebrows drew together in confusion.

"Am I dead?" I asked.

"No," he seemed to force a slight smile, "you're not dead."

My head throbbed as I shivered. I couldn't *remember*.

"It's ok, Freckles," he murmured. "You have a fever."

I managed to get an arm free and reached up to touch his face. He went still, watching me with narrowed eyes. I cupped his face, my thumb stroking across his sharp cheekbone. Something nagged at the back of my mind. How was he here? He didn't move, his eyes fixed on my face as my fingers trailed across his skin before sliding into his hair. It was pulled back, but the wild strands that had escaped felt...wrong. I frowned, but he caught my wrist and pulled my hand away.

"Who am I?" he asked.

I stared at him, trying to wrap my head around that strange question.

"Who are you seeing?" he rephrased, but that wasn't any better.

"Please don't leave." My voice shook.

"I'm not leaving."

"I can't…I can't do this without you." Panic was building in my chest.

"You don't have to."

"No, Trey, you don't understand." More tears slid down my face. "I *can't.* I can't do it. I don't *want* to do it."

He took the blanket in his hand and gently wiped the tears from my face. "I'm not Trey," he murmured. "I'm Lee. I'm your brother's friend."

Terror sliced me into tiny pieces, my breath coming faster. "My brother?"

"Wolf." He watched me carefully as he said it, and I knew I was failing to hide the fear on my face.

"Wolf's here?" I whispered, my voice shaking.

"Well, not here in this cave, but yes."

All of me was shaking, now. "Don't let him see you."

"Why?"

"I can't…I can't watch him hurt you."

"He's not gonna hurt anyone," he said, his brow furrowed.

I pushed away, and he released me, but when I started trying to get to my feet, he caught my arm again.

"Where are you going?" he asked.

"We gotta get the kids somewhere safe." The fear was making me nauseous.

"What kids? Your brother would never hurt a kid."

"It might not be enough." I struggled to focus. This was important.

"What might not be enough?"

"Killin' me." My voice wobbled.

"Freckles, he's not gonna kill you, and he'd never hurt a kid."

"You don't know that," I argued, trying to pull my arm free.

"I've spent the past ten years with him, so I think I can pretty confidently say I do."

I blinked at him in confusion, and he stared back at me. His warm brown eyes looked troubled, and I wanted to see them glowing with sunshine again. I shivered, my teeth clattering together.

"C'mere," he said softly, tugging on my arm.

I let him pull me back into his lap and wrap me in his arms again. I tried to remember what we'd just been arguing about, but it was gone.

"Why do you think Wolf is gonna kill you?" he asked in a soft voice.

"Pa said so," I whispered, trying to press even closer against him as chills wracked my body.

"What'd your Pa say?"

"He said Wolf was gonna come after me and tear me apart." My whispered voice shook. "He said Wolf wants me dead."

He stared at me, studying my face without a word.

"Please, Trey, I can't…if something happens to you—" A sob cut me off.

"Hey," he slid his hands into my damp, tangled hair to grip the sides of my head and tilted my face up to meet his eyes, "nothin' is gonna happen to me."

"Please don't leave me," I sobbed. "Don't leave me alone. I can't do this. I can't…"

"I'm not gonna leave, Freckles," he murmured. "I promise."

I wrapped my arms tightly around his neck, clinging to him as I cried. He was right here, so why did it feel like my heart was breaking?

He hesitated momentarily before wrapping me in his arms and pulling me tighter against his chest. A burst of chills made me shake so hard it felt like my brain rattled. The pain that stabbed through my head was enough to make me suck in a breath and squeeze my eyes shut.

"You're not alone," he said into my hair. "You're not alone, Freckles."

"I'm always alone," I choked out, "and I hate it."

"Not anymore," he said in a low voice.

I shivered and pressed my face against his neck, trying to soak up his warmth. A hand pressed against my forehead again.

"Fuck," he muttered. "Godsdamnit."

He shifted me over, and cold air filled the space his warm body had occupied. I shivered, trying to focus in the dim light. Who…where was I?

"Don't leave," I whimpered.

"I'm not leaving. I'm getting some snow," a male voice answered.

"What?" I mumbled, trying to focus.

A body appeared at my side, startling me, and my lungs turned to stone when I met Juck's gaze. I tried to make myself smaller as I studied his face. What mood was he in? If I didn't get it right, I'd pay for it.

"What's the matter?" he asked.

"Nothin'," I whispered, dropping my eyes. "I'm sorry."

"Why are you apologizin'?"

Fuck, this was a trap. I didn't know. What had I done? I couldn't remember.

"I don't...I didn't mean to," I tried, my voice shaking.

I didn't look at his face, careful to keep my eyes down, but I tried to keep an eye on him in my peripheral vision. His hand moved toward me, and I braced myself for the blow.

"Ember, I am not gonna hurt you."

Fear sizzled down my spine. He knew my name? How did he know my name? Did I tell—

Something cold pressed against my face, and I jerked away.

"I know it's cold," he said, "but we gotta bring your fever down."

Something was wrong with me. What was wrong with me? Fuck, was he going to drug me again?

"I'm fine," I pleaded. "I don't need, please don't—" My gaze searched our surroundings for the small lockbox he kept the narcs in. "Please don't drug me. Please. I swear I'm fine. It doesn't hurt that bad."

Icy cold pressed against my face again, and I tried to jerk away, but I couldn't move. I was trapped.

"Please," I begged, tears gathering in my eyes, "please don't drug me."

"I'm not gonna drug you," he snapped.

Oh fuck, now he was mad.

"I'm sorry. I'm s-sorry," I whispered, squeezing my eyes shut.

The painful cold pressed against the side of my neck, and I cringed.

"I'm just tryin' to bring your fever down," he said in a gentle voice that made me more scared. "I'm not gonna hurt you, Freckles."

I tried to stay alert as Wolf taught me, but a hot, heavy blanket suffocated my mind. I tried to speak and must have gotten words out because someone answered, but I couldn't understand it. My body shivered, and I couldn't make it stop. I needed to make it stop. I needed to keep myself under control.

"I don't want...I don't..." I blinked at the face above me. Words had been slipping off my tongue, but I had absolutely no idea what I'd been saying.

"Hi," the man said.

I knew him, but I couldn't remember how or why. I furrowed my brow.

"I'm Lee." One side of his mouth lifted in a crooked smile.

I frowned in confusion. I was lying on the hard floor, and he seemed to have been lying beside me. Who the fuck was Lee?

"I'm the guy tryin' to keep you alive."

That didn't make any sense.

"It's a much harder job than I expected." His tone was teasing, but his eyes looked worried.

"Am I supposed to feel sorry for you?" I mumbled, annoyed. Was I dreaming?

He blinked, his eyebrows lifting, and then grinned. "Yeah, you are."

My eyelids were so heavy, but I needed to figure this out. I knew him. How did I know him?

"Did you know that man in the cell?" Mac's furious voice ran through my head.

"You were in the cell," I whispered.

"Yep."

There was more, but it danced on the edge of my memory, taunting me. He was in the cell—the cell under the watchtower.

"Why...why were you..." My voice trailed off, my mind spinning.

"I was lookin' for you," he said lightly.

My body went rigid. He was looking for me because he was with...

"Where's Wolf?"

"Hopefully, on his way here," he paused, and a shadow passed over his expression, "though he's probably plotting the most painful way to kill me."

I tried to swallow, but my throat was so dry. "Water?"

"You didn't get enough of it in the river?" he teased, but he stretched to grab something and then handed me a bottle of water.

I tried to sit, but my body was so fucking heavy. He maneuvered me upright, but the movement made the room spin, and my head erupted in pain. I squeezed my eyes shut, wincing.

"You ok?"

I couldn't answer, trying to breathe through the pain in my head. The rock floor was freezing on my bare legs. A hand pressed against my forehead and my eyes popped back open.

"Fuck, you're *still* burning up," he muttered. "I need to get you back to the cabin, but it'll take way too long on foot. Hopefully, your brother gets his head out of his ass, sees the smoke, and figures out where we are."

"How long has it been?" I asked, bringing the water bottle to my lips.

"Been almost a day and a half."

My hand shook, spilling water down my chin.

"Oh, here, I have—"

I glanced at him when his voice cut off, but he was staring at my chest. I looked down, my stomach twisting in panic as I realized the shirt I wore had gaped open, revealing the top of the brand. I moved to yank it closed, but he moved faster and caught my wrist.

"What is that?"

All the lightheartedness had evaporated from his voice, and my lungs seized. I tried to pull my hand away, but his grip tightened. Before I could react, he reached out with his free hand and shifted my shirt. I braced myself, but he just stared, a muscle in his jaw flexing. He dropped his hand, easily undoing another button one-handed, and pulled my shirt open more, revealing the entire hideous mark while I sat there, frozen.

"What is this?" he demanded in a low voice, meeting my eyes again.

I couldn't answer, my heart thundering in my chest. He studied me with his sharp eyes, his hand still locked around my wrist. He looked back at the scar, and I flinched when his fingertips traced the rough, raised skin.

"Is this a 'J'?"

A wave of dizziness washed over me.

"Did Madame do this to you?"

"Please." The word bubbled out of me.

He quieted and studied my face, his jaw clenched tight.

"Don't tell him," I begged in a whisper.

His eyebrows rose, and his voice was full of disbelief as he replied, "What?"

"Please, Lee." I couldn't explain better, but the thought of Wolf seeing the brand made me feel sick. I didn't want him to see just how broken and ruined I was. He would have questions, just like Lee, just like Trey, and I couldn't tell him about all the horrible things I'd experienced or all the awful things I'd done to other people.

"There's no way in fuck I'm keeping this a secret from my best friend about his little sister."

I closed my eyes in defeat and dread, shivering hard. He sighed heavily and pulled me back into his lap. I went stiff as a board against his chest as he wrapped the blanket tightly around both of us again.

"How the fuck did you survive in that river?" he muttered, and I realized his fingertips were drifting across my ribs, slowly tracing them over my shirt. "You've got no fat on your bones."

I tipped my head forward so my hair fell across my face like a curtain, hiding behind it.

"Wolf better bring Sable," he continued. "I need him to stitch up my leg before I lose it as you so kindly predicted."

That caught my attention. I didn't remember saying anything about his leg. I didn't remember he was injured at all. I bit my lip as my power fluttered—weak but alive. My brain felt like it was full of thick mud, but I knew one thing for sure: I couldn't heal him because Wolf could *not* know about my power.

My fingertips tingled. What if he was really hurt?

I can't.

What if I just checked? I could check. He wouldn't even know. My fingertips found a slice of bare skin between his pants and his shirt. He jumped when I touched him but simply muttered something about cold hands.

I tried to focus on letting a tiny bit of my power out, the thinnest little thread that flowed down to his leg. I closed my eyes, and I could *see* it in my mind. The long laceration in his shin was deep and still bleeding. It needed stitches, but more urgently, my powers flared around where an infection was taking root.

Fuck.

There was no running water in this cave—no way to clean the wound like it needed.

I can't.

It might even need to be packed.

I can't.

I'd seen people lose limbs to infection. I'd sawed through bone myself on two separate occasions. It was horrible.

He'll tell Wolf.

It's what Trey would've done.

My brain had no answer to that.

So, I kept letting my power out as slowly as possible to keep him from noticing. I'd never purposefully healed a wound slowly before. It hurt, but I couldn't tell if it was from holding back most of my power or if I was still exhausted from the river. It seemed to take a long time, and my nose started bleeding halfway through, soaking into his shirt where my face was pressed against his chest, but finally, the wound closed without him noticing. I withdrew my hand and let my eyes close in relief.

Stupid.

I couldn't tell if my brain meant me or him, but either way, it was probably right.

CHAPTER 5

I didn't realize I'd fallen asleep until Lee startled me awake when he whistled loudly. An answering whistle sounded, but the rocky ceiling of the cave was spinning, and I couldn't keep my eyelids open.

"What the fuck? Are you bleeding?" I heard Lee demand, his voice distorted.

"I'm gonna kill you," a new voice growled.

"Wolf, later!" a feminine voice snapped.

"I swear she was not bleeding an hour ago," Lee said.

"Where the fuck are her clothes?"

"She went fuckin' charging into the river! I had to get her into something dry!"

Hands maneuvered me onto my back, and I tried to focus, but I couldn't get my eyes to open. I shook with full body chills and cool fingers pressed against my nose and face.

"Looks like it was just a bloody nose, but she's burning up," a low voice said.

"She's been burning up for fuckin' hours. I tried cooling her down with some snowpacks."

"We need to get her back to the cabin as fast as possible."

"Wrap her in that blanket. I'll ride the horse with her."

Even with my eyes closed, the room spun as they bundled me like an infant. The next thing I knew, I was on a horse, galloping through the woods. I tried to focus on who held me, but everything faded away.

෨

I opened my eyes as Wolf carried me to the cabin fireplace while sharply barking orders. His lips pressed together in a flat line, and his eyes flashed as he unwrapped the damp, muddy blanket around me. I shivered hard, my teeth chattering, and barely remembered to cling to the collar of Lee's shirt, ensuring it stayed closed. Kai appeared with a fresh blanket, and the two of them wrapped it around me while Tuck hovered behind them.

"What happened?" Kai asked.

"She jumped in the river," Wolf snarled. "They were at the bolthole."

"Where are the others?" Tuck frowned.

"Coming on foot."

"Was freezing to death part of your genius escape plan?" Kai asked me, but I ignored him.

"Is that her blood?" Tuck gestured to my face.

"Sable said it was from her nose, but it stopped. She's fuckin' burning up."

Kai reached out to me, and I flinched away. He withdrew his hand, eyes narrowing.

"I'm just tryin' to check your temperature," he said.

I closed my eyes. Something happened, but I couldn't quite remember what it was. Something about a cave—

A hand pressed against my forehead, and I jumped.

"Yeah, she's way too hot. Maybe we should take the blanket off."

"I'm pretty sure she's only wearing one of Lee's shirts," Wolf growled.

A short silence fell.

"So, how bad is this gonna be?" Tuck asked dryly. "Bad like The Cedars or bad like Jackson?"

"I might actually kill him this time," Wolf muttered.

"You want some cool washcloths or something?"

"Yeah, probably."

The room spun again as they moved me, making my stomach lurch with nausea. I sucked in a frantic breath through my nose, trying not to be sick. When everything settled enough that I felt safe opening my eyes, I realized I lay on the couch, and Wolf sat beside me, studying my face. It looked like there was a storm raging in his green eyes. For a long time, the two of us stared at each other.

"You grew up," I mumbled.

"Yeah, so did you."

"Don't tell him." Fear seized my lungs, making it hard to breathe.

"Don't tell who?"

I blinked in confusion. What was I talking about? "I dunno."

"It's ok, Em. You're sick."

"I don't get sick."

"This is why you shouldn't jump in freezing rivers," he snapped. "What were you thinking? You almost fuckin' *died*."

"Trey…" I frowned, panic spiking in my chest. "Where's Trey?"

"Who's Trey?"

"Please." I opened my eyes, growing more and more panicked. "I can't…I can't do this. I need him!"

Someone murmured something I couldn't make out, and he glanced at them before returning to me.

"Ok." He reached out and smoothed my hair back from my face. "Ok, I'll find Trey."

I calmed down as I stared at him, my brain struggling to piece together where I was. "You look like my brother."

A corner of his mouth ticked up. "I *am* your brother."

I frowned. "No, my brother wants to kill me."

The pain in his eyes was so sharp. "I don't want to kill you, Emmy."

My lips were so dry. "Don't…don't…" There was something important I was forgetting. I frowned, trying to think straight. It felt like my heart was pounding inside my head. "Where am I?"

"You're safe," he murmured.

Something ice cold touched my forehead, and I cringed.

"Hold still," Kai grumbled. "We need to bring your fever down."

"The fever's back?" I stared at them in horror before attempting to sit. "I need to go to work."

"Whoa." Wolf pushed me back down by the shoulders. "You don't need to go anywhere."

"No, I have to…people are sick. Where are the kids?" I tried to sit again, struggling against his hold.

"What kids?" Wolf asked.

"No one is sick. Just you," Kai said.

"No, I don't…I gotta go check…I have to check…"

"Emmy, you need to lay and rest," a stern voice said.

"I will after this next one, Mac, I promise," I mumbled, trying to push the hands holding my shoulders down off me, even as my eyes closed. "I can do one more."

"You're done," that stern voice said.

"Please get Trey, please. I need…" My voice trailed off as sleep claimed me.

☙

Angry voices cut through the daze I was in.

"—one good reason why I shouldn't."

"Wolf, what the fuck do you think I should've done differently?"

"You never should've taken her into the woods in the first place!"

"Wolf," a new voice said in a stern tone.

"Are you seriously siding with him?"

"What was he supposed to do, let her piss her pants? I think he did the best he could with the information he had, and that's all any of us can do." The voice was feminine and fierce. "He saved her life."

"I *told* you not to trust her!"

"Look, I know I fucked up, alright, but I gotta—"

"She *lies,* and she *runs.* You knew that!"

"Wolf, shut up a godsdamned minute! I gotta tell you something important."

I cracked my eyelids open. Dark, blurry forms were moving around the room by the light of the fireplace. I tried to track them, but the movement made me dizzy and nauseous.

"*What,* Lee?"

"She said your dad told her you were gonna hunt her down and kill her."

The energy in the room shifted in a way that made me try to shrink into the couch.

"What did I just say?" Wolf sounded furious. "You can't trust her."

"I don't think she was lyin', man. She wasn't even talking to *me*. She was so delirious she thought I was someone named Trey, and she kept begging me to hide so you wouldn't kill me, too."

"Trey?" someone asked softly. "Isn't that who she was asking for earlier?"

Someone muttered something too quiet to make out.

"There's more. She's got huge scars all over her back, scars like someone whipped her. And she's got a fucking 'J' burned into the skin on her chest. That's why she didn't want to change her shirt in front of Scar earlier. 'Cause someone fuckin' *branded* her."

The abrupt silence crackled with tension. Panic built under my skin, the pressure almost unbearable.

"Somethin's not right here."

"Lee, she's not—"

"No, don't give me that bullshit. I *know* you feel it, too. It's why you've been in such a pissy mood since we got her. None of this is addin' up. I'm not sayin' she's innocent. I'm just sayin' somethin' is not right."

"She's sort of awake," someone said.

"Ember?"

I tried to open my eyes, but my eyelids were so heavy.

"Can I look at the scar on your chest?"

I pried my eyes open with the burst of fear and adrenaline that question gave me. The one with the long blond hair was leaning over me, his face grave.

"My name is Sable," he said. "I'm a healer."

"Don't," my lips formed the word, but no sound came out.

"I just want to make sure you're alright."

"Don't," I tried again, and my voice rasped to life.

"I'm not going to hurt you."

"No."

He glanced at someone I couldn't see, his eyebrows drawing together. A new face appeared above me, and it took me a few seconds to realize it was Lee.

"Hey, Freckles," he smiled, but it seemed strained. "Can you let Sable take a look at that scar?"

I stared at him.

"C'mon, it'll just take a second. Then you can punch me."

Someone muttered something I couldn't make out, and Lee

winced.

"Alright, fine, you gotta let Wolf work me over first, but I'm sure he'll give you a turn eventually."

I continued to stare at him. The vague fragments of memory flitting through my head were a conflicting mix of fear and something like comfort.

"You back to not talkin' to me? Not even gonna swear at me?"

I flicked my eyes to Sable again as anxiety spiked, and I could see the determination in his eyes. My stomach churned with nausea, and I clutched the blanket to my chest with shaking hands.

"Ember, let him look," Wolf spoke up from where he stood, arms crossed over his chest. His eyes looked angry.

This just kept getting fucking worse, and I knew I wouldn't be able to stop them. Somehow, I'd forgotten how awful it felt to be so alone and helpless. I wished Wolf would have found me six months ago when I had all this fucking emotion locked down and under control. I used to be strong and resilient. Now I was a bird on the ground, my wings torn from me—broken.

"Ember, just let Sable look. He's a healer."

I hated not being physically strong enough to keep people from touching me. My breath started coming faster, and my heart felt like it pounded with a single word: *trapped, trapped, trapped.* A hand landed on my shoulder, and I tried to flinch away, but the fingers tightened, holding me still. My fragile hold on my sanity seemed to snap, and my mind *jerked* away in response, tumbling down a worn and familiar path. I folded into myself like a paper map, buckling on creased edges again and again until I was small and insignificant—until I was *gone.*

My eyes opened, but it was like being underwater and looking up at the distorted surface. My head was quiet and empty. It didn't matter what happened to my body now because I wasn't there.

"Ember?" a muffled voice asked.

"What's wrong?"

"I'm not sure, but she's stopped responding. Look at her pupils."

A bright light shone in my eyes, but I didn't flinch. This place was comforting in a strange way—familiar. More importantly, it was *safe.* Just like always, the words from medical textbooks surfaced as though they'd been waiting for me. They were the ropes I clung to, keeping myself anchored here when the outside world threatened to pull me out.

The sequential steps in evaluating lacerations are first to find and treat serious associated injuries, obtain hemostasis, and look for damage to underlying structures, I recited in my head.

Vaguely, I could hear people calling my name and speaking around me, but I knew better than to respond.

Actively bleeding wounds require hemostasis before evaluation. Hemostasis is best obtained by direct pressure and, when possible, elevation. Clamping bleeding vessels with instruments is generally avoided because of the possibility of damaging adjacent nerves.

"I don't like this," Sable's voice filtered through.

Careful and temporary placement of a proximal tourniquet—

"What's happening?" My brother's voice sliced through the ropes I clung to, making me float dangerously close to the surface again. "Why is she...*gone?*"

Fingers pressed against my neck, taking my pulse. "This seems —it seems like a trauma response."

—may enhance visualization of hand and finger wounds.

Their words became more muffled as I put renewed focus on trying to remember the rest of the text.

Wound evaluation requires good lighting. Magnification can help. A full evaluation may require—

"Lee, you said she hyperventilated earlier?" Sable's voice cut through the fog again.

"Yeah. Her clothes were soaked and fuckin' frozen, and I had to get her in something dry and warm. No, Wolf, don't fuckin' start with me. I don't need any help feelin' like shit. I already feel like a monster for undressing her while she panicked and begged me to stop."

"Fuck, man," someone muttered.

A full evaluation may require—

I tried to remember the rest of the text, but the words wouldn't come. The voices around me rose in volume, dragging my attention away again.

"Wolf!" Sable sounded frustrated. "My point is, think about why your sister might be losing her shit about people taking off her clothes."

Breathing grew difficult again. The air seemed to grow thick with emotion.

A full evaluation may require—

My throat constricted with panic. I couldn't remember—

"Wolf?" a voice asked, maybe Kai, but there was no answer.

The voices were low now, tinged with worry as they faded in and out of my head.

"—to be upset, Wolf," Scar murmured.

I tried to block them out, but despite my best efforts, I began to feel my body again.

"Twelve years is a long time to—."

A full evaluation may require—

"—doesn't change anything." Wolf's voice was hard, now.

"It does, though; she's still your sister."

"And she's still a murderer."

My lungs betrayed me, inhaling a sharp, pained breath, and everyone's eyes snapped to me.

"Ember?" Sable asked. "You back with us?"

Returning to myself *hurt* and made me painfully aware of every part of my body; and as usual, nausea rose and dragged my anxiety with it. I curled my shoulders, trying to shrink back, and hid my trembling hands in the blanket. I didn't look at Sable.

"We didn't look at the scar," he said, calm and quiet. I would've known he was a healer just by his voice. "The only reason we'd ever go against your wishes is if you had a serious injury that needed care."

I stared at the floor, wishing I'd drowned in the river. I hated that my brother was seeing how broken I really was—the paint chipping off and revealing the cracks below.

"Ember."

I tensed at Wolf's voice.

"Why did you go in the river?"

I pressed my lips together and didn't answer.

"No, you don't get to do that. I deserve some answers." His voice sharpened, and he stepped forward, nudging Sable with his leg.

Sable shifted backward, making room for Wolf to sit beside me. My heart started beating faster as I glanced at him. He stared at me with a severe expression.

"Ember, answer me. What were you thinking?"

"Why do you care?" I mumbled.

His eyebrows shot up before his eyes narrowed. "Ember," he snapped, "you could have *died*."

I almost laughed. "So what, it matters *where* I die?"

"What?" he demanded.

"You're taking me to Carth to be killed."

"No, I'm taking you to have a trial," he growled.

"Same thing."

"Godsdamnit, Em," Wolf snapped, "will you just answer the question?"

"What the fuck do you want me to say?"

"I want you to tell me the *truth*," he growled. "Why did you go in that river? Were you *trying* to drown?"

"No," I muttered, which was mostly true.

"Where were you trying to go?"

Home.

"Back to the Vault?" he pushed.

I stared hard at the worn texture of the couch. "Yes."

"Were you torturing people for Madame?"

Shame swept over me, and I didn't answer.

"How long have you been at the Vault?"

I tried to focus on taking deep breaths in through my nose and out through my mouth.

"Ember!" He sounded like he used to when I was a kid and wasn't listening. "Where the fuck have you been?"

My stomach flipped with anxiety. There was a good chance he knew who the Reapers were, their reputation, and what they *did.* "It doesn't matter."

"It doesn't matter?" His voice darkened even further.

"Wolf," Sable warned, placing a hand on his leg.

"I have spent the last twelve fuckin' years searchin' *everywhere* for you after you ran away," Wolf snarled, ignoring him. "So I'd say it *does* fuckin' matter."

"I didn't run away," I repeated wearily, wondering why I even bothered.

"Right, because you were *exiled.*" His voice dripped with scorn.

Hopelessness swept over me. I had no way to prove I didn't run away. It would always be Pa's word against mine, and Wolf would never go against Pa.

"You know, I expected you to have a better lie all planned out after all this time," Wolf said, his voice bitter.

All of this was just so fucking pointless. My entire life was fucking pointless. I had these healing powers, but everyone I ever loved still died. I suffered, but it didn't atone me for anything. I killed Madame. I killed Juck. I spilled their blood and let it stain my soul to keep them from hurting anyone else, but it was always too little too late.

I kept trying to do good, to make up for everything I'd done, but all I brought was death. Maybe I deserved to die for all of it. Maybe that was the only option left for atonement.

But not at Carth.

"I'm not goin' back."

Wolf's eyes snapped to mine. "What?"

"I'm not goin' back to Carth."

My brother's eyes flashed like green fire. "I don't recall askin' for your opinion."

I felt my temper rise in response, and it was such a relief to feel *something*. "If you want a trial, *fine*. Give me a fuckin' trial right here. 'Cause I'm not goin' back there."

"You'll go wherever I decide you'll go," he growled.

"You try to take me back, and I'm gonna fight you every single fuckin' step of the way."

Something like amusement flashed across his face. "I think the six of us can handle you."

Rage burned hot behind my eyes, but my stomach dropped. He was right. They could handle me. I could fight as hard as I physically could, but it would probably still be fucking easy for them to drag me back.

"Has it ever fuckin' occurred to you that you might be wrong?" I seethed.

"Why do you think I'm tryin' to ask you questions?" he snapped. "But you won't tell me anything!"

"You're not actually asking! You're tryin' to manipulate whatever I say into what *you* think happened!"

"That is not true, Ember."

"You *never* listen to me—"

"I listen!" he shouted. "I *always* listened. I listened to you lie over and over, Ember! What the fuck else was I supposed to do?"

"Then why are you asking me any questions at all?" I shouted back. "Why fuckin' bother if you're so sure I'm just gonna lie?"

"Because I keep hopin' one of these times you'll tell me the fuckin' truth!"

Furious tears filled my eyes. "No, you just want me to be a monster so you don't have to feel *guilty*—"

He grabbed the front of my blanket with both hands and jerked me closer, ignoring my flinch, his eyes glittering. "Why the fuck would *I* feel guilty? I didn't do anything!"

"Exactly!" I hissed. "You didn't do a damn thing."

"You *murdered* Dune. What the fuck was I supposed to do?" he snarled.

"You were *supposed* to believe me! You were *supposed* to protect me! All the things you *promised*—"

"Protect *you?* I should've protected Dune *from* you!" he raged.

The pain in my chest was so sharp I almost looked to see if I was bleeding. "How could you think I would *ever* hurt Dune?"

"Because I was *there,* Ember! I watched Dune die lookin' at you with *fear* in his eyes and beggin' you to stop!"

I couldn't breathe again. I could *see* that fear in Dune's eyes as he stared at me. He'd never looked at me like that before. He must have known I was trying to heal him, right? He didn't die thinking I was trying to hurt him...right?

"And then you fuckin' disappeared. I couldn't find a trace of you *anywhere.* I haven't been home in twelve damn years 'cause the council made it real clear not to bother comin' back without you."

"So that's what it is," I realized, exhaustion sweeping over me. "I'm just your key to gettin' back to Carth."

"No! I want to get answers! I want justice for my brother!" he growled, shaking me slightly.

My brother. Not *our* brother. I stared at him, feeling almost as hollow and empty as I did when I stood in Madame's cell. Every ounce of my will to fight seemed to evaporate.

"Fine. Yes, I killed Dune. Yes, I ran away. I'm a lying murderer, so just kill me now and get it over with. Drag my body back and display it for the whole hold to see for all I care."

He stared at me, his brow furrowed, emotion flashing through his eyes. The room was so quiet.

"Why won't you go back to Carth?" Wolf asked.

I was done answering questions. I pulled back, and to my

surprise, Wolf released the blanket. I huddled back in my corner of the couch, wrapping my arms around my legs and burying my face in my knees. No one moved for a long time, and then the couch shifted as Wolf stood.

"Lee, Scar, Sable," he ordered in a clipped voice as he strode away.

I heard the door open and shut and then, after a second, open and shut again. Emotion built in my chest, but my eyes stayed painfully dry.

"Hey."

I startled at the voice so close to me, lifting my head just enough to meet Kai's gaze. He crouched in front of where I sat on the couch, his brows drawn together slightly. He held up a plate with a sliced apple and a sandwich.

"You should eat something," he said.

I buried my face in my knees again. Maybe I'd get lucky and starve to death before we reached Carth. I had no idea how many days had passed since they took me from the Vault, but the last thing I'd eaten was the piece of dried meat Lee gave me. I wasn't sure how long I could go without eating, but the longest Juck ever made me go was three weeks and two days, and I sure felt like I was dying by the end of it.

"C'mon, I made it myself, and everyone says I'm the best cook in this crew."

Someone snorted in amusement from the other side of the room.

"You disagreeing with me, Tuck?" Kai asked.

"Let's just say it's a good thing all you had to do was put some meat between two slices of bread," Tuck answered.

"Well, it's better than whatever stew you made yesterday," Kai shot back.

"I'm not the one claimin' to be the best cook.'"

Kai grumbled under his breath, but their interaction sounded more playful than angry. It reminded me painfully of Mac's—of *my* crew. I just wanted to go home.

"C'mon, Ember, how you gonna fight with Wolf if you don't keep your strength up?" Kai nudged my leg.

I tried to shift farther away into the corner.

"Of course, you're as stubborn as he is," Kai sighed.

"Guess we should've seen that coming." Tuck sounded amused.

"Two Wolfs," Kai muttered, but I heard him stand. "If we

survive this, it'll be a godsdamned miracle."

Tuck huffed a laugh.

"Ember, I'm gonna leave this plate on the couch next to you. Just in case you miraculously come to your senses."

In the silence that followed, my mind drifted, but the cloud of misery hanging over me was full of thoughts and memories of Dune, Trey, Mac, and my crew. Desperate to think of *anything* else, I started reciting a chapter on respiratory infections, which helped. My eyelids grew heavy again. I could hear one of them in the kitchen, and the sound of dishes and cabinets opening and closing was almost soothing. I was nearly asleep when the door opened again. I kept my body still and loose, breathing evenly. If there was anything I was really fucking good at doing, it was pretending to be asleep.

"She asleep?" I heard Wolf ask in a low voice.

"I think so," Tuck answered.

"She didn't eat?" Wolf sounded frustrated.

"Has she eaten anything since we got her?" Scar asked, her voice troubled.

"I got her to eat some dried meat right before she took off," Lee said.

"No wonder she's so tiny," Tuck muttered.

"We can try again when she wakes up," Sable interjected, his voice calm.

"What's the plan?" Kai asked from the kitchen.

"We got movement. So we'll play this like we did in Old Flagstaff," Wolf answered, and the room's energy abruptly shifted to something serious and focused.

"You want me to leave the bait?" Lee asked.

"I'll get in position," Tuck said, his chair creaking as he stood.

I listened with growing dread. I didn't understand what they were saying, but I was confident I wouldn't like whatever it meant. Bait? Who were they trying to trap?

Please don't be anyone from the Vault.

I forced that thought away. I couldn't think about that, or I'd really lose my shit. It couldn't be anyone from the Vault. Maybe it was raiders. Maybe they were just hunting.

"In the meantime, get some rest," Wolf ordered.

Murmured agreements answered him. The couch shifted like

someone sat on the other end, but I still didn't move. I could hear people talking in low voices from the hallway, but soon the room was quiet. I wanted to peek out and see who was sitting on the couch, but I didn't dare. I doubted they'd left me without someone on watch, even if they did think I was asleep.

I focused on breathing deeply and evenly, keeping up my pretense, and listening to the fire crackle in the fireplace. It wasn't long before I pretended myself right into actually falling asleep.

CHAPTER 6

"I love you, Bones." Trey's expression was anguished, tears sliding down his face. "I love you."

"Please! Please don't, please don't," I sobbed, trying to run to him, but my legs were numb and useless.

"I love you," he repeated, his brown eyes fixed on me.

"How sweet," Madame sneered.

"No!"

The gunshot was so loud, and Trey's blood splattered across my face. The light in his eyes extinguished as though someone blew out a candle; he started to fall, and I screamed and screamed—

"Ember!"

I wrenched away from Vulture, gasping in a panicked breath, but I slammed into something hard.

"Em, you're dreamin'. It's just a dream."

I blinked, and it wasn't Vulture who grabbed me and shook me awake. It was Wolf. My stomach flipped with a strange mix of relief and terror. I was still sitting on the couch, now pressed against the back of it, breathing hard. My brother was crouched in front of me, studying me closely.

"It's just a dream," he repeated.

I had a crazed urge to laugh. *If only* it were just a dream. I swiped at my wet face with the sleeve of Lee's shirt, my hands trembling.

"You ok?" a voice asked from behind the couch, and I twisted with a gasp. Lee grimaced at me. "Sorry."

My eyes wouldn't stop leaking. I swiped at them again, sniffing, trying to wrestle myself back under control. They were both silent, watching as I huddled back in my corner.

"I'll sub in," Lee suddenly said. "Wolf, you should get some rest."

"I don't—"

"You *do,*" Lee interrupted firmly.

They glared at each other for a few seconds before Wolf abruptly got to his feet and strode out of the room. I couldn't suppress my surprise, and Lee smirked as he went around the couch and sat close beside me. He threw his arm around the back of the couch, practically around my shoulders.

"You wanna punch me?" he asked.

I cut my eyes sideways at him.

"I'm giving you one free punch, remember?" he grinned.

I swiped at my face again and tried to ignore him.

"Wow, you really are back to not talking to me," Lee lamented. "And here I was thinkin' we'd bonded."

I rested my forehead on my knees again.

"I don't go jumpin' into frozen rivers for just anyone, you know."

I didn't respond, and he fell quiet. Tears continued to spill out of my eyes, dampening the blanket.

I love you, Bones.

"I'm sorry about the cave," Lee said, his voice so jarringly serious I lifted my head. He was staring at me, his brow pinched. "If you weren't in danger of freezin' to death, I never would've…forced you like that."

I stared at him, unsure of how to respond. He took a deep breath, closing his eyes for a second before continuing, his voice even quieter.

"You were talking in your sleep before you started screaming. Sounded like you might've been havin' a nightmare about the cave."

Oh.

I dropped my eyes. "I wasn't."

"What was your nightmare about?"

"Nothin'."

"Lot of this nothin' seems to happen to you."

He'd rolled his sleeves up, revealing part of the tattoo that went down to his wrists, but even in the better light of the cabin, I still couldn't figure out what it was.

"You hungry? We saved your sandwich."

Maybe if I ignored him, he'd shut up. For a minute, I thought it worked.

"You know what's weird? I had this big gash in my leg from somethin' in the river, but when Sable went to stitch it up, it was gone."

I focused on breathing evenly. *Don't react. Don't react.*

"Crazy, right?"

"What's your tattoo mean?" I blurted out the first question I could think of to change the subject, and the grin that crossed his face made me immediately regret it.

"Oh, is that what you were lookin' at in the cave? My tattoo?"

I glared at him, hating the heat rising in my cheeks.

He chuckled and leaned slightly toward me. "It means you shouldn't get tattooed when you're shitfaced."

I glanced back down at his forearm, my brow furrowing as I studied the meandering black ink covering his skin.

"If you want me to take my shirt off again so you can see the whole thing, all you gotta do is ask," he teased, looking far too pleased with himself.

"When are we leaving?" I asked, attempting to ignore him and change the subject.

He paused but then said, "Not sure yet."

His tone was casual—too casual. I remembered the conversation I'd overheard about baits and positions, and my stomach twisted again with fear. He smiled when I made eye contact, his eyes crinkling, but I couldn't read him, which made me more nervous.

"Well, if you're not gonna eat something, you should at least drink something."

He leaned forward, snagged a battered metal water bottle from the floor, and handed it to me. I took it and twisted off the lid, frowning at how my hands shook.

"How you gonna make another escape attempt if you don't eat?"

"What are we waiting for?" I asked, my voice flat.

"You in a hurry to leave all of a sudden? Thought you didn't want to go back to Carth."

I didn't miss that he kept dodging my actual question. I took a final drink of water and handed him the bottle before sliding down into my corner again and resting my head on the arm of the couch.

"That does not look comfortable," Lee remarked.

I closed my eyes.

"You know, you are not what I expected."

Don't ask. Just ignore him. Don't—

"I don't even know what I *was* expecting. Someone a lot scarier looking? Meaner? Taller? A lot stabbier? Less pretty?"

I opened my eyes to see him grinning again. "Give me a knife, and I'd be happy to stab you," I muttered darkly.

"Awww, you sound *just* like your brother."

I glared, but before I could speak, the door abruptly opened, and Sable entered. He was wearing light tactical gear, and snowflakes clung to his long blond hair. His face was grave, and he was carrying a huge gun with a long scope.

"Got the signal," he said.

All of Lee's lightheartedness seemed to evaporate. "I'll wake 'em."

As he vanished down the hallway, I sat up and turned to Sable, trying to look like I wasn't panicking. "What signal?"

He stared back at me, his face impassive. "You'll have to ask your brother."

"Why do you have *that?*" I asked, my eyes dropping to his gun. I knew it was a sniper rifle, but I thought he was a healer.

"I'm a marksman."

"What, like a Ghostmark?" I asked, referring to the legendary group of snipers I'd often heard the Reapers talk about.

"I *was* a Ghostmark, so yes." His expression didn't change, but his voice had an edge.

I blinked in astonishment. The Reapers talked about the Ghostmarks like they were actual ghosts, and I hadn't fully believed they even existed.

Wolf came striding out of the hallway, followed by Scar and Lee. My brother's gaze found me first, scanning me before turning to Sable.

"How many?" Wolf asked.

"They split into three teams. This one's got four or five

scouting."

"Time?"

"Twenty minutes."

"What are you talking about?" I demanded, anxiety thrumming through me.

They all glanced at me and then at Wolf. Wolf studied me, his expression carefully schooled.

"I've got a few questions for Madame, so we're expecting visitors."

I felt my face pale. "What?"

"Lee's in charge of you. Do what he says, and Ember, you try to run again, and I'm tyin' you back up."

"Wait, what... who's comin'?" The panic in my voice was evident as I stood, clutching the blanket around me.

Lee appeared at my elbow, his eyes narrowed at me.

"Stay inside and listen to Lee," Wolf snapped as he grabbed his jacket and a bulletproof vest.

"Wolf—"

"Stay inside," he growled at me and turned to Scar. "You got enough ammo?"

"Madame's dead!" I blurted out, and they all turned to me with predatory focus.

"Since when?" Lee asked sharply at my side, but I didn't look away from Wolf.

"Since a couple months ago," my voice trembled.

Scar made a series of gestures with her hands, and Wolf did some back like they were talking.

"Who's in charge now?" Wolf asked.

"A man named Nemo."

"How'd that happen?" Lee demanded.

"There was a r-rebellion."

"Wolf?" Sable's voice was low.

"Stick to the plan," Wolf said.

"Who's comin'?" I asked again, louder. I stepped toward Wolf, but Lee caught my elbow, preventing me from going further.

"Safeguard crew from the Vault," Wolf answered after a pause.

Fuck. Please, please don't be Mac. "Which one?"

Wolf gave me a funny look, "Mac's."

Panic spiked through me, and the room spun. I must have swayed slightly because Lee's grip tightened on my elbow.

"Don't hurt them!" I gasped out.

Wolf's eyebrows raised as he studied me. Everyone was silent.

"Please," I choked out, trying to breathe normally. "Please, Wolf, I'll do whatever you want. I'll go to Carth, just don't hurt them."

My brother's eyes narrowed. "Why?"

"Please!" I begged.

I knew I was fucking this up, showing my whole hand, but I couldn't come up with a clever plan with this terror thrumming through my veins. I couldn't watch them get hurt or…or worse.

"Who killed Madame?" Wolf asked.

I hesitated, and Wolf's gaze sharpened.

"Ember," he snapped. "You want to protect your friends? Then start talkin'."

"Me," I whispered.

They all wore carefully blank expressions, and I couldn't read them.

"*You* killed Madame?" Wolf repeated.

"Yes."

"How?"

I tried to block the memory of Madame's blood spraying across my face. "They captured her during the revolt."

"I didn't ask how she got taken down. I'm askin' how you killed her. Was it on someone's orders?"

"No," I whispered.

Wolf scanned me again, his eyes narrowing. "*How?*"

My stomach clenched, but I couldn't tell if I was offended he seemed to think I wasn't capable or if it was the guilt and shame at what I'd done. My emotions pulled back like they wanted no part of this.

"I slit her throat." My voice came out steady but so empty.

All three narrowed their eyes, and it felt like being studied by *actual* wolves. I had the panicked thought I wasn't confessing this right. I always went numb. I didn't know how to do it any other way. Was I supposed to cry?

"Those scars on your back, are those whip marks?" Lee asked from beside me.

I nodded, my eyes painfully dry. Sable and Scar glanced

sideways at Wolf so quickly I almost missed it. No one spoke for a few breaths.

"Who whipped you?" Wolf asked, and for a brief moment, genuine fury shone in his eyes.

"Madame." My voice was shaking hard now. "Please, Wolf. Please don't hurt them."

"Weren't you workin' for her?" Wolf ignored my plea.

I nodded, swallowing hard.

"Were you torturing people in the dungeon?" he demanded.

I hesitated again, but then I nodded, shame flooding me.

"Why did Madame whip you then?"

I paused. He was asking *a lot* of questions. He'd said twenty minutes. Surely, he needed to go soon, but they all stood by the door, quietly watching me. Something was off. I scanned their faces again, and a chill washed over me.

"No one's coming," I guessed, nausea churning in my gut.

They didn't answer, but they didn't have to. This had been a trap for *me*, and I'd fallen for it.

Sable glanced at Wolf, and Wolf nodded. Sable slipped out the door, no doubt to tell Kai and Tuck they could stop pretending.

"Why did Madame whip you?" Wolf repeated, his voice dangerous.

Now, my eyes welled up, which only infuriated me further. I jerked my elbow free from Lee and sat back on the couch, pulling the blanket tightly around my body.

"We're not done, Ember," Wolf stalked forward to stand directly before me. "Answer the question."

"Fuck you," I snapped, attempting to blink the tears away.

Wolf leaned down into my space. "Maybe if you would just tell the godsdamned truth for once in your fucking life, I wouldn't have to resort to tricks to get it out of you."

"You wouldn't know the truth if it slapped you in the face," I hissed.

"No, I think that'd be *you*," he stated coldly. "It's always a knife. Is that your preferred weapon?"

My hands were covered in blood, slipping off the handle of the knife as I plunged it into Juck's chest again.

I bit the inside of my cheek hard.

Wolf leaned in even closer, making my heart rate pick up, and growled, "How many people have you killed since Dune, Ember?"

I stared at a spot on the floor and didn't answer.

"How many, Ember? Was Dune even your first?"

Trey's empty eyes surfaced in my mind, and pain stabbed through that empty hole in my chest.

"Ember! Answer me!" Wolf sounded furious.

I spit out the worst insult I'd ever heard the Reapers use, and the shock that flashed across his face was worth it. I didn't have much time to enjoy it, though, because a second later, Wolf seized the front of my blanket and yanked me back to my feet. I flinched with a gasp, certain he was about to hit me.

"Wolf," Lee grabbed my brother's shoulder, and Wolf snapped.

He released me and spun, his fist connecting with Lee's jaw. A sickening *crack* rang out, and Lee went down.

"Wolf!" Scar shouted, lunging forward.

I darted for the unguarded door, abandoning the blanket when someone, probably Wolf, managed to snag it. It was snowing, a slew of tiny snowflakes drifting through the air. Under any other circumstance, I would've thought it was beautiful, but I hardly noticed. I sprinted barefoot through the snow for the trees, Lee's shirt flapping around my mid-thighs. I made it maybe twenty feet before Wolf tackled me to the ground. I gave into my instincts and fought him as hard as I could, even managing to snag one of the knives he had sheathed on his belt before he disarmed me half a second later. By the time I sucked in another breath, he had me pinned.

I shrieked and thrashed, losing myself to fury and panic.

"I thought I taught you better than this." He raised one eyebrow as he easily kept me trapped on the ground. "Guess it wasn't *my* training that kept you hidden for twelve years."

"I hate you!" I spit out at him. "Get off of me!"

He tried to hide the pain that flashed across his face, but he didn't quite succeed. It made guilt and vindictive spite twist together in my chest. A shadow fell over us, and we both peered up to see Kai and Sable.

"Seems like that went well," Kai said dryly.

"Next time you decide to run for it, make sure you have some fucking shoes on," Wolf ordered, swinging off of me and yanking me to my feet, his grip tight around my upper arm.

I jerked Lee's shirt down from where it had ridden up around my waist and exposed Lee's undergarments, wanting to die.

Wolf's disapproving scowl deepened, "And, for fuck's sake, some *pants*."

ଔ

I sat in the small bedroom on the floor against the wall, picking pieces of tree branches and evergreen needles from my wild hair. Scar leaned against the wall, watching me with a mixture of irritation and amusement. The two of us were locked in a ridiculous stalemate, and I bitterly hoped she knew what she was in for because I had *nothing left* but my stubborn fury and I was ready to dish that out in spades.

I was supposed to be changing back into my clothes. I *wanted* to change back into my clothes but refused to change my shirt with Scar in the room. I'd lost the privilege of privacy, Wolf had informed me. So instead, I sat on the floor in my pants and boots, plus Lee's damp, muddy shirt, and started trying to untangle my hair as I pretended Scar wasn't there. We'd been in here for a while.

"Ember, I already know about the scars, so why don't you just get dressed?" she asked for the twentieth time. "I think you know your brother is not gonna be this patient."

Turns out twelve years did nothing to temper my relationship with Wolf. The two of us always managed to get under each other's skin. Dune used to say it was because we were too alike. I was pretty sure it was because Wolf was an asshole.

"You've got maybe a minute before Wolf busts in here and takes matters into his own hands," Scar warned.

I flipped her off, and she sighed heavily.

"Don't say I didn't warn you," she muttered.

Three seconds later, someone rapped on the door. Scar opened it, made a series of gestures with her hands, and then Wolf stepped inside. He looked pissed.

"If you're gonna act like a *child*, I'm gonna treat you like one," he snapped.

"You're already treating me like a child," I snapped back. "I'm not changin' in front of someone."

"Well, you should've thought of that before you tried to run...

twice."

I glared at him. "I told you I'm not going back."

Scar tapped him and then gestured again. He frowned, and she moved her hands again so rapidly it was hard to track. He let out a heavy sigh and pinched the bridge of his nose.

"Fine. You want to wear a wet, filthy shirt? Go ahead. Have fun."

Surprised, I blinked, but he just turned and strode out of the room. Scar turned back to me, her face unreadable, and gestured at me.

"C'mon, dinner's ready."

CHAPTER 7

Wolf and his pack were sitting on the couch and chairs, eating what looked like some sort of stew. My stomach growled, but I ignored it.

"Saved you a spot, Freckles," Lee called, grinning from the couch.

I looked at the small space he gestured toward between him and Sable. *Fuck no.* I went around them and sat on the floor by the fireplace again.

"Wow," Kai said from the other side of Sable. "Lee, you need some snow for that burn?"

Sable chuckled. Wolf didn't react from where he sat in an armchair, but it almost looked like amusement flashed through his eyes.

"Freckles?" Scar asked, raising an eyebrow.

"She told me to stop calling her 'Ember,'" Lee said with a shrug, looking unfazed by my rejection and Kai's teasing.

"What was the name you've been going by, Ember?" Wolf asked, his voice thick with sarcasm.

I didn't answer, pulling my legs in against my chest.

"Bones, wasn't it? Guess it suits you."

I wasn't sure if he meant because I was skinny or because he thought I killed people. Either way, his disparaging tone made tears burn in my eyes. Scar set a bowl of stew on the floor next to me before claiming the last armchair. I ignored it. They ate in silence for a few minutes before Wolf spoke again.

"Maybe you'd actually have a chance at escaping if you ate something."

I ignored him *and* my stomach growling as I tried to figure out how long it'd been since I last ate—an old familiar anxiety raising its head. I painstakingly kept track with Juck, so I knew when to stick with broth and when it was safe to eat regular food. The fear of eating and getting sick was sometimes so intense that the fear itself made me sick. As a healer, I knew getting sick was a natural body function, but I'd been beaten more than a few times for vomiting in the tent or on Juck's bed, and now it was just one more broken thing rattling around in my head.

"I'm only sayin' this 'cause Tuck's not here, but the stew isn't that bad," Kai said.

I quickly scanned the room, realizing Tuck was missing.

"Pretty sure it's just venison, potatoes, and some carrots if that helps," Sable added.

It took about a day and a half to reach the cabin, and Lee said we'd been in the cave for about a day and a half. What had I eaten that day at the Vault? I couldn't remember, and my stomach twisted. I hadn't been eating much. My appetite had been practically nonexistent for the past three months. So what, four or five days since I had an actual meal? How many days had passed since the cave—

"Guess I'm not getting that shirt back, huh?" Lee mused, interrupting my panicked thoughts.

"Guess not," Wolf replied.

"Looks better on her, anyway," Lee said.

"Watch it," Wolf warned, but he was smiling when I glanced at him—a small smile, but it was there.

"You know, I always pictured your sister as a smaller you with longer hair," Lee said. "I was right, but somehow she's a lot prettier than you were with long hair."

"I thought Wolf was very pretty with long hair!" Scar teased, making Lee, Sable, and Kai snicker.

Wolf glared at all of them but just stuffed another spoonful of stew in his mouth.

It suddenly struck me I'd never seen my brother with friends. Had he had friends? He was always taking care of Dune and me, hunting, or helping Pa. In my head, he'd been a grownup for as long as I could remember, but seeing him now, I realized precisely how young he'd been. He was eighteen when Dune died, and he'd started caring for me when he was only eight. I felt a pang of guilt and sympathy I didn't like.

I hate you. My earlier words ran through my head, and the guilt grew.

I tried to picture him with long hair, but I couldn't. I couldn't imagine him ever growing his hair out long. He'd always kept it cut short, controlled, as Carth required of men. Now I realized exactly how much I didn't know him, despite us sharing the same blood. A sickening pit opened in my stomach when I abruptly realized I'd been with Juck longer than I'd been with Wolf. Maybe I was just as much a stranger to my brother as he was to me.

I'd only been at the Vault for about ten months, but my crew felt more like family than my actual blood. The ache in my chest sharpened. I missed them so much. I was still furious at Wolf for making me think he was about to hurt them, but I was relieved they hadn't actually been in danger. It was a confusing mix of emotions.

The sound of boots on the porch startled me. The door opened, and Tuck stepped inside, shaking snow from his curly hair. Lee stood and stretched.

"My turn?" he said.

"Yep," Tuck kicked the snow from his boots. "It's gettin' cold again."

"Perfect."

Lee moved to the door and grabbed his coat. He glanced at me as he shrugged it on, catching me watching him, and winked. I looked away. The stew smelled tantalizingly good. I'd planned to be done with escape attempts, but I wanted to be ready for any opportunity. And as much as I hated to admit it, Wolf was right. I needed to eat to keep my strength up.

Anxiety twisted in my stomach again. Well, it had broth. I could drink the broth, at least.

I picked up the bowl and pretended not to notice everyone watching me. I carefully sipped a spoonful of the broth. It tasted bland, but I preferred that. The Reapers almost always had stew for meals. It was an easy way to make food stores stretch, and I was grateful because I could always get broth when needed. Tuck got himself a bowl of stew and took Lee's vacant seat. They talked a little bit, but not about anything important. Eventually, I tuned them out, slowly sipping my broth and trying to keep my thoughts from spiraling into terrifying what-ifs. I finished the broth in my bowl, and my stomach felt uneasy but not nauseous. I set the bowl of meat, vegetables, and potato on the floor, deciding not to push it.

Scar picked it up and took it to the kitchen without commenting. I wrapped my arms around my legs and listened to the sound of dishes being washed. Wolf and Tuck went outside a few minutes later, and Scar disappeared into the bedroom, leaving me with Sable and Kai. I avoided looking at them, but I was so tense listening for them to make any sound that when the couch creaked, I jumped.

Sable stood still beside the couch, studying me with a serious expression. Kai was still sitting, one arm stretched out on the back of the couch and eyebrows raised at my reaction.

"I'm sorry. I was just about to ask if I could talk to you," Sable said.

Fuck. Now, I regretted eating. I didn't answer, watching him warily. He waited a moment before slowly approaching and sinking to the floor in front of me.

"I know this might be hard for you to believe, but none of us are going to hurt you," he said in his calming, healer voice. "Wolf's only intentions are to bring you back to Carth to have a trial."

Did Wolf's crew know what would happen at the trial? Or had my brother conveniently left that part out? He paused, studying me, and I tried to school my expression.

"I was wondering if you have any specific dietary needs," he added.

Oh great. "No."

"Can you tell me why you haven't been eating, then?" he pushed, and when I didn't answer, he frowned. "If this is a protest, I should warn you we won't let it go on forever."

My temper flared, and I struggled to shove it back down.

"As you know, I'm a healer, so I want to ensure you're alright."

"I'm *fine,*" I said through my teeth.

Behind Sable, Kai snorted, and Sable twisted to glare at him. "Sorry, babe," Kai said, but he smirked at me.

Sable turned back around, and his expression grew more severe. "Like I said, we are not going to hurt you, but we *are* committed to keeping you alive."

Why did it feel so much worse when someone threatened me as if they *cared?* I preferred Vulture's method. At least he didn't dance around it and try to make me feel guilty.

"If you mean you'll put a fucking tube down my throat and force-feed me, then just say that," I repeated Vulture's threat after Trey's death, my voice sharp.

"Good gods," Kai muttered, his eyebrows raising even higher, but Sable's expression didn't even twitch.

"I hope it doesn't come to that, but yes, if you are trying to starve yourself to death and nothing else is working, we will put a tube down your throat."

"I would not advise pushin' us that far, *Bones*," Kai added.

Why was it that I'd spent the last twelve years desperately trying to survive, and now that I'd given up, the universe seemed determined to keep me alive?

"It is remarkable you survived being in that river for so long," Sable said.

I blinked, taken aback by the change in subject.

"Most people would have frozen to death in just an hour, yet you were in the water for almost five hours."

I shifted slightly away from him, dropping my eyes.

"Do you have any theories?" he asked.

"No," I muttered without looking up.

"I suppose it's pointless to ask if you'll let me look at that scar?"

I shifted even farther away, the nausea building.

"Can I show you something?"

I glanced at Sable to see him beginning to unbutton his shirt, and fear spiked in me. What the fuck was he doing? My eyes flicked to Kai, and he must have seen my fear because pity filled his face, which immediately infuriated me.

"He's not gonna hurt you, Ember," Kai said, and then he scowled. "And seriously? You really think I'd just sit here and watch?"

"It wouldn't be the first time," I spit out without thinking.

Both of them went still, eyes fixed on me. Sable had his shirt halfway unbuttoned, but he didn't continue. I bit the inside of my cheek hard and inwardly cursed.

"What does that mean?" Kai asked.

"Nothin'."

"Didn't sound like nothing," Kai leaned forward, resting his elbows on his knees, his eyes narrowing.

I didn't respond, and they shared a loaded glance before Sable resumed unbuttoning his shirt.

"I wanted to show you that you're not alone," he said to me as he slid one arm out and twisted, showing me the back of his shoulder.

I sucked in a breath through my nose as my nausea violently surged.

Stamped into his skin was an old brand, much older than mine, but I recognized it immediately. I'd seen that brand in the skin of more people than I could count. It was the mark of a warlord who went by Mad Dog. Juck used to traffick slaves for him, *a lot* of slaves because Mad Dog went through them quickly. Juck's business profited from that, but something happened between them when I was around sixteen, and Juck never worked with him again. I wasn't sorry about it. Last I'd heard, someone had hired assassins to kill Mad Dog, and all his slaves escaped. I wasn't sad about that, either.

"You know that mark," Kai said.

I met his gaze, and my stomach twisted. Every bit of amusement and concern had vanished, making his blue eyes as cold as the frozen river. Sable shrugged his shirt back on in a smooth, fluid motion and turned to stare at me as well.

"How do you know that mark, Ember?" Kai asked, and his tone made all the hair on the back of my neck stand up.

"Kai," Sable warned.

"Did you work for Mad Dog?" Kai demanded, standing in one fluid, aggressive motion that made me flinch.

"No," I blurted out.

"How do you know it, then?" Kai stalked slowly and deliberately toward me.

"Kai," Sable said louder.

I started scrambling backward, my eyes on his fists clenched at his sides.

"Kai, stop," Sable gracefully stood, putting himself between me and Kai.

I watched him gently cup Kai's freckled face, and Kai finally stopped glaring at me and met Sable's gaze.

"I don't think she was there," Sable murmured, but I *had been.*

I clapped my hand to my mouth and clambered to my feet as nausea surged, and they both whipped toward me. I stared at them, wide-eyed with panic. Kai blinked, his anger swiftly changing to confusion, but Sable must have understood because he immediately seized my elbow and started towing me toward the door. Somehow, I held it in until we got outside, where I heaved up the contents of my stomach into the snow. Sable kept a tight grip on my elbow.

Sable had been one of Mad Dog's slaves.

Did Juck drag him across the desert? Was he one of the sobbing, terrified people I watched get shoved inside the rusty horse trailers? Juck didn't even let them out to relieve themselves on the two-day journey. They were forced to stand in puddles of their excrement. And I'd just watched it happen, too terrified of Juck's wrath even to speak up.

Mad Dog had a harem of female slaves, and his entire garrison was practically a pleasure house. While his lodgings were in the adobe fortress on the surface, the majority of the garrison was underground, and he forced the slaves to dig out more tunnels to expand his hold. I'd never been inside the garrison. Juck always made me stay in his tent under guard when he spent the night inside partaking in whatever Mad Dog offered, but I could guess the darkness underground resembled that awful cell under the watchtower. My stomach heaved again despite being empty now.

"It's alright, Ember," Sable said gently, and shame blazed through me like fire.

I tried to jerk my arm away when I caught my breath. "Let go."

"I don't think so," he replied, but his voice stayed calm.

"What's wrong?" Wolf's sharp voice cut through the quiet.

"Ember's sick," Kai said from the porch.

"Why?" Wolf snapped, sounding closer.

I stayed bent over, my hair hiding my face as I struggled not to cry, spitting bile into the snow.

"Not sure," Sable answered.

Wolf's boots came into view, but I stayed leaning over, trying to hide behind my hair. This was so much worse than when Trey and Sam saw me get sick.

"I showed her my scar," Sable said in a low voice. "She recognized it."

"How?" Wolf asked sharply.

"That's what I want to know," Kai muttered.

"She said she didn't work for him," Sable added.

There was no doubt in my mind now they would know the Reapers and my anxiety grew at the thought of Wolf finding out where I'd been all these years. I hated that a part of me still didn't want my brother to be ashamed of me. He already thought I murdered Dune—that I was a monster—so I didn't understand why I cared.

A hand grasped my other arm and pulled me upright to face Wolf. He frowned, but I could almost believe he looked concerned.

"What's wrong? Why are you sick?" he demanded.

"I'm fine," I choked out.

His eyebrows nearly touched his hairline. "Are you fuckin' serious?"

"This, my friend, is called karma." Lee sounded far too cheerful, and someone snorted a laugh.

"Shut it, Lee," Wolf responded. "All of you, go inside. We'll be right there."

"You sure?" Scar asked.

"Yeah," Wolf's voice sounded strange.

I glanced at him to find him staring at me with a grave expression. He waited until the rest of his crew filed inside and shut the door before he released my arm. I wrapped my arms around my torso, my stomach in knots. I had no idea what he was going to say.

Wolf ran a hand through his hair, opened his mouth, then closed it. He took a deep breath and tried again. When he spoke, he sounded awkward but jarringly gentle at the same time. "Em, are you pregnant?"

I blinked stupidly at him, so taken aback by the question I forgot to answer for a moment. His brow creased in concern.

"No!" I blurted out. Trey and I hadn't used protection, so I had wondered, but I'd bled about a month after Trey's death. It was strange to grieve someone who never existed, but I had.

He stared at me, and his throat bobbed as he swallowed. "You can tell me. I just…I just want to make sure you're alright."

That hurt worse than anything he'd said or done so far because he actually sounded like my brother again. I thought *this* Wolf—the one who cared about me—died on the rooftop with Dune. To my horror, tears filled my eyes.

"I'm not pregnant," I whispered.

"Why are you sick, then?"

I squeezed my arms tighter around myself, trying to hold myself together. "I'm not sick, I'm just—" What *was* wrong with me? I realized I had no idea what to say. "I just *get* sick sometimes."

"Why?"

My entire body trembled. I felt like I was unraveling. Why was this so hard? "Because I'm...sometimes, I get—" I faltered.

"Is it somethin' that happens when you're upset?" he pushed when I didn't continue.

That sounded close to the truth, so I nodded. The muscles in his face tightened, but his expression stayed calm as he studied me.

"You never used to do that. In fact, I don't remember ever seein' you sick before."

I was not about to get into all the little ways Juck had broken me. "I'm fine," I said, my voice ragged.

"You're clearly not." His eyes narrowed, a little bit of frustration and impatience flashing across his face.

"It doesn't matter," I tried again, more desperate this time.

"It matters to me!" he snapped.

"*Why?*"

He blinked, his brow furrowing. "What do you mean *why?* Because you're my sister."

An escaped tear rolled down my face. "You think I *murdered* Dune."

The pain that opened in his eyes was a deep well of emotion. "You're still my sister, no matter what you've done."

No matter what you've done. But how could I convince him I *didn't* do it?

"I practically raised you," he added.

There was no "practically" about it. He did raise me. I couldn't remember Pa ever doing anything.

"That girl you raised is dead." My voice was as empty as my chest.

His nostrils flared, and anger bled into his voice. "Ember."

"No, Wolf, I'm not... I'm not sayin' that to make you mad. I'm just tryin' to be honest. She's gone."

His face creased with a mixture of desperation, fury, guilt, and concern, and his voice shook when he spoke. "Where have you been?

How did you know Mad Dog's mark?"

"Wolf—"

"Who fuckin' branded you?"

I dropped my eyes to the ground.

"Who, Em?" His voice was so dark.

"You brandin' me a murderer hurt worse." The numb words spilled from my lips as I met his gaze again.

He recoiled, horror flashing through his eyes. "I didn't—"

"I knew you'd never believe me," I barreled on. "I knew it when I saw your face on that rooftop. You saw Dune and me, and you decided I killed him, and I knew you'd never even consider anythin' else."

"Ember—" he tried, his voice sharp.

"Wolf, are you actually *listening* or just waiting for me to confess?" I interrupted. "I have no proof other than my word, and I know that doesn't mean shit to you, so what's the fucking point? I'm so… I'm so *tired*."

That muscle in his jaw flexed.

"Just kill me here. Please? I swear, I'm not tryin' to trick you. I just—" my throat constricted, and I struggled to regain my composure. "I can't do this anymore."

"You *want* me to kill you?" His voice had gone eerily devoid of emotion.

I hesitated briefly, my heart clenching at the thought of my crew. "Yes."

He slowly drew his pistol. My heart leapt into my throat, but I didn't move.

"You *want* me to put a bullet in your head right here, right now?"

He placed the pistol gently against my temple, and the memory of Madame doing the same thing to Trey flashed through my head. My eyes overflowed, but I spoke with conviction.

"Yes."

He stared at me, gun still held to my head, his brow furrowing slightly.

"I'm not tryin' to trick you," I choked out. "Just do it."

That muscle flexed in his jaw again, and I closed my eyes, tears rolling down my cheeks. I pictured Trey reaching for me and tugging me into his arms—the last place I felt *safe*.

"Darlin'," I could *hear* his voice, *"darlin', what—"*

The crack of the gunshot made me jump, my eyes popping open. There was no pain. Why was—

I stared stupidly at Wolf, clutching his chest, blood spilling over his fingers. His eyes were looking somewhere over my shoulder at the trees, but as he started to tip, he met my horrified gaze.

"Emmy, run!" he gasped.

I sucked in a panicked breath, and it came out as a scream.

I grabbed Wolf as he fell, trying to slow his descent. He hit the ground on his back with a pained cry, but I was already moving. I ripped his jacket and shirt open as fast as I could and pried his hands away from the wound, replacing them with my own. Warm blood spilled over my frozen fingers as I sent my healing power flowing into him so quickly it hurt.

He tried to grasp my wrist with his bloodied hand, his lips forming words I didn't hear because chaos exploded around us.

Shouts came from behind us, and the door opened, but bullets slammed into the cabin from the trees. I crouched low over my brother as bullets whistled past us, trying my best to shield him. I could feel my powers and his death racing each other. The bullet had gone right through his heart.

"No!" I was sobbing. "No! No, Wolf, please!"

He stared at me, his eyes wide. The tears falling from my eyes were splashing onto my bloody hands.

"Bones!" someone roared, and I glanced up.

Mac stood at the treeline, peering around a tree. I had just enough time to meet his furious gaze before he disappeared back behind his cover as bullets sent pieces of bark flying.

I twisted to look back at the cabin. Wolf's crew were firing from the windows and door.

"Stop!" I screamed, but my voice was lost in the noise.

Tuck stepped onto the porch, holding a fucking huge gun. He planted his feet, and it roared to life, a deafening onslaught of noise. His entire body shuddered with the recoil, but he absorbed it with experienced control as the gun spit casings out like metallic rain. I whipped my head toward the trees, watching in horror as the barrage tore giant chunks from the trees that sheltered my crew.

Movement from the cabin caught my attention again, and under cover of the machine gun, Lee came charging toward me and Wolf. He came within a few feet when his body jerked, blood spraying across the snow, and he fell face-down. I couldn't tell where exactly he'd been hit, but the idiot wasn't even wearing a bulletproof vest. The devastation I felt took me by surprise, and I screamed again and again, tears pouring down my face as I crouched over my brother, trying my best to focus on healing him. Lee turned his head and met my eyes, and his teeth gritted in pain as he began trying to drag himself toward me.

"Stop!" I screamed at him. "Stay there!"

Tuck faltered for a second as a bullet hit him in the arm, but he kept shooting. I turned to the trees again just in time to see Raven go down. Jax's blond head popped up as he ran toward her, and he immediately got picked off and went down. My throat burned from the force of my screams, but they were lost in all the noise. This couldn't be happening. This had to be a nightmare.

The machine gun finally ran out of bullets, and Tuck let out a cry and went down sideways, hitting the porch with a thud that sent spent casings flying.

"Bones!"

My heart seized in my chest at the sight of Griz charging toward me from the trees. He wore tactical gear and held a large rifle in his hands. My eyes widened in panic.

"No!" I shrieked at him. "Griz—"

"Bones, run!" he shouted over me. "Get up—"

A bullet hit him in the shoulder, going through the narrow space of the bulletproof vest with terrifying precision. He grabbed at the wound as he went down on his knees, but a second shot went through his neck, and he fell.

Everything was happening so fast, and I was screaming so hard I felt like I was ripping myself apart. I looked back at the trees to see Mac stepping out—rifle held ready—but he paused as his eyes met mine again, brow creasing like he was confused.

"Mac, no!" I screamed, but a gunshot echoed, and he stumbled backward and fell out of sight.

"NO!" My cry tore something free, and blinding light exploded from my body like a wildfire.

I couldn't see anything, but I could feel them—all the injured bodies dying in the snow. I heard multiple voices swearing and shouting in confusion and fear as my power raced across the ground, gobbling them up and encompassing them. The current flowing through me felt wild and powerful, and Mac's words flashed through my mind, *you're strong enough to cut a path through mountain rock and wild enough to wash everythin' away when you rage.*

For the first time, I felt like that river Mac had described. I was every heartbeat and every breath. I was blood and marrow and bone. I was *life.*

Muscles knit back together, bullets emerged from bloody wounds, and organs wove themselves whole again. All of them were simultaneously healing faster than I'd ever healed *one* person before in my life. I peered down and could just make out Wolf's features in the bright light. His eyes were wide with shock as he stared up at me. The pain came a second later—swift and sharp—tearing my insides until tears streamed down my face, and I gasped in pained sobs; but I held it. I held it until that warmth inside of me sputtered, and the blinding light vanished like a silent thunderclap. Icy cold roared through my veins, and I squinted, trying to focus through the pain that wasn't fading. In the sudden silence, it sounded like my heart was pounding violently in my ears.

"Don't hurt them!" I gasped, and then the ground rushed up to meet me.

CHAPTER 8

I woke up in a strange bedroom.

The ceiling above me was made of wooden planks. The fireplace across the room was built into the wall and framed in smooth river rocks. There was framed artwork hanging on the walls. I managed to turn my aching head to see I lay on a four-poster bed and—

Mac was asleep beside me.

My breath caught, and tears immediately filled my eyes. He sat in a chair beside the bed, his body slumped sideways, and his raven black hair spilled over my pillow. His arm was extended down the bed, his fingertips resting close to mine.

The memory of him getting shot crashed over me.

I twisted, grabbing his hand, and he jolted upright, his wide eyes meeting mine. He blinked.

"Bones—" he breathed my name with so much relief, but I was barely listening.

"Are you ok?" I gasped in a hoarse voice, my eyes running over his body, looking for a bandage or blood or—

"I'm ok," he squeezed my hand hard. "Bones, I'm ok. You healed all of us."

"All of you?" I demanded, my body still thrumming with panic.

"All of us. Everyone is ok," he confirmed, and I realized he was scanning me just as closely. He met my gaze again, and I was struck dumb at the depth of emotion there. "Gods, you scared me."

I stared at him, my heart still racing.

"You've been out for twelve fuckin' days." His voice roughened. "I was startin' to think you weren't ever gonna wake."

I must have heard wrong. *Twelve days?* I shakily sat up, and Mac helped me adjust to lean against the headboard; he didn't let go of my hand even after I was settled.

"You healed all ten of us at once," he continued, and anger filled his face like storm clouds. "Even your brother, who had a fuckin' gun to your head."

Oh fuck.

He leaned forward, a familiar fury igniting in his eyes. "He says you *asked* him to kill you."

My mouth went bone dry.

"Is that true?"

He looked so angry.

"Bones," his voice had dropped to a terrifying, quiet tone, "is that true?"

"Yes," I whispered, realizing I didn't want to lie to him.

Sparks flashed in his eyes, and his jaw flexed. "Did you think we wouldn't come for you?" he demanded.

"I didn't...I don't..." My voice trailed off, leaving a heavy kind of quiet.

"Bones," Mac murmured, his voice pained, "I'll always come for you." His gaze was locked on me, and my throat tightened. "Always," he repeated.

"I'm sorry," I whispered because I had no idea what else to say.

"Don't give up," his voice didn't waver, but it had an edge.

"I tried, Mac, I promise." My voice wobbled. "I tried to escape first."

He squeezed my hand and then took a deep breath like he was trying to calm himself. His exhale sounded shaky. "Sorry, gods. You want some broth? Neena sent me in with this today. I think it's still hot."

He held up a large metal thermos, and I took it gratefully. I rested my head against the headboard and shakily unscrewed the top. The logs shifted in the fire, popping loudly, and as I looked at them, I realized I still didn't know where I was.

"Where are we?"

"Nemo's house."

"Why?" Of all the places I thought we might be, that would not

FANGS

have been one of my guesses.

"Well, your brother and his crew are in the clinic, and we sure as hell weren't gonna leave you there with them. And he pitched a fit about you staying in our bunkhouse, so Nemo offered his spare room as a neutral third party."

"Oh." I didn't know what to think about my brother and his crew staying in *my* clinic. I took a drink of broth, my hand trembling. I felt shaky and weak, but I vividly remembered the feeling of power running through me. I felt unstoppable. I'd never felt anything close to that before. I wondered—

Wolf knew about my powers.

Vaguely, I was aware Mac was calling my name, but panic held me in a tight fist. I didn't know what to do. I'd just handed Wolf even more ammo against me. Now, he had multiple reasons to drag me back to Carth. The Ministry would probably reward him for bringing them not just a murderer but a murdering *witch*.

The memory sucked me in before I could even try to fight it.

"You can't ever tell anyone," Dune's face was grave.

"Why?" I was still beaming, watching the dog that had been almost dead a few minutes ago run in circles around us.

"Emmy," Dune grabbed my hand and squeezed hard.

"Ow, Dune, that hurts!" I cried, trying to pull away.

"Listen to me," Dune hissed, his sandy blond hair blowing across his face. "You can't ever tell anyone. Not Wolf, and especially not Pa."

"But—"

"Promise me."

"Dune, I don't—"

"Emmy, they will kill you!"

My smile fell away. He had to be joking, but this wasn't very funny.

"You know those special meeting nights that the council has on the full moon? The ones Pa goes to and comes back smellin' like ash? Those nights, they take girls and women who they think might be witches, and they burn them alive."

I stared at him. No, he had to be wrong.

"You remember how Mrs. Ammon left to go take care of her sister?"

I nodded, fear and horror churning in my stomach.

"That was a lie. Wolf told me the truth. They burned her."

"Wolf wouldn't—" My voice trembled.

"He doesn't like it, but he said he can't do anythin' to stop it. Not without puttin' himself and us at risk."

"Why'd he tell you, then?" I demanded, hurt.

"When I turned ten, he said I was old enough to know."

I stared at him for a moment longer, trying to believe he was kidding, but he looked scared, which terrified me more than anything.

My eyes welled up. "I don't want to be burned."

Dune pulled me into a tight hug. "You won't," he promised. "Cause it's gonna be our secret—you and me. Nobody else is ever gonna know. Promise?"

"I promise."

I jolted back to the present when someone shook me slightly, focusing on Mac's face hovering close to mine. Concern drew his eyebrows together as I tried to remember how to fucking breathe normally. He was sitting on the bed next to me, his warm hands gripping my shoulders.

"You back with me?" he asked softly.

My hands came up on their own accord and gripped his wrists like I was drowning.

"I'm here. Can you breathe with me?" he murmured, his eyes fixed on mine.

He took deep, exaggerated breaths, and I did my best to copy him, and after what felt like forever, I managed to calm myself a little.

"Better?" he asked, and I managed to nod. He took a breath like he was about to say more, but the terrified words burst out of me.

"What's gonna happen?"

He frowned. "Whaddya mean?"

"Is Wolf gonna take me away?"

His jaw tightened, and his voice came out like quiet steel. "No."

"Are you sure?" I pushed, my stomach roiling. I reluctantly released his wrists, he let go of my shoulders, and both of us dropped our hands into our own laps.

"Nemo is workin' on some sort of deal, but I made it real clear I'm not lettin' anybody take you away against your will."

I wasn't sure if that made me feel relieved or more anxious. "I don't want you to fight with my brother."

"And I won't, so long as he doesn't give me any reason to." He lowered his head, his eyes sharpening into blades that cut through me.

"Will you promise me somethin'?" I pleaded.

"Anything," he said immediately, startling me, then paused. "So long as it doesn't jeopardize your safety."

I grimaced, and the sparks in his eyes started flashing.

"What is it?" he demanded.

"If Wolf gets his way and Nemo lets him take me away—" Mac sucked in a breath, and I held up a trembling hand. "No, just listen. If he gets his way and is gonna take me back to Carth... will you please... please shoot me?"

He recoiled backward as though I'd slapped him. "What the fuck, Bones?"

"Mac, if he takes me back to Carth, they'll burn me alive." My voice broke.

He went still, his eyes locked on mine. "What?"

"They b-burn women they think are w-witches."

The horror on his face hardened into rage, and his nostrils flared. "No, Bones, I am not gonna shoot you."

"Mac—"

He leaned forward and grabbed my face, but despite the anger in his eyes, his hands were gentle. "Listen to me," he commanded. "Your brother is not gonna take you back there. Nemo would never let that happen, and unless Wolf wants a firefight, he has to defer to Nemo. And even if your brother somehow managed to get you out of here, I'd be comin' after him to get you back. So you are gonna stop *askin'* people to kill you, you hear me?"

"There's things worse than death, Mac," I whispered brokenly. The calluses on Mac's palms against my skin reminded me painfully of Trey.

"No." His jaw flexed. "Death is the worst because it's *final*."

A bitter laugh that sounded more like a sob escaped my mouth. I wanted to tell him there was some shit you never fully came back from, but I couldn't get the words out.

He ducked his head a little to catch my eyes again. "I'm fightin' for you, Bones."

My heart lurched, making me lightheaded for a moment. He

studied me, determination in every tensed muscle on his face. I had no idea what expression I had.

"And I'm not gonna stop until you realize you're worth it and start fightin' for yourself," he added in a low voice.

My eyes welled up. This was going in a dangerous direction. I needed to change the subject. My gaze dropped to his shoulder, where I remembered the bullet hitting him.

"You promise you're ok?" My voice wobbled.

When I glanced back up at his face, his expression had softened. He released me and began to unbutton his shirt. My cheeks felt strangely cold now, and I resisted the urge to reach up and touch my face where his hand had been.

He showed me the scar on his shoulder and patiently waited as I examined it.

"I'm sorry I shot your brother."

I looked back up at him, startled.

"To be fair, I didn't know he was your brother when I shot him. Though I still woulda done it even if I *did* know." His face grew stormy. "I'm not gonna hesitate when someone has a gun to your head."

A confusing mix of guilt and fear and something unbearably soft overwhelmed me.

"Wolf told us about your brother Dune."

I lifted the thermos and took another sip of broth, avoiding his eyes.

"When you feel better, we'd like to hear your side of the story."

"What makes you think it's different from his?" I muttered.

He was quiet for a long time, and I wanted to see his expression but wasn't brave enough to look. The fire crackled and popped, tiny sparks dancing in the darkness.

"Bones," he finally said in that soft voice that made my eyes burn, "'cause we *know* you."

Did they? I didn't understand how other people could feel so confident they knew who I was when *I* didn't even know.

Mac rested his hand on the bed and leaned forward again, coming close enough I could smell the peppermint soap he preferred, same as Clarity. "When he told us you murdered your brother, we thought he was fuckin' joking. None of us believe that's what happened."

Oh fuck, Clarity. I started to raise my eyes to his, intending to ask how his sister was doing, but my gaze caught on his chest. He hadn't buttoned his shirt back up, and it was gaping on the opposite side, revealing a scar. I could only see part of it, but it looked like a *word*. I tried to tell myself it was just a tattoo, but I'd seen enough injuries to immediately know it wasn't.

"What's on your chest?" I tried to keep my voice calm, but it shook slightly.

He glanced down at his shirt and muttered a curse, yanking his shirt closed in a move that was painfully familiar. I slowly reached out and curled my hand around his wrist.

"Mac, please. Can I see?" I asked steadily.

He closed his eyes, and I watched his throat work as he swallowed. To my surprise, when he met my gaze again, he only paused briefly before pulling his shirt open. Horror dropped into my stomach like a stone.

Silvery pink scars on the skin above his heart formed the word "TRAITOR."

I instinctively reached out and touched the scars but jerked back when he sucked in a sharp breath. "I'm so sorry," I said, horrified at my intrusiveness. "I should've—"

He caught my hand and lifted it, pressing my fingers against the bare skin of his chest again. I had to resist the urge to shiver—an odd reaction since his skin was so warm beneath my cold fingers.

"It's ok," he said, the words gruff as he released my hand. "Just startled me."

I hesitated but then ran my fingers over the raised scar tissue. It was healed, but it was *new*. This hadn't been there when I healed him from the fever.

"Did Madame do this 'cause Trey and I left?" I whispered, looking up at his face.

His expression was carefully blank, but pain flashed through his eyes. "It's not your fault, Bones."

"Mac—" My voice broke. I looked back at the silvery lines, my heart aching.

"This is nothin' new."

"You're not a traitor." I gently smoothed my thumb over the word, wishing I could erase it with my powers.

"I was to her, and that's a badge I'll wear with honor."

"What else did she do to you?" I doubted Madame stopped there.

"I'm ok, Bones," he murmured, but he wasn't quite meeting my eyes.

I dropped my hand to my lap, forcing myself to be patient. "Mac, what else?"

He stared at the wall for a few breaths before relenting. "She put it on my back, too."

"Can I see? Please?"

His throat bobbed as he met my eyes. We stared at each other for another long moment, but then he unbuttoned his shirt the rest of the way and shrugged it off, twisting to show me his back. My breath caught. The word "TRAITOR" was *all over* his back, but that wasn't even the worst part. Most of them were *old*, with layers and layers of scars.

This is nothin' new.

He'd meant that literally. Madame had been carving this word into him for *years*.

CHAPTER 9

"**D**id Trey know?" I finally managed to whisper, staring at the mess of scars on Mac's back.

"He knew about the older ones," he muttered. "He didn't know she was still doin' it."

"Is it ok if I touch you?" I remembered to ask.

He nodded, then said, "Guess I'm gettin' a taste of my own medicine."

"What do you mean?" I asked as I ran my fingers across the scars, scrutinizing them.

Madame had obviously cut these into his skin with care, and that was worse. The lines were precise and thin, cutting just enough to leave a scar but not enough to leave large wounds—enough to cause pain without a ton of blood. I could practically track her improvement at it across his back. It was so viciously *deliberate*. I'd noticed Madame's skill with a knife in the dungeon. She never hacked at people, always cutting with steady, practiced movements—now I knew what sort of practice she'd done.

"Well, it's not really fair if I insist you be honest about how you're feelin' if I'm not willing to do the same," Mac sighed.

He had intense tan lines on his neck and arms, and I realized I'd never seen him without his shirt. Most people removed their shirts when they were working outside in the heat, but Mac never did. I'd never thought twice about it, but now I understood why.

"How old were you when she started doin' this?" I asked, my

fingers pausing on one of the older scars.

"I'm guessin' Trey told you about my dad?" he asked, and I nodded. "I was seven when he died. I didn't know he was leadin' a rebellion. He kept it all secret so he wouldn't implicate me, but after he passed, Madame threw me in a cell for a few days." He paused. "The one you were in."

The horrible, pressing darkness flashed through my mind, making my skin crawl.

"I was so fuckin' scared. Madame came and visited me several times a day, and sometimes she was nice, almost like a mother, but other times..." I could only see his profile as he stared at the wall, but the muscles in his face were tense. "Other times, she came in with a couple of her men and had them hold me down so she could carve up my back."

"Why didn't anyone stop her?" Fury caught fire in my chest.

"No one knew. Madame did a good job puttin' on an act in front of the hold, presenting herself as someone who wasn't afraid to do what needed to be done for the good of the hold. I was too young to remember, but a gang of raiders blackmailed the previous leader, and for a while, a whole host of raiders moved in and did whatever they wanted. Madame took over by force but framed it like saving the hold. She executed all the raiders terrorizing the people, and everyone was grateful for it."

My fingers were still moving gently across his back, but I wasn't really examining the scars anymore so much as I was just...touching him and trying to provide comfort.

"But then people who disagreed with her started disappearing. She started enforcing strict rules like curfews and limiting food. Her late partner Viper would go out with a crew and return with crates of weapons and more men. Suddenly, she had a small army. I know it sounds real obvious in hindsight, but my dad always said when water heats up slowly, a frog doesn't even know it's bein' boiled to death until it's too late."

I grimaced at the comparison, but I understood it.

"I never liked her, but I never would've guessed she could be like she was under the watchtower—cruel and unhinged." He turned to give me a grim smile. "As you well know."

I dropped my hands from his back and balled them into tight fists in my lap. He scanned my face with a frown.

"What's goin' on in that head?" he asked, buttoning his shirt back up.

"I'm feelin' a lot less guilty I killed her," I muttered.

He blinked. "You felt guilty?"

I tried to push away the memory of how it'd felt to slash that knife through Madame's neck, how the blood had sprayed, and the awful noise she made. "I don't…I don't *like* killin' people." My skin prickled as I remembered the look on his face when he came and got me from Nemo. "And you were so mad."

"Bones," he snapped, "I wasn't mad 'cause you killed her."

I glanced up at him, furrowing my brow slightly. He stared at me, his eyes intense.

"I was mad you took that risk all by yourself. You didn't let any of us help you. You sent Griz on a wild goose chase to get him out of the way, for fuck's sake."

I blinked in surprise.

His eyes narrowed. "Did you seriously think I was mad at you for killin' her?"

"I don't know, you *always* seem mad at me," I muttered.

"Only when you throw yourself in front of every threat like you're the size of Griz." He gave me a stern look, but his eyes looked lighter. "You're not, by the way."

I rolled my eyes, and his lips twitched up. I took a drink of broth, and he studied his clasped hands. When he cleared his throat, I glanced back up at him. He leaned forward slightly, his gaze intense.

"I lost my best friend, my brother," his voice sounded rough, "and I don't want to lose you, too."

The emotion in his eyes startled me. It was like quicksand—if I stepped in, I'd never get back out. Feeling like a coward, I dropped my gaze to my hands.

"Bones," he sounded irritated, "will you stop lookin' so surprised I care about what happens to you?"

I felt my face heat again. "I will when you stop glarin' at me all the time."

He snorted, and I looked back up.

"What?"

"You glare at everybody all the time."

"I do not," I said, offended.

He grinned. "You serious?"

I glared at him, then realized what I was doing and attempted to stop. His grin widened until both dimples appeared.

"Why did you work for her?"

The words tumbled out of my mouth, and I immediately wished I could take them back as his grin vanished, a mix of pain and guilt flashing through his eyes.

"You don't have to—"

"No, it's ok," he interrupted. "I've been wantin' to tell you all of this for a while now. Just never really seemed like a good time." He took a breath and let it out before starting. "When I was in that cell, Ana, Trey's mom, was trying to get custody of me. I guess she was about ready to storm the watchtower even though she was real pregnant with Clarity." He smiled slightly, his eyes sad. "Madame finally told me I could go live with them, but to remember I belonged to her. She threatened to hurt Ana and Trey if I ever went against her, and I was so fuckin' scared of what she might do, I swore I'd do whatever she wanted.

"Most kids join the guards at thirteen, but she came and took me when I was ten. I think she was expecting the other trainees to kill me in the barracks. Maybe she even told 'em to, 'cause they sure as hell tried." His smile was grim. "Once I realized she let the crew leaders make their own rules, I thought if I could just become a crew leader, I could make a place for the people I cared about, where they could be safe. So, I did whatever I needed to do to get it. I killed five of the other trainees, the other *kids,* with my bare hands before they started leaving me alone. I made myself into someone I barely recognized, someone who people feared." He swallowed hard, and I could *feel* his remorse. "Sometimes I think Trey joined the guard 'cause he was afraid of how far I'd go if he wasn't there to stop me.

"Bein' a crew leader became an obsession. It was the only thing I thought about. An' I got it, but Madame was still hurting other people, and everyone thought I'd become a monster. If it weren't for Trey collecting all the other outcasts in the barracks, I probably wouldn't have had much of a crew after training. Ana kept tryin' to talk to me, tryin' to get me to open up, but I spent years ignoring everyone outside my small circle and trying to focus on what I could control. Then Ana died because, despite everything I'd done to keep her safe, I couldn't save her from bleedin' to death in childbirth with Trey and Clarity's baby sister. And Trey..." He smiled, but his eyes were wet. "Trey cared about everyone and couldn't ignore the suffering."

The pieces of my heart ached so fiercely my eyes overflowed again. Mac offered his hand palm up like he did under the watchtower. When I took it, he curled his warm fingers around my shaky hand— quietly comforting.

"I was so angry at him when he got caught passing messages." His voice was rough with emotion. "I was furious he joined the rebels and didn't fuckin' tell me. I was—" He swallowed, his eyes drifting to somewhere over my head, "I was an asshole about it. It felt like after everythin' I'd done and sacrificed to keep him and our family safe—" his voice broke, and I squeezed his hand, tears still streaming down my face. "It felt like he just threw it all away. I was so fuckin' desperate. I contacted someone I knew on Wrangler's crew. I had some savings, so I used some of it to bribe my contact to pass me any info that might be useful. I wanted any sort of bargaining chip I could find. A day later, he radioed back and said he had somethin' huge, but he wanted more for the info. I promised him the rest of my savings, and he told me Wrangler had a lead on Juck's secret weapon."

Even though I knew it was coming, I still felt sick. I didn't blame Mac. I would've done the same thing to save Trey's life. I *should* have.

"I was gonna bargain with Madame for me and Trey to go." He continued, still staring off into space. "But Griz found out and just about kicked my ass. So I told him the crew could vote on it." He shook his head, grimacing. "They voted unanimously to come. So I brought it to Madame, swore I would be personally responsible for Trey, and I'd hand over Juck's secret weapon if she spared his life. She finally agreed, but she made it clear if we failed, we might as well never come back here 'cause she'd execute all of us. Honestly, I would have taken my crew, collected the weapon, and disappeared, but I couldn't leave Clarity behind, and Madame knew that. Trey was fuckin' pissed when he found out what I'd done and what I'd promised Madame. He almost refused to come, but I guilted him hard, using Clarity and everythin' I'd been through as leverage. Trey finally relented, but he was still angry. And then, when we got that safe open and found it empty except for this woman covered in blood," his eyes met mine, sharp with pain, "I thought for sure I'd failed all of them. I would've left you there, but Trey put his foot down. When you ran, and the mercs lost their shit, I realized you must be valuable and thought maybe I hadn't fucked everythin' up. So I took off after you and Trey and caught up to you just after you healed him." He averted his eyes. "I hit you in the back of the head with my gun, and I'm so sorry."

"It's ok," I whispered, and his eyes snapped back to mine.

"It's not ok. I hit you fuckin' hard, and you crumpled so fast I thought I killed you for a second. I probably almost did." He inhaled a deep breath and let it out slow. "Trey lost his shit on me and showed me how you'd just saved his life, but I didn't want to feel guilty, so I just stayed angry."

"I wasn't very nice to you, either," I pointed out.

"At least you had a good reason. Not unreasonable to hate the person who fuckin' kidnapped you and brought you somewhere where you had to watch people get tortured. You healed me in the dungeon, saved my life, and I was still an asshole to you, and I'm so fuckin' sorry."

"Mac." I fixed him with the fiercest look I could muster, with tears still leaking down my face. "I don't blame you. And you already apologized for this."

"I know," he said, his face so serious, "but I didn't tell you the whole story."

We stared at each other for a moment.

"You didn't have to tell me all that. I'm sorry if that sounded like I was...judging you or something," I finally said. "I'm not. I stayed with Juck for twelve years despite...everything."

"You say that like you woulda been free to leave if you wanted." He raised an eyebrow.

"Well, you weren't, either."

He gave me a rueful smile. "I wanted to tell you."

Silence fell, but I didn't let go of his hand, and he didn't pull away.

"How did you find me?" I asked eventually.

"Apple saw them taking you out of the hold." My entire body tensed, but his thumb stroked my hand as he quickly continued, "She didn't try to interfere. She came and got me."

Relief made me shaky as the memory of Zip hitting Apple played through my head.

"We went after you, but they were movin' too fast, and we lost the tracks after a bit. We had to return to the hold, and Nemo got out some old maps of Madame's and found a few places he thought they might use for shelter. Nemo divided everyone up into three teams, and everybody armed up and went out after you. We got lucky that you were at the place we went."

I stared at the floor, my brain piecing together the resources and time Nemo must have used. Would he expect me to pay him back for that?

"What?" Mac asked, and I glanced up to see him studying me.

"That's a lot," I muttered.

Mac frowned, "A lot of what?"

"Resources he used."

"And?"

"Now I owe him for that."

His frown deepened. "You don't owe him. He used all those resources cause someone fuckin' *kidnapped* you."

I raised my eyebrows, my lips twitching with the insane urge to smile again. "What, *you're* the only one allowed to kidnap me?"

He looked surprised, but then a smirk crossed his face. "Yes."

A hoarse laugh escaped my lips, and his grin widened.

"I didn't realize jokin' about kidnapping you was the key to making you laugh," he said, those golden sparks in his eyes warming.

"I have a weird sense of humor."

"I like it."

My cheeks heated, but a tiny bit of warmth seemed to seep into the empty hole in my chest.

"See, now that's *two* nice things I've said to you," he teased.

"Careful, I might get used to it," I warned.

"Good, but like I said, we're always gonna come after you if somebody takes you by force, Bones. And not just our crew. The whole damn hold was ready to tear apart the forest to find you."

I blinked, hoping I didn't look as off balanced as I felt.

"People here care about you," he added, nudging my shoulder.

If he kept being nice, I would lose it again. I seized another question to use as a distraction. "How'd you get Wolf to come back here?"

"We didn't give him much of a choice. We had the advantage of not being shocked by you healing us, so we got the upper hand pretty quick." He hesitated for a brief moment. "I'm guessin' the whole witchcraft thing is why he didn't know about your powers?"

I nodded, my panic spiking again. "Has Wolf…said anything about me healin' him?"

Mac shook his head, frowning. "No, but he hasn't said much."

That did not seem like a good sign.

"The others have asked questions, though. 'Specially Sable."

My stomach churned, and I screwed the lid back on the thermos.

"He's been fillin' in for you at the clinic. You sure you don't want more broth?"

I shook my head and handed him the thermos. He took it but held it in his lap, studying me for a few breaths.

"Sable had a lot of questions about you not eating and getting sick," Mac finally said.

I blanched. "What did you tell him?"

"Nothin'." He frowned at my surprise. "I wasn't about to trust 'em until you woke up and could confirm their story. Besides, all I know is what Trey told me about Juck starvin' you."

He didn't ask, but I could see the question on his face. I twisted the blanket in my hands. *Let 'em in.*

"I didn't understand why I'd get sick…not for a long time. And I was always so hungry I'd eat anything I could when he finally let me." I hesitated, numbness creeping over me as I spoke. "There's somethin' called refeeding syndrome. If someone is starved long enough, their body adapts to conserve nutrients, and if you re-introduce food too fast, it makes their body sick." I paused, my throat tightening. "It's often fatal, so I guess it was probably my powers that helped keep my body alive. But I didn't know any of that for years until I read about it. So I just got sick—a lot. And Juck would get…get real mad if I got sick in the tent. So feeling nauseous started makin' me really anxious. And feelin' anxious made me nauseous, so sometimes I just get…stuck in a loop." I swallowed hard. "The only way I know to keep from getting sick is to not eat. And I know that's not *good,* but I'm so used to feelin' hungry, and I'd much rather feel that than nauseous."

He stayed quiet for a bit, staring down at the thermos in his hands. "You know none of us will ever get mad at you for gettin' sick, right?" He glanced up and met my eyes.

"I know," I held his gaze, hoping he saw the honesty in my face.

"Good," he said gruffly, then paused. "So, your brother and his crew call you Ember…"

It felt so strange hearing him say my real name, and I felt another surge of grief I would never hear Trey say it. "That's my real name," I whispered past the lump in my throat.

"Where'd 'Bones' come from?"

I wrinkled my nose, glancing at him, and his expression quickly darkened.

"Are you serious?" he demanded. "We've been callin' you a name that evil bastard gave you this whole time?"

"I'm sorry," I mumbled.

He sucked in a deep breath, glaring at me for a few seconds, but then he asked, "What name do you want to use?"

I had no fucking idea. "I guess you can call me 'Em' if you want."

"Em," he repeated in his deep voice, and my eyes overflowed. "What's wrong?" he asked, frowning.

I didn't recognize this person I'd become, the soft one always falling apart. "I never told him," I choked out, pressing my sleeves into my eyes.

"You never told Trey your real name?" he guessed, his voice gentle.

I nodded, forcefully choking back sobs, and he didn't say anything for a moment.

"He didn't need to know your real name to *know* you," he said. "He knew you. Names are just words."

I dropped my hands to look at him through the tears. He held my gaze, and it was like staring into a mirror and seeing my grief reflected there.

"Not tellin' him doesn't mean you didn't fully love him," Mac added.

Well, fuck. I didn't realize how terrified I'd been of that until he said it. I pressed my sleeves into my eyes again, my shoulders shaking. After a few seconds, he shifted and carefully wrapped an arm around my shoulders. I cried until I was too exhausted to cry anymore.

"You should try to get some sleep."

"Haven't I been sleepin' for twelve days?" I mumbled.

"You really gonna try to tell me you don't feel exhausted right now?"

He straightened, dropping his arm. When I met his eyes, he raised a questioning eyebrow. I scowled, but I couldn't argue. My entire body ached with exhaustion.

"Besides, you're gonna get swarmed in the morning, so you better get all the rest you can."

"Swarmed?" I repeated, alarmed.

He grinned. "By your crew."

Your crew. Maybe it was the exhaustion, but those two words brought more tears to my eyes, and I furiously blinked them away.

He stood and set the thermos on a small table before grabbing the chair. "I can move this back where—"

"You can leave it there," I blurted out, and he looked at me in surprise. "If you want to."

"You ok?" he asked.

"Yeah, I just..."

"S'alright, Em, you can tell me."

"I don't want to wake up in a different place."

He sat in the chair and leaned his elbow on the bed next to me, grey eyes fixed on me. "You won't wake up anywhere else, I promise. I'll be right here."

I lay back, relieved. Mac picked up a book lying on the small table and flipped it open to a page with a folded corner.

"What are you reading?" I asked.

"Nemo found a whole stash of books in Madame's office." He looked up at me and smiled. "This one's about building greenhouses."

"What other kinda books—"

"No more questions," he interrupted with a smirk. "You're supposed to be sleeping."

I muttered some choice words at him, and he huffed a laugh.

"Hush." His eyes met mine over his book, crinkling slightly with humor.

I glared at him, vaguely remembering him saying that to me months ago while we rode Violet together.

"Don't hush me," I grumbled and was rewarded by another quiet laugh.

In the silence, the only sounds were the crackling of the fire and the whisper of pages turning. He was beside me every time I opened my eyes—a quiet sentinel.

CHAPTER 10

T *he knife slipped in my bloodied hand.*

"Angel," Juck wheezed. "I loved you."

I jerked the knife free from his chest, nearly gagging at the awful squelching sound.

"Trust me, I'm keepin' you safe. The gods gave you to me—"

"Stop," I begged hoarsely, my hands clenching around the knife.

"I'm protectin' you! You don't know what they'd do to you!"

"You hurt *me!" I spit out, shaking.*

"I loved you," he insisted, reaching out to touch my face with a bloody hand. "I only did what I had to to keep my Angel safe."

I stabbed the knife into his chest again, but he caught my wrist and ripped it out with a sudden, horrifying strength. He sat up despite the bloody wounds in his chest and smiled. Pure terror froze me in place.

"You really think it'd be that easy to kill me?"

He jerked me forward by the wrist. My knife was abruptly gone, leaving me defenseless as he shoved me down, and I screamed—

"Em!"

I jolted awake, trembling and sweating. Mac was leaning over the bed, gripping my upper arm.

"It's alright," he murmured. "Just a dream. You're safe."

I sat up with his help. The room was full of dim light, as though the sun hadn't yet peeked out from behind the mountains. I held up my shaky hands, half expecting to see them coated in blood, but there was nothing there.

"You want to talk about it?" he offered in a low voice, sitting on the edge of the bed.

I shook my head.

"You were—"

The door burst open, interrupting Mac. He leapt to his feet and spun to face it, his pistol in his hand before I could even blink. Wolf stood in the doorway, his eyes flashing, and then Sam pushed past him, panting.

"Sorry, he got past—" Sam's words cut off, and his eyes widened as he met mine.

He crossed the room quickly, practically shouldering Mac out of the way to pull me into a tight hug. I could feel his heart pounding in his thin chest. I squeezed him back, my eyes filling with tears again.

"Fuckin' hell, Shortcake," he murmured in my ear. "Are you tryin' to kill me?"

"I swear, I'm not," I choked out.

"Please don't be out that long ever again."

"—a nightmare. She's fine." I realized Mac was saying in a clipped voice to my brother.

I peeked over Sam's shoulder to see Mac had put himself between me and Wolf. In the doorway, I saw Lee and Scar standing in the hallway, watching. Wolf glared at Mac, but his eyes flicked over to meet mine. I couldn't read his expression and quickly hid my face in Sam's shoulder again.

"Your brother might be even more stubborn than you," Sam muttered.

That insane smile spread across my face, and I was glad no one could see it. "You have *no* idea."

"I need to talk to my sister," I heard Wolf growl, and all my amusement vanished.

"Not happening right now," Mac responded.

"She's *my* sister," Wolf sounded furious.

"She doesn't fuckin' belong to you," Mac snapped.

"She doesn't belong to you, either."

"*I* know that."

"I should be able to talk to her alone—"

"You had a fuckin' gun to her head, so no," Mac growled in a voice that made chills run across my skin. "You're lucky I'm lettin' you in the building."

"I was never gonna *shoot* her."

"What's goin' on?"

I peered over Sam's shoulder again and met Griz's eyes. The relief that filled his face made me feel even shakier.

"You're awake," he said, striding into the room with a smile that made my eyes prickle.

Sam released me, and Griz immediately enveloped me in his arms.

"You scared me," he murmured into my hair before turning his head and adding, "Mac, Nemo needs you."

"I'll walk Wolf back downstairs," Mac said, his voice like quiet steel.

Wolf huffed an angry noise, but I heard his footsteps retreat from the room. Mac quietly promised to be back later, and then the door shut. I pulled back from Griz, my eyes scanning him carefully.

"I'm ok, Bones," Griz said. "You healed me and everybody else."

I inhaled a shaky breath and glared up at him. "I'm really fuckin' sick of healin' you."

He grinned. "I love you, too."

Gods, if that didn't take all the air from my lungs. I barely managed to keep myself under control. That's why they felt like family, why this place felt like home—because I loved them.

I seized the first distraction I could think of, desperate to avoid bursting into tears again. "Did I say shit when I was feverish?"

Both Griz and Sam grimaced, and my stomach dropped.

"What?" I demanded. "What did I say?"

Sam looked at Griz, and they seemed to be conversing silently.

"You sure you want to know?" Griz finally asked.

"Please just tell me." I tried to brace myself.

Griz cleared his throat. "Mostly, you kept askin' for Trey, and you got pretty upset about it. You thought other people were Trey a few times. We, uh, let you think Sam was Trey for a while 'cause you were practically hysterical, and holdin' onto him was the only thing that calmed you down."

I glanced at Sam, my face *and* my eyes burning. He wrinkled his nose at my expression, shifting slightly on the bed.

"You just wanted to cuddle," he reassured me. "And I'm always down for bein' a body pillow."

"I'm sorry," I mumbled, anyway.

"It's really ok, Shortcake." His voice softened.

"You thought Nemo was Juck the one time he came in."

My stomach flipped. "What'd I do?"

"You got real quiet and scared, but when he got close, you panicked and started sobbing and—" He broke off and took a breath as his hands clenched into tight fists. "It seemed like you were having a flashback about...something awful he did to you."

Sam muttered something I couldn't make out. I twisted the blanket in my hands, feeling nauseous. I could easily imagine what sort of awful moments my brain picked for me to re-live.

"Was Wolf in here for any of this?" I asked.

"He saw some of it. We let him come in for about half an hour once a day, supervised. You told him he looked like your brother a few times." Griz seemed to hesitate, glancing sideways at Sam.

"What else?" I demanded.

"You asked him where Dune was a couple times."

Oh. I had to work to make my voice come out normal. "What'd he say?"

"He always said Dune was at the market," Griz's voice was so gentle. "He didn't talk to us much but always talked to you. He didn't seem to care you weren't making much sense, and he just went along with whatever you were saying."

I didn't know what to do with that.

"Most often, though, you thought you were under the watchtower."

My stomach churned, but Griz grabbed my hand and squeezed. I met his eyes, startled.

Griz's voice came out rough. "I knew you hated what Madame made you do, but it wasn't until you were feverishly *beggin'* me to get you out of there that I realized you never once asked for help all those months."

The pain in his eyes threatened to undo me, and I dropped my gaze back to the blanket.

"If you *wanted* to ask us for help but didn't feel like you could, I'm so sorry, Bones."

I picked at the blanket with my free hand. "It's not like you could've done anythin' about it."

"Maybe not, but I still wish you'd felt safe enough to ask."

Trey's words echoed. *We're not the Reapers. We've been tryin' to show you that for the past, what, six months?*

"I know you were tryin'," I whispered, misery filling me. "It's my fault I didn't trust you."

"What?"

His voice was sharp enough to startle me. Sam glanced at him, too, eyebrows raised.

"Trey said you'd all been tryin' to show me you weren't the Reapers."

"Did he say it was your fault?"

I backpedaled, trying to remember the exact words Trey had used, "No, not...he didn't say that. He was just frustrated I wasn't lettin' him in...lettin' all of you in."

"If he didn't make it real clear, then let me," Griz gentled his voice, but his eyes were still sharp. "Trust is somethin' that has to be earned, and it takes everybody different lengths of time to get there. There's no right or wrong amount of time, alright? I don't know everythin' you went through with the Reapers, but it's enough to know that you trusting us *at all* means you probably had to fight some fuckin' battles up here." He leaned forward and tapped my forehead with one finger.

I stared at him, tears welling up.

"Trey was a good man. I loved him like a brother, and I miss him every fuckin' day." Griz's voice grew rough with emotion. "When he loved, he loved hard, but he always struggled to understand people who were more guarded."

I didn't know what to say. I felt defensive but also strangely relieved. And that realization came with suffocating guilt. I *should* be defensive of Trey. All he ever did was love me, and he died for it.

"You should talk to Mac about this sometime," Griz continued. "He and Trey butted heads a lot about this."

I blinked, surprised. I'd assumed Trey and Mac knew everything about each other, but then I remembered those scars on Mac's back. *He didn't know she was still doing it.*

Griz released my hand, and the three of us sat in silence for a while. My thoughts tumbled over each other, and I struggled not to cry. After I swiped at my face with my sleeve, Sam shifted, pulled a handkerchief out of his pocket, and handed it to me.

"I'm takin' all your kerchiefs," I mumbled, but I took it.

"You took *one* kerchief almost a year ago," he said, rolling his eyes. "And you didn't take it. I gave it to you."

I barely heard him, my eyes focusing on the slight tremor in Sam's hands. I reached for his hand, and he smiled at me but then frowned when I flipped his hand over and started taking his pulse.

"Are you feelin' alright?" I asked him.

"Are you seriously givin' *me* an examination right now?" he complained.

I studied his face, noting his gaunt appearance with growing worry. "Sam, I mean it. Have you been feelin' alright?"

"Are you tryin' to tell me I look like shit?" Sam demanded.

"You look *sick,*" I snapped.

"You're one to talk," he shot back.

"Children," Griz reprimanded mildly.

"I'm ok, Shortcake, I swear," Sam said, pulling his wrist free from my grip. "Just haven't slept much in the past twelve days."

"How are *you* feelin', Bones?" Griz asked.

I hesitated, still studying Sam and struggling with my compulsive need to lie. "I've felt better."

Sam snorted again.

"Well, I guess that's kinda progress," Griz muttered.

A knock on the door startled all of us, and we looked to see Sable step into the room.

"Hi, Ember," Sable said with a polite smile. "I asked Mac if I could give you an examination, and he said so long as you were alright with it—"

"No," I snapped, my entire body tensing.

Griz and Sam looked at me, eyes narrowed.

"I think all of us would feel better if a healer checked you over," Sable tried.

I looked to Griz for backup, but he was frowning slightly.

"I've been workin' in the clinic with him," he explained quietly, "and he's a good healer. I know *I'd* feel better if a healer made sure you were alright."

"I'm—" I started hotly, but Griz held a hand up, glaring.

"Don't you dare say 'fine.'"

"I was gonna say 'ok,'" I muttered.

"Bones," Griz groaned, scrubbing his hand over his face.

"So what, you're *friends* now?" I demanded, feeling strangely hurt.

"No," Sam answered sharply, but Griz grimaced.

"Look, I can't speak for all of 'em, but Sable seems decent. That's all I'm sayin'," Griz murmured.

"It's your choice, though," Sam said firmly.

I glanced at Griz again, and the clear worry in his eyes cracked through my defensiveness.

"Fine," I muttered.

"You want us to stay?" Griz asked, and I nodded, feeling relieved.

Sable slowly approached the bed when Griz waved him over, looking unbothered by the hushed discussion the three of us had just had about him.

"Alright, I'm just going to start with your vitals," Sable said in a calm healer voice.

He continued to narrate everything he was doing as I grumpily cooperated. Griz and Sam hovered close, watching.

"You had a high fever for eight days," Sable said as he worked. "Your crew said that happens after you use too much of your healing power, but the longest you'd ever been out was four days. Is that correct?"

I nodded, trying to breathe normally.

"Griz told me his theory that you heal yourself as well, but slower. I think he's right. That must be why you survived in that river for so long."

I glanced at Griz, who muttered something about reckless decisions while glaring at me and chewed nervously on the inside of my cheek.

"That's quite incredible," Sable continued, almost to himself. "I wonder if your body can regenerate or if your powers kept your body tissue from freezing?" He paused, and I glanced at his face to see him studying me. "Can I look at the scar on your chest?"

My hands twitched to my shirt collar, and my panicked eyes

found Griz again. He took my hand in his and squeezed it.

"Has anyone ever examined it?" Griz asked quietly. "I mean, a healer?"

I shook my head, my lips pressed tightly together.

"I know how it feels," Sable said, his voice low. "To have a mark on your skin you can never remove, that is a constant reminder of horror and pain." I hated the honesty I could see in his eyes. "I only want to examine it and ensure there were no complications in healing."

"Please, Bones?" Griz murmured.

I swallowed hard, my mind flashing back to Trey standing in the rover headlight, his brown eyes so gentle and kind.

I unbuttoned my shirt with trembling fingers, noting for the first time I was wearing another oversized button-up shirt. I dropped my hands back into my lap and tried to relax my tense muscles. Sable carefully parted my shirt, and when I sensed him go still, I couldn't resist glancing at his face. His eyes were narrowed and angry.

"What was this done with?" he asked in a low voice.

I flinched slightly when his cool fingers brushed my skin. I was *not* going to cry. "Metal fencing."

Griz swore under his breath.

"I could tell it wasn't with a flat iron like mine," Sable said, pressing against the scar tissue as he examined it. "It's too jagged." His voice darkened. "And it was applied with unnecessary force. Most brands only go through the first two layers of skin, but this looks like it went all the way to the muscle in places. Can you feel this, Ember?"

My hands were clenched into fists so tightly it hurt, but I couldn't feel anything on my chest. I thought Sable had stopped touching me, but he looked at me expectantly. I shook my head, my fingernails biting harder into my palms. I remembered Trey gently kissing the rough skin. I'd felt that or, at least, some of it.

I could *not* think about Trey, right now.

"Luckily, only a couple of places appear to have nerve damage," Sable continued. "Did Juck do this himself? Or did—"

I was on my back, kicking in the sand, spraying it into Cobra's face. He swore, releasing my legs to swipe at his eyes, but someone else just took his place.

"No!" I was sobbing in panic. "Please, Juck!"

Whoever was holding my arms snickered.

"Juck, c'mon man," Vulture tried from where Lobo and Vandal held him back. His voice was steady, but his eyes were full of fear. "It's not what you—"

"Shut up," Juck snarled at him.

A sob escaped through my trembling lips, and Juck looked at me from where he stood by the fire, holding the metal fencing in the flames. Tears streamed down my face, but his expression held only cold fury.

"Please," I begged.

He started stalking toward me, the metal fencing glowing orange, and I renewed my efforts to escape.

"Please! Juck, I'm sorry! I'm sorry!"

"You belong to me, Angel," he said in a dark voice as he stood over me. "Don't you ever forget that again." He looked at the men restraining me. "Hold her still."

He brought the crude brand down with such force it felt like it knocked all the air out of my lungs. I couldn't breathe, choking on the blinding pain that seared through my body—

"Bones, breathe."

I blinked, focusing on Griz's worried face. Tears were streaming down my face, and I was gasping in short, desperate breaths.

"Breathe," he murmured, squeezing my shoulders.

Behind him, Sam hovered, his jaw tight. Sable stood on the other side, watching with sharp eyes. I realized I was clutching my shirt closed with both hands, but I couldn't remember doing it. Had I pushed Sable away? My body shook.

"In through your nose, out through your mouth," Griz urged, and I *did* try, but my lungs refused to work.

"She's going to pass out," I heard Sable say as though he was speaking in a tunnel. "Get the—"

৬০

"—all the fuckin' stupid things—"

"Raven."

"Don't you 'Raven' me, Griz. When are you gonna learn to leave well enough alone?"

I pried my eyes open, confused.

Raven and Griz were standing beside my bed. Griz had his arms crossed, face impassive. Raven stood with her back to me, and I couldn't see her expression, but from her violent arm gestures, I could tell she was pissed.

"You wanna go stomp on some anthills while you're at it? Kick some hornet nests? Gods, of all the—"

"Hey," Griz interrupted Raven mid-rant when he noticed me.

Raven whirled, scanning me with sharp, angry eyes.

"What happened?" I asked, my voice hoarse.

"We're surrounded by a bunch of fuckin' idiots, is what happened," Raven snapped, but she stomped over to the bed to tuck the blanket more securely around me.

"You panicked when Sable was examining the brand," Griz answered, frowning. "You passed out."

I winced, the memory smacking me across the face, and Raven muttered something about snakes and grass.

Griz sucked in a breath and let it out in a heavy sigh. "I gotta take care of some stuff. I'll be back later, ok?"

I nodded. After Griz left, Raven stood beside the bed, glaring at me for a few breaths.

"You're ok?" I asked, bracing myself.

"What?" she snapped.

"I saw you get shot." My voice wobbled.

She stared at me, but to my shock, she simply sighed and sat on the bed beside me. "I'm alright, Boney. You healed all of us."

"And Jax?" I wasn't sure why I kept asking the same question. It's not like I thought they were lying to me.

"He's ok, too."

I let out a shaky breath and glanced down at the shirt I wore. "Whose shirt is this?"

"It was one of Trey's."

Oh.

I pressed my sleeve-covered hands against my nose without thinking, but the fabric didn't smell like him. His scent was gone, just like him.

Godsdamnit, I did not want to fucking cry again.

"There's a whole drawer of his clothes at the bunkhouse," Raven said, her voice slightly strained, "if you ever want to go through it."

"I haven't even been able to open his pack," I mumbled, surprising myself.

Raven was quiet while I swiped angrily at my damp eyes with Sam's handkerchief.

"You ever want help with that," Raven began almost hesitantly, "lemme know."

I glanced up to find her looking uncharacteristically serious, something almost *gentle* intermixed with the grief in her eyes. Several tears tumbled down my face, and I quickly swiped them away again as I nodded. I desperately needed to change the subject.

"I really have to pee," I blurted out.

"Alright," Raven said, looking slightly relieved I wasn't bursting into tears, "c'mon, then."

⚬

I thought I was going to pass out on the stairs, but somehow I managed. Raven hovered next to me, but to my relief, she didn't offer to help. As the main floor of Nemo's house came into view, I faltered. I had a fucking *audience.*

Nemo, and a handful of his people, stood around one of the tables covered in drawing plans. Wolf stood at the bottom of the stairs, with Lee, Tuck, and Scar behind him. Sam stood alone and off to the side. All of them were looking at me. I hesitated, briefly considering going back up and just using the damn bedpan.

"Chin up," Raven growled. "Don't let 'em cow you."

I wanted to tell her I was already cowed, but I swallowed hard, lifted my chin, and continued slowly down the stairs. Sam gave me an encouraging nod when I met his gaze. As I finally reached the bottom of the stairs, Nemo approached.

"Well, howdy, Bones," he said, his voice warm. "I'm so glad to see you on your feet."

I didn't know what to say, frozen like a deer in a floodlight.

"You're welcome to stay as long as you need," Nemo continued, and when I glanced up at him, he smiled. "I'll let you get back to it. Just wanted to say hello."

I nodded, feeling awkward. Raven looped her arm through mine and started pulling me toward the door. When we stepped outside, the cool air filling my lungs made me feel like I could finally breathe a little easier. It looked like it was about midday. Several people stopped at the sight of me, smiling and waving. Some took a step toward us like they wanted to come over, but their eyes flicked to Raven, and they quickly continued what they'd been doing. I looked at Raven, too, catching her glaring fiercely at anyone looking at us. My heart ached.

I was shaky and breathing hard when we made it to the outhouse. Raven helped me sit and then frowned at me.

"You're so fuckin' skinny, Boney. When are you gonna start training?"

"Training?" I repeated.

"Training. We gotta get some muscle on those bones since you attract more trouble than shit attracts flies."

My face warmed, but her voice was matter-of-fact, not cruel.

"When you feel better, we're gonna start, alright?"

Training with Raven sounded like torture, but I nodded, anyway. I wasn't dumb enough to argue in my current position.

When we stepped out of the outhouse, Raven abruptly stopped. I followed her gaze to see Jax running toward us, his face panicked.

"Raven," he gasped as he neared. "We need you."

Raven swore under her breath. The worry in her eyes made my stomach clench.

"What's wrong?" I demanded.

"Nothin' you need to worry about, right now," Raven snapped.

"What?"

"Can you make it back to Nemo's house by yourself?" Raven asked, ignoring my question.

"Yeah," I said, hoping it was true. "But what's wrong?"

"Everything's fine," Raven insisted sharply. "You go back inside and tell Sam I had to run. He'll take over."

"But—"

"*Now,* Bones."

I glared at her, but she just took off running. Jax hesitated momentarily, then startled me by throwing his arms around my neck and giving me a quick hug that almost knocked me over.

"Hi, Bones," he said with a shy smile as he pulled back. "Glad you're awake."

"Jax!" Raven barked from where she'd stopped and turned back.

He winced and took off after her. I stood there and watched them disappear, my stomach churning anxiously. What the fuck was that about?

A shadow fell over me, and I turned just in time to see Wolf's eyes glinting as he seized my arm and dragged me behind a nearby cabin.

"Let go of me!" I demanded furiously, trying to jerk away.

He didn't release my arm, looming over me with a fierce glare.

"What the fuck—"

"Did Dune know?" Wolf demanded, his voice sharp.

"What?"

"Did Dune know what you could do?"

I tried to jerk my arm away again, but his grip tightened painfully.

"Ember." His tone grew dangerous. "Did Dune know?"

I swallowed hard, trying to calm down and *think*. "Yes."

Angry pain filled his face. "You told him, but not me."

I pressed my lips together, my legs feeling even shakier.

"Why the fuck did you not tell me?"

"I wanted to—"

"You did not," he practically exploded. "How hard would it be to say, 'I have magic healing powers?' Why didn't you tell me when you were in that cell? When I was—"

"You would've thought I was a witch," I hissed, losing my temper.

"Ember," he snapped, "I *never* would have—"

"Dune thought so, too! He made me promise never to tell you!"

He snapped his jaw shut so hard I heard his teeth click together. The raw hurt in his eyes made mine burn. We stared at each other for a few breaths.

"Do you have any idea how things would've been different if you'd just been fucking honest with me on that rooftop?" he finally asked in a low voice.

"Yes," I snapped, "I would've been burned alive by the Ministry."

He reared back like I'd hit him. "What?"

"Dune told me."

"Dune told you *what?*" He was staring at me with an intense expression I couldn't quite read.

"That the Ministry burns women alive if they suspect they're a witch."

He said nothing for several breaths, and unease started creeping through me. He opened his mouth, then closed it again. When he finally spoke, his voice was rough.

"Em, that's not true."

I blinked at him, my brain struggling to process what he said.

"That's not true," Wolf repeated, his brow pinched together like he was in pain.

"What's not true?"

"The Ministry doesn't burn *anyone* alive."

I stared at him.

"They don't burn *anyone*," he repeated, hurt creeping into his voice again. "You thought I knew this and was just fine with it?"

"You're lying," I snapped.

"I'm not. I swear," Wolf said, his face gravely serious. "I swear, Em, that's not true."

Wolf had to be lying. Dune would never lie to me. I remembered the fear in his face. That was real.

My hands started trembling. "What about the nights when Pa would come home smellin' like ash?"

"He probably smelled like ash 'cause he was standing next to one of the fires on his watch shift."

"Dune said *you* told him this, that when he turned ten, you told him he was old enough to know!" My voice was rising, anger creeping in.

Wolf closed his eyes briefly, his throat bobbing. "If Dune told you that, he was lyin'. I *never* told him that, Em."

"Why the fuck would Dune lie to me?" I demanded, and I could hear the desperation in my voice. I didn't understand what was happening. This didn't make any sense.

"I don't know," he muttered, then his eyes focused back on me, and the pain in his voice speared through me. "How could you think I would just let the Ministry burn you alive?"

I was dangerously close to falling apart and gripped my anger like a lifeline. "Because you let them drag me away and throw me in a fuckin' cell when I was only *ten years old!*" I hissed.

A muscle ticked in his jaw. "What were you doin' with Madame in the dungeon?"

The change in subject threw me off balance, and the nausea surged back.

"You said you were torturing people, so what were you doing?"

I could practically smell the blood and that awful, sickly-sweet smell—

"You can hurt people with your powers, can't you?"

I knew I should say *something* to explain myself, but the shame seemed to seal my mouth shut.

"How the fuck am I supposed to trust you when you still aren't tellin' me the whole truth?" Anger sharpened in his voice again. "How do I know that whole story about Dune isn't another lie?"

I tried to shove all the emotion down before I lost my shit again, trying to tap into the old Bones who could do that on command.

"You wanna know how we found you?"

I glanced back up at him, startled.

"We met up with a woman who claimed she'd seen you. She told us all about how her crew rescued you from mercenaries, but you got her brother killed, and then, if that wasn't enough, you turned her crew against her and got her *exiled*."

Lana.

My mind flashed back to that morning when I was attacked in my own clinic. I could see the two men's sneers and the eager anticipation in their eyes. I could feel the hands that groped my body. I sucked in a desperate breath through my nose, trying to keep from being sick. Part of my mind was raging that she was twisting the story like that, but the majority of me was just so damn tired—tired of trying to prove myself, tired of trying to explain myself, tired of trying. And I could not process the knowledge that Dune, my best friend, had potentially lied to me.

"Well?" Wolf demanded impatiently.

I couldn't do this. My mind and body started shutting down again. The numbness rushed over me like a cold blast of wind, leaving nothing in its wake.

"What do you want to know?" I asked woodenly.

There was a brief silence.

"I want to know where the fuck you've been—"

"With the Reapers." I forced myself to look at his face as I said it, and sure enough, horrified recognition appeared.

"The *raiders*?"

"Yes."

"You joined *the Reapers?*"

"You taught me to survive."

He stared at me.

"So I survived." It was so much easier to talk when I felt empty like this. "I did whatever I had to do to survive, just like you taught me."

"I did not fuckin' teach you to *kill* and *torture* people, Ember!" He looked at me like he'd never seen me before, but all I felt was hollow.

"I did what I had to do."

His jaw worked furiously as if he was so angry he couldn't get the words out. "So you joined the worst gang you could find? The one that raped and killed for fun? The one that tore families apart and sold them to slavers? That's how you recognized Sable's brand, isn't it? Cause you helped *traffick* people like him to Mad Dog?"

I felt removed from my body as if I were watching this play out from somewhere above.

"He was a *child* when he got taken. A *child* when the slavers put that brand on him. A *child* when the Reapers shoved him in a trailer packed with so many people they couldn't even sit down…for *days*."

I had been a child, too, but I couldn't get my mouth to move.

"Do you know what Mad Dog did to his slaves? The *lucky* ones were crushed by collapsing tunnels underground. The pretty ones like Sable's sister, though? He *collected* them," he spit the words out like they burned on his tongue. "Sable got to see her body before they burned it, and he barely recognized her. He would've *died* in those tunnels if he hadn't escaped. And Juck just kept bringin' him fucking truckfuls—"

He cut off abruptly, sucking in a breath, and I tried to brace myself.

"Juck. Is that 'J' on your chest for 'Juck'?"

It felt like I'd fallen into that icy river again, my body numb but somehow still thrumming with pain at the same time.

"Ember," Wolf growled, "tell me you weren't Juck's Angel."

I flinched.

"Is that why you didn't want us to see it?" He was so angry his voice shook slightly. "Are you tellin' me you were Juck's *whore?*"

All the blood rushed from my face at that horrible name. It never seemed to matter how often the Reapers sneered it at me; hearing it always made me sick. The brand on my chest felt like it was burning into my skin all over again. I could see the person Wolf saw, and it wasn't me, but I had no energy to fix it. No matter what I said, he just kept seeing the worst possible version of me, and I was done trying to fight him on it.

"At least Mom isn't alive to see what you've become." Wolf's voice was harsh and bitter.

I remembered Madame slowly shoving her knife into Mist's shoulder and twisting it. I imagined this must be close to what that felt like. I wanted to scream and cry, but I silently bore the pain—just like I always did.

"I have to go," I said numbly, trying again to jerk my arm free.

To my surprise, he let me go, watching me back away with disgust and fury and pain clear as day on his face. I turned my back on him and walked away as quickly as my legs could take me.

That chasm between us felt like it split so wide we might as well have been on two different worlds.

CHAPTER 11

I didn't go back to Nemo's house.

I didn't have a destination in mind, but I wasn't surprised when I found myself standing beside Trey's grave. It smelled like springtime outside. The wind had a hint of warmth, a promise of new life. The patches of snow were worn thin, and the mud squished soft under my boots. Birds sang in the trees. The entire world around me hovered on the verge of exploding with life and growth, and my entire world lay six feet under a pile of dirt.

What the fuck was wrong with me?

Trey would be *furious* at me if he'd witnessed that conversation with Wolf.

I hated that I shut down instead of explaining. Why would I let Wolf think all those horrible things about me? Probably the same reason I couldn't even let a healer examine the fucking brand on my chest. Escaping from Juck didn't fix me. He was dead, and I was still broken.

My legs felt like they were about to give out on me, so I sat. Then I just gave up entirely and lay down, curling up on my side next to Trey's grave. The wet mud quickly soaked into my clothes and hair, but I couldn't find it in me to care. As cold as I felt, it didn't even matter. If I couldn't freeze to death in an icy river, I wasn't going to die lying here in the cold mud, no matter how much I wanted to.

At least, I could agree with Wolf on one thing: I was also glad Mom couldn't see what I'd become.

Dune *lied?*

No. Wolf had to be lying. He had to be. Dune would never, *never* lie to me, especially about something like that. He couldn't have lied because if he did, then everything I went through was even more fucking pointless. If I could've just told Wolf the truth from the beginning, none of this—

I shoved those thoughts down, swallowing the bile creeping up my throat, and clenched my trembling hands. Gods, I wished Trey were here.

I closed my eyes and tried to focus—to see if I could sense any little bit of Trey's spirit. I'd felt *something* in the river and when Wolf had a gun to my head, and maybe it was just because I thought I was about to die both times, but it felt *real*.

Please, Trey. Please don't leave me. I need you.

Only silence answered, and I felt every single one of those broken shards of my heart with agonizing clarity.

I opened my eyes and watched the fluffy clouds slowly travel across the sky. I could hear the horses whinnying in the pasture, the sound of hammers as people repaired a nearby roof, and children yelling and shrieking as they played. The Vault was healing, moving on, rebuilding. Why couldn't I?

Even as I wondered it, I knew the answer. I was stuck here in this mud because every part of me that wanted to *live* was buried in this grave.

ᑐ

"Freckles?"

I cracked my eyes open and stared at Lee, of all people. Behind his head, the sun had moved halfway across the sky. I'd apparently been lying here for a few hours.

He glanced at the grave marker. Realization dawned on his face before he turned back to me. "So this is Trey," he said carefully. "Everyone has been very tightlipped about him. Guess this explains why."

I didn't respond.

"I'm sorry for your loss."

Everyone was sorry. I was so fucking sick of sorry.

"You should probably come inside and warm up," he tried after a moment. "Your lips are gettin' kinda blue."

I closed my eyes again, hoping uselessly that he'd leave.

"Wolf's gonna be tearing this place up lookin' for you in about two minutes."

I doubted it. I was pretty sure Wolf didn't want to see my face ever again.

Lee was talking again, but I tried to tune him out and focus on the sound of the wind in the trees and the feel of the dirt beneath my fingers.

My eyes snapped open when a hand grabbed my arm and hauled me up to sit. The mud released me with a sucking sound, and I met Lee's dark eyes. He crouched next to me, his hand still gripping my arm.

"If you don't stand up, I'm going to pick you up," he said.

"Go away," I said woodenly.

He smirked. "You think I want your brother to cut off my balls?"

He'd said that before—right before I tricked him and ran away. If my brother didn't cut his balls off for that, I was pretty sure it was an empty threat. I wanted to tell him Wolf probably didn't care anymore, but I didn't have the energy.

"C'mon, Ember," he said evenly, "get up."

I tried to yank my arm away. "Go. Away," I repeated. "I'm *fine*."

He didn't release my arm, and his eyebrows raised. "You're *fine*? You're laying next to a grave in the wet mud without a jacket, and it's barely above freezing out here."

"It's not gonna kill me," I said numbly.

He let out a heavy sigh and shook his head. "I'm having' flashbacks to Moab," he grumbled, but he slid an arm under my legs and another behind my back and carefully lifted me. "You and your brother are somethin' else."

I didn't fight him. My head thudded into his chest. He wore a soft flannel shirt instead of the camo uniform and tactical gear he'd been wearing when he fished me out of the river. I felt a flicker of curiosity, wondering what he was talking about, but then it died.

He started striding down the small hill, stepping carefully in the wet mud and slush. "How long has it been?" he asked quietly, but I didn't answer. "Does Wolf know?" He paused again, waiting, before continuing. "Gonna guess that means no." He was quiet for a while before asking, "You love him?"

My mouth suddenly came unstuck. "No, I just like laying in the freezing mud."

He let out a startled laugh. "Alright, smartass, that was a stupid question. I'm sorry," I felt his steps falter. "Ah fuck, ok, Freckles, please don't throw me to the wolves."

I looked up to see Mac storming toward us with a purpose that seemed dangerous.

"Hey, man," Lee said evenly, "I tried to get her—"

Mac reached out as if he were about to wrench me from Lee's arms, but Lee evaded him with graceful movement.

"She's not hurt, but she's cold and covered in mud," Lee said, somehow not backing down from the murderous look in Mac's eyes. "Is there any hot water here?"

"I'm fine, Mac," I muttered.

Mac glared at both of us for a long moment. "No," he said, "but Madame's old place has a tub."

"Can we go there?" Lee asked.

Mac hesitated but finally nodded.

He led the way, and Lee followed. The people we passed gave me wide, concerned looks. Mac stopped, and I realized he was giving one of the older kids a message to pass on to Wolf.

"Tell him I'm here, too," Lee added. "I'm Lee."

The kid looked between Lee and Mac hesitantly. Mac glared at Lee but finally nodded, and the kid took off.

"I'm only lettin' you stay 'cause it'll keep Wolf off my ass," Mac muttered.

"Can't promise that," Lee responded, his lips twitching upward.

Mac glanced at me again, frowning as he scanned all the mud. "Did you fall?"

"She was lying in the mud in the cemetery," Lee said quietly. "I figured I probably shouldn't let her stay there."

Pain and understanding flashed across Mac's face. "Come on, we're almost there."

Madame's house had been gutted, and all her furniture had been distributed to people in need. Nemo had moved all her records and books to his place. There were talks of making her house into a multi-family unit or maybe a school, but it still sat empty. Now that half the hold had been killed or exiled in the uprising, there was no longer a housing shortage.

Mac took a ring of keys out of his pocket and unlocked the door. Warmth washed over me, and I looked at the low fire burning in the woodstove in surprise.

"You're keeping this place heated?" Lee asked, his voice curious.

"Gotta keep the water pipes from freezin'," Mac replied, adding more wood to the fire.

"Ahh, sure," Lee said, slowly turning in a circle to survey the space with me still in his arms.

"Put me down."

He carefully set me on my feet. Pieces of half-dried mud flaked off my body and onto the floor, and I grimaced as I touched the stiff side of my hair. I walked over to the woodstove and huddled next to it, shivering. Mac disappeared into an adjoining room, and I heard water turning on.

Mac returned, striding directly to where I stood by the fire. He stopped in front of me, studying me with his sharp eyes. "What happened, Em?"

What happened? I just found out the one person in the world I thought I could implicitly trust possibly lied to me and set off the horrible chain of events that led to my miserable fucking life.

"They met Lana," I said instead, my voice dull. "That's how they found me."

Mac turned to look at Lee. "You talked to Lana?"

"Guess Wolf told you about that?" Lee asked.

Mac swore under his breath. "What did she say?"

Lee glanced between us, but when I didn't volunteer any information, he sighed and scrubbed a hand through his hair. "Well, she said Ember got her brother killed, and these are her words, not mine, but she said Ember 'fucked her way into the Vault' and got her exiled—"

Mac barked a harsh laugh, interrupting him. "Are you fuckin' serious?"

"That's what she told us." Lee shrugged.

Mac looked at me expectantly as if he thought I would set the record straight, but I just sank to the floor in front of the wood stove. Wolf hadn't mentioned that bit about me fucking my way into the Vault. I wondered who she was telling people I fucked. Mac? Trey? Madame? Nausea washed over me.

"Em," Mac growled, "please tell me you told Wolf what really happened."

I stared at the flames, wishing I were anywhere else. The only thing worse than feeling this grief and emptiness was the embarrassment over feeling it. I *knew* it was ridiculous to lie in the mud next to a grave. I *knew* it was fucking dumb to let my brother believe lies about me. Did they think I *wanted* to be like this?

Mac dropped to a crouch, his eyes flashing as he grabbed my arm. "Godsdamnit, Em."

"Hey," Lee moved closer, "Mac, you need to take a minute?"

"You can fuck off," Mac snapped at him. "You have no fuckin' idea what's happening here."

"So explain it to me."

"You want to know what happened with Lana?"

Mac was on his feet, toe to toe with Lee, before I could blink. Mac was a good five inches taller, but Lee held his ground.

"Her brother disobeyed a direct order from me in a firefight and got himself shot. She blamed Em even though Em had nothin' to do with his death besides just fuckin' being there. Against her will, I might add. I tried to help Lana work through it, but instead, she fuckin' hired two men to attack and *rape* Em."

I squeezed my eyes shut, wrapping my arms around my legs as Mac continued.

"So *I* exiled her. Lana took an oath to do no harm when she joined my crew. She fuckin' knew the consequences."

The silence seemed to last a long time. I laid my forehead on my knees. My mouth tasted like mud.

"Can I tell Wolf what you just told me?" Lee finally asked in a low voice.

"*Somebody* needs to," Mac snapped.

I felt that jab like a kick to my ribs.

Mac took a deep breath and let it out slowly. "We went and took Em by force and dragged her back here on Madame's orders. She didn't want any of it."

A hush fell over the room, heavy and suffocating.

"Em, why didn't you tell your brother what really happened?" Mac asked after a while.

"He doesn't believe me about anything," I muttered into my

knees.

"Well, it's not just you. We were all there."

I didn't reply, feeling stupid. Why hadn't it occurred to me they would back me up? If he only knew what else I'd let my brother think about me.

Mac approached and sank to a crouch in front of me. "Em, you always have us as backup, ok? You don't have to do this alone."

I stared at his boots and hid behind my muddy hair.

"You don't get to take all the blame for everythin', you know. You gotta share with the rest of us," he added in a lighter voice.

I finally lifted my eyes to his, and he gave me a slight smile.

"C'mon, tub's probably full enough." He offered his hands, and I let him pull me to my feet. He frowned. "Your hands are freezing. You better make this a quick bath."

He released me and started leading the way to the bathing room. I halted on the threshold, blinking rapidly in shock. Mac leaned over and turned the water off in the large white tub in a small nook, surrounded by windows with frosted glass for privacy. White curtains lined the windows. Thin strips of light-colored wood covered the walls, and a beautiful old mirror hung above the white pedestal sink. The floor was concrete, but two giant fur rugs covered it. The room was bright, calming, and peaceful—not at all what I expected from Madame. I glanced around, noting the basket of towels and the small table with soap and bottles. This room hadn't been stripped.

"Nemo's lettin' anyone who would like a bath use this room, kinda like a public bathhouse, I guess," Mac said quietly. When I didn't move or say anything, he brought a hand up to rub the back of his neck. "Do you, uh, need help?"

My cheeks heated again. "No."

"Alright, well, I'll wait out here." He went around me and carefully shut the door behind him.

I abruptly turned away from the tub and tried to shut out the painful memories of Trey and I sitting in the bathtub together at the trading post. I tried not to remember his strong fingers rubbing the sore muscles in my back, his hand trailing lightly across my skin, and the soft kisses he pressed to my shoulder.

I rummaged through the few cupboards in a desperate attempt at a distraction. Most of them had towels and soap, but in one, I found a clear glass bottle with a faded label that read "Madame." I opened it, sniffed, then took a tentative sip. Whatever it was, it went down a lot smoother than Mootzie's shit. I stripped off my muddy clothes, braced myself, and climbed into the tub of ice-cold water with the bottle. The freezing temperature reminded me uncomfortably of the icy river, and my teeth immediately started chattering again, so I took a long drink.

I rinsed myself, grimacing as the water turned brown from all the mud. I tried not to think about Madame relaxing in this room, tried not to think about her blood spurting from her neck, tried not to think about the bullet going through Trey's skull, tried not to think about Juck pressing the red-hot metal against my skin, tried not to think about the horror on Wolf's face. The alcohol helped, so I kept drinking it. When someone knocked on the door a while later, I couldn't feel the cold anymore, and the bottle was empty.

"Em?" Mac called at the door. "You doin' alright?"

"I'm fine," I yelled back.

I heard him huff a laugh. "Are you actually, though?"

"I'm great."

"Great, huh?" He sounded amused. "Well, that's good."

I examined the little tray of soaps and bottles. Madame got the nice stuff. There was a bottle marked for hair, so I poured some into my hand. It came out faster than I expected, or maybe I was more tipsy than I thought. Either way, the soap filled my palm and overflowed before I realized what was happening. I swore under my breath, then giggled at my clumsiness. I quickly dumped my palmful of soap into my hair, marveling at how it lathered immediately—much nicer than regular soap.

Then, the scent hit me.

My entire body locked up as Madame's sickly, sweet scent filled the room. I could hear the screams, the desperate pleas, and Madame's cold voice snapping "again." I could smell the vomit and urine. I could feel the blood coating my hands.

I squeezed my eyes shut and tried to breathe. *It's just soap. It's just a fuckin' smell. It's not her.* I tried to lather my hair up faster, but every inhale made the screams in my head louder. I gave up and dunked under the water, but the shallow breath of air I took before I went under did not sustain me long. I broke the surface, gasping in a breath and then choking on the smell. *Fuck.* I couldn't breathe. I had to get out of here.

I scrambled out of the tub. My hair was still sudsy, but I didn't care. I barely remembered to grab a towel to wrap around myself before I darted out of the bathroom.

Lee and Mac had found two wooden chairs somewhere and were sitting in front of the wood stove. They both glanced up and then jumped to their feet when I came flying out.

"The fuck—" Lee started.

"What's wrong?" Mac demanded at the same time.

I stopped abruptly, but the sugary smell started building around me again, and I couldn't *breathe.*

"What's wrong?" Mac was suddenly at my side, gently taking my elbow.

Lee hovered behind him, scanning me carefully.

"The soap," I managed to choke out, fighting my lungs for breath.

"The soap?" Lee repeated, confused.

Mac looked at my hair, the suds that were sliding down my neck, and then his nostrils flared. "Oh fuck."

The room spun, and Mac's hand tightened on my elbow. I couldn't tell if I was shivering or shaking.

"Ok, you still have it in your hair," he said. "If you rinse it out, I bet you won't smell it anymore."

My spine stiffened at the thought of returning to the bathroom, where the smell was so potent. I sucked in a desperate breath through my nose, trying to quell the nausea, but it just made me inhale more of the scent coming from my hair.

"I can't—" I tried to gasp.

"You want me to fill up that bucket?" Lee asked.

"And do what?" Mac asked sharply.

"She could rinse her hair out here."

I sucked in another desperate breath through my nose.

"Ok, yeah," Mac finally said.

He led me to the woodstove, and Lee grabbed the bucket while I tried to get ahold of myself.

"It's ok, Em," Mac said in that gentle voice, and my fucking eyes overflowed.

He wrapped his arms around me, not seeming to mind I was getting soap suds all over his shirt. I clung to my towel and leaned into him, hating that I was falling apart for what felt like the hundredth time.

Lee reappeared quickly, setting a bucket of water on the floor before the wood stove. He handed Mac a chipped mug.

"Here," he said quietly, "I'll wait outside."

"You wanna sit in front of the woodstove and lean over this bucket, and I'll rinse your hair?" Mac asked as Lee left.

I nodded, slowly lowering myself to the floor on my knees, still trying to breathe as shallowly as possible. He crouched next to me, scooped a mugful of water up, and carefully poured it over my hair.

She's not here. She's not here.

"She's not here," Mac murmured. "She's gone."

I meant to say something like, "I know" or "You're right," but the alcohol must have loosened my tongue because what came out was, "She'll never be *gone*."

He poured another couple of mugfuls of water over my hair before he said, "She haunts me, too. I have to bury her again every day, and maybe one of these days, she'll fuckin' stay there."

"What if she doesn't?" I whispered miserably.

"Then I'll try to live with it, knowin' I'm one of the last people she'll ever haunt."

I watched the flames dancing in the wood stove. It didn't seem fair that the monsters I'd killed continued to haunt me, but the one person I desperately wished would stay with me seemed to be gone.

"I think I got all the soap out. Is that better?"

I tentatively inhaled through my nose. I could still smell it, but it was fainter now. I nodded, twisting my hair tightly and wringing the water out. It struck me that I didn't feel anxious being in this very vulnerable position with Mac.

"I wish I woulda protected you better," Mac said roughly. "I wish she didn't haunt you, too."

"There was nothin' you coulda done," I mumbled.

He went quiet as I tried to wring more water from my hair. My stomach settled as the scent faded, but the embarrassment grew. I had to add *soap* to the list of things I couldn't handle. My back ached from staying bent over like this, but the dull ache was so familiar now I barely noticed.

"Does your back ever still hurt?"

My stomach dropped as I realized he was staring at the top of my scarred back, visible above the towel. I quickly shifted so my back faced the fire, and he met my eyes.

He grimaced. "Sorry, I just haven't seen your back since I carried you back from the watchtower when it was bleedin' all over the place."

Cold water dripped down my neck, making me shiver. "It's fine."

"It's not fine," he snapped, but his eyes were pained. "You never should've taken those lashes."

"It wasn't your fault."

"Fault didn't matter." He held my gaze, his dark eyes so serious. "I was tryin' to take some of the hurt."

I stared at him without really seeing him, suddenly tongue-tied and uneasy. *Maybe if you stopped trying to be a godsdamn martyr, you'd see that.* His words from all those months ago ran through my head again. He winced, and I focused on him again, furrowing my brow in concern.

"Sorry, I was just rememberin' some of the shit I said to you," he said, averting his eyes and rubbing the back of his neck with one hand.

"You already apologized for all of this twice," I reminded him.

"I know," he muttered. He let out a heavy sigh and then looked back up at me. "Does your back ever still hurt?" he repeated his earlier question.

I hesitated. "Yeah," I finally admitted.

"What helps?"

"I have an oil infusion," I said, then stopped.

He raised an eyebrow. "But?"

"But I can't really put it on by myself."

Pain flashed through his eyes. "Trey would do it for you?"

I nodded, my heart aching.

"If you feel comfortable with it, I'd help," he said. "And if you'd prefer someone else, you know any of the others would help in a heartbeat, right?"

I swallowed hard. "I don't—" I stopped, desperately trying to figure out what I was trying to say.

You don't ever need to apologize for your scars. These scars are proof that you survived. That you walked through fire, and you came out the other side. You're a godsdamned warrior, Bones, and the most beautiful woman I've ever seen.

I squeezed my eyes shut as though that would do anything against the painful memory of Trey's words.

"He was right." Mac's gruff voice startled me, and it took me a moment to realize it was because I heard it *inside* my fucking *head*.

Inside.

My.

Fucking.

Head.

"What?!" My eyes popped open with a gasp.

He froze, eyes widening. *"Can you hear me?"*

"Yes." My heart was pounding. *"Can you hear me?"*

"Yes." He grimaced. *"I think you've been sending me some of your thoughts."*

"Oh my gods." Panic surged up my throat.

"I swear I'm trying not to hear them." He looked worried. *"It just started during the firefight at the cabin. And at first, I thought I was just imagining it."*

Sending my thoughts? How was this happening? How would I *stop* doing it if I didn't know how I was doing it? My thoughts were the only thing I had that was *mine*. What the fuck was I going to do about—

I forced myself to slam a door on that thought, terrified he might hear it, my heart pounding. For a long time, we simply sat and stared at each other.

"I didn't mean to, uh, overhear that." He paused, and I could feel the weight of his grief. *"But Trey was right."*

I looked away, pulling the towel tighter around my body.

"You know, I'd never seen him in love before. Guess I shouldn't have been surprised that he just knew when he saw you and dove in headfirst. That's how he did every other fuckin' thing." A tiny bit of amusement tangled with the sorrow in his words.

Gods, this pain felt like it might tear me apart.

"I know. Some days, I wonder if it might be possible to die from it."

Why was it comforting to hear he hurt, too? How fucking selfish was that? I shivered hard. *"Can you always hear me?"*.

He started shrugging his jacket off as he answered out loud, "Not always. Seems like I have to be in the same room or at least be able to see you."

He draped his jacket around my shoulders and pulled it shut, buttoning it for me as I worked my arms into the sleeves. The cell under the watchtower flashed through my memory again. Had I ever thanked him for that?

"Thank you for what you did under the watchtower," I said shakily.

He glanced up as he finished buttoning his jacket around me. "I didn't do much."

"You did," I whispered, and his brow furrowed. I struggled to convey what I felt. "I wouldn't... wouldn't have gotten through it... without you."

"I don't think that's true." He gave me a half smile. *"But I'm glad it helped."*

I studied his face. His thick black hair was longer than when we'd first met. It hung in his face and had a slight wave to it. I liked it. It made him look less reserved, but in a good way. He'd let his dark stubble grow out more than usual, and the scar on his cheek disappeared into it.

"Can you hear everything I think?"

"I'm not sure." He grinned, both dimples appearing. *"Glad you like my hair, though."*

I felt my face flame hot, and my eyes narrowed into a glare.

"Less reserved, huh?" His eyes crinkled with humor. *"That's pretty rich comin' from you."*

"What the fuck does that mean?" I demanded.

"It means that most of the time, I have no idea what's goin' on in your head."

I crossed my arms, which were swimming in his jacket sleeves. *"Well, I could say the same about you."*

My powers kept changing, and I didn't like it. Or maybe they were just getting stronger now that I used them more often. I remembered that wild, raw power flowing through me and shivered. I never would've imagined I'd be able to heal ten fatal injuries at once. And now mind powers?

What the fuck were we going to do about this?

"I'm not tryin' to hear your thoughts, I swear," he said. "And I haven't told anyone about it."

My eyebrows raised, unable to hide my surprise.

"I wasn't gonna tell anyone else until I figured out how to tell *you*," he frowned.

"You are...*way* too calm about this."

"Well, I've also had some time to think about it."

"Don't tell anyone," I blurted out.

He frowned. "Why?"

"I just...I need some time."

His frown deepened, and I wondered if he could tell it was only a half-truth. The truth was, I wasn't sure time would make *me* feel any better about this development. I tried to picture my powers forming walls like a golden vault around my mind. If I could keep them behind thick walls and a locked door, maybe I could keep my thoughts in my own head. What if I started sharing my thoughts with others—

"How'd you do that?" Mac asked sharply.

I startled. "Do what?"

"You got real quiet, and then I couldn't hear you for a second."

A flicker of hope stirred in my chest, and I focused again on picturing the golden light of my powers forming thick walls around my mind. I watched him, and all the muscles in his face seemed to tense at once.

"How are you doin' that?" he asked.

"I just pictured my powers like a...a wall around my mind."

His frown deepened.

"Does...does that upset you?" I asked hesitantly.

His eyes flashed to mine for a moment before looking away again. "No, it doesn't upset me." He paused. "But I won't lie, hearing some of what you're thinkin' makes me a lot less worried."

I blinked, taken aback. "Worried about what?"

"You." He fixed me with a pointed look.

"You don't have to worry about me."

He closed his eyes briefly, exhaling heavily through his nose. "You've been a ghost for months, and I had no idea what you were thinkin' or how to help. Of course, I'm gonna worry, Em."

I clutched his jacket tighter around myself, unsure what to say, but then he continued.

"And then, after I finally got you to open up a little and *talk* to me, you fuckin' vanished." He dragged a hand through his hair, leaving it even more disheveled. "When I returned to the clinic, and it was empty, I knew somethin' wasn't right. I tried to chalk it up to bein' paranoid, but then Apple found me, and I almost took off into the woods after you with no weapons or anything."

My chest constricted painfully. "The whole time they were draggin' me away, the only thing I could think was—" I tried to swallow the emotion creeping up my throat, "—you'd probably never know w-what happened. I thought Wolf was gonna kill me, and I—"

My voice broke off as I struggled to keep my composure. Mac offered a hand again, palm up. I took it without hesitation, and he gripped my cold fingers tightly.

I'm not gonna stop. Not until you realize you're worth fightin' for.

"I tried to run." I needed him to know I didn't immediately give up. "I tried to get back here, I promise."

A muscle jumped in his jaw as he studied my face. "Is that when you jumped in the river?"

I grimaced. "I did not *jump* in. I was tryin' to cross. It was my only chance to throw Wolf off."

"Sable said you were in the river for four or five hours," his voice was dark.

I shuddered, remembering how painful the icy cold had been. "I washed up on a tree but wasn't strong enough to get out."

He squeezed my hand a little tighter. "You could have died, Em."

"I know," I mumbled miserably. "I didn't—"

The door abruptly opening startled both of us. My heart leapt into overdrive as Wolf strode into the house, his eyes flashing. He scanned me and Mac on the floor by the woodstove with a thunderous look.

"Get out!" I snapped at him, releasing Mac's hand to clutch his jacket tighter around me.

Behind him, Kai, Scar, and Lee stepped in, and I glared at all of them, horrified.

"Well, this is awkward," Kai muttered.

"Get dressed, Ember," Wolf ordered, his expression growing darker by the second. "We're going back to Carth."

CHAPTER 12

T he panic that surged through my body made me lightheaded, but immediately, Mac was on his feet, standing between me and Wolf, his gun in his hand.

"Like hell you are," he said, and I thought I'd heard Mac angry before, but not like this. His voice was deceptively calm, almost like velvet, but there was a threat in it that made my stomach drop. I realized with a stab of terror Mac still thought I'd be burned alive. Well, maybe I would be. I had no idea what to believe anymore. Either way, Mac was ready to fight to the death in Madame's empty house, and I needed to stop this.

Scar and Kai had their hands on their holstered guns, carefully watching Mac. Lee was hovering in the back, not reaching for a weapon but watching just as carefully. Wolf stood facing Mac, his expression so cold I barely recognized him.

"Get out of my way, Mac," Wolf said in a quiet, menacing voice.

"You're not taking her anywhere," Mac growled.

"I'd rather not have to kill you, but I will." Wolf's voice got even quieter, and my heart stopped.

"Wolf!"

I was on my feet, lurching to get between them, but Mac caught my arm and jerked me behind him.

"They might not burn me alive," I blurted out, panicked. "Wolf said they don't do that."

"What?" Scar demanded, her voice sharp.

"Burn alive?" Kai exclaimed at the same time.

Mac didn't take his eyes off Wolf but spoke in my head, *"What?"*

"Allegedly, Dune told her I'd let the Ministry burn her alive if she told me about her powers," Wolf said before I could explain.

Wolf's crew all looked at me with varying degrees of shock and suspicion.

"Well, that's a new one," Kai said.

"He did," I snapped. "I'm not lying!"

My brother met my eyes, but his gaze was hard. He looked at me like I was a stranger—a monster.

Several things happened all at once. Mac abruptly raised his gun, pointing it directly at my brother's head, which made Kai and Scar both draw their weapons and train them on Mac, but he didn't even seem to notice.

"What the fuck?" Mac snarled. "Say that again, I fuckin' dare you."

I took a panicked step forward, bewildered. I hadn't heard Wolf say anything. If I threw myself in front of Mac, would Scar and Kai shoot me?

"I didn't say anything," Wolf replied harshly.

"Yes, you did." Every line in Mac's body was radiating with fury. "You called your sister 'Juck's whore,' and I'm not gonna let you talk to her that way."

My breath caught painfully, but Wolf stared at Mac, his gaze sharpening like a predator scenting blood.

"I didn't say that out loud," Wolf said slowly.

In the sudden silence, it hit me. *Mac* was hearing *Wolf's* thoughts.

Wait.

Mac was hearing Wolf's thoughts?

Was this *Mac's* power?

Mac glanced back at me, his eyes wide, but Wolf immediately struck. He brought both hands up, caught Mac's arm, and then twisted it around, disarming him so fast I barely saw it. Wolf kicked Mac's gun backward, and Kai stopped it with his foot. Mac quickly retreated until he bumped into me, reaching behind his body to grab my arm with one hand. I abandoned the towel, letting it slide to the floor since Mac's jacket was long enough to reach my mid-thigh.

"Stay behind me." His voice in my head was an order.

"Mac—" I started, terrified.

"Wait, what does that mean?" Scar asked sharply, taking a step closer to Wolf.

"I dunno," Wolf answered, watching me and Mac with narrowed eyes.

"Wolf," Lee tried, his voice calm, "I think we got some bad intel."

"What?" Wolf demanded.

"Lana told us a whole host of shit."

"Like *what*, Lee?" Wolf bit out.

"Like the truth is Mac exiled her 'cause she hired two men to rape Ember."

Everyone's eyes cut to me, and I breathed deeply through my nose, trying not to puke.

"Ember didn't kill Lana's brother, either," Lee continued.

Mac suddenly tensed. *"Em, what the fuck did you tell your brother?"*

His voice was so angry in my head I winced. When I didn't answer, he spun around and grabbed my upper arms tightly.

"What the fuck did you tell him?" he asked in a quiet, scary voice.

I glanced behind him, terrified someone was going to shoot him in the back, but Wolf gestured at Kai and Scar to lower their weapons. They both frowned but obeyed.

"Why does he think you wanted *to be with Juck?"* Mac's voice in my head was a tidal wave of frustration. *"Why did you lie to him?"*

"I didn't...I just... didn't correct him. I keep tryin' to explain, but he wants to think the worst of me, and I'm so... I'm so tired..." My voice trailed off.

Mac stared at me, his face frozen in what looked like angry disbelief.

"Somebody better start talkin'," Wolf growled from behind him.

"I can't," I thought to Mac, suddenly panicked. *"I can't do this, right now. Mac, I can't—"*

"Ok," he interrupted. *"Ok. We just gotta give him somethin'."*

My mind was a hornet's nest buzzing with panic.

"Ok," he said again, his grip relaxing on my upper arms. *"It's ok. I'm gonna help best I can, ok?"*

"Alright, here's the deal," Mac said out loud as he turned around to face Wolf. "Whatever story you've put together isn't the truth."

Wolf's furious eyes narrowed on me again, but Mac continued.

"We're gonna sort it out, alright? But right now, Em needs some fuckin' clothes. So you're gonna have to wait a minute."

"You think—" Wolf started angrily, but Mac interrupted, his voice icy.

"I think, at the very least, you can let her get fuckin' dressed."

Wolf set his jaw, but he stayed silent.

"We can meet you back at the clinic in half an hour, alright?" Mac said.

"Take Lee with you," Wolf said tightly.

I looked at Lee, but he just nodded at Wolf. Mac looked like he was grinding his teeth but finally nodded. He glanced at me and gestured with his head, and I followed him, trying to avoid Wolf, Scar, and Kai as much as possible. Lee trailed behind. I shoved my feet in my boots, not bothering to lace them. It was a cold, silent walk to the bunkhouse. The people we passed gave us odd looks. I knew I probably looked ridiculous in Mac's huge jacket, my bare legs, and untied boots. When we walked inside, Sam, Griz, and Raven did a double take at my appearance.

"What the fuck is...whatever the fuck this is?" Sam stood, his eyebrows almost touching his hairline.

"Are you wearing anything under Mac's jacket?" Raven asked.

Everyone's faces darkened when Lee followed us inside.

"Everything ok?" Griz asked tensely.

"No," I said, and Griz and Raven looked sharply at me.

"Whose question are you answering?" Griz asked.

"Both?" I muttered.

Raven smirked, but the furrow in Griz's forehead deepened.

"Raven, you got any clothes Em can borrow?" Mac asked.

"Em, huh?" Raven drawled, and I tensed, but she stood and gestured. "We'll figure somethin' out."

Raven dug through a dresser in the bedroom before throwing some undergarments and pants at me. I undid Mac's jacket and slid it off, surprised to find I wasn't too concerned about Raven seeing, well, everything. She'd seen it all many times when she was helping me recover.

"Those might fit. We might need to find you some suspenders."

I huffed a laugh, and she did a double take, her lips curling up. The pants were too big, but they stayed on my hips. Raven moved across the room to another dresser, kneeling and pulling open a drawer.

"This is Trey's drawer. You want to pick somethin', or do you want me to?"

I crossed my arms over my naked chest, my heart aching. I could not look through that drawer right now. "You can."

She tossed me a shirt, another one of Trey's old flannels. I pulled it on and then froze. Barely daring to hope, I brought the fabric up to my nose, and immediately, tears flooded my eyes. It very faintly smelled like him, and the scent made my longing and grief roar to life.

"So, do I get to know why you walked in here wearing just Mac's jacket?"

I struggled to keep from falling apart. "It's a long story."

"Can't be that long. I saw him a couple hours ago, and he was wearing it."

I opened my mouth to reply, but she continued.

"And what's with the guard dog followin' you around?"

I made a face. "I dunno. Wolf's makin' him stay with me."

She sniffed scornfully at Wolf's name. "Well, at least he's nice to look at."

I rolled my eyes, but before I could respond, there was a knock on the door.

"Em, you almost done?" Mac called. "We gotta go."

I took a breath, feeling nauseous again. I grabbed Mac's jacket, but before I could open the door, Raven put her palm on it, halting me. I peered up at her in surprise.

"Stop lettin' 'em make you feel small. Speak up and stand your ground. You got backup." I stared at her wide-eyed, and she rolled her eyes at my expression. "Don't look so surprised. I'm on your team, dumbass."

Raven opened the door, and I almost walked directly into Mac's chest. He was holding onto the top of the doorframe, blocking the doorway as he loomed over me, and staring at Trey's shirt, his expression soft and pained. He met my gaze, and I suddenly felt anxious he might not want anyone going through Trey's stuff.

"I'm sorry—"

"It looks good on you," he interrupted, holding my gaze. *"He'd want you to have it."*

I felt my face warm, and my eyes welled up again, but he just pushed off the doorframe. Behind him, Griz and Sam stood with their arms folded. Lee leaned against the wall near the door, observing with arms crossed. I tried to hand Mac his jacket, but he shook his head.

"Keep it so you don't have to walk to the clinic without a coat."

I slipped it back on, rolling up the sleeves so my hands didn't get lost.

"How do you want to do this, Em?" Mac asked.

I glanced up at him. "What do you mean?"

"Do you want any of us to come with you, or would it be easier by yourself?"

I shifted on my feet. If I made it through this without puking from anxiety, it would be a godsdamn miracle. "Is your whole crew gonna be there?" I asked Lee.

"Probably," Lee replied. "We've been invested for a long time."

Well, that didn't fucking help my nerves. I did not want to do this.

"I mean, we're invested, too," Sam said, his voice sharp, "but we're not forcin' her to talk about shit before she's ready."

I felt a swell of gratitude for him.

"You also haven't spent the last ten years lookin' for her," Lee responded.

"I don't think she asked you to do that," Sam snapped.

"Most fugitives don't." Lee's voice was still steady, but something flashed in his eyes.

Sam took a breath like he was about to go off, and I decided I'd had enough.

"Stop," I blurted out. "Just...fine, everybody can come." At least this way, I'd only have to say it once.

"You sure?" Griz asked.

"I gotta take care of some...stuff," Raven said from behind me. "You can fill me in later."

I suddenly noticed Jax was missing. "Where's Jax? Is Clarity—"

"Don't worry about it," Raven interrupted sharply.

"But what about—"

"Don't worry about it," Raven repeated louder.

"Ok," I said quickly, not missing the warning look Mac gave Raven.

"Wolf's gonna be pounding on the door soon," Lee warned.

"C'mon, Shortcake." Sam threw an arm around my shoulders and steered me toward the door. "How bad can it be?"

ᘓ

The energy inside the clinic was so tense it felt like walking into a physical wall. Wolf glared at me from the middle of the room as though he'd been pacing. The rest of his crew sat inside on wooden chairs or leaned against the wall. I put the metal exam table between me and my brother, clutching the edge for support.

Wolf crossed his arms over his chest and planted his feet wide. I felt like I was looking at Pa.

"So once again, you didn't tell me the truth. Gods, I guess I should've expected that at this point."

My breath caught painfully.

"Ease up," Mac snapped at him.

"No, I want to make it real clear," Wolf spat, "this is the last fuckin' time I'm asking you, Ember. So if you're gonna tell me the truth, it better be now."

My stomach churned, and I desperately sucked in a breath through my nose. This was my trial, wasn't it? My mouth went dry, and the anxiety was making me lightheaded.

Wolf stalked forward until he was directly across the table from me, and I took an involuntary step backward, bumping into Sam. Wolf slammed his palms flat on the table and leaned forward, his green eyes hard and focused on me.

"What were you—"

I knew I wouldn't make it to the door, so I spun and heaved into the sink. There was a slight commotion behind me, but I squeezed my eyes shut, my face hot with humiliation. Someone moved beside me, resting a gentle hand on the small of my back, and I peered up to see Griz holding out a clean towel.

Fucking hell. I hated this so much. He hadn't even gotten a whole question out. I turned the water on and cleaned myself and the sink before scooping some water into my mouth and spitting it back out, trying to rinse the sour taste. Griz stayed next to me, and I was so glad I had all of them come. If it were just me facing down Wolf and his pack, I would never be able to do this.

"Was that from bein' anxious?" Mac asked carefully.

"Yeah," I answered miserably.

"Tell him that."

That brought a swell of fear, and I could almost hear Wolf's voice snarling at me not to show any weakness.

"Who the hell was that?" Mac's voice was sharp, startling me.

"The Wolf that lives in my head."

"That didn't sound—"

"Bones?" Griz asked, sounding worried. "You ok?"

I realized I'd been silently leaning over the sink for too long. I forced myself to straighten and turn around. I could feel sweat beading on my forehead, and I wrapped my arms tightly around my body. Wolf's entire pack was on their feet. Wolf was still by the metal exam table, possibly only because Mac and Sam were blocking him. Like they'd formed a human fence to give me space.

"I'm sorry," I said. "I'm...I just...I just sometimes get sick when I'm... I'm anxious."

Wolf stared at me, his face unreadable.

"What were you gonna ask?" My voice dropped to a whisper.

"What were you doing in the dungeon with Madame?" he asked in a slightly calmer voice.

"Madame was t-torturin' people to try and find the leader of the rebellion," I spoke quickly, trying to get it all out. "She would... hurt them, and I would heal them." This time, I was relieved as the numbness started to creep over me. "Then she'd torture them again."

The silence roared in my ears.

"Madame didn't exactly give her a choice," Mac said. "And neither did I."

He stood straight with his arms loose at his sides, his body still between me and my brother like a shield.

"What does that mean?" Wolf growled.

I chewed on my lip, my eyes flicking between the two of them. What was Mac doing?

"Madame made it clear if I didn't keep Em in line, she'd make me and my crew pay. So I told Em she had to *cooperate,*" he spit the word out like it tasted sour. "She never once wanted to be there, never once wanted to be a part of what Madame was doin'." He finally glanced at me, and a corner of his mouth lifted, but his eyes were full of pain and regret. "She cussed me out about it."

"Mac."

"I'm just tellin' him the truth."

"Why did Madame whip you, Ember?" Wolf crossed his arms.

Maybe it was Mac confessing his part or Raven's voice echoing in my head, but I lifted my chin and held my brother's gaze. This was one thing I didn't feel ashamed about.

"I saved a girl she sentenced to death."

"No," Mac cut in, his voice sharp, "for *that*, Madame threw her in solitary confinement for six days with no food or water."

"Mac—" I started, but he kept going.

"*I* was supposed to be whipped, but your sister refused to let that happen and took it on herself." He stepped toward Wolf, and everyone tensed, but Mac's gaze remained locked on Wolf. "That day at the cabin? When she shielded you from gunfire with her own body while she healed you? When she healed every single one of us at the expense of her own self? *That* is who your sister is. *That* is what she's done for this hold again and again. During the sickness, she went out every day and healed until she couldn't even fuckin' walk. Not 'cause anybody told her she had to, but 'cause that's who she *is*."

I had no idea what sort of expression was on my face. I clung to the metal table, my head spinning. I could feel Wolf's crew staring at me, but I couldn't look away from Mac and Wolf.

"The Ember you've been chasin' all this time? She doesn't exist," Mac continued, his quiet voice commanding more attention than yelling. "I doubt she ever existed 'cause I've never met anyone so determined to protect everyone else."

No one besides Trey had ever remembered me like that—like I was *good*—and a small part of me had worried Trey only saw me that way because he looked for the good in everyone. It was much harder to brush away Mac's words. They felt heavier. They felt dangerously like truth.

Wolf and Mac studied each other silently for a few breaths before Wolf glanced over and met my eyes.

"Were you Juck's Angel?" he asked, his voice clipped.

"Yes," I whispered, and a muscle ticked in his jaw.

"When did you join the Reapers?"

The edge of the metal table pressed painfully into my palms as I gripped it. "Juck found me a week after I was exiled."

Something flashed in his eyes at the word "exiled," but he didn't say anything. The silence built into something painful.

"Were you fucking him?" he abruptly asked, his face carefully expressionless.

I sucked in a desperate breath through my nose. The closer I spiraled to unraveling, the more my brother seemed to retreat behind a blank mask.

"Watch it, Wolf," Griz growled, but Wolf didn't look away from me.

"Tell him, Em." Mac's voice in my head was furious. *"Don't let him think you were there by choice."*

"I didn't... didn't *want* to be with him," I choked out.

"That's not what I heard," Wolf replied, his voice maddeningly flat.

I knew the sort of rumors he'd probably heard. I'd had them sneered at me every damn day. The thought of him hearing them made helpless rage ignite deep in my stomach. No wonder he saw a twisted monster when he looked at me.

"You don't know *everythin'*, Wolf."

"Then tell me." Everything about him was blank—his voice, his face. It was like he'd locked everything away.

"What, do you want all the horrible details?"

"If it's the truth, then yes."

A furious desperation to crack through his blank mask gripped me. He wanted to know? He wanted the truth? Fine. Let *him* drown in it.

"Which details do you want, Wolf? You want me to tell you about how *lucky* I was that he only beat me and starved me for the first few years because he thought my powers were tied to my virginity? You want to hear how he was so furious after I tried to run away with my only friend, so convinced we must've been secretly fucking, that he decided to risk it? You want to know I was fourteen when he raped me for the first time? Should I describe how he was still covered in my friend's blood— my friend who was *tortured* for a whole fucking day before he died? You want to know Juck panicked when he realized I was bleeding, that I'd been tellin' the truth about still bein' *pure,*" I spat the word out with venom, "so he cut his arm and told me to heal him? And when I couldn't stop hyperventilating enough to do it, he broke my nose and told me he'd let the Reapers have me as *their* whore if I'd lost my powers."

Wolf's face had paled, and his nostrils flared, jaw flexing. His fists looked like they were clenched as tightly as mine, but I could see the cracks appearing in his mask, and I went after them with a vicious fixation.

"Is that enough *detail* for you, or do you want to hear about the thousands of other times it happened for the next *eight years?*"

Next to me, Sam swore low and furious under his breath. I didn't dare look at any of Wolf's crew, but I could tell they all stood unnaturally still.

"I *know* they said I liked it, that I provoked him, that I got off on him hurting me. I *know* they called me his plaything, his scavenger slut. I *know* they said I was desperate for his dick and that I *loved* him. You think they didn't throw all that shit in my face any chance they got? The *truth* is I gave up." A wild, bitter laugh escaped my lips. "So there— there's your godsdamned truth. The *truth* is I tried to fight like you taught me, and I *lost.* I wasn't strong enough, and he *broke* me. And I *know* I'm pathetic, but I stopped fighting him 'cause it was real fuckin' clear *no one* cared, and *no one* was comin' to save me."

Wolf inhaled sharply through his teeth, and I knew he heard what I didn't say—that I'd realized *he* wasn't coming to save me. He started shaking his head, a slow back-and-forth movement, but the spiderweb cracks in his mask widened until I could see the raw pain underneath. I thought it would make me feel better to force him to understand, but it didn't. The utter silence of the room began to wash away my anger and crush my lungs. Tremors ran through my whole body.

"So yes, I *was* his *whore,*" I spit the word at him, trying to hold onto that anger, and Wolf flinched. "I *was* his *Angel,* and you know what? I spent every day prayin' that maybe next time he'd get carried away and accidentally kill me. At least then, it'd be over. You think I need to suffer for Dune's death? Well, good news, I've been livin' in *hell* this entire time."

I couldn't be in this room any longer. I turned on my heel and fled out the door. No one moved to stop me, and as soon as I was outside,

I started to run.

⟨⟩

I wanted to return to Trey's grave, but I knew they'd look there first. So, instead, I let my feet take me to the stables.

The horses were all in the pasture when I arrived, breathless and shaking. Violet's head popped up as I slid under the fence, and she whinnied at me as she trotted over. She sniffed at Trey's shirt I wore and looked expectantly behind me. The pain in my chest made it hard to breathe.

"He's not comin' back," I whispered, stroking her neck. "He's gone."

She twisted to huff a warm breath in my hair.

"He's gone," I said again, and then I was sobbing.

She didn't move as I buried my face in her warm coat and wrapped my arms around her neck. The future that stretched out before me seemed so bleak. The only life I'd ever dared to want was built in his shape. I couldn't see a future without him. I didn't *want* a future without him.

I heard footsteps approaching, and I felt Violet turn to look, but I didn't lift my head.

"Well, I don't know why you were dreadin' that," a familiar voice deadpanned. "That was so much fun."

I turned to glare at Sam, who was stroking Violet's nose. He dug in his pocket and pulled out another handkerchief.

"How many of these do I have to give you 'fore you start carryin' them yourself?"

"I'm not wearin' *any* of my own clothes," I mumbled, taking it.

"Yeah, when do I get to hear *that* story?" Sam grinned, wiggling his eyebrows.

"There's nothin' to hear," I muttered, wiping at my face.

"I doubt that."

I stared at the mountains, hating that I couldn't stop crying. I wanted to crawl out of my skin and leave it behind. Just talking about the things Juck had done made me feel dirty and broken, like the ragged remains of a baby doll I'd seen half-buried in the ancient rubble of a desert city—once cherished, now trash. How was it fair that Juck was dead, but I would forever be his Angel, the girl he ruined?

"You're not pathetic."

I glanced at Sam when he spoke. He looked more serious than I'd ever seen him.

"A body and mind can only take so much hurt, and anyone who says they could've withstood bein' hurt for that long without breaking is fuckin' lying."

I looked away again, my stomach churning. "I didn't tell him the worst part."

"There's somethin' *worse?*" He sounded horrified.

"Sometimes…sometimes he was gentle and kind." Bile crept up my throat. "When he was like that, sometimes…I think I *did* love him."

I'd never admitted that to anyone, even myself. My hands trembled, and I clenched them into fists, immediately regretting saying the words out loud. What sort of person loved someone like Juck? A fucking pathetic, twisted—

"Emmy," His voice was soft now, and more tears spilled down my face. Hearing him call me that nickname made me think of Dune. "You were a kid—just a little girl who was tortured by a fuckin' monster. The worst kinda monsters twist pain and hate up with love. It's easy to see the bottom of a lake when it's still, but if you stir up the bottom and muddy the waters, it's impossible to see what's really there. It's easy to hate someone who *only* hurts you, so they muddy the waters with love."

He paused, and I glanced at him. He was looking at Violet as he stroked her nose, but there was so much pain in his face.

"My dad used to beat my mom, and I know lots of people have shit dads, but me and my older brother Scout tried so hard to convince her to leave him. Scout even moved to a different hold and worked his ass off to get a house. The plan was for me and our mom to go live with him." He sighed, his eyes far away. "But she changed her mind again and wouldn't leave. She believed our dad had changed and was gonna treat her right this time. Scout couldn't bear to come back, and I couldn't bear to leave her here alone. So I joined the guards, but just a couple months later, she was dead."

I swiped my leaking eyes with his handkerchief again. It was hard to see him like this. He was always so full of laughter and light. Now I wondered if that was *his* mask he wore to hide the pain inside.

"I was so angry at my dad for what he did, but I was angry at my mom for a long time, too. I finally opened up about all of this to Mac,

Griz, and Trey in training, and they helped me realize how manipulative my dad was and how he'd twisted love with pain to trap her. Breaking away from a relationship like that is so fuckin' hard." He paused. "The fact you're standin' here means you might be the strongest person I know —hell, stronger than Griz even."

I didn't feel strong. I hadn't really broken away from Juck. Everything just went to shit, and I did what I had to do to survive. If he'd killed Vulture after he caught us together and the other powered person hadn't interfered, there was a good chance I'd still be with Juck, and that made me feel sick.

Desperate to crawl out of the awful hole I'd fallen back into, I focused on his hands as he stroked Violet. They *definitely* had a tremor. His once tan skin was still pale and tinged with grey, and his blue eyes were sunken and dulled. He hadn't put on any weight or muscle in the past months, and I knew he was trying to. What if he was getting worse? I couldn't heal him. What—

"Oh, for fuck's sake, quit worryin' about me," he said, and he sounded back to his usual annoying self.

"I can't," I snapped.

He grinned. "Cause you *love* me."

"Cause you're *sick.*"

"Sure." He drew the word out slowly.

"Sam, I mean it," I said, frustrated.

"It's ok. You'll admit you love me one of these days. Hopefully, before I die, but—"

His words cut off in a grimace as a confusing mix of emotions choked me—my lips twitching up as my eyes welled up again.

"Too far?"

"You're awful," I mumbled, wiping fresh tears away with his handkerchief.

"I am," he agreed readily, stepping closer and wrapping his arm around my shoulders.

We stood there for a while, watching Violet and the other horses, and the warmth and weight of his arm helped steady me.

"I hate that my powers hurt you," the whispered words suddenly tumbled out of my mouth.

"Well, *I* love that you're still alive," Sam retorted.

"Sam—" My voice broke.

His arm tightened around me. "I'm ok, Shortcake."

"I'm so scared somethin' is gonna happen to you, and I won't be able to heal you."

"If it does, I need you to know it won't be your fault."

"That is *bullshit—*"

"No, listen to me," he turned to face me, gripping my shoulders tightly. There was no trace of humor in his gaunt face. "If I die, and you can't save me, I'm absolvin' you of any guilt."

"You can't—"

"I *can,* and if you insist on blaming yourself, I *will* haunt you." A tiny glint of playfulness appeared.

"At least you'd still be here," I mumbled, thinking of the silence at Trey's grave.

"You say that now," he countered, grinning. "Might change your mind after my ghost knocks all those tiny little bottles off the hutch every damn day."

"Sam, just, please...please promise to tell me if you feel like you're gettin' worse?"

He studied me, his face going serious again.

"Please, Sam?" My voice trembled.

He sighed. "Alright, I can promise that."

We stood in silence for a while longer, just watching the horses. I tried to rein in my fear, but it struck me like a bolt of lightning how terrified I was to lose Sam. I took a deep, shuddering breath and wrapped my arm around his waist, trying to keep myself from clinging to him.

"You can call me 'Emmy'...if you want," I whispered. "Dune used to call me that."

He rested his chin on top of my head, and I could hear his smile. "You tryin' to get rid of 'Shortcake'?"

A small smile crossed my face. "I don't mind 'Shortcake.'"

"Hey!"

We both looked up to see Griz striding toward us. He was studying us carefully, but his voice was casual, as though I hadn't just dumped over a decade of horror on them.

"You two want to come to the canteen for dinner? Bell's about to ring."

They'd been inviting me to dinner for months, and I always said no. But I did not want to sit in the clinic by myself—or worse, alone with

Wolf and his crew.

"Sure," I said.

"I'll bring you—" Griz started before his eyes snapped to my face, full of surprise. "Wait, did you say yes?"

I nodded, unable to resist the slight smile curling over my lips.

"Apple is gonna lose it," Griz warned with an answering grin. "She doesn't know you woke up yet."

"Oh, this is gonna be fun," Sam cackled.

CHAPTER 13

Apple was standing outside the canteen with some other kids, all gathered around Leda and talking a mile a minute. Griz let out a whistle, and Apple turned toward us. When she noticed me, her mouth dropped open, her face visibly paling. I picked up my pace, nervous she was about to faint, but then she burst into tears and charged toward us. I crouched so I could catch her as she barreled into me, her little arms wrapping tightly around my neck.

"Bones!" she sobbed. "I thought you were gonna die!"

My eyes prickled at her distress. "I'm okay, Apple. I'm okay."

She tried to say something but was crying too hard to make it out. I shifted to kneel on the cold ground, holding her tightly as she continued to cling to my neck. I could feel her tears dampening my shirt, but I didn't care.

The other kids surrounded us. More than a few were crying, and I tried to comfort them with one arm as I held Apple with the other. The lump in my throat threatened to choke me.

"It's alright," I promised over and over, smoothing back tangled hair and wiping tears. "I'm alright."

"Don't suffocate her now," Leda scolded as she approached with Jet on her hip, but she was beaming when I met her eyes. "Oh, honey, I'm so glad to see you."

I got to my feet with Apple in my arms, and Leda wrapped both of us in a warm hug. Jet squealed and clumsily patted my face with his chubby hand, drooling around a little tooth I could see peeking out of his gums. The other kids were clinging to my clothes and legs and all talking at once, but despite the complete chaos, I smiled, misty-eyed. This was *home*.

Leda released me, sniffling a little and tucking her long, curly brown hair behind her ear. Then she groaned, "Oh, I'm so sorry, Bones. Jet drooled all over your shirt."

"I don't care," I laughed, gesturing to where Apple had cried all over my other shoulder.

"Alright, kiddos, looks like Neena's about to open the door," Griz announced.

They all pulled back, but Apple's arms tightened around my neck. Griz held his hands out and raised his eyebrows, silently offering to take her, but I shook my head with a smile. The doors opened with a creak, and Neena appeared, grinning at the kids.

As we began to file inside, I glanced around us, and my heart skipped a beat when I realized Wolf and his entire crew were standing off to the side, watching. I quickly looked away.

"Hey." Mac appeared seemingly out of nowhere, scanning me. *"You okay?"*

I honestly wasn't sure, so I shrugged.

"I knew it was bad, but that...that was way worse than I thought."

His voice sounded pained, and I glanced at his face to see pain reflected in his eyes.

"I'm sorry you had to hear all that."

"What?" His eyes narrowed.

"I know it's awful to hear—"

"That's not what I meant." Anger snapped in his voice now. *"I'm not talking about how I felt hearin' about it. I'm talkin' about you fucking goin' through all that."*

I fiddled with the collar of his jacket I was still wearing. *"Oh."*

"The only reason I'm angry right now is 'cause I can't rip Juck into little shreds."

I tried for a smile, but it felt flat.

His eyes softened, and his hand twitched like he would reach for me, but then he stopped. *"You did good today."*

I swallowed hard, trying to keep it together. *"Thank you...for everything you said."*

"I just called it like I saw it."

"You two having a moment?"

Both of us looked at Sam, startled. He glanced between us, eyebrows raised, and I realized Mac and I had been silently staring at each other. Griz was watching, too, and he had a funny look on his face. My heart started galloping in my chest, but Mac grinned.

"Yeah, we were. Rude of you to interrupt, Sam."

"My bad," Sam replied, but he was studying the two of us closely in a way that made me nervous for some reason.

"Don't tell them yet," I begged.

Mac shot me a brief look full of frustration, but in my head, he replied, *"Alright."*

Apple turned her head toward Mac, and he focused on her with a smile.

"You find a baby squirrel?" Mac asked out loud, reaching out to gently tug on one of Apple's pigtails.

She giggled tearfully and swatted at him, and he surprised me by playfully pretending to be knocked backward. It made the lump in my throat worse.

Following the line inside the canteen, I gathered my courage and asked Mac, *"Earlier...did...did you hear Wolf's thoughts?"*

He tensed beside me. *"Yeah."*

I glanced at him, trying to keep my face impassive, but he looked ahead of us into the canteen. *"Mac, I think...I think this is* your *power."*

He finally looked at me, and the discomfort in his eyes made me feel even worse.

"Let's talk about this later."

I chewed on my cheek but replied, *"Okay."*

"Hi, Bones!" Neena smiled at me as we reached the counter and held out a mug of broth. "You want anything with this or just broth tonight?"

"Just broth," I said, touched.

"It's really good to see you," Neena added as she handed the mug over.

My face felt flushed again, but I managed a small smile. As Neena moved on to give Mac his and Apple's rations, I noticed she was missing her ring finger on her right hand. I hadn't paid much attention before, but it looked a couple of years old, and I wondered how it happened. I followed Mac to their table, realizing this was the first time I'd ever sat with my own crew. Granted, I hadn't eaten at the canteen often, but the large room felt different. Someone had hung up a long garland made from what looked like colorful fabric scraps. It draped from the beams in the vaulted ceiling, stretching across the room. It looked cleaner inside, the worn wood floor practically shining. Old tin cans sat on the long wooden tables full of little bouquets of evergreen branches. The entire room seemed brighter and warmer somehow.

Apart from the canteen's appearance, the atmosphere was the most significant difference. Before, the room had been mostly quiet. People kept their heads down and ate quickly before leaving. The loggers and Madame's guards had been loud but in a rough, aggressive way. Now, the room was full of people talking and laughing. Nemo was moving between the tables, talking to people. The kids had their own shorter table now, and they were all sitting at it, giggling and making silly faces as Leda passed out their rations. I glanced at the logger's table. It was pretty empty, with only a handful of people, but Marsh and Silver had taken a seat, and they both smiled and waved when they noticed me. I was glad they hadn't taken Madame's side during the rebellion. They'd always been kind to me.

I sat beside Mac, with Apple still clinging to my neck. "You wanna sit with the kids or with me?" I murmured.

"With you," she mumbled tearfully, finally releasing my neck and clambering to sit beside me on the bench. Griz sat next to her. I started fixing her disheveled pigtails when someone sat directly across from me. I glanced up, and my stomach flipped as I met my brother's eyes. He settled himself on the bench and dropped his gaze to his food. I focused on Apple's hair, registering out of the corner of my eye that Lee and Sable settled on either side of Wolf, and the rest of the pack joined as well. The silence made me want to get the hell out—

"So, where are the rest of you from?" Mac suddenly asked.

I glanced up at him, surprised. His voice sounded strained, but his expression was as friendly as I'd ever seen.

Lee answered, and the rest followed suit. Sable said he was from a town I didn't recognize, and I guessed that was before the slavers took him. I still couldn't look at him. Griz picked up the conversation after that, asking questions and keeping it flowing with help from Sam. I sipped my broth and carefully kept my eyes away from Wolf's side of the table. Apple ate her food while pressed into my side, one hand fisted in my shirt. When I glanced at her, I realized she was scowling fiercely at Wolf and had to fight the urge to smile.

"Bones!"

I looked up to see an older woman whose name I couldn't remember. She stood behind Wolf, beaming at me.

"It's so good to see you out and about," she said with a kind smile.

A shy, answering smile curled over my lips and surprised me. As though the woman had broken some sort of spell, for the rest of dinner, there was a steady stream of people coming over to say hello and ask how I was doing. I couldn't decide if it was nice or uncomfortable. Wolf and his crew seemed to note every interaction carefully, making nerves flutter in my stomach. Did Mac tell people to do this—

"I didn't tell them to do this," Mac immediately replied in my head. *"They're comin' over to say hello and see how you are because they care about you."*

Gods, I forgot he could hear me.

"So, Wolf said they don't burn people alive?" he added.

"I don't know what to believe," I admitted, hiding my face behind my mug as I took a slow drink of broth. *"Dune never lied to me before, and I don't know why he would ever lie about that."*

Mac ate a bite of his food and chewed for a few seconds before asking, *"Could Wolf be lying?"*

"I don't think so," I replied. *"I mean, I don't know, but it didn't seem like he was lying."*

"Would they accept your powers?"

My skin crawled. *"I doubt it. It wouldn't fit with their teachings."*

"What were their teachings?"

"They thought women were lesser, only suitable for havin' babies and takin' care of the home."

His lip curled. *"I've heard of places like that."*

"I'm so confused," I admitted, my eyes prickling. *"I don't understand why Dune would lie."*

He shifted slightly on the bench so that his arm pressed against mine. *"I'm sorry."*

"Mac?"

We all glanced up to see Nemo approaching, his face grave.

"Sorry, but I need to borrow you for a moment," he said.

Mac shot me an apologetic look. "I'll catch up with y'all later," he said out loud.

I watched him leave the canteen with Nemo, the two of them speaking in low tones. Unease and guilt filled me. I needed to tell him about the other powered person. It was urgent. People's lives were at stake. Why hadn't I told him yet? Why did I feel sick with fear when I thought about it?

Even stranger, I wasn't scared by Mac's presence in my head. It was familiar but also so different. The other powered person's presence instinctively terrified me. It felt dangerous, like a predator, like an invasion. So, what did Mac's presence feel like?

I thought about it as I slowly sipped my broth. Mac felt like... nothing—but not in a bad way. That didn't make any sense. Nothing in a good way? That wasn't—

My stomach did a little flip as the realization crashed into me.

No, not nothing. *Me.*

Mac's power—if it was *Mac's* power—felt like mine. That's why I barely noticed it.

What the fuck did *that* mean?

"Freckles? Hey, Freckles!"

I blinked and met Lee's eyes.

"You want some more broth?" he asked.

I glanced at Wolf, but he was simply watching me with an unreadable expression. "What?"

"Do you want some more broth?" Lee repeated, a slight grin crossing his face.

"No," I said, confused. Everyone was looking at me now.

"You were starin' into that mug like you hoped it would magically refill itself." Lee's grin widened.

"Oh." My face warmed. "No, I'm fine."

"Do you often have to stick to broth?" Sable asked from the other side of Wolf.

I set the mug down, still not looking at him, and shrugged.

"Does certain food make you sick?" Lee asked.

"No," I said to my plate.

"You never used to have any problem with food," Wolf finally spoke, his voice low.

My heart was pounding so fast, sending adrenaline surging through me. My body was responding to this conversation like I was about to fight Brimstone again. Movement caught my attention, and I saw Sam standing from where he had sat on the other side of Griz. He strode over and sat in Mac's empty spot, his hand finding mine under the table and squeezing. His thin face was serious again.

"Emmy, c'mon," he said softly.

"Sam—"

"I think it's important," he interrupted.

I stared at him, my heart in my throat.

"If it has to do with your health, it's important," Sable murmured.

Sam squeezed my hand again under the table, his expression expectant and encouraging.

"I'm makin' a guess this is related to the starvation," Sable added quietly.

My spine locked up. Had I said something about that? I honestly couldn't remember everything I'd spit out in the clinic.

"There's something called refeeding—"

"I know," I interrupted, my face heating even more. "And yes."

I gripped Sam's hand as though drowning, but he didn't seem to mind. The table was silent for a moment. Apple wrapped herself around my arm.

"How often were you denied food?" Sable asked.

"I don't know," I mumbled. "Often."

"For long periods?"

"Sometimes, yeah."

"How long?"

I blinked furiously, determined to keep my wet eyes from overflowing. "Three weeks and two days was the longest."

"Prolonged starvation can be devastating to a body," Sable continued, his voice gentle. "Especially for a child."

I pressed my trembling lips together.

"Do you feel like your body still suffers from the refeeding syndrome?" Sable asked after a short silence. "From what I know, it shouldn't be permanent."

"I don't know." I kept my gaze on my empty plate. "If I go t-too long without eating, I get anxious I'll get sick if I eat... and then I get sick because I'm anxious."

"Why do you get anxious about being sick?"

I wasn't going to answer, but the sharp words escaped. "Well, when you get fuckin' beat for puking, you learn to be anxious about it."

Wolf abruptly stood, and I jumped, my gaze shooting to his face. His eyes flashed, but he simply turned and stalked out of the canteen. His crew exchanged silent looks before Scar and Lee got up and followed him.

"If he puts another hole in the wall, he's fixin' it," Sam said.

"What?" I asked, my stomach clenching.

"He punched through the wall earlier," Sam explained matter-of-factly as though that were normal.

"He'll fix it," Tuck spoke up.

"He punched through the wall?" I repeated, bewildered.

"After you left the clinic," Sam said.

"*Through* the wall?" My brain was apparently stuck on this. The wood-paneled clinic wall was not a material easy to *punch through*.

"Well, he did break several bones in his hand," Sable said, also matter-of-factly as though *that* were normal.

"What?" I finally looked at Sable and found him studying me with his pale blue eyes.

"It's alright. I set the bones and bandaged him up."

I hadn't even noticed his hand was bandaged, but I'd been avoiding looking at him at all costs. I exhaled sharply through my nose and stood, gently extricating myself from Apple.

"Where you going?" Sam asked.

"To heal my stupid brother."

౭ఎ

It took me a while to find them. They'd gone into the deserted marketplace. The market only ran three times a week, from morning to afternoon. When it was closed, all the booths were empty. I glanced at the small rectangular booth where a faded green bunting fluttered gently in the breeze, remembering when Griz and I found Jax inside with a bullet in his shoulder. Gods, if we hadn't found him—

I forced that thought away.

Wolf, Scar, and Lee were standing at the far end of the marketplace. Wolf had his back to me, but Scar seemed to be speaking to him with their hand gestures. Lee spotted me immediately, but he didn't warn the others. Instead, he flashed me a crooked grin and watched as I neared. I was almost to them when he finally nudged Wolf. Wolf spun around to face me, and the raw emotion in his face made me falter slightly. It was carefully gone a breath later, his face smoothing into a blank mask.

"Give me your hand," I demanded when I reached him.

His eyes narrowed at me, and his voice came out rough. "What?"

"Your hand," I repeated impatiently, gesturing at his bandaged hand at his side.

"You don't—" he started, but I'd had about enough.

"Wolf," I snapped, "just give me your damn hand."

Lee made a suspicious coughing sound, but I didn't look at him. Wolf glared at me a second longer before slowly giving me his bandaged hand. I took it, carefully unwrapping the bandage and checking to ensure the splints stayed in place. The flesh of his hand was already swollen and darkening with bruises. I cradled his hand in both of mine and let my healing power flow into him, assessing the damage.

He'd broken three bones in his fingers and fractured several in his hand. I was grateful Sable had already set the bones, so I didn't have to move them, but the damage was extensive. My powers painstakingly fused the tiny bones back together, and the swollen tissue began to recede. His breath caught slightly, but I kept my eyes on his hand. The bruising faded, and the skin smoothed over, leaving no sign of the injury.

"The next time you feel like punchin' a wall, at least do it where I could put a fucking window," I muttered.

He didn't say anything, and I glanced at his face. The emotion and pain there made my stomach flip over in panic, so I just released his hand and strode away.

CHAPTER 14

I made it halfway back to the clinic before Lee materialized beside me, scaring me half to death.

"You healed my leg in the cave, didn't you?" he asked, and I nodded, trying to slow my heart rate. "Why?"

I sighed. "Because it was gettin' infected."

"So?"

I gave him a sharp look. "*So?* You could've lost your leg."

"Probably would've made it much easier for you to escape if I only had one leg."

I didn't answer, walking around a particularly deep, muddy puddle in the path.

"Did your dad really tell you Wolf was gonna kill you?"

"What?" I swung my gaze back to him so fast I almost tripped. Had I told him that?

He tilted his head slightly. "Do you remember talking to me in the cave?"

"Yes?"

"Guess you probably wouldn't remember that part, though," he mused. "You were pretty delirious. You thought I was Trey."

I came to an abrupt halt, all the blood rushing out of my face in horror. I thought Lee was *Trey?* What the fuck had I done? What did I say?

"It's alright. You were just very concerned for my safety."

"What does that mean?" I demanded.

"You wanted me to hide so Wolf wouldn't kill me, too."

I stared at him, my mouth dry as sand. "What else did I do?"

"Nothin' happened, Freckles." I hated the pity on his face. "You were sad. You wanted me to hold you, so I held you."

I swallowed hard and lurched forward again. I had no memory of that, and I hated not knowing for sure what had happened. I hated that I just had to trust him. He continued to walk beside me, but I avoided looking at him.

"Griz said he died three months ago."

"I don't want to talk about it," I bit out.

He paused, then said, "Alright."

"Why are you following me?"

"Wolf feels better when somebody's with you," he explained, and I scoffed. "Well, learnin' more about you hasn't exactly eased his mind. Did you really jump into a pit to fight a giant without a weapon?"

"I *had* a weapon."

"A tiny knife?"

I glared at him and found him grinning, eyes crinkled. "I killed Madame with that knife," I shot back.

His eyebrows raised. "Alright, I take it back." He walked beside me for a few seconds before he spoke again. "So, who's Zip?"

For fuck's sake. "Who told you about Zip?" I demanded.

"Oh, Sam mentioned him in passing, and Griz just about bit his head off."

"I'm not talking about him either," I muttered.

"What *will* you talk about?"

"Is stabbing you still an option?"

He laughed out loud. He had a nice laugh, rich and warm.

"I like you," he said, still grinning.

I glared at him out of the corner of my eye, which only seemed to amuse him further. I decided to ignore him for the rest of the walk to the clinic. He didn't seem to mind, walking silently along beside me. As the clinic came into view, I was disappointed no one was waiting for me on the porch. I'd been hoping to have a job to jump into immediately. As I climbed up the steps, I sighed and started mentally running through what cleaning I should tackle first, but when I opened the door, I stopped so abruptly on the threshold that Lee barely managed to avoid walking into my back.

He said something, but I didn't hear it. My eyes were locked on the wall between the wood stove and the kitchen, where the word "MURDERER" was written in giant red letters on the wooden panels. It was fresh—so fresh the red liquid was still slowly dripping down the wall. I don't know how long I stood there frozen before Lee physically moved my body so he could get inside. He released my waist and strode past me, his eyes narrowed on the wall. I finally remembered to breathe and immediately gagged. The entire room reeked of blood and Madame's sickly-sweet scent.

I turned on my heel and retreated outside, somehow not falling down the steps. I stopped beside the apple tree in my front yard, leaning against it with my hand clasped over my mouth as I sucked in air through my nose. Who would do this? Why did the whole clinic smell like Madame? Was that word written in *blood?* My mind shied away from the emotion building inside my chest, floating out of my body again.

A hand touched my shoulder, and I jumped. Lee's mouth was moving like he was talking to me, but it took a monumental effort to force myself to tune in.

"—okay? Freckles? Can you hear me?" Some of the tension in his face faded when I nodded. "There's no one in there. I'm guessin' that's the same scent as the soap?"

I nodded again, inhaling deeply through my nose.

"Any idea who would do this?"

I shook my head.

"How about why?"

I looked away, staring out at the hold. *Why?* That was pretty fucking obvious, wasn't it?

Lee took my free hand, squeezing gently. When I didn't jerk my hand away, he stepped closer and pulled me into a hug. I still had one hand clasped over my mouth and my face pressed against his chest. I stood there numbly, not reciprocating but also not pulling away. My thoughts tumbled over each other like falling rocks.

You were sad. You wanted me to hold you, so I held you.

"What's goin' on?"

Griz's voice was sharper than usual. Lee answered, and I focused on the feeling of his voice rumbling in his chest instead of the actual words.

"What?" Griz sounded furious.

"Go look," Lee said.

"Bones?" Griz asked instead.

I pulled away from Lee and looked at him. Griz studied me silently, but he didn't speak, and that hollow feeling intensified.

"Stay here," he finally said. "I'm gonna go look."

I watched him walk up to the clinic and enter. A dull ringing sound filled my ears.

MURDERER.

Something touched my face, and I jerked away, startled.

"Wait, hold on. Hold still," Lee commanded.

I froze, watching him. He stepped closer again and gently gripped my jaw with one hand while using the other to place a finger on my cheek. His brow furrowed in concentration as he moved his finger toward my chin and then back up toward my ear. Was he drawing something?

"What are you doing?" I finally asked.

"I thought so!" he said.

"What?"

"You have constellations in your freckles." He met my eyes, grinning.

I stared at him.

"I just found Orion."

I continued to stare at him. All the frantic thoughts in my head had come to a screeching halt.

"I swear I found Ursa Minor when we were in the cave."

I blinked, and his grin widened.

"What, no one's ever told you that you have a map of the stars on your face?"

"No," I managed to say.

"Funny, that's the first thing I thought when I saw you." He traced the shape of Orion on my cheek again. "All the beauty and mystery of the night sky right there on your skin."

I'd forgotten how to speak. He shifted to cup my face with both hands. His fingers felt cool on my heated cheeks.

"And those damn green eyes."

Was it my imagination, or had his voice dropped lower?

"Like twin celestial jewels."

"Are you *flirting* with me?" I stepped backward so his hands fell from my face.

He grinned. "Well, you figured it out much faster than your brother."

My brain struggled to process. "You flirt with my brother?"

"I tried, but he prefers blondes," he replied, his voice casual.

My brow creased in confusion. I couldn't tell if he was joking or not.

"I mean, you figured out I was flirting with you before Wolf realized I was flirting with you."

That empty hole in my chest thrummed with pain. "Don't flirt with me."

"Why not?" he gave me a devilish grin.

"I'm not..." What the fuck was this conversation right now? "... available."

He tilted his head slightly, and one of the messy strands of black hair escaping from his bun fell across his face. "Available for what?"

"Anything."

"Not available for *anything*?" His eyebrows raised. "Sounds pretty lonely."

My brow creased even further. What the fuck?

The clinic door slamming shut brought me back to reality. I took a small sidestep further away from Lee as Griz stormed toward us, his face dark.

"Who would do this?" he growled, looking between us.

"No idea," Lee answered.

"I wasn't asking *you*," Griz grumbled at him before looking at me. "Bones, you have any idea?"

I shook my head, feeling a small stab of guilt.

Griz frowned. "We need to get Mac and Nemo."

"I'll go," Lee offered.

The two of us stood and watched Lee stride away. I had no idea what to think about that whole conversation.

"Did you get sick?" Griz asked.

"No," I realized out loud. I'd been too preoccupied with whatever the fuck that was with Lee.

Griz turned to face me, gripping my shoulders with his large hands. His face was so serious. "Are you okay?"

"I don't know," I said, figuring it was probably the most honest answer.

"That scent in there, that's Madame's soap, isn't it?"

I nodded, my throat constricting.

"Someone's tryin' to get to you." Anger flashed through his eyes, and I looked away. "Bones, you swear you don't know who did this?"

"I don't know who did this."

It wasn't really a lie. I didn't know who did this, but I did have an idea. Hawk hadn't said a word to me since that awful night in the dungeon when Mist almost died, but I felt the heat of his hatred any time I made eye contact with him. I wasn't about to name him, though. I had no proof, and besides that, I'd already done enough to fuck up Hawk's life. I didn't want to do anything else.

"You know you're not a murderer, right?" his voice gentled.

I met his gaze again, feeling so damn tired. "I *am* a murderer, Griz. I've killed people."

"I'm not gonna cry over Madame or Juck."

"Do you have any idea how many Reapers I watched die? People I could've saved?"

"I don't think that's the same thing," he argued. "And even if it was, that's on Juck, not on you. Do you think I'm a murderer? I killed people during the rebellion. People I've known my whole life."

"That's different," I mumbled.

He sighed, then surprised me by pulling me into a hug. "It's really not."

I wrapped my arms around his waist, my throat aching. We stood for a long time before I could force the ragged words out.

"I don't *want* to kill *anyone*."

"I know," he said without hesitation, squeezing me tighter. "That's why you're not a murderer, Bones."

"You can call me 'Em' if you want."

He pulled back enough to look at me. "You sure?"

I nodded.

"Alright, Em," he said with a smile.

A couple of minutes later, Mac came running up the path, his eyes flashing with a familiar fury. His voice was curt in my head as he demanded to know if I was okay. I gave him the same answer I gave Griz, and he looked angrier. He paused in front of us.

"You good?" he asked Griz, who nodded.

Mac stormed into the clinic. Nemo and several of his men joined shortly after. It was growing dark now, the last orange and purple glow disappearing behind the mountains. It wasn't long before Wolf and his entire crew appeared. Wolf stopped in front of me, his face serious, and I was acutely aware he knew someone had written "MURDERER" on my wall.

"I've been speaking with Nemo," Wolf said.

My stomach flipped, and my fingers fiddled with my shirt collar, pulling it tighter.

"We've worked out a deal that me and my crew will stay here for two months workin' as security, but the terms are you have to stay at the clinic with us, and you gotta *talk* to me so we can…figure this out. Deal?"

I honestly wasn't sure if I felt relieved or not. "I can't go in there if it…if it smells like that," I said.

"Smells like what?" Wolf asked.

"Like Madame," Griz answered when I didn't say anything.

Wolf gave Lee a sharp look, and I wondered why Lee had left that part out. "What do you mean smells like Madame?" he asked.

"She used this soap that was real strong smellin'," Griz explained. "Whoever did this broke a whole fuckin' bottle of the scent in there." He looked at me. "You can spend another night at Nemo's while we air the clinic out."

Wolf's crew exchanged looks like they were having a silent conversation before Wolf turned back to me. "I don't want you to be alone."

My brow furrowed.

"Somebody vandalized your clinic in a personal attack." He gave me a familiar, exasperated look.

"She won't be alone," Griz said.

Wolf frowned, his eyes narrowing on Griz, but Griz had already turned back to me.

"You ready to head over there?" Griz asked.

"Wait," Wolf interrupted, stepping into my space. "I want to hear you agree to the terms of our deal."

The angry words about where exactly he could shove his fucking deal almost escaped my mouth, but I managed to hold them in. "Deal," I muttered. It wasn't like I had an actual choice.

My brother's eyes narrowed, almost like he knew what I hadn't said. "I always keep my end of the bargain, Ember. I expect you to do the same."

I turned and walked away to avoid saying something I'd regret, and Griz followed my lead. I drew in slow and steady breaths, and I'd cooled my temper a bit by the time we reached Nemo's house. Nemo's guards greeted us quietly. I recognized several of them as guards who found me in Madame's cell, and I couldn't tell if they seemed uncomfortable around me or if I was imagining it.

"Are you staying?" I asked as we climbed the stairs.

"Yep," he replied, and part of me relaxed.

Griz pulled a folded cot out from behind the bed and set it up in front of the door. Once we were both in bed and the light flicked off, my brain seemed to come alive.

MURDERER.

I swallowed hard and rolled over onto my stomach, trying to think of anything else, but every time I closed my eyes, I saw blood—the gaping hole in the side of Trey's head, Madame's neck, the knife in Juck's chest. I flopped into several different positions, but I couldn't get my brain to shut off.

"Griz?" I whispered.

"Yeah?" he answered immediately.

"Do you have any family here?"

"Not anymore, why?"

"I was just wonderin'."

"That why you're tossin' and turnin' over there?" I could hear his smile. "Cause you're wonderin' about my family?"

"No," I muttered. "Just tryin' to…to not think."

"Ah," he said more gently. "You want to hear about 'em?"

"Yeah," I whispered, relieved.

"My grandma raised me. My dad died before I was born, and my mom died when I was two in a farming accident. I don't remember much about her, but I guess she loved to sing." He huffed a quiet laugh. "She was always singin', but nobody minded 'cause she was real good at it. I guess she used to sing when she was out workin' in the fields, and even the animals would get quiet like they were listening, too."

"Do you sing?" I asked.

He laughed. "No, I didn't inherit that trait, I guess. My grandma was a farmer, too, when she was able. She started losing her sight when I was about six. By the time I was ten, I was takin' care of her more than the other way around. I actually liked it, takin' care of her, but she wanted me to go be somethin' more than her caretaker or a farmer."

I remembered all the times Griz nursed me back to health; no wonder he was so good at it.

"My grandma wanted me to get into the guards. I didn't really want to, but I realized if I worked my way up, I could provide her with an easier life in her final years. When I started training, I bunked with three other kids. Two wouldn't stop talking, and one never said a word. Bet you'll never guess who they were."

"Trey, Sam, and Mac?"

"Yep. While I was in training, my grandma's heart gave out, and she passed. I took it real hard. I felt so guilty I hadn't been there. I think that's about when Trey decided we were all gonna be a family since none of us had any."

I felt another stab of guilt that I hadn't bothered to learn anything about them until now. "What about Raven? And...Lana and Exo?"

He didn't answer for a moment. "Lana was Raven's roommate. She didn't want to join the guards, but Exo was her only family left, and she was terrified of being separated from him. They were both Rusters, and her options were real limited. Her choice was to join the guards or join the brothel."

I winced.

"She wasn't cut out to be a fighter, and she was at the very bottom of the pecking order until Raven broke down and took Lana under her wing. But even with Raven's help, she was barely passing and still got beat up pretty regularly. Exo would lose his shit when she got beat up and was obsessed with avenging her, but he was a pretty scrawny kid and always went in way too hot and ended up getting the shit kicked out of him, too. So she stopped telling him about it to try and keep him from gettin' involved and hurt."

"Gods," I muttered under my breath, and he paused.

"That sorta thing is encouraged...or was, I guess. The trainers never intervened 'cause they said it was nature's way of weedin' out the weak. Not many people got kicked outta training, but plenty of 'em quit or died. Things with Lana escalated pretty bad, but she refused to quit 'cause she wanted to be with her brother. Our second year, Mac caught some of the other trainees practically torturing Lana, and he beat the shit out of 'em and told 'em Lana was under his protection from then on. That earned Raven's respect, and I'd known her and Exo from when we were kids, so they just naturally merged with the rest of us."

I lay silently, Lana's red-rimmed eyes full of hatred lingering in my memory.

"Lana was a...complicated person," Griz continued quietly. "She'd been hurt her whole life, and Exo was the only one who tried to protect her before she met us. I dunno what she needed, but I think it was more than we could give her. She got stronger physically but always seemed...on the edge of *somethin'*. Mac and I had a whole conversation a few years ago about what would happen if Exo died." He sighed. "I was afraid she'd snap and hurt herself. I never would've guessed she'd hurt someone else."

I didn't want to feel sympathy for Lana. I still had nightmares about Dale and Pike, but the ache in my chest couldn't be ignored. I knew far too well what layers and layers of pain could do to a person.

"I cared for Lana, but when she asked me to intervene in bein' exiled, I told her I wouldn't. Raven told her the same thing. I guess we all kinda took a step back and really looked at her and saw how she used her pain as a weapon. Not just toward you, but toward everyone."

The pain in his voice was easy to hear, and guilt clogged my throat. "I'm sorry—"

"No, Em," he interrupted firmly. "None of this was your fault."

I stared at the firelight flickering on the ceiling and worried my bottom lip between my teeth. Lana and I seemed more similar than I'd thought.

"I can hear you thinkin' from here."

I huffed.

"What are you thinkin' about?"

"Just...Lana and I... we're not that different—"

"Yes, you are," he interrupted again. "You're practically opposites."

"But—"

"Em, gettin' to know you is what helped me see the kinda person Lana had become. Sure, you both had a lot of hurt, but Lana wielded her hurt, and she was good at manipulating people with it. She thought the world and everybody in it owed her 'cause of what she'd been put through. And then there's you."

The fondness in his voice made my eyes well up.

"You acted like you owed the world every piece of you. And I'm not sayin' that's a good thing, 'cause it's not, but your natural inclination was to give and give while Lana's was to take and take."

"I used my pain as a weapon—" I argued, my voice wobbling.

"No, I think you used your pain as a shield," Griz corrected. "I'm not sayin' you haven't done anything wrong or that you haven't hurt people, too, but at the root of it, the two of you are day and night."

A tear trickled down my face and into my ear.

"She wasn't sorry for what she'd done," he added. "She was angry because she felt like we'd picked you over her. She kept actin' like she'd done nothing wrong, and when we'd remind her, she just brushed it aside."

After a short silence, Griz started telling another story about his grandma, and eventually, his low, soothing voice lulled me to sleep.

CHAPTER 15

Mac came by in the morning shortly after Griz left.

"Me and the crew are goin' out today to pick up some supplies. We'll be gone until tomorrow. Sam's stayin' here, though."

"Oh." He was wearing his tactical gear, which made me feel nervous. "When are you leaving?"

"In a couple hours." He paused. "We got the clinic all cleaned out. Shouldn't smell anymore. We also rigged up a pulley for your loft ladder. Thought you might feel better about sleepin' in the clinic with your brother and his crew if you could pull the ladder up."

Warmth curled in my chest at his thoughtfulness. "Thank you."

"I gotta go help get the rovers ready, but I wanted to come tell you first."

"You'll come say goodbye before you go, right?"

He blinked. "Of course."

I ran a hand through my hair and tucked it behind my ear, a smile creeping over my face. "Okay, good."

He grinned and headed out. After he left, I sat in my bed for a long time, a sick feeling growing in my stomach. I needed to tell him about the other powered person.

Should I tell him before they left?

As soon as I thought it, my hands started trembling, and my lungs seized. Why did this scare me so much? Part of it was because I'd waited so long. I was afraid he'd be angry—justifiably so. I'd put the whole hold at risk by keeping this to myself. I *had* to tell him. He needed to know what dangers could be out there, even if it changed how he felt about me, or he hated me for keeping this secret, or he decided to hand me over in exchange for the hold's safety.

Was that why it scared me? That didn't make much sense since I knew I'd turn myself over if the shadow man showed up and threatened the hold.

I took a deep breath and threw the blanket off. I wasn't going to let Mac and his crew go out blind. I threw on my clothes someone had returned, freshly laundered, and shoved my feet in my boots. Then I headed out, trying to keep myself from imagining the worst possible reactions Mac could have.

The whole crew was in the garage. I walked in, glancing around curiously. I'd never been inside this building. It was a vast space full of more vehicles than I realized the hold had. There were about a dozen rovers, even more single-person four-wheelers, a bunch of dirt bikes, and, most shocking, a fucking *helicopter*. I stopped in my tracks and stared at it.

Griz noticed and laughed at me. "It doesn't work. We don't have the right fuel, and nobody's makin' jet fuel that we know of."

"Mac, Bones is here," Raven yelled, and her angry tone made my stomach twist.

Mac was underneath the rover on his back. He came sliding out, lying on a small-wheeled platform, and stared at me with surprise.

"Hey," he got to his feet, wiping his dirty hands on a rag. "You okay?"

"I need to talk to you," I blurted out before I lost my nerve.

His brows creased, looking worried. "Uh, okay. Lemme just tell Raven to take over for me."

He strode over to speak to Raven in a low voice, and she glared at him like she was contemplating murder. I hoped her anger had nothing to do with me.

Finally, he came back, taking my elbow and steering me outside.

"What's wrong?" he asked in my head.

"Can we go somewhere private?"

His brow furrowed even more. *"Yeah, the bunkhouse is just*

around the corner. That work?"

I nodded, and he released my elbow but walked so fast I had to jog to keep up. We made it to the bunkhouse in record time, and as soon as we were inside, he ushered me to the couch.

"What is it?" he asked, sitting beside me.

My mouth went so dry I could barely swallow. Where should I start?

"Em?" He sounded distressed now.

"Do you think it's possible for me to show *you a memory?"*

"Uh, I dunno."

"Can I try?" I asked anxiously.

He nodded, and I let the memory flood my mind, watching him. His body tensed, his eyes going unfocused, and I knew it was working—no going back now.

I lay on Juck's bed in his tent, sobbing through my teeth. The pain in my arm was so sharp it made me feel like I was going to be sick. Rusty, the man who had filled in as healer before me, was trying to maneuver my arm into the correct position so he could wrap it in a splint, and my body kept moving despite how hard I was trying to hold still.

"You're gonna have to drug her," Rusty finally said, glaring at me. "I can't get her fuckin' arm wrapped up if she keeps jerkin' like that."

I'd never been drugged, and it scared me. I didn't want to be helpless, especially around the Reapers. Juck approached with the needle, and panic grew in me.

"Juck," I got out, my voice raspy and shaking, "please—"

He stopped and sat by my head, gently stroking my hair out of my face. I thought he'd be furious at me for the bike accident, even though it wasn't my fault. I was just the passenger, stuck clinging to Mojave and pleading for him to stop as he sped toward the rocks the Reapers had been using to do tricks on their bikes. But when Juck strode up to the crash where I was half pinned under the bike, screaming in pain, he'd just put a bullet in Mojave's head and then shoved the bike off me, his face full of furious concern. It was one of the rare moments where I felt like maybe part of him actually cared about me, and I hated how desperate those moments made me feel. When he cared for me and was gentle, it was like some pathetic part of me turned weak, and I craved how he spoke and touched me like he actually loved me.

"Don't worry, Angel," he said softly. "I'll take care of you."

"I'm scared." I heard myself sob, reaching up to cling to his hand.

He wrapped his rough fingers around mine and leaned down to press a kiss to the back of my hand.

"Don't be scared. S'alright," he soothed. "You know I'll always protect you."

He freed his hand from mine and took my arm. I jumped at the prick of the needle in my arm.

"Just close your eyes, Angel."

It felt like ice was filling my veins, and terror filled me, but Juck's face was already blurring into darkness.

I thought it would feel like sleeping, like I'd close my eyes and then open them to find that time had passed. Instead, it felt like I was floating in a pitch-black darkness that made my skin crawl. I waited a few minutes, my heart pounding in my throat, but nothing happened. The air around me felt thick, almost like water, but not quite. The darkness pressed in on me, heavy and suffocating. The panic felt like electricity sizzling under my skin as I struggled to breathe.

"Please." I wasn't sure if I was speaking out loud or in my head. "Please help me. Get me out. Please!"

A sudden gust of air floated over me like someone had just run up and stopped before me. I stared wide-eyed into the darkness, my heart tripping over itself in terror. I couldn't see anything, but there was something there—a presence I could somehow sense even though I couldn't see, hear, or feel anyone.

I tried to stay quiet, to hide like Wolf had taught me, but eventually, I couldn't take it any longer.

"Who's there?" I whispered.

It felt like the darkness reached out, an arm and hand forming from nothing but shadows to touch my face. It was a gentle touch, but I still flinched with a gasp.

"Who are you?" I tried and failed to ask confidently.

"I've been looking for you for so long," A velvet voice whispered through my head, and the hair on the back of my neck rose.

I still couldn't see anything, but every instinct that had kept me alive so far was screaming at me to run and hide. Whoever or whatever this was, it was dangerous, but I couldn't run or hide. I was stuck here, trapped by the heavy drugs in my veins.

"Don't be afraid." The voice seemed to attempt to sound comforting, which only terrified me further.

I wrapped my arms around myself, shaking. The voice sounded male and not old, but that was my only impression. I didn't respond, desperately hoping this was a vivid dream.

"You're not dreaming." The voice sounded amused now. "I'm as real as you are."

I could feel his excitement crackling in the air. He seemed to circle me, examining me from every angle.

"I'm nothing," I tried desperately. "I'm no one."

He stopped directly before me, and when he spoke, each word vibrated with fury. "You are NOT no one."

I didn't understand why he was angry, but it didn't matter. I knew how to react to anger. I went silent and still, trying to be small and forgotten.

He laughed darkly, and the sound echoed around in my head like it was taunting me. "Did you really think I could ever forget you, Ember?"

The terror that went through me felt even colder than the narc. My heart was pounding in my throat, and I felt like a rabbit in the jaws of a wolf.

Oh gods, don't think about wolves.

"Do you know me?" he asked.

I shook my head, my lips pressed tightly together. His disappointment washed over me, bitter and lonely.

"What has changed?" he mused, almost to himself. "How are you here?" Strong fingers gripped my chin. "Where are you, Ember?"

I didn't know what to do. Instinctively, I knew not to tell him my location, but I doubted he'd react well if I didn't answer.

"Come now, love, you don't have to hide from me," he crooned, his free hand caressing my cheek. "I don't want to do this the hard way. Just tell me."

Somehow, my mind registered that a crack had appeared in the narc's grip. "I'll... I'll tell you, just... I need some space," I got out.

It was a feeble lie, and I was sure he'd see through it, but he immediately retreated. I took a deep breath and started to pace slightly.

He didn't move, but I could feel his eyes tracking me. My entire body was trembling.

"Should I know you?" My voice shook as I got closer to where I could sense fresh air drifting into the darkness.

"I've known you—"

I lunged for the crack. I heard him yell and felt a hand seize my ankle for a moment, but I managed to kick it away, fighting toward consciousness as hard as I could.

I bolted upright in the real world, my splinted arm screaming in pain at the movement. It was night, and the tent was empty except for me. My heart was pounding with terror so potent that I stumbled out of bed and vomited in the corner. I could hear the Reapers outside laughing and jeering and the faint screams of a woman, and I realized with dull horror I was naked from the waist down.

Out of habit, I quickly buried the evidence of getting sick. Then I stood and found my discarded pants. It was tricky to pull them on with only one arm, but I managed. Then I crawled back into Juck's bed, wishing he hadn't gotten rid of my bedroll. The sheets smelled like him, another reminder there was no escape.

Maybe it was a dream. It must have been a dream. I had no spare energy to worry about a faceless shadow man in my dreams. I was already living in a nightmare.

I opened my eyes.

Mac sat on the couch beside me and stared, his face carefully expressionless. For a long time, neither of us spoke, and my stomach twisted.

"I'm not the only powered person," I finally whispered.

He still said nothing, and I couldn't read his expression. I tried to wait for him to ask questions, but his silence made me uneasy.

"I don't know who he is," I added nervously. "That was the first time I encountered him. It only happens when I'm drugged."

That muscle in his jaw ticked. "But he knows you."

"He said he does, but I have *no idea* who he is. He can… can see my memories, so maybe he just found my name in my head. I don't know."

"You think this… what's happening to me… you think it's *my* power."

"I think so." I desperately tried to read his expression.

"And my power is like his power."

I nodded.

"You're scared of him," he said, staring at me closely. "Are you scared of me?"

"No!" I said immediately. "I'm not scared of you. I don't know how to explain it, but *his* power feels so different from mine, and yours feels… it feels like… me."

He abruptly stood, startling me. He paced the length of the room then stopped at the small window over the kitchen sink, bracing his hands on the counter and hanging his head. Nausea rose, and my fingers twisted the end of my braid repeatedly. He already seemed angry, and I'd barely begun.

"There's more," I whispered.

He turned around and pinned me in place with that unreadable expression, crossing his arms over his chest.

Fuck, I regretted bringing this up, but I couldn't stop now.

"C'mon, Bones. It's fun." Vulture grinned crookedly at me, holding up two vials. "Ever heard of fun?"

I rubbed my arms nervously. I had a rare afternoon of freedom because Juck was gone on a day trip, leaving me under guard of Grip and Vulture. Grip was currently snoring outside Juck's tent, and Vulture had snuck inside, surprising me with two narcs he'd gotten somewhere. I knew many of the Reapers got high for fun, but after my first and only experience with narcs, I didn't want anything to do with them.

"What's the matter? You scared, lil girl?" Vulture gave me a taunting grin. He was only six years older than me, but he loved reminding me of it.

"I'm not scared," I muttered, even though we both knew that was a lie.

"Didn't you have a narc when you broke your arm?"

"Yeah and… I didn't like it."

He rolled his eyes. "You probably just had a bad trip. It's not like the same thing will happen again."

I desperately wanted to believe him. The bruises on my body ached, and all I wanted was to be able to drift away from my real life for a little while. "You think?"

"Yeah, dumbass. C'mon, it'll be fun."

I let him prepare everything, and he showed me how to inject it into the crook of my elbow. I was trying to convince myself this was going to be different, but as soon as the drug hit my veins, I knew I was horribly wrong.

The shadow man swiftly entered my head with brutal expertise. I could feel the anger coming off him in waves, and he didn't even speak before tearing through my memories with what felt like razor-sharp claws. The pain left me gasping for air; writhing on the ground, I had no chance of stopping him. I still couldn't see anything other than what looked like a vaguely human-shaped dark shadow. This time, there was a desperation about him that hadn't been there before. He was muttering to himself, and I tried to pay attention to what he was saying, but I couldn't make out the words. I squeezed my eyes shut and felt him pause. Strong fingers gripped my chin.

"Open your eyes," he growled.

I didn't know why he wanted me to open my eyes, but acting on pure instinct, I squeezed them tighter shut. His claws dug into my skin, and the metallic tang of blood filled the air.

"Open your eyes," he said quieter, but his malice was unmistakable.

Tears leaked down my face, and I was sobbing in gasps of breath through my teeth, but I didn't open my eyes.

"You want to play games, love?" he crooned, caressing my face with the tips of his claws. "We can play games."

He tore his way into my memories again, leaving me screaming in agony, but he was moving slower like something was holding him back.

"You think you can hide anything from me?" His mocking laugh filled my head again. "I will find you, Ember, whether or not you cooperate."

I sensed the crack reappear, but I forced myself not to react. The half dose was leaving my system much faster, and he didn't seem to know anything was different. I waited until he seemed distracted by one of my memories of Dune, and then I fled. He realized what I was doing too late, and his furious voice screaming my name was the last thing I heard before I bolted upright in the real world again.

Beside me, Vulture was half-conscious, grinning at the ceiling with glassy eyes. I barely managed to lean off the bed before I was sick, shaking like a leaf. I knew I needed to take care of the mess before Juck *came back, or he'd add more bruises, but I could only lay there, sprawled on my stomach half off the bed, gasping in frantic breaths of air that left me lightheaded for what felt like forever. Finally, the terror faded enough for me to crawl over to Vulture and curl against him. He didn't even notice my presence, but I didn't care. I just desperately wanted to feel the comfort of another person.*

Mac's emotions felt like a thundercloud in my head, but I frantically grabbed the final memory I needed to show him and yanked it up to play through my head.

I was lying in Juck's bed again, struggling to breathe through the pain in my chest. Tears slowly leaked down my face. Juck was talking to someone, but I had trouble concentrating enough to hear it. I wondered if Vulture was still alive. I doubted it. I remembered Rally's face twisted in pain, the horrible screams that had ripped from him, and the blood—

Juck suddenly appeared above me, and I tensed, biting back a cry of pain at the movement. He stared at me silently for a while, and the swell of fear made me dizzy.

"You in pain, Angel?" he finally asked.

I didn't know how he wanted me to answer that, making me even more panicked. Did he want me to say yes so he knew he'd successfully punished me? Or did he want me to say no so we could move on and never speak of this again?

When he suddenly sat on the bed beside me, I flinched, and more tears slid out of my eyes. He leaned forward and raised a hand. I tried to brace myself, but his hand just gently brushed my hair from my face.

"You know this hurts me even more than it hurts you, right?"

I didn't know how to answer that question, either. I clenched my trembling fists at my sides.

"I promised I'd protect you. You remember that?" His hand stroked down my face so gently. "When I found you wanderin' in the desert?"

I managed a tiny, terrified nod.

"This is me protectin' you, Angel. You're mine, and I'm not gonna let anybody else touch you."

Vulture had to be dead.

He leaned down and kissed me, his lips rough and possessive on mine. My stomach churned, but I automatically kissed him back, a reflex he'd ingrained into me with pain. He smelled like blood and smoke. I squeezed my eyes shut, feeling sick with despair and pain.

"It's alright. I forgive you," he murmured. "I'm gonna get you some medicine."

My eyes popped open. He was pulling back and standing, heading for the small lockbox that held a couple narcs.

"Juck," I choked out shakily, "please don't. I'm okay. It doesn't hurt that bad."

He removed one of the vials, his expression patronizing. "Angel, you don't have to be brave. Let me take care of you."

"I'm really okay. Please. Please, Juck, I don't want a narc." More helpless tears were rolling down my face.

He approached the bed, prepping the needle and ignoring me. I managed to get an arm out from under the covers and hold it up, begging him to stop as pain from the movement screamed through me.

"Please, Juck!" I was sobbing now. "I don't want it! Please stop!"

He easily pinned my arm under his knee, injecting the needle into my shoulder, still smiling as I tried to fight. "It's alright, Angel. I'm gonna take care of you."

I tried to brace myself and be strong like Wolf would want, but I crumbled into pieces instead. I felt the shadow man appear and stand next to where I lay curled in a ball, sobbing. He didn't move for so long I thought maybe he'd left. Then, a hand ghosted over my arm.

"What have they done to you?" he growled.

The darkness seemed to surround me, gently cradling me and turning my body to reveal the "J" burning painfully on my chest. I felt his shock and then his growing fury.

"Who did this to you?" he asked, his voice menacing.

I didn't answer for a moment, but I was so scared and hurt and broken that I turned my head toward him and opened my eyes. Gentle hands cradled my face as he looked through my memories of Juck branding me with his initial while I screamed in pain, but his intrusion into my mind didn't hurt this time. Maybe he was being careful, or maybe it was because I was volunteering the information. I couldn't find the strength to care. His rage grew, but for the first time, it felt like a shelter for me to take refuge in.

"I will kill them for this," he seethed. "You are mine and only

mine."

That sounded eerily similar to what Juck had said, but I shoved that thought aside. I was so tired, and his arms around me didn't feel cold now. They were warm and comforting, and I didn't want to think about the consequences. Someone seemed to care for the first time in a long time, and I wanted to feel that so desperately.

So I didn't fight, didn't try to stop him as I felt him rifling through my memories. My head rested on what felt like a broad chest, my face tilted upward, staring into the darkness where I somehow knew his face was. His arms around me remained gentle despite the anger radiating from him. We stayed that way until I felt the drug begin to fade. I didn't try to escape this time. I just stayed where I was as he started slipping away.

"They will pay, Ember," he promised right before he vanished. "I swear it."

I felt shaky and nauseous as I came back to the present. I'd just shown Mac far more than I'd ever told Trey, and exposing my vulnerabilities like that terrified me. As I opened my eyes, I realized there were tears on my cheeks. Mac still stood by the sink, but as he blinked and seemed to return to himself, his eyes locked on mine, dark and stormy with emotion.

"What happened after that?" he asked.

I twisted my fingers together nervously. "The Reapers turned on each other four days later."

His eyes narrowed. "You think he had something to do with it?"

"He had to. None of it made sense."

"Will you show me?"

I hesitated for a moment but then nodded. I could force myself to endure one more. Mac frowned like he was about to question me, so I quickly pulled up the memory so I didn't have to answer.

I was in the med tent bandaging up a wound I'd just stitched shut when Vulture burst inside. My heart started pounding. We weren't supposed to be anywhere near each other. Juck had made that real fucking clear. The brand on my chest still fiercely hurt, and other more intimate parts of my body ached with pain, all of it a constant painful reminder of who I belonged to. Vulture's eyes met mine for a second, and then he turned to the several injured people in the tent.

"Everybody outside," he ordered.

I stared at him, bewildered. I'd never seen Vulture order people around like this.

"Trust me, you don't want to miss this," he added with a cruel smile before vanishing outside.

I quickly tied off the bandage with shaking fingers as the Reapers began getting up to go outside. This couldn't be anything good. What the fuck was Vulture doing? Did he want Juck to kill him?

When I followed everyone outside, Vulture stood on a pile of broken cement blocks. His eyes found me immediately, and I knew this had something to do with me. Oh fuck. My heart rate quickened until I felt lightheaded and sweat dripped down my back. I quickly glanced around at the growing crowd but didn't see Juck—yet.

"How many of our brethren did we lose to the fever?" Vulture shouted.

I blinked, taken aback. I'd never heard him speak like this before. He sounded like he was pretending to be someone else.

"Well, I come before you to share the truth!"

I tried to catch his eye, shaking my head desperately, but he ignored me.

"Bones has the power to heal wounds magically."

Everyone turned and stared at me, and I shrank backward.

"But Juck only lets her heal himself! She could have saved everyone who fell ill, saved all the people who died in the raid last spring, and healed every horrible, painful injury you've ever had. But Juck kept it all for himself! He forced her to keep this a secret from you because he doesn't care if you live or die. He only cares about himself! You are nothing but disposable game pieces!"

I expected people to start jeering at him, to throw shit and laugh, but the energy in the crowd shifted to something dark. I'd seen the Reapers get riled up about things before, and it didn't feel like this. Something was happening; something was wrong.

"You follow Juck because he claims to be a god, immortal and untouchable, but he is nothing more than a fraud!"

The people around me shifted restlessly, eying each other and muttering to themselves. I slipped backward, to get away from the crowd. This situation would get ugly quickly, and I had no idea what the Reapers would do. I reached the crowd's edge and ran but stopped as I passed a parked bike. A holstered knife was discarded in the sand as though someone had just dropped it there and followed Vulture. I snatched it up, shoving it under the band of my pants and pulling my shirt and jacket over the top.

I was almost to Juck's tent when the first gunshot rang out. It stopped me in my tracks, and I turned and glanced back toward the crowd, my heart in my throat. There was a pause, but then multiple shots rang out, along with voices screaming and yelling. Who were they fighting? Wasn't Vulture trying to get them to turn against Juck? Had Juck shown up? Did he shoot Vulture? Oh fuck, oh fuck.

I ducked quickly into the tent, expecting it to be empty, but stopped so fast I almost fell over. Juck was standing in the tent, quickly packing a bag. He'd turned toward me, drawing his gun, but he lowered it at the sight of me.

"Good girl," he said as his eyes flashed with fury. "We're gettin' outta here. I shoulda put that pup down."

I had to fight to keep from being sick. Fuck fuck fuck. I thought Juck would be out by the crowd, trying to threaten them into submission. The sound of the fighting seemed to be getting louder.

"You got one minute to grab what you want," Juck snapped, startling me from my panicked thoughts. "Then we're gettin' on the bike."

I didn't know what to do. I didn't want to go with Juck, but I was terrified the Reapers would tear me apart. What the fuck was Vulture doing? The brief moment where I hesitated made something dark and ugly cross Juck's face, and my heart leapt into overdrive. I forced myself to move, to go to my small corner and grab a few things. I wasn't even paying attention to what I grabbed. My brain was empty of everything except desperate terror.

"Get your coat," Juck said as he approached the tent doorway. "We're gonna—"

A gunshot echoed, and I jumped with a shriek. Juck stumbled back, his upper arm bleeding, but he recovered quickly, darting around the bed to grab me by the arm, roughly jerking me in front of him. The cold muzzle of a gun pressed against my head as I stared horrified at Vulture standing in the doorway, gun drawn. He looked furious.

"You're done, old man," Vulture said in a soft, menacing voice that didn't sound like him at all.

"Like hell I am," Juck sneered, still holding his gun to my

temple. *"You think I haven't dealt with an uprisin' or two? I've been doing this longer than you've been alive, boy."*

"Let her go," Vulture demanded.

"How stupid do you think I am?" Juck laughed. *"I know what this is about, but you can't have her."* His hand tightened painfully around my arm. *"She's mine—always has been and always will be. The gods delivered her to me. If I die, she dies with me."*

"The gods," Vulture scoffed, a genuinely insane smile crossing his face that made my lungs stop working. *"You think—"*

That was as far as he got before a shot rang out right next to my ear, making it ring painfully. For a terrible moment, I thought Juck had shot me, but before I could process it, I was on my hands and knees in the sand as Juck shoved me down. He crossed the tent to kick Vulture's gun out of his hand. Vulture was lying on his back, his hand pressing against the wound in his shoulder where blood was quickly gushing out. Juck stood over him, gun pointed at his head, and I braced for the shot that would end Vulture's life, but then Juck just started laughing.

"Nah, I'm not gonna give you an easy death," he said in a cruel voice. *"You're gonna lay there and watch me take Bones away as you bleed out in the sand like the trash you are."*

I slid the knife out of the holster and buried it in the sand beside me, my hand still tightly gripping the handle. Vulture said something I couldn't make out, but Juck laughed again, holstering his gun and striding toward me. He bent and grabbed my arm, beginning to haul me to my feet, but I surged up, pulling the knife from the sand and stabbing it into his chest as hard as I could. I aimed for his heart, and the feel of the blade going through his body made me want to be sick. He stumbled backward, and I yanked the knife out and stabbed it in again. Blood started gushing out over my hand.

"Angel," he choked out as he fell backward onto his bed, pulling me with him.

He seemed shocked, like he thought I'd never actually fight back, like he'd broken me completely, and a white-hot rage washed over me. I pulled the knife out and stabbed it in again and again and again. His eyes were wide, and he tried to speak, but he was choking, drowning in the blood that was pouring into his lungs. There was blood everywhere, coating my hands, splattered across my face, and covering the bed sheets. When my hands slipped off the bloody handle, I looked up *at his face and realized he was dead.*

My ears started ringing as I numbly pulled the knife out, but I still heard the horrible squelching sound. I clambered off of Juck's dead body and looked at Vulture. He was staring at me from where he was lying in the sand, clutching his shoulder.

"Angel—" Vulture wheezed.

I dropped the bloody knife, and it fell into the sand with a soft thud.

Angel.

My hands were shaking violently. Vulture had never called me that before, and it was abruptly crystal clear that I hadn't changed a damn thing. I'd just killed a man, and it hadn't changed anything—I hadn't escaped. Juck was dead, and now I was Vulture's Angel.

"Angel, you did it." Vulture was grinning despite the bullet wound in his shoulder. "You killed the bastard."

I backed away, my breath coming in fast, panicked gasps.

"Angel?" Vulture was pulling himself up, his face twisted in pain. "It's okay, baby, you did it. He—"

I backed further away toward the tent door, and I saw the moment he realized I was going to leave him there. I wasn't expecting the hurt on his face to look so raw and real, but it quickly hardened into hatred.

I turned and ran, fleeing into the dim evening light. I heard Vulture yelling in fury, but it was swallowed by the screams and cries of the injured and dying that littered the ground. My feet slowed, and I stared at the bloody scene, horrified. The Reapers had torn each other apart. The sand was stained red, and the smell of blood was thick. A man put a gun to the head of his wounded partner and pulled the trigger without hesitation. They were lovers, and he just... killed him. He met my eyes for a second, and the emptiness in his face scared me worse than anything I'd seen so far. He took a step toward me, but then another gunshot rang out, and his body jerked, blood spraying, and he fell to the side. They were killing each other. Why were they killing each other?

Someone screamed, and it jerked me out of the daze I was in. I took off, my feet flying across the sand. I was panting and sobbing through my teeth, but I didn't stop. I couldn't stop. I just ran, leaving the bloody carnage behind me.

CHAPTER 16

I opened my eyes and immediately bolted to the door, barely making it off the small steps before I was sick. The smells, sounds, and sensations of that day would haunt me forever. I heard the door open behind me, Mac's footsteps slowly approaching.

"You didn't have to show me," he said, irritation coloring his voice.

"I dunno." I took a deep, shaky breath. *"I think it's easier than saying it out loud."*

"Sure, but we could have taken a break or something." He hovered at my shoulder.

"I'm sorry," I thought miserably.

"Are you seriously apologizing for being sick?" I knew he was glaring at me without even looking.

"I should have told you sooner. I should've told you right away. I'm so sorry." I was afraid to look at him, terrified to see what was on his face. If he hated me now, I wasn't sure I could bear it.

"Em," he sounded exasperated as he took my arm, but his hands were gentle, "look at me."

I reluctantly lifted my eyes to his face. He was staring solemnly at me, golden sparks almost glowing in his eyes.

"I don't hate you," he said steadily. "Do I wish you would've told me sooner? Yeah. But I don't hate you. I'm just tryin' to… process all this, I guess."

"I tried to draw him away. That's why I left. He saw the Vault.

When you drugged me. He said he was coming," the words spilled out of me. Was I even making sense?

He held my gaze for what felt like a long time, and I didn't know how to read his expression. Something was lurking in his eyes that made me uneasy, but I couldn't tell what it was.

"I know," he finally said quietly.

I faltered, my mind tripping over those two simple words.

I know.

Know what? He couldn't know about *this*. What the fuck was he talking about?

"You *know?*" I finally got out.

"Trey radioed us."

I stared at him.

"When you were at the trading post."

My mind frantically ran through our entire time at the trading post. Trey must have done it while I was making my infusion with Roe in Zeke's kitchen. He'd told them, and he hid it from me.

"We have a small radio hidden in the bunkhouse," Mac added when I didn't say anything.

Part of me wasn't surprised. Of course, Trey would want to warn his family that they might be in danger, but a much more selfish and broken part of me felt betrayed, and not just by Trey. I'd been trying to figure out how to tell Mac and the crew this, terrified it would ruin everything, and they *already knew*. I'd just been more vulnerable than I'd *ever* been, showing all this shit to Mac, but he *already fucking knew*.

"Em?" Mac asked, gently squeezing my arm, which he still held.

"So, what? You were just waiting for me to tell you so you could act like it was new information?" I knew I wasn't disguising the hurt and anger in my voice, but I didn't care.

"No!" he retorted, his voice sharpening. "I was waitin' until you felt comfortable enough to tell me."

"You waited until I *felt comfortable* enough to show you some of the worst fucking moments of my life, relive all of that shit, and you *already knew?"*

"Well, I wasn't expecting you to *show* me." His eyes flashed with angry sparks.

"Do you seriously think *talking* about it would have been any easier?"

My voice was rising, and I could see people glancing curiously at us. A couple of Nemo's guards were whispering to each other and gesturing at us, and my stomach suddenly dropped.

"Everyone knows," I realized with horror.

"No," he said immediately. "Not everyone, just Nemo and his top people and our crew."

Of course, Nemo knew. No wonder he used up so many resources to *rescue* me from my brother. No wonder Nemo wanted me to stay here. No wonder he was so willing to make a deal with Wolf. When the other powered person showed up looking for me, Nemo could just hand me over like the perfect little bargaining chip I was.

I felt so stupid.

"Em—"

"Did Nemo tell you to keep it a secret from me?" I demanded, my voice shaking.

"He didn't say to keep it a secret; he just didn't want to overwhelm you with everything—"

I yanked my arm free, staring horrified at him with furious tears filling my eyes.

Em, please, just— His voice in my head sounded far more desperate.

I slammed down my mental shield as hard as I could, turned, and fled.

"Em!" he shouted, and I heard him following. "Em, wait, you —"

"Mac!"

I threw a glance over my shoulder to see one of Nemo's top men flagging Mac down. Mac had stopped chasing me, but he stayed in the path, watching me flee as Nemo's guard rushed toward him. I could *feel* him trying to get through my mental shield, but I just turned back around and kept running.

ॐ

I hid out by the wall in a small space I'd discovered between several apple trees, waiting until I heard the rovers leave. It felt childish, but I did not want to see Mac right now. After they left, I stormed back to the clinic. Wolf's entire crew was inside, and it did not improve my mood. The clinic felt so crowded, and people kept fucking trying to talk to me. I eventually just quit responding, and finally, they went quiet, but they still watched me, tracking me around the clinic until I wanted to scream.

To make matters worse, it was a slow day with few people coming in for healing, and whoever had cleaned up the blood and Madame's scent had done a meticulous job, leaving little cleaning for me. After an hour, I couldn't take it any longer and retreated to the loft to scrub the floor just to escape the constant eyes on my skin. I debated pulling the ladder up with me, but that would probably be a step too far. I could *feel* the questions they were all holding back.

It was almost dinner when the door opened, and Sam walked in. I heard Lee greet him, but I didn't come down the ladder.

"Where's Shortcake?" I heard him ask.

"Upstairs," Lee answered, "in a mood."

I barely resisted the urge to pour my bucket of dirty water on top of his head.

Sam appeared on the ladder, looking slightly concerned. "Hey," he said cautiously.

I didn't answer, continuing to scrub the floor with more force than necessary.

"What's wrong?" he asked as he climbed up into the loft.

"You don't have to pretend you don't know everything anymore," I said without looking at him.

He was quiet for a few breaths. "Mac told you about the radio?"

I didn't answer, and eventually, he let out a sigh.

"Do you blame him?" he asked quietly, and I knew he was talking about Trey.

"No," I snapped, which was the truth, and finally looked up at him. "I blame all the rest of you."

He held my gaze, crossing his thin arms over his chest. "You really think you would've reacted well to us sittin' you down and tellin' you what we know?"

"What the fuck do you think I've been doing lately?" I knew my voice was too loud, and everyone downstairs was probably listening, but I couldn't stop. "I've been makin' myself *sick* tryin' to figure out how to tell you, and you already fuckin' knew."

"Why does that matter?" he argued. "It's not like we treated you any different."

"How the fuck am I supposed to know that?" I cried. "How the fuck am I supposed to know Nemo didn't send a fuckin' army to rescue me just so he didn't lose his bargaining chip?"

"What? That's not why we came for you!"

"And how am I supposed to know that's not another lie?"

"We never lied to you! We just didn't bring it up 'cause you didn't, either!"

"*I* was trying to! I was tryin' to convince myself it wouldn't change anything if you all knew!"

"And it didn't!"

"And that's exactly what you'd *want* me to think! Keep me feelin' like I'm not a prisoner! Make me believe I *chose* to stay here."

"For fuck's sake, Shortcake, that's not—"

"For *once*. For *once* in my godsdamned life, I thought maybe I could just be a fuckin' person and not a fuckin' *thing* for other people to *use*—"

"No one thinks you're a *thing!*" Sam's voice rose angrily. "That's a pretty far leap to make there—"

"It's not a *leap*, Sam. It's been my whole fuckin' *life!*" I shouted. "Do you not remember how we met? Cause I sure as hell do! Are you just pretendin' I came here of my own free will?"

He winced.

"I have *always* been a thing, a weapon, a pawn, a *bounty*." I hoped the eavesdroppers downstairs heard that one. "Do you have any idea how it feels always being *used* by people to get whatever *they* want?"

His face contorted as though he was in physical pain.

"And the *only* person I knew for sure didn't see me that way is fuckin' dead." Angry tears rolled down my face. "And for some stupid fuckin' reason, I still haven't learned that nothin' is ever gonna change."

"Shortcake," he said quietly, taking a step toward me, but I threw my hand up, halting him.

"Don't," I choked out. "Go away. I don't want to see you."

"Emmy," he tried.

"Do *not* call me that," I hissed, pointing at the ladder with a shaky hand. "Get the fuck out."

He stood still for a moment, staring at me, but I went back to violently scrubbing the floor, pretending I wasn't still angrily crying.

"Alright. Well. If you need anythin', I'll be at the bunkhouse," he finally said.

I listened to him going down the ladder. There were a few mumbled farewells from Wolf's crew, and then the door shut, leaving behind an awkward silence.

I continued to scrub the floor, eventually managing to stuff the anger and the hurt back down to a simmering emptiness. I was dreading someone coming up the ladder and trying to talk to me, but to my relief, no one did. It wasn't until the dinner bell rang about an hour later that Lee's head cautiously appeared.

"You want to go to dinner?" he asked.

"No."

"Alright," he hesitated. "We'll bring you something back."

I didn't answer, and eventually, I heard him go back down the ladder. It sounded like Wolf's whole pack had left, and I waited for several minutes before venturing down the ladder. The clinic was indeed empty, so I used the outhouse and drank some water before pulling the ladder up with the new pulley system. Once I was safely curled up on my mattress under Trey's quilt, I let myself cry.

I longed for Trey so much it hurt. It stung that he hid this from me, but at the same time, I knew he would have told me on our way back if I hadn't been drugged the whole time. He wouldn't have made me stew about it. He would have been *honest* because that's who he *was*— maybe the only honest person left in the world, and because of me, he was dead.

I knew I was spiraling down a dark hole, but learning Dune lied to me was awful enough, and now *this?*

About an hour later, I heard Wolf's crew come back. Someone quietly called my name from downstairs, but I pretended to be asleep, and eventually, they seemed to give up. I could hear them talking for a long time, but they kept their voices carefully quiet. It didn't matter. I knew they were talking about me, probably making their own plans for what they wanted to do with me because it didn't fucking matter what I wanted. It never did.

CHAPTER 17

I could feel the sun and the gentle wind on my face. The air smelled sweet and floral. Slowly, I opened my eyes and blinked at the landscape around me. I was standing in a mountain meadow, surrounded by wildflowers. The sky above was a bright blue with no clouds in sight. A light breeze blew, making the flowers bob and sway and playing with my hair. I slowly turned, and my skirt swung around my legs. I realized I was wearing a simple but pretty dress made from a fabric with small flowers printed on it.

Something in my chest seemed to tug, pulling my attention away from the flowers to look out into the distance. I froze, my heart pounding at the sight of a figure striding down the mountainside toward me. They were walking directly in front of the sun, making it impossible to see any features, but I immediately knew who it was.

I started to run, and so did he, and by the time we crashed together in the middle of the wildflowers, I was sobbing.

"It's alright, darlin'," Trey murmured, his voice rough with emotion. "It's alright."

"No, it's not fuckin' alright," I sobbed furiously into Trey's shirt.

"I know," he said softly, his strong arms wrapped around me. "I know."

"Please, Trey, I can't... I can't do this without you."

"You don't have to." He pressed a kiss into my hair. "I'm always gonna be with you."

"That is such a load of shit," I sobbed.

He laughed sadly. "I know, but it's the best I can do."

I couldn't speak anymore, sobbing too hard for words. My arms moved up to twine around Trey's neck, trying to pull him closer as though I could physically keep him here with me. He held me just as tightly, and it felt like I was somehow shattering and being pieced back together at the same time.

The wind blew my skirt and hair around us, but neither of us moved.

"Am I dead?" I finally was able to choke out.

"No." He let go of my waist to move his hands up to cup my face, thumbs brushing gently across my wet cheekbones.

I studied his face desperately, trying to memorize every single detail. His soft brown hair fell in waves against his face, and his eyes were just as warm and full of sunshine as I remembered. He smiled that slightly crooked smile that I fell in love with, and those broken shards of my heart ached with excruciating pain.

"I can't do this," I repeated brokenly. "I can't."

"You can," he whispered.

"No, Trey, you don't understand." A sob choked me. "I don't want to."

He leaned down and pressed a gentle kiss to my lips, but I surged upward. He responded eagerly, but I had to break away after a second because I was sobbing too hard. Gods, I was coming apart at the seams.

"Bones—" he started softly.

"Ember," I interrupted, lifting my head to look at him as tears streamed down my face. I was barely able to get the words out between the sobs, but I was determined to do so. "My name is Ember, 'Em' for short."

"Em," he repeated, a hint of that sunshine smile crossing his lips.

Hearing him say my name in this place didn't sound right. It wasn't the same as hearing it in real life, but I knew that was something I'd never get. My face crumpled again, and he gathered me close, pressing a kiss into my hair. I felt him take a breath as if he were about to say something, but we were both startled when the world shifted beneath our feet. I looked up, and my heart stopped in horror as I saw the outline of him beginning to fade.

"No!" I cried, choking on sobs. "Please, Trey! Please don't leave me!"

"I love you, Em," he said, his voice like a whisper of wind.

"I love you, too." I tried to cling to him, but he was wisps of smoke and shadow. "I love you," I repeated desperately, but he was gone.

I opened my eyes to see the dim morning light shining through the loft windows. I was lying on my mattress with tears streaming down my face.

What the *fuck* was that?

Was that supposed to be comforting? Was I supposed to be fucking grateful to get him back for mere minutes only to have him ripped away again? Was that my broken brain's attempt at closure?

If so, it failed spectacularly. All it did was make this world—the one where Trey was gone—unbearable once again.

I decided not to bother getting out of bed.

ဢ

After the morning bell rang, Wolf tried calling my name again. I didn't answer, and he grew increasingly louder and angrier before going silent. I heard someone haul themselves up over the loft railing a minute later. A hand rested on my shoulder and shook me.

"Freckles?"

I opened my swollen eyes to see Lee leaning over me, his face worried.

"You okay?"

"I'm fine," I mumbled, rolling onto my side and turning my back to him.

He was quiet for a few seconds before asking, "You want to come to breakfast?"

"No."

Another pause. "Well, I'm gonna put the ladder down. Can you leave it down so we can bring you some broth?" I didn't answer, and eventually, he continued, "I mean, I *can* climb up to the loft every time but can't guarantee you'll have much broth left by the time I get here."

I wished he'd go away. I hadn't felt this weight of grief since the first weeks after Trey died, and I did not have the energy to talk to him.

"Alright, well, we'll be back, okay?"

I didn't respond, and eventually, I heard him get up and lower the ladder down. Down below, a quiet, heated argument broke out. I closed my eyes and let myself drift away again.

Around noon, Wolf shook me awake.

"Em, you should eat somethin'."

I stared at the rafters in the ceiling, hollow and heavy simultaneously. "I'm not hungry."

"What's wrong?" he asked hesitantly after a pause.

"I don't feel good," I muttered, rolling over and burying my face in my pillow to hide the tears gathering in my eyelashes. It wasn't a lie. My entire body ached.

I couldn't see him anymore, but he didn't move or speak for a long time.

"Can I get you anything?" he finally asked quietly.

I shook my head, tears silently dampening my pillow.

"Okay," he murmured, "well, maybe you'll feel better after some rest."

⁂

I slept all day, interrupted only when I had to use the bathroom or when Wolf or one of his crew would shake me awake and ask stupid questions. Sable apparently handled all the patients who came in, which made me feel even more guilty, but I couldn't do anything about it. The weight of this grief crushed me into my mattress, trapping me.

Every time I fell asleep, I longed to and dreaded seeing Trey again. It had been so *real*. I'd had plenty of vivid dreams, and this was different. I felt the sun and the wind against my skin. I smelled the flowers. He had been there. He'd held me. I wanted to be back there, safe in his arms, but if he vanished again—*when* he vanished again, I wasn't sure I'd survive it.

In the end, my fears were pointless because he didn't return.

⁂

"Em, c'mon." Wolf's voice dragged me from sleep again. "You gotta eat something."

I opened my eyes to see the single bulb lighting up the clinic, and the sky outside was dark. I didn't roll over from where I faced the wall.

"We brought you some fresh broth."

In the long silence, I waited for him to lose his temper, but his voice was even softer when he spoke again, which surprised me.

"You remember that time Dune tried to sneak one of those big orange lizards into our room?"

It was such an unexpected thing to say that I turned and looked at him. He was crouched next to my mattress, his elbows on his knees and a mug of broth in his hand. The corners of his mouth twitched up a little at the memory.

"You were probably three, so I don't know if you remember. Dune was eight. I don't know how the fuck it didn't bite him. He's lucky I found it before Pa did. He thought he could tame it and keep it for a pet. A fuckin' venomous lizard."

I didn't remember that, but it didn't surprise me. Dune loved all animals, no matter how deadly they were. I glanced at Wolf again to see him studying my face.

"You look so much like Mom," he said when I made eye contact.

His earlier words seared painfully through my head. *At least Mom isn't alive to see what you've become.* I swallowed hard and looked away. "Is Mac back yet?"

"No, they had some sort of situation come up."

A sharp stab of anxiety cut through the fog. "What?"

"I don't know the details, but Nemo said it wasn't anything to be concerned about. They'll just be gone a little longer than expected."

I tried to push my unease back down.

"Em, what happened?"

The plea in his voice squeezed my lungs, and I hesitated, but I just—just *couldn't.* "Nothing."

He frowned but looked more sad than angry this time, and guilt seeped farther into my skin.

"Ember?"

Both Wolf and I turned to see Scar appearing from the ladder. She held up a hairbrush and smiled slightly. "Would you mind if I braided your hair? I used to be good at braids, but Sable won't let me braid his hair, so I'm out of practice."

Wolf snorted.

I surprised myself by sitting up. My hair was a mess, tangled around my face, and my back ached—the muscles stiff from lack of movement.

Scar nudged Wolf with her leg, "You git. It's girl time. If you stay, you gotta let me braid your hair, too."

Wolf rolled his eyes, but a genuine smile crept over his face as he got to his feet. Scar plopped on the mattress behind me.

"Any requests?" she asked.

I shook my head slightly.

"Oh, dealer's choice," she mused as she gently brushed out the tangles. "Alright. Let's hope I remember how to do this."

We sat in silence for a few breaths. Below us, I could hear Wolf speaking to somebody, but I couldn't hear the words.

"Did Wolf tell you how we met?" Scar asked quietly, and I shook my head again. "It was, gods, about ten years ago. He was so serious, so determined that he didn't need any help from anybody. He had one goal, finding you, and he wasn't interested in anythin' else. At the time, Lee and I were working with a different group of bounty hunters, but we were hopin' to leave and start our own group. We talked him into helping us with one mission, and in return, we'd help him with one mission." I could hear the smile in her voice. "Of course, he found the guy we'd been tryin' to track down for *months* in just two days. So we parted ways but told him we'd fulfill our part of the deal when he had a lead."

She hit a particularly tangled section of my hair and had to put the brush down to work the knot out carefully with her fingers. "A couple weeks later, he tracked us down and told us he had a lead in Moab. So we set out." She moved on to parting my hair with her fingers and deftly beginning to braid.

Moab. Lee had mentioned Moab when he found me in the cemetery.

"The lead he had was a girl who'd been sold to a whorehouse, so he was already on edge at the idea of you bein' in that situation, which of course, he hid by barely sayin' a word for the three-day journey. And then, when we got there, the girl was gone. The owner said she ran away, but Wolf couldn't let it go. He just kept saying it didn't feel right. We finally spoke to some of the other girls and found out that a week prior, they'd heard the missing girl screaming and found blood in her room and down the hallway.

"Your brother was like a man possessed with that info. He broke into the records and found who had been with her that night. He tracked that asshole down, beat him bloody, and then told him he had two choices. He could talk, or he could die. Turns out the owner charged him triple and let him kill her. I thought for sure Wolf would end him, but he let him go. We were able to find the body based on the info we got. They'd dumped her in a shallow grave outside of town. Animals had gotten to her, so she wasn't exactly recognizable, but she looked enough like you and was the right age and roughly the right size.

Scar's fingers stilled in my hair, emotion clear in her voice. "Wolf stood there staring at the body for a long time. When he finally spoke, I knew shit was about to go south. He told us it was you and took off in our truck without us. By the time we got back to town, he'd killed the man he'd let go *and* the owner of the brothel and told all the girls to run."

I barely breathed as I listened, horrified and captivated at once.

"And Wolf didn't stop there. Next, he got himself drunk off his ass and started a massive brawl at a bar." She made a disapproving sound through her teeth. "Just about got himself killed. Lee and I found him bleeding out in an alley and got him out of there. The whole drive back to New Salt, he kept telling us to let him die, to leave him there, that he'd failed his mission, his family, and *you*. He lost a lot of blood, and I thought he was a goner more than once."

Emotion was welling up in my throat, and I struggled to swallow it down.

"We got him patched up, but he was a broken man. We technically didn't owe each other anythin', but Lee and I couldn't just leave him like that, no matter how many times he told us to. Eventually, we started gettin' through that hard head of his, and he started opening up. He told us all about you, what happened with your brother, and how he didn't know what to do now, so we asked him to join us."

She huffed a laugh as she began to braid the other side of my hair. "We had to ask Wolf about a hundred times before he finally said yes, and I still suspect he only agreed to get Lee to shut up. We were on another mission a year later when we ran into one of the girls from that brothel. She recognized us and wanted to say thank you. Wolf asked her about the girl and turns out they'd been friends. Lee asked if Wolf and you really had the same eyes, and she got real confused before finally tellin' us her friend had brown eyes. I thought Wolf was gonna pass out. He barely made it through that conversation before breaking down."

She shifted from behind me to sit on the floor by the mattress, apparently finished braiding my hair, and I studied her. Her light brown skin made me think of honey. She wore a short-sleeved shirt, and a single glance at her muscled arms would tell me she was a fighter. Her dark brown hair was pulled back in her usual short ponytail. I had to work to hold her gaze because her brown eyes had a warmth that reminded me of Trey.

"We thought he was hurt when he collapsed in an alley, but he just cried and kept saying, 'She's still alive.' And I think that's when I knew I'd stick with him and help him find you, 'cause it was so clear he still loved you so fiercely despite everything."

My throat felt impossibly thick, and a tear escaped and rolled down my cheek.

"He never stopped lovin' you, Ember," she murmured. "He might not fully realize it yet; he's still got a fuckin' hard head, but to the rest of us, it's always been clear as day. It's why we all stuck with him." She hesitated for a moment, searching my face for *something*. "None of us have ever seen you as just another bounty. Even when we thought you were guilty, you were still Wolf's baby sister."

I squeezed my eyes shut. I didn't know if that meant some of them believed me, and I was too scared to ask.

"Also, I think you broke that poor boy's heart."

I opened my eyes. "What boy?"

"Sam. He's just been moping around the clinic."

My shoulders slumped, and I wrapped my arms around myself, my mind replaying the angry words I shouted at him.

"We weren't tryin' to overhear your argument, but, well, it's a small building. And I just wanted to let you know from an outsider's view, it seems obvious your crew loves you as much as we love Wolf."

Tears welled in my eyes, and I bit my cheek hard.

"I know for a fact he's sittin' on the porch right now if you want me to send him up here. Poor boy looks exhausted. I don't think he's been sleeping."

I hesitated for a long moment but then nodded slightly.

"I'll go tell him," she smiled. "Thanks for letting me do your hair."

After she disappeared down the ladder, I carefully reached up and felt the two braids she'd put in my hair. They felt much neater than my regular messy braids. I heard the door open downstairs and tried to figure out what the fuck I was going to say to Sam.

His head popped up over the loft a minute later, and I felt even worse. He looked pale with dark circles under his eyes. His short blond hair was messy, as if he'd been pulling on it.

"I'm so sorry." His voice shook as he pulled himself up and crossed the loft to crouch beside my mattress. "I've never thought of you as a thing, I swear. You've always been a person to me, *always,* but I—"

I interrupted him by throwing my arms around his neck and burying my face in his bony shoulder. He immediately wrapped his arms around me, squeezing me back tightly.

"I'm sorry," he whispered.

"No, I'm sorry." My voice cracked. "I never should've yelled at you like that."

He pulled away to grip my face in his hands. There were tears in his blue eyes. "You are not a thing," he said fiercely. "Not to me, not to anybody else on our crew. I'm sorry Trey was the only one of us smart enough to say it out loud."

"I saw him," I whispered, my eyes overflowing.

His brow furrowed. "Trey?"

"In my dream that night."

He looked confused as if thinking about all the times I woke up screaming Trey's name.

"Not a nightmare." My voice broke. "It didn't even feel like a dream. It felt real—so real. He was *there.* We were together, and then I had to watch him disappear—again."

He dropped his hands from my face, one fist rubbing at his chest. His eyes grew vacant, and his entire body sagged. It was jarring to see—to realize just how much grief he'd been hiding behind his jokes.

"Fuck," he muttered.

"I can't do this, Sam," I whispered through the tears. "I can't."

His throat bobbed as he swallowed hard, and then he wrapped his arms around me again. "You know, his bunk was the one under mine. And I still find myself hangin' over the edge to tell him somethin' I thought of, only to see it empty and remember he's gone." He took a shaky breath. "I think he'll always be the first person I think of when I want to talk to somebody."

"I just want him back," I sobbed. "I'd do anythin' to get him back."

"I know," he whispered. "Me too."

We ended up curled up on my mattress together, both of us consumed by grief, but for the first time in a while, I didn't feel alone.

CHAPTER 18

I squinted in confusion at the bright daylight. What the hell time was it? I tried to shift on my mattress and realized with a start, I wasn't alone. I twisted in a panic, first checking to make sure I was still clothed and then to see who the hell was in bed with me. My fear faded as quickly as it came when I saw Sam curled up behind me, his arm draped over my ribs as he lightly snored. We'd cried together for a long time and apparently fallen asleep. It was the first night in recent memory I hadn't had a nightmare.

My heart swelled. It was strange to know that I loved him. Not in a romantic way, but I did love him. I loved everyone on my crew, but I felt connected to Sam in a way I hadn't felt since Dune died. I stayed half-propped up for a moment, but I didn't *need* to get up yet, so I lay back down and closed my eyes. It was nice to feel another body curled around me.

It was only a couple minutes later that Sam suddenly jerked awake, scaring the shit out of me. I twisted to look at him. He was sitting up, his short hair sticking in every direction, and staring at me with a comical mix of confusion, shock, and panic. He glanced down at his body, seeming to relax when he saw he was still fully dressed.

"That's the first thing I did, too," I said, my voice hoarse with sleep, but that insane smile crept over my face.

His eyes narrowed. "Did you lure me into your bed, you siren?"

"I'm pretty sure this is your fault."

"Well, you can stop looking so damn pleased by it," he

grumbled, but his eyes looked lighter than they had yesterday. He glanced up at the window, looking as confused by the daylight as I was. "What time is it?"

"I have no idea. Did you know you snore?"

He turned back to glare at me. "Yes, Jax loves to complain about it."

"It was kinda cute." I fully grinned now as he blinked at me, eyes widening in outrage. "Like a little baby snoring."

"You know it would take very little effort for me to smother you with this pillow."

I dissolved into silent laughter, and he flipped me off, but he smiled.

"Sorry to interrupt."

I jumped, and Sam swore. Lee leaned his elbows on the loft floor, grinning at us.

"Mornin' sleepyheads," he said.

I glared at him, but Sam rolled his eyes and asked, "What time is it?"

"Just past noon," Lee answered, completely unfazed. "You two slept for almost twenty solid hours."

My eyes widened in astonishment, and I glanced at Sam to see my surprise reflected on his face.

"I volunteered to try kissin' you both awake just in case magic was involved, but everybody else seemed to think you were just tired."

Sam made a funny sputtering sound, his mouth moving like he was speechless for the first time in his life. I pressed my sleeve to my mouth, trying to hide my smile.

"You alright there, Freckles?" Lee looked sideways at me with a smirk.

"Freckles?" Sam finally seemed to remember how to speak. "Freckles!"

As they launched into a heated argument about nicknames, I tried not to overthink how much lighter I felt. Was it normal for a person to swing back and forth between intense emotions like this? Did most people go from wanting to die to laughing? Or was I losing my mind?

I suddenly remembered Leda standing in the clinic, squeezing my hands and telling me she was here if I wanted to talk. I didn't know what had come over me, but I did. I wanted to talk to her. When I stood,

Lee and Sam fell silent, looking at me in surprise. I felt a little dizzy but was sure eating something would fix it.

"Where are you goin'?" Lee asked.

"I need to go talk to somebody," I said, pulling on my boots.

"Who?" Sam asked curiously.

"Leda."

I strode to the ladder, but Lee didn't move, staring up at me from where he still stood on the ladder.

"You should drink that broth first," he said when I raised my eyebrows.

I turned, and sure enough, there was a mug of broth on my dresser. I heaved a sigh but walked over and drank the whole thing. It was cold, but I didn't mind. When I finished, pointedly waving the empty mug at Lee, he finally started going back down the ladder so I could leave.

"You want any company?" Sam asked.

I looked at him and recognized the flash of loneliness in his face from feeling it myself.

"I gotta do this alone, I think." I grimaced. "But I'll be back."

He nodded, then seemed to force himself to grin. "I might get some more sleep then without you hoggin' the covers."

I flipped him off as I started down the ladder and was rewarded by a more genuine smile crossing his face.

Lee followed me to the door, but I stopped in my tracks. *"Alone,"* I repeated pointedly.

I expected him to argue, but to my surprise, he raised his hands in surrender and backed away, letting me continue out the door by myself.

Wolf, Kai, and Sable stood outside the clinic by one of the walls. Wolf had a tape measure, and Sable held a piece of paper. They all looked at me as I came outside, and I didn't miss the surprise and relief that flashed across my brother's face when he spotted me out of bed.

"Hey," Wolf said with a forced casualness that was almost funny. "Nemo found some window panes, and we were thinkin' if you wanted more windows in here, we could probably install them for you."

I stopped in my tracks. Did that mean my brother was letting me stay here? And if he let me stay here, did that mean he believed me? And if he believed me—

"We don't have to," Wolf said, frowning slightly, and I realized I was just staring at him.

"No," I got out, "that'd... that'd be really nice."

The worry in his eyes lightened a few shades.

"Where are you off to?" Sable asked.

"I just have to go talk to somebody," I said, slightly awkwardly.

"Where's Lee?" Wolf's eyes narrowed.

"I told him to stay here. I can go by myself."

"Tuck," Wolf barked.

Tuck unfolded himself from the shadow of the clinic, startling me. I hadn't seen him lounging there on the ground.

"I don't need a guard," I protested, irritated.

"How about a walkin' companion?" Tuck asked with a grin.

He was so tall I had to crane my neck to look up at him as he stood beside me. It made me feel like a child again, glaring up at my big brother.

"This is a personal errand."

"I'm very discreet," Tuck winked.

Why the fuck was my face getting hot? "I don't—"

"Em," Wolf interrupted. "Remember our deal."

I was certain he hadn't said anything about me being followed everywhere by one of his crew when he explained his stupid deal, but I bit my tongue. With an annoyed huff, I started walking, and Tuck fell along beside me. If he thought he could come into Leda's house and listen to our conversation, he had another thing coming.

It was a gorgeous day outside. The sun felt warm, and I realized the last few patches of snow had melted away, leaving behind a thick layer of mud. Many people were out working on their houses and yards, and most said hello to me as I passed. I settled for an uncomfortable wave when they greeted me.

"People sure seem to like you," Tuck remarked.

I didn't answer.

"Nemo told us a little bit about the fever. I like him," he said, gazing around the hold. "Nemo, I mean. He seems like a pretty good person." He huffed a sarcastic laugh. "Though most anybody would seem like a saint after Madame."

I wrapped my arms around myself, trying to contain my shudder. We walked in silence for a while, and just when I started to think it might stay that way, he spoke again.

"So you really thought Wolf was gonna kill you?"

I glanced up at his face. His head tilted as he studied me.

"That's what I was told," I muttered.

"If you thought he was gonna kill you, why didn't you fight when Wolf and Lee took you out of the clinic?"

I didn't answer, angling my stiff steps to put more space between us.

"It kinda seemed like you were just gonna let him kill you."

I shrugged, my fingers tugging my shirt collar closer together.

"Why?" he pushed.

"I always knew he'd find me eventually." My boot slipped in some wet mud, and I flailed my arms to get my balance, but Tuck somehow closed the distance between us in the blink of an eye and caught my elbow, steadying me.

"Yeah, but you didn't have to let him *kill* you," he said, releasing me before I could jerk away.

I pressed my lips tighter together and kept my gaze focused straight ahead.

"And you sure as hell didn't have to *ask* him to kill you."

I winced.

"Hey, Bones!"

One of the blacksmiths was striding down the path toward us, his ruddy face lit up. I tried to remember his name but came up blank. He was probably in his forties with thinning dark hair. I'd healed him before —he'd told me about the Safeguard, but I couldn't remember his name.

"Good to see you!" he said warmly, stopping when he reached us. "You doin' okay?"

I pasted a smile on and nodded.

He glanced at Tuck and then reached out like he was going to take my arm, but Tuck's hand shot out and wrapped around his wrist, startling both of us.

"I was just gonna have a private word with Bones," the blacksmith said, his bushy eyebrows raised as he stared at Tuck.

"Feel free," Tuck said, still friendly but somehow threatening at the same time, "but don't touch her."

"Tuck!" My hands fluttered as I tried to decide if I should grab him or not. "Let him go—"

"No, it's okay, Bones," the blacksmith hurried to say, his gaze swinging back to me and his voice lowering. "I just wanted to say if you ever need help—with *anything*—all you gotta do is ask." He cast a not-so-subtle glance at Tuck, who finally released his arm. "Anytime."

My fingers twisted the ends of my hair as I swallowed hard. I couldn't even remember this man's name, and he was offering to help me escape my brother and his crew if need be.

"Thank you," I managed to say. "I'm alright, but I'll keep it in mind."

The blacksmith studied my face for a moment longer, but then he nodded. "Good. Well, I'm glad I ran into you. Been meanin' to get over to the clinic to say hello."

I fiddled with my shirt collar and tried again to smile.

"Have a good one," he added, nodding politely at Tuck before continuing down the path.

"He never would have, you know," Tuck said, and I swung my gaze back to him, my brow furrowing. "Wolf. He never would've shot you. He was just tryin' to call your bluff."

"I wasn't bluffing," I retorted, my voice rising. "And do not fucking do that again. If I don't want someone to touch me, I will fucking handle it."

"Who tried to touch you?"

I gasped and lurched away, crashing into Tuck, who caught me. Pressing my hand against my pounding heart, I righted myself and glared at Lee. The asshole grinned back at me.

"Stop. Doing. That," I hissed.

"Lee," Tuck added, his voice stern. "For fuck's sake."

"Sorry," Lee smirked, looking not at all apologetic. "It's just too easy."

I straightened my shirt and started walking again, wishing they'd both leave me alone. Instead, they fell in on either side of me.

"Why weren't you bluffing?" Tuck asked after a blissful few seconds of silence.

"What?" I snapped at him.

"Why did you *want* Wolf to kill you?"

"I don't want to talk about this." I wrapped my arms around myself.

"Lemme guess, you think you're a lost cause? Unworthy?" Tuck continued, ignoring me.

I opened my mouth and then snapped it shut again.

"You make mistakes, so you think you're damned?" Tuck added, and I struggled to keep my face blank.

"You keep fallin' off the narrow path that leads to righteousness?" Lee chipped in.

I stole glances at both of them, unnerved at how they knew these specific fears.

"How do you know where that path is, Ember? Whose map are you following?" Lee raised an eyebrow when I met his gaze.

I came to an abrupt stop. "What do you mean 'whose map'?" I sputtered. "There's only—"

"Does that map have one path for good and one path for evil?" he interrupted me, his gaze so intense on me that it made me want to shrink. "One way to paradise and one way to torment?"

"What else—"

"Why do you deserve to die, Ember? Did you kill Dune?" Tuck asked.

"No!" I blurted. Was this an interrogation?

"Then why?"

"Because I'm not *good*."

My fists clenched at my sides, my entire body feeling abruptly unsteady. They both stared at me, their faces solemn, and I wished I could take the words back. Why had I said that?

"Carth really fucked you and Wolf up, didn't it?" Tuck's voice gentled, and my fingernails bit into my palms. "All that religious bullshit about good and evil bein' absolutes. Do you know anyone who is *only* good or *only* evil?"

Juck's face sprang to mind, but so did my confession to Sam. Juck was evil, but he hadn't *only* tortured me. He'd loved me, too, muddying the waters like Sam said. I bit my lip, staring at the ground.

After a moment, Tuck continued, "Your brother spent so much of his life strugglin' to reach some unachievable level of perfect. He thought the fact he struggled meant he was damned, but strugglin' is just part of being *human*. His obsession with rules and order didn't make him a better person or the world around him better. It just made him mistrust his own intuition. It made him fuckin' miserable. You want to know why he isn't dragging you back to Carth right now? It's cause he started trusting his gut."

"I'm not tryin' to be perfect," I said to my boots, "I'm just tryin' to make up for…for everythin'."

"Balance the scales?"

I glanced at Lee, but my feeling of relief that he understood died when I saw the amused and irritated look on his face.

"Yeah, we know all about the fuckin' scales. Your brother wouldn't shut up about them for *years*. So I'm gonna ask you the same thing I asked him. Who's holding the scales? Is it you? Is it the Ministry back in Carth? Is it one of the gods?"

I stared at them, unsure of what to say. They both looked so damn serious.

The stray hairs escaping Lee's top knot waved around his face in the breeze. "Look, this is just my opinion, but I think if *you're* not the one holding the scales, it's all just bullshit. Who are you lookin' for approval from? Cause the only person who can give you that is *you*."

I blew out a shaky breath, feeling suddenly exhausted, but before I could say anything, a shout interrupted us.

"Bones!"

We all turned to see Cloud running down the road toward us, his eyes wide. My heart lurched.

"What is it?" I asked sharply.

"It's Nemo," Cloud gasped as he reached us. "He just collapsed."

The three of us ran the entire way to Nemo's house. By the time we got there, I was panting and shaky, and, to my annoyance, Tuck and Lee had barely broken a sweat. Wolf and Kai stood outside Nemo's house like they were waiting for us.

"Sable's upstairs with him," Wolf said immediately.

I didn't hesitate, I ran up the wooden steps of his porch, feet pounding, and darting through the door. The fear seizing me was far more intense than I would have expected. If Nemo died, what would happen to the Vault? Would everything fall apart?

Nemo's guards were standing inside the main room. As I approached, they all looked up at me, their faces a mix of relief and wariness.

"He's upstairs," said one.

I dashed up the stairs. Smith, the guard, stood outside a door at the far end of the hallway and beckoned me forward. When I entered the simple yet cozy bedroom, Sable looked up from where he leaned over the bed, checking Nemo's pulse. Relief nearly choked me when I saw Nemo awake and alert.

"Howdy, Bones," Nemo murmured. "Sorry if I gave you a scare."

"He's stable, but I think he may have some internal bleeding," Sable said gravely. "He mentioned being tortured, and I think there might be some residual damage."

I made my way to the opposite side of Nemo's bed from Sable, but I hesitated, my hands hovering between hanging at my sides and reaching out toward him.

"Can I?" I asked hesitantly.

Nemo blinked, his brow furrowing slightly. "Go ahead, Bones."

I gently wrapped my hands around his forearm, hoping no one noticed how they trembled, and let my healing power flow through me. My powers surged to several places in his body, carefully healing many lingering injuries. I remembered how battered he'd been that last time Madame had summoned me, and I'd refused to heal him. I hadn't even checked on him after that. He must have been in so much pain for the past few months, but he hadn't come to me for healing either.

"Suppose I shoulda come see you sooner," Nemo said.

I kept my eyes down, shame eating away at my insides, as I double-checked to make sure I'd healed every injury. "I don't blame you."

"Whaddya mean?" Nemo asked.

"I just mean...I don't—" I swallowed hard. "After...after what I did, I understand."

"Bones—" Nemo began in a gentle voice, but I panicked.

"I don't blame you," I said again quickly, backing toward the door. "You're healed, but you should rest."

"Bones, wait," Nemo called, but I darted through the door, startling Smith.

I didn't *run* down the hallway but walked as fast as possible.

"Ember?" Sable called behind me, but I didn't stop.

As I quickly descended the stairs, I internally cursed at all the people still standing in the main room. Wolf, Kai, and Lee stood just inside the front door. Everyone was staring at me expectantly, and I tried to paste a normal expression on my face.

"He's okay," I said, "but he needs to rest."

I strode past my brother and his crew and out the door. I made it a couple steps before all three were at my side.

"What's wrong?" Wolf asked.

"Nothing."

"Em," Wolf sounded irritated, "c'mon, what's wrong?"

"Nothing!"

"This feels kinda familiar for some reason," Kai mused.

"You know, I was thinkin' the same thing," Lee responded.

Wolf shot them a withering look. "Em, just tell us what happened."

"Wolf, nothing happened. I'm just going back to the clinic," I said in my best attempt at a normal tone of voice.

"Do you think they're related?" Kai asked.

"The resemblance is uncanny," Lee grinned.

"Both of you, shut up," Wolf barked.

"Ember!"

We glanced back to see Sable jogging toward us, and I cursed under my breath. I sped up, but Wolf caught my wrist and jerked me to a halt.

"Wait," he snapped at me.

"Let go," I snapped back.

"Ember, Nemo would like to talk to you," Sable said when he caught up to us.

"I'll talk to him later," I lied.

"I think it would be beneficial," Sable pushed.

"I have shit to do," I said through my teeth, trying to wrench free from Wolf's grip.

"What happened?" Wolf asked Sable without releasing me.

"Nothing happened," I snapped. "Wolf, let *go* of me!"

"This remind you of that time Wolf had a bullet in his leg and kept insisting he was just a little sore?" Lee asked Kai.

"See, I was thinking about the time he concealed that stab wound, just about bled to death, and Sable almost murdered him," Kai answered.

Wolf glared at them, but Sable's lips were twitching upward, and the other two idiots were grinning widely.

"Ember, Nemo would—" Sable began.

I pulled the oldest trick in the book. I pointed behind them with a gasp, my eyes widening in terror. Wolf released my arm as they all spun around, hands going to their respective weapons, and I didn't waste any time. I took off toward the clinic.

"Are you fucking kidding me?" I heard Wolf yell, and laughter erupted.

I glanced back to see Kai and Lee laughing hard as Lee gripped my brother's arm. Wolf and Sable looked less amused.

"Let her go. She earned that one," Lee said.

I kept running, but I couldn't stop the manic grin that came over my face. As I approached the clinic, Scar and Tuck stood on the porch, eyes narrowing.

"What's going on?" Tuck asked.

"Where's everyone—" Scar started.

I darted past them into the clinic and went straight up the ladder, only to come to an abrupt halt when I saw Sam sleeping in my bed.

Oh, right. I'd forgotten about Sam.

I couldn't stop grinning like an idiot, so I kicked off my boots and shrugged out of my jacket before crawling in next to Sam. He opened his eyes slowly and then visibly startled at the sight of me climbing into bed with him.

"What—" he started, his voice hoarse with sleep.

I curled into him, hiding my face in his shoulder. His arms slowly wrapped around me. Neither of us spoke as I tried to catch my breath and stop fucking smiling.

"So, is this a thing we do now?" he finally asked, sounding sleepily amused.

"Guess so," I tried to say casually but started giggling silently.

Sam pulled away and looked at me, but his worried expression faded to relief when he saw I was laughing.

"What's going on?" We heard Tuck yell from the porch.

"Wolf just got hoodwinked by his miniature," Kai howled.

Sam raised an eyebrow, a crooked grin crossing his face. We could hear them continuing to tease my brother outside, and eventually, Wolf started harassing them back. Sam and I listened to them insult each other, attempting to stifle our laughter with Trey's quilt. I expected Wolf to march inside and drag me down the ladder, but the door didn't open.

"So, what the hell just happened?" Sam asked after the commotion outside quieted.

I groaned and pressed my face into the pillow, my voice coming out muffled. "I healed Nemo. He collapsed 'cause he's been hurt for the past three fuckin' months. Internal injuries from… from Madame."

"Oh shit."

"He's fine now," I added.

"So…why were you running?"

Talking with my face hidden in the pillow was easier. "Nemo wanted to talk to me, and I… panicked."

"I'm shocked," Sam deadpanned.

"Shut up," I mumbled.

"What did he want to talk about?"

"I told him I didn't blame him for not wanting me to heal him after… after I helped torture him."

"He said he didn't want you to heal him?"

Hidden in the pillow, I grimaced. After a few seconds of silence, Sam sat up, ripped the pillow away, and smacked me in the back of the head with it. "So you made assumptions *and* ran away?"

"No," I lied stubbornly.

"Fuckin' hell, Emmy." He glared at me. "You are *always* jumpin' to assumptions and runnin' away."

I jabbed a finger into his side.

"Ow!" he yelped dramatically. "I think you just broke my rib."

"I did not," I muttered.

"How would you know?"

"I'm a healer, I'd fuckin know."

He snorted, and the corner of my mouth lifted slightly. He motioned for me to lift my head and replaced the pillow, then flopped on his back beside me.

"You know you can always do this, right?" he asked.

"Do what?"

"Tell me shit."

"Why? So you can yell at me?" I grumbled.

"I'm not yellin' at you. I'm *gently* tellin' you that sometimes you're a big ol' dummy."

I huffed. "I'm not good at talking."

"Well, I'm excellent at talkin', so I'll help you get better."

I choked on a laugh. "Just cause you talk all the fuckin' time doesn't mean you're *good* at it."

He grumbled about how mean I was, but I suddenly remembered the question I'd meant to ask.

"Where did Mac go? Why aren't they back yet?"

I felt him stiffen and quickly lifted my head to look at him. He grimaced at me.

"What?" I demanded. "Where are they?"

"We got a distress call from Lana."

I stared at him, sure I'd heard him wrong. "From *Lana*?"

"I'm sorry," he said, "It wasn't a secret, but I kinda forgot to tell you with everything goin' on. She's apparently real sick—on her deathbed."

"*Lana?*" I repeated.

"Look, what she did to you was horrible, but she's our family. Mac couldn't let her die alone, and Raven and Griz wanted to join."

"They're not bringing her back for me to heal?" I felt strangely numb.

Now Sam looked surprised. "We'd never ask you to do that after what she did to you."

I stared at him without really seeing him, my mind whirling.

"What's goin' on in that head?"

"Why aren't you going?"

He smiled, but it looked pasted on his face. "I know if I caught it, you'd probably kill me yourself."

I stared at him, struggling to pull in a deep breath as my throat ached. I saw his pain through the fake smile and the joke. It obviously hurt him that he couldn't say goodbye to someone he considered his family. I tried to push away the suffocating memory of being pinned to the floor. Lana had hated me, still hated me based on what she'd told Wolf and his crew, and while I wasn't exactly a fan of hers, I couldn't entirely blame her. She'd lost her twin brother.

Was I seriously considering this?

It's what Trey would've done.

"Shortcake?" Sam asked, his brow furrowing.

"Would they bring her back if I wanted to heal her?"

"You don't—"

"*Would* they?" I interrupted.

He hesitated for a few seconds. "Yeah, probably."

"Can we send them a message?"

"Okay, wait, are you sure about this?" He sat up, his face serious. "She'll probably still hate you. Maybe more if you save her life."

"I know."

"You don't have to feel guilty. Lana made her choices, and she knew the cost."

I swung my legs over the side of the mattress, getting to my feet. "I know," I repeated.

"Emmy, I'm serious."

I shoved my feet into my boots. "I am, too."

He studied my face with narrowed eyes. "You're absolutely sure?"

"Yeah."

He heaved a sigh. "Alright, well, let's go to the bunkhouse."

৬৩

Wolf and his whole pack were outside measuring and marking the outside of the clinic for the new window. I let Sam do the talking, but annoyance stabbed me at feeling like I had to get my older brother's permission to leave my own clinic.

The radio was hidden in a small secret compartment in the wall of the crew's bunkhouse. Sam gave me a basic rundown of lingo, including Lana's call sign of "Nightshade" and Mac's call sign of "Alpha Leader."

"Nightshade? A poisonous plant, really?" I asked dryly, and he shrugged. "What's mine, Shortcake?" I added curiously.

"No, yours is Sunshine."

My eyebrows raised, and his smile turned sad.

"Trey."

My eyes filled with tears, and he caught my hand, squeezing it gently before returning to the radio. With a practiced ease, he pushed a series of buttons on the radio and handed me the worn pair of headphones.

"Mac should respond soon."

Sure enough, after about thirty seconds, Mac's voice crackled in my ears. "Go for Alpha Leader."

Some tight knot in my chest loosened at the sound of his voice. I pushed the button on the walkie and spoke into it, trying to keep my voice steady. "Alpha Leader, it's Sunshine. Over."

"Go ahead. Over." His terse voice replied quickly.

"I just found out where you are. Over."

There was a pause.

"I'm sorry I couldn't tell you myself. Over," Mac replied.

"I'm not upset. Bring Nightshade home, and I'll heal her. Over."

There was another pause.

"Say again. Over."

"Bring Nightshade home. I will heal her. Over," I repeated.

"Are you sure? Over."

"Yes... I mean affirmative. Over."

I glanced up at Sam in the pause.

"He's probably gonna want to talk to me," Sam said.

"Requesting contact with Shadowfox. Over," Mac finally said.

"Are you Shadowfox?" I asked Sam, raising an eyebrow.

He grinned. "Yes, I am."

I handed over the headphones.

"This is Shadowfox. Go ahead, Alpha Leader. Over," Sam said into the radio. He listened for a moment, nodding. "Affirmative. Over." Whatever Mac said next made him roll his eyes. "I copy. Over." He was quiet for longer this time, but then he grinned and eyed me in a way that made me suspicious. "Sunshine appears sober and has at least *most* of her wits about her. Over."

Now, *I* rolled my eyes.

"Roger that. Over and out." Sam waited a moment before removing the headphones and turning the radio off. He blew out a dramatic breath and looked at me. "I hope you know what you're doing."

"I have no idea what I'm doing," I replied.

"Great," he drawled. "This oughta be fun."

CHAPTER 19

W̲e were returning to the clinic when the dinner bell rang. As we neared the small building, I realized Wolf and his entire pack were standing outside, clearly waiting for us. They all seemed to be frowning at me, and I remembered that I'd practically fled from them earlier.

"Ember, Nemo wants to speak with you," Sable said as soon as we were close enough to hear him.

"Perfect, we're on our way there now," Sam replied.

I nearly wrenched my neck, twisting to look up at him, incredulous. He grinned, completely unrepentant.

"Oh," Sable didn't even try to hide his surprise.

"We'll meet you at the canteen," Sam added, looping his arm in mine and towing me past the pack. "Save us some of that bread Neena's been bakin' all day!"

"What the fuck are you doing?" I demanded once we were out of earshot.

"Mac gave me a message for Nemo, and you need to talk to him, too, so two birds, one stone."

"I don't want to—"

"I know you don't *want* to, but you gotta stop fuckin' running away, Shortcake."

My body wasn't sure if it wanted to puke or kill him. "Sam—"

"I'll be right here. You can do this."

I fell silent, my stomach churning. Sam pulled me along, moving far too quickly, and soon Nemo's house appeared. Nemo's guards watched us go up the stairs, frowning, and I wondered if they ever worried that I'd kill him.

Sam pushed open the door when Nemo's weak voice beckoned us inside. He looked surprised to see us, but his smile was warm as he pushed himself up to sit.

"Sam, Bones." His eyes lingered on me. "Glad to see you. Bones, I wanted to speak with you real quick."

I kept my lips pressed together and tried to brace myself.

"Bones, I don't blame you for what Madame did," he said, his voice so gentle. "That's not why I didn't come to see you."

Why did it feel worse when people didn't blame me? What the fuck was I supposed to do with all this guilt?

"It was two-fold, really," Nemo continued. "I figured you needed some time to heal as well. I didn't want you to have to deal with these injuries so soon after, uh, everything. The second reason is I have a —" He cleared his throat and ran a hand through his thinning white hair. "I deeply dislike doctors and clinics and most medical things—not 'cause of you. It's somethin' I've dealt with for most of my life.

"You're actually the first healer I've been able to let examine me in, well, many, many years. When I fell ill with the sickness, I didn't summon you. I convinced myself I could ride it out." He grimaced. "The folly of man, I suppose. Smith was the one who discovered I was ill and sent for you. Your healin' power is an incredible thing, Bones. Even under the watchtower, when you would heal me, it was such a welcome respite from the pain. Not just 'cause you healed my physical body, but 'cause you poured your emotions into your power."

My heart beat faster as I stared at him.

"I could feel your regret, your horror, your pain at what you were forced to do. While you were healin' me, it was more than just the pain easing. It felt like comfort, like somethin' so powerful it created a shelter from everythin' for a moment." He smiled, his eyes damp. "If you hadn't been there giving me that respite, I don't know if I would've been able to withstand the pain. I might've broke and given up names, and more good people would've died."

He paused, regarding me as I struggled to keep from losing control of my emotions.

"I know it wasn't just me, either. I spoke to Mist to see if she felt the same when you healed her. She brought it up without any prompting. She got real fierce defending you. Seems she assumed I was contemplating punishin' you, and she was not gonna stand for that." He smiled again, and the kindness there made my eyes spill over. "I believe everyone you healed in that room felt the same. They knew your pain and felt your comfort. You probably gave more people the strength to hold fast than you even realize."

Mist. I hadn't checked in on her, either. Sam shifted closer, and I noticed he was offering another handkerchief. I took it with a watery look of gratitude.

"Trey knew you would play an important part in freeing the hold from Madame. He told me many times you weren't just healin' people. You were giving them hope. When he came and told me he was going with you so he could help you get away from Madame, I was initially reluctant to let you go. He made it clear he wasn't askin' for permission but lettin' me know as a courtesy."

I was really crying now. Sam wrapped an arm around my shoulders.

Nemo cleared his throat again, and pain filled his face. "He made me promise if somethin' happened and the two of you got dragged back to the Vault, I would do everythin' in my power to make sure you survived. He was willin' to sacrifice his life for the people here, but he was adamant that we couldn't let Madame kill you—kill that hope you'd given so many."

The pain in my chest was unbearable. So many emotions were raging through me. Fury, grief, and love all intermingled together. Sam wrapped his other arm around me, too, and I could hear his unsteady breaths.

"In the end, I couldn't do much since Madame had me locked away, but I wanted you to know that Trey understood the risks when he chose to help you escape." There was a short pause. "I spoke briefly to Mac before they departed, and he informed me he told you about Trey's radioed message."

I tensed.

"He didn't have time to give me all the details, but he said you were very upset that he didn't tell you sooner. I'm afraid that'd be my mistake. I hoped to give you some time and instructed the others to wait." He let out a heavy sigh. "I hope you will forgive an old man's misguided attempt to protect you."

Sam's arms tightened around me. I took a deep, shuddering breath and raised my head, wincing slightly at the state of Sam's shirt from my tears. Nemo smiled sadly as I met his gaze.

"That's all I wanted to say, but if you ever have any questions, you're always welcome, Bones."

"Ember," I said hoarsely.

Nemo's eyebrows raised in question.

"My name is Ember."

He smiled, his eyes warming. "Ember it is, then."

"Oh, I almost forgot," Sam said, his voice almost as hoarse as mine, "Mac had a message for you."

Nemo looked surprised but gestured for Sam to continue.

"Emmy asked him to bring Lana back so she could heal her, so they're comin' back with her."

Nemo glanced at me, but he didn't look surprised. "Thank you, Sam. I'll make the necessary arrangements. Are they leaving today or tomorrow?"

"Tomorrow morning."

Nemo nodded, his eyes going slightly distant. "Alright. I'll inform the others."

"Have a good night, sir," Sam added, pulling me toward the door.

We didn't speak until we stepped outside of Nemo's house. It was darker than I'd expected outside. We'd been there for a while. Sam sucked in a breath and let it out in a gust.

"Well, that was... a lot."

"I don't know if I can do dinner, now," I said shakily.

"Honestly, me either," he muttered.

"Can we go home?"

"Yeah," he took my hand and squeezed it. "Let's go home."

When we entered the clinic, Tuck glanced up from where he was sitting by the wood stove, paging through a book. His eyebrows raised as he took in our slightly disheveled, tear-streaked faces.

"Everythin' alright?" he asked cautiously.

"Why aren't you at dinner?" I blurted out, startled to see him.

His eyebrows raised even further, glancing between the two of us. "Wolf set up a rotating guard to make sure somebody is always here watchin' the clinic."

"Oh," I mumbled, hoping I didn't look as confused as I felt. "Well, we're goin' upstairs."

Tuck stared at me for a second but then smirked and got to his feet. "I think I'll sit outside. Get some fresh air."

I didn't understand the look he gave me, but I headed for the ladder. Sam followed me up, and he spoke as soon as we heard the door shut.

"Yeah, he thinks we're fuckin'."

I almost tripped over my own feet. "What?"

Sam grinned. "Tuck. He thinks you just told him to get out so we could *do it*."

"He does not!"

"I'd bet you anything he does."

I gaped at him. "Well, we're... we're *not*."

Sam laughed out loud. "*I* know that."

The uncertainty that crashed over me made my stomach twist, and it must've been written all over my face because he quickly sobered.

"It's alright, Shortcake. I'm pretty sure we're on the same page."

"What page?"

"Well, I'm not gonna lie, you're beautiful and kinda mean, which is my type." His grin was cheeky as I glared at him. "But I feel like we've fallen into... I dunno, something more like siblings, I guess? Like me and Raven. I love her, I'd do just about anythin' for her, but the thought of kissin' her makes me feel..." he made a face "...kinda queasy."

Relief made me dizzy. "Yeah," I got out, unsure if I wanted to laugh or cry. "We're on the same page."

He gave me a dramatically outraged face. "How dare you feel queasy at the idea of kissin' me!"

I sat on my mattress, pulled off one of my boots, and chucked it at him. He caught it easily, grinning.

"I'm gonna tell Raven you said the idea of kissin' *her* makes you queasy," I threatened.

"Trust me, she probably feels more queasy than I do about the idea."

I snorted, pulling off my other boot, and he plopped on the mattress next to me.

"So," he said, suddenly serious, "some powerful mind reader is hunting you?"

The casual way he brought it up made my body break out in chills. I had to remind myself I already knew he knew, but it didn't stop my body's panicked response.

"Yeah."

"That's pretty fucked up."

"Yeah."

"Do you really think this Mental Menace will slaughter everyone if we don't hand you over?"

It took me a moment to get the words out. "I don't know."

"You know we'd never do that, right?"

"*I* would."

"Well, that's—" he broke off, staring at me. "Wait, what do you mean *you* would?"

"Sam, if he comes here and threatens to kill everyone, I'm gonna hand myself over."

He stared at me. "What? Weren't you just *furious* thinking that's what Nemo would do?"

"No," the realization crashed over me as I spoke out loud, "It wasn't about giving me to him. It was about using me like a...a game piece." I swallowed hard. "You all made me feel like a p-person again, and I thought I was findin' out it was a trick, that nobody *really* saw me that way."

He was quiet for several breaths. "I'm glad we made you feel like a person again 'cause that's how we've always seen you."

"I know," I said, managing a watery smile.

"But can we go back to the part where you're planning on handin' yourself over to the Mental Menace?"

"I'm not *planning* on it, but I'm not gonna just sit here and hide if he threatens to hurt people."

"There's no fuckin—"

"*Sam,*" I interrupted fiercely, "I will do *whatever* it takes to keep him from killin' anyone here."

He glared at me, but I saw the flash of fear in his eyes. "Alright, let's make a deal," he said, his voice rough.

FANGS

I eyed him warily. "What?"

"If it comes to that, and you're gonna hand yourself over, take me with you."

"I can't—"

"No, Emmy, listen. I keep tryin' to build my strength back up, but it doesn't seem to work. I get tired so easily, I can't fight in hand-to-hand combat, and my hands shake too much to shoot accurately." His voice broke slightly. "Do you know how much it killed me that I couldn't go with them to get you back? I had to sit here and *wait*."

This guilt was going to eat me alive. "I'm so sorry, Sam, I—"

He grabbed my hand and squeezed it hard. "I don't regret it. I'd do it again, even knowin' the outcome. But at the same time, it kills me how *useless* I am."

"You're not useless," I whispered.

"I'm useless as a Safeguard, and that's just a fact." His eyes held mine with an intensity I hadn't seen before. "I can't go on missions 'cause I'm a liability, but I can find new ways to help. And if you're gonna just sacrifice yourself, I can at least come with you so you don't have to do it alone."

My eyes overflowed. "He might hurt you. He might *kill* you."

"I'm willing to take that risk."

"Sam, I can't...I can't let you get hurt for me."

"Emmy," his voice was so quiet and pained. "You're askin' me to be alright with *you* gettin' hurt for *all* of us, and I'm not gonna try to talk you out of it 'cause you're stubborn as a fuckin' mule, but gods, please let me come with you."

"The last time I let somebody come with me—" I choked out, but I couldn't finish.

"I know," he squeezed my hand hard again. "But he made that choice, and I'm makin' this one. Please, don't take that choice from me. I don't have many left."

I stared at him with tears sliding down my face, but my protests died at the tears glimmering in *his* eyes. He was letting me see this pain he'd been carrying, and I hated that he felt useless, that his only available option was *this*. His throat bobbed as he swallowed hard, but then he shifted and, with his free hand, pulled *another* handkerchief out of his pocket and handed it to me.

"Besides, if I don't come with you, who's gonna supply you

with all these quality kerchiefs?"

I couldn't tell if I was laughing or crying as I took it and wiped my wet face. It was a familiar feeling, the nausea of fear and the relief and gratitude all mixed together. I wanted to refuse, but I kept wrestling with the memory of Trey telling me I was trying to control everything.

Finally, I let out a shaky breath. "Ok."

His eyes lit up. "Yeah?"

"On one condition."

"Ok, let's hear it."

"You have to promise to try to stay alive." My voice wobbled, but I held his gaze.

He suddenly held up his free hand with only his little finger sticking out. "We'll swear an oath."

I furrowed my brow, confused.

He rolled his eyes at me. "C'mon, gimme your finger."

I copied him, and he gripped my little finger with his, wrapping them together. "I swear I'll try my damndest to stay alive." He looked at me expectantly.

"I swear I'll let you come with me," I said shakily.

He squeezed my finger once more and then released it. "There's magic in that oath, so don't you dare break it."

Fifteen minutes later, the door burst open, and Wolf must have fucking sprinted up the ladder with how fast he appeared. Sam and I jumped, staring at him—me from where I sat on the mattress against the wall writing in the healer's notebook, and Sam from where he was lying beside me, tossing a pair of rolled-up socks in the air like a ball.

Wolf went from furious to confused to irritated at a speed that made me dizzy. "Brought you both some dinner."

He stalked over to hand me my broth and tossed Sam his ration. Sam was grinning madly, and Wolf glared at him, his jaw flexing.

"We're not fucking," I stated calmly.

Wolf's head snapped toward me. "What?"

"Sam and I," I took a sip of broth, "we're not fucking."

Wolf looked at Sam.

"What are you lookin' at me for? She's not lyin'," Sam said, sitting up to unwrap his food.

Wolf glared at us a moment longer before storming back to the ladder and disappearing. We listened to the clinic door slam shut.

"What are you gonna do when you *do* want to fuck someone?" Sam asked, taking a bite of his sandwich.

Pain stabbed through me, but I forced myself to push it down, to pretend like the thought of being intimate with someone didn't make the broken shards of my heart dig deeper into my flesh.

"Convince you to create a diversion?"

I didn't have to pretend to laugh when he nearly choked on his food.

CHAPTER 20

S am left a few hours later. I almost asked him if he wanted to stay, but I hesitated, unsure of the boundaries in this new relationship we'd defined. For a moment, he paused, too, almost as though he wanted to ask something, but then he just smiled and wished me a good night. I heard him say goodnight to Wolf and his crew downstairs and head out.

I sat upstairs on my mattress, trying to ignore the crushing weight of being alone pressing in on me again. I could hear Wolf and his crew talking downstairs but couldn't find the courage to join them. They all still felt... like strangers. They were loyal to my brother, and I didn't know what my brother thought of me now. I remembered him saying his terms were that I *talk* to him, and my skin prickled with dread. No one else seemed to find talking as difficult as I did.

Maybe no one else was quite as broken as I was.

I changed into my sleep shorts and shirt, nervously keeping an eye on the ladder, and climbed into bed. Usually, I would go downstairs and wash my face and teeth, but like a coward, I just burrowed under Trey's quilt.

I hoped I didn't dream about Trey again.

I swallowed hard.

I hoped I *did.*

๑๖

I woke up mid-scream to someone shaking me and yelling my

name.

I tried to scramble away, still seeing Juck's face, still sobbing broken pleas.

"Ember!"

I blinked, abruptly registering Wolf gripping my upper arm, his eyes flashing.

"I'm sorry, I'm sorry." The words tumbled out in a panic.

"Em, it's just a dream," he said, but his voice was angry, and I cringed.

"Wolf, you're scaring her," I heard someone say, and as my eyes darted around the room, I realized Scar was standing on the ladder, watching us.

Wolf was crouched on the floor by my mattress, still gripping my arm. One of my candles sat on the floor beside him, illuminating the small dark loft. My chest was heaving with sobs, and I attempted to get a hold of myself.

Wolf turned back toward me, his eyes sharp, and I dropped mine to the floor. As I woke up more, I wished I could disappear. Wolf released my arm, and I thudded into the wall behind me. I quickly righted myself, my face burning. I hadn't realized how much I'd been trying to pull away from him.

"Emmy." His voice had gentled, and it only made me feel shakier. "It's alright. It was just a dream."

I wrapped my arms around my torso, trembling. In the silence, we listened to the ladder squeak as Scar returned downstairs.

"Sorry," I finally managed to get out. "I'm fine."

He didn't respond, and I couldn't help thinking of all the times in the past twelve years I'd woken up from nightmares and wished for him so badly that it hurt. Now he was here, but everything was all wrong, all fucked up.

"No, I'm sorry," he said finally, shifting to sit beside me on the mattress. "I shouldn't have yelled. You were just—" he faltered for a moment, "—just beggin' Juck to stop."

It felt like all the blood rushed out of my face, and I clapped a hand to my mouth, sucking in deep breaths through my nose. The two of us sat stiffly side-by-side for a while as I slowly moved past the urge to be sick. I was about to tell Wolf he could go back downstairs if he wanted, but then he began to hum.

I'd tried to remember the song he used to hum many times in the past years, but it was like a forgotten word that taunted me from the shadows of my memory. The longer I went without hearing it, the less I could remember how it went. As soon as he started humming it, it flooded back to me, and all that bottled-up emotion escaped.

Wolf had always been there for me at night when I had nightmares, no matter how awful I'd treated him during the day. I couldn't remember Pa ever comforting me, and Dune slept like the dead. Wolf was the one who always woke up and rubbed my back or held me and hummed. He said it was a song Mom sang when he had nightmares.

I didn't know my mom, though, and her memory didn't comfort me. For me, it had only ever been Wolf.

I tried to cry quietly, angling my face away from the candle, but a sob choked me, and he stopped humming. I tensed, but then a warm arm wrapped around my shoulders as Wolf shifted closer, and that was all it took for me to unravel completely.

I covered my face with my hands as huge sobs shook me, but I leaned into him. His arm tightened around me, tucking me against his side, and I felt his cheek rest on the top of my head. He started humming again, and I knew no matter what happened between us, I'd at least have this moment with the brother I remembered.

I woke up at dawn all by myself.

I was tucked into my bed, so I assumed Wolf must've untangled himself after I fell back asleep. I lay there momentarily, watching the early morning sunbeams play on the rafters. My heart felt... raw, but I *felt* it. It didn't feel like I had an empty hole in my chest. The grief was still there, an ever-present ache, but this felt a tiny bit like... new growth.

I took a deep breath and sat up. My braids from Scar were falling out, and I knew my hair probably resembled a bird's nest. I had to

—

The door below crashed open, making me jump. I heard Wolf say something in a sharp voice along with someone else, but then a body scrambled up the ladder at an inhuman speed and crashed into me, knocking me back onto my mattress. My brain struggled to register the chaos as I stared wide-eyed in horror at the person leaning over me.

It was Clarity. Tears spilled down her gaunt and ashen face, and her entire body was shaking.

"—tangled in shadows. They hunger. I see her path. They hunger for marrow and bone—"

I could barely understand the frantic words that were spilling out of her mouth. Behind her, Wolf and Lee appeared, grabbing her and trying to pry her off me, but she let out a blood-curdling scream.

"It's ok!" I shouted, waving them away. "It's ok!"

They released Clarity but didn't step back, looming over the two of us with matching dangerous expressions.

I managed to push her off enough to sit up. Clarity huddled beside me, babbling words that didn't make sense and shaking like a leaf.

"Clarity?" When she didn't respond, I gently took her face, holding it still until her wild eyes finally met mine. "Clare? Clare, can you hear me?"

Her body went so abruptly still that my heart stopped, sure she'd just had some sort of stroke, but then her hands gripped my wrists with an unnatural strength. She blinked, and I couldn't contain my gasp as her brown eyes vanished, swallowed in black. There was no white, no iris, just like when my eyes had glowed golden, but Clarity's eyes were full of a deep, empty darkness. It leaked from her eyes in thin black tendrils.

"She is the ember that ignites the pitch, and the loom is weaving the strands of the flux."

It was still Clarity's voice, but something about it made all the hair rise on the back of my neck. Before I could react, she blinked again, and her brown eyes focused on me, her brow drawing together.

"Bones?" she asked, like *she* was confused about *me*.

I gaped at her, speechless. She had her back to Wolf and Lee, so they hadn't seen her eyes change. Had I imagined it?

"I did it again, didn't I?" Clarity whispered before I could remember how to form words, and she burst into tears.

I reacted instinctively, pulling her into a hug and holding her. She was still trembling, and my mind was spinning through every possible disease and disorder I'd ever read about. I could feel all her bones protruding through her skin. Something was wrong, *terribly* wrong.

My fingers rested on the bare skin of her shoulder, and I tentatively let my healing power flow into her. It felt different from all the times I'd healed her before, but I couldn't figure out why. Still, her body responded positively to my power. I couldn't pinpoint any injury or infection, but I felt her strength returning. She let out a shuddering gasp, and I pulled back enough to look at her face. Her eyes were wide, shock written all over her face, and I *watched* her color return, and her cheeks fill out again. It reminded me of when I healed Zeke's little boy, Roe, from that terminal disease, but it wasn't quite the same. For one, there was no sign of a disease *at all*.

The way her body absorbed my power was...

I frowned. It *almost* felt like what I would imagine healing an elderly person and making them young again would feel like, but I couldn't reverse the body aging. I couldn't make skin more elastic or stop muscles from shrinking, just like I couldn't make amputated limbs grow back.

Wolf muttered a curse, and I remembered he was in the room. I stole a glance at him and Lee. They were watching us closely with similar expressions of astonishment.

"Did you heal me?" Clarity whispered, her eyes still huge.

"I...I don't know," I admitted, frowning. "Clarity, how long—"

"I'm so sorry," she interrupted, her eyes filling with tears again.

"Why are you sorry?"

"I shouldn't be here," she continued as though I hadn't spoken, glancing nervously at Wolf and Lee. "Raven is going to kill me."

Fury immediately filled my veins. "What?"

She met my gaze, looking alarmed, then shrank back at whatever expression was on my face.

"Raven *knew* you were sick?" I demanded, my voice too loud for the small space.

"It's not their fault," Clarity whispered.

"They *all* knew?"

My fists clenched in my lap, trembling with rage. My crew knew Clarity was like this, was obviously ill, and they hid *it*?

"Bones," Clarity's voice trembled, and the plea cut through my anger. "Let me explain."

The door opened, and running footsteps entered the clinic. Lee glanced below.

"It's Sam and Jax and that girl who's scared of us," he said.

Clarity muttered a curse, and I gave her a sharp look, but Sam's head popped over the loft.

"Fuck," he gasped, clearly winded. Then he glanced at my face and grimaced at my furious expression. "Fuck."

"Sam, move," someone said.

He climbed the rest of the way up into the loft, edging around Wolf and Lee, and Sky's head appeared from the ladder. Her hair was growing back after being crudely shaved before they threw her in the Pit, covering her head in tight black curls. She froze when she realized Wolf and Lee were upstairs, her eyes widening.

"Sky, it's ok," I said, trying to temper my anger. "Come over here."

Wolf and Lee stepped backward, pressing themselves against the eaves to give her more room. Sky hesitated a moment longer, but then she scurried up the ladder and darted to where I sat on the mattress. I hadn't seen her since before Wolf stole me away, and I took a second to scan her. Like all the kids, she'd put on some much-needed weight, and her brown skin was glowing with health. If only her mental and emotional wounds were that easy to heal. She wedged herself behind me and eaves like she was trying to hide, but then she shuffled forward enough to grab Clarity's hands.

"Clare, are you ok?" she whispered.

Jax followed her up, his eyes wide and nervous. Sam sank on the mattress beside me, and I turned to him.

"What the *fuck*—" I started angrily, but Clarity gripped my wrist and stopped me.

"No, wait, don't be mad at them," she whispered, her brown eyes—Trey's eyes—still swimming with tears. "It's my fault."

I stared at her, hurt and guilt filling my chest. "Why didn't you come to get healed?"

"I couldn't bear to face you," she whispered.

The pain in my chest squeezed my lungs. I was right. She blamed me for Trey's death and—

"It's my fault Trey's dead," she continued, and then her eyes overflowed again.

I blinked, my brow furrowing. Sky wrapped her arms around Clarity, holding her tightly.

"What?" I finally managed to get out, my head aching with confusion.

"It's my fault," Clarity repeated through sobs.

"Clare, it's not your fault," Sam said, his voice gentle.

"No, it's not," Sky affirmed.

Jax crouched beside Sam. He didn't say anything, but his face was so serious. I had no idea what was going on.

"What are you talking about?" I demanded. I knew my voice was still too angry by how Clarity winced. "It's not your fault, it's *mine.*"

Clarity's eyes snapped to mine, a hint of matching anger flashing through them that surprised me. "No, Bones, I *saw* Trey's death, and I failed to stop it from happening."

"Saw? You mean you were there?" Did she see me just standing there like a fool when Madame killed her brother?

"No, I mean, I *saw* it weeks before it happened," she bit out through sobs. "I saw Madame kill him, and I thought if he left with you, maybe he'd escape that fate, but it did *nothing—*"

Her voice broke, and she covered her face with her hands. I turned to Sam, anger and confusion making me nauseous.

"Ok, we don't know what's happening," he said quickly, his blue eyes full of regret. "Clarity's been... seeing things. And a lot of those things seem to come true. Like... like she's seein' the future."

"And you didn't tell me?" I couldn't let this go.

"Emmy," he said quietly, his face uncharacteristically serious, "you were barely able to get out of bed."

"So?" I demanded. Did they think I was too weak? That I wouldn't be able to heal Clarity? How many more seriously ill people did they turn away because I was so pathetic—

"You needed time, and we weren't even sure you'd be able to heal her."

"I asked them not to, Bones," Clarity choked out. "It's not their fault."

"I don't need you to screen my patients, Sam," I said through my teeth. "I'm the only one who would know for sure—"

"You were a fucking *ghost,*" Sam interrupted me. "You weren't sleepin', you barely ate, you didn't say a word to anybody, you—"

"What if she'd *died?*" My voice shook with the force of holding back all the emotion in my throat.

"I knew I wasn't gonna die," Clarity tried to interject.

"That is bullshit," I snapped. "You can't—"

"Bones, please don't be mad," Jax said in a low voice, and when

I glanced at him, the pleading look in his eyes made me feel worse.

"Alright, hold up." Wolf startled all of us. He pushed himself off the wall and beckoned at me. "Em, come outside a minute."

I debated refusing, but Clarity was sobbing again, and the other three were either glaring or looking close to tears. I let out a sharp sigh and got to my feet, following him down the ladder. Lee came after me, walking outside with the two of us.

Wolf halted under the apple tree, hands on his hips as he surveyed the hold. I stopped an arm's distance from him, but of course, Lee halted directly beside me, throwing his arm over my shoulders. I shoved him away and stepped out from under his arm, glaring, but he just grinned and stuffed his hands in his pockets. Gods, and I thought *Trey* had no concept of personal space.

"Seems like a lot is goin' on here," Wolf said, turning to study me.

I didn't answer.

"If that girl is seein' the future, I assume that's a new development?" he asked.

I nodded, but then a surge of panic went through me as I remembered that moment in Madame's old house when Mac heard what Wolf *wasn't* saying aloud.

"Have you ever met anyone else with powers?"

I didn't answer.

"Does anyone else here have powers?"

I knew what he was fishing for, and he knew I knew, but I pressed my lips tightly together.

"Ember," he sounded irritated, "I'm tryin' to understand what's happenin' here so I can *help* you."

"Why?"

His eyebrows raised. "Why what?"

"Why bother? Aren't you still plannin' on dragging me back to Carth?" I tried to keep my voice even, but it shook.

He studied me silently, and I couldn't read his expression. "I'm reservin' that decision for the end of the two months."

"And I'm just supposed to fuckin' wait and *trust* you?" I demanded.

"Yes."

I stared at him, my temper boiling.

His eyes narrowed. "What?"

"I'm just tryin' to decide if you think *I'm* stupid or if you're a hell of a lot dumber than I remember."

Lee let out a noise suspiciously like a laugh, but Wolf's temper rose to meet mine.

"Ember—"

"I *don't* trust you, for the record. Or your crew." I snapped.

Maybe I imagined the hurt that flashed through his eyes because he just sounded angry when he spoke. "You trust these people more than your own brother?"

"*These* people believe me."

"What do you think these two months are for?"

"I don't fuckin' know, Wolf!" I threw my arms up in the air. "To torture me?"

"We made a deal, remember? You said you'd talk to me, Ember."

"I might have to tell you everythin' about *me,* but I am not draggin' anybody else into this."

"So there are others, then," Wolf raised an eyebrow, the corner of his mouth ticking up.

I bit the inside of my cheek hard to keep from swearing. Godsdamnit, I hated that he could still back me into a corner so fucking easily.

"Mac has some sort of power, doesn't he?"

I glared at him and didn't answer.

"What doesn't make much sense is that no one else seems to know," Wolf continued like I was participating. "Like you and Mac are keepin' it a secret."

"I'm not talking to you about Mac," I said through my teeth.

"Em, all I'm tryin' to get at is if you and Mac are keepin' somethin' a secret from the others, I would guess you have a pretty good reason for it. And if you have a good reason for keepin' it secret, don't you think your crew had a good reason for keepin' that girl's powers a secret from you?"

I felt my cheeks heat up, and a familiar stubbornness filled me. "It's different."

"Why?"

"Because it's Clarity."

"Why does that make it different?"

I wrapped my arms around my torso, trying to physically hold myself together. My voice came out wobbly. "Because she's Trey's sister."

Realization flashed through his eyes, and he studied me quietly for a few breaths. "I would guess if her health started going downhill, they would have immediately told you."

He was right, and I hated it. I wished he would stop making so much sense and just let me be mad.

"Ember, I'm not tryin' to dig up information on your friends for whatever horrible reason you've got in your head. I've got no beef with any of them."

"Well, I'm sorry if I don't trust the person who snuck in here in the middle of the night and abducted me at gunpoint."

Lee wasn't even trying to hide his grin now. Wolf noticed and shot a dirty look at him.

"Look, man, I'm not gonna lie; it feels good to see you have to deal with this mini version of you."

Wolf and I glared at him, but he just shook his head, chuckling. Wolf heaved a sigh and turned back to me.

"All I'm sayin' is that if more people are developing powers, this is much bigger than you and me."

Developing powers.

How was this happening?

My stomach suddenly dropped, and all the blood rushed out of my face with it. What would the other powered person do when he found out about Clarity? About Mac? Clarity was possibly *seeing the future.* People would kill for that kind of power. No, people would do much worse than kill for that kind of power. I tried to swallow the urge to be sick. What if he put out a bounty for them? Would Wolf go for it?

"What's wrong?" Wolf asked.

My brother would never traffick people with powers, right? He'd been so angry about what happened to Sable. It was a risk, but I needed to know for sure.

"I just know what kinda bounty someone would pay to own a person with powers."

Wolf's brow furrowed, but then I watched the realization dawn on his horrified face. "Is that what you think I'd do? Traffick people with powers? Ember! What the fuck?"

It was a relief to know he was telling the truth despite the guilt I felt for asking. "I don't know. I don't know you."

"We're very selective in what jobs we take. There's gotta be proof that a person committed a crime, a *violent* crime. We only hunt the worst kinda people. The kinda people who like to *hurt* others."

People like me. That's the kind of person he thought I was. It stung, which frustrated me. I *knew* that's what he thought of me, so why did it keep fucking hurting?

"Did any of the Reapers ever show signs of powers after you healed them?" Wolf asked abruptly.

His question startled me, but then I felt my cheeks warm. "No," I hesitated, "I didn't use my power on them."

There was a pause.

"I thought you were their healer."

My voice came out wooden. "Juck made me keep my powers a secret. I only healed him and two other men who knew. I was just a regular healer for everyone else."

He was quiet for what felt like a long time. I didn't dare look at his face.

"Did any of those three ever show any signs of power?"

Did he think I was *giving* people powers? Was I? *Oh fuck.* Horror rushed through my body, paralyzing me. What if I had given Juck powers? No, what if I *did?* What if he had a power that revived him? What if he was out there right now—

"Em, calm down," Wolf said, stepping toward me.

I held out a shaking hand, wordlessly pleading for him to stop, and he did. "You think *I'm* giving people powers?"

"I don't know," he replied evenly.

Fuck. I couldn't breathe. Wolf took another step toward me, but I retreated, and he halted once more, glancing at Lee. The responsibility of bestowing powers on potentially everyone I'd ever healed felt like an entire mountain dangling over my head and threatening to crush me. My vision swam. People were going to be hurt and *used,* and it would be—

Warm hands cradled my face, and I blinked in surprise at Lee's face close to mine.

"What do you hear right now?" he asked in a low voice.

"What?" I choked out.

"What do you hear? Tell me."

I stared at him, confused, but I tried to focus. "Birds?"

"Good. What else?"

"Why?"

"Just humor me a second, Freckles," he murmured. "What else do you hear?"

"Dog barking?"

"Good. Give me three more."

I had no idea what he was doing, but I strained my ears, "People workin' on that roof, the wind..." I paused, listening. "Somebody laughin'."

He grinned at me like we were both in on something, but I had no idea what it was.

"What are you doin'?"

"You breathin' easier?"

I wrinkled my nose, confused, but I *was* breathing easier.

"It's a trick Sable taught us," he explained, still holding my face. "Focusin' on stuff you can hear or see or taste or *feel*," his thumbs stroked across my cheeks in emphasis, and goosebumps rose on my arms, "can help distract your brain when you're panicking."

I bit my lip, torn between feeling annoyed and embarrassed.

"What scared you just now?" he asked, lowering his voice.

I tried to step back and pull my face out of his hands, but his fingers tightened. It wasn't enough to hurt, but enough to hold me there.

"Yes, I am holdin' you hostage until you tell me," he smirked.

I glared at him as fiercely as I could manage, but he didn't release me. I knew better than to test my strength against his, so I gave up and whispered, "What if Juck is still alive?"

He blinked in surprise. "He's not."

"How do *you* know?"

"I know 'cause we came across what was left of the Reapers' camp probably a couple days or so after the fight. I looked at Juck's dead body myself."

The relief that surged through me made me shaky.

"He's definitely dead, Em," Wolf added, reminding me he was *also* here.

I pulled away from Lee again; this time, he let me go, smirking. My whole face felt hot.

"You know how I've always been good at trackin'?" Wolf asked, and I nodded. "I usually just...get a sense of where to go, at least a general direction. But with you, there was *nothin'*." He frowned. "For twelve years, it was like you'd just vanished. Until one day, it came out of nowhere. I was mid-sentence and suddenly knew we had to go west. We followed the trail, and it led us to the Reapers."

I stared at him, unease trickling through me.

"I can't say for sure, but it seems like I sensed you again when... when Juck died."

I wrapped my arms around my torso. "What does that mean?"

"I don't know," he said, his voice solemn.

I wished Mac were here.

The clinic door squeaked as it opened, and we all turned to look. Sam stood on the porch, staring at us with a frown.

"Is Sam sick?"

I glanced at Lee when he spoke, surprise giving way to guilt. "Kinda."

"Have you tried healing him?" he pushed.

"Yeah." I turned back toward the clinic, but Lee caught my arm.

"What happened?" he asked. "You couldn't heal him?"

I narrowed my eyes, studying his expression. His voice had a strange tone. I glanced at Wolf and caught him studying Lee, too.

Lee sighed like he was annoyed with both of us. "If she couldn't heal Sam, maybe it's the same reason she couldn't heal Dune."

Oh. I barely resisted cringing, my eyes darting to Wolf again, but he was looking at Lee. "It's not the same reason. Sam—"

"—saved her life like the fearless, noble hero he is," Sam finished, coming to a stop beside Lee, his hands in his pockets and a wide grin on his face.

"How?" Wolf demanded.

He was looking at me when he said it, but I couldn't get any words out around the lump in my throat.

"Well, we didn't finish that story... about when she jumped in the Pit," Sam said, raising a hand to scratch his head.

"You said she was fine," Wolf growled. "Sounds finished to me."

"She *was*... eventually."

A muscle jumped in Wolf's jaw.

"I'd get to the part where you finish it, then," Lee muttered.

"Well, uh, Brimstone kinda beat the shit out of her. Broke her arm, and what was that thing that happened to your lung?" Sam turned to me.

"It collapsed," I mumbled, eyeing Wolf's darkening expression warily.

"Yeah, that. Her lung collapsed, and she couldn't breathe. She was dying on the clinic table, so I took a gamble and asked her to direct her power through me to heal herself. And it worked," Sam grinned again, but I could see it for the mask that it was, "because I am a motherfuckin' genius."

Wolf turned his furious gaze to me, but for a moment, I saw a flash of worry and fear so deep it took my breath away.

"So what, it made you sick? Her power?" Lee asked.

"Not sure," Sam shrugged like it was just a minor inconvenience, and my anger surged.

"Yes," I snapped, "it did. It sucked the fuckin' life out of him, which is why it's *never* happening again."

"Shortcake—" Sam tried to interject, but I ignored him, turning to my brother.

"That never happened with Dune, so I *know* it's not the same thing."

Wolf studied me, his jaw still tight. "You don't think it could've happened, and you were too young to remember it?"

I hesitated. I'd never thought about that, but then I remembered how it'd felt when I tried to heal Dune. "It felt completely different. When I tried to heal Sam... after... it felt like hitting a wall, and I couldn't get through it. With Dune," my voice grew hoarse as I tried to control my emotion, "it felt like I was just pouring everything into him, and none of it was... was sticking."

"Sticking?" Wolf repeated.

"Usually I can... feel it... the injury or the sickness. My power goes right to it, and it feels... contained. But with Dune..." I struggled to find the words to convey how it felt. "With Dune, it felt like pouring something into a bucket only to find out it was actually a sieve."

They all studied me silently. The grief for Dune ached in my chest, right next to my grief for Trey.

"But it hurt Dune," Wolf finally said roughly.

I nodded, but then Lee spoke.

"Did it hurt when she tried to heal you?" he asked Sam.

"It didn't hurt me, but it hurt *her,* " Sam answered quietly.

"I healed Dune lots of times before," I added, surprising myself. "Anytime he had a scrape or a cut... I never had a problem healing him."

Not until it really mattered, anyway.

"Will you tell me what happened?" Wolf asked.

I glanced up at him, familiar fear twisting in my gut, but there wasn't rage or anger lurking in his eyes like every time he'd questioned me before. His expression was calm, though all the muscles in his face were pulled tight.

"With Dune?" he added, even quieter.

Maybe it was because he was clearly trying, or because this wasn't planned and I didn't have time to work myself up about it, or because we were outside under the budding apple trees in the fresh air. Whatever the reason, the words came. They were shaky, but they came.

"He wanted me to try healing bigger wounds, but I was scared. We'd been arguin' about it for weeks. He came and found me after you left to go hunting and was... was being so strange. He wouldn't let it go. He'd never been so... intense." I hesitated briefly, then decided to be honest. "He reminded me of *you.*"

Wolf winced.

"It made me mad. I told him to leave me alone, and I started walking away. He yelled my name, and when I turned back, he had the knife." My voice grew shakier. "I didn't think he'd hurt himself, but he said somethin' about how he was doin' this for me. I started runnin' back, but before I reached him, he *stabbed* himself. I panicked and tried to heal him, but it just...did nothing. And he started screamin' that I was hurtin' him, but I couldn't stop tryin' to heal him 'cause there was so much...so much blood, and I knew if I didn't save him with my power, he'd d-die."

Wolf's expression looked like it'd been carved from solid rock while my eyes filled with tears.

"I didn't know what to do, so I started screamin' for you, but Dune grabbed my arm and... *snarled* at me to keep my promise and not tell you about my powers. And then you came, but you looked at me like... like I'd *done* it..."

My voice trailed off as I struggled to control myself. Sam

stepped closer and wrapped an arm around my shoulders.

"When you asked me what I'd done... I knew... I knew there was nothin' I could say. Not without breakin' my promise to Dune. You were lookin' at me like you didn't even know me. An' I just... just panicked and ran."

Wolf closed his eyes, and his throat bobbed as he swallowed. When he opened his eyes again, they looked wet.

"Thank you for tellin' me," he said, monotone, before turning and striding back to the clinic.

Lee hesitated briefly, then followed. Sam and I watched them go, standing together under the tree. I took a deep, shaky breath and tried to calm down.

"Good job," Sam said, his voice serious. He smiled when I glanced at him, but he looked sad. "See, you're gettin' better at talkin' already."

I scoffed and looked away.

"I'm sorry I didn't tell you about Clarity," Sam continued. "I wanted to... so many times. We all did, but she kept making us promise we wouldn't, and Mac said unless it was an emergency, we needed to respect her wishes." He paused. "It's probably good you found out, though, 'cause I think Raven was about a day away from exploding."

"Is that why she's been so mad?" I asked, still trying to blink away tears.

"Yeah," he huffed, "I thought she was gonna kill Mac when he told us they were bein' sent out."

That made sense.

"Well, she was also pissed about leaving you here with your brother's whole crew."

I looked at him in surprise.

"I know she doesn't always show it, but Raven might be the most loyal person I've ever met. Once you're in, you're in. And unless you do something despicable like Lana, you'll be in with her forever."

A group of chickens moved slowly down the path, clucking softly.

"Wolf thinks I'm givin' people powers," I whispered.

His eyes lit up in a way that made me nervous. "I want one!"

"Sam, if I *am*, I'm not doing it consciously!" I snapped.

"Well, then tell your subconscious to get on it!"

I rolled my eyes and turned toward the hold. "When do they get back?"

"Tomorrow afternoon or evening."

I took a deep breath. "Ok."

"Uh, have you told your brother about Lana yet?"

I furrowed my brow. "No?"

"Well, seeing as they met her and now they know she lied to them…they might not be, uh, thrilled."

Oh right.

"Also, Jax is pretty sure you hate his guts now."

My eyes widened. "What?"

"He thinks you're furious about Clarity."

I frowned. "I *am* furious about Clarity, but I don't hate Jax."

"Well, you might want to tell him that 'cause the poor kid's a mess."

I heaved a sigh and started trudging back up to the clinic with Sam following. Wolf was sitting in one of the wooden chairs, his gaze fixed on the floor. Scar stood beside him with her hand on his shoulder. Lee had pulled another chair up to Wolf, leaning close and speaking in a low voice. Sable and Kai stood against the wall together, Sable's head resting on Kai's shoulder. Tuck was sitting in another chair, oiling one of his guns. They all went quiet and looked at me when I came in, and I had to fight the urge to shudder at the weight of so many eyes. The clinic was not big enough for this many people.

I stopped without warning in the middle of the room, Sam bumping into me. "Mac and his crew are bringing Lana back here. She's really sick. I told them to bring her back so I can heal her."

The shocked silence didn't last long.

"You what?" Lee was the first to speak, and his voice was dangerous.

"Ember—" Wolf growled.

"I'm not askin' for your permission," I interrupted. "Just tellin' you as a… a courtesy." With that, I turned and retreated up the ladder, ignoring the angry questions being shouted at me.

Clarity, Sky, and Jax were all still huddled on my mattress. Jax clambered to his feet and approached me, his eyes wide and miserable.

"Bones, I'm so sorry," he mumbled.

"It's alright, Jax." I softened my voice. "I'm not mad at you, I swear."

His eyes widened even further, and he glanced at Sam and then back at me. His dark blue eyes were full of tears. "So you're not gonna kick me out of the crew?"

I blinked, taken aback. "What? No!"

"Jax, you're never gonna get kicked out, bud," Sam said, and from his gentle but exasperated tone, this was not the first time they'd had this conversation.

"But Lana—"

"Lana tried to hurt her. It's not the same." Sam interrupted.

"But my brothers—"

"Jax." Sam stepped into his space and grabbed the teenager by the shoulders, his face serious. "You are not responsible for what your brothers did."

Jax's lip trembled, and I glanced between the two of them, bewildered. Sam noticed and pulled Jax into a hug, mouthing the word "later" to me over his head. I nodded and turned to where Clarity and Sky were still huddled on my mattress, taking a deep breath. It wasn't hard to understand why Mac would've insisted they respect Clarity's wishes—most of her life had been dictated by someone else.

"I'm sorry for bein' an asshole," I said, shifting slightly on my feet.

"I'm sorry for keepin' secrets," Clarity whispered.

"Just... please, if you don't feel good, come see me. Please." My voice grew even more hoarse.

Clarity's eyes overflowed again. I moved forward until I could crouch before her, offering my hands like Mac always did. She gripped them immediately.

"Trey's death was not your fault, Clare." My voice wobbled dangerously. "Don't put that on yourself."

"Then you can't put it on yourself, either," Clarity said through the tears, squeezing my hands.

I smiled, but it felt stiff. "Tell me what you've been seeing."

CHAPTER 21

Clarity's visions were jumbled, similar to what she said to me. She saw bits and pieces of imagery that made no sense—all of it wreathed in shadows. If Mac's power felt like me, Clarity's power felt like the opposite.

It felt like *him.*

I tried to force that thought down.

The clearest visions she'd had were the vision of Trey's death and the vision of me running. She saw mine when she touched my arm in the clinic a few days before I left. Her vision showed me hiding supplies in my mattress and my plan—or lack thereof. Then she kept getting little flashes the entire week leading up to it. I remembered how I'd had that sensation of spiders crawling on my skin several times and fought the urge to shudder.

"Trey and Mac were about ready to confront you. They were so mad you didn't have a solid plan," Clarity said.

"Oh, they weren't the only ones," Sam muttered.

I ignored him. "Do you remember anything you said earlier?"

Clarity shook her head, frowning.

"Something about ember igniting pitch and a loom weaving... something."

"Ember... that's your name, isn't it?" Clarity asked hesitantly.

I winced. "Uh, yeah. You can call me that or Em... if you want."

Sky's lips moved as she mouthed, "Em."

"You also said something about bones...shadows hungering for bones?"

"So both of your names were in there?" Sam asked, and his tone was so intense I glanced at him. He was looking pointedly at me.

"What, you think it's about me?" I asked.

Sam's eyes narrowed. "Yeah, what a wild leap, thinkin' a prophecy that mentions both names you go by could be about you."

I elbowed him, and he grunted.

"What *exactly* did I say?" Clarity demanded, her eyes huge.

"Shadows hunger for marrow and bone. Um, the ember igniting the pitch and a loom weaving..." I tried to remember the word she'd said. It wasn't one I recognized.

"Flux."

We all jumped and looked at the ladder where Lee was casually lounging, his elbows resting on the loft floor again.

"Will you stop fuckin' doin' that?" I snapped... *again*.

"Doin' what?" he asked, eyes widening with fake innocence. "Remembering things you forgot?"

"Fuckin' sneaking up on me!"

He grinned in a way that made me want to throw something at him.

"What does that mean?" Clarity asked.

"Flux?" Lee asked, and she nodded, biting her lip. "I always knew it as meanin' somethin' flowing. Like a tide." He fixed me with a pointed look. "Or an icy river current."

I glared at him.

"That doesn't make any sense," Clarity murmured.

"No offense, but nothin' you said made sense," Lee replied, still grinning.

"I've been seein' so many shadows lately," Clarity continued, ignoring him.

My skin crawled. Shadows hungering for me? That was easy to interpret. I glanced at Sam and caught him giving me a questioning look. He didn't know about the shadows part, but I wasn't sure he needed to in order to put two and two together.

"What's that look for?" Lee asked.

Why did it seem like Lee never missed a thing?

"Nothing," I snapped. "Go away."

Instead, he pulled himself fully up into the loft. I felt Sky tense beside me, and I gently touched her hand. She glanced up at me, and whatever she saw in my face seemed to make her relax a little. She shuffled closer and leaned into me, so I wrapped an arm around her shoulders.

"Clarity also said, 'I see her path,' and 'she is the ember who ignites the pitch,'" Lee continued like he was a part of our little group. "You think she meant Freckles?"

Sam glanced at me but, to my dismay, nodded.

"Could this be tied to whoever vandalized the clinic?"

Sam's eyes focused on him, and I could practically see the gears in his head turning. "Could be."

"Any progress on that?"

"Wait," Clarity interrupted, frowning, "someone vandalized the clinic?"

"Someone wrote 'murderer' on the wall in blood," Lee answered.

They all looked at me expectantly, and I hated being the focus of everyone's attention. "For the last time, I don't know who did it. Stop askin' me."

"Not any progress, no," Sam answered. "Mist was missing a few bottles of scent, but she's not sure when they disappeared. And Sierra Crane was outside gardenin' most of the evening and said she didn't see anybody go in or out."

"Who?" I asked.

Sam frowned at me. "The older lady who lives across from you."

"Oh," I mumbled. I had no idea who my neighbors were.

"She's gettin' up there, so I don't know how reliable a witness she is," Sam continued.

"I think it's a good idea if you don't go anywhere alone for a bit," Lee told me.

"I don't need a guard."

Sam narrowed his eyes at Lee but sighed and said, "No, I think he's right, Shortcake."

"You don't know for sure any of that stuff is about me," I argued. "Sometimes I have to leave in the middle of the night or real sudden. I'm not gonna wait for someone to come with me."

"Don't make me sleep in front of the door," Lee warned.

"Mac and everybody will be back tomorrow," Sam quickly cut in as I sucked in a breath to go off on Lee.

"Oh, that reminds me, I gotta go finish somethin'," Jax blurted out, scrambling to his feet and darting for the ladder.

I waited until I heard him leave before I turned to Sam. "What was that with Jax earlier?"

He let out a sigh, bringing up a hand to scrub through his short hair. "Jax's two older brothers were two of the kids who attacked Mac in training." He glanced at Lee, and I heard what Sam wasn't saying—two of the kids Mac was forced to kill with his bare hands. "At some point, his mom died, leaving Jax an orphan. We didn't know he existed until after we finished training. One night, Jax broke into the bunkhouse determined to kill Mac with nothin' but a rusty wrench, but once he got inside, he couldn't do it. He went to leave and accidentally woke Mac up, and then he broke down and confessed everything. Trey, of course, immediately petitioned to add him to our crew, and Mac agreed. He's been with us ever since, but he's still afraid of getting kicked out."

My heart ached. Of course, Trey would take the kid who snuck in to kill someone under his wing. No wonder Jax had been Trey's constant shadow. I took a deep, shaky breath.

"Are they seriously bringin' Lana back?" Clarity asked, her eyes on me.

"Yeah," I said, but Lee's expression darkened, so I hastily changed the subject. "The brothel's not still operating, is it?"

"Nemo left it up to us," Clarity said, fiddling with a loose thread on her shirt. "Some people are still workin', but mostly 'cause they want to." She glanced at me and caught the question on my face. "I think some just don't know what else they could do. That's what the rest of us are tryin' to figure out." Her mouth twisted in a bitter smile. "I couldn't keep workin' when I was havin' fits from touchin' people."

I remembered how she'd avoided touching me that day in the clinic, and I opened my mouth to ask another question, only to be interrupted by the breakfast bell. The day hadn't even fucking started yet.

"Clare, you want to go to the canteen?" I asked.

Clarity shook her head, glancing at Sky. "We should get back."

"I'll walk you back," Sam said. "I gotta check on Jax, anyway."

"And I'll walk Freckles to breakfast," Lee volunteered far too cheerfully.

As Lee put it, Wolf and the rest of his crew left the clinic earlier to give us "privacy," which made me roll my eyes. I knew he reported everything he heard to my brother. I walked silently, my brain turning the events of the morning over and over. My skin seemed to buzz with a restless anxiety I couldn't shake, and it put me on edge.

"Whatcha thinkin' 'bout over there?" Lee asked.

"Nothin'," I muttered.

"Oh, don't give me that bullshit."

I couldn't get a good read on him. At first glance, Lee appeared to be an open book, but I was starting to realize how guarded he was. The jokes and the flirting were distractions—a sleight of hand.

"C'mon, Freckles," he coaxed, slinging his arm around my shoulders again.

I cut my eyes sideways to glare at him, my temper immediately flaring. "Why do you care so godsdamned much?"

He stopped abruptly, his hand tightening on my shoulder to make sure I stopped, too.

"Why do I care?" he repeated, his eyebrows raising.

I pulled away from him and crossed my arms, waiting.

"You're seriously askin' me why I care?"

"Do you get this friendly with every bounty you catch?"

"Only the pretty ones." A smirk lifted one corner of his mouth. "Why? Are you jealous?"

I sputtered angrily for a moment. "What? Why the fuck would I be jealous?"

"Seems like you're always watchin' me," he grinned.

"Because if I don't, you fuckin' sneak up on me!"

"Uh-huh." He winked.

"What I'm gettin' at is, you can cut the act," I seethed. "I know you're just my brother's spy, and you're here to report everything I say and do so you can quit pretending."

"You think I'm pretending?" His eyes narrowed.

"Just spy on me from a distance and quit talking to me."

"Are you serious?" he asked with a hint of anger.

"Yes," I snapped. "Leave me alone."

"Sorry, Freckles, but I'm not gonna do that." His eyes flashed.

"You're not my brother!"

"No, and thank the fuckin' gods for that," he shot back.

That stung—stung enough that I struggled to keep my hurt from my face, which annoyed the shit out of me. I shouldn't care what Lee thought of me. He blew out a frustrated breath, seized my arm, and dragged me into a narrow alleyway between two buildings.

"What—"

He moved so fast, and suddenly, my back was against the wall, and his palms were flat against it on either side of my head, caging me in. I gasped, and his pupils expanded.

"Don't you dare do that," he said in a low, angry voice.

"Do *what?*" I snarled, my heart pounding.

"Take that to mean I don't care about you!"

I hated that he saw that emotion on my face, so I went on the offensive. "Don't act like you know me."

"I know you," he growled.

I scoffed.

"I've spent the last ten years hearin' all about you. I know you."

"No, you fuckin' don't 'cause *that* girl in all of Wolf's stories? She's fuckin' dead."

He stared into my eyes as I tried to shove all the emotion welling up back down.

"Then who are you?"

The bitter words escaped my lips. "I'm just Juck's whore."

His eyes flashed so angrily I couldn't help flinching when he moved. He froze and then continued moving his hand to grip my chin gently.

"I never want to hear you call yourself that again," his voice was dangerous. "Do you hear me, Ember?"

"Did you tell my brother that?" I couldn't resist snapping.

"Yes," he replied immediately. "I told him if I ever heard him say it again, I would kick his ass."

I tried to swallow past the lump of emotion in my throat. I hadn't expected that.

"You were a *victim.* A fuckin' *child.*"

I tried to turn my head, unable to hold his heated gaze, but his fingers tightened on my chin.

"You are not the things that were done to you, Ember."

KL SPEER

His voice was unbearably gentle. I jerked my chin away, and this time he let go.

"Well, I don't need you hoverin' over my shoulder all the godsdamn time. Go do somethin' else."

The muscles in his jaw flexed while he stared at me. "I can't."

"I don't care what Wolf ordered you—"

"It's not just for Wolf. It's for *you*." I scoffed, but he cut me off by leaning in even closer. "When you were burning up with a fever in that cave, you sobbed in my arms and begged me not to leave you alone because you were always alone, and you hated it."

I stared up at him, eyes widening.

"And I'm glad I'm not your brother," he added even lower, "'cause I think about kissin' that smartass mouth of yours far too often."

My eyes flicked to his mouth before I could help myself, my stomach swooping with something I tried to convince myself was horror. His lips curled into a smug smile, and my eyes shot back to his.

"I don't hate bein' alone," I blurted out the lie nervously.

"No offense, Freckles, but I'm more inclined to believe you when you're delirious."

"I don't," I tried to insist.

"There's nothin' wrong with not wanting to be alone," he murmured, his eyes searching mine. "From what I know, you've been alone for a real long time."

My stupid eyes were filling with stupid tears. "I'm not—"

"Available?" he finished with a smirk. "For anything?"

"I'm b-broken," I whispered, my voice shaking. "I can't... I'm not... I tried to tell him—Trey. I *knew* he'd end up d-dead 'cause every... everyone—"

I pressed my lips together, trying to get control over myself.

"Freckles," he murmured, shifting to lean on one hand so he could brush my wild hair out of my face with the other. "You don't have to do that. You're not gonna scare me off if you cry."

"Madame shot him right in front of me," the words tumbled out of my mouth. "She put a gun to his head and told me it was my fault and p-pulled the trigger."

He stayed still, watching me with those dark eyes, waiting.

"I tried to heal him, but I c-couldn't. It was t-too late, and he... he was gone, and I can't... I don't—" I dissolved into sobs, and Lee pushed off the wall to pull me into his arms.

"I'm sorry," he said.

I wrapped my arms around his waist and tried to muffle my sobs against his chest. He rested his chin on top of my head and held me. I lost track of time as we stood there, but eventually, we started hearing people leaving the canteen and heading to work or home. I lifted my head, alarmed, but he just shuffled us farther into the little alley, turning so his body hid me from view. If anyone looked between the buildings, he would look like a dark shadow leaning against the wall.

"We can—" I started to whisper, frantically swiping at my eyes, but he slid a hand against my wet cheek and into my hair, tilting my head up to look at him. His dark eyes glittered in the dim light.

"No. You don't have to pull yourself together. If anybody comes down here, I'll tell 'em to get lost." My lips parted slightly in surprise, and I saw his teeth flash as he smiled. "I told you you're not alone," he reminded me. "Not anymore."

I stared up at him, desperate to ask but terrified to know his answer. "Do you believe me?" I finally got the words out. "About Dune?"

He smiled a soft, sad smile, "Freckles, I always knew you were innocent."

My eyes overflowed, and he pulled me close again. A tiny glimmer of light that felt dangerously like hope flickered. If Lee never believed I was a murderer, maybe I had a chance. Maybe I could find some way to convince my brother I wasn't a bad person.

I just had to convince myself first.

CHAPTER 22

E ventually, I seemed to cry myself out, but I still didn't move for a while. Lee's arms were warm around me, and when did I start craving touch like this?

You sobbed in my arms and begged me not to leave you alone.

I had no memory of that, and I hated not knowing what else I'd said while I was feverish. The embarrassment lingered, but at the same time, I couldn't help looking at Lee in a different light. I didn't know what to do with any of these revelations.

I pulled away, fishing one of Sam's handkerchiefs out of my pocket and trying to dry my wet face. Lee stayed leaning against the wall, waiting. He didn't say anything, but he also didn't seem impatient at all.

"Be honest," I finally said, looking up at him. "Do I look like I've been crying?"

He studied my face. "Your eyes are kinda red and puffy, and you look sad."

I grimaced.

"Still beautiful, though," he added with a crooked smile.

I glared at him. "Quit."

"Not my fault you're so damn cute when you blush."

"Lee," I snapped, my face growing hot, but he just grinned at me, completely unrepentant.

"Bones?"

I peered around Lee to see Apple standing a few feet away, her eyes huge and worried.

"Hi, Apple," I said, hoping I sounded close to normal. "Are you okay?"

She looked between me and Lee and didn't answer.

I moved around Lee and approached her, concerned. When I knelt before her, she wrapped her arms around my neck again.

"Are you—" I started

"Are *you* okay?" she interrupted in a fierce whisper that Lee definitely could still hear. "Did he hurt you?"

"No," I quickly assured her, pulling back to see her face.

Apple scrunched her nose in a fierce scowl aimed over my shoulder, and I fought the urge to smile.

"I was... feelin' sad, and Lee was talkin' to me. I'm okay, Apple."

She looked back at my face, studying my expression solemnly. "Sad about Trey?"

I had to swallow hard before choking out, "Yeah."

The well of pain and grief in her blue eyes was far too deep to exist in a child, and I felt a stab of guilt that I hadn't checked on how the kids were handling Trey's death.

"I miss him." I forced myself to not hide the tears in my eyes. "All the time."

"I miss him, too," she whispered, then her little face crumpled.

I gathered her up in my arms and stood, holding her tightly as she sobbed into my shoulder. Lee moved silently to my side and put an arm around my waist, helping support me. It made me feel even shakier, tears sliding down my face. How many tears did I have to cry before they finally dried up?

After a while, Apple raised her head and noticed Lee, her body tensing.

"Hi," Lee said, his voice gentle and playful. "I'm Lee, and you must be the Queen of the Vault."

"I'm not the queen," she said, her little voice hoarse.

Lee clutched his chest and gasped. "You're not?"

She giggled a little, resting her cheek on my shoulder, one hand absentmindedly playing with my hair as Lee reenacted pulling out a pretend map and asking Apple silly questions about castles and dragons until she was giggling too hard to speak.

"You want to come to the clinic with me?" I asked Apple as Lee folded up his invisible map.

"Yes," she chirped. "Wolverine has your broth."

A startled laugh escaped me. "You mean Wolf?"

She grinned. "That's what I said!"

Lee grinned wickedly. "Well, we don't want to keep Wolverine waiting."

When we arrived, Wolverine, Kai, and Sable were installing my new window. Sam and Scar stood off to the side talking, and Sam's entire face was lit up in a way I hadn't seen for a long time. I brought Apple inside the clinic and then stopped in my tracks. The new window faced south, and the sun was *beaming* inside. I didn't think one window would make that much difference, but the clinic felt warmer and homier.

"Wow," Apple breathed.

I stepped into the middle of the light pouring through the window. The sun warmed my face, and tears filled my eyes again. I'd never see Trey's sunshine smile warm the clinic again, but I would think of him every time the rays shone inside like this.

Apple suddenly wrapped her arms tighter around my neck and pressed a sloppy kiss to my cheek. I turned to look at her, startled.

"What was that for?" I asked, trying to muster a smile.

She gazed back, solemn again. "Cause I love you, and you looked sad."

My chest ached but with a surprising softness alongside the sharp pain. I set her on the counter to give my arms a break but stayed right there.

"I should've told you this months ago, but I'm so sorry I didn't stop Zip from hittin' you." The words tumbled from my mouth, and her eyes widened. "I should've protected you from him better, and I never should've yelled at you like that. I didn't mean any of it. I was just... just so scared he was gonna hurt you even worse." My voice wobbled. "I knew Zip wasn't a good person, and I never should've stayed with him. But that's on me. You're not responsible for me, okay? I'd never forgive myself if somethin' happened to you 'cause I... I love you, too."

She watched me with those huge, serious eyes, but when I reached the last part, her entire face lit up, and she threw her arms around me again.

"I forgive you," she said, so sweet and innocent, which only made me cry harder.

After a few seconds, I forcefully choked my tears back as she released me and took a shaky breath. I needed a mindless distraction. I ran my hand over the counter and frowned at the layer of sawdust from the window installation coating my palm.

"I'll get the broom!" Apple said with a grin.

❦

As the day progressed, I became more nervous about seeing Lana again. Wolf and his pack prowled restlessly around the clinic, muttering to each other. Apple stayed for most of the day, chattering at me or Sam. It was late afternoon when we finally heard the rovers approaching.

"You ready?" Sam asked in a low voice.

I nodded, chewing on my cheek, and we walked toward the main gate. Unsurprisingly, Wolf and his entire crew followed along. When we neared, a single rover was just pulling in. Mac was driving, and his eyes immediately found me. He parked but didn't get out. Nemo approached and spoke to him. Sam and I started moving closer, and fear gripped my lungs. Where were the others?

Nemo met my eyes and beckoned to me. I picked up my pace.

"Lana and the others are outside the hold. They didn't want to bring her in here while she was still ill just in case she's contagious," Nemo said, and the relief made me shaky. "Mac can bring you to her to heal, and then you can all come back in."

I nodded, already climbing into the rover, but as I sat, I glimpsed Wolf and Lee striding forward, their faces dark.

"Sam, can you—"

He glanced behind him and made a face. "Yeah, I got it."

He intercepted my brother and Lee. Thankfully, they stopped, but both of them glared at me.

"Ready?" Mac asked, and I nodded.

The rover peeled out again, swinging in a loop and heading for the open gate. Riding in the front felt strange, but I was grateful I didn't have to sit in the back and think about Trey.

Once we hit the trees, Mac suddenly pulled over and stopped. I looked for the other rover, but it was just us. I turned to Mac, confused, but he was getting out of the rover.

"Mac, what—"

He came around to my side and opened my door. "I just...I gotta talk to you," he said, his voice tight.

I fumbled to unbuckle and climbed out, my heart rate picking up again. He paced away and then back to stand in front of me, running his hand through his messy hair. For several seconds, we just stared at each other.

"Em, I'm so sorry," he said, his voice low and hoarse and full of pain.

My mind began to run through horrible possible scenarios. Raven was hurt. Griz was dead. What else—

"You're not a pawn or a prize or a *thing*," he continued fiercely, and my stomach lurched as I realized he was talking about the fight we'd had before he left. "I should've told you right away that I knew about the other powered person. I didn't think about how it might look to you—like we were tryin' to trick you—and I'm so fuckin' sorry."

I could *feel* the warmth curling in my chest. "Mac—"

"Sam radioed and told me what you'd said to him, and I wanted to come right home to make sure you knew I'd never let anyone use you like that. I know I fucked up by draggin' you here, and I'm so sorry, but I swear, Em, I will *never* let *anyone*—"

I interrupted him by stepping forward and catching his hands. He gripped mine back tightly. His emotion felt like a tangible thing that swirled around us, and it was so apparent he'd been working himself up about this the entire time he'd been gone. For the first time, I felt I was comforting him instead of the other way around.

"It's okay. It's okay, Mac," I said softly. "I'm sorry I freaked out —"

"Don't apologize, please." His voice in my head was rough.

"No, I shouldn't have assumed the worst about you like that. You've done nothin' to make me think that about you."

His eyes narrowed into a glare. *"That's not true."*

"Mac," I glared back, exasperated. *"You've apologized enough."*

"I don't think I'll ever be able to apologize enough," he said, and the raw honesty in his voice made my eyes well up.

"I forgive you for all of it," I held his gaze, hoping he saw and felt my sincerity. *"I don't hate you, remember?"* I tried to smile.

He let out a heavy sigh, squeezing my hands. *"I thought I'd fucked everything up,"* he admitted.

"That was on me, not you," I found myself saying, the urge to explain surprising me. *"Once I stopped and thought about it, I realized how stupid it was. I just got scared and panicked...and I hate feeling scared, so that made me mad. I promise I know you'd never do that."*

We both fell silent, studying each other. Mac's eyes were less guarded than I'd ever seen as if he was deliberately opening himself up and allowing me to *see* him. It was an openness that reminded me of Trey, and I hesitated as the pain swelled. He didn't move, didn't draw back. He just waited as I tried to breathe through the grief and find the strength to look.

Bones, let 'em in.

Why was all of this so *hard?*

I gathered my courage and peered into Mac's eyes, but it wasn't like gazing into Trey's eyes. As soon as I looked, I *felt* the connection between our powers, as if we were woven together. His emotions washed over me, and I could *feel* his regret, concern, and pain. I took a breath to say something, but then another emotion *jolted* between us like electricity, the strength of it so familiar and *terrifying*—

I jerked away like I'd touched a hot iron, and he immediately released me.

"I'm sorry," I said, my heart in my throat, unsure what I was apologizing for.

His face had gone carefully blank. "It's okay."

I stared at him, trying to figure out what the fuck just happened.

"Sorry, I lost my shit there," Mac said like he was forcibly lightening his voice.

"You've seen me lose my shit enough times," I managed to say. "I owed you at least one."

He let out a startled but genuine chuckle, and some of the weird tension seemed to melt away.

"So, Lana?" I asked, desperate to keep the weirdness from returning.

He sobered immediately. "Are you sure you want to do this? I don't want you to feel like you have to heal her."

"I know. I *want* to."

He looked away and let out a heavy breath. I waited, but he said nothing, and I started getting nervous.

"Are you mad at me for doing this?" I asked tentatively.

His head snapped back up. "No, I'm not mad." He smiled, but there was something sad about it. "Just..." He dropped his eyes and scrubbed a hand through his hair again. *"None of us deserve you."*

My brow furrowed. "What does that mean?"

Instead of answering, he returned to the rover and opened my door. I followed, climbing back in and looking at him expectantly.

He shut the door and leaned on it, finally meeting my eyes again. "It means you're a damn good person, Em."

I frowned, but he walked around the front of the rover and climbed into the driver's seat. He didn't look at me as he started the rover and began to drive again.

"Mac, what's wrong?" I finally asked.

He glanced at me briefly. *"Just been a rough couple days."*

I felt a stab of guilt for taking off on him and then hiding so he couldn't talk to me again before he left. I hadn't set out to purposefully hurt him by doing it, but I had.

"So that's where you were," he said, his voice a little lighter, *"Apple trees by the wall. Adding it to the list."*

"The list?"

He glanced at me again, and he was almost smiling this time. *"I'm gonna figure out all your hidey-holes, and you better believe I'll come find you when you try to disappear."*

I remembered how he promised to always come for me, and that soft emotion swelled again.

"You can try," I said loftily, hoping it would make him smile.

I was rewarded with a grin, not a full one that showed his dimples, but a genuine smile. *"Is that a challenge, Ember?"*

A shiver ran down my spine at his use of my full name, confusing me. I didn't usually like being called "Ember," probably because Wolf only used it when he was pissed at me.

"I'm just sayin', I'm good at hiding."

"I know. It drives me crazy."

I laughed, and finally, those dimples peeked out as he smiled wide.

"Things go okay while we were gone?" he asked after a moment.

I had to stop and think back to when he left, trying to remember everything that had happened, and grimaced. My fight with Sam, that dream about Trey, Nemo, nightmares—

"So, no," Mac interrupted, a worried crease forming between his brows, and I realized he'd been listening to my list. *"This gonna be a longer conversation? Cause we're almost there."*

"Yeah," I carefully tried to keep Clarity from my head. I didn't want to open that can of worms right now. *"We can talk about it later."*

"I should warn you, Lana is... not happy about this."

My anxiety surged at the serious look in his eyes. *"Is she... aware of what's happening?"*

"Enough to know you're involved."

I winced.

"She's..." he trailed off, his mouth pressing into a hard line. *"I just want to remind you that you don't have to do this."*

"What symptoms does she have?" I needed to think like a healer. It was easier to ignore my own emotions that way.

"Started with a fever and vomiting, I guess. Now she's real weak, can't keep anything down, and the fever comes and goes." He paused. *"It reminds me of the sickness, which is why I didn't want to bring her into the hold like this."*

"Is anyone else feelin' sick?" I asked, dread creeping over me as I remembered how quickly the sickness had swept through the hold.

"No, and we've been tryin' to be careful, but you should probably check everybody before we go back." He gestured up ahead, and I saw part of the other rover between the trees. *"You ready?"*

I nodded. The worry lines on his face deepened, but he didn't say anything. We pulled up beside the second rover to see Raven and Griz sitting in the front. Griz's face broke into a smile, his white teeth flashing against his dark brown skin as he ran a hand over his close-cropped black hair. Raven didn't smile, but the tension in her face eased. She flicked her long black hair behind her shoulder. The bare side of her head looked freshly shaved.

"Hey, Em," Griz called.

"Took your sweet time, Mac," Raven grumbled, but her eyes scanned me carefully like she needed to ensure I was alright.

I hopped out, and Griz enveloped me in a warm hug. "I'm sorry we didn't tell you about the radio."

"It's okay," I assured him.

"You sure about healing Lana?" he added quietly in my ear.

Did *anyone* think this was a good idea besides me? "Yeah," I said, hoping I sounded like I believed it.

Raven had also climbed out of the rover, but she crossed her arms and glared at me. "You've made a lot of stupid decisions, Boney, but this one might take the cake."

Guess that answered that question.

"Good to see you, too, Raven. I'm great, thanks for askin'," I surprised myself by saying.

Her eyebrows rose, but her mouth twitched.

"Well, you ready?" Griz asked.

I nodded and followed him to the backseat of the second rover. They had converted the seat into a makeshift bed, and Lana lay in a pathetic ball on a pile of blankets.

She was asleep, but her face was sunken and pale and shiny with sweat. Her lips moved, muttering something too faint to make out. She hadn't been as muscular as Raven before, but she'd looked strong and healthy. Now, I could see her bones protruding, and my stomach dropped. Part of me had wondered if she was faking, but there was no faking this level of illness.

I took a deep breath and climbed into the backseat, kneeling beside her and gently peeling the blanket back. She shivered violently, and I maneuvered her arm out and covered her back up, trying to focus. I wrapped my hands around her arm and let my healing power flow.

I immediately knew it was the same thing as the sickness from before. My powers collided with the darkness oozing through Lana's body, and it immediately fought back. I gritted my teeth. It was strong, and I couldn't tell if it was worse than all the previous versions or if I'd forgotten how it felt. If this damn sickness was going to keep coming back, it needed a name. My mind idly ran through possibilities, trying to distract myself from thinking about who I was healing and the strain on my powers.

"I like that one," Mac suddenly said.

I blinked and looked up at him. He was standing outside the rover with Raven and Griz, watching.

"Which one?"

"Shadowbane Fever."

I managed a half smile. *"Alright."*

"Is this how it always feels?" he asked, his brows drawing closer together.

"What?" Why was I getting tired so quickly?

"Healing this. Does it always feel like this for you?"

"Some are worse than others, but yeah." His arms crossed, lips pressing tightly together. *"What's wrong?"*

"You did this for months." He sounded angry. *"You did this over three hundred times."*

"I *know*, but why are you mad about it?" I snapped.

"What?" Griz asked, and I realized with a sinking feeling I'd responded out loud.

My eyes darted between the three of them. Raven and Griz stared at me with furrowed brows, and Mac had gone perfectly still.

"What do you want to tell them?" Mac asked.

I sucked in a breath and let it out. "Just tell them."

"Tell us what?" Raven snapped.

"Who are you talkin' to?" Griz asked.

"She's talkin' to me," Mac answered.

Raven and Griz both turned to him, eyes narrowed. Mac shifted on his feet, his hands curling into fists and then releasing again.

"I can... hear and communicate with some people's thoughts." When Raven and Griz just stared, he added, "It just started recently."

"I asked him not to tell you," I inserted before I lost my nerve.

"Why?" Raven demanded.

Griz glanced between me and Mac, silently studying us.

"Because I was scared," I admitted. "I know what some p-people can do... when they find someone with powers."

They all went quiet, and when I glanced back at them, they appeared to be having a silent conversation. I could guess what it was about.

"I know about Clarity," I said.

All three looked sharply at me with various degrees of surprise and alarm. Raven immediately turned to Mac, radiating anger.

"I fucking told you," she hissed at him.

"Raven, hold on," Mac ordered, returning to me. "What happened?"

I explained what happened that morning and how I'd healed Clarity. Raven asked a lot of questions, and I didn't know how to answer most of them. The fear in Raven's eyes made me feel oddly protective. Mac tried to apologize again, but I cut him off, letting them know I *did* understand why they wanted Clarity to feel in charge of her own life.

"Just don't hide sick people, please? I can't..." my voice wobbled, "I can't heal 'em if they're dead."

"I'm sorry, Em," Griz murmured.

"I never wanted any of this to be a secret," Raven fumed.

"That's true," Mac said, sounding tired. "Raven was against all of this from the beginning."

"Guess I'm not done apologizin' yet, am I?" he added in my head.

"I'm not that mad...anymore."

He sighed, rubbing his forehead.

"So that's what's been goin' on between you two?" Griz asked. "You've been having mental conversations?"

I nodded, but Mac gave Griz a look I didn't understand.

"Who can—"

Lana suddenly surged upright, her wide eyes full of a familiar ice-cold fury focused solely on me.

"You!" she shrieked, then launched at my face.

CHAPTER 23

I released Lana's arm, trying to bring my hands up to shield myself, but she hit me with so much force that both of us toppled out of the rover on the opposite side from where the others stood. I hit the ground hard with Lana on top of me. My scarred back spasmed in pain, and all the air whooshed out of my lungs. I was so distracted by not being able to breathe that Lana was able to rake her fingernails down my face.

She was screaming, but if she was screaming words, I couldn't understand them. I finally gasped in a breath and got my arms up over my face as she clawed and scratched my flesh like a feral cat. Then, just as suddenly, she was gone, ripped off me by Mac, who pinned her to the ground with Raven's help. Griz dropped to my side, swearing furiously.

"Fuck, Em! Okay, hold on. Let me get the kit." He jumped to his feet again, darting to the rover.

I sat up, my back shrieking in pain, and gingerly touched my face with shaking fingers. It felt like she'd left long scratches on my forehead and cheek. My fingers came away bloody, but the cuts felt shallow.

"Em!" I realized Mac was *shouting* at me in my head. *"You okay?"*

"I'm okay," I assured him. *"It's just a scratch."*

Griz appeared at my side again, a first aid kit in hand. "What the *fuck,* Lana?" he thundered, but his hands were gentle as he pressed a clean rag against the bleeding wounds on my face. His eyes, dark with anger, met mine. "Did you hit your head?"

I shook my head, listening to Raven yell at Lana. "They feel pretty shallow," I reassured him.

He carefully cleaned the scratches on my face, my eyes smarting at the sting. Lana finally stopped shrieking in the background, and I could hear Mac talking in a low, angry voice. Griz's lips were pressed in a thin, flat line, and maybe I imagined it, but he seemed to avoid my gaze.

"How do I look?" I asked, hoping to lighten the mood.

He studied the jagged scratches on my cheek and sighed. "Like you got in a fight with a cat."

I gave him an exaggerated frown. "A *cat*? C'mon, couldn't it be a cougar?"

His eyebrows raised slightly as he finally met my eyes. "You wouldn't have much of a face left if you got in a fight with a cougar."

"Wow," I drew the word out. I tried to raise an eyebrow, but that hurt. "Okay, fine. Can we at least say it was a bobcat?"

He stared at me, his eyes narrowing. "Are you *joking* right now?"

I smirked at him.

"Mac, I think Em must've hit her head," Griz yelled over his shoulder.

Mac was at his side in seconds, his face worried. "She hit her head?"

"She must've 'cause she's makin' fuckin' *jokes*."

Mac's brow furrowed, but his eyes lightened. "You're right, must be pretty serious," he drawled.

"Probably on death's door," Griz agreed, his lips twitching.

"Oh, for fuck's sake," I rolled my eyes, but a grin crept across my face.

"You okay to stand?" Mac asked, holding out his hands.

I nodded and took them, trying not to wince as the scars on my back screamed at the movement. Mac moved to take my elbow, frowning, but my eyes immediately went to Lana.

She was sitting on the ground with her hands bound behind her back and dirt smeared across her face. Her eyes were flashing with anger and focused on me. Raven was standing between Lana and me, her stance defensive, like she was *protecting* me.

I stepped toward them, but Mac's hand tightened on my elbow. "What're you doin'?" he asked.

"I wasn't done healin' her."

"Well, you're done now," he scowled.

My eyes narrowed, and I tried to keep my voice even. "Mac, I'm not gonna let her go off and infect people."

"I don't care."

"No." My voice came out harsh and shaky. "You don't get to tell me who I do and don't heal."

Guilt flashed through his eyes, and a muscle flexed in his jaw as we stared at each other, but after a few seconds, he relented, "Fine, but Griz and I are holdin' her down this time."

I nodded, and Griz got up to put the first aid kit back in the rover. When they approached Lana, she started snarling at them, but they ignored her, each of them taking an arm and holding her as she thrashed. I took a deep breath as she started screaming, reminding myself that they weren't hurting her. Still, when I sank to my knees beside her, my hands shook as they wrapped around her arm.

"You fuckin' bitch," she hissed as my healing powers flowed into her. "Don't touch me. Don't touch me! I don't want Juck's whore —"

I winced, but at the same time, Mac growled, "Lana! Call her that again, and I'm leavin' you in these woods when she's done."

Lana went silent, but then she started to cry, which was worse. "I'm sorry! I'm sorry! I just... you picked *her*. You fuckin' *left me*... how could you—"

She broke off, sobs shaking her shoulders. I saw Mac lean forward and murmur something into her ear, and a sudden flash of anger went through me. Lana's eyes snapped to my face, her red-rimmed eyes full of hate. I looked away, focusing on smothering the remaining bits of Shadowbane. After it disintegrated under my healing powers, I released her and got to my feet. Mac and Griz released Lana, and I beckoned Mac to follow me with my head as I moved back toward the rover.

"Can I check and make sure you're not sick?" I asked as he approached.

He nodded, and I took the hand he extended. His hands were so large, dwarfing mine, and the comfort I immediately felt made me feel unsteady. I stared at our joined hands, suddenly overwhelmed with how much I'd misjudged Mac from the very beginning. My healing powers touched his skin briefly and then vanished, and I had no idea how or why, but I knew he wasn't infected.

"You're not sick," I said, willing my voice to be steady. "I should check—"

His free hand touched under my chin, nudging my head up to meet his eyes. He was frowning, his brows drawn together.

"What's wrong?" he asked.

"I'm so sorry I was so awful to you," I blurted out, miserable.

His brow furrowed even more. "What?"

"When we first met," I whispered. He was still holding my hand, and his knuckles rested gently under my chin.

His eyebrows raised, and amusement warmed his voice as he said out loud, "When we first met, I kidnapped you. I think you had every right to hate me."

"I'm glad you kidnapped me," I confessed.

One side of his mouth tipped up. *"I won't lie, I am, too."*

"You make me feel safe." I had no idea why the words kept pouring out of me, but I couldn't find it in myself to regret it when his eyes softened, and his fingers tightened on my hand.

"You'll always be safe with me, Em," he murmured.

I stepped into him, pulling my hand free so I could wrap my arms around his waist. I felt his surprise, but it quickly faded to something warm as he hugged me back. I'd never initiated hugging him, but all this emotion was drowning me, and it wasn't the emotion from the past few months. It was something softer and warmer, and I needed a rock to cling to.

That's what Mac was—my rock.

Why did it feel like I was going to cry?

"You sure you're okay?" he sounded worried.

I squeezed him tightly for two more seconds and then forced myself to release him and take a step back. *"I'm okay. What happens now?"*

"Now we go back to the Vault. Lana's probably gonna be under house arrest for a bit while we figure out what to do with her."

"House arrest where?"

"Not sure."

"But not the cells?"

"No." His eyes softened. *"Not the cells."*

I let out a shaky breath, relief coursing through me.

"Can I look at those scratches?" he asked out loud.

"Uh, sure."

He stepped close again, taking my face in his hands and turning my cheek toward the sunlight peeking in through the thick canopy of evergreen trees. His touch was gentle but confident. His brow furrowed as he peered at the scratches, anger tightening in his jaw.

"Maybe we'll match," I said.

He met my eyes, "What?"

"Matching scars," I clarified, gesturing to my face.

"I hope not for your sake," he said lightly, but there was a pain there I didn't miss.

"I like your scar," I blurted out.

His eyebrows raised, but he didn't look convinced. Why was I saying all this shit? My face was getting hot, but I wasn't about to back down now.

"I do! It looks good on you."

His lips twitched. "Did you just compliment me?"

I tried to smirk, but it felt more like a genuine smile. "Don't get used to it."

He gently turned my head like he was trying to look at the back of it. "Gods, you sure you didn't hit your head?"

I huffed a laugh, and he was grinning when he turned my head back.

"I don't think these will scar," he said, his eyes returning to the scratches on my face, "but they're gonna look dramatic until they heal." He slowly released my face like he was hesitant to do so. "Alright, you wanna check the others?"

Raven and Griz were clear, too, so we loaded up and headed back to the Vault. Raven and Griz drove with Lana, and Mac drove with me. I realized for the first time Mac's rover was full of building materials. Those must have been the supplies they originally set out to get.

"Well, guess I better fill Sam, Jax, and Clarity in when we get back," Mac said. *"So what happened while we were gone? I know about Sam, but what happened with Nemo?"*

I told him about Nemo collapsing and our conversations. That led to what happened with Clarity, which led to my conversation with Wolf about Dune. He made me repeat the words Clarity had said several times, frowning. By that time, we were pulling up to the gate, which was slowly opening for us. Mac pulled in and parked, and I glanced up and immediately caught my brother's eye. His expression quickly moved from surprised to furious, and he started storming toward the rover.

"Here we go," I muttered, unbuckling.

"What the *fuck* happened?" Wolf snarled as he reached the rover,

"I'm fine," I said firmly.

"You're fine? You have claw marks down your face!"

I expected him to yank me out of the rover, but he simply steadied me as I hopped down. He continued ranting and insisting Sable examine me, and eventually, I caved and agreed, hoping it'd make him shut up.

I glanced up at Mac as we headed back to the clinic. "See you later?"

"I'll come by after I get things sorted with Lana and Nemo," he promised.

"Good," I replied mentally, and he smiled.

Sam was at the other rover talking to Raven and Griz, but his worried eyes followed me. I gave him a little wave, trying to convey I was okay. I let Wolf lead me away, and Lee and Scar joined us, demanding to know what happened. So I explained it *again*.

Wolf muttered something I didn't catch. He was still holding my arm but was more supportive than forceful. My back ached in a way that made me feel slightly nauseous. When we arrived at the clinic, Sable, Tuck, and Kai sat on the porch. They stood as we neared, their eyes narrowing on my face.

"I'm fine," I repeated for the third time, annoyed.

"Sable, can you—" Wolf started.

"Of course," Sable interrupted him.

All of them followed us into the clinic. I tried to insist on standing but was bullied into sitting in the damn exam chair. Sable scrutinized the scratches, even pulling out a special pair of glasses that magnified his eyes and made him look like a giant owl so he could check to ensure no dirt or foreign substances were lodged in the cuts. He *was* a good healer, thorough and gentle, which made me even more uneasy around him. Why the fuck was that?

"Does anything else hurt?" he asked after picking a few things out of the cuts with tweezers.

My back twinged, but I ignored it. "Nope."

He started cleaning up the supplies he'd used, and I slid out of the chair, realizing I was alone with Wolf and his entire crew for the first time since the cabin. The urge to flee to the loft swelled, but I was tired of hiding upstairs in my own clinic. All of them were looking at me, though, and I desperately needed something to do, so I turned and went back to my old failsafe, re-organizing the damn tincture bottles.

After a while, they stopped standing there staring at me. Kai moved to help Sable clean up. Wolf sat in a chair and started taking apart his gun. Tuck and Scar went back outside, and Lee appeared at my side.

"You want help?" he asked, grinning.

"No," I muttered.

"How are you plannin' on reaching the ones on the top shelf?" He leaned on the hutch, crossing his arms.

"I stand on a chair."

"Or you could take advantage of havin' someone with longer arms," he countered, reaching up to pluck a bottle off the top shelf and waving it at me.

Gods, this was way too familiar.

"Fine," I said, the word coming out shorter than I meant.

He raised his eyebrows but didn't comment as he pulled the bottles off the top shelf for me. He even got a rag and dusted it, and I tried not to think about the last time I organized the hutch while my body hurt and Trey tried to get me to sit after Pike and Dale—

I shoved that memory away where it could fester somewhere quietly.

"What sort of sickness did Lana have?" Sable asked after he finished cleaning up.

I glanced over at him to see him leaning against the counter. Kai stood beside him, his arm wrapped around Sable's waist as he gently kissed his temple. I quickly looked away, my heart aching.

"The same one that hit the hold last fall."

"Fever?" Sable asked.

"Yeah."

"You have a problem with us, Ember?"

Kai's sharp voice startled me, and I turned around to see him staring at me with a fierce expression.

"What?"

"Kai," Sable murmured, but Kai ignored him.

"Do you have a problem with me and Sable bein' together?" he asked.

I glanced at Wolf, bewildered, but Wolf was also looking at me sharply.

"No?" I got out, confused.

"Why do you keep avoidin' us, then?" Kai pushed. "Lookin' away like you can't stand to see us?"

Oh.

"I know what sorta bullshit Carth shoved down your throats," Kai continued. "About what kinda people can be together—"

"No," I interrupted him, guilt and pain twisting together in my chest. "No, I don't believe in that shit."

All of them silently stared at me, waiting.

"It's just... hard... hard to..." I swallowed and turned back around to the hutch. Maybe if I didn't look at them, it'd be easier. "Seeing the two of you makes me miss my... my..." I fiddled nervously with the label on a bottle, my eyes welling up. "My person."

I sensed the energy in the room change, but I didn't turn back around.

"I'm sorry."

Kai's low apology startled me enough to glance back. I'd half expected him to make a joke or be an ass, but his expression was solemn.

"I shouldn't have assumed," he added, scrubbing a hand over his face.

"I don't think Ember ever did anything the way Carth wanted her to." Wolf's voice was quiet but heavy.

I met his gaze, and the emotion there made my stomach flip nervously. I wasn't entirely sure *what* emotion I was looking at on his face, but he paused, and all of me went still and quiet, waiting to see what he was debating telling me.

"Just a few days before... Dune," he faltered slightly, "one of the Arbiters came by and told me if I didn't make you fall in line, they would do it for me."

Do it for him? "What does that mean?" I whispered.

"Probably some sort of public humiliation. Maybe a caning. If that didn't work, they would have taken you away from me so they could fully break you."

His tone was so steady—like he was talking about the weather. I stood frozen in place, staring at him as my mind raced. The Ministry had always scared me, especially the enforcers in their black robes and faceless masks, and I'd tried to avoid them as much as possible. I didn't remember a kid ever getting in trouble like that before. I had vague memories of adults chained on their knees to a platform, a scroll or something around their neck for everyone to read their transgressions. Wolf never let me go near them, and I'd never seen a caning. I'd never heard of a kid being taken away, either. Where would they be taken?

"They took kids?" I heard myself say.

"Yes," Wolf said, holding my gaze with unwavering focus. "If the parents were unfit or noncompliant, they took them, and then they sterilized both parents so they couldn't have more children."

The edge of the bottle I held was digging into my palm, but I couldn't move. *Sterilized?* His entire pack was quiet and watching, but none of them looked surprised, so they'd obviously heard this before.

"They made a special exception for me," Wolf continued, his voice flat. "The Ministry, in their infinite wisdom, deemed me unfit to ever have offspring and sterilized me before they sent me out lookin' for you."

I scanned everyone's faces, trying to figure out if this was some sort of trick or manipulation to get me to do something. But they just stared back at me, their faces grave.

"Why?" I got out. "Why you? What about Pa?"

"When I begged Pa not to give you to the Lopez family, Pa made it clear you were my responsibility in every way, Ember."

I couldn't breathe. Wolf had been *eight* when he became my caregiver, then eighteen—*eighteen years old*—when they took his choice to ever have children.

"Lopez?" I repeated numbly. I remembered a row of little girls, their hair in neat braids, frowning at me when I raced past them with Dune.

"Mrs. Lopez had a stillborn a few months earlier. She wanted to take you, but I…" he roughly cleared his throat. "I didn't want to lose you."

My hands were shaking. "Why are you tellin' me this?"

He took a slow, deep breath and then said the last thing I was expecting. "I don't know." He paused. "Because it's the truth? Because when I said you had to talk to me, I didn't mean you had to do all the talking? Because I wanted you to know? Because you said you don't trust me, and I'm tryin' to be honest?"

"Because you're tryin' to trick me into something again?" I couldn't help adding.

He winced. "No. I'm not tryin' to trick you again."

"Told you that would bite you in the ass," Sable muttered. He smiled at Wolf when Wolf glanced at him, but Wolf didn't return it.

"Yeah, well, you're usually right," Wolf said, and the pain in his voice startled me.

I didn't understand the tension that filled the room. Sable and Wolf held each other's gazes and watching them made me feel like I was intruding on something private.

"Wolf," Sable finally murmured. "We're movin' forward, remember?"

"I know," Wolf replied. "I'll just always wish I would've listened to you a lot sooner."

I glanced around at the others. Kai was looking at the floor, his jaw tight. Tuck and Scar leaned against the wall, quietly watching Wolf. Lee was looking at Wolf as well, but with an intense focus that made me look closer. His hands clenched at his sides and then released. I thought he'd been joking about flirting with Wolf, but it felt like the room was full of tangled emotion.

I turned around and went back to dusting the shelf, my mind whirling. I wanted to know more about Wolf's relationship with his crew and about Carth, but at the same time, I felt like I needed to be in a quiet, dark room to process what I'd just been told. Pa's face rose in my mind, dragging with it the pain and hurt. What was he doing right now? Did he look like an old man? Was he still on the council? How could he let Wolf go through all of that?

Wolf had to grow up even earlier than I did. My throat constricted. *Sterilized.*

Lee bumped me lightly with his hip. "Where do you want these vials?"

I directed him where to put them, and he went back to teasing me like nothing had happened. I wanted to throw something at him, but I also realized my hands had stopped trembling. It was almost more annoying that he could distract me so easily. I wondered if he told Wolf or anyone in his crew about how I broke down in tears in the alley earlier. His hand landed on the small of my back, and I met his eyes.

"You okay?" he asked, low.

Godsdamnit, he was attractive. My eyes flicked to his lips before I could help myself, and they curled into a smirk.

I think about kissin' that smartass mouth of yours far too often.

Before I could answer him, the door opened to reveal Sam. My relief quickly died at the look on his face.

"I need to talk to you," he said, his voice tight.

My stomach sank as I followed Sam outside to stand under the apple tree where we'd been just this morning, talking about Clarity and Dune. He ran a hand through his short hair and met my gaze, and the hurt and anger on his face made my breath catch.

"You were so angry at me for keepin' Clarity a secret, but you and Mac were keepin' secrets, too?"

He phrased it like a question as if hoping I would tell him he'd misunderstood.

"Yes," I whispered, feeling like absolute shit.

His jaw flexed as he stared at me.

"I'm sorry," I added. "I should've told you."

"Yes, you damn well should've. This trust thing has to go both ways. You can't demand honesty and not give it in return."

"I'm sorry," I repeated helplessly.

"I get why you were scared, but were you really scared of *me*? Did you think I would hurt Mac with that knowledge?"

"No," I mumbled. "I know you wouldn't."

"Then why didn't you tell me?"

"I don't know." The raw hurt on his face was too much, so I looked at the ground. "I just... everything is changing. I feel so out of control, and... keepin it to myself... kinda helps. I'm so... so scared of what will happen to him and Clarity if..." What had Sam called him? "...if the Mental Menace finds out. It wasn't *you*."

He sighed, then stepped forward and hugged me. I wrapped my arms around his waist and held him tightly.

"I'm so sorry, Sam," I said into his shoulder.

"It's alright," he murmured, resting his chin on my head. "I get it… it just… still hurts."

"I swear I'm trying," I said, miserably desperate for him to understand. "I swear, Sam, I'm just—"

"No, I know you are," he interrupted, his voice firm. "I know you are, Emmy."

He pulled back but took my face in his hands, tilting it up so he could examine the scratch marks Lana had given me.

"So Lana is still as delightful as ever," he said with a hint of his dry humor.

"Will you forgive me?" I blurted out.

He blinked, surprise in his eyes. "Of course I forgive you."

Relief made me feel shaky, and whatever expression was on my face softened his eyes. He leaned in and pressed a kiss to my forehead.

"You know I'll always love you," he smiled at me when he pulled back. "I don't make pinky promises with just anyone."

"I love you, too," the hoarse words tumbled out of my mouth.

Emotion filled his face, and I remembered how he'd teased me in the horse pasture. *You'll admit that you love me one of these days.* I tried to brace myself for a big reaction, but thankfully, he just gave me a crooked grin and slung an arm around my shoulders.

"Of course you do," Sam said, and the words were flippant, but his eyes stayed soft. "I'm lovable as fuck."

CHAPTER 24

S am returned to the clinic with me, and I loved him even more for keeping up a steady stream of small talk with Wolf and his crew. I didn't see Mac before the dinner bell rang, but Griz and Jax joined us as we walked to the canteen with Wolf's crew. Apple came running down the path as soon as she saw us, throwing herself around my legs. She was excited to see Griz again, attacking him next and squealing as Griz tossed her into the air. Then, Apple shocked everyone by demanding a shoulder ride from Lee.

"Of course, Your Majesty," Lee immediately replied, making her giggle.

When we arrived, Nemo was making rounds in the canteen. He looked much better, walking straight and steady and greeting people with his usual energy. He smiled and waved when he saw us, and I managed a smile in response that didn't feel too forced.

Apple sat between me and Griz again, but she entertained the entire table by chattering about anything and everything. Apparently, she was no longer afraid of my brother and his crew. I took a full ration along with broth and ate most of it without feeling sick. Sam was flirting with Scar, who seemed amused. She had to be at least ten years older than him, but she wasn't shutting him down. I kept looking for Mac, but he never appeared.

"Where's Mac?" I asked Griz as we walked back to the clinic after dinner.

"Dealin' with Lana," he muttered.

I wasn't sure what that meant, but his body language seemed closed, so I didn't push. I turned to go up the path toward the clinic, but Griz, Sam, and Jax didn't follow. When I paused, turning to look back at them, they simply called a hasty goodnight and continued down the main path toward the bunkhouse. For a second, I stood there debating on tagging along behind like a lost puppy, but they were striding quickly away and speaking in low tones to each other. So, instead, I reluctantly followed Wolf and his crew into the clinic.

They were at ease in my space, but they'd been staying here for two weeks without me. They pulled out the wooden chairs and sat talking to each other. Tuck, Lee, and Scar started playing a game of cards. Lee attempted to coax me to join, but I declined, opting to do some laundry in the sink. I listened to them talk and laugh with each other as I scrubbed my clothes, and I felt *weird*.

I wished I could be at the bunkhouse. When I was with my crew, I felt like I was *with* them. They were my crew. But separated like this, the doubts crept in. I wasn't actually alone this time like I'd been after Trey's death, but somehow, I felt even lonelier surrounded by Wolf and his crew. They were tight knit, just like Mac's crew, but I had no idea where I fit into their group. Prisoner? Bounty? Murderer? Wolf's little sister? I still didn't know how to process everything Wolf had told me about Carth.

When I finished my laundry, I bundled it in my arms to take upstairs, but I paused at the ladder momentarily, feeling awkward. "Um, goodnight."

Wolf and his pack all looked up at me.

"You're going to bed?" Wolf asked, his brow furrowing, and I nodded.

"Kinda early," Lee added, flashing a grin.

Wolf rubbed his chin and glanced at Scar. "You're welcome to join us if you want."

"I'm tired, thanks," I rattled off the excuse before fleeing up the ladder.

The cloud of misery around me seemed to grow thicker as I hung up my wet clothes to dry. It didn't help that my back fiercely ached. I changed into my sleep clothes and dug through my pack to find my oil infusion. I couldn't put it on my entire back, but I could at least get the places I could reach. I emptied the bag, but it wasn't there. I frowned, trying to remember where I'd put it.

My eyes suddenly landed on Trey's pack sitting against the wall, partially buried under my old blanket.

It was in his pack. Grief surged up to join the heavy emotions already crushing me as I remembered the last time he'd rubbed it into my skin. Our last night together hadn't been beautifully memorable. We'd both been exhausted. He helped me with the oil, kissed me goodnight, and took the first watch.

I wasn't sure it would have been any better to have known, but I did wish that we had spent our last night curled up together, holding each other close.

The grief threatened to choke me as I knelt in front of his pack and slowly opened it. I pulled out clothes that still faintly smelled like him, and that lump in my throat grew harder to ignore. All our camping supplies were here, and I hated how things like a simple cooking pot and a chunk of flint could make my eyes burn. I sorted through them, finally finding my oil infusion wrapped in one of his shirts, but as I unwrapped it, something fluttered to the floor. I stared down at the small, fat square of folded paper. It looked like it had been folded over on itself until it couldn't fold anymore.

Slowly, I unfolded it, my heart thudding in my throat. A full sheet of scrawled words came into view, and my hands trembled as I held it open and began to read.

Darlin,

I hope you never have to find this letter, but I'm writing it just in case. You're currently sleeping in the bedroll across the campfire from me, and gods, you are so beautiful. I keep looking up and getting distracted by how much I want to pull you into my arms.

But if you're reading this, it means things didn't end well. It means I'm gone.

I think I know you well enough to guess you're probably blaming yourself, and I need you to stop doing that, alright? It's not your fault, darlin'. I hope we have a good, long life together, but any amount of time I got to love and be with you is worth it. No matter what happens. I used to have all these grand ideas about going off and seeing the whole world, but then I looked into a pair of the most beautiful green eyes, and everything changed. You once told me you felt like you could never be enough, but you are, darlin'. I got my whole world, Bones, because my whole world is you.

I also have to confess that I radioed Mac from Zeke's and told him about the other person. I hope you can forgive me, but I couldn't leave them unprepared. Mac is a good man, and I trust him with my life. He'd never use this against you, and I hope, fuck, I hope if you're reading this, you're back at the Vault. I hope you have all of them around you and that you're all helping each other through this. Promise me you're letting them in, darlin'. It's okay to need them, and they'll need you, too.

Fuck, this is the hardest thing I've ever had to write. It kills me knowing if you're reading this, you're hurting. I wish I could comfort you. I wish I could hold you and promise you everything will be alright. When Mac was missing his dad, my mom used to say there's something beautiful about how our bodies return to the dirt. All of us are made up of life that came before, and all life to come will contain pieces of us. So look for me in the apple trees, the dandelions, and newborn kittens. You'll find me wherever there is life.

One thing I know for sure is that I will forever be drawn to your light. I'll find you somewhere out there again—maybe in another lifetime.

If you're not at the Vault, find a way to contact Mac. You don't have to be alone. Mac will always be there for you if you let him.

I love you, darlin'. I'll never be able to say it enough. I love you, I love you, I love you.

Always yours,

Trey

I sat there, staring at his name with tears rolling freely down my face, but out of habit, I carefully controlled my breaths to keep from making any noise.

I wished I hadn't found it.

I wished I'd found it sooner.

I wished he was here.

I wished I'd never fucking met him.

Trey knew I'd be *hurting*. Despite all my attempts to explain, he still didn't realize that losing him would *destroy* me. "Didn't end well?" What a fucking stupid description of the *agony* that was his death. The thought of us finding each other in another lifetime didn't bring comfort; it just made me hate that version of me who got to have him. The rage and the grief were so twisted together I couldn't see where one started and the other ended.

Did other people feel like this?

Other people lost loved ones during the rebellion. Other people were grieving—my *crew* was grieving—but they appeared to be continuing on and healing. What was I doing besides losing myself to emotion or losing myself to numbness? These violent swings in emotion kept knocking me off my feet. Was it because of Juck? I'd had to learn the hard way that expressing my emotions led to pain. I had to feel less to survive, but I didn't know how to feel *less*, so instead, I felt *nothing*.

Now, I felt everything, and it was tearing me apart.

I slowly leaned forward until I folded in half over my knees, the letter still clutched in my hand. I couldn't move, frozen in place as the pain poured out of me. I had to be dying. I was no stranger to pain, but no person could endure, could *survive* feeling pain like this.

My mind knew what to do. It wanted to retreat down that worn path to the empty, quiet place in my head where I'd hidden from Juck so many times. I didn't fight it. Maybe I could stay there forever. A lifetime of feeling nothing had to be better than this.

I closed my eyes. My mind was already pulling away, folding into itself again, the pain fading. I didn't even have to recite medical textbooks to keep myself anchored. I sank like a stone.

ᘒ

"Ember?"

A hand wrapped around my wrist, and for a moment—a single desperate second—I thought maybe I would open my eyes and see Trey.

Instead, I met Mac's dark gaze.

We weren't in the loft. Darkness surrounded us, but it wasn't empty. Golden light twisted around us, flowing from our bodies. It reminded me of when light would emanate from my skin, but this was different. Instead of beams or a glow, it was thin and sparkling like a thread made of flecks of pure gold. The threads flowed from our skin and around the two of us, moving gracefully in a way that reminded me of the Northern Lights. I'd never seen this before, but I instinctively knew it was my magic—it was *our* magic. Mac was gripping my wrist, holding me in place, keeping me from falling farther into the deep darkness below. His eyes flashed fiercely, reflecting the golden threads that danced around us.

"Come back," he said in my head.

I stared at him, tears still leaking from my eyes, but they drifted around my face instead of falling.

"Ember, come back," he repeated.

I couldn't muster the energy to explain that I wasn't strong enough. I couldn't face that pain anymore. It was too much. *I* was too much, slowly drowning on dry land while everyone around me continued to breathe.

"Then lean on me; let me carry you for a while," he said, and the emotion in his words colored the darkness a deep midnight blue. *"I know it hurts, but if you lock everything away, you'll lose all the beauty, too. So lean on me—I can take it."*

As though he commanded them, the golden threads began to weave together, forming a cord twining around his arm, moving down toward his wrist and my hand. I watched numbly as my golden threads did the same. The thicker the cord, the brighter the light became, and when the two cords of woven magic met where Mac's hand still tightly gripped my wrist, the light flared, blindingly bright. When it faded, there was no sign of where the cords had joined. It was like they had fused into one, binding the two of us together with one long, continuous flow of magic.

Somehow, I knew if I wanted to pull away, I could; the magic would release me. The magic between us seemed to pulse like a heartbeat; whatever this binding was, it *lived.* Pulling away would hurt us both; severing our connection would be like sawing off a limb. I stared into Mac's grey eyes and knew he was aware of it, too. He knew I had the power to hurt him, but he still waited.

"Em," his voice was rough, *"please let me in."*

His pain flowed through our magic and crashed into me, stealing the air from my lungs. The weight of his grief, fear, regret, and guilt would have been enough to bring me to my knees, but it was his crushing loneliness, like an echo of my own, that broke me.

I instinctively reached for him with my free hand, wrapping my fingers around his wrist. I wasn't so much trying to reach for help as I was trying to ease that pain in him, but the relief that filled his eyes was impossible to miss. He pulled, and I moved toward him like we were floating in water. The golden magic between us grew brighter again as I neared him, and just before I reached him, everything went white.

I opened my eyes with a gasp. I was still kneeling on the loft floor, folded in half, but Mac was beside me with one arm around my back and the other gripping my hand. The letter lay on the floor in front of us. Awareness and pain poured back into my body, and my muscles tensed at the onslaught. Mac shifted to pull me upright, and I winced at the pain in my back, but then he was crushing me against his chest, his arms wrapped tightly around me, anchoring me with his entire body.

"I'm here," he murmured in my head. *"Let it out."*

Another crack in the dam. Pain and grief poured from my body in sobs, but the weight of his arms soothed the sharpness. I wanted to be done. I wanted to pack this grief into a neat little box and tuck it away, never to be seen again, but it was everywhere, in my blood and bones.

"I know." I could hear the pain in his voice. *"I know. I loved him, too."*

Eventually, the flood eased, and I returned to the quiet loft and Mac. He sat on the floor, leaning back against the wall, and I was sitting between his legs, curled into him. His arms were solid around me, and my face was pressed into the crook of his neck. My senses flooded with the smell of mint from Mist's soap, and his chest rose and fell beneath me as he breathed. My arms had wrapped around his neck at some point, and my entire body felt like liquid.

"What happened?" I mumbled.

"I felt you," he answered, emotion roughening his voice. *"I dunno how. I was talkin' to Nemo, and suddenly I felt your pain and then... nothin'."* His arms tightened around me. *"You were just gone. Scared the hell outta me. I thought you fuckin' died."*

We didn't speak for a while, just breathing together. My eyes found the discarded letter on the floor.

"Did you read it?" I whispered.

"Yeah," he answered, the single word heavy with guilt. *"I'm sorry, I was tryin' to figure out what happened."*

"It's okay," I mumbled, mostly relieved I didn't have to explain what the letter had said. *"You were in my head?"*

"I came to find you," he explained quietly. *"You weren't responding to me, and I... or maybe these powers knew what to do. I can't really explain it. Felt more like instinct than anything else. I had to search for a while, though."* I felt a tiny hint of amusement. *"Figures that you'd be good at hidin' in your head, too."*

"Where's Wolf?"

"They're out on the porch. I told 'em I needed to talk to you privately."

Relief flowed through me that they weren't downstairs waiting to come up and demand what was wrong with me *now*.

"I can hear his and Kai's thoughts, now," he added.

I sat up, reluctantly pulling away. *"You can hear both at once? Without even seeing them?"*

"Yeah, it's loud."

I frowned, but he spoke out loud.

"Do you want to talk about this?" he asked, tapping the letter on the floor with his fingertips.

The raw hurt rose again so swiftly I was unprepared. "I tried to tell him so many times... what would happen if I lost him. I t-told him it would d-destroy me, but he still... he still didn't—"

I pressed my lips together, inhaling shakily through my nose. Mac offered a hand, palm up, and I took it gratefully.

"Trey always had so much hope in the goodness of people," he murmured, his eyes on our entwined hands. "And Ana and I... I think we instinctively tried to shield him to keep that hope alive. After Madame carved up my back the second time, he marched to her office and told her to stop. He was fuckin' nine years old." He huffed a weary laugh. "He thought it worked, but really, I just stopped tellin' him stuff 'cause I was scared Madame would hurt him. He had such a big heart and was determined to make a change, but he viewed a world where things were different—simpler and easier. Maybe we shouldn't have shielded him as much as we did. But he was always just... just..."

"A dreamer," I whispered, the ache in my chest growing sharper.

He glanced up and met my eyes. "Yeah. A dreamer."

We sat in silence for a long time before he spoke again.

"Maybe we need the dreamers to inspire us. Maybe the rest of us need to see somebody reach for the stars before we realize how much we want 'em, too."

Silence fell again, but it wasn't uncomfortable. As the adrenaline from the grief faded, exhaustion swept in.

"I think you're a dreamer, too."

I shot Mac a skeptical look. I was still sitting between his long legs, and something about his knees creating a makeshift wall around me made me feel safe.

His lips twitched up, but his eyes were serious. "I do. You were just trapped in nightmares for so long you forgot what other dreams were possible."

I stared at him, emotion welling up in my throat again.

"Then Trey, with his big dreams, swept in and reminded you." My eyes overflowed, and he winced. "I feel like I'm always making you cry."

"No," my voice wobbled as I realized out loud, "you're always *letting* me cry."

A strong emotion swept across his face, and when he spoke, his voice was rough again. "I can take it, Em."

"I know," I said because it was true. I thought about what I'd realized out in the woods. "You're my rock."

He went still, and his throat bobbed as he swallowed. "I'm your rock?"

"Every time I feel like I'm comin' apart, you're there," I fumbled to explain, tears still dripping down my face. *"You let me hold onto you when I need it, but you never hold me down."* I sniffled, using my free hand to swipe my face with one of Sam's handkerchiefs. *"It was harder to... to talk to Trey about this kinda shit."*

Mac squeezed my hand gently. *"I can't speak for you, but I know I struggled to tell Trey about the hard shit 'cause he always took my burdens on like they were his. I don't think he even realized he was doin' it. I know it came from his heart. He wanted to fix things. He just... didn't understand that sometimes things weren't as simple as he wanted 'em to be."*

Guilt swept through me, and he frowned.

"I'm not sayin' he was a bad person, Em. He was a good person, a damn good person, but he was still a person. *He wasn't perfect. Nobody is."*

My conversation with Tuck and Lee about good and evil and scales swept through my head. Trey was at least a better person than I was. Maybe if I just lived like *Trey* was holding the scales—

"I don't think Trey was a better person than you," Mac interrupted.

I raised my eyebrows, a humorless laugh escaping my lips.

"Why would he be a better person?" Mac pushed.

I stared at him with so many reasons running through my head that I couldn't even pick one. He sighed, his eyes narrowing into a familiar, exasperated expression.

"The only person who's lived your life is *you.* So why the hell would you try to make decisions based on someone else?"

"Because he was a *good* person," I whispered.

"You're a good person, too."

I started shaking my head, but he caught my face and held it still.

"Ember, you are a good person." His voice was firm, eyes flashing.

"I'm not—"

"Stop," he interrupted and pulled my face toward him.

For the briefest moment, I thought he was about to kiss me, and my stomach launched into the stars with, what? Fear? Anxiety? Something else? But he just pressed his forehead against mine. His eyes were so close I could see the shades of gold surrounding his pupil.

"You are good, Em," Mac murmured, and I could feel the warmth of his words against my skin. "You're not a *perfect* person, but you're a *good* person. I've never been more sure of anything in my whole damn life."

I bit my bottom lip to keep it from trembling. I could *feel* his sincerity, but not from his expression or his words; I could *feel* it the way I could smell the woodsmoke in the air, the way I could feel the worn wooden floor under my fingers.

"I can feel you, too," he murmured in my head. *"I can feel your confusion and pain like it's my own."*

My heart tripped over itself. What exactly had our magic done inside my head?

He released my face and sat back against the wall, running a hand through his dark hair so it fell to one side.

"It's gettin' late. Let's try not to worry about it too much right now, alright? You should get some sleep."

I took a deep breath and nodded, trying to push all my worries back down. I met his eyes and managed a slight smile. "Thank you… for bein' my rock."

When his sharp eyes grew soft, the difference was so noticeable, and it made me feel unsteady again. He stood and offered a hand to help me up. "I meant it when I said I'll always come for you, Em."

I let him pull me up, and a tangible shiver raced across my skin. It felt like a promise—like an oath—and the emotion accompanying it almost overwhelmed me again. He stooped, picked up the discarded letter lying on the floor, and held it out to me. I took it to my dresser and placed it inside the top drawer.

"You want me to send anybody in?" Mac asked.

I shook my head, leaning against my dresser. The *last* thing I wanted was to answer questions from my brother or his crew.

"You know where to find me if you need anything." He seemed to be hesitating by the ladder, cool tendrils of his worry drifting around me.

"I know." I took a deep breath, trying to exude calm confidence. "I'll be alright. Night, Mac."

He stood for a moment longer, then smiled. "Night, Em."

CHAPTER 25

"Em, you have a patient."

I cracked my eyes open, blinking in confusion at the daylight. Wolf was crouched next to my mattress, shaking me gently.

I sat up, rubbing my gritty eyes as Wolf disappeared down the ladder. I peered over the loft's edge to see Smith, and adrenaline jolted me awake. He was pale-faced and cradling a broken arm. I quickly got dressed, went downstairs, and tried to pretend that Smith wasn't still looking at me with a wariness that hadn't faded since he found me sitting next to Madame's dead body.

"Sorry, Ember," Sable said. "I thought it might be easier for you to heal him than for me to splint his arm."

"No, that's fine," I said, still raspy with sleep.

All the bedrolls were put away. It looked like it was past breakfast. Had I slept that late?

I gestured at Smith to sit in the chair while I washed up at the sink. The ice-cold water on my face helped wake me up. When I returned to where Smith sat in the chair, I hesitated at his side, my eyes scanning his arm.

"I'll have to set the bone before I can heal it," I told him, trying to keep my expression even as he stared at me. "It will hurt."

"Alright," he muttered.

I pulled over the little rolling table that fit over the exam chair. "Can you put your arm here?"

He grunted in pain but managed to get his arm onto the table. I steadied myself and carefully put my hands on his arm, my powers tingling in my fingertips, and moved his arm as quickly as I dared. He swore through his teeth, gripping the arm of the chair with his good hand. When my powers felt the bone line up, they rushed through, mending the bone and healing the injury. He swore under his breath again, but it sounded less pained this time. I let go, and he experimentally lifted his arm and flexed his hand.

"Is there any remaining pain?" I asked.

"No," he answered gruffly.

"You're good to go, then." I returned to the sink and washed my hands, but when I finished, he was still standing by the exam table, watching me. "Did you need anything else?" I asked, trying to keep my unease from my voice.

"I just wanted to say…" he hesitated, shifting on his feet. "I hope you're… feelin' better."

I stared at him, unsure of how to respond. What did he want to hear? *Don't worry, I don't feel like murdering anyone else?* "Um, thanks," I mumbled.

For a few uncomfortable seconds, he didn't move, but then he forced a smile, said thanks, and left. I wiped down the exam chair, pretending I didn't see how Wolf and his crew were studying me.

"What was that about?" Lee asked.

"What?" I didn't look up from what I was doing.

"Who was that guy?"

"Smith, he's one of Nemo's men," I answered, moving to the sink to wash my rag.

"Does he have a problem with you?" Wolf asked, his voice sharp.

I didn't turn around. "I don't know."

"Ember," Wolf sounded frustrated, "we're never gonna find who vandalized the clinic if you don't tell us what's goin' on."

I shut the water off and attempted to wring every tiny drop of water out of the rag, stalling. My stomach flipped uneasily at the realization that Wolf had made it his mission to find whoever vandalized the clinic. He rarely failed when he focused on finding someone, and he'd only gotten better if the stories were true. "I don't think it was Smith."

"Why was that whole exchange so weird, then?" Lee demanded.

I took a breath, feeling tendrils of shame creep in, but I forced myself to turn around and meet six pairs of narrowed eyes. "Because he found me in Madame's cell after I killed her."

"But you don't think he wrote 'murderer' on your wall?" Wolf's eyebrow raised.

Because you clearly are one, my brain filled in for him. I tried to breathe evenly, to keep the pain and guilt from my face, as I turned to hang my rag up to dry. "No."

The silence thickened, and I studied the clinic, trying to find something to do to keep my hands busy. Wolf's crew did more cleaning than I expected, which was helpful but also annoying when I desperately needed something to do. Vulture's crew hadn't cleaned a damn thing.

I swallowed hard, pushing down the memory of the manacle around my ankle.

"Mac came by earlier, but we didn't want to wake you. He said they're busy tryin' to get a hold of their contacts from Angel City on the radio." He huffed a humorless laugh. "I told him good luck."

I glanced at him, wondering if I was supposed to know what that meant, "Why?"

Wolf's brow furrowed. "Because of the uprising."

"Did our radio towers get damaged during the fight?" I asked, confused.

Wolf frowned. "Not the uprising here, the big one... in Angel City."

I'd never been to Angel City, but the Reapers had loved asking if that's where I came from, thanks to Juck's nickname. I knew the Voiceless had a base there and that it had once been an enormous city in the Before. Since then, most of the ruins had been swallowed by the ocean. Rally once told me the best scavengers there would dive from a boat to swim through the underwater ghost city, looking for anything of value.

"What uprising?"

"Seriously?" Wolf looked strangely shocked, and I felt I was missing something.

"I haven't heard anythin' about an uprising," I said, defensive.

"The people overthrew the Voiceless."

My eyes widened.

"It wasn't as bad as the Sin City Uprising, but it was still a bloodbath."

I knew Sin City had another large Voiceless base, but that was about it. "What happened in Sin City?"

Wolf's brow furrowed even further as he stared at me. "You've never heard of the Sin City Uprising?"

"Obviously not, or I wouldn't be askin'," I snapped.

"It was about ten years ago. The people formed a resistance and fought back against the Voiceless, but they were badly outgunned. The Voiceless slaughtered them all and anyone who was even the slightest bit related or connected to the resistance."

I stared at him, processing that. I knew the Voiceless were spreading like a toxic weed, but I had no idea they were powerful enough to have uprisings against them.

"They killed everyone—the elderly, children, pregnant women. Thousands of people died, Ember," Wolf added like he was disappointed in me.

"Well, I'm sorry the Reapers never told me," I snapped.

"You didn't even hear them talk about it?"

The only time the Reapers spoke to me was usually to call me names or taunt me or worse. I couldn't count how many times someone told me in detail what disgusting things they wanted to do to me as I tried to bandage them up or stitch their wounds. I heard bits and pieces about other things happening, but usually it was shit about warlords or other gangs. After a few years, unless someone spoke directly to me, I retreated into myself and didn't listen to anything happening around me. I used to look forward to the evening bonfires because that was when I would hear exciting tidbits about the world, but after Rally's death, I did everything possible to get out of going to them. I hated how often I forgot he was gone and searched the faces for him, but worse was how Juck started acting at those bonfires. He'd always sat next to me and sometimes demanded I sit in his lap, but after Rally, it was like he wanted to flaunt me in front of the gang. His hands would be all over me, and the Reapers would stare. I'd never felt more like his whore than I did in those moments. But I wasn't going to tell my brother any of that.

"No," I muttered.

"What about New Seattle?" he crossed his arms over his chest.

I had no idea what he was talking about. I glanced at the others and found them watching with expressions similar to Wolf's.

"The Minnie Riots? The Badland Ambush? New York?"

I felt more and more stupid. I'd never heard of any of these.

"How the fuck did you not know anything that was goin' on around you? Phoenix fell just five years ago. Didn't the Reapers stick around that area?" Wolf sounded more shocked than mean, but my hackles rose even more.

"Juck never said anythin' about any of that."

"So you have no idea the Voiceless have been tryin' to take over?"

"No 'tryin' about it," Lee muttered. "They *are* takin' over."

I felt the blood leave my face. Juck had talked about the Voiceless a lot, but mostly, he went on and on about his take on their religion. He'd never said anything about battles or uprisings.

"It's not her fault, Wolf."

All of us looked at Sable, startled.

"He kept her isolated. She'd only know what he chose to tell her."

"Yeah, but what about the past year? You never even heard people at the Vault talking about it? *I've* heard people here talking about it, and I've only been here a few weeks."

My eyes were prickling now, and guilt began creeping in. Maybe Juck kept me isolated, but I hadn't realized how isolated I'd continued to keep myself after I got away. I hadn't spared a single thought about what could be happening in the world.

Wolf appeared to be waiting for an answer.

"I didn't hear anyone talking about it."

"Not even at the canteen?"

"I didn't go to the canteen," I mumbled. "Sam brought my food here."

"Sounds right," Kai muttered, and I attempted to ignore him.

"What about your patients or your crew? They never mentioned it?"

"I didn't *talk* to people, Wolf," I snapped.

"At all?" Wolf looked so confused. "You never *stopped* talking when you were a kid."

Anger flashed through me. "I told you, I'm not *her*."

"Wolf," Scar murmured.

Wolf turned his head and looked at her. She said something to him in that hand language they used, and he scrubbed a hand through his hair and let out a heavy sigh before he replied. I glanced at the rest of his pack, noting how they were all watching my brother, concern and care clear on their faces. It was the least guarded I'd seen any of them, and it struck me like a bolt of lightning that they really did love him. They cared about him. They were a family.

Part of me was glad, relieved that he had them.

A more selfish and dark part of me seethed. I hated that Wolf found a family and got to spend the last decade with them. I hated that they were looking at *him* with sympathy, clearly concerned about how he must feel hearing about his little sister's horrible life. How sad for Wolf to have to listen to this shit.

I was the one who had to fucking *live* it.

"Where are you going?" Wolf asked, his voice sharp again, as I started toward the door.

"Breakfast," I said without looking back, slamming the door behind me.

Warm air greeted me outside, but it did nothing to ease the chill that clung to me. I wrapped my arms around myself, focusing on holding myself together.

"Ember!"

My stomach dropped at the sight of Sable jogging to catch up.

"I'll walk with you," he said as he reached me.

"You don't have to do that," I replied stiffly.

"I want to."

Fucking great. I continued on, my arms still wrapped around my torso, trying to stay an arm's length away. Sable kept pace beside me but said nothing for several agonizing seconds.

"I wanted to apologize."

I stole a glance at him through my hair. He was looking at me with a serious expression, and nausea swept over me.

"Kai is…very protective of me…and *us*, but he's overreacted several times, and you did not deserve that."

I didn't answer, staring at the muddy path as though it needed my undivided attention. I knew he wanted a response, but I had none.

"You seem…uncomfortable around me," Sable finally continued. "If I've done anything to make you feel that way, I'd like to apologize for that, too."

I wished I was anywhere else. "I'm not," I lied.

"Ember," his tone was gently reprimanding, "that's clearly a lie."

"Haven't you been listening to Wolf? That's what I do," I muttered, my tone bitter.

He huffed a laugh through his nose. "If you want my opinion, I think you do lie a lot, but not about the things Wolf suspects."

I never would have imagined anything worse than my older brother finally hunting me down, but Wolf showing up with a whole crew of people who thought they knew me and were *invested*—that was worse.

"My theory," Sable continued after I didn't speak, "is that it has something to do with the fact that Wolf lost his head when you first told him you'd been with the Reapers and that he brought me and my past into it."

My shoulders were so tense it felt like they were up around my ears.

"If that's true, I want you to know I don't hold it against—"

"Don't," I blurted out.

He raised an eyebrow. "Don't what?"

Don't forgive me. I longed to shout; instead, I bit out, "I don't want to talk about it."

"I know it's not easy," he said, his voice frustratingly steady, "but I don't want there to be any bad blood between us."

"There's not," I said, trying to inject as much force into my voice as possible. "I'm fine."

He frowned at me. "Is it because I'm a healer?"

"It's not *anything*," I snapped.

His brow furrowed even more, but I picked up my pace. There were countless things I would never be able to forgive myself for from the past twelve years, but the dozens of times I did nothing as the Reapers shoved screaming people—mothers and *children*—into those trailers and delivered them to a monster felt the most unforgivable.

I glanced behind me to see Sable trailing behind, frowning sadly, making guilt spike through me. No wonder Kai thought I was such a bitch. Even if I wanted to, I'd never be able to accurately explain the agony of having every single door from my past ripped off the hinges, exposing all the horrible ugliness inside. I *was* trying. I was trying so damn hard, but Sable and Mad Dog—it was too much.

I went around the corner of a house and walked straight into a body. I bounced off and would have fallen on my ass if the person hadn't grabbed my arm and caught me.

"Sorry," I hurried to say, but the rest of my apology died on my lips as I met Hawk's dark gaze.

"You're sorry," he repeated with a smile that didn't come anywhere near his eyes.

"I am." My voice trembled. "I'm so sorry, Hawk—"

His grip tightened painfully on my arm as he jerked me closer and got in my face, fury flashing through his eyes. "I don't want your apologies, Bones. You ruined—"

"Hey!" Sable called from behind me, his voice sharp.

Hawk straightened, an amicable mask quickly sliding over his face. "Sorry, Bones, I should've been watchin' where I was going better." He smiled politely at Sable, but his grip on my arm tightened even further. "Sable, isn't it? I'm Hawk."

Sable didn't respond, and Hawk's fingers squeezed until I had to focus on keeping the pain off my face.

"You sure you're okay, Bones?" Hawk asked, and that smile was still on his face, but his eyes were hard as his fingers crushed my arm. "Sorry again for bumpin' into you."

"It's okay." I hoped my voice sounded steady. "My fault."

He finally released my throbbing arm, still smiling, and I had to resist the urge to rub it.

"Well, have a good day."

He stepped around me, nodded politely at Sable, and disappeared. I didn't move for a few seconds, trying to breathe normally.

"What was that about?" Sable asked.

"I just walked into him."

I forced my feet to move and pushed the side door to the canteen open before he could ask any more questions.

"Hi, Bones!" Neena called from where she was chopping up some vegetables in the warm kitchen. She had her long black hair in one thick single braid today. "There's a pot of broth on the stove and some leftovers on the shelf."

I fixed myself a small plate as Sable lingered quietly near the door. I saw Neena glance at him curiously a few times.

"You want to pull up a chair and eat in here?" she asked as I ladled some broth into a mug.

"Uh, sure," I said, mostly to put off walking back to the clinic alone with Sable.

I found a chair and pulled it up to the metal table she was working at. Sable silently did the same, sitting beside me. I awkwardly used my left hand to hold my fork, letting my aching right arm rest in my lap.

"Where's Neka?" I asked between bites.

"Meeting with Nemo about the crop rotation. They're finalizing their plan for this spring." She glanced at Sable and explained, "Neka is my twin brother."

"Is it just the two of you working the kitchen?" Sable asked.

Neena smiled. "Most of the time, it's just the two of us, but more people come in a few hours before meals so they can help. Our moms were in charge of the kitchen before us, and we took over for them after they passed."

I saw Sable notice her missing finger.

"It's okay," Neena said, noticing as well, "you can ask."

"I'm sorry." Sable grimaced. "I'm a healer, so I notice those things."

"Madame took my finger," Neena said. "She suspected her partner was poisoned by a man named Hojo who worked in the kitchen."

I almost dropped my fork, my stomach roiling.

"She took my finger as punishment for allowing it to happen in my kitchen."

"Was he poisoned?" Sable asked, his voice utterly devoid of judgment.

Neena studied him for a second before simply replying, "Yes."

I blinked. That was news to me. Trey had implied that Viper died of the fever, but maybe he didn't know.

"It wasn't Hojo, though," Neena continued, sorrow coating her words. "He took the fall for me."

"What happened to Hojo?" Sable asked.

"Madame killed him."

"I'm sorry to hear that," Sable murmured.

"He was a good man," Neena smiled, but her eyes were wet. "He never broke under Madame's torture."

I shoved another forkful into my mouth, the food tasting like ash, and abruptly stood. "Sorry." I hoped I sounded normal. "I just…I should get back."

Neena nodded, her expression hard to read. Sable stood as well, thanking Neena politely, but I bolted out the door. I strode as fast as my legs could carry me, sucking in breaths through my nose and letting them out of my mouth as I tried not to picture Hojo's gaunt, broken body. Nemo's words from the other day suddenly rose in my head.

I believe everyone you healed in that room felt the same. They knew your pain and felt your comfort. You probably gave more people the strength to hold fast than you even realize.

Gods, I hoped that was true.

"Ember?"

I heard Sable jogging to catch up with me again and swore darkly under my breath.

"Based on your reaction, I'm guessin' you were there for that."

I didn't answer, still speed-walking down the worn dirt path.

"It doesn't seem like Neena blames you," he added.

"She might not know," I bit out.

"Do people not know?" he sounded surprised.

I shrugged. I had no idea who knew what. It wasn't like I was going around asking.

"I would be willing to bet most people *do* know," Sable said. "Nemo has been pretty transparent about things from what I've seen."

Great.

He didn't say anything for a while, simply matching my fast pace. "You know, when I first met Wolf, he was consumed by guilt," Sable suddenly said in a low voice. "Most of it was guilt over things he never had any control over, but he was allowing it to fester into something deadly." He paused. "You remind me a lot of how he was then."

I really fucking wished they would stop comparing me to my brother.

"Wolf and I were together for a while," he added, and *that* shocked me enough that I glanced at him. He smiled slightly at my expression. "We weren't a good match, or maybe it was just the wrong time. He couldn't get over his guilt, and I let my trauma get between us. It reached a point where we knew if we stayed together, it would ruin any chance of us staying friends."

His voice was even, but I could feel the heaviness in him.

"I loved your brother—I'll probably always love him—but he lost years to his guilt and trying to follow the teachings from your hold. Neither of us wants to see you take the same path."

My lips twisted upward in a bitter mockery of a smile.

"What's that look for?" he asked quietly.

I didn't answer.

"Ember, we're concerned about how you close yourself off to everyone—"

My temper boiled over, and I came to a stop, the words pouring out of me. "I'm not my brother. I'm not even the girl he told you stories about. How many fucking times do I have to tell you all? *That* girl is dead. I'm whatever broken pieces were left, and trust me, *I* don't like how I put myself back together, either!"

He held my gaze. The wind blew our hair around our faces. Somehow, it made him look even more beautiful while making me feel like a mess.

"You should hate me! Do you know how many people I watched Juck shove in those trailers? How many people I ignored when they begged me for help? How many people I watched Juck drag out and beat or cut their tongues out or…or *worse* because they *annoyed* him?"

"You were a child, Ember," he said, his voice soft.

"I could've done *something*," I hissed. "I only tried *once*. I should've tried every damn time."

"And what happened the one time you tried?"

I fought the surge of nausea at remembering Juck's reaction and focused on Sable. His calmness enraged me. "It doesn't matter. What matters is that I put my safety over hundreds of people…of *children*."

"If Juck hadn't been there—if it was just you and you could freely choose, would you have still done nothing?"

"No," I snapped, horrified.

"But you weren't in control, were you? You didn't have a choice. You couldn't stop what was happening. Only Juck could do that, and *he* decided to hurt people, not you."

"Do you honestly expect me to believe *you* wouldn't have done anything?"

Pain filled his face. "Yes, because that's exactly what I did for years."

We stared at each other for a few breaths.

"In Mad Dog's garrison, the guards often came into the slave quarters at night and took slaves for many disgusting reasons. Sometimes, it was to punish someone who was too difficult or loud. Sometimes it was to find someone to fuck. Mad Dog had my younger sister in his harem, and I was determined to get out and rescue her. So, those nights when the guards came? I didn't try to interfere or defend the other slaves. I stayed quiet and small and tried to be invisible." Pain deepened in the lines of his face, and I struggled to push down the memories of all the times I tried to do the same. "And after I discovered she was dead, I made my escape alone. I didn't try to take anyone with me. I saved only myself."

The memory of Vulture's face when I left him bleeding out in Juck's tent flashed through my head, and I bit my lip hard.

"I nearly let the survivor's guilt destroy me," he continued quietly. "I became a Ghostmark. I killed *hundreds* of people simply because someone paid me to do so. Maybe they were guilty, maybe they were innocent; it doesn't really matter. I took their lives because I didn't value mine." He paused, smiling sadly. "And then I met this handsome broody stranger obsessed with finding his little sister, and I realized I had the power to be the person I needed when I was helpless...to be the person *my sister* needed when she was helpless."

I'm not your sister, I wanted to snap, but I didn't.

He cocked his head slightly. "Why did you take on caring for all the orphans? Why did you jump in that pit to save Sky?"

I pressed my lips together. I didn't know why I did those things. I just knew I couldn't *not* do them.

"Why do you want me to hate you?" he pressed.

"Please leave me alone," I said, my voice trembling.

When I turned and strode away, I could have cried with relief that he didn't try to follow.

CHAPTER 26

I went to my hiding spot in the apple trees by the wall. The tree buds looked like they were seconds away from bursting into blooms. I sat under one of the gnarled trees and leaned against the trunk.

Maybe Sam was right; maybe I did always run away.

I sighed and hugged my legs to my chest, dropping my forehead onto my knees. I don't know how long I sat there, letting my mind drift before I felt him approaching. I didn't know *how* I felt him approaching, just that I did.

"See? That list is comin' in handy already," Mac said as he sat next to me.

I huffed without raising my head.

"I was waitin' for you and Sable to get back, but then he came back without you. I almost shot him first and asked questions later."

I turned my head so my temple lay on my knees and looked at him. He met my eyes and raised an eyebrow.

"So, Sable wanted to talk to you?" he asked.

"Yeah," I mumbled, then switched to mental communication without a second thought. *"He wanted to know why I disliked him."*

Mac was quiet for a few breaths. *"Do you not like him?"*

Instead of answering, I let the memory of him showing me his brand and the Reapers trafficking people to Mad Dog play through my head. It was strange how quickly I was getting used to this form of communication with Mac, and even stranger was how comfortable I felt with it.

"Fuck," he muttered.

"How's Lana?"

His eyes narrowed at the change in subject. *"Angry, but healthy."*

"What's gonna happen to her?"

"I think next time we go to Lone Pine, we're gonna drop her off, but we gotta meet a contact of Nemo's in Liberty first. We're leavin' later this afternoon. We'll be gone for three nights."

I felt a pang of disappointment.

"Does this have to do with the uprising?" I asked.

"Kinda. We're trying to build a better radio tower to reach farther." He hesitated, then added, *"Sam's comin' on this one."*

My head shot up. "What?"

"This contact…well, he knows Sam. We could do it without him, but it's gonna be a helluva lot easier if Sam comes."

Fear made my skin prickle. "Is it going to be dangerous?"

"Shouldn't be, but you never know."

I stared at him, my mind whirling, but none of the frantic things I wanted to say came out of my mouth.

"I'll keep him safe, Em," he murmured.

I swallowed hard and forced myself not to beg him to order Sam to stay here.

"You know, this is what the rest of us have to deal with all the time, knowing people might get hurt and not being able to heal them magically."

"I hate it," I muttered.

He snorted, shaking his head, then added, "Oh, Raven wanted me to tell you that when we get back, you're starting training."

I groaned.

"I'd say you'll be fine, but I don't want to lie."

He was smiling wide enough that both dimples were out. I tried to jab him with my elbow, but he caught it with one hand, still grinning.

"Just think, you might be able to land a hit like that with some training," he teased.

"Oh fuck off," I grumbled at him, but with no heat in it.

"I could hear Sable's thoughts when he came back," he said suddenly, still holding my elbow. *"He was worried about you. I don't think he holds any grudges against you for the things Juck did."* His face

grew serious. *"Which is good 'cause he shouldn't. If he did, he and I would be havin' a talk."*

"Mac—"

"Trey mentioned a few times that you were lookin' for atonement."

My stomach lurched.

"And I'm just wonderin', if no one blames you, who are you lookin' for atonement from?"

"Some people do *blame me,"* I muttered, careful to keep Hawk's face from my thoughts.

"Blame you for what?"

"For doing whatever I was told, even if it hurt someone else."

"Seems shitty to blame the person who didn't have a choice."

"I did have a choice, Mac, and I chose myself."

"I don't think it's that simple." He released my elbow and spoke out loud, "Do you remember when I came into the clinic and questioned you about…well, the escaped prisoner who turned out to be Lee?" He waited until I nodded and continued, "You said somethin' to me I haven't been able to forget."

I couldn't remember what I'd said at that moment. Mostly, I remembered Mac trapping me against the sink and my confusion over why Trey hadn't taken the opportunity to lie to Mac and hurt me back.

"You said, 'Why are you in here using your scary asshole act on me?'"

I stared at him, my brow furrowing, and his lips twitched up.

"Em, most of the people here thought I *was* a scary asshole, but you saw right through it."

I stayed quiet, just watching him.

"I'm not sayin' I've never been an asshole. I have, and I'm sure I'll be one again, but you were right. The scary asshole thing was an act… one I'd been doin' for so long I forgot it wasn't who I was or who I wanted to be. It was just the only thing I could do to survive and keep people safe." He ran a hand through his unruly hair, exhaling heavily through his nose. "I'll carry remorse about the other kids I killed as long as I live, but I didn't start those fights. I didn't attack them or plan on killin' them. They made their decisions, and I was forced to make mine. I don't know if either of us were 'good' or 'bad,' just kids put in a desperate situation by adults who *did* know better." He paused, raising an eyebrow. "Sound familiar?"

I grimaced and didn't answer, but we both knew it did.

"So I'm just sayin' I know a little bit about bein' forced to become something you're not to survive and how hard it is to let that person go when it's safe."

I stared at the dry leaf crumbling to tiny pieces in my hands. I had no idea what to say.

"Just think about it, alright?"

I reluctantly nodded, then changed the subject. "Did you get a hold of your contacts in Angel City?"

He frowned and shook his head. "No, that's why we're trying to get a stronger radio signal goin'. I'm guessin' most of their radio towers are down, so they're probably stuck usin' the smaller radios. Nemo was lookin' through some of the old logs, and it sounds like before they got those towers operating again about fifty years ago, the Vault had no contact with most of the larger strongholds."

"I didn't know the Voiceless were takin' over," I admitted. "Juck talked about them a lot, but he never said anythin' about uprisings or battles."

He looked surprised, but it felt less judgmental than Wolf's reaction. "What'd he talk about then?"

"Their beliefs and shit. He used to be one of them."

Mac's eyebrows almost launched off his face. "Juck used to be one of the Voiceless?"

"That's what he told me."

He frowned. "And they let him leave?"

"He said they parted ways, but I think there was more to it. He was always real careful to keep us from ever crossing paths with them. One time, we saw a couple of prophets in a town, and he nearly wrenched my arm off, dragging me in the other direction."

Mac's eyes went distant. "Interesting."

"Sometimes it feels like nothin' in my life makes sense," I mumbled, plucking at some fresh shoots of grass.

"Just sometimes?"

His wide smile was contagious. I liked this side of him when he was relaxed and teasing. I noticed his smile widening and remembered he could hear me. I vividly pictured myself flipping him off, and he laughed out loud.

His laughter cut off abruptly, and I looked up in alarm to see him clutching his head, his eyes screwed shut in pain.

"Mac?" I lunged toward him, intending to grab his bare forearms, but he held out a hand, stopping me.

"I'm alright," he groaned.

"Yeah, looks like it," I snapped, hovering next to him on my knees.

He made a choked sound that might have been a laugh. "Just gettin' hit with a lot of thoughts at once."

It took my brain a moment to catch up—*other people's* thoughts. He was hearing other people's thoughts.

"How many people are you hearing at once?" I asked.

He grimaced. "All of 'em, I think."

"All...of the crew?"

"Nope. The whole hold."

My lips parted in shock as I stared at him. I tried to imagine hearing over a hundred people's thoughts at once and felt nauseous.

"Started happenin' early this morning. So far, I've managed to kinda force 'em back, but—" His voice cut off again as he winced.

"What if I...try to help? Maybe my powers can help?" I asked, fidgeting anxiously.

"Can't always rely on your powers," he said through gritted teeth. "Gotta figure this out."

I sat beside him, feeling helpless as I watched sweat bead on his forehead, his muscles tense, and his jaw clench. It felt like a long time before he let out a shaky breath and opened his eyes. They still looked pained.

"Better?" I asked, my eyes wide with worry.

"A little, yeah," he mumbled. "Quieter, at least."

I forced myself to go silent and wait, resisting the urge to examine him as my fingers twitched. After a few more minutes, he pulled a handkerchief out of his pocket and wiped his brow.

"What the fuck is happening to me?" he muttered.

Maybe the relief from seeing the pain fade from his face made me lightheaded, but the teasing words tumbled from my lips. "Well, you see, when a boy becomes a man, there's this thing called puberty—"

His head snapped up to look at me, and the expression on his face was so full of stunned disbelief that I started laughing, unable to finish my sentence. His dimples appeared as he grinned.

"You're funny," he said, and there was an odd note in his voice. "How'd I not know that?"

My laugh faded. "Nothin' felt funny for a long time."

I watched his throat bob as he swallowed. "Until Trey?"

When would his name stop hurting? "Until all of you."

He smiled, but it looked sad. "Makes sense," he said in a low, rough voice.

I focused on him, trying to keep from falling apart at the thought of Trey. He was breathing a little fast, and his face looked clammy. I desperately wanted to take his pulse, but I wasn't sure—

He held his wrist out to me like an offering. I glanced up at his face to see his brow slightly furrowed as he studied me. "You're worried about me."

It wasn't a question, but at the same time, it was. I took his wrist, my eyes narrowing into a glare as I pressed my fingers against his artery. "Quit lookin' so surprised that I care about what happens to you," I parroted back the words he'd said to me in Nemo's spare room.

He huffed a laugh, a smirk curling across his lips as he repeated my words back to me, "I will when you quit glarin' at me."

I tried to keep glaring, but my smile ruined it. His heart rate was elevated but not dangerously so.

"Am I gonna live?" he deadpanned.

"Unfortunately." I released his wrist, warmth creeping into my chest at his chuckle.

"You feelin' ready to go back?" he asked. "I wanted to show you somethin' before we left."

As we neared the clinic, I stared in confusion at the chaos outside. My whole crew was there chatting with Wolf's crew. Griz and Sam were holding rakes and standing beside giant piles of dead brush by the empty patch next to the clinic. Wolf and Raven were taking measurements, and Kai wrote down the numbers they shouted.

"What is happening?" I asked, glancing up at Mac.

"Well, I know Trey was planning on fixing up the garden for you this spring, and it just so happened Nemo found some polycarbonate sheets Madame had dumped in one of the storage rooms. So, I thought

I'd look into building a little greenhouse to go with the garden. We got some more polycarbonate on our last trip and—uh, you okay?"

I'd stopped halfway up the hill, biting my cheek hard as I willed my expression to stay steady. "You're buildin' me a greenhouse?" I managed to ask.

"If you want one." He frowned, his eyes suddenly uncertain.

I remembered him sitting next to my bed in Nemo's spare room and reading a book about greenhouses; I wanted to ask him if he'd decided to build one before or after that moment, but I wasn't brave enough.

"I'd love a greenhouse," I choked out.

"Why are you blocking me?" he asked in a low voice, stepping sideways like he was shielding me from the others.

I blinked. I wasn't trying to block him, just trying to keep from bursting into tears. "I'm blocking you?"

He nodded, and I tried to relax my grip on myself. Immediately, tears started sliding down my face, and I huffed in frustration. His eyes widened.

"Why are you crying?" His voice grew more worried.

"I'm not," I tried to protest, tears sliding down my face.

His eyebrows raised, but one corner of his mouth lifted.

"I'm not... I'm not *sad*," I fumbled to explain. "I don't know why I'm cryin'."

Emotion filled his eyes. "Happy tears?"

"Is that a thing?" I swiped at my face, desperately trying to stop.

"Yeah," he murmured. "Yeah, it's a thing."

"What'd Mac do now?" Sam asked with a grin, appearing beside Mac.

He was already in his tactical gear and looked happier than I'd seen him in a long time.

"He's buildin' me a greenhouse," I said, still trying to wrap my head around it.

"You mean *we're* building you a greenhouse," Sam scowled, crossing his arms. "I refuse to let Mac get all the credit."

I let out a watery laugh, and Sam threw his arm around my shoulders, pulling me up the hill.

"C'mon, I'll show you what we're planning."

☙

They left a couple hours later. I made Sam promise to be careful so many times that by the end, he shouted, "Okay, Mom!" After the gate closed behind them, I didn't move, trying to convince myself I wasn't on the edge of panicking.

"Ember?"

I glanced up to see Nemo. He offered me a smile that I attempted to return.

"We've been working on turning the Pit into a nice space for folks to hang out, and it's finally finished. So I was thinkin' we could have the first bonfire tonight after supper. I hope you'll consider joining us."

"Oh, um, I'll think about it," I responded, and he smiled and moved on to tell the others.

"A party, huh?" Lee appeared at my side and draped his arm around my shoulders.

"I guess," I said, slightly distantly.

"What, you don't like parties?" he teased.

"I've never been to one."

"Well, it's settled; you're comin' tonight."

I raised my eyebrows and finally focused on him. He was grinning widely.

"I should probably stay at the clinic."

"Why? So you can sit in there and worry about Sam?"

I crossed my arms and glared at him.

"C'mon, Freckles, it'll be fun," he coaxed.

"What'll be fun?" Wolf inserted himself, his eyes narrowing on Lee's arm around my shoulder.

"The bonfire tonight!" Lee didn't seem bothered by Wolf's glare in the slightest. "Help me convince Freckles to go and not sit at home and sulk."

"You should come, Em," Wolf said, his eyes earnest. "We're all gonna go."

I wavered. I didn't want to sit at the clinic by myself, but I also didn't have any of my crew to be a social buffer.

"You know Apple will lose her mind," Lee added, and I couldn't argue with that.

৶

It was a busy day at the clinic. An illness was going around the little kids and the older folks, keeping me working constantly. I had to admit it was helpful to have Sable organize people, check vitals, and handle any minor issues. He didn't speak to me unless necessary, but he was polite and calm when he did. I tried to ignore the guilt.

I wished Kai was giving me the silent treatment, but unfortunately, he expressed his anger over my treatment of Sable by constantly making little needling comments that set my teeth on edge.

"Oh so you *do* know how to say 'thank you,'" he said after I thanked Leda for bringing me some fresh herbs.

"You're good at lying, can't you at least pretend to be nice?" he asked after I responded curtly to a tearful mother's heartfelt thanks.

The day passed quickly, though, and soon the supper bell rang. I reluctantly joined Wolf's crew, heading to the canteen. Lee immediately threw his arm around me again, and I'd never admit it, but it strangely helped ease my nerves. Apple came flying down the path when she saw us and, as Lee predicted, lost her mind when I told her I was going to the bonfire. She had to run back and tell all the kids, who shrieked and ran around like wild things until Leda finally corralled them into a line again.

I took my regular seat at our table and then realized if everyone did the same, I'd be the only person on the table's far side. I hesitated, but Lee immediately sat beside me, and Wolf sat on my other side. Scar sat across from me in Wolf's usual spot, and Sable, Kai, and Tuck took their usual seats. Apple wedged between me and Lee, and I was grateful because she happily filled any silences. I nibbled at my food. The absence of my entire crew hit me hard. Three nights alone with Wolf and his crew felt like an insurmountable obstacle.

"Hey, can I talk to you for a second?" Wolf asked when we stood to head to the Pit.

My stomach churned, but I nodded, and we both fell back a little from the rest of his crew.

"I wanted to apologize," he said in a low voice, and I glanced at him in surprise. "I shouldn't have reacted the way I did to you not knowing what was goin' on in the world. It wasn't your fault, and I'm sorry if I made you...feel shitty."

"It's okay," I said automatically.

"It's not okay," he corrected, but he didn't sound mad.

I didn't answer, unsure of what to say to that.

"I also wanted to apologize for all the shit I said when you first told me you'd been with the Reapers. I was out of line. I said some really fuckin' awful things to you, and I'm so sorry, Emmy."

I kept my gaze on the path ahead as we walked, my fists clenched tightly at my sides.

"Mom would—"

"No!" I finally looked at him, the word bursting out of me in panic. "Don't. It's fine. I forgive you."

"Em—"

"Please, Wolf. I can't—" I swallowed hard. "Can we not talk about this right now?"

He was quiet for so long that I glanced at him. He was frowning at me, but he looked sad.

"Alright," he said in a low voice. "But later, okay?"

I nodded, relieved, and wrapped my arms around myself. If this was indicative of how these three nights were going to go, I was fucked.

My stomach tied itself in a knot as we approached the pine trees surrounding the Pit. I hadn't been here since the night I jumped in the Pit with Brimstone, and it was affecting me more than I'd expected. When we stepped through the trees, I came to an abrupt halt. The Pit was gone entirely…filled in and leveled out. In the middle of the area was a bonfire. Nemo and Smith and several other people were standing around it, admiring their work. The area around the fire pit had many log benches for seating and lanterns hung on poles.

It looked lovely and peaceful—as if the brutal murders that occurred here were nothing more than a bad dream.

My fingernails bit into the palms of my hands as I stared at the fire pit, remembering the horrible crack when Brimstone snapped that man's neck like a twig, Sky's freezing fingers clutching my shirt, the terror she exuded, the realization that I was dying as Brimstone's hands squeezed my throat—

"You makin' escape plans, or are you actually stickin' around for once?" Kai asked as he passed, and I forced my feet to move.

No one else seemed bothered, but I scanned the group for Sky and wasn't surprised when I didn't see her. I wondered if anyone else here had ever seen one of the sentencings. From what I gathered, most decent people said their goodbyes to those sentenced beforehand and didn't attend the event.

I sat on one of the logs beside Wolf and rubbed my arms. Nemo and a few others had pulled out some musical instruments and played them quietly from a corner. Apple bounced between us and the other kids as they played hide and seek.

I wondered if we were sitting near where I'd lain in the Pit in the freezing rain and waited to die. I rubbed my arms again.

"Here."

I jumped. Wolf stood before me, offering a mug of steaming liquid. I took it, frowning.

"What's this?"

"Peppermint tea." Wolf returned to his seat beside me and gestured to where Neena and Neka were pouring steaming water into mugs for people. "You keep rubbin' your arms, so I figured you were cold."

I wasn't really, and I hadn't even noticed I'd been doing that. I forced a smile. "Thanks."

He tilted his head and looked more closely at me, but to my relief, Scar plopped on the seat beside my brother and started talking. I sipped my tea and scanned the area. Lee and Tuck were talking to a group of the remaining loggers; the kids were still running around shrieking and laughing, and Sable and Kai were snuggled together on a bench.

I meant to look away, but I watched, transfixed, as Sable tugged Kai closer by his jacket collar and kissed him. Kai smiled against his lips and tilted his head, his hands tunneling into Sable's long hair. Kai broke their kiss to say something that made Sable laugh, and then Kai kissed him again even harder.

Grief swept over me like a wave.

I just wanted Trey. I wanted him here. Gods, I wanted him here so fiercely it was a physical ache in my chest. I didn't care about the letter. I didn't care about any of the things I'd been angry about.

I made myself finish my tea before I stood. "I think I'm gonna head out."

Wolf's lips pressed into a thin line.

"You sure?" Scar asked, her head tilting.

"Yeah, I'm tired." I pasted a smile on my face.

"You want me to walk—" Wolf started in a low voice.

"No, it's okay," I interrupted, my fingers twitching. I hoped I didn't sound as desperate as I felt. "I'll be fine by myself. It's a nice walk."

He opened his mouth like he was about to argue, but Scar gently nudged his leg. He glanced at her and then back at me, and his expression shuttered. "Okay, well, we won't stay out long."

I ducked my head and hurried back down the path. I hated that I was proving Kai right. I hated the disappointment in Wolf's eyes. I hated that I felt guilty for leaving without telling Lee. I hated that I couldn't stop caring what they thought of me.

It was a long walk back to the clinic, and I wasn't surprised when my feet veered off the path home and brought me to the cemetery. It was quiet over here, but I could still hear the kids laughing and the faint sound of the music. I stood next to Trey's grave and wrapped my arms around myself, but my eyes remained painfully dry. My memories of the Pit were impossible to separate from Trey—his rage interlaced with gentleness as he carried me home, the raw honesty cracking through his voice, the entire world falling away when the soft curve of his lips met mine.

When the world ended, humanity didn't. I often longed for the Before I read about in books, but some people had to wake up the morning after the world's end, get out of bed, and continue living. How did they find the strength to survive with the knowledge of precisely what they'd lost?

I tried again to feel *something,* any little bit of his spirit, but nothing came. My shoulders slumped, and my entire body felt so heavy. I wished I could sink into the dirt—

A sound from behind me made me spin around just in time to see a person step out of the darkness. They strode toward me, and I froze, my eyes locked on the dark silhouette.

"It's just me, Tuck," a deep voice said.

Relief surged through me, making me dizzy, but on its heels came anger. I glared at him as he stopped at my side.

"You okay?" he asked.

"Did you follow me?" I snapped instead of answering.

"I was just gonna make sure you got back safe, but I started gettin' worried."

"Did Wolf tell you to follow me?" I demanded.

"He wants to keep you safe—"

"If you're going to be overbearing assholes, you could at least be *honest* about it," I hissed, pushing past him and storming out of the cemetery.

I thought I heard him chuckle, which made me angrier. He followed me back to the clinic but didn't come inside. I darkly hoped he got eaten alive by mosquitos, but the clinic's quiet felt oppressive as I washed my face and teeth. I flicked the light off, climbed the ladder, and mechanically changed into my sleep clothes before climbing into bed. It wasn't much longer before Wolf and the others got back.

Tuck greeted them from the porch, and Wolf asked if he was successful. My face heated as Tuck explained that I saw him in the cemetery.

"Was she okay?" Wolf asked.

"She wasn't cryin', just standin' there. I probably should have left her alone, but she didn't move for so long I got worried. Once she saw me, she got mad. Said we were 'overbearing assholes.'"

Someone said something too quiet for me to hear.

"Kai, cut it out," Wolf's voice was sharp. "You're not helpin'."

"All bets were off as soon as she started treatin' Sable like shit," Kai shot back.

"Why don't you yell a little louder? I'm not sure the *entire* hold can hear you." Lee said dryly.

Their voices quieted to a low mumble where I couldn't make out any words. I stared at the ceiling, embarrassment and anger and hurt and pain all fighting for my attention. When Wolf came up the ladder to check on me a few minutes later, I closed my eyes and pretended to be asleep. He hovered over me for several seconds before going back downstairs.

My eyes opened, staring unseeing at the ceiling, alone once again.

CHAPTER 27

I wasn't sure what woke me.

I opened my eyes, and my heart stopped at the sight of a shadowy figure standing over me in the moonlight. I stared at them, my body locked in frozen terror, and tried to convince myself it was Wolf or one of his crew. I couldn't see a face because they were standing with the moon behind them. Nothing happened for the longest few seconds of my life. Then, the shadow moved. I sucked in a breath to scream, but liquid suddenly poured over my head, choking me. I lurched up to sit, coughing, and screamed as soon as I could breathe.

Below me, commotion exploded. The ladder rattled as someone climbed up to the loft. I tried to open my eyes, but the liquid ran into them, forcing me to close them again. I tried to wipe my face, but my hands were also coated, and as I gasped in a breath, I gagged on the scent of blood.

"Fuck! Emmy!" Wolf's shout sounded frantic. He swore again as he crashed to his knees beside me and yelled, "Sable!"

I was shaking, trying to hold my breath, and desperately trying to wipe the blood out of my eyes. Wolf was trying to help, wiping my face with rough fabric and demanding to know if I was hurt.

"Someone's here! Someone—" I gagged again at the smell, realizing with horror that it wasn't just blood. It was Madame's scent, too.

I lurched sideways, barely managing to be sick on the floor instead of my mattress, steady hands catching me and holding me up.

"We've got you, Ember," Sable's calm voice murmured, and I felt his cool hands searching my face and head for an injury. "No one is here."

"Is she hurt?" I heard Wolf snarl.

"I don't think so?" Sable replied, his voice terse.

"Get it off," I gasped as soon as I managed to stop retching. "Get it off!"

"What happened?" Wolf snapped, but he sounded more worried than mad.

"Please, get—get it—off!" I choked out, still desperately trying to wipe my face, and my hair was *drenched*. I retched again, my head swimming as I fought to breathe.

Together, they maneuvered me down the ladder. Next thing I knew, I was sitting on the counter next to the sink, and a dripping washcloth was wiping the blood from my face. I was finally able to get my eyes open and realized Wolf stood on one side of me, holding me upright while Sable wiped the blood off my face. Both of them were smeared in the blood that covered me. I shook uncontrollably, breathing in short gasps, and all I could smell was Madame and blood.

My stomach heaved, and I clasped a hand over my mouth to avoid getting sick again.

"It's okay, Em," Wolf murmured, but his voice was rough.

"Here, lean her over the sink," Sable ordered.

The room spun as I moved, and then I was leaning over the sink while someone poured water over my head. I clung to the side of the sink and closed my eyes so I didn't have to see the red water running from my hair and down the drain. Madame's scent was getting slightly fainter, but it was still there. I realized I had my jaw clenched tight, trying to keep my sobs contained.

"Not sure this is gonna come out of this quilt."

I straightened so fast I knocked the bowl in Sable's hand into the sink with a clatter. I twisted to look at Kai, my stomach somewhere on the floor, to see him holding my quilt, *Trey's quilt*, covered in dark red blood.

"No," I whispered.

I pushed away from Wolf and strode toward Kai, only partially aware of the water running in rivulets down my neck and clothes. He handed over the quilt when I reached for it, his brow furrowed. I turned around and returned to the sink, feeling like I was floating outside my body again. Wolf was saying something, but my ears were ringing too loudly. I dumped the quilt in the sink and started trying to scrub the blood out. Someone touched my elbow, but I jerked away. I had to get the blood out. I had to. I couldn't lose this quilt. I just…I just couldn't.

There was so much blood, and the quilt was so large that I struggled to get the whole thing rinsed. The red faded to pink, but I couldn't get the entire thing clean. I lost track of how many times I rinsed it, but I couldn't get all the pink out.

"Em." Wolf's voice was so gentle.

"Don't," I said through my teeth.

I felt him hovering at my side, watching me try to squeeze the water out of the quilt. Everything blurred as tears filled my eyes, and soon, I was sobbing too hard to see what I was doing.

"Let me try, Ember," someone said, prying my hands from the quilt.

"Here, I got her some clothes," someone else said.

Wolf half pulled, half carried me to a corner, barking at everyone to turn away, and Scar appeared before me. She towel-dried my hair like I was a child as I sat on one of the wooden chairs and cried, covering my face with shaking hands.

"Let's get you in some dry clothes," she murmured.

I realized she was watching me warily as though expecting a fight again, but I didn't have a single spare fuck to give about my scars at the moment. I stood and pulled my shirt off. I watched her eyes flick down to see the brand; her nostrils flared, and her eyes hardened, but she just handed me a dry shirt.

"What happened to your arm?" Scar asked suddenly.

She carefully ran her fingers over a ring of dark bruises on my upper arm. My brow drew together as I stared at it. I had no fucking idea where it'd come from.

"These look like fingerprints," she added, meeting my gaze.

The fury in her eyes startled me. Fingerprints? I pressed my fist hard against my breastbone, rubbing it. Had someone grabbed my arm—

Hawk.

Hawk had grabbed my arm. I remembered how much it had hurt as his grip tightened. I hadn't even noticed the ache in my arm until now, but I was so accustomed to bruises—

"Ember?" Scar caught my attention again. "Did someone do this?"

I bit my lip hard and pulled away to put on the jeans she'd found in my dresser, but I saw her expression darken. She'd given me the sleeveless shirt Trey had found for me when I first came here. I hugged myself, covering the bruises with my hand and shivering.

"Here, Em." Wolf reappeared and draped Mac's jacket that he'd lent me the other day over my shoulders.

I put it on and pulled it tightly around me. It smelled like Mac, and that comforted me. Kai was scrubbing my quilt in the sink. Sable, Lee, and Tuck were missing. Wolf and Scar ushered me outside, the three of us sitting on the porch. Scar lit a lantern and set it on the worn wooden floor.

"What happened, Em?" Wolf asked.

I glanced at him. His gaze was intense, his jaw tight, and his entire body felt coiled like a spring. I ran my fingers through my damp hair, working out the tangles.

"Someone was in my room," I said, my voice shaking.

"In the loft?" Wolf's brow drew together.

"I w-woke up, and they were standing over me. I couldn't see their face. They dumped the b-blood on me."

"No one went up or down the ladder." Wolf frowned.

"Were any of the windows open?" Scar asked in a low voice.

"No," Wolf answered. "They don't open."

In the silence, pain began to pound behind my eyes.

"Could it have been a nightmare?" Wolf finally asked.

"That blood was very real," Scar said. "Just like those bruises on your arm are very real, Ember."

I winced as Wolf demanded, "What bruises?"

"She has dark bruises on her arm like someone grabbed her," Scar answered, her voice dark.

"Em—" Wolf started furiously.

I turned toward him, wrapped my arms around his neck, and pressed my face into his shoulder like I used to when I was little. He froze briefly, then slowly wrapped his arms around me, holding me tight. I squeezed my eyes shut and wished I was still a kid and Wolf would fix this—would fix everything like he used to.

"Who grabbed your arm, Emmy?" Wolf finally asked, but his

voice was more gentle this time.

I hesitated, then whispered, "Hawk."

I felt his entire body tense again, and he went unnaturally still and silent. If he and Scar spoke again, it wasn't out loud. Eventually, the door opened, and Kai quietly announced he'd gotten the blood out of my quilt. Voices approached, and I recognized Nemo, Sable, and Tuck.

"Can you take her so I can talk to Nemo?" Wolf said to someone. He pried my arms from his neck. "I'll be back, Em."

I wasn't at all surprised when Lee sat in his place. He wrapped an arm around my shoulders and tucked me tightly against his body. I rested my head on his shoulder, wondering when Lee's presence had become comforting.

Nemo and a few of his men entered the clinic with Wolf and his crew, casting curious glances my way. I pretended not to see them. I let my eyes close, suddenly exhausted.

I wished I hadn't given them Hawk's name. I didn't *know* he was the person who did this. Hawk might hate me, and rightfully so, but to do something like this? The rage in his eyes flashed through my memory, and I felt sick. When did I start assuming people *wouldn't* do the worst possible thing?

I closed my eyes again, listening to Lee's heart beating in his chest. We sat there for a long time, and I drifted into a half-asleep daze.

"—like to use my spare room again, you're welcome to."

"You goin' right now?"

"Yes, Smith is roundin' up a few more men."

"You can go with him if you want," Lee said in a low voice. "I'll take her to Nemo's."

"Don't leave her alone," Wolf warned.

"I won't."

Lee stood, hoisting me into his arms. His steps were so graceful and smooth. I knew he was taking me to Nemo's house, and I was strangely unbothered. Part of me was annoyed that Lee had somehow weaseled his way into my circle, but most of me was just relieved. I kept my eyes closed as Lee spoke to one of Nemo's men at the door, who escorted us to the spare room. Lee laid me on the bed, and I listened to him speak in low tones to the guard as he built a fire in the fireplace. Finally, I heard him bid us goodnight, and the door shut quietly behind him.

I couldn't hear Lee walking, but when I opened my eyes, he stood beside the bed. We stared at each other for a moment, and I didn't know how to interpret all the emotion flickering through his eyes, but I did know one thing.

"Will you stay with me?" I whispered.

"Of course," he said. "Smith said there's a cot—"

"No," I interrupted, "will you sleep in the bed? With me?"

His eyebrows raised, a tiny smirk appearing. "Do you *want* your brother to kill me?"

I did not want to worry about my brother right now. "Please, Lee?"

His amusement disappeared. He ran a hand through the hair escaping his bun, took a deep breath, and released it in a rush. "Guess you better start planning my funeral then."

He sat in the chair and started taking off his boots. I was still wearing Mac's jacket, but I had no plans to take it off. I scooted over as Lee climbed into bed beside me, also still fully dressed.

"What kind of flowers do you want?" I asked as he settled on his back, hands tucked behind his head.

He frowned at me, his brow furrowing in confusion. I stayed sitting, leaning on one hand. It was kind of nice being able to look *down* at someone for once.

"For your funeral," I clarified.

He blinked in surprise, then grinned. "Forget-me-nots."

"Myosotis asiatica?"

"Are you tryin' to put a spell on me?" he asked, eyebrows raising.

"That's their name. I use them as an astringent in poultices, and their oils can be used as an antidote to some poisons."

"I'd love to tell you I knew that, but I just think they're a pretty color."

"They are a pretty color," I agreed.

"Are you gonna sit there and lecture me about the medical properties of pretty flowers, or are you gonna come over here?"

A flutter of nerves came to life in my stomach, startling me, but I forced myself to lay beside him. *You asked him to do this,* I reminded myself, annoyed. I lay on my side, facing him, and he rolled over to his side to do the same. There was a whole foot of space between us, full of unspoken questions.

He lifted a hand and gently brushed my hair back, his fingers tracing a shape on my cheek, and his eyes narrowed in concentration.

"What are you tryin' to find?" I asked.

"Cassiopeia," he answered. "There, right here!" His fingers traced a jagged line from my nose to my cheek. "Found her."

"Her?"

"According to an old myth from Before, she was a queen who angered the gods," he murmured. His eyes met mine. "The gods put her in the sky as punishment and sentenced her daughter to be sacrificed to a monster."

"What happened?"

"The princess was chained to a rock for a sea monster to devour, but a hero rescued her and killed the monster."

His voice had a dark edge that made me instantly wary. I studied his face, trying to understand what he was feeling.

"So the gods from the Before weren't much better, then," I finally said.

He smiled, but it didn't reach his eyes. "Gods are just monsters by another name."

I opened my mouth to ask another question, but he grabbed my waist and pulled me, sliding my body closer and wrapping me in his arms.

"You should get some sleep," he murmured, his legs entangling with mine. "Those damn roosters will be crowin' soon."

I curled into him, selfishly enjoying the feeling of another body against mine. The scent of peppermint soap lingered on Mac's jacket, and with my eyes closed, it almost felt like Mac was holding me. Butterflies filled my stomach, and I tried to rationalize them away. *You just miss Mac and the crew, and you're starved for touch. That's all.*

Still, the heavy, crushing loneliness felt farther away.

⌒

"Darlin', open your eyes."

Trey's warm brown eyes greeted me. I stared at him, my lips parting in surprise.

"Look around us," he murmured.

I turned my head, staring at the dark, shadowy shapes of the trees surrounding us. We stood in the woods at night, arms around each other, swaying as though we were dancing. But what caught my attention were the tiny golden lights drifting around us.

"Fireflies," he whispered.

I gasped, watching them flit around us like glimmering magic. Eventually, I realized I didn't know where we were. My brow furrowed in confusion. How did we get here?

"It's alright, darlin'," he said, his voice soft. "I just wanted to see you."

Something flitted on the edge of my mind, and I tried to pull away. His arms tightened around me, pain flashing through his eyes.

"Please, Em. Stay with me?"

I stopped pulling away. Our feet continued to move, turning us slowly in a circle, but the pain didn't leave his eyes.

"What's wrong?" I asked.

"Nothin'." He smiled, but it looked forced. "Just missin' you."

I frowned and opened my mouth to ask why he was missing me if I was right here, but the memory of his bloodied face suddenly hit me like a fist. I came to an abrupt stop, horrified.

"You died. You're dead." My voice shook.

"Em—"

"How are you here?" Anger swiftly filled me, burning with savage, painful fury. "Why can't I ever feel you when I need you?"

His eyes closed, long lashes sweeping across his cheeks, and his throat bobbed. "I'm sorry."

I jerked away, and this time, he let me go. His hands fell to his sides, and the pain in his face speared through me, but I wasn't done.

"I can't keep doin' this. I can't get you back for little moments just to lose you again." Tears rolled down my face. "I tried telling you, but you still don't get it. I can't...I can't keep puttin' myself back together. This is killin' me—"

"I'm sorry. I'm so sorry." His voice came out harsh and desperate. "If only you knew how sorry I am."

"Why can't I feel you?" I meant to sound angry, but my voice broke.

"It's complicated," he whispered, still frozen where I left him. "I shouldn't be here, but I can't help myself."

His handsome face blurred as tears filled my eyes. *"Can you come back? If I can see you here, does that mean you can come back? Can my powers...can I bring you back?"*

The pain that filled his face was a tangible thing, and I knew the answer before he shook his head. Grief rushed over me, filling my lungs and bringing me to my knees. He crouched beside me, resting a gentle, almost hesitant hand on my back.

"Then take me with you," I begged through the sobs. *"Don't leave me here. Please, Trey, I can't—I can't—"*

He gathered me into his arms, pressing a kiss into my hair. *"I'm so sorry, love."*

I went still, my heart leaping into my throat. For a few seconds, I remained frozen, my mind spinning, and then I abruptly pulled away, staring wide-eyed, my chest heaving with breaths that didn't bring me any air.

Only one person had ever called me that.

Only one.

And it wasn't Trey.

"Ember—" he started, his eyes sharpening on my expression.

"You're not Trey," the words fell out of my mouth in numb disbelief.

Everything seemed to be suspended momentarily as if the entire world around us had held its breath. Then, the fireflies, the woods, everything vanished, leaving us in a terribly familiar darkness. He didn't move from where he was still crouched, watching me warily, and fury flooded my veins—so hot I thought I might burst into flames.

"How dare you," I seethed, scrambling to my feet. *"How dare you use his face."*

He slowly got to his feet but stayed where he stood. *"Ember—"* he tried again. His face remained Trey's, but that was not Trey's voice.

"He is not a fucking puppet for you to play with!"

"I didn't intend to trick you," he said, his voice steady but with a thread of something sharp.

"Stop using his face!" I lunged toward him, and he tried to step back, but I caught his arm.

I didn't have a plan, just rage, but as my hands touched his skin, golden beams of light flared, cutting through the darkness in every direction. I gaped at them, but he cried out as though in pain, stumbling to one knee. Under my hand, Trey's wrist dissolved into shadows, revealing a pale, thinner arm. My heart pounded so loud it drowned out everything else as my eyes followed his arm; the rest of the shadows fell away like a curtain, and I stared at the man who appeared before me.

His hair was pure white, hanging around his face in loose curls, but he looked about the same age as Wolf. The planes of his face were sharp and angular, almost as though he'd been cut from rock. His eyes were jarringly blue. I'd never seen him before.

"Ember," his voice came out pained, "I'm not your enemy."

"Not my enemy?" I repeated in disbelief.

"Just let me explain."

"Was that you? In the flower field?" I demanded, feeling like I teetered on the very edge of a precipice.

He held my gaze, his expression impassive, but something flickered in his eyes. "Yes."

"Was it ever Trey?" My voice broke, but I didn't let go.

He paused, his throat working as he swallowed. "No."

A tear ran down my cheek, quickly followed by another. "How did you get in my head?"

"You reached out. You were reaching for…him."

I stared at him, horror and pain and anger drowning me. "And you saw an opportunity."

"You shut me out—"

"You fucking terrorized me!"

Anger sparked in his eyes. "You have no idea what I've done for you."

"What does that mean?"

"I've been trying to keep you safe," his voice rose.

"Well, you've done a real shit job of it!" I hissed.

"You think you know—"

"How does pretending to be Trey keep me safe?" I interrupted, so angry my voice shook. "I don't want your fucking protection. I want you to leave me the fuck alone!"

He stared up at me, and I watched his blue eyes harden like a door slamming closed.

"Do not tempt me to take more drastic measures," he said in a familiar silky tone.

"Who the fuck do you think you are?" I tightened my grip on his *arm, golden light flaring. "You don't scare me anymore. You try to find me, and I will kill you."*

A cruel smirk crossed his face. "Are you truly so eager to have nightmares about killing me?"

I opened my mouth to snap a retort, but he continued.

"Just like you have nightmares about that knife in Juck's chest? Or the blood spurting from Madame's neck?"

Fear turned my veins to ice, but I refused to back down. "I'll gladly have nightmares if it keeps you from hurting anyone else."

He laughed softly, making the hair stand up on the back of my neck. "Love, you think I don't know what happened tonight?"

I sucked in a breath through my nose. "Was that you in the clinic?"

He scoffed. "No."

I was beginning to feel nauseous, and I desperately tried to pretend I wasn't. He suddenly got to his feet gracefully, and I flinched but still gripped his arm. His eyes narrowed, and he stepped into my space. Now that he was standing, I realized how tall he was. Shadows still covered his lower body, but they recoiled from my light. I was very aware I had no exit plan. I was afraid to let go of his arm since that seemed to give me a slight advantage, but I also desperately wanted to leave.

"The scent of Madame's soap is all it takes to break you, yet you threaten me," he murmured. "I still can't decide if you are brave, foolish, or both."

"Says the man who hid behind shadows and threatened me," I sneered, my temper flaring.

His expression grew darker, and my heart leapt into my throat. My stupid mouth.

"You know nothing," he said in a soft voice that made chills run across my body. "You think you don't need my protection, but you have no idea what sort of monsters exist in the dark."

"No, I don't want your protection—"

His cold fingers seized my chin. "What you want does not matter. You are mine."

"I am not yours," I spit out defiantly despite the fear coursing through me.

His smile didn't reach his eyes. "He's dead, Ember, and he's not coming back."

Pain stabbed through me. "It doesn't matter. I'll always be his."

His eyes flashed, and the darkness pressed in, heavy and suffocating. "You would devote yourself to a man who died and left you here alone?"

"He didn't choose to die!"

"He didn't fight it, either."

"His death started the rebellion," I parroted Nemo's words even as they hurt. "He helped free people!"

The shadows around him writhed and grew, and my golden light suddenly seemed small. "Well, that is the difference between us, then," he murmured, leaning closer, "because I would let the whole world burn rather than abandon you. I would never make you beg to follow me into death. I would never promise to love you and then leave you."

I stared at him, my heart pounding. I wanted to scream at him, but I hated the tiny selfish part of me that ached with pain—that wished Trey had felt that way.

"So remember that the next time you decide to label me a villain, Ember," he said in a soft, dangerous voice, and then he vanished like smoke.

CHAPTER 28

I bolted upright in bed, gasping in panicked breaths.

"What the fuck?" a sleepy voice mumbled beside me, and I gasped, lurching away. "It's Lee, Freckles. It's Lee."

I couldn't respond, too focused on trying to breathe. The bed shifted as he sat up, and his warm arms encircled my shoulders. I gripped his forearms and tried to stop shaking.

"It's alright, you were just dreamin'," he murmured into my ear.

I shook my head. No, that was not a dream.

"You're safe, Freckles." He sounded a little more awake now. "I'm right here."

He squeezed me tight, and a pained sound escaped my lips. He immediately released me.

"Did I hurt you?" he demanded.

"My back's just sore," I whispered.

"Your back is sore?" he repeated. "Is that normal?"

I nodded, but I didn't want to talk about my back. "It's fine."

He sighed but gently wrapped his arms around me, tugging me back onto the bed and pulling the blankets around us again. It looked like it was almost dawn, and the dark sky was beginning to lighten. He wrapped his body around mine, and I rested my head on his shoulder, clenching my trembling hands.

What the fuck was that? Maybe it *was* a dream?

No, I knew better. It was never Trey.

Tears filled my eyes. I wasn't sure if it was better or worse that it had never been him. Had he tried? Was it even possible?

What had Sam called him? The Mental Menace? Menace was right. I was furious that he'd pretended to be Trey. He'd fucking *kissed* me, and I'd kissed him back. He said, "I love you," for fuck's sake. Seeing Trey had destroyed the fragile progress I'd made, sent me down a dark spiral *again,* and it wasn't even him. I wanted to scream or burst into tears, or maybe both. I thought I had a decent grasp on what Menace wanted and how he would act, but now I was confused again. Every other time I'd interacted with him, he'd been arrogant, reckless, and entitled. He hadn't been any of those things while pretending to be Trey. If he hadn't slipped up and called me "love," I might have never figured it out. My skin crawled. How long would he have kept pretending?

Lee shifted, and his fingers gently brushed away tears. "You want to talk about it?"

For a brief second, I considered it. We were entwined together, and I felt safe, warm, and comfortable with him. It would be nice to get all of this out of my head, and maybe it would ease the pain of my heart breaking all over again.

But I hadn't told Wolf anything about Menace, and I wasn't sure if I *should.* It wasn't something to dump on Lee with no warning. I couldn't forget they were bounty hunters.

"Freckles?" Lee murmured.

"Just a bad dream," I whispered, more miserable tears escaping. I wished Mac or Sam were here so I could talk to one of them.

We lay quietly until I finally managed to calm down. An embarrassed flush crept into my cheeks. I was so fucking sick of crying.

"You want a distraction, then?" he asked in a low, suggestive voice, and my stomach lurched for a very different reason.

"What kind of distraction?"

"Whatever kind you'd like."

Fuck he was smooth. "What if I want you to do a flip?"

"Then I'd do a flip." I could hear the smile in his voice.

"What if I want you to sing?"

"Then I'd sing."

My skin felt heated, but I could feel the tidal wave of grief I was barely holding back.

You would devote yourself to a man who died and left you here alone?

I shoved away the memory of Menace's words, but I couldn't deny I had no idea if it was even possible to move on from Trey. Part of me longed to be touched, but how could I let someone else touch me after Trey? How could I touch someone else after Trey? The thought of caring about someone, loving someone like I'd loved Trey, seemed impossible. My eyes filled with fucking tears *again*.

Sounds pretty lonely, Lee had said, and he was right.

Maybe I was cursed always to be alone. I got a handful of days of bliss with Trey, and maybe that was all I'd ever get.

"Hey, talk to me," Lee whispered.

"I can't, Lee," I said, my voice wobbling. I wasn't sure if I meant talking or…distractions. Maybe both.

His arms tightened around me, though I noticed he carefully avoided pressing on my back. Neither of us spoke for a while, and I tried my damndest to stop thinking, swallow back the tears, and pretend the fragile scaffolding I'd managed to re-erect hadn't just come crashing down.

"You're not alone, Em," Lee murmured. "You're not alone, alright?"

I pressed my face against his shoulder and didn't respond.

ॐ

"—wasn't there?"

"Couldn't find him anywhere."

"But no one went through the gate?"

"Not according to the guards."

I slowly opened my eyes, squinting at the daylight streaming through the windows. Wolf, Lee, and Sable stood before the fireplace, speaking in low voices.

"So he just vanished?" Lee sounded frustrated.

"He's gotta be in the hold somewhere," Wolf answered. "I'll find him."

"Did he say anything about motive?" Lee asked.

"Nemo said Hawk was arrested for being part of the rebellion. He doesn't know for sure if Hawk was tortured. He wasn't injured when they freed him."

"Could be harboring a grudge," Sable murmured.

"Hawk was close with a woman who was tortured, so Nemo's

fetching her to see if she has any answers."

Mist. Oh fuck, I felt sick.

"Tell me again what you saw, Sable," Wolf ordered.

"Not much. Ember was pretty far ahead of me, but when I rounded the corner, he was holding her arm and speaking to her real close. It definitely looked aggressive, but then he acted like nothing was wrong." His voice grew dry. "And I know this will probably shock you, but Ember wouldn't talk about it."

Wolf muttered something I couldn't make out, and Lee snorted a laugh.

"I thought it looked like he was gripping her arm pretty tight, but she didn't really react, and she never acted like it hurt afterward."

"Scar said the bruises were *purple*," Wolf said.

"Well, maybe she'll have more to say now," Lee said. When I glanced at him, I realized he was looking directly at me, one eyebrow raised.

Wolf and Sable both turned around to look at me, and I fought the urge to pull the blankets over my head like a child.

"Morning, Ember," Sable said as the three approached the bed. "Can I take a look at the bruises on your arm?"

I stared at them with my lips pressed into a flat line. This was not how I wanted to start my morning.

"Ember," Wolf warned.

"They're just bruises," I muttered.

"Ember," Wolf repeated, his voice sharpening.

I huffed a frustrated breath and sat up, unwrapping myself from Mac's jacket I'd cocooned myself in. Sable took a seat on the bed in front of me as I let the jacket fall from my shoulders, revealing the dark bruises. Wolf made an angry sound through his teeth.

"Gods," Sable muttered as he gently took my arm and inspected them. "Why didn't you say anything?" When I didn't respond, he pushed, "What did he say to you?"

"That he didn't want my apologies," I muttered.

"Why?"

"Because Madame used me to torture Mist in front of him." My voice sounded dull and flat.

"Why did you say you didn't know who was vandalizing the clinic?" Wolf demanded.

"I don't know if it was him," I said, twisting the blanket in my fingers.

"You could've at least named him as a suspect," Wolf snapped.

"I already fucked up his life," I mumbled.

"That doesn't mean he's allowed to fuck up yours," Wolf shot back.

"Wolf," Sable murmured.

Wolf took a deep breath and let it out slow, but I kept my eyes on my hands. A rooster crowed somewhere outside.

"Well, he's disappeared, so that's not helping him look innocent," Wolf said, his voice calmer.

"Was it actually your back hurting last night, or was it your arm?" Lee abruptly asked.

I blinked up at him. "My back."

Lee frowned, pointing at my bruised arm. "You're seriously gonna tell me that doesn't hurt?"

"I didn't notice it."

His eyebrows arched, and simmering silence filled the room. They were waiting for me to explain, but I had no idea what to say.

"What's wrong with your back?" Wolf finally asked, his voice rough.

My face was so hot. "It just hurts sometimes."

"The scars," Lee added quietly, and Wolf's expression twisted.

"Do you have any salves to put on it?" Sable asked.

"I have an oil infusion," I mumbled.

"I have an ointment I picked up from a healer in New Salt," Sable said. "It's helped us a lot with aching muscles. Would you be willing to try that?"

I nodded, hoping that would satisfy him, then blanched when he pulled a small tin out of the satchel he carried. I hadn't expected him to have it with him. My panicked gaze met my brother's worried eyes.

"Please, Em, can you let him look? If it's hurting you, you need a healer."

My fists clenched in my lap. I wasn't getting out of this without a massive fight. "Fine."

"Can I stay?" Wolf asked.

I wanted to say no. I knew if I said no, he would leave, but the pleading look in his eyes filled me with even more guilt. I could see my brother clearly in those green eyes, and it extinguished my protests. So I nodded and turned my back to them, holding my shirt over my chest as Sable pushed the back of it up. I tried to steel myself, but the sharp intake of breath I heard from Wolf stabbed through me. Sable didn't say anything for a moment.

"Did they have to use stitches?" Sable asked, and I nodded. "I'm going to touch your back, alright?" he warned, but I still cringed when his fingers made contact with my scarred skin. He moved his fingers along the scars, pressing lightly, and then his fingers paused. "Did the stitches rip at some point?"

"Yes," I mumbled.

"How did that happen?"

I tried to breathe evenly, but my voice came out shaky. "Madame summoned me before it was fully healed. I passed out, and Mac had to carry me back. At some point, the stitches ripped."

Either Lee or Wolf muttered something in an angry voice.

"Did you put anything on it?"

"A poultice with horsetail."

"Good choice. Okay, I'm going to put some of this salve on. It might feel cold," Sable warned before smoothing the salve onto my scarred skin.

I bit my lip hard, my head tipped down so my hair fell forward and shielded my face. Everyone was so quiet behind me.

"Does this hurt here?" Sable asked, pressing hard on my back, and I arched away with a hiss of pain. "Gonna guess that means yes. The scar tissue is so thick here, but a massage a few times a day might break up that tissue and relieve some pain."

The thought of someone touching my back multiple times a day made me feel ill. "It doesn't hurt that bad."

Sable pressed in on another spot, and my body betrayed me, flinching away. "Not that bad, huh?"

I tried to yank my shirt down, but he didn't let go.

"Hold on, Ember, I'm almost done."

I gritted my teeth and forced myself to stay still, embarrassed tears in my eyes. I hated this. I hated the eyes on me. I hated the hands touching me. I hated the pity I knew I would see in their faces. I hated revealing this weakness. Sable's hands traveled toward my lower back, still rubbing in the salve, but the panic built until I couldn't take it anymore.

I abruptly scrambled away across the bed to stand on the other side, pulling my shirt down. My face was on fire, and I was breathing in shaky gasps. Sable sat frozen, salve still on his fingers, watching me. Lee's eyes were sharp on my face, and Wolf's brow was drawn as he glanced between me and Sable.

"I can't… I'm fine. It's fine." I choked out.

The silence only lasted a couple seconds, but it felt like hours.

"Okay," Sable said, his voice soft. "Well, I'm going to leave this salve with you, and if your back hurts, have someone help you put it on. I'm always willing to help, but it's okay if you'd prefer someone else. If you can handle someone massaging those scars that hurt, I really think it could help."

"Okay," I said automatically, grabbing Mac's jacket from the bed and pulling it back on as though it were armor.

Sable held the tin toward me, and I shoved it into Mac's pocket. Wolf and Lee were silent, but the tension radiating from them practically crackled in the air.

"Any word from Mac?" Lee asked, breaking the silence to my relief.

"Nemo said they were gonna meet their contact today," Wolf answered.

I felt a surge of anxiety for Sam. I hoped their meeting went smoothly. Someone knocked on the door, and then Kai poked his head in.

"Nemo's back with Mist."

༄

We filed downstairs and into one of Nemo's meeting rooms. Mist was sitting at the table, and she looked much better. Her hair was longer and worn loose, hiding where her ears had been, and her face had filled out. She smiled at me as I entered, and I attempted to return it.

"Hi, Bones. Or should I say, Ember?" she asked.

"Either one is fine." I tugged my shirt collar closer together.

"Mist, this is Wolf, Sable, Lee, and Kai," Nemo said, gesturing to everyone. "Wolf is Ember's brother."

Mist smiled politely at them as we all sat.

"Well, I wish we were meeting under better circumstances, but Mist, we wanted to ask you about Hawk. Have you noticed anything unusual about his comings and goings lately?"

Mist frowned and shifted slightly in her seat, "I haven't spoken to Hawk in a couple weeks."

Nemo looked surprised. "Oh, I thought the two of you were close."

Mist glanced at me, her expression twisting, and my stomach sank. "We were, but we had a bit of a falling out. What is this about?"

"We have reason to believe he might be involved in an attack on Ember last night," Nemo said gravely.

Mist's gaze snapped to me. "What happened?"

"Someone got into the clinic and dumped a large volume of blood mixed with Madame's soap scent over Ember's head."

Mist's eyes widened. "Blood from where?"

"It's gotta be animal blood," Wolf answered. "Unless you've found some dead bodies."

We all swung our gazes back to Nemo, who shook his head.

"Wait, more of Madame's scent?" Mist rested her elbows on the table and massaged her temples.

"Have you noticed any missing?" Nemo asked.

Mist grimaced. "No, but I packed up that scent and put it in my storage shed." She glanced at me again. "I can't stand smelling it, either."

My stomach churned.

"I hate to pry into your business, Mist, but did your falling out have anything to do with Ember?" Nemo asked, his tone regretful.

Mist sighed. "Partially, I guess. I've just needed some… space." Her eyes glimmered with tears. "I broke and gave Madame his name when she was torturing me."

The pain in her voice made my throat ache, and shame swallowed me.

"When Bo—I mean Ember wasn't there, it was… so hard to keep from breaking. I always thought I could withstand something like that, but you don't know until it's happening." She wiped her eyes with her sleeve. "Hawk wanted to fix it, but I have to figure it out by myself. He made a few negative comments about Ember, and I got angry and told him he had no idea what she did for me in that room." She looked at Nemo with a grim smile. "You know."

Nemo nodded, his eyes sliding to me, but I glanced at my brother. He didn't look confused or shocked, so maybe they'd already talked about this while I was unconscious.

"I can't imagine him doing something like that to Ember," Mist continued. "But I don't know… he's hurting, and what happened in that room… it changed us."

"He grabbed her arm the other day, grabbed it hard enough that he left big purple bruises." Wolf crossed his arms over his chest.

Mist looked from him to me, her eyes widening.

"Do you have any idea where he might be?" Nemo asked, his voice gentle. "We haven't been able to find him."

Mist frowned. "I don't, but I can help you look."

"That'd be great, Mist," Nemo said, then he looked back at me. "I'll let you go, Ember. The breakfast bell should be ringing soon."

I stood, and Wolf, Lee, Sable, and Kai stood, too. My head was full of thoughts about Mist and Hawk.

"Em!"

Wolf's call startled me back to the present. We were outside, and I'd started toward the clinic, but the four of them were standing on the path, watching me.

"Where are you goin'?" Wolf asked, a familiar edge to his voice.

"The clinic." I furrowed my brow. Why was he talking to me like I was trying to get out of my chores? It made my hackles rise, and I tried hard to keep from reacting.

"No, it's breakfast time." His eyes narrowed into a glare. "You need to come eat."

I'd genuinely forgotten where I was going, but the way he was talking ignited my stubborn anger. "I'll get something later."

He stalked toward me, and I had to fight the urge to retreat. "No, you're coming now."

"I can make my own decisions, Wolf."

His face darkened. "You clearly can't take care of yourself," he said in a low, angry voice as he approached me. "So, no, I don't think you can make your own decisions."

"What are you so fucking mad about now?" I snapped, my temper leaking out.

He stared at me, eyes flashing. "You're supposed to be talking to me, to be tellin' me the truth. And you still aren't."

"When have I not told the truth?" I threw my arms out, frustrated.

"About Hawk and your arm!" he snapped. "Why would you hide —"

"I wasn't tryin' to hide it!" I fumed.

"Really," he drawled, the word oozing with sarcasm.

Behind him, Sable, Kai, and Lee approached, their eyes flicking between the two of us.

"I'm not lyin'," I tried and mostly failed to temper my voice.

He scoffed sarcastically, and the hurt that went through me nearly bowled me over. Why did it bother me if he didn't believe me over this one stupid little thing? He didn't believe me about a lot of far bigger things.

"Fine," I hissed, recklessly ignoring the anger darkening his expression. "Don't believe me. Believe whatever you fucking want. That's all you do, anyway."

"That is not fair, and you know it, Ember Cutler. Now get your ass over to the canteen so you can eat something."

"I'm not hungry," I spit out, stepping backward.

"Wolf," Sable's voice sounded like a warning.

"I'm not askin'," Wolf's voice dropped to a dangerous growl.

"Wolf!" Sable caught Wolf's arm as he started to reach for me.

Wolf spun on his heel but stopped just as quickly as soon as he faced Sable. They stood there, staring at each other, Sable's hand still wrapped around his upper arm. The tension felt thick.

"We can bring her food back," Sable finally spoke, his voice low.

Wolf jerked free and strode off toward the canteen without even glancing back.

"Two godsdamn Wolfs," Kai muttered, stepping closer to Sable. "You okay?" he asked in a lower voice. Sable nodded, giving him a wan smile.

I started back toward the clinic, and Lee began walking with me. I halted, still brimming with frustration. "Lee, please, just go to the canteen."

His eyes narrowed, hurt flashing across his face, but from behind him, Kai spoke up, "Tuck's there, Lee. She'll be fine."

I didn't wait, turning and striding away. I waited on edge for Lee to ignore me, but when I glanced back, he was walking toward the canteen with Sable and Kai. Embarrassment itched across my skin. Why couldn't I get along with my brother? And while I was at it, why couldn't I just let a healer put fucking salve on my back? It'd only been one day without my crew, and I already missed them so much it hurt.

When I approached the clinic, Tuck was sitting on the porch. He frowned. "Where's everybody else?"

"Going to breakfast," I muttered, stomping up the steps and slamming the door behind me.

The new window was open, letting cool, fresh air in. I couldn't smell the blood or Madame's scent anymore. My quilt was neatly folded on the exam table. I carefully spread it out, checking for the bloodstains, but Kai had removed them completely. My chest felt tight.

The door opened, and I glanced up, but it was just Tuck. He approached the table, still frowning, as I folded my blanket.

"What's goin' on?" he asked.

"Nothin'."

He exhaled heavily through his nose. "Lemme guess. You got in a fight with Wolf?"

I chewed my lip and didn't answer.

"Look, you probably already know this, but your brother does not handle feelin' helpless very well."

I turned and started flipping through my notebook to see if I needed to restock any of my tinctures.

"He's worried about you," Tuck added after a few seconds.

"I can take care of myself," I muttered, trying not to think about how I'd completely fallen apart and begged for help last night when I was covered in blood.

"Wolf used to say the same thing," Tuck sounded amused. "Then he'd get a dead-end lead on you and end up gettin' shitfaced and starting a brawl."

I tried not to think about how I'd gotten shitfaced and tried to fight Brimstone.

"When I first met him, it was right after Moab. Scar told you about that, right?" I gave a short nod, and he continued. "He was real fucked up, and not just physically. He thought you were dead; he'd been shot three times, and the grief and trauma of it made him lose the ability to speak. I'd heard *about* him but never met him. Scar and I go way back, and I was between jobs, so she asked if I wanted to join her new crew with the infamous Wolf Cutler."

I shot a startled glance at him, and he grinned. "Yeah, your brother made quite the name for himself. I've never met anyone who could track a person down so fast. I was a cocky bastard and made the mistake of underestimatin' him once I saw he was all bandaged up and couldn't speak. We went out to a bar one night, and some guys started tryin' to pick a fight with him. I tried to step in and help, and they thought I was his bodyguard." I must have looked confused because he paused, then explained, "In our line of work, the strongest survive. He had a reputation of bein' dangerous, but he *looked* weak—covered in bandages and unable to speak. If he *had* hired a bodyguard, it would mean he *was* weak, and whoever took him down could take his place."

My fingers had stilled on the pages of my notebook as I listened. These stories they were sharing about Wolf brought up so many complicated emotions I couldn't even begin to sort through.

"Your brother went outside and beat the shit out of all three men with one arm in a sling and without saying a damn word." Tuck huffed a laugh. "It was one of the most badass things I've ever seen, and people in New Salt still talk about it. Though nobody besides our crew knows he almost died from internal bleeding afterward."

My heart lurched, and I tried to calm myself down.

"Honestly, I think he was even scarier when he didn't speak, but only our crew knew why. Scar taught him and the rest of us sign language, but it was almost a year before I heard him speak out loud." He paused again, and I glanced over to see him smiling sadly. "He's a good man, your brother, but he's got his demons. Try not to judge him too harshly."

I turned back around, flipping the pages without really seeing them.

"So why aren't you at breakfast?" Tuck asked.

"Just didn't want to," I muttered.

"Alright."

I glanced at him, startled.

"If I know anything about you Cutlers, it's that you won't ever do anything unless you want to, so if you don't want breakfast, I'm not gonna try to talk you into it," he said, heading toward the door. He paused on the threshold. "Let me know if you need any help with anything."

In the silent, empty clinic, I shut the notebook with a loud thud and leaned my elbows on the counter, digging my fingers into my hair. What the fuck was wrong with me? All I wanted was to be *normal*. I felt like that feral kitten from the barn, biting every hand regardless of whether they were trying to help or hurt. Would I have still been like this if Dune hadn't died? If I hadn't been exiled? If I had never met Juck?

I hissed a frustrated breath through my teeth. The door abruptly opened, and I turned, expecting to see Tuck or maybe my brother, but instead, Mist stepped through the door. I froze, but she quickly crossed the clinic and approached me, catching my hands and squeezing.

"Are you okay?" she asked, her wide eyes worried.

"I'm fine," I said, startled.

"Bo—Ember, did Hawk really hurt you?" Her distress bled into her voice.

"He just grabbed my arm, Mist, I'm okay."

She studied my face, and the silence stretched.

"I'm sorry," the whispered words slipped out of my mouth, and her eyes widened. "I'm so sorry, Mist. I should've... I should've—" A sob choked me, and she released my hands to hug me as the tears I'd held back all morning escaped.

"It's not your fault, Ember," her voice was tearful but firm.

"I can't... I hate myself for... for hurting you—"

"You didn't hurt me," she corrected me. "You *never* hurt me, Ember. You kept me from breaking completely."

"I never... never stood up to her," I sobbed.

"If she knew what your healing power did for me... and all the others... I think she would have stopped summoning you," Mist said, her voice gentle. "Every time you healed us and gave us a moment to breathe, you stood up to her."

"I didn't—"

"If you need to hear it, I forgive you. I don't blame you, but you have my forgiveness."

I didn't feel I deserved that, but I didn't say anything. After a moment, I pulled away, and she let me go. I dug one of Sam's handkerchiefs out of my pocket and swiped at my face.

"Can you tell me everything that happened with you and Hawk?" Mist asked.

I took a deep breath, and then I did. I didn't leave anything out, and the furrow between her brow deepened as she listened. When I finished, she stared thoughtfully at the exam table for a few seconds.

"I could see him grabbing your arm, but the other stuff? That seems so out of character for him. Even if he was real mad."

I didn't know what to say, so I shrugged.

"I checked the bottles," she added. "There's a good dozen of Madame's scent missing."

I sucked in a breath, trying to soothe the nausea.

"They won't get any more, though. I poured the rest down the outhouse hole." She grimaced. "Smells like someone made shit cookies."

A wild, potentially manic giggle escaped my lips, and she looked at me in surprise. I tried to stop, pressing both hands over my mouth, but the hysterical laughter kept coming.

"You okay there?" she asked, but a wide grin spread across her face.

"Shit. Cookies," I got out.

Mist started laughing, too, and soon, we were both clutching our stomachs, tears of laughter streaming down our faces. The door opened, and we both looked over to see Tuck standing there, his eyebrows nearly touching his hairline.

"What the hell?" he asked.

Neither of us could answer him, and he glanced between us, his lips twitching even as his brow furrowed.

"Should I be worried?"

"Shit cookies!" Mist wheezed through giggles.

The baffled look on his face set us both off again.

CHAPTER 29

Maybe laughter was its own kind of healing magic because I felt much better after we managed to calm down.

"You want to go out for drinks tonight?" Mist asked, swiping at her face. "I don't know about you, but I could use a drink."

"I'd like that," I said, warmth curling in my chest.

"Hell, why wait? You want to go at noon?"

I grinned. "Yes."

She laughed. "Alright, I'm gonna go do a little bit of work, and then I'll see you in a couple hours."

Mist gave Tuck a little wave as she left. He returned it, looking amused. I took a deep breath and went back to working on my inventory. The sunshine poured in through the window Wolf installed, warming my skin.

As though I'd conjured him with my thoughts, the door opened, and Wolf and the rest of his crew entered. Wolf approached, his lips pressed firmly together, and handed me my breakfast.

"Why didn't you notice your arm hurting?" he asked in a strange, flat voice.

I blinked, startled enough to be honest. "I'm used to hurting."

He stared at me for several breaths, his expression closed, but his eyes raging with emotion. Then he turned and stalked back out of the clinic. I stood holding my food, staring at the door, and hating the uncertainty coursing through me.

"He's trying," Scar murmured as she passed by to go to the sink.

I turned to see the rest of the crew watching me, and my heart tripped over itself. I dropped my eyes and unwrapped my breakfast.

"How's your back feeling?" asked Sable.

I kept my eyes on my food but paused to think about it. It still ached, but it was duller now. "Little better."

"Good." Sable sounded pleased. "You can keep that salve."

I inhaled my food so I could get back to work. Scar and Lee went outside. Sable asked to help, so I gave him the job of making more tinctures to soothe a cough while I started cleaning the inside of the cabinet that housed my tools. Kai helped Sable with the tinctures, and Tuck sat in a chair and started oiling one of his guns. After we all worked in silence for a while, my tense shoulders dropped back down, and I stopped twitching whenever one of them made an unexpected noise. A few patients came in with minor injuries. I rarely had super busy days now that the hold population was smaller. Time passed quickly, and soon Mist was striding through the door again.

"You ready?" she asked with a grin.

When we stepped outside, Wolf, Scar, and Lee looked up from their seats on the porch.

"Where are you goin'?" Wolf asked.

"Out." I inwardly winced as the word came out curt, and Wolf's eyes narrowed.

"We're gettin' some drinks at Hydro," Mist clarified.

Wolf's expression didn't lighten, and I had to remind myself I was *not* asking for his permission. I was an adult, and I could make my own decisions.

"Be back later," I said as breezily as I could manage, catching Mist's elbow and tugging her down the steps.

"Ember—" Wolf started to growl but cut off with a grunt as someone elbowed him in the ribs.

I kept going, my ears straining for any sound behind us, but when I finally glanced back, they were still sitting on the porch. I let out the breath I hadn't realized I'd been holding.

"Your brother seems like... a lot," Mist said.

"That's 'cause he is," I muttered.

"Makes sense that he's protective, though," Mist added, and I glanced at her in confusion. "Since someone's been attacking you?" She raised an eyebrow.

I blew out an annoyed breath. "Yeah, I guess."

Mist laughed lightly. "Well, c'mon, we're gonna go have fun for a couple hours, and we're not gonna think about brothers, exes, blood, or dungeons."

"What about shit cookies?" I cut my eyes sideways with a smirk.

She playfully shoved me. "Don't get me started giggling again."

⟳

Hydro felt different in a nice way. A mix of people sat inside, and the low murmur of conversation filled the room. Some of Nemo's guards were present, but the clientele wasn't primarily guards like before. Everything looked clean and bright.

Mist and I sat at the bar, and the drinking began. It was soon clear that Mist was drinking to forget just as much as I was. She made a game of it, and after a couple drinks, I realized I was having *fun*. My body felt loose and relaxed, laughter flowing and grinning so hard my cheeks hurt.

"This is so much better," I told Mist.

"Better than what?" She wrinkled her nose in confusion.

"Without Zip."

Understanding flashed across her face. "You caused quite a stir by pickin' him."

I winced and took a large drink.

"Hawk told me Mac asked him and his crew to keep an eye on you if you were there with him," she continued, and my heart started beating faster. "He asked the foreman, Silver, to keep an eye on you, too. I guess he made it pretty clear he'd fuck Zip up if he hurt you."

"You sure it wasn't Trey?" I asked, eyebrows raised.

"No, definitely Mac. I just heard rumors when I was in the dungeon, but I heard Mac beat the shit out of him while you were in solitary."

I stared at her. "What?"

She shrugged. "I don't know if it's true, just heard there was a brawl at Mootzie's cause Mac and Zip got into it."

I dropped my head into my hands, letting my hair shield my face, and tried to remember if Mac had looked beat up when he brought me water and food in that cell. I hadn't noticed anything visible, but the light was so dim and I was so panicked.

"Heard another rumor that Zip was found with a bullet in his head in the woods," she continued, her voice casual. "Guessin' that was you or Trey."

"That one was Trey," I got out.

"Good riddance, I say," she muttered, taking a drink.

I stared down into my drink, miserably replaying the events of that night. I hadn't even tried to fight back when Zip cornered us in the woods. I'd immediately started trying to manipulate the situation, to find a way to cooperate, to put my head down and *survive*. I'd done the same thing with Madame when she had a gun to Trey's head.

"Wow, I know how to bring the mood down," Mist groaned.

I forced a smile that felt stiff. "No, it's okay."

"Fuck, and I said we weren't gonna think about exes."

I tried hard to shove all those dark thoughts back down. "I don't know if we've drunk too much or not enough."

She laughed and waved her hand at the bartender. "I vote not enough."

Several drinks later, I couldn't remember why I'd been sad earlier. Mist and another woman were drunkenly singing a ridiculously lewd song, and I was laughing as I watched when a familiar voice spoke near my ear and scared the shit out of me.

"Havin' fun?"

I yelped, twisting on my stool and forcing Lee to catch me before I fell.

"Stop fuckin doin' that!"

"What? Keepin' you from fallin' on your ass?"

"No, sneakin' up on me!" I glared at him. "You need a damn bell."

"A bell?" His eyebrows rose.

"To jingle," I tried to pantomime a bell ringing, "when you walk."

He grinned. "I'm offended you think I'd make a bell ring by walking."

I still sat on the stool, but he stood between my legs, holding onto my waist, and I kind of liked it.

"We need you back at the clinic," he said, his eyes still sparkling merrily, "but I'm thinkin' you might be too inebriated to heal—"

"I can heal just fine."

I slid off the stool, and the room tilted. Lee caught my arm as I listed to the side, trying to steady myself.

"Yeah, I'm doubtin' that."

"Oh fuck you," I said, jabbing a finger into his chest.

"Whassgoinon?" Mist asked, slurring the sentence into one indistinguishable word.

"We need Freckles at the clinic," Lee answered.

Mist squinted at him. "Freckles?"

"Your drinkin' buddy," Lee grinned.

Mist glanced at me, realization dawning across her face. "Freckles!"

"Don't you start." I glared at her, but she just giggled drunkenly.

"You need a hand gettin' home?" Lee asked, and it took me a second to realize he was talking to Mist.

"I'm not goin' home yet," she threw her arm around the older woman she'd been singing with.

Lee laughed, "Alright. Have fun."

He wrapped an arm around my waist and steered me toward the door. It felt like we were moving far too fast, the world around us blurring.

"If you can't heal, that's okay. Sable can stitch the kid up."

"What kid?" I demanded.

"Uh… one of the older ones? Colt?"

"What happened?"

"He said he was practicing knife throwing."

"The fuck?" I stumbled over something, and Lee's arm tightened around my waist.

"Don't worry, I already volunteered to teach him."

I came to an abrupt halt, glaring at him. "Don't give my kids knives."

He grinned at me. "They already have knives. I'm just gonna teach 'em how to use 'em right."

I scowled and shoved him away, wobbling, but stayed on my feet. "I can walk just fine by myself."

"Can you?" he chuckled.

I started moving, concentrating hard to go in a semi-straight line. Lee walked next to me, looking increasingly amused.

"Quit smil—"

My foot went into a small hole, and I went down on my ass. He didn't even try to catch me, watching with a shit-eating grin.

"Fine, huh?"

I swore at him, and he laughed again.

"You're walkin' like a baby fawn."

I tried to keep glaring at him, but for some reason, that struck me as hilarious, and I erupted into giggles again. His eyebrows raised again, and he grinned crookedly.

"Baby fawn," I repeated, tears of laughter filling my eyes.

"C'mon, Freckles," he pulled me up and wrapped his arm around my waist again.

"You don't need to say 'baby,'" I tried to explain, still giggling. "Fawn means baby. You're sayin' 'baby baby.'"

"Drunk you is a lot more fun than drunk Wolf."

"I'm a lot more fun than Wolf *all* the time," I corrected him, tilting my head to grin at him as we walked.

"That might be true," he agreed.

I studied his face as he smiled at me. It was really unfair how attractive he was. His full lips curved into an amused smile as I blatantly admired him. His cheekbones were so high, and I loved how they caught the light and highlighted the sharp planes of his face. He raised an eyebrow.

"Something on my face?"

"Your cheekbones."

His other eyebrow raised. "My cheekbones?"

I abruptly stopped walking and shifted to face him. His other hand caught my waist, steadying me as I reached up to hold his face in my hands.

"These." I stroked my thumbs along the pronounced bones.

His eyes darkened, his fingers flexing on my waist, but his voice seemed deliberately light when he spoke. "How much did you drink?"

"Enough to not think about dungeons and exes," I parroted Mist's words.

"Dungeons and exes," he repeated thoughtfully.

"Not Trey." I paused, realizing how much easier it was to say his name when I was drunk. "Zip."

"Wait, Zip is an ex-boyfriend?"

"Not anymore, 'cause he's dead." It really wasn't funny, but I started giggling again. I dropped my hands from his face, but he didn't let go of my waist.

"How'd he die?"

"Trey shot him." I shrugged, then noticed a group of chickens nearby. "Look at that rooster!"

Lee glanced at the chickens with a frown. "How come?"

I screwed up my face in disbelief. "Cause he's so pretty!"

He snorted. "No, how come Trey shot Zip?"

"He hit me. No, wait, that was before. It was—" I cut off abruptly as it finally occurred to me in my drunken state he would not be happy about this.

Lee's fingers tightened on my waist. "It was why?"

I wrinkled my nose. "I don't want to tell you."

His eyes narrowed into slits. "Why?"

I needed to—fuck, what did Sam call it? De-something. I stood on my tiptoes and twined my arms around his neck, watching his pupils dilate in surprise.

"Don't be mad at me, right now," I pleaded. "You can be mad at me tomorrow."

He didn't respond for a moment, but then he sucked in a deep breath through his nose and let it out his mouth. "That's not fair," he said, but his voice sounded lighter. "You know I can't stay mad when you use those big green eyes on me."

I widened my eyes even more, hoping I looked pathetic and not ridiculous. He groaned, which I assumed meant I was successful.

"C'mon, we need to get to the clinic before—"

"Oh fuck!" I gasped. "I forgot about Colt!"

I took off and heard him swear as he scrambled after me. He caught up fast and ran beside me, holding my forearm so he could pull me upright every time the world started tilting. As we approached the clinic, I saw Wolf, Scar, and Tuck standing on the porch. I stopped in the yard, bending over with my hands on my knees, trying to catch my breath, but that threw me off balance, and I almost went face-first into the dirt. Lee caught my arm again as I giggled breathlessly.

"What the fuck?" Wolf snapped.

"Yeah, not sure how helpful she's gonna be," Lee said.

"I'll be fine!" I shoved away Lee's hands, striding unsteadily toward the porch.

"You're drunk," Wolf said, disapproving like I was still ten years old.

"I knoooow," I drew the word out as I went past him and into the clinic.

Sable and Kai looked at me, eyes narrowed, then at Wolf. Colt was sitting in the exam chair with tears on his face, his bloodied hand wrapped in a bloody cloth.

"Guess I'm stitching—" Sable started, but I interrupted.

"No!" I pointed a finger at him, scowling. "I got it."

I didn't miss the disbelieving looks they both gave me, but I marched over to the sink and grabbed the soap, only to immediately drop it in the sink. I swore under my breath and snatched it, only to have it squirt out of my hands and across the floor, stopping by Sable's boot. Sable picked it up, his fucking perfect eyebrow arched, and I started giggling again. He walked over and deposited the soap into my hand.

"I can stitch—" he tried again.

"I said, I got it!"

Thank the gods, I managed to wash my hands without further incident. Colt watched me with wide eyes as I approached him, wincing as I smacked my hip on the corner of the exam table.

"Bet you a drink this does not end well," Kai said, not even trying to whisper.

I ignored him as I gently took Colt's bloodied hand. The large gash in his hand healed quickly, leaving a faint scar. I carefully inspected it to ensure it looked okay, then released him. He thanked me and clambered down from the chair. Wolf and his entire pack were staring at me, eyebrows raised, so as I backed toward the sink, I smugly flipped them all off with both bloodied hands.

"Alright, I take it back," Kai smirked.

Lee, Tuck, and Scar grinned, but Sable and Wolf continued to frown.

"How much did you drink?" Wolf demanded.

"Enough to not think about dungeons and exes," Lee answered for me.

"Yeah," I chirped, "that much."

"You should drink some water," Sable said as I scrubbed my hands.

"Okay, mom," I muttered.

Someone behind me snorted. I scrubbed off all the blood and then nearly fell over as I bent to dry my hands on the towel. Kai lunged toward me, but I caught myself giggling when he scowled.

When I headed for the door, Wolf snagged my arm. "Where the fuck do you think you're going?"

"I saw some wild plantain outside the other day, so I'm gonna harvest it."

He frowned but released me. They followed me outside like ducklings as I wandered around the clinic collecting the broad leaves. They were strangely quiet, just watching me, and eventually, I couldn't take it any longer.

"So who's fucked who?" I asked, gesturing to all of them.

"Ember!" Wolf barked as the others let out surprised bursts of laughter.

"What?" I grinned as my brother's face reddened. "I'm just curious."

"Wow," Tuck said dryly, raising his flask toward Wolf before taking a sip, "you are fucked, my friend."

That made me start giggling again, and Wolf ran a hand through his hair with a groan. I tripped on a stick, and Scar caught my arm, steadying me. Impulsively, I threw my arms around her and hugged her. She let out a startled laugh and hugged me back.

"I thought we weren't talkin' about exes," Lee chimed in.

I made a face. "Oh, right." I paused, staring into the distance. "Do you ever get scared that something's gonna bite your dick when you're peeing in the woods in the dark?"

Lee and Tuck laughed so hard they folded in half.

"Em, what the fuck?" Wolf sounded horrified.

"Not somethin' I have to worry about," Scar answered, and we smirked at each other.

"I never did *before*," Kai muttered. "I'm gonna think about it every time now, though."

"Drink more water," Wolf ordered, handing me the water cup he was carrying around.

I rolled my eyes, but I took a drink, watching over the rim of my cup as they kept staring at me. "Why are you all lookin' at me like that?" I finally snapped.

"Like what?" Lee asked.

"Like you've never seen me before."

"Well, we've never seen you this... uh... smiley," Kai said.

"Well, maybe you should try bein' less of a dick," I shot back, making Lee snort.

"Kai did scrub all the blood out of your quilt," Wolf reminded me.

That sobered me slightly. I wrinkled my nose and looked back at Kai. "Okay, yeah. Thank you for doin' that."

His eyebrows raised, but he simply replied, "You're welcome."

"How come that quilt is so special?" Tuck asked.

"It was Trey's," I answered, my voice wobbling.

Tuck's eyes softened. "Ah."

"You want to tell us about him?" Wolf murmured.

"Nope," I answered quick, dropping to pick some more plantain.

"Em—" Wolf started gently, but I could not do this, right now.

"Please, Wolf, I just... I just want to be *not* sad for *one* day."

Wolf stared at me, his throat working. When he spoke, his voice came out rough, "Okay."

They all looked at me with heavy sadness in the brief silence, and I wracked my brain for something to chase it away.

"I want to hear the most embarrassing stories about Wolf."

"Oh, buckle up," Lee said, grinning as Wolf groaned.

"We got plenty of those," Kai agreed.

They launched into stories, and I listened with rapt attention as I worked, slowly putting together who my brother had grown up to be. They painted a picture of a man who was smart and stubborn as hell, who was serious until you got to know him and discovered his dry sense of humor, a man who sometimes took things too literally and had trouble shifting his focus, a man who could not and would not be stopped when he set his mind to something; and a man who loved his friends like family.

I healed a few people between stories, and by the time the dinner bell rang, I was mostly sober. In the dining hall, Nemo came by and gave us an update about Mac and the crew. When he told us that everything was going according to plan and they would be back tomorrow, I couldn't stop the wide smile that spread across my face.

I didn't stop smiling until we returned to the clinic. I stopped short at the sight of my bed on the main floor, surrounded by bedrolls.

"Why is my bed down here?"

"Cause someone fucking attacked you last night." Wolf sounded exasperated. "You're not sleeping upstairs by yourself."

I glared at him, anxiety crawling back up my throat. "I want to sleep in the loft."

"Why?" he asked, but in a much more gentle way than I was expecting.

I shifted on my feet and picked the most uncomplicated reason to give. "I'll probably have nightmares and wake you up."

"No offense, Freckles, but you wake us all up from the loft, too," Lee said, nudging me with his elbow and my face heated.

"Can you sleep down here tonight? We can talk about other options tomorrow." Wolf's voice was even, but there was an edge of tension in it. I glanced up at him, and I couldn't deny the worry in his eyes.

"You can't snore louder than your brother if that's what you're afraid of," Kai added.

"Shut it, Kai," Wolf rolled his eyes.

"You want all of us to cram into the loft with you instead?" Tuck asked, smirking.

I had no doubt they could keep this up for hours. I blew out a frustrated breath and gave up. "Fine."

As annoyed as I felt, the relief that swept across my brother's face made me feel *good*.

CHAPTER 30

I did some random cleaning to kill time and channel my anxiety into something productive until bed. Wolf and his crew did their usual evening routine of playing cards, but they did so on the porch since the bedrolls and my mattress were already laid out on the floor. I sternly reminded myself we'd been sleeping in the same building for days. The only change was that I was on the same floor now. It wasn't like I thought any of them would hurt me. It just felt... intimate. I liked the separation of my loft. It made it easier to keep them all at arm's length. Well, except for Lee, who had somehow become the exception.

It was just getting dark when they came inside, and Wolf asked if I was ready for bed. I knew they were going to bed earlier than usual for my benefit, but I pretended not to notice. I went upstairs and changed into my sleep shorts and oversized T-shirt. When I came back down, I noticed for the first time that they all just changed in front of each other, simply turning their back for a bit of privacy. I washed my face and teeth in the sink, and when I turned around, I caught Lee watching me from where he was unbuttoning his flannel shirt, revealing the muscled plane of his stomach. His heated gaze was on my bare legs, but it crawled upward until he finally met my eyes. My eyebrows raised, but he didn't look even slightly embarrassed that I caught him. Instead, he held my gaze, and his dark eyes flashed with a challenge. Uncertainty swept over me, and I hesitated, but he cocked an eyebrow and smirked, and *something* came over me. My body flooded with warmth as I raised my hands over my head and stretched, knowing my shirt rode up and exposed my midriff and my breasts strained against the fabric. His throat worked, and his eyes moved across my body, lingering on every curve like a caress. A new tension stretched taut between us when he met my gaze again, sending a shiver across my skin.

Wolf began talking, breaking the spell. I climbed onto my mattress, unsurprised, to find that Wolf was on my right and Lee on my left. Tuck waited by the light switch until everyone was settled and flipped off the light. In the darkness, my anxiety about these new sleeping arrangements seized control again. I burrowed under my quilt and pretended I was up in the loft. I'd been so tired earlier, but now I was wide awake. Time slowed to a crawl as I lay awake under my quilt, listening to everyone's breathing even out in sleep, but I couldn't get my body to relax.

I pulled the blanket off my head and looked over at my brother. In the dim light of the woodstove, his sleeping face looked peaceful. I turned to the other side and bit back a startled curse when I met Lee's dark eyes.

He grimaced and mouthed the word "sorry." I glared at him, but that only made him smile. We lay there silently, watching one another for a while. My anxiety seemed to settle a little, and I wondered again when his presence had turned into something comforting.

He shifted and reached out toward me. I narrowed my eyes suspiciously but didn't move. He brushed a stray piece of hair from my face, and then his fingers lightly trailed down my cheek. His hand was warm, and the physical touch made my lungs ache with longing. He gently brushed his thumb across my lips, and a shiver ran over my skin.

I think about kissin' that smartass mouth of yours far too often.

He smirked like he knew I was remembering what he'd said and stroked his thumb across my lips again. Impulsively, I captured his thumb with my lips and pulled it into my mouth, trying not to laugh when his eyes widened in shock. I swirled my tongue around his thumb, and his entire hand flexed, his eyes darkening. I pursed my lips around his finger, sucked lightly, and *heard* his breath catch.

He pulled his hand back, and I released him, but my smirk died at the intense look on his face.

"Outside. Now," he breathed.

I blinked, suddenly anxious. I couldn't tell if he was mad, but I got to my feet as quietly as possible and followed him to the door, picking up my boots. Somehow he opened it without making a damn sound. I stepped outside and shoved my feet into my shoes, and he shut the door behind us and did the same. Then he strode to me, grabbed my wrist, and tugged me along with him. My stomach sank. He sure seemed angry.

He found a quiet, narrow space between two buildings, one of which I was pretty sure was still empty. He marched into the shadows, dragging me behind.

"Lee—" I tried nervously.

He spun around. "Are you tryin' to kill me?" he demanded, eyes flashing.

"No—"

"What the fuck was that?"

Anger flared. "What, so you can flirt with me, but I can't flirt with you?"

He stared at me, disbelief written all over his face. "Freckles, flirting is harmless fun. That was way more than flirting."

The embarrassment and rejection stung like a fresh wound. I crossed my arms across my chest and spoke stiffly, "I'm sorry I misread things. I won't do it again."

His brow furrowed, and he just stared at me again. When he didn't say anything after several breaths, I went to walk around him to go back to the clinic, only to get spun around again. My back hit the wall, and his entire body pressed against me.

"No, godsdamnit, you're not walkin' away," he growled in my ear, making goosebumps break out across my body. "You are unbelievable. Did you seriously take that to mean I didn't want you?"

My skin flushed hot with frustration. "I don't know what the fuck you want, Lee!"

He seized my wrist and dragged it down and—*oh*. My hand slid across his hard length, straining against his pants, eyes widening. I had to resist the urge to squirm to alleviate the sudden ache between my legs.

"Does *that* feel like I don't want you?"

"So why the fuck did you yell at me?" I hissed, jerking free before I did something stupid like stroke him.

"I did not *yell* at you," he pulled back just enough to look me in the eyes. "But I was playin' in the shallows, and you fuckin' jumped off the cliff. I'm tryin' to be careful with you—"

"I don't need you to be *careful* with me," I snapped.

"You're still grieving," he said, his face grave. "I'm gonna be careful."

"Well, maybe I just want to forget about everything for a little bit. Maybe I just want to fuck someone. Have fun."

He frowned. "So what, you just want some casual sex?"

I stared at him, my chest heaving. "That's all I have to offer, Lee."

"But you *are* offering?"

"I just..." I struggled to get the words out past the lump in my throat, "I just want..."

"What do you want, Freckles?"

"I just want someone to touch me," I finally got out miserably. "I'm so tired of bein' *alone*—"

His lips crushed into mine as his body pressed me against the wall, yet I couldn't help but notice he was being careful of my back. I was startled for half a second, but then I kissed him back just as fiercely. I pushed myself onto my toes so my hands could slide into the wild hair escaping the tie holding it. He ground his hips into me, making every nerve ending in my body come alive.

"I'm more than willin' to touch you," he rasped. "You wanna feel good, Freckles?"

I arched into him, seeking that friction, but he interrupted me by seizing my hands and pinning them against the wall above my head. One large hand easily spanned both my wrists, holding me in place while he reached down to grip my chin with the other. I stared at him as he tilted my head up, breathing hard, my entire body thrumming with need.

"I want an answer, Freckles," he purred. His voice sounded dark, but it didn't scare me. Instead, heat pooled in my stomach and smoldered through my veins. "You wanna feel good?"

"Yes," I whispered.

"Yes, what?" The asshole's mouth twisted in a smirk.

I glared at him. "What? Do you want me to say 'please'?"

His smirk widened. "A little politeness never hurts, but no, I want to hear that mouth describe all the things you want me to do."

"My *smartass* mouth?" I cocked an eyebrow, experimentally tugging against his grip on my wrists, but he didn't budge.

His eyes looked black in the dim light, and he smiled wide, his teeth flashing. "Yes, that one."

I could feel my doubt, self-consciousness, and grief threatening to rise, but I had just enough alcohol left in my system to ignore it.

"I want you to make me come until I'm dripping all over your fingers," I breathed, my mouth curling into a smirk when surprise flashed across his face again.

"Smartass, filthy mouth," he teased, grinning.

My nipples drew tight, and he released my chin to kiss my neck, still pinning my wrists to the wall. He wasn't particularly tall, but I was particularly short, and he easily took control of my body. His teeth nipped my skin where my neck met my shoulder, and I gasped, but his tongue followed, soothing the pain away. His free hand slid down my body, stroking my sides, and even though he stayed on top of my shirt, his touch made me shudder. My tongue traced his lips, demanding entry, and he parted them for me. When I brushed his tongue with mine, he made a low sound in the back of his throat that made me ache. I wanted more. I wanted him to touch me everywhere, to chase away the heavy sorrow on my skin. I wanted to feel good without any strings attached. No deep emotions, no baring of my soul, just pleasure.

His tongue stroked into me mercilessly, and I tilted my head, deepening the kiss. His hand moved from my side to my breasts, fingertips trailing over my hard nipples and tracing circles around them. The worn fabric of my sleep T-shirt made just enough of a barrier between our skin to be tantalizing. His mouth abruptly left mine, and I gasped as his lips closed over one fabric-covered nipple, his tongue flicking out and twirling, wetting the thin fabric enough to cling to my skin. When his mouth moved to my other breast, the cool night air mixed with my wet shirt made a moan escape from my mouth. He repeated his ministrations to my other nipple and grazed the hard nub with his teeth, making me jolt and my core throb. He chuckled, and then he was kissing me again, tongue insistent and demanding. Every time I moved, my wet shirt dragged across my nipples, and I had to bite back a whimper.

His hand traveled down to grip my ass, pulling me even tighter against him. "I've been dreamin' about getting my hands on you like this," he groaned.

"Then put your hands on me," I demanded.

"Gods, you're bossy," he mused, pulling back to grin at me.

"You told me to tell you what to do." I tried to pull my wrists free again, but his grip tightened. I glared at him, but he just looked amused. "If you're not up for it, I'm sure I could go wake up Tuck," I added with false sweetness.

Emotion I couldn't quite read flashed through his eyes, but it was gone as quickly as it came.

"Don't put words in my mouth," he said smoothly, and then he grabbed the waistband of my sleep shorts and yanked me closer, his hand gliding south. "These damn shorts."

"What's wrong with my shorts?"

"You look good enough to eat is what's wrong with them."

A shiver went through me at his words, then his fingers grazed across my clit, and I gasped, bucking my hips.

"You're so wet for me, Freckles," he groaned, his breath hot against my neck.

"Don't—" I shuddered as his fingers moved, thumb circling my clit, "—stop."

"Stop what?" His fingers went still, and he grinned mischievously at me.

"You're so mean," I hissed.

"Maybe I just like seein' you all flushed and worked up and beggin' me for it," he murmured in my ear.

"I am *not* beggin'—" I gasped as he plunged a finger inside of me.

He kissed me again, mouth open and wanting, and I gladly gave him everything. I longed to touch him, but every time I tried to pull my hands free, his grip just tightened on my wrists.

"I think you're already drippin' all over my fingers." His teeth grazed my earlobe.

"Don't you dare stop."

"So bossy." He nipped at my neck again.

I tilted my hips, and his fingers hit a spot that made me gasp.

"Oh fuck!" I whispered frantically.

"Right there?" he purred, curling his nimble fingers and making every part of my body seize.

"Lee! Oh gods, yes."

His fingers picked up the pace, thumb rubbing against my clit, and within seconds I strained against his hold on my wrists, lightning flashing white behind my eyelids. I gasped in a breath, but his mouth captured mine, muffling my cries. His tongue thrust into my mouth, mimicking the stroking movement of his fingers. He tilted his head, fastening his lips and pressing me harder against the wall. I could barely breathe, my entire body rigid and trembling as the pleasure washed over me in waves.

As the heady rush began to fade, a thought occurred to me, and my eyes popped open in a sudden panic. I broke our kiss and looked down at my body, terrified I would see my power lighting up the entire alley like a beacon, but there was no glow emanating from my skin and no golden light surrounding us. I froze, trying to process the twisted mess of emotion that swept over me. Lee's fingers stilled, and he pulled back enough to see my face.

"Are my eyes glowing?" I asked in a hoarse whisper.

His brow furrowed. "No?"

I tried to swallow the lump in my throat. "Oh," I said in a small voice.

"You okay?" he asked, breathing unsteadily.

"Yeah," I lied, and then my face crumpled.

"Hey," he murmured, releasing my wrists and withdrawing his hand from my shorts so he could wrap me in his arms. "What's wrong?"

"I'm sorry," I sobbed into his shoulder, hating myself.

"You don't need to apologize, Freckles."

"I hate this," I managed to get out. I had to believe that Trey didn't realize how much losing him would destroy me. I had to believe he didn't know I would be so broken.

I would never promise to love you and then leave you.

I hated Menace for those words he'd planted in my head. I hated that he made me resent Trey for dying—as if he had any fucking control over what happened.

"I'm guessin' that's the first time you've been with someone since Trey?" Lee asked softly.

I nodded, squeezing my eyes shut as fresh sobs choked me.

"It's okay, Freckles." He pressed a kiss to my hair and then my forehead. "It's okay to grieve."

All of me wanted to withdraw, to get out of here and create some space so I could go cry alone, but something held me back.

It's okay to need people. Trey's voice echoed in my head, and I wondered with sudden horror if he'd been trying to prepare me for losing him.

I would never promise to love you and then leave you.

I shoved that cold voice out of my head and wrapped my arms around Lee's neck. He pulled me close, murmuring soft, gentle things, and I cried.

"I'm sorry," he said after I managed to calm down a little, and the sadness in his voice was enough to make me look up at him.

"For what?" I asked

"Just… everything," he sighed, raising his hands to cup my face. "We should go back before Wolf comes out on the warpath."

I followed him back to the clinic, adjusting my rumpled clothing and swiping my wet face as I went. As I climbed back onto my mattress, Wolf stirred and sat straight up, his eyes narrowing.

"I just had to go to the bathroom," I lied in a whisper, and his face relaxed.

I bunched Trey's quilt in my fists and pulled it up to my face, closing my eyes. I felt wrung out physically and emotionally. I wasn't sure how I'd feel about what I'd done with Lee tomorrow. I wasn't sure how I felt *right now* about what I'd done with Lee. No, that was a lie. I felt everything: grief, desire, guilt, fear, attraction—all of it together at once.

I jumped when a hand touched my arm, but when I peeked out, Lee had scooted slightly closer, his dark eyes on me. His arm slid further under my quilt to find my hand, lacing our fingers together and making my chest ache.

It's just physical. I tried to remind myself, but my fingers curled around his, anyway.

CHAPTER 31

W hen I woke the next morning, Wolf was already out of bed and building up the fire. My head throbbed with pain as I sat up, a reminder of how drunk I'd gotten yesterday with Mist. Most of Wolf's crew was still asleep, but I glanced at Lee to see he was awake and looking up at me. My face heated as we locked eyes, the memory of what we'd done last night sizzling in my mind—intensified by the fact I'd broken down in tears *again*. The urge to drop my eyes, shrink back, and push him away felt like it was choking me, but I forced myself to tilt my chin up and hold his gaze. A corner of his mouth lifted, and his eyes shone with approval.

I climbed out of my mattress, stepping carefully over sleeping bodies, squinting through my headache. I shoved my feet in my boots and headed outside to use the outhouse, but Wolf followed me outside.

"How you feelin'?" he asked.

"Headache," I muttered, rubbing my arms covered in goosebumps. I hadn't grabbed my coat as I'd planned to run to the outhouse and back, and the morning air was heavy with a chill that coated the ground in frost.

"Here," Wolf shrugged out of his jacket and handed it to me with an exasperated glare.

"I'm just—" I tried to protest.

"Just take it, Em," he said, but a smile lurked in the corners of his mouth.

I took it, eyeing him as I shrugged it on. Things felt... different this morning, and I wasn't sure why. I tried to remember everything I'd said yesterday, and while some of it made me cringe, nothing stood out as particularly meaningful. When I left the outhouse and returned to the clinic, he was still standing on the porch, watching and waiting.

"I don't think someone's gonna attack me in the outhouse," I said, unsure if I was annoyed or amused.

He frowned. "That's where I'd hide if I were tryin' to get someone."

I wrinkled my nose. "Please tell me you wouldn't be in the hole."

He huffed a laugh, "I've hid in worse places."

"Gross."

"Come inside. We'll get you some medicine for your head."

"It doesn't work."

He stopped and turned back to me, his brow furrowed. "What doesn't work?"

"Pain relievers." I grimaced. "They don't do anything to me. The only thing that works are narcs, but I can't take those, either."

"Why?" he asked.

I hoped I concealed the surge of panic as I fumbled slightly. "They make me sick," I lied, internally wincing. I hadn't thought before bringing up the narcs. Hopefully, my old excuse would hold.

"Well, that sucks," Wolf said, surprising me.

"Yeah, it does," I agreed, relieved.

I followed him inside, my mind drifting back to Menace. What had he said? I'd shut him out? Is that why he could only reach me if I were drugged? Or if I was reaching for Trey?

You have no idea what I've done for you.

My stomach did a nauseating flip. What had he done? And how did I shut him out? Was I still doing it? I hated not knowing. I hated how that conversation had thrown me off kilter.

Who the fuck was he? What did he want?

"Ember!"

I jumped and looked up at my brother, who was standing by Sable, looking at me with raised eyebrows.

"What?"

"I just said your name about six times," he grumbled. "I asked if you wanted to go to breakfast."

"Oh, sure."

"First, have someone put some salve on your back," Sable said, his expression firm.

I swallowed hard. "It doesn't—"

"I can tell when it hurts," he interrupted me. "You walk differently."

I took a deep breath, unreasonably angry that he could tell, and lied, "It really doesn't hurt."

Sable's eyes narrowed, his entire expression darkening. Wolf glanced at him, and a corner of his mouth lifted, which irritated me even further.

"Now you've done it," Kai said, quietly sing-song, and Tuck snorted.

"You've been the only healer here, so the others have deferred to your judgment about your health." Sable's voice was so stern it reminded me of Pa. "But you're not the only healer here now, and I can see through your bullshit."

Everyone looked amused, as if this was entertaining, and I bristled. "I don't—"

"I've seen you put your own health at risk about two dozen times since I met you, and it's clear you've been abusing your role as a healer to avoid being examined by anyone. I cannot, in good faith, let that continue."

I gaped at him, at a loss for words. How *dare* he—

"I'm not trying to antagonize you. I'm trying to do *my job*." Sable crossed his arms over his chest, staring at me. "You should know that since you're also a healer."

I glanced at Wolf, but he shook his head. "I agree with Sable, Em. You can't keep treating your body like it's invulnerable."

"I'm not!" I snapped.

"You are."

I sputtered for a moment. "I don't have to listen to any of you. This is *my* clinic—"

"You do, actually," Kai cut in from where he was leaning against one of the wooden braces holding the loft up. When I met his gaze, he smirked like he was enjoying this, which made my blood boil. "You're Wolf's ward for these two months," he said.

"I am not a child!" I seethed.

"Then stop acting like one," Kai shot back.

Well, fuck my good morning. I thought we were on better terms now. Why were they pulling this bullshit now?

"Is this just because of the fucking bruises?" I asked Wolf, my voice sharp with irritation.

"Em, this isn't a punishment," he said, and I hated that the gentle tone of his voice made my eyes prickle.

"This is not a punishment," Sable agreed, his voice softening slightly. "You said you're used to hurting, and I believe you. I believe you didn't notice the pain in your arm because you were forced to learn how to ignore pain, but now you need to re-learn how to recognize your body's limits. We're going to help you do that."

"I don't want your help," I ground out, hating how exposed I felt.

"I know," Sable replied, "but it's not up to you."

I turned to Wolf again, trying to calm myself down. "Wolf, I really don't—"

"Emmy, all we're asking is that you get some salve on your back," he cut me off. "Do you want me to help you? Or maybe Scar? When your crew returns, you can have one of them do it if you want."

My eyes found Lee. He was hovering near the sink in the kitchen, his face grave. He was the only one who didn't seem amused by this. When he met my gaze, he grimaced.

"Lee can help me," I said, pretending not to see the shock and suspicion in my brother's face.

Wolf's eyes narrowed as he turned toward Lee, but I stormed up the ladder and waited. There was a whispered argument downstairs, but after a couple of minutes, Lee appeared, frowning at me. He pulled himself into the loft and crossed the barren floor to stand before me.

"Not a fan of bein' used as a pawn to get back at your brother," he said in a low voice.

"I'm not," I muttered.

He raised an eyebrow, and I realized he was partly right. I knew it would bug Wolf the most if Lee helped me, but the primary reason was genuine.

"Okay, it's not *just* that," I sighed and lowered my voice, "You're just... I get least anxious about you..." my face felt hot "... touching me."

His expression lightened as he pretended to be shocked. "You don't say?" he teased, but I couldn't muster the energy to be playful.

"What do you think?" he asked after a few moments. "Is it okay if I put that salve on?"

I took a deep breath and turned around, holding my shirt against my chest, my heart rate increasing despite my best efforts. I waited for him to lift the hem of my shirt, but instead, he leaned down and gently kissed my shoulder. I sucked in a startled breath, but his lips touched my neck next, and my knees felt suddenly weak. He slid a hand into my hair, gathering the thick waves into one hand and using his hold to turn my head so he could kiss my neck again. My eyes fluttered closed as he explored my skin with his lips and tongue.

"I don't think... this is how you... do the salve," I managed to whisper.

"Maybe not the way Sable does it," he murmured against my neck. "I like doing things my own way."

He kissed my neck again, just under my ear, before releasing my hair. I heard him open the tin, and then he lifted my shirt and spread salve over my scars, his fingers gentle. Every so often, he leaned forward to kiss my shoulders or neck, and I eventually realized he was doing so whenever I started to tense up—he was trying to soothe me.

"I want to kiss every freckle you have," he said low in my ear.

"I have freckles everywhere," I whispered, curling my lips into a smile.

His hands slid from my back to trail across the bare skin of my stomach. "And I'm gonna find 'em all."

I let my head fall back to rest on his shoulder, a shiver running through me at the heated promise in his words. *You're just starved for touch.* I told myself as my entire body felt alive under his fingers. *It doesn't mean anything.*

"We better go back downstairs before somebody comes up here to check on us," I said.

"I'll go down. You should get dressed," he said, releasing me, but when I turned around, he stepped into my space, seizing my face with both hands and kissing me until I was breathless. Then he pulled away, a smug smile on his face.

I stared at him, trying to catch my breath, and he winked before disappearing down the ladder. *It's just physical.* I reminded myself sternly, turning to pull my clothes out of my dresser. *It means nothing.*

෨

Breakfast was quiet at our table. I refused to acknowledge Sable and Kai, gave Wolf and Scar one-word answers, and tried to pretend I wasn't acting like a sullen child.

The quiet continued at the clinic. I had no patients to distract me, so I threw myself into cleaning. It felt like the first day with Wolf and his crew in the clinic all over again—me cleaning and all six of them watching me like hawks watching a mouse. I ran out of things to clean and started re-organizing the tincture bottles for the hundredth time... this week.

"Didn't you just do this yesterday?" Tuck asked, breaking the silence.

I clenched my jaw and didn't respond.

"Pretty sure you did it the day before that, too," Kai said.

"Pretty sure I've seen you do this at least six times," Wolf added.

I set the tincture bottle I held on the shelf with more force than necessary.

"Leave her alone," Sable said. "She does it when she's nervous."

For fuck's sake. I turned on my heel and stomped to the door.

"Where are you going?" Wolf demanded.

"To check on Clarity," I said without looking back, slamming the door behind me.

I didn't get far before I heard someone catching up to me. I glanced back, assuming it would be Lee, but instead met Wolf's angry gaze.

"Ember," he snapped, "will you quit throwing a temper tantrum?"

"I'm not," I snapped back.

He let out a sarcastic laugh. "You forget *I* was the one who always had to deal with your temper tantrums? I know one when I see one."

My face heated, his words stinging unexpectedly. "Well, good news, you don't *have to* deal with me anymore."

"What?"

"I'm not your burden to bear anymore."

He swore under his breath and grabbed my arm, forcing me to

stop and face him. "What?"

"Do you need me to spell it out for you?" I hated the angry tears pricking in my eyes. "No one is making you *deal* with me. I don't know if you're a fucking masochist or what, but you don't *have to* keep parenting me anymore. I'm not a child."

His brow furrowed as he stared at me, but he said nothing. The longer he waited, the more frayed I felt.

"Do you think I hated raising you?" he finally asked, a rawness to his voice that startled me.

"Didn't you?" I shot back.

"No, Em." His eyes were pained. "No."

We stared at each other for a few breaths.

"I hated having no fucking clue what I was doing. I hated that I lost my temper so much. I hated that you didn't have Mom, who would've done a hell of a lot better job than me, but not you. Never you."

I looked away, trying to hold myself together, and he released my arm.

"Did you always think I hated raising you?" He sounded gutted. "I mean, did you think that before Dune died?"

I wasn't sure I could speak, so I just shrugged. The silence continued for a long time, but I stubbornly refused to look at him.

"You were so small," he finally said in a rough voice. "Any time I put you in the cradle, you'd just cry and cry. Pa said you'd cry yourself to sleep eventually, but I couldn't just lay there and listen to you sob. So I'd get up and bring you back to our pallet and hold you, and you would immediately grab my shirt or my finger." His voice grew more choked. "Then you would fall asleep, so long as I was there next to you, and you could hold onto me. I was so terrified of your trust in me, but at the same time, I loved you more than I ever knew it was possible to love someone."

"I always felt like a burden," I said, low.

"You weren't a burden." His voice cracked. "I always assumed I'd have children in the future, and now that I won't get that chance, I'm even more grateful I at least got you."

I stared hard at the mountains, but my voice wobbled when I spoke, "Did you—"

"Wolf! Bones!"

We both whirled around to see Lee and Smith running toward

us. My heart slammed into overdrive.

"Mac's crew is under attack," Smith reported, his words clipped with worry.

"What?" My stomach was somewhere on the ground.

"By who?" Wolf immediately asked.

"The Voiceless," Lee answered, his face sharp with urgency. "Nemo wants to know if we can go."

"Gear up," Wolf ordered without hesitation, and Lee immediately took off and headed back toward the clinic.

"I'll tell Nemo. We'll meet you at the gate," Smith said, relief visible in his ruddy face as he left.

Wolf started striding toward the clinic, and I had to jog to keep up.

"I'm coming with you," I said.

"No," he replied, his voice stern.

"Wolf, I can help!"

"No."

"If someone gets hurt, I can—"

"You're not gettin' anywhere near the Voiceless, Ember."

"Why?" I demanded. "I've seen them before—"

He stopped in his tracks and seized my shoulders. His face was serious, and I saw fear flash through his eyes. "They're lookin' for you, Em. They put out a bounty for you. Now that I know about your power, I understand why, and I won't risk it."

My mouth dried as fear went through me like a lightning bolt, but I forced myself to shake it off. "I don't care. I'm not stayin' here."

"You think this is a coincidence that they're attacking your crew, right now? They're baiting you. They *want* you to come."

"Wolf, I can't stay here if my crew is in danger!" I tried to say it fiercely, but my voice shook.

"We have Sable. He can stabilize any injured people until we get them back here."

"Wolf, please!" I was clinging to his forearms now.

"No, Em," he released my shoulders, his voice gentling. "I'll bring 'em back, okay?"

I opened my mouth to beg him, but he took off at a sprint. I scrambled after him, swearing, but he was faster than me. By the time I reached the clinic, panting and nauseous, they were just finishing strapping on their gear, faces grave.

"I'm comin' with you!" I said between gasps.

All six of them simultaneously gave me the exact same stern and furious expression.

"Absolutely not," Lee snapped.

"No," Sable said at the same time.

Scar and Tuck looked at Wolf, but he was shaking his head as he buckled his tactical vest. "No, Em."

"I can help!" I protested, panic choking me.

"Ember, I said no." Wolf's voice sharpened. "Will you just listen to me *for once!*"

"You can't force me to stay here!" I raged, losing myself to desperation. "I'll follow you—"

Wolf stopped what he was doing to glare at me. "Don't you dare," he growled.

"I'm not staying behind! My crew might be *hurt,* and—"

Wolf strode up to me and grabbed my wrist, jerking me further into the clinic, and I assumed he was going to speak to me privately.

"Wolf, I really can—"

My words cut off as he grabbed my other hand and brought it around one of the wooden posts holding up the loft. I realized far too slowly that he was zip-tying my hands together. I tried to jerk away, but he was too strong, and the ties cinched tight on my wrists.

"Wolf!" I snapped, straining against the ties, layers of panic rising to choke me.

"I meant it, Em," he said firmly. "I'm not lettin' you anywhere near the Voiceless."

"Okay, I'm sorry. I won't follow you. Just please cut me free." I hoped I sounded calm.

"Yeah, I know better than to believe that," Wolf said, grabbing his gear.

"Wolf, I'm serious." My voice shook. "Cut me free."

He ignored me, continuing to get ready, and I realized he wasn't fucking around. He was going to leave me here tied up. My stomach flipped inside out.

"Wolf!" He didn't even turn around to look at me. "Wolf! Please!"

He walked to grab his pack and a long, deadly rifle. The rest of his crew stood by the door, watching quietly. I met Lee's pained eyes, desperate.

"Lee, please don't leave me tied up. Please don't—"

My pleas cut off in shock as he turned his back on me and stepped out the door. Tears sprung to my eyes as the door swung shut behind him. Panic was building in my chest, and I met Scar's gaze.

"Scar, p-please, I'm not… not lying—"

She shook her head, her expression closed. "It's safer this way. I wouldn't put it past you to follow us."

"I can't… I can't be trapped in here—" I gasped.

"Wolf," Sable murmured.

"I'm not risking it," Wolf said, his voice a firm order.

Sable glanced at me again and frowned.

"Just sit tight, Em. We'll be back," Wolf said.

"Wolf, don't do this! Don't leave me here like this!" Tears spilled down my face. "I'm gonna… I can't be tied up! I swear I'm not lying—

Wolf started ushering the rest of his crew out the door, ignoring me, and I lost it.

"I swear to the gods, if you leave me here like this, I will never forgive you!" I shrieked.

Wolf turned and met my eyes briefly, but he just closed the door, leaving me a prisoner in my clinic again. For a moment, I stood frozen in disbelief, my eyes finding the space by the door where Vulture had sat and watched me work with Trey's blood staining my clothes and a manacle on my ankle.

Panic abruptly swallowed me. I fought against the ties, sobbing and trying to get my hands free until my wrists were burning with pain and slippery with blood. Like an animal caught in a trap, the only cohesive thought in my head was that I *had* to get free.

The next thing I knew, I was on the ground, resting my forehead against the wooden beam and sobbing hard. I hated Wolf for leaving me like this, but Lee turning his back on me hurt worse. At least now, I knew if it came down to me or my brother, Lee would always choose Wolf.

If any of my crew were killed—

I barely managed to choke back the bile in my throat, breathing in deeply through my nose, but my breath was coming faster, and I couldn't stop it. I tried to do Sable's trick of listing things I could hear, but Trey's bloody face filled my vision and—

⁊

"Em? Em, wake up. Please wake up!"

I cracked my eyes open and met Apple's tearful gaze. I lay in an awkward pile on the floor of the clinic with my hands still zip-tied around the beam. My wrists smarted with pain.

"Em! Em, can you hear me?"

Apple's little hands were on my face.

"I'm okay," I choked out.

"What happened?" she demanded, her little brow furrowing furiously.

"Wolf tied me up," I explained numbly, managing to sit up.

"Why?" she gasped, and I could see the betrayal I felt reflected in her eyes.

"So I couldn't go with them." My head pounded. "Apple, can you cut the ties?"

She nodded, her face serious, and got up to find a knife. It took her a while to cut through the plastic cord, and I tried to brace myself for getting accidentally cut, but the first time she slipped and nicked my wrist, I jumped. She immediately burst into tears, and I had to calm her down before convincing her to keep going. She got me a couple more times, the knife sliding on the zip tie, slippery with my blood. Finally, the ties fell off, and I brought my hands up to inspect my bloody wrists. I winced at the large amount of blood staining my sleeves. I'd put deep gashes in them from yanking against the ties and a couple lacerations that probably needed stitches. I shakily got to my feet and stepped around the beam, grimacing more at the blood smeared across the floor.

"How long has it been since they left?" I asked.

Apple wrinkled her nose like she was thinking hard. "Twenty hours?"

I looked out the window at the sunlight, lips twitching wearily at her attempt. It looked like it'd been maybe a couple hours.

Apple followed, attached to my side, as I went to the sink and started woodenly cleaning out the wounds on my wrists. The deepest lacerations were still bleeding a fair bit, but I wasn't going to deal with stitching myself up right now. My body would probably heal the wounds before I bled *too* much.

I've seen you put your own health at risk about two dozen times since I met you. Sable's earlier words ran through my head, but I shoved them away.

It hurt as I washed the wounds out, but I barely noticed. I felt removed from myself again. I understood why Wolf tied me up when he first abducted me, but tying me up *now?* I'd *begged* him not to, but once again, he saw my panic as manipulation. I couldn't keep doing this. I couldn't keep ripping out bloody pieces of myself to show him if he was going to pick and choose which ones he thought were real. I got my left wrist bandaged, but then I fumbled with the bandage on my right.

"Can I do it?"

I glanced at Apple, who looked up at me with huge, solemn eyes. I dropped into a crouch and held out my wrist, instructing her how to do it as she clumsily wrapped it for me.

Once it was tied, I got to my feet, jaw set with grim determination. "Go find Leda, okay?"

"Where are you going?" Apple whispered.

"To Nemo's," I answered.

෧෨

Nemo's house was full of people. They all looked startled when I came storming in, but no one stopped me. I found Nemo in his office with Smith and a handful of other people gathered around the large radio, their faces grim.

"What's happening?" I demanded.

The people around Nemo stared at me with wide eyes, but Nemo was studying me carefully, frowning. I knew I looked crazed. I'd tried to clean myself up a little, but my eyes were red and swollen, both my wrists were bandaged, and there was blood smeared on my clothes.

"What happened to your arms?" he asked.

"Nothing," I bit out. "What's happening?"

Nemo glanced at Smith and then moved around everyone to approach me.

"Come speak with me privately for a minute," he said, gently taking my elbow.

I debated refusing to move until someone updated me, but the kindness and patience in Nemo's face took the wind out of my sails. I nodded, and he steered me out of his office and into the kitchen. It was a small, enclosed space but cozy and homey.

"Ember, what happened to your arms?" Nemo asked again.

"It's just a cut," I said stiffly.

His eyebrows drew together. "On both wrists?" When I didn't answer, he pressed, "Did someone attack you again?"

"No."

His frown deepened. "Is it self-inflicted?"

"No! I mean...not intentionally..."

He simply studied me.

"Wolf tied me up in the clinic because I threatened to follow them," I finally admitted, hating that my voice wobbled.

The anger that filled his eyes surprised me. "He tied you up?"

I nodded. "I...sort of panicked and, um, fucked up my wrists."

"Can I see?" he asked, gesturing to my wrist.

The urge to flee filled me, and I hesitated but then slowly unwrapped the bandage on my left wrist and let him examine the lacerations I'd put in my skin. His jaw flexed, and his eyes narrowed as he inspected the wounds. I hadn't expected him to be angry on my behalf, and it flooded me with something like relief.

"I'll speak to him," he finally said, meeting my eyes. "This is unacceptable."

For some reason, that made me start crying—fat tears rolling down my cheeks—and his eyes softened.

"My father abused me for years," he said as he re-wrapped the bandage on my wrist. "I was often tied up, and to this day, someone grippin' my arm tight is still enough to bring up all that panic and fear."

I sniffled, watching him and wondering if that had anything to do with why he disliked clinics and healers.

"I know Madame and Vulture chained you up in the clinic," he added. "While I have the power to do so, I'm gonna make sure that doesn't happen again, alright?" He glanced up at my face, waiting until I managed a tiny nod. "Your brother is a good man, I think. I don't think he meant to hurt you, but even good men can make mistakes." He gave me a slight smile. "As I have many times."

He tucked the bandage in and released me, opening his mouth as though he would speak and then closing it again with a sigh. I pulled my arm back, waiting to see if he had more to say.

"I had a daughter," he finally said, his voice soft and pained. "I lost her and her mother when she was only eight. You remind me of her, and I must admit I occasionally find myself takin' the role of a protective father, and I apologize for that."

I wondered if this was what it felt like to have a father who cared, and my heart ached. The words spilled out of me in a shaky whisper before I could stop them, "My dad hated me."

The grief in his eyes made mine burn. "Parents not lovin' their children is somethin' I'll never understand. I'd do most anythin' to have mine back." He paused. "I think it's pretty clear your brother loves you, even if he makes mistakes."

I hesitated but then spoke, "Wolf said the Voiceless put a bounty out for me."

He took a deep breath and let it out slowly. "I figured they would eventually."

"Do you know why?" I asked, my stomach churning.

"The Voiceless are all about power, but they have none to wield besides fear. Their leader, he has a sort of power, but it's nothin' like yours." He paused, his face grave. "I would imagine he either wants to use you somehow... or kill you."

I shuddered. "Juck said he used to be part of the Voiceless."

Nemo's eyebrows raised. "Really?"

"Do they let people just... leave if they want to?"

Darkness flashed across his face again. "No."

I frowned, my mind spinning. It felt like the Voiceless had been lurking on the edge of my life for a long time, and I gathered the courage to ask a question that had been bothering me. "Does the Voiceless leader... could he be the one with mind powers?"

Nemo shook his head, but the unease on his face didn't provide much relief. "No, he doesn't have any powers like that. I'd never heard of such powers until Mac told me."

I stood silently for a few seconds. "You... you seem to know a lot about the Voiceless..."

It wasn't a question, but it was. He studied my face for a moment. "I was also a part of them, but not by choice. I escaped. Many are not so lucky." He took a deep breath. "I will share my story soon, I promise. With all of you."

I had a million questions, but the sound of running footsteps stole our attention. The door opened, and Smith stuck his head in.

"They're on their way back," Smith reported, worry evident in his voice. "They've got wounded."

My stomach dropped.

"Let's go to the gate, Ember," Nemo said, calm but grave. "Smith, alert the others."

CHAPTER 32

I couldn't stand still by the gate, so I paced, nervous energy running through me like an electric current. Apple came and tried to join the waiting group, but I got Leda to take her and the kids back to the canteen. I wasn't sure what was coming, and I didn't want them to see.

On one of my turns, I spun and nearly ran directly into Clarity. I stopped with a gasp, but before I could say anything, she seized my hands, her eyes going wide and completely black.

"Beware the gentle hand. The shadows cloak its biting smile!" she babbled.

"Clarity—" I tried to pull away, but her grip was painfully tight.

"The loom has woven a tapestry of lies," she continued, her voice rising hysterically. "These shadows owe him no allegiance."

I could hear the rovers approaching, and my heart leapt into my throat.

"In silence, the snare is set!" Clarity cried. "The snare is set!"

"Clare, it's okay," I tried to soothe her.

Her eyes returned to their normal color, but Nemo, Smith, and the other guards were all staring.

"Clarity!" Sky appeared, panting. "Sorry, Bones, she's so fast."

"It's okay, just... get her out of here."

Sky wrestled Clarity back as she continued to shout nonsense at me. I'd have to explain to Nemo what *that* was, but I focused on the gate slowly opening. The first rover roared through with Mac driving, and I almost burst into tears when I saw he looked bloody but mostly uninjured, but any relief I felt evaporated as I realized someone was lying unmoving in the backseat. I started running, vaguely registering that Wolf's rover came next, but Lee was driving it, and all the occupants were slumped over. Griz drove Wolf's second rover inside with more unmoving bodies, and Raven followed in the last rover containing her and Jax. They both looked rough but okay.

That meant—

"I'm sorry, Em," Mac's voice was desperate and rough. *"I tried to keep him safe."*

Oh fuck, Sam.

I scrambled into the rover almost before it stopped and hovered over Sam, fear choking me. His face was so grey, his body limp and eyes closed, but there were no injuries I could see.

"What happened?" I demanded, my shaking fingers trying to find a pulse in Sam's neck. It was so faint.

"We managed to take out their leader, but he was rigged with some sort of chemical weapon… or something. As soon as he fell, this thick black fog started hissing out of him like a fuckin' smoke grenade," Mac said.

"Never seen anything like it," Griz added gravely from the other side of the rover.

"It didn't hurt any of us except Sam and your brother's whole crew… minus Lee," Mac continued.

I glanced over at my brother's rover to see Lee bent over Wolf's unconscious form, and my heart felt like it was about to explode from pounding so hard. I needed to focus.

"Em, you can't—" Mac reached for me as I gripped Sam's wrists.

"Don't you dare try to stop me," I snarled at him.

He looked startled at my ferocity but withdrew his hands and didn't argue.

I called my healing power and let it flow into Sam, bracing myself for the pain of hitting that wall. *Please, please, please*—

I gasped as my powers connected with something, but it wasn't the barrier I'd felt before. It was a nauseatingly familiar roiling darkness that fought back—the Shadowbane. I poured my power into Sam, determined to win, and after several minutes, I felt it begin to shrink. I stared at Sam's face, barely daring to hope, but I could see the color returning to his face and his chest rising and falling as he began taking deep, steady breaths.

"Oh my gods," I breathed.

"Is it working?" Mac demanded, and I realized he had crammed himself into the backseat with us.

"It's working," I choked out.

The darkness vanished, but a wave of sudden, intense nausea went through me. I released Sam's arms, and my hands felt numb and prickly as though I'd slept on them funny, but I didn't have time to dwell on it because Sam opened his eyes and slowly focused on me with a grimace.

"Guess this is the part where you say 'I told you so,' ain't it?" he mumbled.

I threw my arms around him, squeezing him tight as I burst into tears.

"Did you... heal me?" he asked, hugging me back and sounding confused.

"I healed you," I sobbed.

"Em, your brother—" Griz started, and I jerked upright again.

"Let me out," I told Mac, pushing him gently but urgently.

He stepped out of the rover but caught my hands; his gaze focused on the bandages around my wrists.

"What happened?" he demanded, eyes flashing.

"Later," I said, pulling my hands free.

He glared at me, but I darted around him and ran to my brother's rover. Lee looked up and met my eyes, his usually tan face pale.

"I'm so sorry—"

"Do *not* talk to me," I hissed at him as I went around the other side to where Wolf was slumped in the passenger seat.

"Freckles, please? I'm sorry. Fuck, I'm so sorry."

I set my jaw and ignored him as I grabbed Wolf's wrists and let my healing power flow. It felt the same as with Sam, the same as with Lana, the same as with the whole fucking hold. It was the Shadowbane. I was sure of it.

"What the fuck happened to your wrists?" Lee leaned across Wolf's body like he was trying to examine my bandaged arms.

"Stay away from me," I snarled at him, and his eyes snapped to my face.

I didn't try to hide the pain and hurt and fury roaring through me as I held his gaze, and his face creased with distress. *Good.*

Mac appeared at my side, his entire body radiating tension. "What's goin' on?"

I wasn't sure if he was talking to me, but I had to focus on healing Wolf. The Shadowbane was fighting hard. It took a long time to crush it, but finally, that darkness vanished. I didn't move for a second, breathing hard.

"Em—" Wolf's voice was weak, but the color had returned to his face, and his eyes were open.

I released him without a word, and Mac took my elbow, steadying me as I moved to the backseat where Sable and Kai lay. Sable was closest, so I healed him first. I tried to ignore the nausea and the pounding in my head when the Shadowbane vanished.

"Em—" Wolf tried again as Sable slowly sat up with a groan.

"Don't you dare speak to me," I said through my teeth.

"Em, what the fuck happened?" Mac demanded in my head.

"I'll tell you...just... let me finish." Sweat trickled down my neck.

I felt him grumpily agree, and when Wolf tried again to speak to me, Mac snapped at him to shut up and let me focus.

As soon as Kai was healed, I started to storm to the other rover but took one step and had to cling to Mac's arm as the world spun violently.

"Ember, are you hurt?" Sable asked, his voice hoarse.

I glanced up to see Wolf, Lee, Sable, and Kai all peering at me, their faces a mix of worry, guilt, and regret. It didn't make me feel better. It made me want to cry, and that made me angrier.

"Fuck *all* of you."

I forced myself to start walking toward the other rover, but after a few steps, Mac was supporting most of my weight.

"Em, please?" He sounded so worried.

"They tied me up in the clinic." I knew he could feel my pain and fury and panic from the memory.

"They what?" he demanded, his fury rising.

"Let me finish healing first," I begged, trying to focus as my vision swam. *"I... I need you."*

He didn't respond, but his arm tightened around my waist, and he didn't let go as I healed Scar and Tuck. By the time I finished, my legs were trembling like they had after a full day of healing the sickness. Mac didn't hesitate, crouching to sweep an arm under my knees and lift me like Trey had done countless times. His face twisted in a worried frown.

"Ember, wait."

Wolf was on his feet, holding the rover's side for support. Mac paused for a moment, glancing at me.

"You want to talk to him?" Mac asked.

"No," I said fiercely.

"Em, c'mon—"

Mac started striding away with me in his arms. I heard Wolf shout after us, but I didn't look back, anger simmering in my veins.

"You want to go to the clinic? Mac asked.

"No." I didn't want to see my brother and his crew at all. "Can we go to the bunkhouse?"

"Of course," he murmured.

I lay my head on his shoulder and wrapped my arms around his neck. Nausea came and went in waves, and I closed my eyes, trying to breathe deeply through it.

"I can't tell what you're feelin'," Mac said quietly. "Did healing them... hurt you?"

"I think I'm just tired."

He was quiet for a few breaths. "You sure?"

"I'm okay, Mac," I murmured.

"So your wrists..."

"Wolf zip-tied me to one of the beams so I couldn't come with them. I... panicked... and fucked up my wrists trying to get free."

I could feel the rage radiating from him.

"I was so scared you all were hurt or... or worse," I admitted.

He took a deep breath and let it out slowly. *"I won't lie, I'm glad you didn't come with 'em, but tyin' you up... that's fucked up."*

"I could've helped," I said with a deep pang of hurt.

"I know you could've," he replied. *"But I think the Voiceless... I think they were lookin' for you."*

My skin crawled. *"Wolf said they were."*

"What?" Mac said out loud, his voice sharp.

"He said they have a bounty out for me."

"When the fuck was he plannin' on sharin' that?"

I opened my eyes so I could look up at him. His eyes were full of furious golden sparks, and I almost grinned. It was nice to not be on the receiving end of that look.

"I am not constantly mad at you," he rolled his eyes.

"Anymore," I corrected, my lips twitching. *"And that's all I know, but Mac, that weapon they used... it was the Shadowbane."*

I felt him tense, but his steps remained steady. "I was afraid of that."

"They weaponized it?" I asked, half hoping he would tell me I was wrong.

"Seems that way."

Fuck.

"Did it feel different from when you healed Lana or the rest of us?" Mac asked.

"Maybe?" I admitted, trying to keep most of the details out of my thoughts. I wasn't entirely sure why I was concealing it, but I didn't want him to worry. *"It was strong... stronger than Lana's."*

His jaw clenched, but he fell quiet. We reached the bunkhouse a few seconds later.

"You want to lay down?" Mac asked. "You can take my bunk."

"Will you sit on the couch with me?" I asked.

"Of course," he replied.

He carried me over and sat me on the couch before sitting beside me. I felt his surprise as I curled into his side, but it faded to a happy warmth. He slid an arm around my shoulders and shifted closer so I could lay my head on his shoulder. I felt awful, nauseous, shaky, weak, and exhausted. I'd never felt *sick* any other times I healed people from the Shadowbane. Tired? Yes, but not sick. I was grateful he was letting me lean on him.

"You sure you're okay?" he asked softly.

"I'm really glad you're home," I whispered.

His arm tightened around me. "Me too."

I wanted to keep talking to him, but I must have dozed off shortly after that because the next thing I knew, quiet voices were speaking around me. I kept my eyes closed, listening.

"—talk to Nemo soon," Griz said.

"He can wait," Mac replied, his arm tightening slightly around me.

"She okay?"

"I dunno," Mac's voice was so low I almost didn't hear it. "She said she was tired."

"You sure it didn't hurt her to heal me?" Sam spoke up, his voice rough.

"It didn't seem like it did," Mac responded. "Last time, it was real fuckin' clear it was hurting her."

There was a brief silence.

"Nemo lit into Wolf," Griz sounded darkly pleased.

"Good," Mac growled.

"There was blood all over the floor," Griz added. "Nemo said she probably should've had stitches."

The door creaked open, and then a feminine voice gasped.

"It's okay, Clare," Mac said in his soft voice. "We're all okay."

"I saw something right before you got back," she said, her voice trembling. "I don't remember all of it, but…"

"Is Em okay?" Raven cut in as Clarity's voice trailed off.

"Okay enough to eavesdrop, apparently," Mac answered.

I huffed, prying my eyes open. "Not my fault you're all bein' so damn loud."

Mac chuckled, but Clarity's eyes were swimming with fear.

"Are you okay?" she asked.

"I'm just tired," I tried to sound reassuring.

She moved through the crew to sit beside me. "Do you remember what I said?"

"Um, you said 'beware the shadows,'?" I tried to remember what else she'd said, but I'd been so focused on the rovers.

Clarity worried her lip between her teeth.

"What's wrong, Clarebear?" Mac asked.

"I don't know. I just… I just keep feelin' this sense of… of doom," she admitted.

"Isn't that kinda normal now?" Raven asked, and I'd never heard her speak so gently before.

Clarity frowned, and she looked so miserable that my heart ached. "Yeah, but this is worse than normal."

The door opened again, and Jax popped inside. "Mac, Nemo wants a debrief."

Mac sighed but removed his arm from around my shoulders and stood. Sam immediately took his place, and I turned to examine him more closely. Sam rolled his eyes and held out his wrist.

"Okay, fine, check me over."

I smacked him in the shoulder. "Don't pretend you didn't just almost die, you dumbass."

"For the record, I was not expecting chemical warfare."

"Black fog came out of his body?" I asked as I took his pulse.

"Out of his mouth and nose and ears and eyes," Griz answered. "Sam and your brother's crew all dropped immediately. Except for Lee."

"What'd the Voiceless do then?" I asked, my heart pounding.

"They left," Mac answered from where he lingered by the door.

I met his gaze, my anxiety spiking at his grim expression.

"I'll be back soon," he added before slipping out the door.

I turned my attention back to Sam. His vitals and appearance were about the same as before he'd left. He was still skinny and gaunt, nowhere near his regular, healthy self, but he didn't look like he was seconds from death anymore. I frowned. It was like I'd healed the weaponized Shadowbane, but *only* that. I hadn't healed any of the damage I had done to him when I healed myself through his body.

"Can I try something?" I asked him.

He narrowed his eyes, brow furrowing, but nodded, so I wrapped my hands around his forearm and let my healing power flow into him. Immediately my powers slammed into the wall, the pain making me suck in a breath through my teeth.

"Shortcake?"

I ignored him and kept pushing, my heart sinking. Why was it different before? Why had I been able to heal the Shadowbane but nothing else? The pain built, and tears gathered in my eyes, but I stubbornly kept going. Until Sam jerked his arm away, and golden light poured out of my hands, filling the room with blinding light before vanishing.

I blinked and blinked, and as my vision slowly cleared, I saw the others doing the same. Raven was tearing a bandage off her arm, and Griz lifted his bloodied shirt to look at his side. Jax's fingers searched his forehead.

"Well, that's one way to heal all of us," Raven muttered, showing the new scar on her bloody arm.

"Don't fucking do that again," Sam snapped, and I winced as I met his furious expression. "For fuck's sake, Emmy!"

"I don't understand why it worked earlier," I said, hating how helpless I felt.

"Fuckin' hell," Sam growled, but he dug a handkerchief out of his pocket and handed it to me. "Your nose is bleeding."

I pressed the handkerchief to my nose and scanned their worried expressions with guilt.

"Did you heal a bunch this morning?" Griz asked.

I shook my head, but then I noticed Clarity wringing her hands together, her face tense. "Clare, it's okay. I didn't get a lot of sleep while you all were gone," I hoped my face wasn't turning red as last night's escapade flashed through my mind, "so I might just be tired."

"Did you tell them about the attack?" Clarity asked, then cringed as everyone started demanding answers.

I sighed but told them about the attack at the clinic. I glossed over the details of how I lost my shit, but even still, when I finished, there was a heavy, tense silence.

"They still haven't found Hawk?" Griz asked, his voice dark.

"No."

Raven abruptly turned and stormed out of the bunkhouse. I glanced back at Griz, alarmed, but he was following Raven, a grim look on his face.

"Where are they going?" I asked nervously.

"To kill Hawk, I'd guess," Sam muttered.

"I don't know for sure it was him!" I protested.

"I bet it was," Sam said.

"Why?" I demanded.

"Because he was talking shit about you, and Mac already had a talk with him."

"Why did no one tell me?" I snapped.

"Because we handled it." Sam glared at me.

I leaned forward, my head in my hands and my elbows on my knees, letting my hair fall forward to shield my face.

"Anything else happen while we were gone?" Sam asked after a moment.

"Nemo turned the pit into a gathering space." My stomach churned.

"Sky hates it," Clarity said in a low voice.

I straightened, grimacing. "I didn't love it, either."

"How about you, Clarity?" Sam added. "What've you been up to?"

Her smile looked brittle, and she gave a half-hearted shrug. "Not much. Just hanging out with Sky and having nightmares about shadows."

I took a closer look at her appearance. Clarity's curly brown hair hung limp around her face, and her clothes were disheveled. I still didn't know her *that* well, but it suddenly occurred to me she usually looked more put together.

"Clare, are you okay?" I asked her.

She gave a slight nod, but her eyes were dull. I caught her hand and squeezed, and she finally seemed to focus on me. I knew she wasn't working at the brothel anymore, so why was she still living there?

"Why don't you move into the bunkhouse?" I asked her.

"I'm already enough of a burden," she mumbled.

"You're not a burden," I said, my voice firm. "Plus, if you stayed here, Raven would be around here more."

Sam gave me a sharp look, but I ignored him. I had a feeling I knew what arguments to use on Clarity—the same ones I knew would work on me. Sure enough, her cheeks reddened, and she averted her gaze. "I'm not asking her to stay with me."

"I know," I assured her. "But I doubt she'd stop coming even if you told her to. So why not move in here? You know Trey…" My voice cracked. "Trey would be so happy if you did."

Her eyes filled with tears, but she blinked them away, chewing on her lip for a moment. "Okay."

Sam sat up straight, and his eyes were wide when I glanced at him. "Okay?"

Clarity gave him a small smile. "Okay."

"Let's go pack up your stuff!" Jax leapt to his feet, beaming.

Clarity's smile grew slightly at his excitement. "Alright, let's do it."

The two of them left, Jax chattering happily, and Sam turned to me as soon as the door shut behind them.

"How the hell did you do that?" he demanded. "We've been tryin' to get Clarity to move in here for *years*."

I smirked. "Gotta know the right buttons to push."

His eyes narrowed. "You *would* know. The two of you are both stubborn as fuck."

I snorted, but my amusement swiftly died. "There's somethin' else that happened," I said, and Sam's face went serious at my tone. "You know how I told you I had a dream about Trey...a good dream?" He nodded. "I had another one... but it... it wasn't actually Trey."

"What do you mean?"

My voice grew progressively hoarser as I explained what had happened and how Trey had actually been Menace the entire time. I told him how my powers washed away his disguise and described his appearance to Sam, but he didn't recognize him. By the time I finished explaining, his expression was furious, and I was crying.

"I wan—wanted it to be... to be him."

"Of course you did," he murmured, hugging me. "I would've, too."

"I haven't told Wolf anything about this," I added. "I don't even know if I should."

"Me either," he muttered, running a hand through his short hair. "I can't believe he fuckin' tied you up."

"Yeah," I agreed faintly, the hurt flooding back.

He laced his fingers with mine and squeezed. After a few seconds, I rested my head on his shoulder. As we sat in comfortable silence, it struck me that I would never be able to return to life before I had this crew—this family.

More importantly, I didn't want to.

CHAPTER 33

Boots on the small steps outside caught our attention. The door opened, and Sam and I glanced up just in time to see Wolf walk through the door. Before I could react, Sam leapt to his feet, eyes flashing.

My brother held up both hands, palms facing us. "I'm not here for trouble."

Sam scoffed, positioning himself between my brother and where I sat frozen on the couch.

"Ember, are your wrists okay? Nemo said they might need stitches," Wolf asked.

I stared at my hands and didn't answer.

"I'm not sorry for trying to keep you safe, but I am sorry I tied you up."

Sam let out an angry noise from between his teeth.

"C'mon, man, I'm trying here," Wolf's voice sounded tense.

"You're gonna have to try a helluva lot harder," Sam snapped.

"I was tryin' to keep her safe," Wolf's voice rose. "She was threatening to follow us. Would you have wanted her there with the Voiceless?"

"No, but I never would've considered tyin' her up!" Sam shot back.

"What the hell else was I supposed to do? I didn't cinch 'em tight enough to hurt her. She would've been fine if she hadn't freaked out! Why the fuck did you do that, Em?"

Before I could even consider answering him, Sam exploded. "Are you fucking serious? When we first found her in that safe, she'd been in there with her hands zip-tied for *days*. She was fucking chained up in the clinic for over a week after Madame killed Trey! Chained! When we finally got her out eight days later, she was still wearing the same clothes stained in Trey's blood. So you tell me why you think she might've fucking panicked about being tied up in there!"

Halfway through his rant, I glanced up at them, stunned horror at Sam's tirade making me feel numb and weightless. Sam was glaring at Wolf, but Wolf's eyes were closed, and one hand pinched the bridge of his nose. My shoulders rose and crept forward, trying to retreat into myself. I hated that his expression made *me* feel guilty.

Wolf was quiet for a long time. "Em, I'm sorry," he finally said.

"I *begged* you." The words bubbled out of me, and I wanted to be angry, to scream at him, but instead, my voice came out thick with tears. I wished I could be more like Raven—fierce and strong. All I did was fucking cry lately, and I was so sick of it.

"I know," my brother's voice was steady, and mine was anything but, "I thought you were just trying to manipulate me."

I let out a bitter laugh, furiously wiping away tears. "All I've done since you got here is tell you the fuckin' truth, but you're never gonna believe me, are you?"

"That's not fair," Wolf argued, "Intentionally not tellin' me shit is the same as lyin'."

"I only haven't told you shit 'cause I fucking *can't*!" My voice rose.

"What? You can't just *talk?*" Wolf crossed his arms.

He didn't say it cruelly, but the question *hurt,* and I immediately lashed out. "I dunno, can *you?* Real convenient of you to forget about all those months when *you* were too broken to *talk.*"

His mouth pressed into a flat line as his ears turned red, and I saw the same hurt I felt flash through his eyes, but it didn't make me feel better.

"You know what? It doesn't matter. How about we make this real easy and just never speak again."

"Ember—"

I stood, strode into the bedroom, and slammed the door. I leaned against the door in the dark room, holding my breath as tears rolled down my face.

"For the record, I knew maybe an eighth of all this before you got here and even fewer details." I heard Sam say, and I could tell his voice was still angry, even muffled through the door. "The only one of us who knew more was Trey, and it took over six months for him to be there for her before she could tell him what happened. I don't think you realize how hurt she was when we found her. You've seen some of her scars, right?" There was a brief pause. "Well, the worst scars she has are ones you and I can't see, but Juck put 'em there just as much as the brand on her chest. You demanding she tell you all this on *your* time is like demanding a man without legs move across a room. Sure, he can get down on the floor and drag himself across with his hands, but it's gonna hurt, and it's gonna be fuckin' hard, not to mention humiliating. And how do you think he's gonna feel if you don't acknowledge any of that and instead just get annoyed at how long it took?"

Wolf said something that I missed, but Sam wasn't done.

"You're lookin' at all the shit she's *not* doin' or *not* tellin' you and completely missing how fucking hard she's working at what she *is* doin' and tellin' you. And lemme tell you, she's workin' fuckin' *hard*. You have to make a decision, man. Is she your sister who you want back in your life, or is she your prisoner who you're turning in for a bounty? Cause she can't be both, and you can't keep going back and forth between the two. It's not fair to her."

His words felt like they smacked me upside the head. That was a big part of why I kept feeling so off balance with Wolf, wasn't it? I could never tell if I was his sister or his prisoner. I wrapped my arms around myself and tried hard to keep my sobs quiet. I'd never heard anyone defend me like this until Mac stood up to Wolf and, now, Sam.

Mac had told me they knew me, and I believed it now.

"Alright," Wolf finally said, his voice so low I almost couldn't hear him. "I'm gonna head back to the clinic." He paused. "If she doesn't want to stay there for a while, I understand."

Sam muttered something, and I heard Wolf walk to the door. As soon as I heard the front door shut, I opened the bedroom door, startling Sam, who had been reaching for the handle.

"Sorry, hope I didn't overstep," he said, frowning at my tear-streaked face, but I threw my arms around him and hugged him again. He squeezed me tightly back.

"Thank you," I whispered hoarsely.

"Anytime, Emmy," he murmured.

We stood there for a few seconds before returning to the couch. I didn't doubt that any of my crew would stand up to Mac in a situation like that. I also knew Mac would never, but while these realizations were comforting, they also hurt. I couldn't stop remembering Lee just turning away from my pleas and leaving me behind. Vulture had always deferred to Juck and had followed Juck's orders, even if it actively hurt me. I wasn't going to be with someone like that again.

Sam sighed and wrapped an arm around my shoulders again. "I don't think your brother meant to hurt you, but the fact is he did, and now he's gotta deal with it."

I leaned my head on his shoulder. "Can I stay here tonight?"

"Of course," he answered immediately, then added in a lighter tone, "You wanna squeeze into my top bunk with me?"

"I might." A smile tugged at my lips.

The door opened again, and Mac, Griz, and Raven came in, their faces grim. My heart lurched.

"Did you find him?" I asked.

"No," Griz muttered.

"Why didn't you tell me about the attack?" Mac asked, crossing his arms, his gaze fixed on me.

"I was going to," I explained. "Just, a lot of shit happened, and then you had to talk to Nemo."

He let out a heavy breath. "Well, that's true." His eyes went distant, and his jaw flexed. "If Hawk knows what's good for him, he'll stay gone."

"We have good news and bad news," Sam announced. "Which one do you want first?"

Raven sat heavily on the couch next to me. "Good news."

Sam grinned. "You'll like this, Raven. Shortcake convinced Clarity to move in here."

"Really?" Mac asked, his face brightening.

Raven twisted to look at me, and the fragile hope in her eyes made emotion well in my throat. "She's movin' in?"

"Jax took her to go pack," I said, smiling.

Raven grinned, glancing up at Mac. I followed her gaze to see Mac grinning, too.

"How the fuck did you manage that?" Mac asked.

"Just a little emotional manipulation?" I wrinkled my nose.

"I'll take it," Raven said.

"What's the bad news?" Griz asked.

"The bad news is the Mental Menace has been pretending to be Trey in Shortcake's dreams."

Three pairs of horrified eyes snapped to my face.

Wearily, I recounted both dreams, though I didn't get into the details of what Menace had said about Trey. When I finished, Sam, Raven, and Griz angrily went off, raging about what they wanted to do to Menace. Mac, however, was still quiet, leaning against the wall, his eyes on me. Feeling guilty, I met his gaze.

"What'd he say that you aren't tellin' us?" he finally asked in my head.

I swallowed. *"I don't think I can say it."*

"Can you show me? Like you did before?"

I swallowed hard and let the memory run through my head. His hands dropped to his sides, fists clenching tight enough to make his knuckles white, and his nostrils flared. The anger emanating from him felt hot enough to spark a fire.

"That is so fucked up." His eyes flashed. .

"So what does he want?" Raven asked, cracking her knuckles aggressively.

"I have no idea," I admitted.

"Before, he seemed intent on coming here and getting you, right?" Mac asked, and I nodded. "But he didn't say anything about that this time?"

I shook my head, realizing with a sinking feeling I was now responsible for the Voiceless *and* Menace potentially attacking the Vault.

"Em, you're not responsible for what others choose to do," Mac said out loud.

"Alright, I see how this whole mind-reading thing is gonna be real fucking helpful with you," Sam muttered, and I elbowed him. "Quit stabbin' me with your pointy elbows!"

"You want to stay here tonight?" Mac asked.

"If that's okay," I said, feeling weirdly nervous.

"Of course, that's okay. You're welcome anytime."

"Wolf came in here while you were all gone," Sam said, and the room erupted into angry questions again.

Sam explained what happened with my brother, and I rested my head on the back of the couch, feeling drained. Why was I so tired? I carefully pulled up my mental shield, doing my best to ensure there weren't any cracks. Mac's eyes shot to mine suddenly, and I knew it must be working. I attempted an apologetic smile and let the shield drop enough to speak to him.

"I thought I should probably practice shielding... maybe it will help keep him out."

His expression relaxed. *"That's a really good idea."*

"Tell me if it slips?"

He nodded, and as the four of them talked, I tentatively let my mind go back to healing Sam, my brother, and his crew. I wasn't sure exactly what happened, but it'd almost felt like...

No, I must've imagined it. My powers had proved deadly to the Shadowbane over and over again. It must've been the adrenaline and the stress of healing while furious at my brother and his crew.

My skin crawled, the sensation like something slithering just under the surface, and I had to fight the urge to shudder. It had to be my imagination because it wouldn't make any sense if the Shadowbane infected *me*.

I fell asleep on the couch shortly afterward, sleeping hard until Griz woke me up after the dinner bell rang. I didn't feel like going to the canteen and potentially seeing my brother or Lee, so Griz fetched dinner rations for Sam and me. After dinner, Clarity arrived with her things and a very nervous-looking Sky in tow.

"I'm only stayin' here if Sky can, too," she declared, eyes flashing in a way that reminded me of Mac.

"Of course, Sky can stay here," Mac immediately answered, and the flurry of unpacking and setting up the bunks began.

Clarity took Lana's old bunk above Raven, and Sky took Exo's old bunk above Griz. Raven smiled more than I'd ever seen, practically beaming. She seemed to take every opportunity to touch Clarity, resting a gentle hand on her arm or brushing hair from her face. I had suspicions about Raven's feelings for Clarity, but they seemed obvious now. Clarity was comfortable with Raven, but I wondered if she realized precisely how Raven felt about her.

Sky stayed close beside me or Jax for most of the evening, but she slowly relaxed. She was still jumpy, but she'd spent enough time around Mac, Sam, and Griz to know they wouldn't hurt her. As the others figured out how to string Clarity's red silk curtains from the ceiling to give her some privacy, Sky huddled closer to where I sat on the couch. I shifted to wrap an arm around her thin shoulders, and she curled into me like a cat. With her head shaved, she'd been all sharp angles, but now her head was covered in little corkscrew-shaped black curls that softened her appearance.

One bunk bed remained for me, but I knew it had been Trey's bed. The grief rose, flooding through me. I wasn't sure I could sleep there, not without falling apart. Maybe I'd sleep on the couch, though I wished I had my quilt.

I paused. I could go get it.

My stomach twisted at the thought of seeing my brother and Lee, but anger washed it away. I didn't need to hide in the bunkhouse and sleep without a blanket because mine was at the clinic. They couldn't make me stay there. If they tried to keep me, Mac would break the damn door down.

I glanced at the doorway to the bedroom, where I could just see Mac and Jax, but they were all holding parts of the curtain in the air as Raven screwed hooks into the ceiling. I didn't want to bother them to ask if they'd walk me there like a child.

"You feel like takin' a walk?" I asked Sky instead.

"Where to?" she asked.

"I want to grab my quilt out of the clinic." I watched panic flash across her face and reassured her, "You don't have to come inside."

A small smile crossed her lips. "Okay."

As we put our boots on, Mac noticed us.

"Where you two goin'?" he asked.

"I gotta grab something at the clinic, and Sky's walkin' with me."

"You want more company?" he asked, a worried furrow between his eyebrows.

"No, we'll be okay."

He frowned but didn't push. "Okay."

"Come lookin' if we aren't back in fifteen," I added, managing a half smile.

"I'll come lookin' if you aren't back in ten," he promised.

When we stepped outside, the sun had almost disappeared behind the mountains, and the sound of frogs croaking was practically deafening.

"Must be spring," Sky said, rubbing her arms and shivering.

It was chillier than expected, and Sky only wore a thin T-shirt. I shrugged out of my sweater and handed it to her. She tried to protest, but I glared at her until she gave in and put it on. Goosebumps covered my arms, but I'd survive.

After a few seconds, Sky ventured, "Do you think the others—"

A shadowy figure appeared directly in front of us, materializing from *nothing*. Sky and I both came to an abrupt halt, and I grabbed her arm, ready to run, but the shadow seized my shoulders, and suddenly, we were *falling* through darkness. I tried to scream, but there was no air in my lungs; it felt like we were turning inside out. When it finally stopped, we were still in complete darkness, but there was a ground beneath my feet, and the sickening sensation had stopped. I finally managed to gasp in a lungful of air and screamed. The sound echoed around us in a horrifying way that seemed vaguely familiar. Sky was sobbing, and I pulled her tightly against my body. As the echo of my scream slowly faded, a dark laugh sounded from somewhere to our left. I jerked Sky behind me, turning to face the noise, my heart in my throat.

Light flared, blinding me, as a match lit a lantern, and once my eyes adjusted, I met Hawk's eyes. He looked awful. His face was pale and thin, and the whites of his eyes were red. As he moved, his motions were jerky and unsteady. My breath started coming faster as I realized where we were—the solitary cell far below the watchtower. Sky and I were inside the cell, and Hawk stood outside the bars, sneering at us.

"Hawk." My furious voice shook. "What are you doing?"

"I'm executing justice, Bones."

"Let Sky go," I snapped. "She hasn't done anything."

Sky stepped out from behind me, and Hawk's eyes widened like he hadn't noticed her, shock flashing across his face.

"What the fuck is she doing here?" he demanded.

"I don't know," Sky said, her voice trembling. "I was walking with Bones."

Hawk turned a furious glare at me. "You would find a way to

fuck this up, wouldn't you?"

"Me?" I cried. "You're the one who fucking dragged us here!"

"No," he said in a cold voice. "I brought *you* here, and just like always, you dragged an innocent person down with you."

My breath caught painfully in my chest.

"Hawk, please," Sky begged. "Please let us go."

He looked at her, and honest regret filled his face as he set the lantern on the floor and drew his pistol. "I'm sorry, Sky. I can at least grant you a quick death."

"What?" she gasped, and panic lanced through me.

"Hawk, she's innocent!" I shouted as Sky began to cry. "Just let her go. You can do whatever you want to me. Just let her go."

He started pacing, bringing a hand up to rub his forehead, and the pistol he held glinted in the dim lantern light. He muttered to himself, but I couldn't make out the words. I took a breath and attempted to *think*. A rumpled bedroll and a pack were on the floor in the hallway. I spotted a mug and a metal fork on the floor against the hallway wall.

"Have you been living down here?"

He glanced at me but didn't respond.

"If you let us go, you could come home." I softened my voice.

He started laughing, and the manic sound gave me chills. "They'll never let me back in the Vault."

"I could vouch for you. You haven't done anything past forgiveness yet, Hawk."

He swung suddenly toward us, and I lunged in front of Sky. Hawk slammed into the bars, the pistol clanging hard against the metal and making my ears ring. "I don't need your forgiveness, Bones," he snarled.

"Okay," I said, my voice shaking despite my best efforts. "Okay, you're right. You don't need my forgiveness."

He stared at me, his eyes wide, and I noticed his pupils were fucking *huge* like he was high on something.

"You have a power, don't you? You can... travel between places?"

"The gods gave me the means to bring you down," he sneered.

"Not Sky, though. She's innocent."

"No, Bones, don't!" Sky sobbed.

"Just let her go," I pleaded. "You're not a murderer, Hawk."

"No, *you're* the murderer!" he shouted, spittle spraying from his mouth.

Sky shrieked in terror, clinging to me.

"I am. You're right. I'm a murderer." I struggled not to cry, to *think* like Wolf taught me.

Hawk stepped backward, but the despair that filled his face made my stomach drop. "I'm sorry it had to end this way, Sky."

"Hawk, please," Sky begged, her voice panicked.

"Nemo sealed off this place." Hawk waved the pistol in a vague gesture around us. "No one will find you, maybe for decades. This will be your tomb."

I was struggling to breathe now. "Hawk, please. Mist still believes in you—"

His face twisted with fury, and I knew I'd fucked up by bringing up Mist. "Don't you dare say her name," he hissed. "I *loved* her. I had our life all planned out, and then *you* ruined everything."

"I'm sorry," I whispered, tears rolling down my face. "I'm so sorry."

"You stole everything from me." His voice shook. "So I'm gonna bury you where no one will ever find you."

He lifted the gun and pointed it at me, but Sky darted around me, throwing her hands out like she could catch a fucking bullet.

"No!" she screamed, and I think I was screaming too as I lurched forward, trying to snag the back of my sweater she wore.

The gunshot cracked like thunder, but at the same time, *fire* exploded from her hands.

I instinctively jumped backward, away from the blistering heat, and gasped as the fire completely enveloped Hawk's body. He screamed, beating at the flames consuming him. His gun clattered to the floor, but I focused on Sky.

She stood wreathed entirely in flames as though she was a creature made of fire and ash. The flames didn't seem to be hurting her like they were Hawk, but as she turned toward me, I realized she was clutching her chest where blood dribbled from a gunshot wound. I darted forward and grabbed her arm with one hand, only to release her with a cry of pain as the fire seared my skin.

"Bones!" she shrieked, her wide, terrified eyes reflecting the orange flames covering her.

"Put the fire out, Sky!" I cried, cradling my burned hand. "I can't touch you!"

"I can't!" she sobbed.

A part of my brain registered how strange it was that the blood simply ran down her skin, unaffected by the flames. I glanced at my hand, but the blistering burn covering my skin was very real.

Sky stumbled to one knee, gasping for air.

"Sky! You have to try! Try to put it out!" I pleaded.

"It's not... not working!" she wheezed.

I knew I should calm down; a good healer would be calm and talk her through this, but my heart was in my throat, and she was bleeding out, and I couldn't touch her because she was fucking *on fire*.

"Please, Sky! Put it out!" I hovered next to her helplessly.

"Help me!" she begged, blood dribbling from her lips.

"I can't!"

The flames surged even higher as though fueled by the panic I could see on her face. She crumpled to the ground; I forgot and tried to catch her again, hissing in pain and jerking back as my skin burned again.

"Sky!" I screamed.

She lay on her back with her face twisted in pain, struggling to breathe. I could see her fading away. The bullet wound looked like it'd probably gone through her lung. I tried to summon my power, to heal her with a burst of light like I'd done to other people before, but nothing happened.

"Sky, please try!"

Her eyes closed, tears still sliding down her face as her breathing turned into a gurgle. I screamed in frustration as I tried and failed to summon the golden light to my hands without touching her.

"Sky, no!"

It was just seconds later that her chest stilled and didn't move again. The flames abruptly extinguished, and I quickly grabbed her arm, bracing myself for it to be hot, but it wasn't. I shoved my healing power at her, but like with Trey, it simply evaporated into the air instead of seeping into her skin. She was dead.

I pulled her limp body into my arms and held her, sobbing broken apologies. Her clothes had burned away. She would be cold in this horrible cell. I tried to wrap my arms around her more, to keep her warm, ignoring the small part of my brain reciting the symptoms of shock at me.

The light in the room began to fade, and I glanced up. Nausea surged as I realized the lantern was lying on its side, broken, and the remaining light was coming from Hawk's burning body. He'd fallen against the rough rock wall, his body slumped to the side, disintegrating into char and ash. The smell suddenly hit me, and I gagged at the scent of burning hair and flesh. My throat ached from the smoke.

The fire faded to embers, throwing the room into darkness. I stared at the flickering orange glow, silently begging it to stay, even as my mind shied away from the horrible knowledge of what it was.

It flickered again, then went out.

CHAPTER 34

I sobbed myself into a state of panic where everything felt like a dream. Sky's body grew cold, but I couldn't let her go. I didn't want her to lay naked on the cold, rocky floor. I don't know how long I sat like that, but it was long enough that her body began to stiffen as rigor mortis set in. Why couldn't I summon my power and throw it when I *needed* to? Why was I always so useless when it mattered the most?

"*Ember!*"

I straightened, gasping. Was that real? Was I dreaming—

"*Ember! Can you hear me?*"

I stopped breathing, every part of my body straining to focus on the faint voice in my head. "*Mac?*"

"*Oh gods, Em, where are you?*" His desperate voice grew louder as I focused on it.

"*In the cell. Under the tower. Hawk had a power. Mac, he killed —killed her. Sky. Sky's dead.*" I choked out, hoping I made any sort of sense.

"*Hawk?*" The single word vibrated with fury.

"*He's dead, too.*"

"*Hold on, Em, we're comin',*" he promised fiercely. "*Hold on, ok?*"

"*Please hurry,*" I sobbed.

"*I'm comin', sweetheart. Hold on.*"

Sweetheart? He'd never called me anything like that before, but I clung to his words like a lifeline. He kept a steady stream of narration as he gathered people to run for the watchtower. I cradled Sky and listened. Nemo had sealed the tunnel exceptionally well, and Mac went quiet as he worked with the others to break the wall down. It felt like forever, but finally, I realized the darkness was growing lighter. I fixed my eyes on it, relief flooding me, and then Mac spoke in my head again.

"We're almost through, Em."

I stared at the bobbing light reflecting on the walls, something cold creeping over me. *"You're not through yet?"*

"No, almost."

Bile crept into my throat as I realized the light wasn't approaching from *up* the stairs. It was coming from *below.*

"Someone's comin'!" I told Mac, my voice frantic.

"What?" he demanded.

"Someone's coming from… from below." I scurried backward, hauling Sky's body with me until my back hit the rocky wall.

Mac swore, and I felt his surge of fear. The light grew brighter, illuminating the blood covering Sky's body and my clothes and hands. I glanced at where Hawk's body had fallen, but the charred lump almost made me sick. I pulled Sky's body tighter against me like I was trying to protect her.

"Almost through!"

A body stepped into view, a giant hulking shadow that strode toward me with a swinging lantern in hand. A key flashed in the dim light, and as the person ducked to unlock the cell door, the light shone on their face. I stared dumbfounded at Sax, Madame's right-hand man—the man who dragged me down to this cell the first time—the man who whipped me. He'd gone missing along with Zana, the third council member, after the rebellion. He met my wide eyes with his familiar impassive stare, as though he hadn't just appeared from possibly hell itself. For a few dizzying seconds, I questioned if I'd been locked in this cell the entire time, vividly hallucinating everything from the past several months, but Sax's salt and pepper hair was longer and wilder, and Sky's body was cold in my arms, and Mac was *shouting* my name in my head.

"It's Sax! It's Sax!" I shouted back as he unlocked the door and pulled it open.

"Hold on, Em! Hold on!"

"What do you want?" I shouted at Sax as I scrambled sideways until I hit the corner, dragging Sky with me.

He didn't answer as he caught my ankle and jerked me toward him. I managed to kick free and dropped Sky, pain and guilt stabbing through me as her body slumped to the floor. I leapt to my feet, but he immediately trapped me against the wall. I lashed out and hit him hard in the jaw, and his head snapped to the side, but he just turned back and gave me a grim smile.

"Mac!" I shrieked.

I tried to hit him again, but he caught my bandaged wrist and forced it down; the lacerations on my wrist burned with pain as he squeezed. His strong arms clamped around me, pinning my arms to my sides and lifting me off my feet. I kicked and thrashed, slamming the heel of my boot into his shin over and over as he carried me out of the cell.

"No!" I screamed.

"Em!" Mac sounded frantic.

"Let go of me!" My heel connected with his kneecap, and he let out a grunt of pain. My brief sense of accomplishment vanished as he shifted, one thick arm coiling around my neck in a chokehold and tightening like a snake. I gasped and clawed at his arm as he cut off my air, but he didn't even flinch. Black spots filled my vision.

"Mac!"

I'm coming! I'm—"

ᏳᏌ

I woke up in a tent.

A face appeared over mine, and it took me a few seconds to recognize Zana, the third council member. Her head was no longer bald but covered in short, dark hair. She looked thinner and rougher, but it was undeniably her.

"Good mornin', Bones," she said with a grin that reminded me of Madame. "Bout time you joined the party."

My panicked eyes scanned the tent, but it was empty except for us. I shifted and realized metal handcuffs bound my bandaged wrists in front of me. I tried to sit up, but she shoved me back down with one hand and held me there. I stared at her, my heart thudding in time with my pounding head. I'd barely interacted with her at the Vault, and I didn't know her well enough to anticipate what she'd do. She'd always seemed more like Madame than like Nemo, and she was clearly working with Sax. Did they know I'd killed Madame? Was this revenge?

"What do you want?" I asked, my voice raspy and hoarse. My throat ached.

She sighed, tilting her chin in a strange, almost playful way. "So many things."

I stared at her.

"Oh, you mean with you?" she grinned. "Well, I could think of several fun things to do with you, but unfortunately, I'm to deliver you in one piece."

The hair on the back of my neck raised. "Deliver to who?"

"The God of Death." I must have looked as startled and confused as I felt because her smile turned wicked. "Aww, sweet thing, you didn't know? The God of Death himself promised to elevate whoever fetched you to godhood."

I could only stare, speechless.

"Unfortunately, we will have to travel with those Voiceless creeps, but it's a small price to pay for immortality."

"He's lying," I said, trying to sound confident, but my voice shook. "That's impossible."

"A year ago, I would've said it was impossible to heal another person just by touching them, but here you are." She leaned down and tapped me on the nose with one finger.

"No one is immortal," I tried.

"How do you know?" Her head tilted as she studied me.

I hated that she was looming over me while I was stuck lying on my back. It made me feel completely powerless. "Are the Voiceless here?" I asked, ignoring her question.

"They will be any minute."

I forced my spinning mind to focus with a monumental act of will. "How did you know where I was?"

She grinned. "Did you think Hawk unraveled all by himself?"

"What do you mean?" I breathed, my heart lodging itself in my throat.

She narrowed her eyes as she held my gaze, and I was about to ask again when pure terror seized me, so potent I immediately was sick. I barely managed to roll on my side so I didn't vomit all over myself. When I glanced at her, trying to catch my breath, her nose wrinkled in disgust.

"What just happened?" I choked out.

"You're not the only one with powers anymore, sweet thing." She smiled wide, showing all her teeth.

I stared at her in horror.

"I can manipulate emotions," she bragged.

Oh fuck.

"You made Hawk hate me?" I whispered.

Her head tipped back as she laughed, the mockery clear. "Oh, he already hated you. I just turned the dial up a little and *suggested* he bring you to that cell."

I had to breathe deeply through my nose for a moment. "He killed Sky because of you!"

She shrugged. "Am I supposed to know who that is?"

Every part of her radiated indifference like Sky's life meant nothing, and I snapped as rage roared through me. I lashed out with my leg and connected partially with Zana's shoulder. She grunted but immediately blocked my next attempt. The next thing I knew, she'd shifted to pin my thighs under her knee. I brought my cuffed hands up to shove her, but she caught my wrists and forced them to the ground above my head. I couldn't help the hiss of pain as she manhandled my bandaged wrists, but I still fought to escape.

Zana leaned down, her grip like iron, and her mouth twisted in a smirk. "Your fear is delicious. It's really too bad we don't have time to play. I'd love to see how much fear I could squeeze out of you."

My temper surged, and before I could think better of it, I spit in her face.

Her grin faded as her eyes narrowed into cold slits. She brought one hand up to wipe the spit from her face and then suddenly struck, slamming her fist into my stomach and forcing all the air in my lungs out in a pained wheeze. I struggled to gasp in a breath, but she wasn't done. Zana seized a handful of my hair and yanked my head back as she leaned in.

"I was gonna make this quick, but I think I'll play a little after all."

With a vicious twist of my hair, Zana slammed the back of my head into the ground. Stars burst in my vision, and before I could recover, her hands were around my throat, squeezing with no mercy. Her smirk dimmed in my vision as her grip tightened.

"Goodnight, sweet thing," she crooned, and darkness swallowed me.

⌒∿

I woke up in a different tent and stared at the canvas ceiling in confusion. This tent was more like the tents the Reapers had used, with a tall wooden pole holding up the ceiling—a pole to which my hands were handcuffed behind my back.

I sat up, my head and throat aching, and squinted in the dim light. Before I could get a good look around the tent, a shadow moved toward me, and a strangled shriek escaped my lips. A dirty, white, tattered robe came into view, and then the person crouched before me, revealing the horrifying face of a Voiceless prophet. I pressed against the pole, trying to get as far away as possible, but there was nowhere to go. He looked like a man, beard stubble poking out from the thick white paint that coated his face. His eye sockets were blackened with what looked like ash, creating the illusion of a skull, and streaks ran down his face from sweat or tears. The customary black thread stitched his lips closed, and the holes pierced in his skin were red and irritated. Dried blood and who knew what else crusted the thread.

His mouth opened slightly, and his tongue pressed a wet knot of black thread out between his lips. He lifted pale hands with long fingernails and calmly picked at the knot as I watched in disgust. It took him almost a minute, but he got it untied, then grabbed one end of the thread and *pulled.*

My stomach churned as the black thread began sliding from the puncture holes in his lips. It caught often, blood trickling from several of the holes, but he never even flinched. My entire body itched to clean out the wounds.

The thread finally came free, and the Voiceless smiled, flashing yellowed teeth.

"Ember Cutler," he said in a thin, raspy voice that made all my hair stand on end.

"So not voiceless after all," I scoffed hoarsely with far more bravado than I felt.

He smiled wider, and more blood dribbled from the holes in his skin. "Our voices are for the gods alone."

I glanced pointedly around the tent. It was empty except for us.

"Gods… and goddesses," he said reverently, and fear coursed through me.

"I am not a goddess," I snapped.

"The prophecy states that to fulfill the covenant, the Goddess of Life must unite with the God of Death. Their union shall forge a new era, cleansing the ashes of Before and igniting the embers of genesis."

I stared at him, my heart pounding.

"I am the Prophet Talmar. I bandaged your burned hand and re-bandaged your wrists." His eyes narrowed. "How did you come to be injured?"

I wiggled my fingers, realizing one of my hands was wrapped in gauze, but I was more concerned with what he'd said before.

"What do you mean, 'unite'?" I demanded.

He smiled. "A union of flesh and blood. Your children shall inherit the earth."

A union of flesh and blood.

A roaring sound filled my ears.

Your children.

I wanted to appear strong and defiant, but my body started trembling as the horror of what he'd just said slowly registered. I thought I'd experienced the worst ways I could be used, but this was a whole new level of fucked up I had stupidly never considered. They wanted to *breed* me like an animal to their God of Death in hopes that our children would also have power? I sucked in a breath through my nose, trying to keep from being sick.

"No," I choked out. "Fuck, no."

He made a disapproving sound through his teeth. "It has been written."

"By *who?*"

"By the High Priestess."

I had no idea who that was, but a new fear stabbed through me. I had to make sure these assholes did not find out about Clarity. She'd already experienced someone else controlling her body, and I would do anything to keep it from happening again. "I'd rather die," I hissed.

"It matters not what you want, Goddess. We serve a greater purpose than ourselves." He smiled like he thought his words were comforting. "It is a great honor to be the bride of Death and carry his children."

That sounded like some Carth bullshit, and I couldn't help the bitter laugh that escaped my lips. "I'd rather *die,*" I repeated.

Talmar pursed his lips and tilted his head, studying me. "The God of Death is the one who blessed you with your sacred healing powers. You were always meant to be his Goddess, and without him, your powers will corrupt. You feel it, don't you?" He leaned forward slightly, reddened eyes fixed on me. "The darkness in your veins?"

I bit the inside of my cheek hard, willing myself not to react, but it felt like something slithered beneath my skin as though summoned by his words.

"Even now, your healing power weakens. If you continue on this path, your body will decline, and you will become a harbinger of sickness and death. Only by submitting to this union can you ensure the protection of yourself and those you care for."

Fear choked me, but there was no way I would *submit* to this.

His eyes dipped down, and a terrifying expression flashed across his face. He moved, and I flinched, but he grabbed the front of my shirt and pulled it down to reveal the brand on my chest. I tried to jerk away, but his other gloved hand grabbed my arm, holding me in place with a grip that felt inhumanely strong. His eyes hardened, and he gently ran his fingers over the mark, ignoring me as I tried again to yank my arm free. When he raised his head, the muscles in his neck strained against his skin, and his nostrils flared as he bared his teeth.

"The traitor has claimed your flesh?" he snarled.

I shrank back from that rage, my head spinning. Traitor? Before I could speak, a pained expression crossed his face, and he pulled my shirt back up with an unsettling tenderness and released my arm.

"Forgive me, Goddess." His bloodshot eyes held mine, and I realized they were hazel. The color made him seem more human, but the frenzied light that shone in them made my blood run cold. "Did I hurt you?"

"What do you mean, 'traitor'?" I asked shakily instead of answering.

"Juck." His face twisted like he'd bitten into something sour. "He heard the prophecy, along with several other *faithful* members, and then he deserted his post. I can only assume he thought if he found the Goddess of Life first, he could finally achieve the godhood he so desired."

My mind flashed back to that moment in the desert, the shock and excitement that had filled Juck's face as I healed Grip. I thought I was showing him I could be useful so he wouldn't kill me, but instead, I just demonstrated that I was exactly the person he'd been searching for.

"He said I was an angel," I heard myself say as though I was floating outside my body.

Talmar hissed angrily through his teeth, startling me enough to look at him. The muscles in his neck corded again as he clenched his fists. "He knew you were no such thing."

I had no idea what to do with this information. Juck *had* wanted to be a god. He'd repeatedly told me he was a god, the divine, and I was his angel.

"He should have worshiped at your feet," Talmar continued, stroking my arm. "Now you are where you belong, among your devoted."

I jerked my arm away. "I'm not an angel *or* a goddess."

His brow furrowed, lips pressing tightly together for a second before he sighed. "I see we have our work cut out for us."

"What the fuck does that mean?" My hackles rose.

He pressed a hand against his heart momentarily. "You should have been raised among us with the knowledge of your true purpose. You've long been neglected, left to grow wild in ignorance." His tone was patronizing, and it set my teeth on edge. "But the God of Death guides our hands, and we shall mold you into the vessel you are destined to be."

I had to stop thinking that events in my life were the worst they could possibly be. The universe seemed determined to prove me wrong. He waited, staring into my eyes like he expected my undying gratitude and oath of devotion to the God of Death, and I *did* have some words for him—just two.

"Fuck. You."

His expression hardened, and he abruptly stood, making me cringe, but he just strode to the tent's entrance and left. Alone, I slumped against the pole, my body shaking. I had to get out of here. It felt like I'd gone in a horrible circle—I'd escaped the oppression of Carth, where my sole purpose was to submit and have children, only to end up in the exact same role for a fucking *god*.

"Mac? Mac, can you hear me?" I tried, desperate, but there was no answer.

I didn't know what to do.

Had Wolf known the details? Had he known what the Voiceless wanted with me? I remembered the fear that had flashed through his eyes when I threatened to follow them, the grim determination on his face as he left me restrained in the clinic. Fury and guilt twisted together in my chest. If he knew, why didn't he just fucking *tell* me?

The tent flap abruptly opened, and I went cold all over as Talmar and another Voiceless entered, dragging a *child* with them.

"Let go! Let go of me!" the child sobbed.

They shoved the small body forward—hard enough that the child sprawled on the ground at my feet. The child lifted their head, and I stared in horror at the familiar tear-streaked face, the wide hazel eyes, and the head of soft black curls.

"Roe?" I gasped.

CHAPTER 35

"**S**ara?" Roe cried, scrambling to climb in my lap, wrapping his thin arms around my neck. His entire body shook as he sobbed into my shoulder.

It hadn't been *that* long since Trey and I stayed at the Outpost and met Zeke and his little boy Roe. I'd healed Roe from a terminal illness, and I remembered their beaming faces as they waved goodbye to me and Trey.

I strained against the metal cuffs keeping my hands behind my back, desperate to wrap my arms around him. "Roe, what are you doing here? Where's your dad?" I asked, frantic.

"They killed him," he sobbed.

Fuck. Zeke had been so kind to me and Trey, and he'd loved his son more than anything. I glared up at the two Voiceless, full of fury. They stared back at me, their expressions blank.

"What the fuck are you doing?" I snarled.

"Providing incentive," Talmar answered, and my stomach dropped.

"You're threatening a *child?*"

"What happens to this child falls on you, Goddess. Submit, and he won't be harmed."

Tears of helpless fury filled my eyes. I'd been so relieved it was just me. I could fight if they were threatening me, but not if they were threatening Roe. I couldn't sacrifice him to save myself.

"Fine," I seethed.

Talmar smiled, and the satisfied victory on his face made me want to scream.

"Uncuff me," I demanded.

I didn't think they would, but Talmar shocked me by pulling a key from his pocket and crouching to unlock the manacles. As soon as they fell away, I wrapped both arms around Roe and held him tightly.

"Do not try to run," Talmar warned. "There are guards at the door. We leave at first light."

I didn't respond, and after a brief pause, they both left.

"Did he call... call you 'Goddess?'" Roe asked in a shaky whisper.

I winced. "Yes, but my real name is actually Ember. You can call me Em."

"Where's Flint?"

Pain lanced through me, and for a second, I considered lying, but I knew trying to shield Roe from the truth would do little to protect him.

"His real name was... was Trey, and he's dead," I whispered, my voice cracking with emotion.

Roe wrapped his arms tighter around my neck, and when his shoulders shook, I realized he was crying again. I smoothed back his unruly curls, tears brimming in my own eyes. I felt the urge to promise him I would keep him safe, that I wouldn't let the Voiceless hurt him, but I kept my lips pressed tightly together. I couldn't truthfully promise him that. I had very little control over anything, right now.

Roe cried himself to sleep. I had so many questions, but I didn't wake him up. He looked exhausted, with dark circles under his eyes. I tentatively let my powers flow into him, but besides some bruises and scrapes, he was unharmed, and there was no sign of the illness I'd healed months ago. I healed the few minor injuries he had, remembering the joy on Zeke's face when I healed Roe and the tenderness as he held his son, and grief overwhelmed me. He was dead—most likely because of me.

How did the Voiceless find them? Had they followed us there?

I swiped my wet face on my shoulder. Little did Talmar know that dragging Roe into this just made me more determined to get us both out. There was no way in hell I was going to submit to the God of Death and have his children.

I'll always come for you, Em.

Mac's voice ran through my mind, and my eyes overflowed

again. I knew he would come for me. I had no doubts about that, but would he find me in time?

I struggled to my feet and gently maneuvered Roe to the bed of furs in the corner. He let out a little whimper but didn't wake up. I crept over to the tent flap, carefully peering through the crack. I could see at least one guard standing outside—another of the Voiceless. How many were here? I thought there were only seven of them. I tiptoed back, examining the inside of the tent. It was large but only contained one bed made up of furs. I searched for anything that could be used as a weapon but found nothing. They'd even taken the handcuffs with them. I returned to Roe and tried to think. The Voiceless had freed me, so either they believed I wouldn't try anything now that Roe was here, or they were setting a trap.

They said we were leaving at daybreak. Was right now the best time to take them by surprise, or were they out there just waiting for me to try to escape?

I took a deep breath. I didn't have enough information. I didn't know how many Voiceless there were or if others traveled with them. I needed to wait. I would risk it if it were just me, but I needed to be smarter. I had to protect Roe.

I climbed into the furs next to Roe, and he startled awake. "It's ok, Roe, it's Em," I whispered.

It was getting cold. I lay beside Roe, giving him plenty of space and ensuring he had most of the furs, but he immediately shifted closer and curled into me. I could feel him trembling. I tentatively wrapped my arms around him.

"I'm so sorry, Roe," I murmured, guilt running through my veins like poison.

"I want my dad," he whimpered, and then he started sobbing again.

"I know," I choked past the lump in my throat. "I know, but you're not alone, ok? I'm here, and I'm gonna..." I hesitated, trying to figure out how to reassure him without lying. "I'm not gonna leave you, and we're gonna try to get away."

Maybe wishful thinking, but I was going to try to believe it. *You're only stuck if you believe you're stuck.* A bittersweet ache went through me at the memory of Trey's words. I still thought that was the stupidest thing I'd ever heard, but here I was trying it.

"Ok," he sobbed.

I gently ran my fingers through his curls, and without thinking, I started humming Wolf's song. It took a long time, but eventually, his sobs died. Even after I knew he'd fallen asleep, I kept humming, hoping Wolf's song would also soothe *me*.

⌒

"Wake up."

I jolted awake to see a Voiceless leaning over me and barely resisted the urge to scream. It was still dark but with a rosy hue that meant the sun was beginning to rise. Roe's fingers dug into my skin as he clung to me.

"We're leaving soon," the Voiceless added.

This wasn't Talmar, but this Voiceless had also removed the black thread from his lips. I sat up, pulling Roe with me, and climbed out of the bed. The Voiceless beckoned to us, and I reluctantly followed him out of the tent. Outside, I had to work to keep my expression blank. There were so many Voiceless—at least a dozen of them. They were packing up the camp, but everyone who noticed me immediately sank to one knee and pressed their fist against their chest. The hair on the back of my neck prickled.

"Why are they doin' that?" Roe whispered.

"Ember is the Goddess of Life," the Voiceless leading us turned to say. "To disrespect her is to disrespect the God of Death himself."

Roe looked up at me, eyes wide, but after the Voiceless turned back around, I rolled my eyes and shook my head slightly. Roe's nose wrinkled in confusion.

The Voiceless led us to the dying fire. Roe and I huddled together, trying to keep warm. He wore a jacket, but I was still in my tattered T-shirt. My burned hand and my wrists ached, but Talmar's bandaging looked neat and clean, so I didn't unwrap them. Roe suddenly tensed, and I peered up to see Sax striding toward us. I pulled Roe behind me, but Sax offered a jacket to me. I didn't move for several breaths, glaring at him, but he waited, no expression on his face. Finally, I reached out and took it, noting that it looked like *his* jacket. He turned and left, and I pulled it on. I didn't want his jacket, but it *was* warm. It was also large enough to wrap around Roe *and* me. I glanced up and saw Zana standing across the campsite, her arms crossed, and eyes narrowed at me; I looked away.

Another one of the Voiceless brought us some food—a chunk of bread and cheese. Roe and I ate together, watching as the rest packed up camp. I tried to count how many Voiceless I could see, but it was hard to keep track of them, much less tell them apart. I assumed they were all men, partially because they looked like men but more so because I doubted the Voiceless would ever let a woman be a prophet. They reminded me of ants, scurrying around and packing up, all identical and working in tandem without saying a word. I didn't see anyone besides Sax and Zana who weren't wearing the tattered white robes.

Another Voiceless approached, leading a horse. This one still had his lips stitched shut, but he gestured toward the horse, and I stood, pulling Roe with me. He frowned and made a gesture like he didn't want Roe on the horse with me.

"He's riding with me," I said, trying to channel the authoritative way Mac spoke.

His eyes flicked to me, and he continued to frown, but finally, he nodded. I helped Roe on first and then climbed on behind him. This saddle was smaller than the one Trey and I had used, but Roe and I fit easily, and I wrapped Sax's jacket around us. The Voiceless broke down the tents and loaded everything into packs carried by a team of mules. There were six other horses, all ridden by Voiceless. Everyone else traveled on foot. I counted at least fifteen Voiceless, and my heart sank. How the fuck were we going to get away?

We set out going roughly south, a long train of horses and people walking. One of the Voiceless walked in front of our horse, holding the reins.

"How did they find you?" I asked Roe, pitching my voice low enough that the Voiceless couldn't hear.

"I don't know, but I heard them talking about a trail," Roe whispered back.

My heart sank. Did they follow a trail left by me and Trey? "Did any of them hurt you?"

He shuddered. "They hit me a few times."

My blood boiled, and I muttered a curse through my teeth.

"Are you actually a goddess?" he whispered.

"No, I'm just a person."

He was quiet for a while. "How do you know?"

"Well, I'm pretty sure I can die," I answered, realizing that beyond that, I had no idea.

"Who is the God of Death?"

I shivered. "I don't know."

Where were they taking us? Juck usually talked about the Voiceless in Sin City, but after my conversation with Wolf, I realized I had no idea where the God of Death might be. The scope of how much I *didn't* know felt overwhelming. Talmar had seemed willing to answer all my questions last night. Maybe I could get more answers.

"Hey, you," I called, my eyes on the Voiceless holding the horse's reins.

He turned and stared at me, but his lips were stitched closed. I decided to try, anyway.

"Where are we going?"

He looked behind me and signed something with his hands. I glanced back to see a Voiceless with unstitched lips riding toward us. I recognized Talmar as his horse fell alongside ours.

"What is it you need, Goddess?" he asked.

It was so strange looking at them in the daylight. They were still horrifying with their stitched lips and blackened eyes, but they looked more like what they actually were—creepy-ass men with peeling face paint and tattered robes.

"Why hasn't everyone removed their..." I gestured to my mouth.

"Not everyone has earned that privilege," he answered.

I wasn't sure I wanted to know *how* that privilege was earned. "Where are we going?" I repeated my original question.

"To the God of Death."

I huffed an annoyed breath. "*Where* is that?"

"The Sanctum."

I glared at him. Was he doing this on purpose? "For fuck's sake, *where* is that?"

His expression remained steady, seemingly unbothered by my attitude. "It has been known as 'Sin City,' but the God of Death has renamed it the Sanctum."

Finally, an actual answer. I remembered Wolf talking about the Sin City Uprising. How long ago had he said it'd been? Ten years?

"Renamed is a shitty way to describe slaughtering innocent

people and seizing control."

"They would not have been harmed if they had not resisted."

I bit back my fury and instead asked, "Who is the God of Death?"

He blinked, a hint of surprise in his eyes. "You do not know the God of Death?"

I glared, waiting.

"The God of Death is the head of the seven gods, the one true God. Only he can grant the honor of his true name."

This speaking in cryptic, non-answers thing was going to be the death of me. "Ok, who are the other gods?"

He frowned as though he disapproved of my ignorance but answered, "the Goddess of Fertility, the God of Fire and Destruction, the Goddess of the Harvest, the God of Knowledge, the Goddess of Love and Beauty, and the God of Justice and Order."

Now, I frowned. The people of Carth worshiped the God of Justice and Order, calling him the true god, but I had no idea he was one of the seven Voiceless gods. Carth had always portrayed the Voiceless as barbaric heathens—a laughingstock. Did *they* know they shared the same god? Then, another thought occurred to me. "You already have two goddesses. Why can't one of them be the Goddess of Life?"

He gave me a pitying look, and my hackles rose. "Fertility and the Harvest are not the same as Life."

"You mean you twisted your made-up religion to fit the story you chose."

"You have the power to heal, and yet you think this is made up?"

"The people at Carth certainly think so," I shot back.

A knowing sneer crossed his face. "Yes, the Justice Keepers, with their narrow minds and rigid laws, believe they alone hold the truth, but they are looking at a tiny fragment of a greater whole. They are like children holding a pebble and believing it to be the entire mountain. They have forsaken the other gods in their ignorant pursuit of a world already lost. We see the pebble, the mountain, and the entire cosmos beyond."

"Good for you," I muttered under my breath, then louder asked, "How many Voiceless are there?"

He smiled wide, cracking open the healing puncture wounds on his face again. "We are in the tens of thousands."

All the blood drained from my face. I felt Roe twist to glance up at me, but I just stared at Talmar. He had to be exaggerating. That couldn't be true. Talmar studied me, his smile turning smug at my reaction, and I tried to school my expression.

"Are the other gods at Sin City?" I hated that my voice shook.

"The Sanctum," he corrected. "No, they have been separated, but the God of Death plans to unite them all."

"What do you mean, separated?" I asked, narrowing my eyes.

"The gods were once united in purpose, but over time, the other gods were swayed by earthly desires and corrupted. The God of Death saw the impending decay and sought to correct them, but they turned against him. He was forced to leave, to bide his time and gather a devout force to restore balance. The Voiceless are His chosen ones, destined to cleanse the world in preparation." He paused, and that feverish light in his eyes shone brighter. "You were always meant to be the guiding light, Goddess, a beacon of creation and renewal. But when the gods fell into discord, you were lost in the chaos." He leaned even closer as we rode beside each other, and I instinctively tried to lean away, clutching Roe tightly. "You are not just a part of this, Ember; you are the very heart of it. Life and Death are two sides of the same coin, and with your return, balance shall be restored."

Breathe. I tried to remind myself as my head spun, but the fuzziness of panic crept closer.

"So I'm just as powerful as your God of Death if we're two sides of the same coin," I tilted my chin as I glared at him.

He gave me a patronizing smile as though I was a child. "Your power is great, Goddess, but do not mistake your strength for equality. Even life must bow down to death. Your power is meant to serve as a complement to His."

Furious tears burned in my eyes. Of course. That's what I always was, a tool for other, more powerful people to use. "If the God of Death is so powerful, it seems pretty fucking lazy that he didn't fetch me himself."

His expression darkened, and I knew I should have watched what I said, but my temper was slipping. "He did not come because He did not need to. He asserts His will through us, His prophets."

"Or he doesn't even exist."

His knuckles cracked as he gripped his reins tighter. "You may be the Goddess of Life, but you owe your God your respect."

"I don't owe *your* god shit," I snapped.

The Voiceless leading our horse turned and signed something to Talmar.

"Yes," Talmar answered him, staring pointedly at me, "this resistance is a sign that Ember's pride blinds her to the truth. It is our duty, painful though it may be, to guide the Goddess back to the higher path the cosmos has bestowed upon her."

I pulled Roe tighter against me as my heart tripped over itself.

Talmar smiled, baring his yellowed teeth. "Do not fear the sacred rite of correction, Ember. Through suffering comes purification, and through purification comes understanding."

I understood plenty. I understood the fear tactics. I understood the threat. I understood that we needed to get the hell out of here.

When I didn't say anything, Talmar continued. "The God of Death is very real, just as these gifts he has blessed us with are very real."

I glanced at him as he removed his single glove and pulled the sleeve of his robe up to his shoulder, and then I stared. My brain couldn't understand what I was seeing. Instead of flesh, his hand and arm were *metal*. It began at his shoulder, hydraulic pistons softly hissing as it moved. What appeared to be metal tendons flexed, the hand opening and closing with a humanlike dexterity, and thick black tubes ran down the metal arm like veins. The metal was dented and scratched as though battle-worn.

"It is through the God of Death's power that we have been blessed with augmentation—a holy union of flesh and the divine. These enhancements are the instruments he has gifted us to bring balance to this world teetering on the edge of chaos."

"Did he *gift* it after you lost your arm, or did he chop your arm off to *gift* it to you?" I muttered.

"It is a small price to pay," Talmar replied.

I assumed that meant the God of Death wasn't providing prosthetics to the disabled, but I pressed my lips together.

"These gifts bless us with a fragment of the God of Death's power, lending us his speed and strength. The Black Veil, those who have proven their unwavering devotion to the God of Death, are even gifted the ability to block or sense the astral plane."

"Are you one of The Black Veil?"

"It is my deepest desire to achieve such a blessing."

"So, no, you're not," I sneered. "The God of Death couldn't even send his most devoted to fetch me?"

Anger flashed in his face, but he seemed to swallow it down. "One of The Black Veil was with us, but he was unfortunately slain in the skirmish with the Vault's Safeguard."

He must have been the one whose body released the Shadowbane. "Do all the Black Veil turn into fucking biological weapons?"

"Yes," he said so calmly that a shiver went down my spine.

"That is so fucked up," I muttered.

"Even in death, the Black Veil carry on their divine work."

I wanted to ask how they surgically implanted a device to go off after death and how they kept the Shadowbane contained, but he spoke again.

"Juck was a member of the Black Veil, which is how he kept you hidden for over a decade. I would assume that—"

"Juck wasn't a biological weapon," I interrupted.

"He fled before that enhancement was gifted."

"Wait, what do you mean, 'kept me hidden'?" I remembered Wolf saying he couldn't find me until Juck's death.

"He could shield himself and any near him from the Astral Plane." Talmar looked as though he'd swallowed something sour. "It is one of the greatest honors to be gifted such an ability."

"What is the astral plane?" My entire body had gone numb.

Talmar frowned again, looking dismayed. "The Astral Plane is another realm that only the divine can access. It has no limits, no boundaries, and transcends our mortal senses. Your power flows through the Astral Plane and into you. Have you never experienced it?"

I swallowed hard and asked, "Can the God of Death access it?"

"Of course," Talmar answered instantly.

I felt the blood rush from my face. Was Menace the God of Death? That sounded an awful lot like the place I went while drugged—the place where Menace always found me.

"What does the God of Death look like?" I got out.

"None may describe the God of Death," Talmar said sternly. "Those blessed enough to see his face swear an oath of silence."

Of fucking course.

Nemo had told me the god of the Voiceless didn't have powers like Menace. He could've been wrong, I supposed. I wasn't sure I could explain why, but Menace had always seemed separate from the Voiceless to me. For starters, I was sure if he was the God of the Voiceless, he would've said so—over and over. The Voiceless seemed to get off on talking about their religion.

Unless Menace was also a prisoner?

I chewed on my lip. How would the Voiceless keep him a prisoner? He seemed far too powerful.

Should I try to contact him? My stomach flipped with anxiety. I didn't know if I *could*, much less if I *should*. Would he help me? He would probably rage against someone else claiming I belonged to them. Unless he *was* the God of Death.

Was this what he was trying to protect me from?

I clenched my jaw, fighting the urge to scream in frustration.

"Did you have any further questions?" Talmar asked.

"No," I ground out. I wanted him to go away.

Thankfully, he bowed his head and slowed his horse, returning to where he'd been riding.

"Em?" Roe whispered, his voice full of anxiety.

I glanced at him, hating the fear that was pinching his little face.

"This is bad, isn't it?"

I sucked in a breath and let it out slowly. "Yeah."

"Are they gonna hurt you?"

"I'd rather they hurt me than you," I muttered.

He fell silent for a few breaths. "I'm scared."

"Me too," I admitted.

He gripped my hands tightly, and I squeezed them back, and then we both fell silent. He fell asleep again soon after, but thankfully, my fear was enough to keep me awake. Time seemed to crawl by, and I couldn't decide if that was good or bad. The Voiceless were moving quickly but weren't rushing, which told me they didn't believe anyone was pursuing them. I wondered where on earth the watchtower tunnel came out. It could be anywhere. How the fuck would Mac find—

Wolf.

My breath caught. If anyone could find me, it would be my brother. My heart ached as I remembered how I'd thrown his own trauma in his face and the cruel last words I'd said to him.

How about we make this real easy and just never speak again.

I forcefully swallowed the bitter tears in my throat. Trying to be inconspicuous, I pulled some long hairs from my head, letting them drift into the bushes. I could, at the very least, try to leave him a trail.

CHAPTER 36

We rode until the sun began to set in the sky.

I was exhausted, my entire body aching from sitting in the saddle for so long. Roe and I huddled together under guard as the Voiceless set up the camp. I was looking forward to food and sleep, but when Talmar approached, something in his expression made dread fill my stomach.

"I'm sure you must be exhausted," he said, "but before we rest for the evening, we must begin the rite."

"What?" I snapped, instinctively pulling Roe tighter against me.

"The rite of correction," he explained patiently. "Do not fear for the child, Ember. This is just about you."

That was weirdly relieving, but fear still made my hands tremble.

"Follow me, please," Talmar instructed.

I forced myself to let go of Roe, but he clung to me.

"No!" he cried, panicked. "No, don't take her!"

"She will return soon, my child," Talmar said, motioning to one of the Voiceless who had been guarding us.

The Voiceless grabbed Roe with a familiar-looking metal hand. How many of these assholes had cybernetic parts?

"It's ok, Roe," I said, hoping I sounded confident. "I'll be back, ok?"

He simply sobbed, weakly fighting against the hold. I followed Talmar into the trees, trying to breathe evenly. Soon, I heard running water, and we went down a steep embankment toward a wide river. As we reached the shore, I realized five of the Voiceless stood up to their waist in the water, watching us. Thank the gods, they still wore their white rags. Talmar stopped at the bank and turned to me.

"You may undress or remain clothed; the choice is yours."

"Clothed," I bit out.

He took my elbow without commenting and began pulling me into the river. It was cold. Not as cold as the half-frozen river, but still cold enough to make me gasp. My boots slipped on the rocks, but Talmar's grip tightened on my elbow. The five Voiceless watched as Talmar led me to the middle of their half-circle and then stopped. The current tugged at my legs.

"God of Death, we invoke you as humble vessels awaiting your will," Talmar began. "May your shadows guide us and bear witness."

I pressed a trembling hand against my breastbone, trying to steady myself.

"Ember, Goddess of Life," Talmar turned and stared at me, his eyes like two black holes in his face. "You stand before us with a heart hardened by pride and defiance. You have turned from your divine path and rejected the sacred union with your God."

The other Voiceless stepped forward, closing the circle around me.

"Wait," I gasped, holding out a hand. "What are you... what are you—"

"Only by accepting death can one truly honor life," Talmar intoned over me.

Hands grabbed my upper arms and head and *shoved* me underwater.

I fought them instinctively, but there were too many of them, and they held me firmly in place. I opened my eyes, squinting in the dim, murky light. I could see the light reflecting on the surface above me, but so many hands restrained me. My lungs began to scream for air, and my struggle grew more desperate as I panicked. Just as I thought for sure my body would give in and try to breathe, they hauled me up out of the water.

I gasped in a lungful of air.

"Pain is but a fleeting moment in the eternal expanse of existence. Through suffering, we are cleansed, and through trials, we are purified."

They shoved me underwater again. This time, I forced myself not to fight and let my body go limp. I half hoped they would pull me up if it appeared that I'd lost consciousness, but they continued to hold me under. I waited, panic building despite my best efforts, and soon, instinct seized control. There was no reaction as I kicked and scratched, and they still didn't pull me up. Hard as I tried, I couldn't stop my body from attempting to gasp in a breath. Water rushed into my lungs, and it *hurt*. I was drowning. I was fucking drowning—

They pulled me back up, holding me upright as I retched up water from my lungs, my eyes and nose streaming as I sobbed and tried to breathe.

"Embrace this pain, Ember, as the shadows lead you back to the light of humility."

I went under again.

I lost track of how many times they half-drowned me, but it seemed to last *hours*. The sun set lower and lower until the surface was just as dark as the blackness underwater. My throat felt raw, my chest ached, and I thought if the water didn't kill me, the panic might. I fought them the whole time, but I stayed silent every time they hauled me back up, simply puking up water and gasping in air. I knew better than to beg them to stop.

"You cannot escape this destiny, Ember. You must find the peace that comes from submission, the power that comes from surrender to the will of the Divine."

When they dragged me to shore, I couldn't even manage to stand because my legs trembled so badly. I stayed on my hands and knees where they left me, gagging up water and shivering, my wet hair plastered to my face.

"Ember, do you renounce your defiance and embrace your sacred duty as the Goddess of Life, destined to become the God of Death's bride?" Talmar asked.

Talmar and the other five stood before me, staring with grave expressions. Their wet robes clung to their bodies, and I counted two metal legs and three metal arms. I spit a mouthful of river water and bile in his direction.

Talmar sighed like I was a rebellious child. "The sacred rite of correction shall resume tomorrow."

Two of the Voiceless stepped forward and grabbed my arms, half carrying and half dragging me back up the embankment. Roe was waiting inside our tent, his face pale, and he gasped when the Voiceless dragged me inside. They dropped me to the ground and left, and Roe crashed to his knees next to me.

"Em! Em, what happened? Are you ok?" he cried.

"I'm ok," I said through chattering teeth. My voice was hoarse. "I'm ok, Roe."

"Why are you all wet?"

"Went for a swim," I said, my lips twitching up in an insane smile.

Roe stared at me, his little brow furrowed with confusion.

"I'm ok," I tried to reassure him. "Just cold and wet."

He looked frantically around the tent, which looked the same as last night. "I don't think there's any spare clothes besides that jacket." He pointed to where Sax's jacket lay on our bed of furs.

"It's ok," I mumbled. "I'm just gonna rest a bit and then figure it out."

Roe hovered anxiously over me. "I think you should get up, Em."

"I will." My eyes closed. "Just gimme a second."

"Em." His voice sounded like it was coming from far away. "Em!"

I wasn't sure if I was half asleep or in a state of shock. I couldn't stop shivering, and my body felt completely drained, reminding me again of when I was healing the Shadowbane the first time. I could hear Roe calling my name every so often, and I tried to reply, but I couldn't tell if any words made it past my lips.

Someone hauled me up to sit, and my body felt weirdly boneless. I couldn't get my eyes open.

"Don't…you doing? You……that!" Roe's frantic cries faded in and out of my head.

A thread of panic trickled in, but my body refused to move. It felt like I was spinning endlessly, and everything faded away again.

෨

"Ember? Can you hear me?"

I cracked my eyes open to see the blurry face of a Voiceless. I gasped, attempting to scramble away only to realize he was firmly holding my arm and Roe was sitting on the other side of me.

"It's alright, Ember," the Voiceless said, and I realized it was Talmar. "You're safe."

I stared at him, my heart in my throat. I was lying in the bed of furs, and Roe was clinging to my shirt—my *dry* shirt.

"Can you sit up?" Talmar asked.

I sat up with his help. I felt shaky and weak, and the room spun for a moment. I was wearing dry clothes that I didn't recognize. Bile burned in the back of my throat as vague memories returned. Had Talmar undressed me?

"I have some stew for you." Talmar picked up a bowl from the floor and scooped up a spoonful, holding it out to my lips as though I were a child.

I was so taken aback that I opened my mouth and let him feed me a spoonful of stew. It was warm and flavorful and awoke my intense hunger. He tried to feed me another, but I turned my head away.

"I can do it," I said, my voice hoarse.

"Let me care for you, Goddess," he said softly, making all the hair on the back of my neck stand up.

"I can do it," I repeated fiercely through my teeth.

He looked disappointed but handed me the bowl. I took it, noticing that my wrists and burned hand had been neatly bandaged again. I glanced at Roe and noted that he didn't have any food.

"Did you eat?" I asked him.

He shook his head, his eyes darting to Talmar.

"He may eat after you, Goddess."

"He eats now," I said as authoritatively as possible with my raspy voice.

Talmar's eyes narrowed, but he dipped his head after a breath. "As you wish."

I waited until he stood and left the tent before I set the bowl down and turned to Roe. "Are you ok?"

Roe looked up at me, his lip trembling. "I'm ok."

"What happened?"

"I couldn't get you to wake up," he whispered. "He came in and took your clothes off, but he put dry ones on. He was angry about the scars on your back."

The tiny bit of stew I'd eaten threatened to come back up.

"He bandaged your arms and carried you to the bed, then he told me to watch you while he got food."

Roe's face was pale, his dark eyes wide. He looked like he was a second away from bursting into tears. I reached out and took his hands, squeezing. "I'm ok, buddy."

"I don't like them," he whispered, tears welling up.

"Me either," I muttered.

Talmar reappeared with another bowl of stew. He handed it to Roe, picked mine up from the floor, and held it out to me again.

"You must eat, Goddess."

"Don't call me that," I snapped, but I took the bowl.

"Whether you like it or not, you are our Goddess." He stroked my arm, and I tried to subtly shift away. "But if you prefer, I can call you Ember."

I gripped the bowl so tightly my knuckles turned white. "What the fuck are you doing?"

His brow furrowed as though confused by my anger.

"You nearly *drowned* me."

"What?" Roe gasped.

"The rite of correction is not meant to harm you, merely to cleanse you. What you experienced was intense, yes. The sensation of drowning was a direct confrontation to your mortality, a reminder that life is fragile."

I scoffed.

He smiled and the patronizing expression reminding me of Juck. He reached out again, combing his fingers through my tangled, damp hair. "You have undergone a great ordeal, and now it is my duty to ensure you are comforted as well as corrected. The water has done its work, and now you must be restored for the path ahead."

"Don't touch me," I gritted out.

"We are bound to ensure you are cared for," he murmured in a soothing tone, ignoring me. "None of us are permitted to touch you intimately."

I tried to shift away, but his fingers tightened painfully in my hair, and panic sparked in my brain. "Let go of me!" I shrieked.

The tent door whipped open, and Sax stooped over to fit his tall frame through the entrance. Talmar released my hair, dropping his hand into his lap and pressing his lips together as he regarded Sax with narrowed eyes.

Sax scanned the tent, his face unreadable as usual. "Orin is lookin' for you, Talmar."

Talmar let out a sharp breath through his nose, but he stood. "Make sure she eats," he ordered before pushing past Sax to exit the tent.

Sax stepped into the tent, moving to stand in the center where the ceiling was the highest. He stared at me as I stared at him. He was probably around the same age as Pa, somewhere in his fifties. His greying hair was long enough that it almost brushed his shoulders, and a grizzled beard covered his jaw. He'd never been a clean-cut figure, but he looked wilder than he had at the Vault—skinnier, too, but I knew from being manhandled that he was still stupidly strong. His hands curled into fists at his sides, and I remembered how he'd knocked me out with one blow in Madame's dungeon after I refused to heal Nemo, how he'd stripped the skin off my back with that whip—

"Eat," he commanded in his gravelly voice.

"Fuck you," I snapped, and beside me, Roe let out a distressed squeak.

Sax's expression didn't change. "Don't push me, Bones."

"Or what? You gonna hit me again? Whip me again?" The rage building inside my ribcage felt unbearable.

"If you wanna protect the kid, you better learn to keep your mouth shut," he stared hard at me as Roe cringed into my side.

"If you touch him, I will kill you," I snarled. "Just like I killed Madame."

He didn't react, so either he already knew, or he didn't care. "Use your head, Bones, and fuckin' eat."

I glared at him, wishing I could light him on fire like Sky had done to Hawk, but I forced myself to continue eating the stew. He stood like a statue, watching me, and I hoped he could feel the heat of my hatred. Apparently, he couldn't because, after a few seconds, he spoke again.

"You keep fightin' them, and this is gonna get even worse for both of you," he said, low.

A wild laugh escaped. "Oh, should I be like you and just roll over and show my belly like a *bitch*?"

His face reddened. "Bones, you better—"

"Or do you just like bein' other people's lapdog?"

My mouth was running too fast to catch. His eyes flashed, a muscle in his neck going taut, and I instinctively shifted to put myself between him and Roe. I expected him to retaliate with his fists, but he just stood there, jaw clenched.

"They wanted to know every single detail," he finally said, even quieter. "All about you and Trey and everythin' that happened. They know all of it, Bones."

I gaped at him, too angry for words. What the fuck did that mean? Was he threatening me or warning me? Before I could figure it out, Roe let out a choked sob, and I looked down at him. He was clinging to his bowl of stew, eyes wide, and tears rolling down his face.

I wrapped him in my arms, ignoring Sax in favor of comforting Roe. After a few minutes, Sax simply turned and ducked back outside. Roe and I sat in the dim light without speaking for a long time before we eventually resumed eating.

"We should get some sleep," I whispered once we'd finished, and he nodded.

I waited until he climbed under the furs before blowing out the lantern. Then I waited some more until his breathing evened out before I quietly sobbed myself to sleep.

ᆼᏬ

The next day was exactly like the last. A Voiceless woke us up, and we ate, mounted our horse, and rode until sunset. The closer to sunset it got, the more my nausea grew. They tried to feed me, but I couldn't eat. Thankfully chugging an entire cup of water seemed to appease them even though it left a bitter taste in my mouth. When Talmar came and got me, I was shaking. Roe sobbed and had to be restrained again, and I didn't have the energy to try to reassure him. I assumed we were again going to the river we'd been traveling alongside, but Talmar led me deeper into the woods. We found the other five standing in a small clearing, waiting. Talmar ushered me to the middle of the circle again, and I tried to brace myself.

"God of Death, we invoke you as humble vessels awaiting your will," Talmar recited again. "May your shadows guide us and bear witness."

I scanned the other Voiceless, trying to figure out what horrible thing they would do this time.

"Ember, Goddess of Life," Talmar said, but I didn't bother looking at him. "You stand before us with a heart hardened by pride and defiance. You have turned from your divine path and rejected the sacred union with your God."

I swayed where I stood, the clearing warping in my vision before snapping back to normal. I grimaced, shaking my head slightly, trying to clear it.

"Only by accepting death can one truly honor life."

Another wave of dizziness hit me and brought me to my knees. The Voiceless didn't move, but their eyes seared into my skin. What the fuck was happening? I stayed kneeling on the ground, my fingers digging into the dirt like I could anchor myself. The outlines of the Voiceless blurred and doubled, the colors growing blindingly bright.

"What?" The word slid out of my mouth and shattered into a million pieces on the ground. I squeezed my eyes shut hard and opened them again. My fingers were no longer digging into the rocky dirt, they were digging into Juck's dead body.

I shrieked and jerked away. My hands were covered in blood, and I wiped them frantically on my pants. Then in one blink, it was gone. Panting, I met Talmar's gaze, and he smiled.

"You drugged me." I think I managed to say, but another wave of dizziness had me squeezing my eyes shut again.

"Darlin'?"

My head shot up, and I stared at where Trey stood in the clearing, smiling gently.

"You ok?" he asked, his brow furrowing.

I stared silently at him. This was a trick. It had to be. It was Menace again.

"Hey," he moved forward and crouched before me, taking one of my hands. I could feel the warmth of his skin, the brush of calluses. "What's wrong?"

"I know it's not you," I whispered.

He frowned. "What?"

"Stop pretending to be him. I know it's not him."

"Bones, what are you talkin' about?" His hand brushed my hair back from my face, and I couldn't resist leaning into his hand, tears prickling in my eyes.

"It's not real. It's not real." I whispered.

"Hey, c'mere," he said, pulling me into his lap and wrapping his strong arms around me.

I covered my face with my hands, trying to remind myself this was not Trey. He kissed my hair and then my cheek.

"You're shaking," he said.

A sob escaped my clenched teeth.

"Look at me," he murmured, pulling my hands from my face.

I stared into his soft brown eyes, brimming with sunshine, love, and concern.

"What's wrong, darlin'?"

"You're not real," I meant to shout, but it came out faint.

He frowned, confused, and there was a little bit of hurt in his eyes that stabbed me through the heart. "Bones, c'mon, it's me."

I scrambled out of his lap and backed away. "No. No, it's not."

He stepped toward me, and when I retreated again, he stopped. "Bones? Hey, what—"

A gunshot echoed, and he stumbled backward. His hands pressed against his heart, where blood was rapidly running through his fingers and down his arms. Instinctively, I ran toward him, my heart in my throat.

"I love you," he rasped out, those brown eyes locked on me.

"No! Trey!" I lunged for him as he began to fall, but he vanished into black smoke.

A swell of dizziness rushed over me as I landed empty-handed on my hands and knees from my momentum. I gasped in air, trying to keep from being sick.

It's not real. It's not fuckin' real.

"Emmy!"

My heart stopped at the sight of Dune running toward me. His entire face lit up in a smile. I'd had plenty of dreams and nightmares about my brother in the past twelve years, but never this clear. I'd forgotten he had a single freckle on his right cheek and a tiny gap between his two front teeth. He came right up to me as I huddled frozen on the ground and grabbed my hands, pulling me to my feet.

"C'mon, let's go!" He grinned. "What are you sittin' on the ground for?"

"Dune," I breathed, squeezing his hands in mine. It felt real. *He* felt real.

"Hurry up, we gotta make it to—"

Like a vengeful ghost, Madame appeared behind my brother with a wicked grin. I only had time to suck in a gasp before she slashed the knife she held across his throat. Dune's hands tightened on mine, his face a mask of horror and fear as blood sprayed.

"No!" I screamed, stumbling under Dune's weight as he tipped forward.

I managed to get him to the ground and glanced up, looking for Madame, but she was gone. It was just me and Dune. I fumbled for the wound with my bloodied hands, trying to call my power, but there was nothing. No warmth resided in my chest. It was *gone*.

"No!" I gasped, tears flowing down my face.

"Ember!"

Wolf ran toward us, and the fury on his face made my panic surge.

"I didn't—" I began, desperate.

He shoved me so hard that I fell onto my back. I watched, stunned, as he gathered Dune's bloody body into his arms, glaring at me through his tears.

"Murderer!" he snarled. "I hate you! I hope you die!"

"Wolf! Please—"

Both of my brothers vanished in black smoke.

I sat up, pulling my knees against my chest. "It's not real. It's not real," I sobbed.

"Em?" A gentle hand on my shoulder made me cringe, but I met Mac's worried gaze. "What's wrong?"

I knew it wasn't real. I *knew* it wasn't real, but I lunged forward and wrapped my arms around him. He folded me into his arms, and I clung to him, sobbing.

"Talk to me, sweetheart," he murmured into my hair. "What's wrong?"

"Get me out of here," I begged him, the line between reality and nightmare blurring.

"Ok, c'mon." He pulled me to my feet, urgency filling his voice. "We gotta hurry, there's—" He made a horrible pained noise, and I stared, uncomprehending, at the blade protruding from his chest. "Em," Mac gasped, "run."

The blade suddenly withdrew, and Mac stumbled to one knee. All of me froze in horror at the sight of *myself* standing behind him, holding a bloody knife. I met my own eyes, and the horrible version of me smiled.

"No," I sobbed, dropping to grab onto Mac, but as soon as I touched his skin, he vanished into black smoke.

One by one, I watched everyone I loved die.

I tried to tell myself it wasn't real, but did it even matter? I still saw every single one. I still heard them gasp their last words or beg me for help. Real or not, I knew their deaths would forever be carved into my mind. They saved the worst for last, and after Zip stepped out of the shadows and snapped Apple's neck as she screamed for me, I broke. I collapsed onto the ground and sobbed hysterically in a tight ball.

Gentle hands pulled me upright, and I tried to jerk away, my eyes squeezed shut. I didn't know who this would be and couldn't watch anyone else die.

"Hush, it's over now," a familiar voice soothed.

I cracked open my swollen eyes and stared at Talmar.

"Ember, do you renounce your defiance and embrace your sacred duty as the Goddess of Life, destined to become the God of Death's bride?" he asked.

"Fuck you!" I spat between sobs.

The sun was beginning to rise, and the soft pink color of the sky felt jarring. Had we been out here all night long? I tried to get to my feet, but the slightest movement made the world tilt and spin. What the *fuck* did they drug me with?

"Your fury is understandable," Talmar said, his voice low and gentle as his human hand brushed my tangled hair from my face. "The visions of mortality are a harsh but necessary purification. They strip away the illusions of this world and force you to confront the inevitable death that awaits us all." He caught my wrist when I swatted his hand away and leaned in, his eyes wide and earnest. "You want to protect those you care about? The only way to do so is by accepting your destiny."

"Get the fuck away from me," I hissed, trying to jerk free.

His jaw set as he studied me, a vein in his forehead pulsing, but the emotion filling his face looked like disappointment.

"Come, Ember, let us go back to the camp so you may rest." He got to his feet and offered me his hands, but I scrambled backward away from him. He dropped his hands, fists clenching at his sides, and drew in a deep breath. "Ember, come."

I snarled a string of curses at him through my tears. I couldn't shake myself free from the drug's grasp, and the bloody visions played over and over in my head. After a moment, Talmar exhaled sharply through his nose and moved toward me. I tried to fight him, but he lifted me into his arms and began carrying me back to the camp, ignoring my efforts to escape. When we reached the camp, he set me on the ground beside the fire, knelt in front of me, and began to wipe my face with a wet cloth. I tried to shove him away, but another Voiceless grabbed my wrists and held them firmly. I struggled briefly, but I was too exhausted to fight for long, and I eventually gave up and let him clean the dirt from my face.

When he brought me back into the tent, Roe immediately began demanding answers, his voice high-pitched with panic. Talmar answered him, but as soon as I was placed on the bed of furs, I curled into a ball. After silence fell, I felt Roe shaking me, tearfully calling my name, but I couldn't respond. I just cried, my breath still coming in short, frantic

⁊

The sun was bright when I opened my eyes next, and by the stifling heat of the tent, I guessed it was around midday. I felt nauseous and shaky as I sat up. The tent was empty, and I felt a stab of worry for Roe. Where was he? I tried to get to my feet, but the room spun and blurred, and I ended up back on my ass.

Someone stepped into the tent, and I slowly focused on Sax's face. He was crouching in front of me, his familiar impassive expression firmly in place.

"Where's Roe?" I demanded.

"He's fine," Sax replied, offering a waterskin. "You want some water?"

"Is it fuckin' drugged again?" I snapped.

Some sort of emotion flashed across his face. "No."

I hesitated, but the thirst was enough to force me to trust him. He stayed crouched on his heels as I drank.

"We're stayin' here today, campin' overnight, and then moving on in the mornin'," he informed me.

I drank my fill and then handed him back the skin. He took it, but didn't move, and unease slid through me as we stared at each other.

"Alright, it *was* drugged," he admitted gruffly.

Panic surged through me, and I lunged away intending to make myself vomit up the water. I couldn't see everyone die again. I couldn't do it. But Sax caught my arm, and jerked me back.

"Bones!" he snapped holding me in place, "It's not the same thing. This'll just help you sleep."

I stared at him in horror, and a little crease appeared between his eyes.

"The fuck?" I got out.

"Just sleep," he commanded. "It's alright."

"Fuck you, you fuckin'… " my voice was already slurring, my sight getting fuzzy around the edges.

"Just lay down, Bones." Hands pressed me back down into the furs, and my eyes fluttered closed.

༄

I woke to someone shaking me and sucked in a terrified gasp at the sight of Sax's face illuminated by a lantern and hovering over mine. He quickly covered my mouth, muffling my shriek.

"Hush," he growled at me, removing his hand. "I'm tryin' to help you."

The tent behind him was dark, but Roe was hovering at his side, eyes wide. My brain moved sluggishly, but the past events trickled in.

"Help me like how you *drugged* me earlier?" I hissed.

"Bones, get up. We gotta hurry." Sax held out my boots.

I sat up and snatched my boots from him with a glare, shoving my feet into my boots and struggling to lace them up with my shaky fingers.

"Why?" I managed to ask.

"We're gettin' outta here."

I paused, staring at him. He met my suspicious gaze, and something like guilt flickered in his eyes.

"I didn't sign up for this religious shit," he finally said.

"So why don't you just *use your head* and leave?" I threw his words back at him, my voice flat. "Why bother with us?"

He shifted slightly on his feet. "I ain't sayin' I'm a good man—"

My eyebrows raised, and a sarcastic laugh escaped my lips.

He shot me a glare. "Even I have my limits, alright? You really think Trey and Mac were able to sneak past me to come bring you food and water in solitary?"

I bit back the flood of furious words I longed to spit at him and continued lacing up my boot. A tiny flame of hope stirred, and I tried to squash it. I glanced at the door and was startled at the sight of two Voiceless lying motionless just inside the tent.

"The guards," Sax explained, following my gaze.

"Are they dead?"

"Yes," he said with no emotion.

I didn't feel any either, simply nodding and shrugging on his jacket. Once I was ready, Sax led the way. I saw the pistol in his hand and couldn't bring myself to care if he shot anyone with it. I grabbed Roe's hand and held it tightly as we crept through the dark camp; my heart seized at every little sound, but we made it to the woods.

"C'mon," Sax said, his gravelly voice low. "We gotta run. Try to put as much distance between—"

"I knew you'd turn on us," Zana said in a smug voice as she stepped into the moonlight, "you dumb fuck."

Sax stepped in front of me and Roe. I couldn't see any Voiceless, but the woods were so dark.

"You think I don't know you've been messin' with my head?" Sax growled.

I peeked at Zana from around Sax's massive body and watched surprise flicker across her face.

"I know it's been you makin' me feel all this guilt," Sax continued. "Thing is, I don't fuckin' care. This ain't worth it, Zana."

"Immortality isn't worth it?" Zana sneered. "You've always been—"

Sax moved fast for such a big man, lifting his pistol, and the gunshot deafened me. Roe flinched in my arms and let out a little cry, but I stared transfixed at the dark stain oozing through Zana's jacket over her heart.

She looked down at it and then back up at Sax, betrayal, fury, and fear in her eyes, but Sax turned to me and Roe and roared, "Run!"

I didn't hesitate. I took off, dragging Roe with me. Eventually, he got his feet under him, and we ran hand in hand through the dark woods. Behind us, shouts and angry cries rose. The Voiceless had discovered we were gone. More gunshots rang out, and I realized Sax wasn't with us, but I didn't stop.

Something flew past us, moving so fast I thought it was some sort of vehicle, but I skidded to a stop when a Voiceless appeared in our path. Roe stumbled, and I jerked him up, spinning to drag us in a different direction. Another Voiceless voice appeared. Roe started screaming, and I realized they were all around us, trapping us.

"No," I panted.

"There is no escape, Goddess," one of them said.

They moved forward, hemming us in until they were close enough to pull us apart. Roe and I both screamed and fought, but then a familiar prick and rush of ice-cold startled me. I caught a glimpse of a syringe, and my stomach dropped.

"No!" I shrieked over and over, but I could tell my voice was already slurring. Beside me, Roe had gone limp in the arms of another Voiceless.

I tried to claw toward him, but the world tilted and went black.

CHAPTER 37

"Ember!"

I opened my eyes and stared at the face over me. Menace was crouched beside me, leaning over my body, blue eyes full of rage.

"Where are you?" he demanded.

"Are you the god of the Voiceless?" I rasped instead of answering.

He blinked, brow furrowing. "What? No."

I stared hard at him, trying to discern whether he was telling the truth.

"I'm not their god," he repeated, disgust clear in his voice. "Why?"

"You're not the God of Death?" I pushed, my voice hoarse but fierce.

His jaw muscles tensed, and my heart leapt into overdrive.

"Oh my gods, you *are.*" Furious tears started rolling down my face.

"No," he snapped. "I am *not* a part of the fucking Voiceless, But..." he hesitated briefly. "But I...I am the God of Death."

"That doesn't make any fucking sense!" I struggled to sit, but he grasped my arms and pulled me upright.

"Where the fuck are you?" his voice sharpened.

"With the Voiceless," I choked out, and the shock and horror that filled his blue eyes looked *real.*

"What?" he snarled, his grip tightening on my arms. "How the *fuck* did this happen?"

"They took me, and I can't—" I broke down in sobs.

"Ember," he growled, shaking me slightly. "I need to know where you are."

"I don't know where we are!" I cried.

"Listen to me," he said, his voice urgent. "Can you focus?"

I tried to shake the cobwebs from my head and focus on him.

"This is important." His severe tone made my skin break out in chills. "The god of the Voiceless is a fraud."

The only word I could get out was, "What?"

"He is nothing, simply a man who uses tricks to fool his followers into believing he is a god. He wants you because then he will have a little bit of power and the potential to have children *with* powers."

"So there isn't a prophecy?"

He gave me a sharp, bitter smile. "No, there *is* a prophecy."

Horrible understanding crashed over me all at once. "But it's about you, not him."

He released me and stood without answering, but his silence and his rigid posture said everything.

"Oh my gods," I whispered.

"There are powers at play here you know nothing about."

Tears continued to roll down my face as I stared at him. All I could think about was all the times he told me I *belonged* to him.

"Have you reached the desert yet?"

"Why the fuck would I tell you?"

Anger filled his face. "What? We don't have time—"

"How are you any better?" I snarled through my tears. "You've lied to me, threatened me, told me over and over that I *belong* to you—"

"So you'd rather go with the Voiceless?" His voice was ice-cold. "Go to their false god and let him fuck you until you're with child over and over? Is that the life you want?"

I tried to stay fierce and angry, but sobs escaped, and terror made my legs weak. "So, what? I should let *you* do it?" I choked out.

"Ember!" He leaned down to grip my chin hard and forced me to meet his eyes. "Listen to me. If I had wanted you *here,* if I had wanted to fulfill this godsdamned prophecy, I would have brought you here a long time ago. Now answer the question, have you reached the desert yet?"

I stared into his blue eyes, blazing with anger, and gave up. "N-no, we're still in the mountains."

"Ok, that's good." He released my chin and straightened. "He's close, then."

"Who?"

He stared at me, and I didn't know how to read the expression on his face.

"I need to know if I can trust you," he finally said, and I *felt* his power stir to life—shadows emerging to twine around his legs—but after everything he'd put me through, that statement infuriated me.

I scoffed, furious. "You need to know if *you*—"

"Ember," he interrupted me, his voice thundering through the darkness. "This is much bigger than just you and me. To defeat the Voiceless, we have to form an alliance."

I took a deep breath and tried to choke my anger down. "What does that mean?"

"I can share some information with you, but you have to allow me to place a string in your head."

"What the fuck does *that* mean?"

"It's a small bit of my magic." He glanced away, and I noticed his ears were pink. "When I was a kid, the best way I could describe my magic was like strings connecting me to other people. I could use them to control other people, or I could cut them and leave pieces of myself with them, giving me a smaller bit of control without contact. I started calling them 'strings,' which just stuck."

I stared at him, my heart rate picking up speed. "String like a…a puppet?"

He winced. "I know this requires a large degree of your trust. I am only taking this precaution because this knowledge does not just endanger you or me. In this case, the string would simply prevent you from sharing the information I give you."

"How am I supposed to know you aren't lying, that you won't use this string to control me?" I snapped.

He took a deep breath and let it out. "I don't know."

I tried to think, tried to imagine what Wolf would do. "Is there anything you can tell me? Information you can give me in exchange for my trust?"

"I can tell you that I could easily force this string into your head, but I won't."

Fear made my head swim, and I scrambled to my feet. "That doesn't fuckin' help."

He sighed. "I can show you my true self," he said in a low voice.

"I can already see your true self."

"No, you see my ideal self," he corrected me, and then shadows seemed to pour from him.

He disappeared from view as the shadows enveloped me, and I could've sworn they caressed my face as they passed. As they faded, I stared at the person who emerged. He had the same face, stark white curls, and bright blue eyes, but the tall, graceful body and lean muscles were gone. He was thin and gaunt in a way that reminded me of Sam, but much worse, and sat in a wheeled chair. I dragged my eyes back up to his face to see him watching me. His mouth twisted in a bitter mockery of a smile.

"Behold, the terrifying figure of the God of Death."

"Are you sick?" I blurted out.

"Yes," he answered, eyes fixed on mine. "My powers are killing me."

I felt a prickle of horror for him. "Why?"

"Because I need you."

"What?" My voice sharpened.

"Our powers were never meant to be separated," he said. "They need balance."

My eyes narrowed. That sounded like what fucking Talmar said. "And how would they be balanced?"

"I don't know," he admitted, surprising me.

"Then how do you know my powers would help you at all?" I demanded.

He studied me for several breaths, then sighed, closing his eyes like he was resigning himself. "Because you've healed me before," he murmured.

"When?" My heart was pounding so fast. "I've never seen you before."

"When you tried to heal Dune."

When you tried to heal Dune.

Dune.

The words echoed around and around my head, but it was like they couldn't sink in. I couldn't understand them.

When you tried to heal Dune.
Tried.

I realized in a removed way that shadows were back, but not to disguise him. They wrapped around me as I swayed, forming a solid seat as my knees gave out and gently lowered me into it. He didn't move from where he sat, but his eyes watched me carefully.

"I...knew Dune," he finally said after a long time of me sitting frozen, staring at him. "We were friends. I had to leave Carth abruptly when you were still a baby, and I was upset. I didn't want to go. I was a child who didn't fully understand this power. I accidentally left a string in him. I didn't even realize I'd done it until later when I accidentally slipped into his mind. I should have removed it and left, but I was...I was lonely, and he was playing with you."

I wasn't sure I was still breathing.

"I had no one, and I was so sick." His voice grew harsh. "But when I was in Dune's mind, I could pretend I was still...that I had a family. I thought I was going to die, and I justified what I was doing with the fact that soon I would be dead and gone." He paused. "Then I saw you heal for the first time."

I started shaking my head as though I could keep his words from reaching me.

"I knew the prophecy. I knew who you were. I knew what it meant."

"No," I whispered.

"I told you not to tell anyone. I made up a story about the people of Carth burning witches and made Dune believe it, too, so he would keep your secret when I wasn't there."

"No," I repeated.

"The Voiceless have eyes and ears everywhere, even in Carth. I knew they would come for you if they caught even a whisper of your power."

I stared at him in horror.

He visibly swallowed before continuing, "I tried to help you practice with your power. I thought you'd be safe if I could help you get strong."

"Please," I interrupted, tears slipping out of my eyes, "please tell me you didn't... didn't..."

The pain that filled his face made him appear brittle as glass. "I made Dune stab himself."

I dropped my head into my hands, sucking in deep breaths and trying to keep from splintering into pieces.

"I had no idea your healing power would flow through the string and into me instead of Dune. Being filled with your power, being *healed* —it was such a shock that I didn't react until it was too late. You started screaming for Wolf, and I panicked that you would reveal yourself. So I told you not to tell him and left, but I now know that Wolf arrived, and you didn't try again to heal Dune." His voice grew even more rough. "I felt him die, and I knew it was my fault."

I abruptly stood and paced away from him, pressing a trembling hand to my mouth as tears continued to roll down my face.

I didn't kill him.

I didn't kill Dune.

It wasn't my fault.

The knowledge didn't bring me any relief, though—just more grief.

The ground shifted beneath my feet, and I realized with horror that the narc was beginning to wear off. I turned back to Menace to see him in his perfect form again, swiftly approaching me.

"We don't have much time," he said urgently, grabbing my arm. "You have to decide. Do you trust me or not? There's more…so much more, but I can't tell you unless you let me put that string in you. I have to protect the people *I* care about."

I hesitated briefly, but now that he'd opened these floodgates of truth, I had to know more, desperately *needed* to know more.

"Ok," I whispered. "Ok, I'll trust you, but I swear if you—"

"I won't," he interrupted fiercely. "I swear."

His hands settled on either side of my head, and shadows filled his eyes, slowly swallowing the blue until there was only black—just like Clarity's power. Then I felt it, a shimmer of darkness sliding through my veins, and it felt so similar to the Shadowbane that I almost jerked away.

"Wait," he suddenly spoke sharply, and his voice sounded both close and far away, crackling with power that made the hair on my arms stand up. "You have—"

৶

"Em? Em, please wake up. Please. Please don't be dead!"

I dragged my heavy eyelids open and stared at the sky, slowly lightening with the dawn through the bars of a cage. I tried to move, but my body was still partially paralyzed by the narc. I managed to turn my head to see Roe sitting beside my cage and gripping one of my hands. Relief filled his tear-stained face when he met my gaze.

"Em!" he sobbed. "Are you ok?"

"M'ok," I mumbled.

"They killed Sax," he said through sobs.

Sax. Sax was trying to help us, but he failed. He killed Zana, and the Voiceless killed him, and now it was just me and Roe.

Roe let out a squeak of terror, and Talmar crouched beside him. He was frowning, an icy anger crackling in his eyes. *Fuck.*

"Ember," he began, and the cold tone of his voice made my hands start shaking, "running was a grave mistake. You cannot escape your destiny, and all you have proven is your own weakness and lack of understanding. As you continue to delay the inevitable, you bring more suffering upon yourself."

"Is it inevitable if it can be delayed?" I mumbled without thinking, then winced. I'd gotten too used to speaking freely.

Talmar stood, towering over us with a furious expression. Then he turned and *kicked* a booted foot hard into Roe's ribs. All the air rushed out of Roe's lungs with a pained gasp, and his hand was ripped from mine as he fell backward. Before he could get up, Talmar was kicking him again and again.

"No!" I shrieked, forcing my numb body to lurch upright. "No! No! Stop! Please stop!"

Talmar withdrew, and with horror, I noted there was blood on his boot. Roe didn't move.

"I had hoped it wouldn't come to this, but your defiance comes at a cost. There are consequences to each act of rebellion. If you persist in this, the consequences will be severe." He gestured at Roe, who was curled in a ball, gasping sobs. "Do not mistake my mercy for weakness. The child will suffer if you continue to challenge your divine purpose."

Tears streamed from my eyes as I clung to the bars of my cage and stared helplessly at Roe. I knew better than to run my mouth, especially with Roe here.

"I'm sorry." I forced the words out, the lie bitter in my mouth. "Please forgive me, Talmar."

He stared at me, his expression unreadable. I couldn't tell if he believed me, but I put my all into keeping my expression contrite.

"This is your last warning, Ember," he finally said. "You will accept your fate or suffer the wrath of the God of Death. The decision is yours but know that we are watching and will act accordingly."

I bowed my head in what I hoped looked like an act of submission.

"You shall remain here until we are ready to depart," he finished before standing and striding away.

I waited until he was a safe distance away before scrambling to the corner of the cage closest to where Roe lay.

"Roe, can you hear me? Roe!"

He moved agonizingly slowly but lifted his head and looked at me. His face was already swelling, and his nose and lip were bloody.

"Oh my gods," I sobbed, horrified. "I'm so sorry, Roe. Can you come here?"

Roe pushed himself up, tears sliding down his cheeks, and managed to drag himself back to me, one arm wrapped around his ribs.

As soon as I could reach him, I took his arm and let my healing power flow. Talmar had broken two of his ribs, his nose, and a part of his skull was fractured. Relief filled his face as my magic healed his injuries. Once fully healed, I pulled him as close as possible, hugging him through the cage. His body trembled as he clung to me.

"Roe, listen to me," I said in a low voice. "You have to get out of here. They're going to keep hurting you. You need to get away and *run*. Don't stop until you literally can't keep going. Then find a small shelter and sleep a little, but don't make a fire."

"Em—" he tried to interject.

"Don't make a fire for at least three days; you have to run as far as possible. Pick a mountain and go toward it to make sure you're not going in circles. Try not to leave tracks."

"Em, I can't!" he whispered through tears.

"You *can*," I said firmly. "You fought a horrible sickness that was tryin' to kill you for *ten years*, Roe. You are so much stronger than you think."

He stared at me, shaking.

"My friends from the Vault might be searching the woods. Or my brother Wolf and his crew. You can trust them. Do not come back here, no matter what you hear. Even if you hear me screaming, *do not stop*. Do not trust the Voiceless, no matter what they say."

"I don't want them to hurt you," he whispered, eyes huge with fear.

"I know, but they're gonna hurt me whether you're here or not, and it will kill me if they hurt *you*." My voice broke, tears brimming in my eyes.

"I'm scared," he confessed.

"I am, too, but we both need to be brave, ok?"

He took a deep, shaky breath. "Ok."

"If you take off Sax's jacket, you can prop it up here and make it look like you're just sleepin' under it." I glanced around the camp. They still had probably an hour before the camp was packed up. "How good are you at throwing?"

"I'm pretty good." He puffed out his thin chest a little. "I killed a prairie dog with my slingshot."

"That's amazing," I whispered, trying to muster a smile. "Ok, I need you to find a small rock and throw it as hard as possible at the mules to create a distraction. As soon as the mules freak out, you go straight to the woods and don't stop running, ok?" I reached through the bars and squeezed his hands. My voice wobbled, but I managed to continue, long-forgotten words suddenly surfacing in my head, "You can do this. My brother used to tell me that bein' brave doesn't mean you aren't scared; it means you're scared, and you do it, anyway."

He squeezed my hands back, tears still in his eyes. Then he let go and found a small rock in the dirt.

"I'm gonna keep looking at you so they don't suspect us," I whispered. "Make sure no one's watchin' you."

He sat, quiet and alert, for almost a full minute before he moved, chucking the rock hard and then huddling down. It clattered somewhere in the distance, and he winced. "I missed."

"It's ok. Count to a hundred and try again."

I watched his face as he concentrated. A Voiceless walked past us, carrying buckets of water. Their eyes scanned us carefully, but then they moved on. Roe's fingers dug another rock out of the dirt. He bounced it in his palm, testing the weight, before closing his fist around it. He scanned the camp without moving his head, and I pleaded with my power, the universe, the gods, and whoever would listen that Roe would get safely away.

Roe moved swiftly, flinging the rock as he bit his lip in concentration. I heard the mule bray, and chaos erupted.

"Put the jacket up and go," I hissed at him as I turned around and moved to where I hoped I was blocking him from most of the Voiceless' view. I held onto the bars and craned to see where the mule was trying to break free of the pack line, hoping I looked appropriately surprised and curious. Several of the Voiceless glanced at me, but then they went back to struggling with the mule. I forced myself to count to a hundred before I turned back around like I'd lost interest. Sax's jacket was propped up like Roe had curled into a little ball; I lay in my cage next to it and closed my eyes, straining my ears for any sound of alarm.

Please. Please. Please. I begged to the rhythm of my pounding heart.

It took the Voiceless at least half an hour to get the mule line back under control. A Voiceless approached at one point, and I sensed them standing over me. I kept my breaths as even as possible, clenching my shaking hands. It felt like they stood there for an eternity, but finally, they moved away. It was another hour before they had everything packed up, and as I watched them secure the final things to the mules, I prayed I'd given Roe enough time. I couldn't forget how fast the Voiceless had moved through the woods with their cybernetic limbs.

Someone approached my cage. "Wake up, Ember."

I sat up, rubbing my gritty eyes as he unlocked the door and beckoned me to crawl out. I did so, watching as the Voiceless glanced at Sax's jacket.

"Get up, child."

I stood, shakily stretching my cramped limbs and watching the Voiceless stare at Sax's jacket. When nothing happened, he walked closer.

"Boy! Wake up."

He nudged the jacket with his foot, and it collapsed inward. He snatched it up and stared at the empty spot beneath it before his eyes flashed to me. I had planned on acting shocked, but I couldn't help the victorious smile that crossed my face.

There was no sign of gentleness or compassion in Talmar's face as the Voiceless, furiously holding my arm, explained Roe was gone. His metal hand grabbed my arm hard, yanking me toward him.

"Where is the boy?" he hissed.

I didn't answer, and I heard the pistons in his arm move as his grip tightened until I was gasping in pain.

"I don't know!" I shrieked when I couldn't take the pain any longer.

For a moment, I thought he would hit me, but he just shoved me back into the cage and locked it. He shouted orders at the three with cybernetic legs to search the surrounding woods. Seeing them run in the daylight was even more horrifying than in the dark. They moved so inhumanely fast. I huddled in a ball in my cage, my arm aching with pain and straining my ears for any noise of Roe screaming or crying. After about ten minutes, the three returned empty-handed.

The Voiceless had a fierce argument, half out loud and half with signed gestures, but I understood enough to figure out they were trying to decide if they should stay and search for Roe or keep going. When they landed on the decision to keep going, tears of relief filled my eyes, but my stomach sank at the dark look on Talmar's face.

He jerked me out of the cage by the wrist. "It seems you have not yet grasped the severity of your situation, Ember," he snarled as he marched me to my horse. "We have given you every opportunity to accept your role with dignity, yet you continue to defy your God."

We stopped beside my horse, and he leaned in close, spraying spittle on my face as he hissed out the words.

"You have chosen your path, and mark my words, by evening's end, you will beg for the mercy you so foolishly squandered."

CHAPTER 38

I waited until midday before I made my move. I wanted to get as far away from Roe as possible, but I was not about to go quietly. Talmar thought I was uncooperative before? I was going to make every single one of these assholes regret coming on this mission.

They stopped at midday for a rest, and the Voiceless dismount. The one leading my horse dropped the reins and began to walk back to grunt at me to get down, but as soon as he'd turned his back on the reins, I kicked my horse as hard as possible. The poor thing reared back on its hind legs, knocked the Voiceless off his feet, and bolted, bowling over a few more Voiceless who didn't get out of the way fast enough. We thundered down the path, and I let the horse take the lead, ducking low in the saddle to avoid branches and clinging to the saddle horn for dear life.

I glanced back once to see they were pursuing me on their horses, and I urged mine faster. The reins were dragging on the ground, out of reach, and I hoped the horse wouldn't step on them and fall. We slowly outpaced the other horses, and for a moment, elation seized me. I was getting away! If I could lose them somehow in the woods, maybe I could find my way back to the Vault and—

Movement at my side caught my attention, and a strangled cry escaped my lips when I saw one of the metal-legged Voiceless running alongside my horse. He grabbed the trailing reins and pulled back, and the horse fought him but slowed.

No!

He had his hands full trying to stop the horse, so as soon as I was pretty sure I wouldn't *die,* I bailed off. I hit the ground and rolled, tumbling down the steep mountainside and picking up speed until I slammed into a tree. I didn't move for a second, trying and failing to gasp in a breath, and that was all it took for the metal-legged Voiceless to catch up to me. He seized my arm and yanked me to my feet. I fought him, and the black threads on his lips strained as he hissed out an angry noise. I wasn't *winning* by any means, but he struggled to get me back up the ridge. I landed a lucky kick right to his groin, and despite the metal legs, he was still a man between them because he crumpled with a groan.

I took off, but a second enhanced Voiceless caught me seconds later. This one was bigger than the first and threw me roughly over his shoulder. I tried to kick and scratch, but my attempts barely got his attention. He carried me back to my abandoned horse, where Talmar was waiting. The Voiceless dumped me on the ground, and I stayed there as Talmar loomed over me, his eyes narrowed with fury. As my heart pounded in my throat, I wondered if he'd expected this to be easier—if he'd expected *me* to be easier. Maybe I would have been if I hadn't met Trey and my crew. If the Voiceless had found me right after I killed Juck, I would've already been mostly broken, and I doubted it would've taken much to finish the job, but I'd had time to heal and get a taste of life and love and freedom, and I wanted *more.*

"Get up," he snarled.

I didn't move.

Talmar gestured at the Voiceless who'd carried me back, and rough hands grabbed my upper arms and hauled me to my feet. I saw Talmar's windup and tried to brace myself. The blow caught me across the face, snapping my head backward and making me stumble into the big Voiceless behind me.

"No more," he hissed, his face contorted with rage. "We can no longer wait until evening for you to face the consequences of your defiance. Your insolence must end *now.*" He glanced at the Voiceless behind me. "Bind her."

He turned on his heel and mounted his horse as the Voiceless wrenched my hands back and began tying them with what felt like a rope. He cinched them painfully tight, but I pressed my lips together, refusing to make a noise. He knocked me to the ground after binding my hands so he could bind my ankles as well. Then he picked me up and threw me over the back of my horse like a dead deer. I hung there, blood rushing to my head, and tried to breathe as we returned to the rest of the Voiceless. I reminded myself over and over that at least Roe was safe and that they couldn't hurt him. I was infinitely familiar with pain. I could handle pain. This would not break me.

"You're a river. You don't break, you bend."

As we approached the others, I could hear hammering. When we came into view, I realized they were hammering long metal stakes into the ground. Each stake had a leather strap attached to it, and my entire body started shaking. Still, when they pulled me down and untied me, I fought, aiming for eyes and groins and flinging handfuls of dirt into their faces. I used every dirty trick I could remember Wolf teaching me, but I was no match for a dozen Voiceless. They overpowered me, securing my wrists and ankles to the leather straps and forcing me to lay spread-eagle on my back in the dirt. I snarled up at them, trying to focus on how many were bloodied, disheveled, and panting rather than the restraints on my body. Talmar appeared above me, and I was viciously pleased to see he had a fat, bloody lip.

"God of Death, we invoke you as humble vessels awaiting your will," Talmar recited with cold fury. "May your shadows guide us and bear witness."

I spat out every horrible curse I knew, and a vein pulsed in his forehead.

"Ember, Goddess of Life," Talmar continued, raising his voice over my swearing, "you stand before us with a heart hardened by pride and defiance. You have turned from your divine path and rejected the sacred union with your God."

I tried to brace myself, even as each breath came jagged and uneven.

"Tonight, you face the consequence of your defiance. You have challenged the will of the God of Death, and you will atone in agony."

I tried to suck in deeper breaths, shaking. *You don't break. You don't break. You don't break.*

"Your body has previously been claimed by another who defied the will of the cosmos and the God of Death. Your soul is stained with his defiance, and your flesh still bears his mark, but today, you shall be reforged."

My body went cold all over. *No. He couldn't mean—*

A Voiceless stepped forward. He met my frightened gaze as he knelt in the dirt beside me and pressed his fist against his chest, head bowed. Then he straightened, grabbed the front of my T-shirt, and ripped it open to my navel.

Panic stole all the air from my lungs, and tears rolled down my face. Talmar approached, his eyes hard and unforgiving, and my eyes locked on what he held in his hand. It was a metal branding iron—a real one—and a sob escaped.

"May this symbol forever serve as a reminder that your mind, body, and soul belong to the God of Death. As this brand burns away the mark of the traitor, may it also burn away your pride and your resistance, may you be purified through fire, and may the God of Death look favorably upon your sacrifice."

Talmar turned and held the brand out. A Voiceless stepped forward, lifted their metal arm, and *flames* shot from their palm like a blow torch. I watched the metal slowly begin glowing orange, gasping in panicked breaths. *You don't break. You don't break.*

All too soon, Talmar turned back to me, holding the glowing brand aloft. I couldn't make out the symbol from where I lay, but I knew it was something worse than Juck's initial.

"Prepare yourself, Goddess, for the mark of reclamation."

There was no hesitation, no guilt, no regret in Talmar's expression—just a feverish light shining in his bloodshot eyes. I sobbed through my teeth as I clenched my jaw and tried to brace myself as Talmar slowly lowered the brand, but the second the burning metal pressed into my skin, a scream of agony ripped out of me. The horrifyingly familiar smell and sound of my flesh burning choked me as I tried to suck in a breath, but I couldn't breathe. I couldn't—

I jerked back to consciousness at the sensation of my pants being removed. I immediately started kicking, my bare foot smashing into the face of a Voiceless, but the pain in my chest hit me, and I almost passed out again. As I struggled to stay conscious, my ankles were seized and rebound.

Talmar appeared above me and smiled.

"Fuck...you," I got out through my teeth.

He crouched beside me, still smiling, and I knew something worse was coming. "As I told you, it is forbidden for us to touch the

Goddess of Life intimately," he said softly, and bile surged up my throat. "So I shall offer my body to the God of Death. I shall be his vessel as he claims your body for his own."

"No," the hoarse word escaped despite my effort to keep my mouth shut.

He gently stroked the side of my cheek, and I jerked my head to the side. "I warned you, Goddess. I gave you so many chances to avoid this fate." He grabbed my chin, forcing me to hold his gaze. "We *will* break you, Ember. Continue to defy us, and we will strip away every last shred of dignity until you understand the futility of your resistance."

There was no point in holding back anymore. I shoved down all the horror and fear at what was about to happen and let unfettered rage take control. "The only thing you're a vessel for is your tiny *dick,* asshole!"

The red veins in his eyes seemed to protrude even further as rage filled his face, but the cruel excitement in his eyes scared me the most. He stood and turned to the surrounding Voiceless, raising his arms to the sky. "By the power vested in me as a prophet of the Voiceless, I call upon the God of Death to descend upon this humble vessel. Through me, the God of Death shall claim the flesh of the Goddess of Life and bind her soul to his eternal will."

"You do not break. You bend."

I squeezed my eyes shut. The panic was breaking through the rage now, building and burning in my chest worse than the pain from the brand. I felt him approach, and the tattered pieces of robe brushed across my bare legs.

"Let this be your final lesson in humility, Ember," Talmar said low in my ear. "Or else I shall invoke the God of Death into every single prophet here, and we shall take turns until you are begging to submit."

His metal hand grabbed my bare upper thigh, and panic exploded in my brain. Everything went white.

෨

I woke to the incessant buzzing of flies. The sun was high overhead, shining brightly on me. I went to sit up, but the pain in my chest made me halt with a gasp. I raised shaky fingers to touch my chest where the pain *screamed,* but then I remembered, my body stiffening at the memory of being restrained, the brand, and then—

I squeezed my eyes shut and sucked desperate breaths in through my nose. When I was certain I wasn't going to be sick, I braced myself and sat up, wincing in pain, and froze. My bare legs were *covered* in blood. Each breath I took sounded far too loud as I slowly lifted my eyes and stared in numb horror at the carnage surrounding me.

For a long moment, my eyes couldn't process what I was seeing. I was no longer restrained, but there was blood *everywhere,* and the flies were thick. My gaze caught on a severed hand lying a short distance away, and it slowly dawned on me that I was looking at *pieces* of bodies. Pieces. As though the Voiceless had exploded. Even the metal prosthetics hadn't withstood whatever happened, chunks of torn metal and frayed steel tendons mixed in amongst the flesh. I got to my feet, shaking, and slowly turned.

Talmar's eyes were bulging in what looked like fear as they stared up at me from his severed head. There was no sign of the rest of him.

I turned and retched, but there was nothing left in my stomach. A ringing sound filled my ears as I fought to catch my breath, and everything in my head went quiet. Some deep-seated animal instinct seized control, narrowing everything down to only crucial steps to survival.

I was alive.

I was barefoot and half-naked.

I needed clothes.

Slowly, I walked through the bloody gore, searching for my pants. Several coyotes lurked on the edges of the camp, watching me. A few of the braver ones seized chunks of remains and darted into the trees with them. Above me, in the sky, several hawks and other birds of prey circled. There would be more predators soon, lured by the smell of blood. I finally found my pants, partially buried under the remains of a Voiceless. I pulled them free and did my best to shake them off. New holes looked like they'd been *burned* through the denim. I glimpsed Sax's jacket, lying on a discarded pack, and pulled it on. I found my boots next, my socks neatly tucked inside. I struggled to put them on as my hands violently shook.

Slowly, something began to cut through the shock. It was similar to the ringing in my ears but more melodic. As I finished lacing my boots, my eyes moved of their own accord to the gory remains of a shoulder attached to the shredded pieces of a metal arm, and in a strange dreamlike state, I reached down and fished through the blood and flesh until my fingers touched something hard that made my healing power jolt. I pulled it out and stared at the small object in my bloody hand. It looked like a rock—a black rock that was flat on one side and jagged on the other. It glinted slightly in the sun as I turned it, but I would have described it as unremarkable—except for my blood *singing* as I held it.

I glanced down at the gore at my feet. I couldn't tell if it had been embedded in the shoulder or just buried in the mess, but something still called to me. I stood and moved forward, my boots squishing until my feet stopped. I couldn't see anything, but again, I reached down, and my fingers immediately closed around something hard buried in the carnage, sending another jolt of power through me. Again and again, my feet moved until finally, I stood with eleven rocks in my bloody hands, and whatever was driving me vanished. I stared at the rocks for a moment longer before shoving them into a small inner pocket that buttoned closed in Sax's jacket, and then I started walking in no particular direction. It didn't matter *where*, so long as it was *away*.

I stumbled through the brush like a drunk but stayed on my feet. The sun had begun to set before I became aware enough to realize I should have taken one of the horses. I hesitated, wondering if I should go back, but the thought of returning to all that blood and—

My feet lurched back into motion. No, I couldn't go back.

As the sun set, it became increasingly difficult to see where I was going. I often fell, tripping over sticks or slipping on uneven ground, and the pain in my chest made it hard to breathe, but I kept dragging myself up and putting one foot in front of the other. I had to keep going.

Eventually, I fell, and my shaky arms gave out when I tried to push myself up. I closed my eyes, trying to catch my breath. I'd rest for a moment—just a moment.

The next time I opened my eyes, it was daylight again, midday by the sun's position. The sight of my bloody body and clothes immediately made me retch again, but nothing came up. I needed to find water. Water and food.

I got to my feet and again focused on just putting one foot in front of the other. I found a craggy mountaintop that looked familiar and pointed my body toward it.

One more. One more. I chanted in my head with every footstep.

I was almost at the top of a ridge when I slipped on loose gravel and tumbled down the entire distance I'd worked so hard to climb. My palms stung as I pushed myself up, leaving bloody handprints in the dirt.

Keep going.

I found a stream and drank from it, washing my hands and arms as well as I could. My palms were covered in scrapes, tiny pieces of gravel embedded in my skin.

The grade grew steeper, and soon, I was on my hands and knees crawling up the mountain. Every single muscle in my body ached with pain, but I kept going.

One more.

One more.

One more.

The sun was beginning to set when a noise registered in my head. Something was running, crashing through the woods toward me. I twisted, and a strangled scream escaped my lips at the sight of a body charging up to me. They grabbed my upper arms, and I fought to get away, panicked.

"Ember! Ember, it's Sable!"

I finally focused on the face before me, taking in the familiar long blond hair and pale blue eyes. Sable. It was Sable. He let out a piercing whistle and then focused on me again.

"You're safe, Ember. It's just me, it's Sable." He paused, worry and rage deepening the furrow in his brow, but when he spoke again, his voice softened. "Emmy, can you hear me?"

I realized I had frozen like a frightened deer, just staring at him and panting. I couldn't think straight. My head felt like it'd been stuffed full of straw.

"It's okay, Emmy," he said, even softer. "You're safe."

I started shaking like my entire body was seizing, and his grip tightened on my arms, lowering me to sit on the ground as my knees gave out. He crouched before me, sharp eyes scanning me carefully, but stopped on my chest.

"Emmy, can I look at that wound?" he asked, but the words made no sense, bouncing around in my head until they shattered.

After a moment, he reached out, watching my face, but I just stared at him. Slowly, he parted Sax's huge jacket and peeled one side of my torn T-shirt back. He went still, staring. Then he peeled back the other side, and his pale eyes lit with rage. Part of me realized this would normally make me panic, but I felt nothing.

"They branded you on top of the other one?" His voice was a low snarl.

I couldn't answer him. It felt like I'd lost my voice, not from hoarseness or sickness, but like it was *gone*. He pulled Sax's jacket closed, and his cool fingers gently prodded my swollen, bruised face, feeling for broken bones.

"I think you're in shock," he said after a few seconds, "I want you to lay down so I can—"

He'd begun attempting to lay me on my back, but my body panicked and fought him, clawing at his arms and trying to stay upright. He stopped, eyes narrowing on my face. A muscle flexed in his jaw, and his eyes hardened, but his voice was still soft when he spoke.

"Okay. It's okay, Emmy, you don't have to lie down."

He whistled again, the loud noise making my ears ring.

"You're safe, Emmy," he repeated. His hand curled around one of mine, and I clung to it. "I'm here, you're safe." His voice roughened, and I glanced up at his face.

The tears in his furious eyes startled me. He'd always been calm and collected, but he was neither, right now. I knew I should apologize for being such a bitch to him. I should explain myself. I should tell him how sorry I was for what Juck did to him, but none of those words made it out of my head.

Instead, I just tipped toward him like all the strength had fled my body at once. He wrapped his arms around me and held me where I'd fallen against his chest. I didn't move, closing my eyes and trying to stop shaking. He kept murmuring that I was safe, and I believed him.

He whistled again, and this time someone whistled back.

"Wolf is comin', okay?"

We sat there for a long time. Every so often, a whistle would echo through the trees, and Sable would whistle back.

"Slow down," Sable suddenly said sharply. "I think she's in shock."

I opened my eyes and met my brother's horrified eyes. He slowly lowered himself in front of us, scanning me carefully, a landslide of emotion all over his typically stoic face.

"Is she hurt?" he asked, anger and fear crackling in his voice.

"I haven't fully checked," Sable responded, his voice dangerous, "but they branded her again…over top of the other one."

Wolf sucked in a breath, his nostrils flaring. "What?"

Sable pried my clenched fists from his shirt and shifted around to my back, quietly explaining to me what he was doing as he peeled my shirt back again. "The symbol of the Voiceless."

My brother's jaw clenched tight, and he kneeled before me with unnatural stillness as he stared at the mark. The air seemed to pulse.

My lips moved, and my hoarse voice came out. "You came."

Wolf's eyes met mine again. "Of course, I came." His voice was low and rough.

"Roe?" I whispered.

"Roe?" he repeated, and a trickle of dread cut through the numbness.

"He's out there. You have to find him." My voice shook, rising higher.

"Okay," he said immediately. "Okay, describe him to me."

"Ten, but he looks younger. Black curly hair and brown skin. Skinny. He's scared. He's just a kid."

"Okay," Wolf's eyes were sharp. "We'll find him."

Another whistle rang through the trees, and Wolf whistled back.

"The others will be here soon, and then we'll start searchin'. When did you last see him?"

"I told him to run," my hoarse voice grew more ragged. "I don't know…I don't know how long—" My words abruptly cut off as panic swelled.

"More than a day?" Wolf pushed.

"Yesterday morning. I think." It felt much longer. "We rode half a day."

"Any idea which direction you were goin'?"

"I don't… I don't know." Why hadn't I paid attention to which direction we were going? I knew better—

"It's alright, Emmy. We'll find him," Sable murmured from where he still sat behind me. His chest against my back was the only thing keeping me upright.

Wolf glanced up at him and then back at me. "We'll find him," Wolf repeated, taking one of my hands and squeezing it. "It's okay. We'll find him."

"Wolf."

All three of us looked up to see Kai and Scar. Their grim faces darkened even further as they scanned me.

"We found the Voiceless camp."

"How many?" Wolf growled.

"Hard to tell. They're all dead, but, uh, there's no bodies," Kai answered, his eyes darting to me for a moment.

I closed my eyes.

"What do you mean?"

"I've... never seen anythin' like it." Scar's voice was low. "Just... bits and pieces of bodies and... other things."

"How far?"

"About thirteen miles northeast."

"We've got another missing person," Wolf said, quickly relaying my description of Roe. "We need to retrace their route. We gotta get her back to the Vault, though."

My eyes flew open. "No! No, I'm not going back without him. He's just a kid."

There was a brief silence as I held my brother's conflicted gaze.

"Okay." Wolf finally conceded. "We'll stay together."

"They had horses at the camp," Kai said.

Their voices blurred together into noise as I stared at the trees. At some point, someone handed me a water bottle, and I drank some, moving on autopilot. Then Wolf's hand gently touched my arm, getting my attention.

"Can you walk?" he asked.

I nodded, trying to convince myself I could. I got my feet under me, stood with Wolf's help, and immediately pitched forward into darkness.

CHAPTER 39

The dark, shadowy shapes of trees looked ominous in the flickering firelight, but above the trees, stars filled the night sky like a million shards of broken glass. I lay there, admiring them, when everything suddenly came crashing back to me. I bolted upright with a gasp that turned into a hiss as my muscles seized at the pain in my chest. I curled inward, trying to breathe. Fuck, I'd forgotten how much it hurt.

A hand landed on my shoulder, holding me in place as I tried to scramble away. Sucking in a breath to scream, I twisted and met Wolf's wide eyes.

"It's me! It's just me, Em," he was saying, quiet and urgent. "Sorry, it's just me."

It was dark, and I had been lying in a bedroll on the ground. I couldn't see anyone else around the campfire, just me and my brother. I relaxed, trying to slow my breaths and pounding heart.

"The others are out lookin' for Roe," he said. "We're workin' in shifts."

Both my hands were bandaged up past my wrists. I held them up, staring at the tips of my fingers sticking out.

"Sable had to pick a lot of gravel out of your palms," Wolf explained.

"I fell," I mumbled.

"That was our guess." He paused. "Your wrists looked better, though."

That moment he left me tied up in the clinic felt like it was years ago instead of days. I gingerly touched my chest and realized they'd bandaged that, too. I dropped my hand back to my lap.

"As soon as one of 'em picks up a trail, they're gonna get me," Wolf said after a few breaths. "I'll find him, Em. I promise."

"Don't promise that," I said. I couldn't get my hopes up. I couldn't.

"Emmy, we're gonna find him," Wolf repeated, his voice fierce.

I glanced up at his face and could feel hope digging its claws into my heart, but I tried to ignore it.

"Do you want some water?"

I nodded, and he fetched a bottle of water and opened it for me. I fumbled with my bandaged hands but managed. When I was done, I gave it back, and a heavy silence fell. I stared at the fire, knowing he was going to ask what had happened. I might as well get it over with.

"Did you know what the Voiceless wanted with me?" My voice sounded hollow.

"I knew they wanted you brought back to Sin City," he said cautiously.

"I'm supposed to be the God of Death's bride."

His brow furrowed over his flashing eyes. "What?"

"There's a prophecy. They were gonna bring me back to have his children."

He stared at me, nostrils flaring and a muscle flexing in his jaw.

"The Voiceless think I'm the Goddess of Life." I could tell that my flat, wooden tone was scaring him, but I couldn't do anything about it.

"So what, they were gonna force you to…" His voice trailed off like he couldn't bear to say it.

"Fuck him until I was pregnant over and over? Yeah."

A strong gust of wind made the surrounding trees creak, breaking the silence with the eerie sound. Wolf stood, and the abrupt movement made me flinch. He didn't move for a moment, staring at me, his trembling hands clenching and unclenching at his sides. Then he paced away, running a hand through his hair. I jumped when he let out a yell and lashed out, his knuckles smashing into a tree trunk over and over, making the entire tree shudder. I huddled into a small ball and watched him—my eyes painfully dry. When he finally stopped, he paced away again and stood with his back to me, swiping at his face with his sleeve. The emotion pouring from him was its own kind of storm—a much more normal reaction than the nothing I felt. It was several minutes before he returned, and I could tell by the way he was holding his arms that he'd hurt his hands again.

"Did *you* know about this?" he asked, his voice ragged.

"No."

"Can I sit with you?"

When I nodded, he carefully stepped over the bedroll and lowered himself next to me. I tried to take his bloody hand, and he pulled away, frowning.

"You're injured, Em."

"Please?" I whispered.

He hesitated a moment longer but finally gave me his right hand. I healed his injuries, slow but steady, through my unbandaged fingertips.

"You just don't seem very surprised," he said, low.

I gestured for his left hand. He let out a heavy breath and gave it to me.

"I'm not surprised."

"Why?" His voice cracked.

Part of me wanted to scream the words at him, but exhaustion pulled at my bones, and the words came out so empty. "Because this is my life."

I finished healing his hand, and we sat side by side in silence for a while as he took deep breaths with shaky exhales. His emotions were wild again, raging around us, and if he was a storm, I was a hollow tree awaiting my fate.

"Mac said someone named Sax took you?" he asked once he calmed down again.

"Yeah. He brought me to Zana. They both worked for Madame. They gave me to the Voiceless because the God of Death promised to make them gods if they turned me in."

"Is that... possible?" Wolf sounded hesitant.

I shrugged. "I dunno."

A log popped in the fire, sending a spray of orange sparks, and I waited.

"What did the Voiceless do to you?" His voice was rough with emotion.

There it was. "Where do you want me to start?"

"At the beginning, I guess?"

So I told him, the words falling from my lips, rocks tumbling down a hill. I told him about Roe, the rite of correction, and the ways the Voiceless had tried to break me and get me to submit. He had to get up and pace for a while, but he didn't punch any more trees. Once he returned, I told him about Sax trying to help us and then about Zana and her powers. That led to me backtracking to explain why Hawk went crazy, but then I faltered.

"Did you find Sky's body?"

"Yeah," Wolf answered, his tone softer than I expected. "I'm so sorry, Em."

"She had fire powers," I stared at the flickering flames of the fire, remembering how she'd *become* a living flame.

"That explains a few things."

Explaining how Sky saved my life, and then I failed to save hers was harder to get out, but I did it. A stab of guilt and grief pierced through the numbness. I should've been able to heal her. I knew I *could*. I *could* make golden light explode out of me and heal everyone it touched. Why did I—

"What happened after the Voiceless brought you back... after Sax?" Wolf prodded.

I took a shaky breath and told him about Roe getting away, Talmar's rage, and my escape attempts, but then the words became more difficult to get out.

"They strapped me down and... and branded me again. I passed out... and then I woke up to... they... they were..." I tried to hide my shaking hands in my lap.

Wolf radiated pure fury the same way the fire radiated heat. "Did they rape you?"

I sucked in a breath through my nose and let it shakily out through my mouth. "He said he was invoking the God of Death into his body so he could touch me. He said if I didn't submit, he'd let *all* of them..." I broke off, trembling. Beside me, Wolf was bristling with violence, and I struggled to finish. "He was going to, but... I don't think... I don't know what happened. I woke up and... the Voiceless... they were..."

I hunched forward, curling inward, as the horrible realization dawned on me. I killed the Voiceless *with* my healing powers. I'd somehow twisted it into something dark and deadly—the one *good* thing about me that helped, healed, and brought life. I thought hurting Sam while healing myself was the worst thing I could do, but this?

"Did you kill them with your powers?" Wolf asked, and he still felt coiled tight as a spring, but his voice was strangely calm.

Was he looking for the final evidence that I needed to be dragged back to Carth? Everything Menace had told me suddenly flashed through my head. I hadn't killed Dune, but Wolf didn't know about Menace, so how would I even explain? I had no proof of Menace either, and Wolf would probably think I was lying... *again.*

"Emmy?"

"I... I don't know..."

"I hope you did."

I looked up at him, startled by his low, savage tone. He watched me with a mix of turbulent emotions, but he almost looked *proud.*

"What?"

"I hope you killed them with your powers," he repeated, holding my gaze. "You defended yourself, and I'm fuckin' glad those monsters are dead."

I stared at him.

"What are you thinkin', right now?" he finally asked.

I had no idea what to say. I had a million thoughts crashing through my head, but my mind was somehow empty at the same time.

"There's no right or wrong answer, Em," he added. "I genuinely want to know."

"I don't want to kill people." The words tumbled out of my mouth. "I want to be *good.*"

I couldn't read the emotion in his eyes, but he reached out and gently gripped my bandaged hand. "Emmy, I don't think you murdered Dune."

I stopped breathing, certain I'd heard him wrong.

"I don't understand what happened, but I don't think you murdered him." He paused, pain and regret filling his eyes. "I'm sorry I thought you did for so long. I'm sorry for all the horrible things I said to you. I'm sorry I didn't trust you or believe you." His voice grew rougher. "You're right. I promised to protect you, but I didn't. I turned my back on you, and you suffered… suffered so fuckin' much because of it."

Emotion was pouring off him, and I felt *nothing*.

"I'm sorry," I whispered.

He frowned. "Why are you apologizing?"

"I don't know why I do this."

"Do what?" His brow drew together.

"Go numb." I gestured vaguely to my face.

"Numb?"

"It's like my emotions just… just shut off. I know it makes it seem like… like I don't care, but I do. I really do. I promise."

His eyes softened, but his shoulders sagged. When he spoke, his voice sounded thick with emotion. "It's okay, Em." He paused, taking a deep breath. "As you know, sometimes my words just…shut off. It's like I get trapped in my head and can't speak. Scar taught me sign language, which…gave me a voice when I lost mine, but sometimes I couldn't even do that. It's gotten a lot better, but I've been workin' on it for years with my crew."

For twelve years, I'd pictured Wolf as a terrifying, deadly force stalking me, trying to get close enough to sink his fangs into me and tear me apart. Now I tried to picture the real Wolf, eighteen years old, grieving his brother and being sent out into the desert to search for his sister—entirely alone and knowing that if he didn't find me, he'd lost the only family he'd ever get to have. A fissure ran down the numb shell I was stuck inside.

"I'm glad you found them," I whispered.

He smiled slightly. "I think it's more they found me."

A whistle echoed from the woods, and Wolf's head snapped up. He whistled back, and then another whistle answered.

"They found a trail," he said. "Lee's comin' to replace me."

Lee.

My stomach did *something* I couldn't interpret.

"Don't hold it against him," Wolf said, and I glanced back at him. He was grimacing. "All of 'em chewed me out about leavin' you tied up in the clinic, but I've never seen Lee this angry. He's barely spoken to me since."

I didn't know what to do with that. Wolf got up and started grabbing his gear. Even though I was watching for him, it still startled me when Lee silently materialized from the woods. He met my eyes, and the intensity there made my heart pick up speed.

Wolf crouched in front of me, blocking my view of Lee. "I'll be back," he promised. "I'm gonna find him, Emmy."

He smiled, and it was a smile I must have seen hundreds of times. It was the smile I got when he would give me a dandelion or when I would successfully land a hit in training. It was all Wolf, all my brother, and the words bubbled out of me, shaky with emotion.

"I don't hate you."

He went still, his eyes locked on mine.

"I'm sorry I said it," I whispered. "I don't hate you. I've never hated you."

He gently took my face and kissed my forehead, and a bittersweet emotion cracked that fissure wider. When he pulled back, his eyes were wet.

"I've never hated you, either," he said, his voice rough. "I wanted to sometimes but could never quite manage it."

My lip trembled, and I took a shaky breath.

"You should try to rest, okay?" he added. "I'll be back."

I managed a nod, and he released my face and stood. He approached Lee, who was waiting with a closed expression. Wolf clapped a hand on his shoulder, leaned in, and began speaking to him, too quiet for me to hear. Lee sighed and replied, and the two of them conversed briefly. Some of the tension between them seemed to ease.

Wolf disappeared into the woods as silently as Lee had appeared. Lee stayed on the other side of the campfire, but his eyes found me again, a muscle flexing in his jaw. Emotion started to trickle back into me, prickly and uncomfortable.

He slowly moved around the fire toward me and crouched at my side. His dark eyes glittered in the firelight. "I'm sorry," he said, his voice low. "I fucked up."

I didn't answer, my head a mess of hurt.

"Please, Ember, tell me how to make it right."

"You left me there," the bitter words escaped.

"I know." The two words were heavy with guilt and regret. "I'm so sorry. I'd do anythin' to go back and do it all over."

I pressed my lips together, sorting through my tangled emotions, but he shifted to his knees.

"I'll grovel on my knees if that's what it takes." His low voice was rough. "I can't lose you."

The way my chest ached—not the brand, but my *heart*—it was almost like... like...

"I know you said you can't offer me anythin', but gods, Ember, I'll take whatever you're willing to give me."

Fuck. I *liked* him. That's why it hurt so much. Whatever this was between us, it wasn't just physical. Maybe it'd never been just physical. He made me feel safe. He coaxed me out of my head and away from the ledge every time I was in danger of falling apart. He saved my life, kept me company, and made me laugh.

"Why are you calling me 'Ember'?" I asked.

His throat bobbed as he swallowed. "Doesn't feel like I deserve to call you a pet name."

The emotion filling my chest scared me, but it was *soft*. It was nothing like how I'd felt about Trey. There was no deep well of emotion opening up in my chest to swallow me whole, and that knowledge was strangely reassuring. Maybe... maybe it was okay to *like* him.

"I like it when you call me 'Freckles,'" I whispered, my eyes prickling.

He shifted closer, gently resting his hands on my knees, all of him intensely focused on me. A light flickered to life in his eyes, like hope. "Freckles, please forgive me."

"I forgive you."

He blinked, his lips slightly parting before he recovered. "Are you sure?"

"Sorry, did you want to grovel some more?"

He blinked, then gave me a devilish smile that made my blood heat. "I'm more than willin' to stay on my knees in front of you."

"Smooth," I said dryly, but the wave of relief made me feel almost drunk.

"Don't blame me," he murmured, gently taking my face in his hands, "I'm addicted to you."

I arched an eyebrow, "Addicted?"

"Helplessly." He leaned in closer, and my heart went into overdrive. "Addicted."

His lips brushed gently across mine, and I wrapped my arms around his neck, pressing us closer. Moving hurt like hell, but I tried to ignore it. I wanted this moment. I wanted him. After everything that had just happened with the Voiceless, it felt fucking powerful to make a choice—to *have* a choice. The pain couldn't control me, just like the Voiceless couldn't control me.

Then I shifted, and pain made stars fill my vision. My entire body locked up. Maybe the pain was stronger than I thought.

"Freckles? Hey, you okay?"

"Yeah," I panted, trying to hold my body still. "Just moved the wrong way."

"Oh fuck," he pulled back to glare at me. "You should not be moving."

"I want to move," I protested.

"No. I'm a fuckin' asshole."

"Lee, it's okay—"

"There's no rush, Freckles. I'm not goin' anywhere."

I tried to protest, but he got up and put more wood on the campfire, brought me some food and water, and then, after I ate, tucked both of us into the bedroll, gently wrapping me in his arms. I lay on my side, facing the campfire, and he curled up behind me, one arm cushioning my head.

"I'm sorry I was so difficult in that cave," I murmured.

"Don't apologize. I understand why," he said low in my ear.

"I should've said this sooner but thank you for saving my life."

His free hand lazily traced the freckles on my cheek. "You're welcome."

My eyes fluttered close as his fingers moved across my skin. He murmured the names and stories of constellations he found until I drifted away again.

ॐ

"Em?"

I opened my eyes and blinked at the face hovering over me. Then it registered who it was.

"Roe!" I sat up, my breath catching from the pain of the movement, but it didn't stop me from throwing my arms around him. "Oh my gods, Roe!"

He clung to me, and I could feel his tears dripping onto my neck. "Are you okay?" he choked out. "Did they hurt you 'cause I ran away?"

"I'm okay," I said, relief making me shaky. "Are you okay?"

FANGS

"Yeah." He sounded as shaky as I did. "I had to climb a tree to get away from a bear, though."

My arms tightened around him as fear shot through me. I glanced up to see Wolf watching us, a soft emotion on his face.

"Thank you," I said, tears filling my eyes.

"You're welcome, Em," he murmured. "He's okay, just tired and hungry and a little scraped up."

I held him tightly, taking his hand to send my healing power through him, healing every little scrape before pulling away. "Let's get you some food," I said.

"I got it," Lee said, crouching beside me, his hand gently brushing against mine. "Hi Roe, I'm Lee. You hungry?"

Roe glanced at me, wide-eyed.

"It's okay," I said softly.

"This is your brother?" he asked, glancing up at Wolf.

"Yeah, he's my big brother," I smiled a little. "He's a pain in the ass, but you can trust him."

Lee snorted, and Wolf rolled his eyes when I glanced at him, but his lips twitched upward. Roe flashed a nervous grin and finally released me, following Lee. Sable appeared at my other side and crouched, scanning me.

"Time to change those bandages," he said. His tone was calm and professional, but he watched me warily.

I swallowed my pride and fear. "Okay."

The flash of surprise that went through his eyes was gone as quickly as it came. "You can stay sitting up," was all he said.

My hands were healing quickly, and Sable didn't take long to re-wrap them. However, changing the bandage on my chest was a slow, painful process. I thought I might faint at one point, but Wolf crouched behind me and steadied me. Finally, Sable got the bandage off and frowned as he examined the brand.

"There's no sign of infection," he said, but his expression remained dark.

"What is it?" I asked, trying to breathe through the nausea.

"It's the symbol of the Voiceless," he said, his voice clipped.

I wasn't sure what that looked like, but my skin crawled, knowing I'd been marked as their property.

"I'm gonna clean it out as best I can and re-bandage it, but I'll have to do some more work on it when we get back to the Vault."

I sucked in a deep breath. "Okay."

"It's gonna hurt," he warned.

"I know."

I kept my jaw clenched so tight it ached by the time he was done. Wolf held my hand, not complaining as I nearly crushed it. I didn't make any noise, but tears of pain poured down my face.

"You're doin' great, Emmy," Sable murmured at one point.

I glanced at my brother to see something soft and pained on his face as he studied Sable, but then he swallowed hard and looked back at me. By the time Sable finished, I was exhausted. Roe hovered beside me as the others packed their little camp with the stolen horses and mules. There were enough horses for all seven of us to have our own, but Wolf took one look at my drooping eyelids and told me I was riding with him. I didn't argue. I did not want to go tumbling off the horse again.

"How far away are we?" I asked as Wolf settled in the saddle behind me.

"Probably about three days ride," he answered, clucking at our horse to start moving.

Wolf and I took the front, then Lee, Roe, Sable, Kai, the string of mules and the extra horse, and finally, Tuck.

I wanted to ask him some more questions, but I fell asleep almost immediately and didn't wake up until we stopped at midday. After a brief rest and some food, we saddled back up. Roe was with Lee now since he'd been close to drifting off earlier, and when I glanced back about ten minutes later, he was already asleep. Lee gave me a soft smile, and I returned it, feeling lighter than I had in a long time.

"So Mac can read minds, huh?" Wolf suddenly asked.

I froze, unsure of how to answer him, and he huffed a laugh.

"He told us, Em. It's okay. He had to explain how the hell he knew where you were."

"How did you find me?" I asked the question that had been plaguing me.

He was quiet for a few breaths. "What does it feel like when you use your powers?" he asked in a low voice instead of answering.

I frowned in confusion. "Um, warm. It feels like this warm, golden light goes from my chest, down my arms, and out my hands. Why?"

"I've always been good at tracking, but this felt... different." He paused. "We got through that wall in the tower and found you gone. Nemo told us there was a vast network of caverns and tunnels under the watchtower. He advised Mac not to follow that way because he'd get lost, but I..."

I glanced up at him to see him frowning.

"I could *see* this faint golden glimmer disappearing into the darkness. No one else could see it, but it looked like a thin, shimmery golden thread. I said I was going through the tunnels. Nemo didn't like it, but he didn't try to stop us. Mac said he'd take the rovers and go above ground, and me and the Fangs took the tunnels. I swear—"

"The Fangs?" I interrupted.

"That's the name of my crew," he explained.

My heart started beating faster, and a faint memory came back to me. "The Fangs...are you the ones who took down Mad Dog?"

He hesitated a moment. "Yes."

I stared at the passing trees without seeing them. I remembered now. I remembered Juck talking about the Fangs, one of the most sought-after groups of bounty hunters, talented trackers who never failed, and lethal killers who were capable of taking down an entire garrison by themselves. Rumors of who paid the Fangs to take out Mad Dog had been flying, and the delicate balance of alliances had become even shakier for a while. Juck had bitched about it—how so many jobs were put on hold because no one was sure if the warlords were going to turn on each other.

"Was it a job?" I whispered.

"No," Wolf sounded darkly pleased. "That was revenge."

I sat quietly, absorbing that. It was jarring to think of my straight-laced older brother executing someone out of revenge, but I had to admit I was still holding onto assumptions about him. We'd both changed so much in the past twelve years, and I couldn't blame him. Not after what Sable had gone through—Sable *and* his sister.

"Sable and I...we bonded over the fact that we'd both lost our sisters," Wolf finally added in a low voice. "He didn't ask us to help him take Mad Dog down. We volunteered."

"Did you free the slaves?"

"Yes."

I tried to swallow past the lump in my throat. "The first time

Juck took a load of slaves to him, I'd only been with him for about a month. I tried to sneak out at night and open the trailer, but I got caught. In front of all the Reapers, he stripped me naked and beat me with his belt until I passed out." I pressed my trembling lips together.

His arms tightened around me, and I could hear his teeth grinding. We rode in silence for almost a full minute before I spoke again.

"Do you ever feel guilty about killin' people? Even bad people?" I whispered.

He was quiet for a few seconds, then answered, "Yes."

"I do, too," I confessed.

"About Madame?"

"And Juck."

"You killed Juck?" he asked.

I couldn't tell from his voice what he was thinking, but I wondered if he was remembering how they found Juck's dead body. "Yeah."

"Good," he said in a low, vicious voice.

It felt like a weight fell from my shoulders, and I took a deep, shaky breath. Trey and my crew had all said similar things when they found out I killed Juck, but for some reason, Wolf's reaction was the one I'd needed.

"Wait, go back to the tunnels," I said, realizing I'd derailed what he'd been trying to tell me. "You saw a golden light?"

"Oh, right. So I saw the thread and somehow *knew* it was you. So I followed it. The tunnels, more like caverns, had so many branching paths, but that golden thread led us straight through the maze. When we got aboveground, I thought for sure it'd fade in the daylight, but it didn't. It led us to you. In a few places, it got snarled, and once it disappeared, but I found it again. It stopped at the Voiceless camp, though. I don't know why it didn't show me where you were in the woods."

"Do you think it's a power?" I asked, my mind spinning.

"It felt... otherworldly, but..." he made a frustrated noise. "I don't know how to describe it, but it felt so familiar at the same time."

"I understand that," I murmured, thinking of Mac.

"So it's me, Zana, Mac, Clarity, Hawk, and Sky who got powers?"

I remembered Hawk's screams, and my stomach turned. "As far

as I know."

"We should probably have a serious talk with Nemo when we get back."

I made a noise of agreement, but my mind drifted back to Menace. I wished I would have asked him his name. I desperately wanted to ask Wolf about him. If he'd been friends with Dune, Wolf would have known him. But before I said anything about Menace to my brother, I needed to talk to Mac.

Mac.

I could still hear the fear and desperation in his voice as he called to me when Sax was taking me away. He was probably beside himself, and I wanted to let him know I was okay.

I'm comin', sweetheart. Hold on.

The eleven stones still hidden inside my pocket seemed to hum and pulse, almost like a heartbeat. I pressed my palm against them, willing it to stop, and after a moment, the sensation faded away. I struggled to swallow, my mouth suddenly dry. What the fuck were they? I hadn't said a word about them to anyone, and I didn't really know why. It was almost like... like the stones themselves didn't want me to reveal their presence.

I shivered.

"You ok?" Wolf asked.

"I'm fine."

CHAPTER 40

It was another day before we reached my crew on the radio. Mac's voice sounded fierce as he demanded to talk to me, although talking to me probably didn't ease his worries much since I immediately burst into tears when he asked if I was alright. Wolf gave him a rundown of what happened, my injuries, and where we were. My crew had gone southwest, but Mac promised to be back at the Vault by midday tomorrow when Wolf told him we'd be arriving.

I couldn't sleep enough to ease the exhaustion running through me. I couldn't tell if it was just from my body trying to heal the burn on my chest or the ordeal or something else.

You were always meant to be his, and without him, your powers will corrupt. You feel it, don't you? The darkness in your veins?

I tried to tell myself Talmar was lying, twisting things as he attempted to manipulate me, but I felt *weak*—just like he'd said I would.

If you continue on this path, your body will weaken, and you will become a harbinger of sickness and death.

This nausea was just my anxiety. It had to be.

Roe slowly opened up to Wolf and his crew, and I had to admit it was cute to see them interacting with him. All of them were more at ease around a child than I would have guessed, which was a pleasant surprise. Sable and I seemed to call a truce. I let him re-bandage the brand every day and didn't fight him about examining me, and he seemed careful only to do what was necessary. Wolf relayed to the rest of the crew what I'd told him on the first night, thankfully while I was sleeping. After that,

I noticed Kai stopped glaring at me and seemed to make more of an effort not to be a dick. And Lee was Lee. He returned to teasing and flirting as though nothing had happened, but we had no more opportunities to be alone together.

My nightmares grew worse. I woke up screaming every night, sometimes more than once, and I hated that it made Roe cry every time. I tried to remember how I'd managed to keep my jaw clenched shut after Trey's death, but maybe my body had reached its threshold for stuffing down hurt. Wolf was always there to calm me down, though, and I fell back asleep every night to him humming, but Talmar and the Voiceless continued to haunt me. I started dreading nightfall and tried to sit by the fire and keep myself awake as long as possible in the evenings. I could tell everyone knew what I was doing, but they didn't mention it.

"Em, wake up."

I straightened with a gasp, my heart slowly calming as I realized I was still on the horse with Wolf.

"Look," my brother said, raising a hand to point ahead.

The Vault was below us, nestled in the small basin between the mountains, and my heart swelled at the familiar sight of the tall metal walls and even the fucking watchtower in the middle. *Home.* The Vault was home.

"Mac must've beat us back," Wolf said, gesturing to where I could just barely make out the rovers parked inside the gate.

"Mac?" I tried, wondering how far his power reached.

"Em!"

His familiar voice filled my head and brought tears to my eyes. *"Hi,"* I managed to get out.

"Are you back?" he demanded.

"Almost."

"Fuck, I need to see you," he sounded agitated.

"What, speaking to me telepathically isn't enough?" I teased, but the urgency in his tone made me feel unsteady.

"You'd think it would be, but it's really fuckin' not," he said with humor, but it still sounded strained.

"I'm really okay, Mac."

"Em," I felt the jolt of pain and fury that went through him, *"you're not okay. They fuckin' tortured you."*

"Okay, true," my mouth was so dry, *"but I'm feelin' so much*

better now that we're almost home."

"I hope you're prepared 'cause there's a whole damn welcoming committee for you."

I grinned.

"I'm gonna try real hard not to be a pain in the ass, but I might have trouble lettin' you out of my sight for a while."

"Understandable," I said with a laugh, and it struck me how that statement didn't make me angry or afraid—just loved. *"I can't wait to see you."*

His smile felt so warm, even though I couldn't see it. *"I can't wait to see you, too. I'm gonna go let everybody know you're almost here."*

Even without him actively speaking inside my head, I could *feel* him—that golden thread running between us and binding us together. I hadn't realized how much I'd missed it. The connection was so comforting—it felt like belonging, like home.

An hour later, we arrived at the gate, and I gasped as it opened to reveal a massive crowd of people. Most of them were standing back, though, with just Nemo and a few of his men and my crew waiting near the gate. Wolf and I rode up to them, and Mac stepped forward, his intense gaze fixed on me. All of me felt shaky as Mac reached up toward me and helped me dismount, but my feet didn't even touch the ground. He pulled me against his body and held me in a fierce hug, with his arms wrapped around my lower waist and my legs dangling. My arms went around his neck, and his face burrowed into my hair. Pain stabbed through my chest, but I just closed my eyes and pressed my face against his neck, breathing through it. I was starting to love the smell of peppermint soap. Neither of us said anything, but our emotions were a sudden summer storm raging around us. I could feel his heart pounding in his chest, his overwhelming relief that I was home, and a soft, tender concern.

"Mac, put her down." Sam sounded annoyed.

Mac took a shuddering breath and set me on my feet. *"Welcome home,"* he said, smiling wide enough that both dimples popped out.

Sam elbowed him out of the way a second later and hugged me. Raven surprised me by going next, gripping my shoulders and scanning me closely.

"I'm so sorry about Sky," I whispered, unable to help myself.

"For fuck's sake, quit apologizin' for shit you didn't do," she muttered, but her eyes were softer than I'd ever seen.

Clarity openly cried as she hugged me. Griz hugged me so gently it made my throat ache. Apple flew across the patchy grass, threw herself into me, and sobbed. Jax beamed, and Nemo smiled, and all of them looked so genuinely *happy* to see me. In return, I managed a shaky smile and called Roe over from where he was huddled by Lee. Apple clung to my neck as I introduced Roe to everyone, stumbling slightly over Trey's name as I explained how we'd met. Roe attached himself to my side, his fingers clutching my jacket.

"In a few minutes, I'd like everyone to come to my house to get all the details straight," Nemo said.

My stomach churned, and I crouched on the ground to set Apple on her feet. She didn't let go of my neck, leaning into me as she and Roe silently studied each other.

"Sorry I can't hold you longer," I said. "You're just gettin' so big, my arms get tired."

Truthfully, I felt weak and shaky, and I desperately hoped I just needed some more rest.

"Where am I gonna live?" Roe asked abruptly, and his voice was so small and scared that it broke my heart.

"You're welcome to stay with me for now," I said. "We don't have to figure it all out right this second, okay?"

He nodded, but the fear in his face didn't fade.

"You want to come swing with me?" Apple asked him abruptly.

A month ago, Leda had convinced Mac and Griz to hang a crude swing in one of the taller pine trees. It wasn't anything special, just a thick rope with a large stick tied to one end, but the kids loved it. Roe glanced up at me, frowning.

"It's okay, you can go play," I smiled.

Roe gave Apple a shy nod and followed as she led the way, already talking a mile a minute. Wolf talked quietly to Mac and Nemo while the rest of the Fangs unpacked the horses. Sam sidled over and wrapped an arm around my waist.

"You sure you're feelin' okay?" he asked, a slight furrow between his brows.

I leaned into him gratefully. "I'm tired, and most everything hurts," I said honestly.

"Let's head to Nemo's," he suggested, "We can sit on his comfy couches and wait for everyone."

I nodded and let him tell Mac what we were doing, but as soon as they heard the plan, my entire crew elected to walk to Nemo's with me. I didn't mind; I was grateful for their company. The walk wasn't very long, but by the time we got there, I felt even worse, shaky and nauseous.

"Em, you okay?" Griz asked with a frown.

"I don't feel great," I admitted.

"You look pale," Raven said bluntly.

"You look like you're about to be sick," Mac muttered, scanning me closely.

"I might be," I muttered.

Sam started climbing the handful of steps leading to Nemo's porch, but I stopped, clinging to the rough wooden railing. The stairs looked impossibly steep.

"What's wrong?" Mac asked, his voice sharper.

"I'm sorry," I mumbled, unsure why exactly I was apologizing.

"Em, what—"

Could anyone else hear that ringing noise?

"Em? Em! Grab her—"

⌒

"—know you well enough to tell when there's something you want to say."

A bitter laugh.

"Wolf, c'mon, what is it?"

"I told her the other night."

"Told her what?"

"That I don't think she killed Dune."

"Oh shit. How'd she react?"

"She didn't."

"What do you mean?"

"I mean, she didn't react, and then she apologized for not reacting. She said she doesn't know why, but a lot of times, she goes numb and doesn't feel anything."

A soft, knowing sigh.

"I'm such an asshole."

"Wolf—"

"I should've listened to you. You were right. You're always right."

"Wolf—"

"I've fucked this up every step of the way, Sable. She was right. I didn't want to feel guilty. I *did* want her to be a monster cause if she wasn't, that meant everything...*everything*—"

I managed to pry my heavy eyelids open, alarmed at the pain in my brother's voice. It took me a second to realize I was in Nemo's spare room again. I scanned the room, finally finding Wolf standing by the fireplace with Sable. He was leaning against the wooden mantle, one hand covering his face. Sable stepped forward and caught Wolf's wrist, pulling his hand away from his face.

"Wolf, listen to me," Sable said, his voice firm but kind. "You've made some missteps, but you're here. She's here. You have another chance to make things right."

They studied each other for a long time, and the emotion filling the room made me feel like I was intruding on something private.

"Is that how you feel?" Wolf asked, but the question was gentle.

"I don't want to make this about me," Sable said in a low voice.

"Sable," Wolf's voice was so *soft,* "you caring about her, too, doesn't make this about you."

"It's hard... to separate the two now," Sable confessed. "Sometimes I can't remember Hattie's face, and when I try to picture her, I just see Ember."

"You've been lookin' for her with me for a long time. I'd be more worried if you didn't care about her."

"I know. I just would never want Hattie to feel *replaced.*"

Wolf stepped closer to Sable, and I watched him tenderly brush Sable's hair back, tucking it back behind his ear. "I know I didn't get to meet Hattie, but from what you've told me, I'd guess she'd only be happy to see you take care of another little sister who needs it."

I watched them with an ache in my throat. I'd never seen my brother like this with anyone. I'd genuinely not paid much attention to the teachings of Carth, but I tried to imagine how it'd been for Wolf, constantly being told that a part of himself he had no control over was something bad, that any love he felt was twisted and wrong. I'd seen the twisted and wrong kind of love. *That* kind of love had been beaten into my body, mind, and soul. That kind of love was all I knew until Trey.

"Speaking of..." Wolf looked up and met my eyes, grinning. "Mornin', Emmy."

I flushed at being caught eavesdropping, but Wolf didn't seem mad. Sable straightened and strode toward me, scanning me closely.

"Good morning, Ember. How you feelin'?"

I made a face in answer. "What happened?"

"You passed out," Sable answered, frowning as he took my pulse from my wrist.

"No shit," I couldn't help saying, the corner of my mouth lifting.

Sable smirked, glancing at Wolf. "That smartass trait really must be hereditary."

Wolf snorted, but the smile on his face was soft.

Sable grew solemn again as he turned back to me. "You didn't get a fever, did you? After you... used your power?"

I didn't miss the hesitation, but he was right. I'd been out of it after leaving the Voiceless camp, but not feverish. I must have expended a lot of power taking out the Voiceless, but no burnout fever followed. I swallowed hard, trying to keep from picturing the bloody mess. Was it because I'd... I'd killed them instead of healing?

I realized Sable was still waiting for an answer and shook my head.

"Correct me if I'm wrong, but based on your vitals, I would guess you still aren't feeling great?"

"Might be the... the brand," I mumbled.

"I suppose," Sable replied, his tone doubtful.

"What do you mean, the brand?" Wolf asked from where he'd perched on the end of the bed.

"If her powers are working on healing the brand, the constant healing could be draining her."

"So she might feel better once it's healed?"

"I would hope so."

I didn't miss the look Sable was giving me. He suspected there was something more, but I did not want to dwell on what I'd done to the Voiceless *or* the possibility that I was sick or, as Talmar put it, *corrupted*.

"Time to change the bandage?" I asked.

"Yeah, you ready?"

I nodded and slowly sat up, trying to brace myself for the pain.

The bandage didn't cling quite so badly this time, but cleaning it still hurt like a bitch.

"I owe you an apology, Em," Sable said suddenly, causing Wolf and I to look up at him in surprise.

"For a long time, your brother would hide wounds from me, and I had to push him constantly before he let me help him. It drove me crazy." He glanced at Wolf with a wry smile, and Wolf's ears turned red. "You are like him in so many ways, and I think I instinctively started bein' pushy with you like I would with him, but that wasn't fair to you. You're not him, you didn't know me at all, and you have a lot of understandable trauma about being touched. I should have been more patient, and I'm sorry."

I glanced between Sable's serious, sincere expression and Wolf's guilty one. "It's okay," I whispered, my throat constricting. "I'm... I'm so sorry about Juck—" a sob choked me, "and your s-sister—"

"Emmy," Sable took both my hands and squeezed them gently. "What Juck did was not your fault. You were a victim just as much as I was." He glanced at Wolf. "Wolf told me about the beating you got the time you tried to free the slaves and I wish I'd been there. I wish I could've killed him for it."

"Me too," Wolf said viciously.

"When I think about all the times you were so fuckin' close by and knowin' he was trying to throw us off—"

"Wait, what?" I choked out.

Sable shot a stricken look at Wolf. "Shit, sorry, I thought you told her about that."

"S'alright, I was going to." Wolf sighed and turned to me. "Juck gave us several bad leads about your location. Claimed he saw you in a bunch of different places, but they always ended up being dead ends." His voice cracked. "And the whole time, he had you *right there*. You were so close, and I didn't know. He was just fuckin' toyin' with us."

I squeezed my eyes shut. The knowledge that I could've been rescued, that he'd been so close more than once, hurt just as bad as the burn on my chest. I hated that all of us had just been pawns in other people's games.

"I'm so sorry, Em."

The pain in my brother's voice made me open my eyes. His face was a map of guilt, and my eyes overflowed as I freed one hand from

Sable and took his, squeezing hard. "It wasn't your fault, Wolf," I managed to say. "It wasn't your fault. None of it was your fault."

We sat in silence for a while, all of us grieving what could have been. Eventually, Sable let out a deep breath and released my hand to reach for the bandages so he could re-bandage the burn.

"Wait... I... I want to see it."

Wolf and Sable exchanged a look, but Wolf got up and fetched a small mirror hanging on the wall. He handed it to me, and I stared at the reflection of my pale face. My eyes looked large on my thin face, and a yellow bruise lingered on my cheek. I took a breath, attempting to steel myself, and angled the mirror down.

My chest was a mess. The skin around the brand was swollen and inflamed, with the brand itself red and blistered. A familiar ringing filled my ears as I numbly studied the shape. It resembled an "X," but with the top and bottom closed, forming two triangles meeting at their points. A horizontal line slashed through the middle where the points met. This new mark was larger than the "J" and covered most of it, but the shiny scar tissue of the "J" was still visible inside the triangles, with the tail of the "J" curling out from the bottom.

It was clearly made with a branding iron. It looked far more legitimate than the crude brand Juck had given me and more like the brand on Sable's shoulder. The whole thing was made of sharp, aggressive lines. It looked like a brand you would find on an animal, which made me feel even worse for some reason. It was horrible and ugly and—

The door burst open, and I jumped, but Mac stood there, breathing like he'd run up the stairs. Wolf and Sable were on their feet, snapping questions at him, but Mac ignored them, striding up to where I sat frozen on the bed, still holding the mirror. He sat on the bed beside me, his eyes on the burn, rage flashing across his face, but then he looked up and met my gaze. He reached out and cupped my face, thumbs gently brushing away tears I hadn't realized were leaking down my cheeks.

"Trey said it first, but you really are a godsdamned warrior, Em," he said in my head.

I sniffled and tried to contain myself, but the memory of Talmar's words flashed through my head—*may this symbol forever serve as a reminder that your mind, body, and soul belong to the God of Death.*

"The only thing this mark is a reminder of is how you fought back, and you *won,"* Mac said, his voice fierce. "I hope whenever the Voiceless see their godsdamned mark, they think about how you beat them."

I couldn't hold his gaze. I dropped my eyes only to catch the reflection of my chest in the mirror again. I pushed the mirror away from me, letting it fall flat on the bed. It felt so fucking dumb to even think about physical appearance right now, but a part of me hated that the horror I'd gone through was so *visible*—that they'd disfigured my body in such a prominent and permanent way. I had secretly hoped the "J" would fade with time, but I doubted this would. I'd be lucky if it healed flat. I hated that I felt so *ugly*.

"Em." Mac's voice was soft in a way that made my stomach flip. *"You're beautiful in a way that won't ever change, no matter what scars are on your body.* His voice grew rougher, and I glanced back up at him, very aware of his hands holding my face. *"I've seen the stars countless times, but every night, their beauty still finds a way to surprise me—like my mind can't fully remember how lovely they are, no matter how hard I try. Every night, they still have the power to take my breath away."* The golden sparks in his eyes practically glowed. *"That's the kind of beautiful you are, Ember. You're not beautiful* despite *these scars. You're just beautiful."*

I couldn't respond, tears spilling down my face and my lungs struggling to function, but in a very different way than normal. This wasn't panic; this was something else. The rough calluses on his hands were gentle on my heated skin, and I could *feel* the conviction he spoke with and the warmth and tenderness in his chest as he looked at me.

He leaned in even closer, and my breathing hitched. For a wild second, I was sure he was about to kiss me, and I couldn't tell if it was fear or a terrible want running through my veins. But he just pressed his forehead against mine and closed his eyes, inhaling a deep breath that sounded unsteady, before pulling away and dropping his hands.

"Sorry to come barging in here," he said out loud in a lighter voice. "I felt your emotions, and my feet started movin' before my brain could catch up."

"It's okay," I whispered automatically, feeling slightly lightheaded as I realized Sable and my brother had left. It was just the two of us.

He seemed to realize that at the same time I did, and his face grew serious again. "I'm so sorry I didn't get to you in time."

"It's not your fault, Mac."

"I know, but gods, it kills me that I didn't get through that damn wall sooner." His face twisted with pain.

"I don't think any of us would have guessed that Sax would appear from underground like a damn prairie dog."

He smirked slightly at my attempt at a joke, but the pain lingered in his eyes. "We had that meeting with Nemo while you were out. Wolf told us everything you'd told him, and Roe was able to fill in some missing details, so I think we got a decently clear picture." He ran a hand through his hair, his jaw flexing. "A fuckin' horrible picture."

"There's more," I said, my heart rate picking up as his grey eyes snapped back to mine.

I told him about Menace, the horrible part he'd played in my life with Dune, and what he'd told me about the god of the Voiceless and himself. I hadn't been sure if he'd placed the string, but I got my answer when I tried to tell Mac about it. My mouth didn't move. I opened my mouth and closed it again. My jaw worked just fine. I tried again to speak, but my jaw refused to move.

"You okay?" Mac asked, his brow furrowing.

The sensation of something foreign controlling my body made my skin crawl. I tried to do it mentally, but again, it was like the words were locked in my brain.

"Em?" Mac was studying me closer, looking concerned.

"Sorry," I got out. "Sometimes it hits me that all of that was... was *real*, and it's..."

"A fuckin' nightmare?"

"Yeah," I whispered.

"So Menace just told you all that as a gesture of trust?" Mac asked.

"I think so."

"What was he gonna do afterward?"

"I have no idea." I tried not to feel guilty about the slight lie. If I *could* tell him, I *would.*

"Well, I don't trust him," he muttered.

"I don't fully, either, but if I'm bein' forced to choose between him and the Voiceless, I'm gonna choose him."

Mac's hands clenched in his lap, and his jaw worked, but he

didn't speak.

"We have to make sure neither of them finds out that you, Clarity, and anyone else have powers now," I whispered.

"Why?" he asked, his voice tense.

"Because who knows what horrible plans they'd make for the rest of you!"

"Em," he sounded frustrated, "you don't have to do this alone. If they know other powered people exist, maybe they'd think twice about trying to take you again."

Fear made my stomach churn. "No. They can't know."

"Em—"

"*I* did this somehow," I whispered, desperate. "I don't know how, but I think I gave you powers, and that means I'm responsible for what happens to you because of it."

"That is bullshit," Mac snapped. "Ember, you can't take all that on yourself."

"I have to protect all of you," I insisted, setting my jaw.

"No, you don't," Mac glared at me. "We're a *team*. We work *together*."

"Mac, I can't let any of you get hurt. I can't." My voice broke, and his glare softened slightly.

"That's not somethin' you can control, Em."

"But I have to try!"

"No, you have to let us in. Let us help you. We're so much stronger together."

I pressed my lips into a flat line, sucking in a deep breath through my nose.

"You've got a big leg up on us for having dealt with this magic for so long, but you have no idea how to work as a team." He held up a hand, halting me as I sucked in an angry breath to go off. "That's not a judgment on you; it's just a fact. This is *my* strength. I know how to work as a team. I know how to teach you to work as a team. You can teach us about magic. We play to our strengths."

Gnawing doubt settled in my stomach. I had no idea how to teach anyone about magic. I knew almost nothing, and each conversation with Menace proved that more. I was useless.

"You're not useless," Mac interjected.

"I don't even know how *my* magic works," I mumbled.

"We'll take it one day at a time, okay? I bet you know a lot more than you even realize."

I blew out a shaky breath and nodded.

"You should get some more rest."

"Will you stay?" The words slipped out before I thought them through, and his eyes darted to mine. "You don't have to if you're busy," I quickly added, my face heating. "I'm sure you're busy."

He tilted his head slightly, eyes focusing sharply on me, and I knew he heard the things I wasn't saying.

"I'll be fine," I tried to sound more confident.

"You can tell me when you don't want to be alone," he said, his voice gentle. "I'm never gonna judge you for that, and if you ever want me to stay, all you have to do is ask."

It took a few seconds, but finally, I whispered, "I don't want to be alone."

"Then you won't be," he said simply. "Do you—"

A knock at the door startled both of us.

"Can I come in?" Sable called.

I sighed but called him in. He gave me an apologetic smile.

"Sorry, I still need to bandage you back up, and Lee would like to come in."

We were all quiet as Sable bandaged my chest. When he finished, he glanced at Mac.

"Give me a couple minutes, and I'll switch with Lee," Mac said.

Sable nodded and left after cleaning up his supplies. I glanced at Mac to see him frowning.

"What's wrong?" I asked.

"Nothin's *wrong*," he said in a low voice. "Just weird that I can hear the thoughts of every single person in this hold... except for Lee."

I stared at him, my brow furrowing. I couldn't deny that it *was* weird.

"Your brother trusts him with his life, though, and maybe more importantly, he trusts Lee with *you*."

Panic raced through me, and I slammed down my mental shield before thoughts of Lee surfaced. Mac looked sharply at me, and my face grew hot, but I couldn't think of anything to explain why I'd just locked him out of my head.

"What's goin' on?" he asked finally.

"I'm just… tryin' to have a *little* privacy." I didn't mean for it to come out short, but it did.

His nostrils flared and hurt and guilt flashed through his eyes. "Right. Well, I'll send Lee in."

"Mac, wait, I—"

"It's okay," he interrupted, already moving toward the door. "You're right. You do deserve privacy." He paused in the doorway and smiled, but it looked stiff. "I'll see you later."

"Mac—"

The door shut behind him. I let out a frustrated breath, annoyed at myself. It wasn't his fault he could hear my thoughts. I didn't have to make him feel bad about it—especially after he came in to comfort me and said some of the sweetest, most beautiful things. My stomach churned with guilt.

The door opened a few seconds later, and Lee walked in, but he wasn't alone. Wolf and Scar were with him. They asked some more questions, clarifying things that Roe had said. I answered as honestly as possible but kept Menace out of it. I knew the longer I went without telling Wolf, the messier it would be, but I wanted to get Mac's opinion first. After a while, my eyelids began to droop, and Wolf shooed Lee and Scar out so I could rest. I was grateful that my brother stayed, pulling up a chair and grabbing a book from Nemo's shelf. He glanced up at me and gave me a slight smile.

"Go ahead and sleep, Em," he said. "I'm just gonna sit here and read, okay?"

I hummed sleepily and closed my eyes, listening to the pages turn and the low hum of the eleven stones hidden inside a pair of socks in the dresser.

CHAPTER 41

T he brand healed far more slowly than the first one. The whole damn hold seemed to band together in agreement that I shouldn't heal unless it was a life-or-death emergency. Wolf refused to let me return to the clinic, insisting he had a good reason. He got a secretive smile every time he said it, so it was clearly something *good,* but whatever they were doing kept everyone busy. Sam and Clarity hung out with me the most. Mac came by every day but only stayed for a few minutes. The space between us felt strained, and I didn't know how to fix it. Someone was always with me until the third day when Sam had to leave after breakfast. He promised to come back when he could, but an hour crawled by as I lay in my bed—an hour of replaying everything that had happened with Talmar and the Voiceless.

Eventually, I couldn't take it anymore. I got up, put my boots on, and tiptoed down the stairs. Nemo was meeting with his guards in the main room, but I skirted the wall and slipped out the door, not wanting to disturb them. It was cloudy and drizzling slightly, but the weather matched my mood. I visited Violet first, but she wasn't in the field, or the stables, and several other horses were missing, off being used for something. I lingered near the fence, trying to figure out where to go. I wasn't supposed to go to the clinic yet. I took a deep breath and let it out. There was one place I needed to visit.

My heart ached as I walked through the small cemetery. I found Sky's grave quickly; the bare dirt was a dead giveaway. The other graves, including Trey's, were covered in green now, but there were two fresh ones—one for Hawk and one for Sky.

I knelt beside Sky's grave and placed my little handful of wildflowers I'd gathered on the dirt, my eyes filling with tears.

"I'm so sorry, Sky," I whispered. "Thank you for saving my life. I'm so sorry I couldn't save yours. I should've...I should've been able to —" my words cut off as I tried to keep the sobs contained. "You mattered, and I'll carry you with me forever." I fiercely swiped my sleeve across my eyes. "I'll make sure no one ever forgets you."

Then there were no words at all, just tears and grief, and I hoped if her spirit lingered here, she could sense my sincerity. Words felt like such a meaningless thing to offer, but they were all I had. After a while, I pushed myself up and walked the familiar path to Trey's grave. I stood beside it, staring at the simple marker. I knew it wasn't fair that I was carrying all this hurt and anger that it had never been him in my dreams, but that didn't change the fact that I *hurt*.

"I wish it would've been you," I whispered, tears and rainwater dripping off my chin, "at least once."

I would never promise to love you and then leave you.

I squeezed my eyes shut, fighting for control. The worst part about grieving Trey was that the only person I wanted to talk to about it *was Trey*. I wanted to pour it all out to him, to feel his comforting arms around me, to lean on him, to let him support me—all the things he'd wanted me to do. What a fucking cruel twist of fate that I only felt ready to do so after he died.

"You just can't resist torturin' yourself, can you?"

I choked on a gasp and spun around to see Raven standing a few feet away, her arms crossed. She raised an eyebrow at me as she strode forward, passing me and continuing toward Sky's grave. I hesitated, then followed. When I caught up, Raven crouched beside Sky's grave, adding a single yellow buttercup to my little bouquet.

"You bring these?" she asked.

"Yeah," I mumbled.

Raven rested her elbows on her knees and fell silent. The half of her head that wasn't shaved faced me, and her long black hair hung over her face and hid her expression, but I could feel her pain. I watched her, my heart aching, wondering if she had any other family left alive or if Sky had been the last one.

"When she was four, I convinced her that buttercups were where butter came from, and she ate a whole bunch. Turns out, buttercups are toxic, and she fuckin' puked all night long. My aunt just about tanned my hide." Raven's voice shook slightly. "She hated buttercups after that, and me and my other cousins used to leave them everywhere for her to find—just being lil' assholes. She'd get so mad." She paused. "I saw this one on my way to the garage and figured if she ever expected me to put flowers on her grave, it'd probably be buttercups."

She fell quiet, and when she didn't move after a minute, I couldn't just stand there silently any longer. I crouched next to her, gingerly wrapping an arm around her. I kept my eyes on the flowers, watching raindrops run down the petals. I tried to brace myself for her to shove me away, but she didn't.

"Our moms had a falling out. They were sisters and fought constantly, but this time, it was bad. They stopped talkin', and we just didn't really get to see each other much. I didn't see them at all after I joined the guards, so I didn't know my aunt turned into an addict and stopped takin' care of my cousins. By the time I tried to reconnect, she didn't want anythin' to do with me. When she was thirteen, she left home to move in with her boyfriend—a grown-ass man."

I wasn't sure if I'd ever heard Raven talk this much before, so despite my feet going numb and the cold rain slowly soaking into my bones, I didn't move, listening.

"Her boyfriend was an asshole. He started pimpin' her out to the guards so they'd look the other way when he and his asshole buddies smuggled drugs in. Somethin' happened one night—shit went south, and her boyfriend shot one of the guards. He was killed by another guard, but they still arrested Sky and charged her with all the crimes her boyfriend had been committing. She was in the cells for almost a whole fuckin' year, and I didn't even know she'd been thrown into the Sentencing until she came runnin' screamin' for Trey 'cause you were dying in the Pit."

I swallowed hard, sorrow and rage entangling around my ribs. Even without knowing the details of Sky's story, I wasn't surprised. I'd known what sort of story she'd have, and I hated that. I remembered Wolf remarking I didn't seem surprised about what the Voiceless wanted. Of course, I wasn't. None of this was a surprise. When you were small and weak, you always found yourself under someone's boot. I hoped in her final moments, when she'd burned Hawk to ash, she felt powerful and feared—at least for a moment.

I took a breath, but Raven's sharp voice cut me off.

"Don't apologize."

I snapped my mouth shut so fast my teeth clicked together, but she startled me by huffing a laugh. When I glanced at her, she rolled her eyes.

"You gotta stop bein' so predictable, Boney." Before I could think of a response, she was standing up and hauling me with her. "C'mon, you look like a half-drowned cat."

I scanned her wet black hair sticking to her face and the rainwater or perhaps tears clinging to her eyelashes. "You're one to talk," I grumbled.

"You know, gettin' yourself kidnapped by a cult is a pretty fuckin' dramatic way to try and get out of training," she remarked as we walked back down the hill.

A startled laugh escaped my lips. "Well, it worked, didn't it?"

"Not on your life. You're startin' as soon as you don't look like a strong gust of wind might blow you over."

I snorted, trying to push down the fear that I wouldn't shake this weakness—that this was something else. *Without him, your powers will corrupt.* Was that just more bullshit, or was it actually true? If it was true, was it talking about Menace, or was it the fake God of Death? My life was complicated enough without fucking prophecies breathing down my neck.

We were a couple houses away when we saw Kai and Sable burst out of Nemo's home into the drizzle. My stomach dropped, and I felt Raven tense, but Kai spotted me and shouted at Sable. They both started storming toward us, the relief in their faces changing to anger.

"Fuck," I muttered out loud.

"Where the fuck were you?" Kai demanded as he reached us.

"I—"

"I asked her to come to the cemetery with me," Raven interrupted. "I didn't realize she was a prisoner."

Kai's sharp glare snapped to Raven. I glanced between them, uncertain if I should step in.

"You didn't think to leave a note?" Kai gritted out.

"Next time, I'll submit a written request so you can shove it up your—"

"Sorry!" I blurted out. "I'm sorry!"

Kai's angry face almost matched his hair, and the smirk on Raven's face didn't help.

"Kai," Sable put a hand on his arm, but he frowned at me. "You scared us, Ember. No one knew where you were, and we couldn't find you."

Real guilt stabbed through me. "Sorry," I mumbled.

"Let's go inside," Sable sighed.

"I gotta head to the garage," Raven said, meeting my gaze, still smirking unapologetically. "See you later, Boney."

Nemo glanced up when Kai, Sable, and I came in, and the deep furrows in his face relaxed at the sight of me. I attempted to give him an apologetic smile, and he gave me a warm one in return. My boots left little puddles of muddy water on Nemo's stairs.

"You were at the cemetery?" Sable asked as we walked down the hallway.

I nodded, hoping they wouldn't press. I felt physically and emotionally exhausted. Thankfully, they were quiet. Sable got to work changing the bandage while Kai glared at me with his arms crossed. Sable was finishing up when the door opened, and Wolf walked in.

"I got somethin' for you," he said, grinning.

He walked up to the bed, and then, from behind his back, he pulled out a dandelion.

I stared at the small yellow flower, my heartbeat slowing as it thudded in my ears. I could see Trey's sunshine smile and warm brown eyes. What had he written in that letter? To look for him in the dandelions? That I would find him wherever there was life?

I looked at the flower, but all I saw was a painful reminder of everything I'd lost.

The tidal wave of pain crashed into me, sent me tumbling underwater, and then I was sobbing.

I was vaguely aware of Wolf sitting beside me on the bed and asking me questions in a concerned voice. I sat cross-legged on the bed, hunched over with both hands covering my face. I couldn't answer them. I could only sob. The bed shifted, and a warm arm wrapped around me.

"I'm here, Emmy," my brother murmured. "I got you."

I curled into him, clinging to his jacket, and cried into his chest. It was a long time before I finally cried myself out, my body-shaking sobs slowing to hiccupy gasps. Wolf held me tightly, his cheek resting on top of my head. Eventually, I realized that Sable was sitting on my other side, and Kai was in the chair.

"You want to talk about it?" Wolf asked, his voice gentle.

I didn't answer momentarily, but then the hoarse words escaped. "I miss him so much."

"Trey?" he asked, and I nodded, squeezing my eyes shut as fresh tears rolled down my face. They were silent for a few seconds before Wolf said so gently, "I'm sorry you lost him."

That apparently opened the floodgates because the words suddenly came spilling out of my mouth. Tearfully, I told them about Trey, about saving his life, the kittens and the dandelions, and how he had my back every time I needed him despite how cruel I was to him. I told them about our escape and capture. I told them about his death. I wasn't sure why the words were coming to me now, but I didn't try to hold them back.

"He healed *me*. I was so fucking stuck just tryin' to survive, and he showed me how to *live*. He never...never gave up on me, and he...he had every right to. He was always kind—*always*—and so patient. When I got swept away in that river, I realized I didn't care if I died anymore." My voice was a broken, fragile thing. "I was so tired of fighting to survive when all surviving did was *hurt*, and I thought maybe...maybe if I died, I'd see him again."

They were quiet for several breaths.

"Is that why you asked me to kill you?" Wolf asked roughly.

I hesitated, then mumbled, "Partly, yeah."

"Do you still feel that way?" Kai surprised me by asking.

He was leaning forward in the chair, his elbows resting on his knees. His freckled face was solemn, but his eyes were no longer angry. I took a moment to think about it, and the answer came far more quickly than I expected. No, I didn't want to die. I wanted to be here. I wanted to get to know my brother and the people he called family. I wanted to hear Apple giggle, kiss Lee again, help Roe find his place at the Vault, make Mac smile, and let Raven teach me how to fight the Voiceless. I wanted to keep healing people. I wanted to *live*.

"No." My voice came out thick with emotion. "I don't feel that way anymore."

I didn't miss the shaky breath my brother released or the way his arms tightened around me. "Good, because I need your help figuring out why the fuck Pa lied to both of us."

I pulled away enough to look up at him, my eyes widening. He told me he believed I didn't kill Dune but believing me about what happened afterward—believing *me* over Pa was something entirely different, something I never expected him to do.

He believed me.

He *really* believed me.

I must've said it out loud because he smiled sadly and said, "I really believe you. I'm sorry it took me so long to get here."

I threw my arms around his neck and hugged him, tears streaming down my face. I had my brother back.

I had my brother back.

I could barely breathe through the sobs. I hadn't realized how much this would mean to me, or maybe I'd refused to think about it since it seemed impossible. All I knew was the emotion flooding me was overwhelming. It felt almost as strong as the grief over losing Trey, but instead of pain, it was *joy.*

"I missed you so much," I sobbed into his shoulder.

"Em, you have no idea how much I missed you." His voice was choked with emotion.

The stubble from his beard scratched my face, and my chest ached from pressing against him, but I didn't care.

"So…guess we're not gettin' that bounty after all?"

Wolf and I pulled apart, and both looked at Kai. Sable stood beside him, tears on his face, and Kai's eyes were damp, but he was grinning at us.

"Don't make me kill you," Wolf warned, but when I glanced up, he was smiling, and his face was wet.

I noticed the dandelion discarded on the bed and snagged it, tucking it behind my ear like I used to when I was a kid. Wolf noticed and grinned at me.

"As if I haven't heard that threat a million times," Kai scoffed. "You gotta come up with some new ones, man."

"I'll work on it," Wolf said dryly.

CHAPTER 42

I thought I struggled with nightmares before, but they paled in comparison to my nightmares now. I woke up screaming so often I didn't know how I was going to move back into the clinic because no one would get any fucking sleep. I tried to avoid being alone as much as possible, but I knew that wasn't sustainable. After about a week, I forced myself to ask for a little more space. Wolf and my crew had been taking turns sleeping on the cot in Nemo's spare room with me, so I started with nights, figuring at least I would be asleep for most of it.

Instead, I just stopped sleeping.

Wolf took one look at the dark circles under my eyes the following day and tried to insist on having someone in the room with me again. I finally convinced him to let me keep trying, but the few times I did manage to fall asleep, the nightmares I woke from made sleep impossible again. Wolf stubbornly started sitting outside the door so he could hear me and come in and wake me up. He looked almost as exhausted as I did, and I hated it.

After several nights of this, I was lying in bed, staring at the ceiling, when there was a soft knock on the window.

Confused, I sat up and almost screamed at the sight of Lee perched on the windowsill of the second floor like an overgrown bird. I stomped to the window to open it for him.

"What the fuck are you doing?" I hissed.

"Comin' to see you," he whispered with a devilish grin.

"What's wrong with the door?"

"Wolf's sittin' outside of it."

"So?"

"So, I don't want him to know I'm in here," he smirked.

I blinked. "You can't be serious."

He slid inside the window, effortlessly contorting his body to fit through the space. I leaned out the window, looking at the straight drop to the ground. There were no handholds I could see.

"How the fuck did you get up here?" I asked.

"I'm a man of many talents."

Before I could even fully turn, he was pulling me into his arms, lips hard and hungry on mine. I gasped, and he took advantage of the moment to deepen the kiss, his tongue tangling with mine and sending shivers down my spine. His fingers tightened on my waist, and a whimper escaped my throat.

He broke our kiss to shush me, his dark brown eyes glinting with his grin.

"Are you insane?" I breathed as my brain jerked back into gear. "My brother is right outside the door!"

His gaze darkened to a smolder that made me *ache*. "So be a good girl and stay quiet."

He kissed me again, and the memories that haunted me were lost to the sensation of his hands sliding down to palm my hips and his mouth taking my lower lip between his teeth. I threaded my hands into his hair and pressed myself harder against him. He broke our kiss to groan a quiet curse.

"You remember when you took my thumb in your mouth?" he asked, his thumb brushing across my lips.

I nodded.

"I almost lost it right there." His eyes were locked on my lips. "All I could picture was how pretty that smartass mouth would look wrapped around my cock."

Heat sizzled through me. There was a desperation in him I liked. There was no sweet lead-up, no tender moments, and that was exactly what I needed. I pulled him into a kiss again, letting my hands trail down his stomach to dip below his shirt. He groaned against my mouth as I slid my hands across the plane of his stomach. He was so warm, as though fire ran through him, and I wanted that fire to devour me.

Lee released me for a moment to shuck his shirt off and drop it on the floor before grabbing my waist and sealing his lips against mine again. He backed me toward the wall beside the door, and once I was leaning against it, his fingers hooked in the waistband of my sleep shorts.

"These damned shorts," he said, flashing me a sinful grin, and then he slowly slid them off my hips, crouching as he went.

I sucked in a breath, feeling a flash of self-consciousness as I stood half bare against the wall, but he ran his hands up my calves, coming to land on the backs of my thighs, his fingers tightening on my skin like he was physically holding himself back.

"Gods, you're perfect." His eyes were hungry as he gazed at me. "I want to taste you. I want to feel you come apart on my tongue."

"Lee," I breathed, my entire body pulsing with heat and want.

He stayed crouched on the ground and looked up at me, the firelight highlighting his cheekbones and casting shadows on his face.

"What do you want, Freckles?" he asked in a low, sensual voice that made the throbbing ache between my legs worsen.

I could see the desire in his eyes. He wanted me, but he was giving me a choice. It made me feel powerful in a way I hadn't experienced before. The Voiceless and their God of Death thought I was a game piece they could move across the board, a body they could use and control, but I'd *fought,* and I *won.* And now I was here with this man who teased and flirted mercilessly but also cared for me when I was at my most vulnerable and spent his time hanging out with me so I wouldn't be alone.

"I want you to do what you want with me," I whispered, surprising myself. I wasn't sure why I was giving him back the control he'd given me. Maybe it was a test. Maybe I wanted to see what he would do with it. Maybe a part of me liked the way he'd dominated me, pinned me to the wall, and fucked me with his fingers until I was dripping—just like I'd asked.

His grin became downright feral. "Careful what you wish for."

He leaned forward and pressed a kiss to my stomach, right below my navel, and it struck me.

I *trusted* him.

That was it. I could hand him control because I knew he wouldn't hurt me with it.

"Tell me." I barely recognized my breathless whisper.

He glanced back up at me, his eyes so dark it almost reminded me of that moment when darkness had filled Menace's eyes, shadows swallowing the brilliant blue. He raised an eyebrow, clearly waiting for me to continue.

"Tell me what you're gonna do to me."

His teeth flashed as he grinned. "You wanna know what I'm gonna do to you?" His hands slid from the backs of my thighs to the front, slow and tortuous. "First, I'm gonna fuck you with my tongue right here against the wall." He shifted even closer, pressing a kiss to my inner thigh, urging my legs apart. "And you're gonna be a good girl and not make a sound."

I sunk my teeth into my bottom lip, electricity zipping through my veins.

"Right, Freckles?" His hands were sliding higher, so close to where I desperately wanted them.

"Yes," I whispered.

He locked eyes with me, and then his mouth closed over my center. I sucked in a breath and then bit my lip again, trying to stay quiet as his tongue swirled around my clit. His eyes crinkled with amusement, and he slipped a finger inside of me. My entire body tensed, clenching with pleasure as he stroked my walls. Despite his words, he moved at a leisurely pace, almost torturously slow. I squirmed above him, grinding against his face, desperate. He hummed low in his throat, and the vibration against my clit made me gasp.

"Fuck," I panted, my voice barely a whisper.

He added a second finger, curling them inside me, and the heat built and built, but he kept me teetering on the edge, slowing down every time I neared the peak.

"Lee," I begged.

He grinned up at me. "What do you say?"

"Are you fucking kidding me?"

"You want to come?"

That look on his face was fucking *wicked*.

"I *want* to *stab* you," I gasped as his fingers curled again, making my legs tremble.

"Huh, guess not then," he purred, leaning forward to suck my clit into his mouth.

I barely managed to swallow the cry that tried to escape. If he just kept doing *that*—but he released me again.

"Thought you were gonna be a good girl for me."

I was so close, and then he kept snatching it away. I *did* want to stab him, but I had to admit, this game of control, the push and pull—it was *fun*. When I couldn't take it any longer, I surrendered.

"Please, Lee," I gasped. "I want to come."

His eyes crinkled with amusement at me, but he didn't hesitate. He grabbed my right leg behind my knee and slung it over his shoulder, and his tongue moved across my clit as his fingers picked up the pace.

In seconds, I was a quivering, shaking mess, whispered pleas escaping my mouth as I barreled toward release. I sunk my fingers into his hair, my head tipped back against the wall, and my jaw clenched to stay quiet. When his fingers curled perfectly again, I shattered. My fingers tightened in his hair as he licked, his fingers pumping in unison.

"Oh gods, oh gods, oh gods," I babbled in a frantic whisper as white-hot pleasure rolled over me in waves.

As I came down, he withdrew, looking smug. "Stay there," he ordered, getting to his feet.

I wouldn't have been able to move if I wanted to. My legs felt wobbly. So I stayed leaning against the wall, catching my breath and watching as he took all the pillows off the bed and placed them on the floor.

"What are you doing?" I whispered.

"I want you on your hands and knees, and you're gonna want to brace yourself on something besides the floor." He smirked.

I looked at the bed and then back at him, raising an eyebrow.

His smirk turned into a grin, and he walked over to the end of the bed, leaned over, and placed his hands on the mattress. Then he started moving back and forth, mimicking thrusting. The bed immediately began to squeak alarmingly loud, and I shot a panicked look at the door—terrified Wolf would come bursting in at the sound.

"That's why," Lee whispered as he approached me, and the desire burning in his eyes made my core throb again despite the wetness from my previous release still coating my inner thighs. He tugged me toward the pillows, pulling me in for a savage kiss before murmuring against my lips, "On your knees, Freckles."

I lowered myself onto my hands and knees, but I twisted to look behind me as he removed his belt and dropped his pants. I stared at the silver piercing in the head of his cock, and my entire body felt flushed and tingly. He gripped his shaft and pumped it a few times, and I could see a bead glistening on the tip near the silver barbell. The firelight highlighted the dark tattoos on his chest and arms and the muscles that rippled as he moved. He approached like a cougar stalking its prey, dangerous and lethal and utterly focused on me.

"Now," his voice was a low growl as he lowered himself to his knees behind me. "I'm gonna fuck this perfect pussy with my cock."

"How are you gonna fuck me?" I whispered, smiling like a fool.

The heat coming from his body seared my skin, and I shuddered as he dragged his cock through my wetness, that silver barbell grazing my clit and making me moan. I felt him line himself up at my entrance, and then he leaned down, his chest against my back.

"Hard," he said low near my ear.

Before I could catch my breath, he thrust into me, one hand gripping my hip and the other twining into my hair and pushing my head down onto the pillow. The impossible fullness and slight pain stole the air from my lungs. Without breaking his rhythm, he released my hip and found my clit, stroking it with his skillful fingers as he pounded into me. Each deep thrust made his piercing rub against my upper walls, and soon, I was unraveling.

I clenched around him, my legs shaking, and buried my face in the pillow to muffle the cries I couldn't control as I went over the edge. He didn't let up, continuing his brutal pace. My lungs forgot how to work as all my focus narrowed on the almost overwhelming pleasure. Nearly as soon as my release faded, another began to build. I pushed my hips back into him, meeting his thrusts and urging him deeper. His hand released my hair and skimmed under my sleep shirt to capture my nipple, tormenting it between his fingers just hard enough to make me moan into the pillow as I came again, harder and wilder than the first.

After it faded, I sagged onto the floor, but he wasn't done with me yet. He pulled out and flipped me onto my back, pushing my legs up to almost fold me in half. He entered me swiftly, slamming into me again, and pushed my shirt up enough to reveal my breasts. I couldn't help noticing he kept my shirt covering the thick bandage on my chest, but I forced myself not to dwell on it. It was easier to forget when Lee's mouth closed around my nipple, his fingers rolling the other—hard. I bit my lower lip, trying to stay quiet, but the coiling heat in me was almost too much.

"Lee," I whispered raggedly. "Oh my gods."

His mouth came off my nipple with a popping sound. "You look so pretty taking my cock," he groaned, his dark eyes on mine.

His fingers stroked my clit again, and I slid my hands down to my nipples, rolling them hard like he had, my chest heaving.

"Fuck." His sharp eyes were fixed on my hands on my breasts.

The heat coiled tighter and tighter, and I arched off the floor, my ankles around his neck. I felt like I was going to explode.

"I can't," I panted. "It's too much."

"Yes, you can," he said through gritted teeth, "come for me again, Ember."

My body obeyed, tipping me into an ecstasy that swallowed me whole. I bit down on my fist to contain my cries while lightning filled my veins, and it just kept coming. Lee groaned, something I didn't catch, and shuddered as he thrust into me one more time, his cock pulsing. The shockwaves continued to rock through me for a few more seconds, and I whimpered around my fist.

For a moment, neither of us moved, breathing hard, and I did a quick scan with my eyes to make sure my powers weren't making me glow. They weren't, but I was prepared for it this time. Lee pulled out and gently lowered my legs. I couldn't quite read the expression on his face as he got to his feet and held out his hands. I took them, and he pulled me upright, then crouched to sweep me into his arms. He carried me to the bed and laid me down before fetching the pillows from the floor. I watched him, my heart in my throat at the combination of his sudden tenderness and impassive expression. After he replaced the pillows, he slid still naked into the bed and pulled me against his chest. Both of our hearts were thundering.

"Are you ok?" he asked in a low voice. "I didn't hurt you, did I?"

Warmth swelled in my chest, startling me. "No, you didn't."

He propped himself up on his elbow to look at me, his face serious.

"I promise you didn't hurt me," I repeated, softer.

"I didn't hurt your chest?" he pushed.

"No. I'm ok, Lee."

He looked so worried I took his face in my hands and pulled him close to kiss him. He responded with a gentleness that was anything but *casual.* Our lips broke apart, but our foreheads stayed pressed together.

"That was fuckin' amazing," he finally murmured.

"That piercing is...real nice," I grinned.

He finally grinned back, a little bit of the smug cockiness returning. "I know."

I rolled my eyes, but I huffed a laugh.

"Gods, your smile," he said, brushing my wild hair out of my face and tucking it behind my ear, "might be the most beautiful thing I've ever seen."

I felt my cheeks warm, and he cradled my face with his hand. His eyes were soft, but there was still pain lingering there, and I couldn't figure out why.

"Are you ok?" I asked.

"No," he said seriously, and my stomach dropped, "I've been fuckin' devastated by my best friend's little sister."

"Don't do that!" I smacked his shoulder as he laughed silently. "You scared me."

He pulled me tight against his chest again, and I melted into him. His fingers traced gentle circles on my back, carefully going around my scars.

"You remember how Sable said massaging these scars might help?" he asked quietly.

I nodded, my stomach clenching at the memory—the horror in my brother's face.

"I'd be more than willin' to do that for you."

I hesitated, insecurity raising its ugly head. "Are you sure?"

"Of course I am. Why wouldn't I be?"

"It's just...I know they're..." I paused, remembering Trey's words with a stab of pain. "... not pretty," I finished lamely.

"They're just scars, Freckles."

I tilted my head up to see him frowning at me.

"I'm not put off by your scars if that's what you're asking," he added, a corner of his lip twitching up. "Thought that was pretty clear."

I huffed. "My shirt stayed on."

His eyes narrowed. "Yeah, so your bandage didn't get fucked up."

"Oh."

"Yeah, *oh.*" His face was a mask of disapproval.

I wrinkled my nose at his glare and started over. "That'd be nice...if you wanted to do that."

"I'll wait until the burn heals. Just in case massaging the scars makes them sore."

"Ok," I whispered.

My definition of "casual" was getting harder and harder to hold on to, but I pushed that thought away. We lay in silence for a long while, his fingers continuing to move across my back. My eyelids began to droop.

"Can you stay?" I mumbled, half asleep.

"I can't stay the whole night," he answered regretfully. "Too risky."

I frowned, my arms tightening around him.

"I can stay for a little while, though." He pressed a kiss to my temple. "As long as I can."

I wasn't sure how long that ended up being because I fell asleep just minutes later. When I woke up in the morning, he was gone, but I didn't have a single nightmare.

⁊

After that, Lee snuck into my room every few nights. Our trysts were always full of need and passion, and I tried to keep a wall up between him and the softer emotions I was experiencing more and more often, but that line felt blurry at best. It didn't help that his presence kept the nightmares at bay. I tried not to overthink why.

I kept my shield up whenever I was around Mac, even though I hated the way it made him pull away from me. I wasn't entirely sure why I didn't want him to see anything about Lee and me, but I didn't want anyone to know. That was a line I couldn't cross. Other people knowing would make everything far too real, and besides, my brother would *kill* him.

I could tell Sable was suspicious. Lee asked for pointers on massaging my scars, and Sable gave them to him, but after, I felt him watching us more often. I hoped he didn't tell Wolf.

It was another week before Mac came and found me in Nemo's kitchen, eating breakfast by myself and looking over Sable's notes in the healer notebook. When I saw him in the doorway, my heart stuttered strangely in my chest.

"Hi," I said, closing the notebook and studying his expression.

He looked...off. I couldn't tell why or how, but he seemed upset.

"Are you ok?" I asked when he didn't respond.

"Why have you been blocking me?" he asked, ignoring my question. His voice was rough.

I felt my cheeks warm as guilt settled like a stone in my stomach. "Mac, I just—"

"Is there somethin' going on between you and Lee?"

The guilt intensified, and I fell back on anger as a crutch. "I don't think that's any of your business."

His face darkened, his grey eyes flashing. It was a very familiar expression, but it made me realize I hadn't seen it in a long time—at least, not directed at me.

"I don't trust him," he growled, stalking into the room toward me.

"Why?" I was glad I was sitting. Otherwise, I might have retreated. "Just because you can't hear his thoughts?"

"I don't know," he admitted, like not knowing made him angrier. "I just...have a feeling."

I flattened my lips into a thin line, my eyes narrowing.

"I know," he snapped, running a hand through his hair. "I just...I don't know. There's just something."

"Mac—"

"I saw him climbing down from your window the other morning," he interrupted.

My face felt like it was on fire. I stared at him, my mind spinning, but unable to think of a single thing to say. He stared back at me, emotion raging in his eyes.

"I don't want you to get hurt," he finally said in a low voice.

"Mac, you can't keep me from ever getting hurt again," I said, a little snappier than I meant to. The memory of him feverishly promising not to let anyone hurt me again ran through my head.

A muscle flexed in his jaw.

"Lee's not going to hurt me. I trust him," I tried, a little softer, but if anything, it seemed to make him angrier.

"Do you really think *you'd* be able to tell?" he snapped.

I reeled back, hurt filling my chest. "What the fuck is that supposed to mean?"

"Em, you went from Trey to *Zip*, for fuck's sake. I can't—"

"I knew what Zip was. I'm not dumb!" I snarled, angry tears welling in my eyes.

"I know you're not dumb! I'm saying sometimes I think *good* scares you, so you run away to what's *familiar,* which is someone who's gonna treat you like shit!"

A bitter laugh escaped my mouth. "Oh, so you think I'm broken."

"Ember!" he growled. "That's not what I meant."

"Is that how you see me? As someone so damaged you have to step in and *protect* me from myself?"

"If you're askin' me to stop trying to protect you, that's not somethin' I can do." He took a step closer, eyes glinting.

"I killed over a dozen Voiceless by myself," I shot back. "I don't need your protection."

"And you've had fuckin' nightmares about it every single night since then!"

I snapped my jaw shut, panic creeping over me. Did he see my dreams?

"Yes," his voice lowered, and his dark tone made my skin prickle. "I am seein' your dreams. I have them with you every damn night."

I could only stare at him in horror.

"I know what kind of nightmares you're having, Ember." He stepped closer and leaned down to brace his hand on the table by my plate. His face was so close to mine, the golden specks in his eyes glowing. "I see the things they do to you in your dreams. I see the Voiceless stalk you, hurt you, violate you, and I'm fuckin' *helpless* to do a thing about it. But I also know your worst nightmares aren't about what *they* did to *you*."

"Stop," I whispered.

"The ones that scare you the most, make you sick, and keep you awake at night? Those are the dreams about what *you* did to *them*."

I sucked in a ragged breath, my hands clenching in my lap.

"I *know* you can protect yourself," he said quietly, his eyes searching mine. "But I also know it *kills* you to have to hurt people. Even people who are fuckin' monsters, who are *torturing* you. So if I can be your sword, I'm gonna fuckin' do it. If I can kill the monsters for you so you don't have to carry that burden, I will."

My fingernails dug into my palms, but my mouth didn't move. Tears ached in my throat, but they weren't from anger now.

"Trey made me swear to watch over you if something happened to him, and I will die before I break that oath."

The pain in my chest made it hard to breathe. I wasn't sure why those words hurt so badly, but I was speaking before I could think. "So that's why you've done everything? Because you promised Trey?" My voice shook. "I'm just a *job* for you? A *task* that Trey saddled you with?"

"No!" His voice rang out angrily, and his hand moved toward me at the same time.

I flinched instinctively, and he recoiled, pain and horror washing over his face.

"Em," he said with urgency, "it's me. You know I'd never hit you, right?"

I stared hard at the floor. I hated feeling so off-balance with him. The ground I'd established as steady was shaking, and I didn't know how to fix it.

"Ember," his voice was fierce. "Look at me."

I couldn't. I couldn't because I would fall apart if I looked at him.

Slowly, he lowered himself until he was on one knee by my chair. His hands moved toward me slowly, and he gently took my face and tilted it up to meet his eyes. I'd never seen the ocean, but I imagined it would look like his eyes—roiling and dangerous.

"I can't promise that I will never hurt you because I'm a fuckin' asshole, but I can promise that I will *never* hit you. It doesn't matter how angry I am. I will *never* fuckin' hit you."

I pressed my trembling lips together.

"I don't care if you never believe anything else I say, but please believe this." The pain in his eyes was deep. "I've done everything because you *mean* something to me. I swore that oath to Trey because I would've fuckin' done it anyway, even if he didn't ask, and he knew that. He wouldn't have asked if he thought otherwise."

I stared at those stormy grey eyes, and it felt like my golden powers were filling that empty hole in my chest. His thumbs stroked my cheeks.

"I don't think you understand, Em. I will do anything for you," his voice was just above a whisper. "*Anything*. Not because of Trey. Because it's you."

I squeezed my eyes shut, but a tear escaped. He brushed it gently away.

"If you want to be with Lee, I'm happy for you, but if he ever hurts you, I *will* kill him."

I suddenly remembered what Mist had said about Mac and Zip getting into a fight. My watery eyes opened. "Did you beat the shit out of Zip when I was in solitary?"

He smiled, but the dark violence in it made my breath stutter. "Yes."

"You didn't look hurt...under the watchtower."

"I wasn't hurt. He barely got a few hits in." He said it so casually. "But I should've killed him. Don't think I'll make that mistake again."

I shivered and watched his pupils dilate as he tracked it. Then he abruptly tilted his head, his eyes going distant.

"Sam's comin' to see what's taking so damn long."

"What?" I whispered, my head still spinning.

"I'm supposed to be bringing you back to the clinic." He stood and offered a hand.

I took it and let him pull me to my feet, but he didn't release me. My pulse quickened as he brought my hand up to his face and gently pressed his lips to my knuckles. I could feel the raging sea in his eyes inside of my chest, emotion and magic crashing over each other. His eyes abruptly widened, breath catching.

"Your eyes are glowing," he murmured, something like awe in his voice.

I forgot how to breathe. "Are you sure?"

His lips twitched up. "Pretty damn sure. They look like liquid gold."

Every thought seemed to empty out of my head, leaving only the pounding of my heart echoing in the empty chamber.

"That might be the most beautiful thing I've ever seen," he said, stepping closer and ducking his head to study them. "Has that ever happened before?"

His face was so close to mine my legs felt shaky. "A couple of times," I managed to say, my voice hoarse.

His eyes narrowed on me, and I braced for more questions. Then, he straightened and released my hand, taking a step away. A second later, I heard boots approaching the door. Sam popped his head in and frowned at us.

"Mac, what the fuck? We're all waitin' for you two."

Mac grinned, and it looked a little sheepish. It was an adorable expression on his usually serious face. "Sorry, got distracted talking."

Sam rolled his eyes, "Well, c'mon."

As we followed him out the door, I dropped my shield enough to ask Mac, *"Are my eyes still glowing?"*

He glanced at me. *"No, they're green again."*

"I can't wait to see your face, Shortcake," Sam said, dropping back to wrap an arm around my shoulders.

"Why?" I asked, suspicious.

"You'll see," Sam grinned.

CHAPTER 43

S am talked me into letting him tie a handkerchief around my eyes before we could see the clinic. He took my hand to lead me, but after I stumbled several times over obstacles, he "didn't notice," Mac took my other hand, lacing his fingers through mine and making my heart skip. His hand was warm and callused. Sam was still talking, but I wasn't listening because all my focus was on Mac's hand in mine. As if he knew, he slowly stroked his thumb across the top of my hand, and my entire body erupted in goosebumps.

Sam stopped, and I was so distracted I nearly walked into him. "Ok, are you ready? Wait, Mac, can you take the blindfold off? I want to see her face."

I had no idea what I was about to see, and it was making me more nervous. Mac moved around behind me and placed his hands on my shoulders.

"You ready?" he leaned in to ask low in my ear.

My body was ready for *something*. I felt like I might combust, and it confused the shit out of me, but I nodded, anyway. Mac began to untie the handkerchief, and then the blindfold fell away, and I stared at the scene in front of me, my lips parting in astonishment.

My crew, Wolf, and the Fangs all stood outside the clinic, grinning at me, and I didn't know where to look first. The clinic was *bigger*. They'd put a whole fucking addition on. It looked like at least one more room and easily doubled the size of the building. On the other side, a cute little whitewashed wooden fence surrounded the garden plot, full of neatly raised garden beds. Tucked in the corner was a small greenhouse with see-through walls and a tin roof.

I stared, and I stared, my mind refusing to acknowledge what I was looking at was real. Vaguely, I could hear Sam asking me something, but I couldn't focus on the words.

"Em?" Large hands gripped my shoulders, and a face appeared before me, blocking my view.

I focused on Mac, noting how his brow was creased and his eyes were studying mine like he was worried. It was only then I realized tears were streaming down my face.

"Are these happy tears?" he asked softly.

I nodded, still too overwhelmed to speak. Sam gave a dramatic sigh on the other side of him and handed me a handkerchief.

"You want to come take a closer look?"

I nodded again, wiping my face, and he smiled.

"C'mon." Mac laced his fingers in mine again and tugged me forward up the slight hill.

I wanted to keep holding his hand, but Wolf hugged me as soon as I reached them, pulling me away.

"Come look inside first," Wolf said, grinning.

He led me inside, and still, all I could do was stare. They'd put in two more windows, and the warm sunlight beamed in from multiple directions.

"All the windows open so you can get some air in here in the summer," Wolf explained. "And over here, we have the addition."

He led me to where the hutch had previously resided, but they'd removed the wall, creating a large entryway to the addition. I glanced back at the large empty space to the left of the front door to see the hutch in the corner with the stack of wooden chairs. The new addition had a hallway that led to three different doors. Wolf opened the first door and led me in. My dresser stood against the wall, and my mattress sat on a new handmade bed frame. There was *another* window in here. It smelled like fresh-cut wood.

"This is your room," Wolf said. "We put a lock on the inside of the door so you can have some privacy when you need it."

"We made you a new bedframe, too," Mac added from where he leaned on the doorframe. "Since Madame took the last one after you left."

"There's a trundle underneath," Wolf crouched to lift Trey's quilt and show how another bed could roll out from under mine. "I wasn't sure if Roe would be movin' in with you permanently, but this gives you an extra bed if you need it."

This was only the first of three rooms, and I was already struggling to process the amount of thoughtfulness they'd put into it.

Wolf led me out to the second door in the hallway. "This is an extra bedroom. We figured some of us could sleep in here."

It was empty except for a few bedrolls, but there was a fourth window. All the natural light made my heart feel like it was about to explode out of my chest.

Wolf opened the last door. It was a smaller room with no windows, but two cots were inside.

"This can be whatever you want. Storage, a room for patients to sleep, a private exam room—anything. The only thing these new rooms don't have is electric lights, but we can add those once we get the materials," Mac said.

"We put the rest of the bedrolls up in the loft, so we'll be out of the way in the main room," Wolf added.

"Em, come see the garden now!" Apple chirped from the door.

In a daze, I followed her outside to the garden. The beds were formed from neat piles of dirt, ready for planting. The fence had a gate that shut and locked to keep the free-roaming animals out. Leda and baby Jet stood in the garden talking to a woman I didn't initially recognize.

"Em, do you know Vale?" Leda asked, gesturing to the other woman.

Jet reached for me, so I took him from Leda and turned to Vale. She was older, probably in her fifties, with greying hair and fine wrinkles across her skin. She looked familiar, but I couldn't place her. Her expression bordered on stern, but her face softened as I met her eyes.

"You saved my life during the rebellion," she said quietly. "A merciful action since I was not one of the rebels."

I remembered. She had been lying on the ground near the watchtower with a giant hole in her abdomen. Jet babbled at me and waved his chubby fingers.

"Vale has been working with Nemo, and they've come to an understanding," Leda said firmly. "Let the past stay in the past."

They both watched me as though waiting for me to speak, as

though my opinion mattered, and I fumbled for what to say. "It's behind us."

Leda beamed, and Vale seemed to grow misty-eyed.

"I'm one of the heads of agriculture," Vale continued after clearing her throat. "So I was just discussing with Leda what things you could plant here. Herbs would be useful for the clinic. It's a little late in the season, but we can plant a few things, and we have an abundance of wildflower seeds if you would like some of these to be flower gardens for summer. And before winter, we can try planting some cold-hardy greens in the greenhouse."

I nodded, pretending all her words hadn't blurred together.

"You should step in the greenhouse," Leda said, grinning as she took Jet back from me.

Obediently, I stepped into the greenhouse. The door shut behind me, muffling the outside noise a little, and I took a deep, shaky breath of the warm air, which smelled like fresh dirt and cut lumber, earthy and sweet. Behind me, the door opened.

"Warm, isn't it?" Mac said.

I turned to face him. He was leaning on the doorframe, watching me.

"This is…a lot." My voice wobbled.

"You deserve it," he said without hesitation.

"I don't…no one's ever…" I bit my trembling lip.

He pushed off the doorframe and approached to wrap an arm around my shoulders. "You deserve it," he repeated firmly.

A lump rose in my throat as I realized picturing the future was no longer impossible.

It just looked different.

The grief rose up, and I fought the urge to stuff it back down, remembering what Mac said—that locking away the pain would also lock away all the good, the beauty of what Trey and I had. I'd desperately wanted a future with Trey, but I would never get it. I'd loved him—I would always love him—but he was taken from me, along with all of those hopes and dreams. I let that truth settle in me, heavy as a mountain. Mac's arm tightened around me, anchoring me, and I leaned into him and wrapped my arm around his waist. My heart ached, but I didn't break.

"Em!" Apple burst into the greenhouse, her little face scrunched indignantly, "Roe said you healed him with a magic potion!"

"No, I didn't!" Roe followed on her heels, equally indignant. "I said you made a magic potion and then healed me!"

"What if you each get a little bottle and make your own magic potion?" Mac suggested.

"Out of what?" Apple breathed, her eyes widening.

"Anything—dirt, plants, little pebbles, water. Everything has magic in it."

They both stared at him with huge eyes for a second before taking off and shrieking ideas at each other. Mac grinned after them.

"That should keep 'em busy for at least five minutes."

"Maybe three," I said hoarsely, and he grinned so wide both dimples appeared.

෨

The afternoon was a blur of re-organizing things, people coming in and out, and sunshine pouring into the clinic. Before I knew it, the dinner bell was ringing.

"Em, you ready to go to dinner?" Wolf yelled from outside.

"Give me a minute," I yelled back, still trying to finish grinding up some dried bark.

It took me another five minutes to finish my task, and I quickly put everything away. I took a second to stop and look around the clinic—so bright and cheerful and *home*. I was *happy*.

As I washed my hands, looking out one of the brand-new windows, nausea suddenly flooded me. I braced myself on the edge of the sink and breathed deeply through my nose. I thought it was passing and began to turn, but it surged so violently I had to spin and vomit into the sink.

As I struggled to catch my breath, I stared without blinking for so long my eyes began to ache. I had to be seeing wrong. I finally blinked my dry eyes, but nothing changed. There must have been something in the sink I didn't notice—some dirt or something. I wiped the back of my shaking hand across my wet mouth and examined it. Horror rooted me to the floor as I stared at the *black* sludge slowly running across my hand. It was thick and viscous, sliding across my skin like oil, nothing like the consistency or color of regular vomit. It dripped into the sink and joined the dark, glistening pool of the same foul substance. My mouth tasted like *ashes.*

I stood there and stared at it for a long time before woodenly turning the water on and rinsing it down the drain. Then I rinsed my mouth and washed my hands. My reflection stared back at me in the mirror, slightly pale and eyes wide, as I dried my hands.

It's nothing. I tried to tell myself. *I must've eaten something weird.*

But my hands continued to shake as I hung up the towel, and the nausea still lingered faintly. I forced myself to take a deep breath and walk to the door. As I reached for the doorknob, I froze again, staring at my arm. I could've sworn I just saw a dark shadow slither under the skin of my forearm.

The door abruptly opened, and I jumped back with a gasp. Lee stood in the doorway with a furrowed brow and a confused grin.

"Sorry, did I scare you?"

"Yeah," I rubbed my forearm, trying to erase the prickling sensation, and forced a smile.

He stepped inside and let the door shut behind him so he could pull me into his arms and kiss me. I kept my lips closed, worried he might notice the taste of ash that lingered in my mouth, but he didn't seem to mind. Instead, he gentled his lips and transformed the kiss into something sweet. It took me by surprise, and I melted into his arms.

We were playing with fire, inching closer and closer to the boundary I'd erected in my head. I'd admitted to myself I liked him, but I'd caught myself almost telling him more than once. The way his eyes crinkled in the corners with laughter, the wicked corner of his mouth lifting into a smirk, the feeling of his thick, silky hair in my fingers—I was starting to crave all of these things. Just thinking about the secret touches we shared under tables and behind closed doors made my heart race. There were still times when he seemed distant or sad, and I found myself wanting to be the one he confided in. I wanted to ease whatever troubled him, carry some of the burden, take some of the hurt.

"You keep lookin' at me like that, and we're not gonna make it to dinner," he murmured.

My cheeks warmed as I realized I'd been gazing at him like a starry-eyed fool, but I grinned. "I can't help it; you're just so nice to look at."

"Well, *I* can't help it, I'm naturally beautiful."

"I guess we're both doomed."

Something dark flashed through his eyes, but a second later, it was gone. He kissed me again, his warm hands cradling my face, but he pulled back far too soon.

"C'mon, we gotta go to dinner," he grinned at my scowl.

Wolf and my crew were lingering at the base of the hill. They looked up as we appeared.

"Gods, finally," Kai complained. "I was starting to plan a search party."

I flipped him off, and he grinned as he wrapped an arm around Sable's waist. Then I noticed who was standing beside Raven, and my face lit up.

"Clare, are you joining us?"

Clarity smiled back at me as our group began walking toward the canteen. "I was bribed. Neena allegedly made cookies."

Raven smirked. "Sweets are her weakness."

Clarity glared playfully at her. "You swore you wouldn't tell!"

The rest of the group walked ahead of us, chattering and laughing. Sam and Lee were laughing with Jax and Scar. Griz, Wolf, Tuck, and Mac were discussing upgrading the rovers. Kai and Sable were in their own little world.

Raven leaned in close to Clarity as the three of us walked, speaking so low I almost missed it. "No shame, Clare, you know I love sweets too."

Clarity's cheeks flushed red, and Raven's grin was downright sly. I clamped my lips together to hide my smile. I didn't need to know the details to know they weren't talking about food any longer.

Outside in the warm sunshine, it was easier to pretend I hadn't just vomited something straight out of a nightmare. Guilt pricked at me. I knew I should tell my crew, but maybe it was nothing. Maybe it'd been a trick of the light.

Without him, your powers will corrupt.

I violently shook my head, sending my hair whipping across my face as if that would get Talmar's words out of my mind.

"You good, Boney?" Raven asked, startling me back to the present.

"Sorry," I forced a smile. "Bug flew in my face."

A harbinger of sickness and death.

Despite the warm sunshine, chills ran across my skin, and I clenched my jaw. *No.* This was what the Voiceless wanted. They wanted to get in my head. They wanted me to panic enough to come crawling back, promising to submit. How many times did Juck use similar manipulations? It was probably nothing. It was probably all in my head.

I took a deep breath and forced myself to tune back into Raven and Clarity's conversation, smile, and laugh like everything was normal.

If it happened again, *then* I'd tell someone.

BONUS CHAPTER

— MAC —

G riz found me in the garage swearing at a rusted bolt on
the rover.

"What'd that bolt ever do to you?" he asked, one eyebrow raised
as he leaned against the wall.

I set my jaw and put all my weight on the torque wrench again.
He watched me in silence, but as usual, his thoughts rang loud in my
head.

*He better tell her before she gets in too deep with Lee. Damn,
that bolt really is stuck. How long before he asks for a blowtorch? If I
throw this at him, will he catch it?*

I internally rolled my eyes and put out my hand, catching the
apple without looking. Griz's favorite part of my new mind-reading
power was throwing random shit at me without warning to see if I could
catch it.

"Nice catch," Griz grinned.

I gave up on the bolt and sat up, chucking the apple back at him.
"You have somethin' you wanna say?"

"I probably already said it, didn't I?"

I glared but didn't correct him. I *had* already heard it in his head.

"She's happy," I muttered. "I'm not fuckin' it up."

"What about you?" Griz asked.

I wiped my hands on a rag and played dumb. "What about me?"

"Don't you deserve to be happy?"

I glanced up at him and smiled a wide, toothy, completely fake smile.

"That's so fuckin' creepy, man."

"You ever seen her eyes glow gold before?" I changed the subject as I got to my feet.

"Gold?" Griz raised his eyebrows. "Only when she healed me and Jax by the watchtower. Caught a glimpse of 'em right before she turned into a living sunbeam."

I hummed thoughtfully and moved past him to put the wrench away.

"How come?"

I could feel his eyes boring into me and hear all the speculation running through his head—each one more ridiculous than the last. I leaned my hip on the workbench and raised an eyebrow.

"No, I'm not tryin' to awkwardly ask if she's secretly smitten with you," I huffed, but I couldn't help the grin pulling at my lips.

"Look, if you give me nothin', I'm gonna make assumptions," he grinned back. "And she *is* secretly smitten with me, so tough luck, fucker."

I rolled my eyes. "I'd rather she be smitten with you than fuckin' *Lee*."

"Do you think Wolf knows?"

I barked a laugh. "No. There's no way he knows."

"How the fuck does he *not* know?"

That was a good question. My whole crew had figured it out without me saying a word. It really wasn't hard. Wolf was real fucking perceptive, so how he didn't notice Ember's cheeks going pink when Lee whispered in her ear or Lee being glued to her side or the way their eyes seemed to always find each other across the room was beyond me.

I shrugged.

"Guess everybody's got a blind spot," Griz muttered.

"Mac?" Raven's yell came from outside, and it had a hint of urgency that made me head immediately to the door.

"What?" I asked as I strode outside, scanning for any sign of a threat.

"Em needs some help at the clinic!" Raven reported, her voice clipped.

I didn't wait; I took off running. I skimmed through the thoughts nearby, trying to figure out who was with her and why she needed help, but found nothing. The clinic finally came into view, and my stomach dropped when I realized Wolf's crew wasn't outside. Where the fuck were they? I burst into the clinic, scaring Roe and Apple, where they were lying on the floor drawing with charcoal on some paper.

"What's wrong?" Apple demanded, sitting up. Roe copied her, his eyes wide as saucers.

"Nothin', it's ok. Nothing's wrong. Where's Em?" Nothing looked out of the ordinary.

"In our room," Roe answered timidly.

"You kids stay here, ok? Everything's fine." I tried for a friendly smile, but they both frowned at me.

I strode into the addition and up to her door, rapping gently on it.

"Come in," she called from inside, and just the sound of her voice eased some of my tension.

I pushed the door open and stepped into her room only to freeze on the threshold, the words I'd been about to say stuck in my throat.

Ember stood with her back to me—her bare, unguarded back. My eyes followed the curve of her spine and mapped the exposed, scarred skin she worked so hard to hide. The scars weren't just lines—they crawled across her freckled skin like barren, twisted branches. I'd seen her back bloody and shredded, but somehow this was worse. A bleeding wound was temporary—these marks had been carved into her with a cruel permanence—and they should have been mine.

Her hair cascaded down her back in damp, unruly waves as though she'd just bathed. The jeans she wore were too big for her slight frame and belted tightly around her waist. Her ribs jutted out like monuments to the hunger she'd been forced to know so intimately. Looking at her, one could easily misjudge her as fragile, but she was tough—tougher than anyone I'd ever met. You didn't survive this world by being soft, and she was a survivor.

"Sorry, Raven, I know you're—" She turned as she spoke, holding a towel over her naked chest, and as soon as our eyes locked, she froze like a deer in headlights. Her eyes widened, panic flickering in them.

"Hey, sorry, I should've announced myself." I kept my voice

steady as I held her gaze. "Raven said you needed help?"

"Oh." Her voice was flustered and uncertain. "Um, sorry... I just thought... Raven was gonna... I saw her and asked, um..."

I could practically see her scrambling for composure. Her cheeks were painted in a rosy pink, and I fought the smile that tugged at my mouth. Her blush undid me every time.

"Em, it's ok." I softened my voice. "What did you need help with? Your back?"

"You don't have to—"

"Ember," I interrupted, my voice low and firm. I stepped further into her room, gently closing the door behind me. I waited until she met my eyes to continue. "I wouldn't be here if I wasn't ready and willin' to help."

She caught her bottom lip between her teeth.

"If you want someone else, that's ok," I said in her head. *"But I'm more than willin'."*

I could practically hear Griz snorting in amusement at that.

"Are you sure?" she asked.

"I'm sure. Your back hurtin'?"

She let out a breath, and her shoulders slumped a little. *"Yeah."*

I glanced behind her at the bottle of oil on her dresser. "That it?" I gestured toward the bottle, and she nodded. I strode over and grabbed it, noting the orange flower petals floating in the clear oil.

"Calendula?" I asked, holding up the jar as I approached.

Her beautiful eyes widened. "Yeah." She paused. "How did you know?"

"You made a shit ton of these this past winter. How would I not?"

She stared at me, her brow slightly furrowed like she was trying to figure something out.

"Alright, tell me what to do," I added when she didn't say anything.

She instructed me on how to apply the oil, clutching the towel to her chest and stumbling slightly over her words. My heart broke as I watched her steel herself before she turned and revealed her scarred back as though bracing herself for my reaction. A shimmering wall of solid golden power hid her thoughts from me. I hated that she'd learned to block me so fast; I hated that she felt the need to.

Gently, I gathered her thick hair and tucked it over her shoulder, and her little shuddering breath almost brought me to my knees. The oil pooled, glistening, and I warmed it in my hands before gently touching her skin. She flinched slightly, making my gut twist, but I didn't stop. I worked the oil into the scar tissue slowly, my movements deliberate, willing her to know there wasn't a single thing about her that repulsed me, not an inch that didn't command my respect. She tipped her head down, hiding her face behind her hair, and I longed to tell her, to make her understand her scars didn't make her any less—they made her *more.*

Slowly, her muscles relaxed under my fingers. I added a little more pressure, trying to erase the ache with my thumbs. I wished I could take all of it—all the pain, all the hurt, all the years she spent being chipped into smaller and smaller pieces. She told me she was broken, but the fact she was here with this map of violence covering her skin and still so much kindness and care in her heart meant she was fucking *unbreakable.*

A goddess remade piece by piece, scar by scar, into something achingly beautiful.

"That feel ok?" I asked, and even in my head, my voice sounded slightly hoarse.

"Yeah." Her voice was soft—the single word packed with emotion.

Her muscles were hard where they should have been smooth as if they were trying to protect themselves from more damage. Under the rough scars, I could feel the muscles straining to hold together what had been torn apart. The worst of it was across her lower back, where the stitches had ripped, leaving a jagged line. The whip had bitten into her so deep since she had little fat or muscle to protect her, and the way her flesh had knitted itself back together looked more like survival than healing.

The memory assaulted me—shoving my way through the crowd to see her dangling from her cuffed hands on the whipping post, her back a shredded, bloody mess. Trey lifted her up, trying his best to avoid the wounds on her back as I uncuffed her hands. I remembered how my hands shook as I tried to unlock the cuffs and how Trey's voice cracked with fear as he begged her to open her eyes. I remembered sitting beside the table where she lay unconscious and taking her limp hand, my thumb gently tracing the welts on her wrists from the cuffs. I remembered wanting to put a bullet in Madame's head for what she'd done. I fucking should have. Instead, I took my fury out on Zip after Trey told me how the asshole hit Ember hard enough to knock her out.

I'd more than repaid the favor.

My hands followed the stiff muscles, and under my fingers, they became loose and pliant. I wanted to lean down and kiss the back of her neck and run my hands through her thick hair. I wanted to devour her, taste all her sighs, and hear her gasp my name. I wanted to explore her entire body with my hands, my mouth—

I shifted slightly, trying to inconspicuously adjust myself. Getting an obvious hard-on was an asshole move, and I wanted her to feel safe to ask me for help with anything.

I didn't want to stop, but I was running out of oil to rub in. Reluctantly, I dropped my hands. "That feel any better or does—"

She turned to face me, and her eyes were full of tears.

"What's wrong? Did I hurt you?" I demanded, my blood suddenly running cold.

"No!" she said quickly. "That was...really nice. And...I am just..." A tear spilled over, and she practically growled in frustration. "I am so fucking sick of crying."

I attempted to hide my smile. "It's ok if you cry."

"I don't *want* to," she muttered.

My hands moved with a mind of their own, finding their way to her face. Her soft skin against my rough hands made a quiet ache settle in my chest. I kept finding myself here, gently cradling her cheeks, even though I knew I shouldn't. Something about how her face fit so perfectly in my hands as if it were shaped just for me. It was becoming a habit or perhaps an addiction to hold her like this and feel her pulse thrumming with life beneath my fingers and my magic racing to the surface as though it recognized her. It felt like holding a godsdamned fallen star in my hands.

Her emerald eyes always went wide, emotion flashing through them like lightning—there and gone before I could get a good look. She never pulled back or spoke, like she was waiting for me to say something —and gods, I wanted to. I wanted to tell her how breathtaking she was, how she was everything I didn't deserve and everything I wanted. I wanted to tell her holding her like this was like holding the last bit of warmth in a cold, cruel world. I wanted to tell her these moments felt like

I was stealing something sacred, but it was a crime I would commit again and again just to feel the curve of her cheek against my palm.

Instead, I asked, "Where's your brother?"

She blinked. "He's meetin' with his crew about something. Why?"

"Nobody was here guarding the clinic."

"Raven *was* here," she replied, her brows pulling together and a familiar stubborn light igniting in her eyes.

I had a pretty damn good idea why Raven switched places with me. As if Griz playing matchmaker wasn't enough.

"Well, I guess you're stuck with me now," I sighed, shaking my head with an exaggerated frown.

"Ugh," she groaned playfully.

"What were the tears for?" I asked, softer.

The vulnerability in her eyes seemed to freeze, hovering between letting me in and retreating behind that wall. I reacted instinctively, gently stroking my thumbs down her cheeks.

"Don't shut me out, Em," I murmured.

Her pupils dilated as my thumbs moved across her skin. "I don't know how to explain it," she whispered.

"Would it be easier like this?" I asked in her head.

"Maybe?" She frowned. *"I just...felt...connected. To you. I felt your emotions about my...my scars."*

I fought to keep from reacting, but my heart started hammering in my chest. *"Was that good or bad?"*

"Good." Her voice wobbled.

The words rushed to the tip of my tongue, suddenly desperate to pour from my mouth, but a loud knock on the door startled both of us. I dropped my hands and took a step back, and just like that, the spell was broken.

"Em?" Apple called. "Can we get some more paper?"

I stepped out to help the kids, giving her some privacy to finish getting dressed. She emerged a few minutes later, and the rest of the evening was mundane—domestic even. Wolf and his crew returned shortly after sunset, and I exchanged pleasantries with them, pretending not to notice how Lee's hand lingered on the small of Ember's back.

When I stepped outside, the cool evening air did little to ease the weight of everything I didn't say. Inside the clinic, I heard her laugh, the sound like sunlight breaking through the clouds, and my feet stopped. I lingered on the small, rickety porch, listening to that beautiful sound and remembering the silence of those first few months. I'd tried so damn hard to hate her, but her hollow gaze haunted me. The moments she would spark to life and fight me, her eyes flashing with defiance and rage, were a relief. I preferred her like that—those moments when she seemed *alive*, even if it was fueled with fury at me.

I could carry the weight of these unspoken words if it meant she was happy. For now, it would be enough to love her in silence—in the spaces between words.

ACKNOWLEDGMENTS

How on earth we've made it to the acknowledgements for my *second* book is beyond me. Equally astonishing is that I published *Bones* only ten months ago.

It has been an *extraordinary* ten months.

Thank you to my husband Aaron for being my reference for everything from boxing moves to particle physics. Thank you for always helping me with my website when my brain refuses to compute anything I'm looking at. Thank you for all the times you have spontaneously told me you're so proud of me, for running interference with the boys when I'm in editing mode, and for sending me every real life person who reminds you of one of my characters. I like you and I love you.

Thank you to my seven-year-old for telling so many people, "My mom wrote THE *Bones* book!" It usually leads to me awkwardly explaining to someone in the library or the grocery store what you meant, but the pride and excitement you radiate is always crystal clear. I'm sorry you can't read it until you're forty-five years old. Thank you to my four-year-old for keeping me company and being my snuggle buddy while I write. I'm sorry for always waking up so early (again, you do not *have to* get up with me at the crack of dawn), but the fact that you will still grumpily follow me downstairs and snuggle with me is one of the sweetest things. I love you both all the way up to the moon and back.

Thank you to my best friends, Amy, Jason, and Steph for always being so excited and telling so many people about my book. If you found *Bones* in one of the Minneapolis Little Free Libraries, you have Amy to thank for that. Thank you, Amy, for every time you took the boys to the park so I could write. Thank you Amy and Steph for putting up with me texting you spoilers because I couldn't help myself. You're the best, and I love you.

Thank you to my brother Brad who again devoured the beta version of *Fangs* in a ridiculously short time. Again, I'm so sorry you read that spicy chapter while sitting in our parents' living room with Dad trying to talk to you about lawnmowers. Thank you to all my family members who have supported me by buying *Bones* even though it's not your type of book *at all*, and hopefully you never ever read it.

Thank you to Elsa Portman for being my ride or die fellow author friend. It is so much fun navigating this with someone else in the same boat. Thank you for always being willing to rant about grammar, discuss penis piercings, and exchange all of our smutty scenes like kids passing notes in class.

Thank you to everyone on my Discord server. I'm so grateful that I got to meet all of you through this! Thank you to Abby for helping me set the server up and answering all my dumb questions about how the hell to use Discord. Thank you to Maria who *made an actual map* of the Vault with mapmaking software so I could draw my map with an actual sense of scale. She also gets recognition for being the first to get a *Bones* tattoo. What is my life?! Special thanks to Alisha and Priscilla for not taking advantage of me accidentally in my sleep adding them to secret discord channels full of spoilers. True MVPs.

Thank you to my wonderful beta readers: Abby, Alisha, Amy, Brad, Brandy, Casey, Emma, Jess, Juliana, Kaiti, Libby, Maya, Miranda, My-The, Paula, Rania, Sarah, Stephanie, and Florence. Even though I knew it would happen (after my experience with *Bones*), seeing *Fangs* evolve and improve *so much* due to your feedback and critique is incredible. I'm so grateful for all the time you dedicated. Thank you to all my ARC readers for your early reviews, your posts, your messages, and especially your wild theorizing in the Discord ARC channel. It was an unbelievable experience watching that unfold and hearing all your ideas and *definitely not* evil cackling as I did so.

Thank you to everyone who took the time to send a message or email after reading *Bones*. They always made my entire day. Thank you to everyone who made posts, videos, reels, fanart, and/or reviews. I don't think I will ever be able to express how much that means to me.

Thank you to Jaime, my editor, for taking me back as a client after I used an unholy amount of adverbs and broke your heart with the ending of *Bones*.

Thank you to Sam whose Facebook post caused me to sell out of every copy of *Bones* that I had on my site and led to a serendipitous get-together in my hometown. I'm so glad I got the opportunity to hang out with you and your kids!

Thank you to Britney whose bookstore Good Girls Bookshop in Kalispell, MT is the first and (currently) only brick and mortar store to sell copies of *Bones* and *Fangs*!

I could keep going for pages, but really thank you to everyone who has read these books and waited patiently (or not patiently!) for the next one. I've found the best group of readers, and I am so lucky.

Love,

Kelsey

ABOUT THE AUTHOR

Kelsey Speer is an author and artist who lives in Minneapolis, Minnesota with her husband and two children, but she grew up in the remote mountains of Montana where the story of The Bones Series primarily takes place. With a background in graphic design, she is always creating something. Thanks to that creative spirit, she has explored numerous artistic mediums from embroidery, drawing, costumes, painting, ai art, fancy cakes, and the color of her hair, but the one she always comes back to is writing.

Kelsey started writing her first novel when she was twelve years old. Tragically the pink floppy disc containing it was lost. Since then, she has started writing many different books, and after finally getting officially diagnosed with adhd as an adult, she actually finished one.